*She stopped ten paces from the Guild House gate, which gaped at her, silent as an unanswered question.*

The moment Jehane Mor broke cover, slipping out of the shadows and toward the unlit entrance, she caught movement from the corner of her eye. Her head whipped around as a dense inky blot, with long tendrils trailing beneath it, detached from an eave diagonally opposite the gate. The tendrils exploded toward her in a jet of black matter, and she sprang back, gathering her power to counterattack—only to drop to the ground for the second time that night as an arrow sang.

But the unseen archer was not aiming at her and the arrow flew true, piercing the attacker's ink-black core. The creature shrieked, one long, keening whistle, before folding in on itself and collapsing to the street.

Jehane Mor rose to her feet, taking in the stain of black matter oozing across the cobblestones as the archer jumped neatly down from a vine-hung balcony half a block away. He fitted another arrow to the string, quartering the street and surrounding roofs with his eyes as he walked toward her, but it was not until he drew near that she recognized Tirorn of the Derai.

"Darkspawn," he said.

# By Helen Lowe

*The Wall of Night*
THE HEIR OF NIGHT
THE GATHERING OF THE LOST

THORNSPELL

# HELEN LOWE

# THE
# GATHERING
## OF THE
# LOST

## THE WALL OF NIGHT
### BOOK TWO

**HARPER** Voyager

*An Imprint of HarperCollinsPublishers*

**HARPER Voyager**

*An Imprint of* HarperCollins*Publishers*
10 East 53rd Street
New York, New York 10022-5299

Copyright © 2012 by Helen Lowe
Cover art by Greg Bridges
Map by Peter Fitzpatrick
ISBN 978-0-06-173405-2
**www.harpervoyagerbooks.com**

First Harper Voyager mass market printing: April 2012

Harper Voyager and ) is a trademark of HCP LLC.

Printed in the U.S.A.

10  9  8  7  6  5  4  3  2  1

The Gathering of the Lost *is dedicated to the memory of the 181 people who lost their lives in the Christchurch earthquake of February 22, 2011.*

*And also to the police and fire service personnel, the urban search and rescue services from many countries, and to the Student Volunteer Army, the "Farm-y Army," and all those individual people who pitched in and made the difference, most particularly on and after February 22, but also following the September 4, 2010 and June 13, 2011 earthquakes.*

# Acknowledgments

When I wrote the Acknowledgments for *The Heir of Night* (The Wall of Night Book One), I said that "writing the first book in a series is always a major undertaking." Well, as I have found out, writing a series is a major undertaking, and the second book is as significant, if not more so, than the first. In the case of *The Gathering of the Lost*, the natural pressure on the second-in-series to keep the momentum of the first book going was compounded by the fact that in the year from September 4, 2010, my home city of Christchurch suffered three major earthquakes (7.1, September 4; 6.3, February 22; 6.3, June 13) and over 8, 000 noticeable recorded aftershocks, many of these significant events in their own right. Living in this environment, and in particular dealing with the citywide and property-level damage that followed both the February 22 and June 13 earthquakes, all made for a challenging writing environment.

So there are people I would like, and need, to thank, who have made a difference in getting this book written under extremely difficult circumstances.

Firstly, my lead editor, Kate Nintzel of HarperVoyager USA, for her patience, understanding, and encouragement under very trying circumstances. But also, for her love for and understanding of the story and what I am trying to do with it. Thank you, Kate, for always being part of the solution.

And to the UK team at Orbit, particularly Bella Pagan and Joanna Kramer, who have also been consistent in their concern and support.

I also owe particular thanks to my agent, Robin Rue, and her assistant, Beth Miller, who were always there to help keep the writing path as smooth as possible.

One of the consequences of both the February and June earthquakes was liquefaction, a phenomenon where the ground turns to slurry, and silt and floodwater are spewed to the surface. Our property was relatively hard hit, and so I would like to thank the forty-five people who turned out over three days to help us dig out in February, including my cousin Christine, and friends Joffre, Janine, Peter, Irene, Petra, Kayley, Andrew, Susi, Tina, Paul, Dave, James, and their friends and roommates, and all the helpers from Aikido Shinryukan Canterbury.

I also need to thank all those who helped again on June 13: Joffre, Dave, Caroline, Susi, Peter, Fitz, Ram, Shane, and Chris—as without their help I would not have met my July 1 deadline for completing this book.

Other, equally valuable disaster assistance that helped me to keep going and keep writing in 2010-2011, was provided by Lou Stella, Wen Baragrey, Jacqui and Colin Church, and Jenny Grimmett and Mike Elston. I also very much appreciate the three-week, dedicated writing retreat offered by Mary and Frank Victoria, as the time away from continual aftershocks enabled me to really get traction on finishing the book. My very sincere thanks to you all.

A writer always owes profound thanks to those who read the raw manuscript and offer constructive feedback—in this case, Andrew Robins, Irene Williamson, Peter Fitzpatrick, and Chris Whelan. All provided invaluable insight and assistance, for which I am extremely grateful.

Publication day, coming after months and years of hard work, is always an exciting moment. As part of the launch fun around *The Heir of Night* (The Wall of Night Book One) I ran a competition on my blog, with the winner's name to be used for a character in *The Gathering of the Lost*. The winner was Jan Butterworth. Jan, I hope you enjoy the appearance made by your character.

Last but not least, and as always, I wish to thank my partner Andrew for his unfailing encouragement and support. Good times, bad times—what more can you say?

# Contents

## PART III: *The Border Mark*

## PART IV: *Midsummer*

## PART V: *Summer's End*

# THE
# GATHERING
## OF THE
# LOST

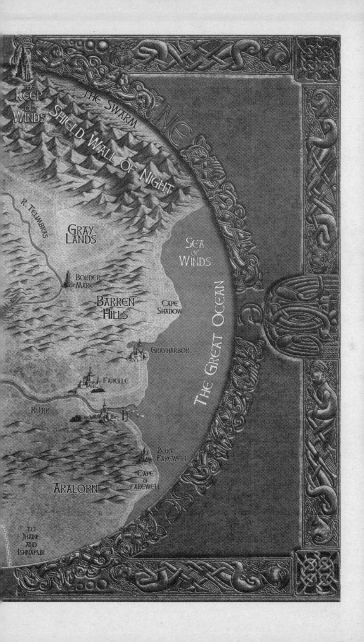

# Prologue

✦═══❖═══✦

Malian's dream was darkness: blackness without stars, water without light, a tower without a shadow that she remembered climbing—but that too fell away as she plummeted, diving head first through the dream. She kept her eyes open, remembering the crow in the shadow tower, the one that had told her this was something she would need to learn how to do.

The crow had been right, Malian thought, not that it helped when the universe of her dream was devoid of light.

*"It is not the eyes."* The voice of Nhenir, the legendary helm that had once belonged to Yorindesarinen, the greatest of all Derai heroes, was a mixture of light and dark, speaking into Malian's mind. *"Your inner awareness must be open: you must learn to eat the dark lest it eat you."*

Malian did not answer as she plunged deeper, and then deeper again into the well of her dream. Mind, heart, and soul, she felt as if she were made of darkness—but was that not fitting since her name was Night?

She was far, far down in the dream before she saw light, a single star drowned at the bottom of the well. She turned toward it and the light grew, finally becoming a torch that gleamed white in a crystal bracket. Malian caught at it with her mind and stepped forward—into the center of an enormous cave that was ringed with more torches.

The cave was so vast that both its roof and the light were lost in the darkness overhead. But the space surrounding Malian was not empty: thousands of warriors lay all around her on stone biers. All were armed, but their helms and weapons, like their companion beasts—horses, hounds, and even the occasional hawk—were disposed around them. They looked exactly, Malian thought, like the depictions of legendary heroes in ancient sepulchres. Yet these warriors were alive: she could see the steady rise and fall of their breath.

"Asleep," Malian whispered, "they're all asleep."

Slowly, she paced their silent rows—and saw young faces and those that were older, keen faces and grim, worn faces and sad. Every face looked resolute, as though some grave purpose had brought them to this one place, and a great many, Malian noticed, were beautiful, the men and the women alike.

The crystal torches were spaced evenly around the cavern, with a gonfalon hanging beside each light. Malian did not know either the runes or the heraldic devices depicted, but saw that every pennant was colorful and finely wrought. Far down the length of rows, in the very heart of the cavern, three great standards rose on staves of yellow, white, and bright red-gold. The banners were worked in the colors of fire, and their brilliance both dazzled Malian and drew her close.

The central banner and the highest of the three was vermilion silk with a pattern of silver and gold flames at its center. Living fire, Malian realized, when she finally stood below it, and with some kind of creature, a serpent or perhaps a lizard, coiled at the heart of the conflagration. The eyes of the lizard, too, were burning coals.

It's just a banner, Malian told herself, only a device.

She would never say now: *It's just a dream.* For her kind, there was no such thing. She looked away with an effort, turning her eyes to the banners on either side. The one on her left was orange and gold and fiery rose, all three colors shifting and weaving together with a fire bird device extending its full length. The bird's wings were like knives, its tail a fall of shooting stars. The banner to Malian's right bore a bird device as well, partially concealed by folds in a fabric that was both intensely white and indigo-blue as the hottest flame. The brilliance hurt Malian's eyes, so she looked down at the biers instead, one beneath each of the blazing banners.

All three were draped with rich cloth that matched the standard overhead—but for the first time in all that vast hall, two of the three biers stood empty. Armor and weapons alone were laid out on the central plinth and the one immediately to its right. Malian considered them, her brows drawn together, before turning to the bier beneath the white-hot banner. The warrior who lay there was armed like all his companions, but a coif of silver mail covered his head and chin, and a naked sword was set upon his breast. His gloved hands curved around the hilt and his expression was full of grief and weariness, the folded lips stern.

The mail of the coif was cunningly wrought, a master smith's work, but the sword was plain, with a simple guard and straight blade that was dull as pewter. Clearly, though, the man was a leader, despite the plainness of the sword. The runes worked into the cloth on which he lay, as well as his position beneath the standard, led to that inevitable conclusion. Although perhaps, Malian decided—with a quick glance at the bier's empty companions—he had not always been the only leader.

Her eyes returned to the sword, because there was something about it despite the unadorned simplicity—something that drew the eye and asked to be grasped, held aloft and wielded against one's foes. Malian half extended her hand, even though she knew that grasping the sword might trigger some warding spell.

*"It is not yet time."* The voice spoke out of the flames on the central banner and Malian snatched her hand back. Her eyes flew to the creature in the fire's heart and saw that the watching eyes were no longer fiery coals, but had grown dull.

"Time for what?" Malian's dream voice echoed in the vastness of the chamber.

*"The Awakening. But it is not yet time and you are not the one appointed. So who are you then, that steps so boldly into my ages-old dream?"*

Malian knew that it was dangerous to reveal her name— but it could be even more dangerous not to, caught in so deep a dream. Her heart was racing, but she raised her chin. "Malian of Night is my name and I, too, dream."

Silence fell all around her and the fire in the torches lengthened, growing brighter. When the voice spoke again, it held a note of wonder: *"Malian. Who named you, child?"*

What an odd question, Malian thought, astonished. "I don't know," she said finally.

*"It is not,"* the voice reflected, *"a name that belongs to Night."*

Malian could not recall ever having thought about her name before, but it certainly wasn't a common Night form. "No," she agreed. "Does it matter?"

*"I would be interested to learn who it was that gave it to you,"* the voice replied. *"When you find out, you must return and tell me."* Malian heard a note beneath the unhurried, reflective voice that she could not quite identify, although she thought it might have been excitement.

"I may not be able to find you again," she said.

*"I think you know that you will,"* the voice replied. *"You are very strong, for all your youth. Besides, it will be easier if I wish to be found."*

Did you wish to be found this time? Malian wondered. She decided to be bold. "Who are you? And who are they, all these warriors? What are they doing here?"

*"They are sleeping,"* the other replied, *"until the hour and the time appointed, which is not now. Your name would mean something to them, too, though—as would the name of the one who gave it to you. It could be . . . a very great gift."*

Malian shook her head. "You talk in riddles," she said. "But one gift deserves another: you still have not told me *your* name."

Humor tinged the voice's reply. *"You still have not told me who named you. So: a riddle for a riddle, an answer for an answer, a gift for a gift. You know my name already for it is also your name—although you might not recognize it as such."*

Malian ran a hand over her hair. "I'm not sure that you play fair," she said ruefully. "Is that a prerogative of age?"

*"My dear,"* said the voice, *"it is not that I am old. I am dead. I died a long time ago, so that they might live."*

Malian reflected that she might have erred, after all, in venturing so deep within the Gate of Dreams, where the dead were always more powerful than the living.

*"Generally,"* the voice continued, *"I am not kindly disposed toward those who disturb my dreams, but you I could almost like, despite your youth."* A ghost of a laugh shivered through the cavern. *"Besides, you bear a good name."*

"And," Malian suggested, "may be able to discover something that interests you?"

*"And,"* the voice answered, laying a fine emphasis on the word, *"you have powerful friends beyond this Gate of Dreams. They have been tolerant of my presence here; I do not wish to test their goodwill. The other reason is also worthy of consideration, of course."*

"Of course," echoed Malian. She took a step back, away from the biers and the banners. On impulse, she bowed. "Farewell," she said, "until we meet again."

*"Farewell, namesake."* The torches snuffed out so that Malian was again in darkness. She reached upward with her mind and back all the long way that she had come—and realized that she was far deeper in than she had thought.

*"You must learn to be less reckless, child."* The voice whispered around her, dry, but a little amused as well, and Malian was given a sudden boost, so that instead of climbing against the weight of darkness she arced through it like a comet. *"You are strong, yes, and young, but the Gate, too, is strong, its depths more profound than you can imagine. And not all those you may meet here are disposed to be . . . kind."*

The voice snuffed out as the flames had done, and Malian breached the surface of the darkness like a diver, to find herself standing before the main gate of the Keep of Winds. The keep cleaved the dream realm like the prow of a great ship, yet the Derai world massed behind it was as closed to her now, even in the realm of dreams, as it was in the waking world.

"Exile." Malian whispered the word to herself, but the echo came back from the keep's height: *exile-exile-exile!*

This time, it was Nhenir's voice that spoke into her mind. *"There is no part of the Gate of Dreams that is more closely warded. The barriers flung up when the Derai first arrived here have endured, and the two realms, the world of the Derai and that of Haarth, have not bonded. They overlap, but no more than that, a schism that is even clearer here on the dream plane than it is in the physical world."*

The dream was thinning, Malian thought, the Keep of Winds and the Derai world withdrawing into the whiteness. She could hear the bluster of the wind over the Winter Country and smell the smoky interior of a Winter lodge. Yet still she lingered, unwilling to cross back. "So even here," she said, stifling a rush of grief and loss, "I cannot enter my own world anymore."

*"Not unless you force a way through, which I don't advise until you have learned to conceal your use of power rather better than you can now. Even then, you would risk drawing attention—and creating a greater rift between Haarth and the Derai."*

And my reason for leaving the Wall, Malian reflected, was to disappear out of sight and mind among the lands of Haarth. Not without regret, she released the dream and opened her eyes to the smoky darkness of the lodge. She grimaced, feeling the cold of the frozen ground rising through the layers of felt and fur piled on the floor as she lifted Nhenir from her head.

The fire was a dull glow, turning the leather and felt-hung walls to sepia, but Malian felt the touch of Kalan's mind before she turned her head and saw him by the fire pit. Swathed in furs, his shadow hulked even larger against the lodge wall. *"You went too far,"* he said abruptly, but Malian could hear his fear. *"The contact between us broke. I know we've both learned a lot from the shamans this winter and you have Nhenir . . ."* His mind voice trailed off as he shook his head. *"You still need to be careful."*

"I know." He could speak directly into her mind, but she could not respond in kind as she could with Nhenir—and as both of them had been able to do with Tarathan of Ar and Jehane Mor, the heralds of the Guild, when beyond the Gate of Dreams. The lack of reciprocity was a bitter frustration for Malian, and a danger, too. All the histories made that clear, even though they also indicated that the two-way link could well come with time. But what, Malian thought, if it does not, especially since we are not to remain together once the thaw begins?

*"Did you find anything?"* Kalan asked, still silently, because there were some things they tried never to speak of openly. *"Any sign at all of the sword and shield?"*

Malian shook her head. She had felt drawn to the sword on the sleeper's breast, but Yorindesarinen's armring had not burned with silver fire as it had when she found Nhenir. The helm, too, had not given any sign of recognizing the sword—which it would have if the sleeper's blade *had* been Yorindesarinen's famous, frost-fire sword.

*"You have the armring,"* Kalan replied. If he had spoken aloud his tone would have been heartening. *"And Hylcarian said that all the lost arms would be rousing themselves to answer your need, as Nhenir did. So it has to be just a matter of time."*

*"Besides, you already have me,"* Nhenir pointed out. *"And I am the greatest of the three."*

*"Also the most modest?"* Malian queried silently. She got up and sat close to Kalan, so that she could whisper a description of the cave and the sleepers without fear of being overheard. His eyes widened as he listened.

*"It's like something out of the oldest stories. But the sword you saw, you're sure that it wasn't Yorindesarinen's?"*

"It was too plain, and didn't have any qualities of either frost or fire . . ." She let her voice trail off, and he nodded.

*"That namesake business, though—that's really strange."* His look was curious. *"And you really don't know who named you? What about a naming ceremony sponsor?"*

Malian shook her head, because if she had a sponsor, no one had ever told her—and not every Derai child, even those of the Blood, had a ceremony and a sponsor in any case. She remained silent, watching the flicker of the flames and listening to the roar of the wind. Linden, the spring-singer of Rowan Birchmoon's clan, had told them this might be the last storm before the snowmelt began. "And once the floods that follow snowmelt are done," she had added, "you can begin your journey south."

Our separate journeys, Malian thought now, feeling hollow. She and Kalan had argued against being split up, each sharply aware that the other was all they had left of the Derai world, but the Winter leaders had been adamant. "If those you flee seek a girl and a boy together," Linden had observed in her gentle way, "then the wise course must be to send you south by diverse routes—and to different destinations."

"Besides," the oldest of the shamans, Wolf, had added, "both smoke and stars show you following disparate paths to your power. Best, then, that we not meddle."

He was Rowan Birchmoon's great-uncle, Malian had discovered, his eyes shrewd in a face that was a mass of weathered seams—and his was the final ruling. So as soon as the weather allowed they would leave as part of separate hunting parties, each band following a distinct tributary of the Wildenrush south toward the River. A journey across the Wild Lands, Malian thought, which Linden says will take most of the summer. Yet only a few short months ago I believed that no one ever went there.

Despite the separation from Kalan, she felt a thrill of excitement. "One day," she said, "I should like to go as far as Ishnapur and look out on the great sea of sands."

"We should go there together," Kalan agreed. "One day."

They fell silent again, listening to the snowstorm buffet the lodge roof and scream around its entrance. *From Ij to Ishnapur*, Malian thought dreamily—and Linden will go with me as far as the Wildenrush, so that I may continue what I have begun and learn to read the patterns of smoke and stars like a shaman.

A vision of the cave of sleeping warriors filled her mind again, wavering into the Keep of Winds emerging out of mist and darkness. I must never forget why I am here, she told herself—that my duty to Night and to the Derai Alliance is why I follow this path. "We mustn't change," she said, quick and fierce, then wondered if the need to say the words at all was driven by her fear that Haarth *would* alter her. She saw the same thought reflected in Kalan's face as he studied hers.

"We may have to," he said slowly, "to survive where we're going." His eyes held hers. "But we must never change to each other."

No, Malian thought silently, but if we alter in other ways . . . She shivered as the wind gusted again, shaking the lodge.

Kalan built up the fire. "Spring coming or not, it's still freezing. Sometimes, I think I've forgotten how to be warm." He remained crouched on his heels, watching the flames lick across the dry wood and spark along a smear of resin. "When I was in the Temple quarter there were stories told. About the Lost."

"The Lost?" Malian asked, her inner sight flashing to the cave of sleepers again.

"Renegades. Priest-kind—those with old powers who managed to flee the Wall and disappear into Haarth."

As we're doing, Malian thought. Her warrior upbringing made her wrinkle her nose at the association, before she reminded herself that she, too, was priest-kind now. "I thought the fugitives were always caught and brought back?"

Kalan shrugged. "I've heard rumors that some find sanctuary well beyond the Wall, although it's probably just a story we spin to delude ourselves there's hope. But you should know, just in case."

In case I'm recognized as being warrior Derai, Malian wondered, and vengeance is sought against me for wrongs done on the Wall? These Lost would have to know who I am for that—although I suppose if they include seers in their number, they well might. Then again, if the Lost exist, they *are* still Derai. They might want to return home, if a path of honor opened for them.

And, she reflected, narrowing her eyes on this possibility, the Alliance is going to need all of those with the old power that it can get, even if most Derai on the Wall don't realize it yet.

The day when they did was probably some way off though, as was the time when she and Kalan, let alone anyone else, could even contemplate returning. Kalan grinned when she said so aloud, but soon afterward they both yawned and burrowed into their separate piles of furs. Kalan's breathing deepened quickly, but Malian kept thinking about the cave with its crystal torches. Time after time, she traversed the rows of sleeping warriors and wondered what it all meant: who were the sleepers and why had her seeking taken her there—and where exactly was *there*?

I know I went deep within the Gate of Dreams, she reflected, but are the sleepers of the present, the future, or the past? And why is *my* name a riddle to the power that guards them? Malian half thought that Nhenir might respond, but the helm remained silent even when she stretched out a hand and touched its curved surface. It was only when she was almost asleep that the ghost of a whisper crept into her mind.

*"You stood in the long ago past, so deep and so long ago that you frightened even me. The dream touches on the present and the future, too, but as for the puzzle of your name—even I cannot resolve that."*

Riddles, Malian thought drowsily, before she let sleep

take her—and so did not hear when the helm spoke again, a shiver across the blizzard's roar.

*"I wonder, Child of Night, if you could have returned so easily, despite your strength, if you had not had help? And how could you possibly understand the wonder of the help that you received? But then,"* Nhenir continued, meditative, *"she always was disposed to be kind—although that is something the Derai have chosen to forget."*

# PART I

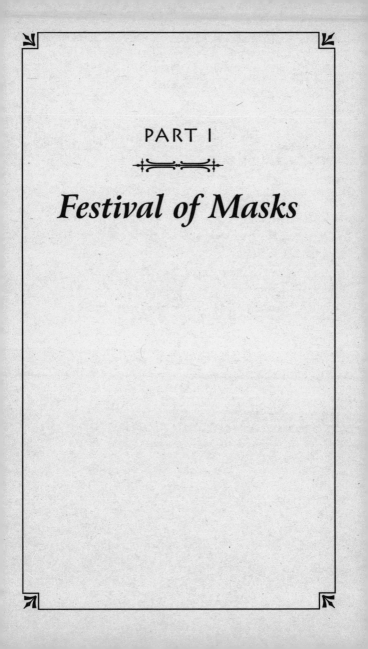

# *Festival of Masks*

# 1

## The Road to Ij

$S$ pring came to the River in a flurry of blustering winds and driving rain that turned the local roads into quagmires and hurled the first fragile blossoms to the ground. Two heralds were blown out of the city of Terebanth with the weather and turned east toward Ij, following the great Main Road that had endured since the days of the Old Empire. At any other season a river passage would have been faster, but the combination of contrary winds and spring floods, fed by snowmelt in the headwaters of the Ijir and the Wildenrush, would keep the merchant galleys in port for at least another month. And unlike the adjoining local roads, the Main Road was well paved and drained and would not turn to mud in the spring rain.

Even so, it took the heralds the best part of a chill and dreary month to complete their journey. The rain continued, steady and unrelenting, and they slept in small wayside inns or camped in the leafless woods. Both heralds were swathed in thick gray cloaks, but they and their horses were equally sodden by the time the first watery sunshine appeared, just before the toll bridge and the great Patrol fort at Farelle.

The bridge, with its seven great arches spanning the river, was a relic of the Old Empire. Together with the fort, it marked the last stop before Ij, which lay an easy, two-hour ride away. The floodwaters had finally begun to recede and the riverbank was lined with barges, while mules, wagons, and foot travelers crammed the bridge. The heralds stood up in their stirrups, trying to make out why the flow of people and goods had slowed to a trickle.

"Something on the far side," the first one said, while his companion angled her horse toward a solitary traveler coming toward them. His garb and the lute on his shoulder suggested a journeyman minstrel, and his progress was steady despite the crowd, although he seemed glad to stop in the lee of the herald's great, gray horse.

"'The whole world comes to Ij in the springtime'—isn't that what they say?" He addressed the gray-clad rider cheerfully. "Just my luck to be going the other way as the festival's beginning! But Arun-En, on the Wildenrush, has lost its minstrel and someone must take her place." He settled the pack on his back into a more comfortable position.

"Safe journeying," the herald said politely. "But what is holding up the Ij-bound traffic?"

The minstrel pulled a face. "Oh, it's some bunch of uncouth foreigners from northern parts who don't understand civilized ways and have taken issue over the tolls. The Patrol were shifting them out of the way as I came through, so things should start moving soon. Mind you, it did look like the Patrolers might have to bang a few heads there for a time, but it didn't come to that in the end."

He raised one hand in cheerful salute and carried on west, against the current of travelers. His prediction proved true, for the congestion on the bridge began to ease and the trickle through the tollgate became a steady flow just as the rain began again. The heralds held up their official sigils as they reached the far end of the bridge and were waved through, but they, like most others, glanced curiously at the small band of foreigners who had objected to paying the toll. A mounted unit of the Patrol had moved the strangers to one side and were watching, silent behind their visors, as a harassed looking clerk related the lawful charges. It was clear that the foreigners either did not understand or chose not to—and that the Patrol were leaving the business of explanation to the clerk and would only intervene if violence was threatened.

The heralds exchanged a glance before the woman of the pair turned her horse and rode over. Her hair, within the shadow of her gray hood, was fair, her gray-green eyes tranquil. "Greetings," she said to the clerk, her tone as calm as her expression. "You appear to be having some difficulty. Perhaps I can assist?"

The clerk turned, wiping the fine beads of rain from his face, and bowed low when he saw who had addressed him. "Greetings, your honor. Serivis of Farelle at your service. I am trying to explain the tolls to these foreign folk but they don't seem to understand our language very well. Or don't want to," he added darkly.

The herald nodded. "Jehane Mor," she murmured, "of the Guild House in Terebanth." She studied the strangers, her expression thoughtful, and they stared sullenly back. She counted fourteen in their band, all well armed and with two or more horses for each rider, and understood why they would have blocked the bridge once stopped—and why the Patrol had not moved away as soon as the bridge was cleared. "They are Derai, I believe," she said to the clerk, "from the Wall of Night, far to the north. Many of them do not speak our River tongue, but as it happens, I speak theirs."

"*Do* you?" exclaimed Serivis. "That is wonderful! At least, that is, if your honor is willing to speak with them?"

"Gladly," the herald replied, smiling. "Greetings," she continued in Derai, addressing the warriors in front of her. "Honor to you and to your House."

The nearest Derai looked at her from under his brows. He was a bull of a man, very tall and heavily muscled, especially across the shoulders, and his expression was far from pleasant. "Light and safety on your road," he grated out finally, just before his silence became outright insult.

She inclined her head. "I am Jehane Mor, of the Guild of Heralds. Perhaps I may help resolve your difficulty here?"

"Difficulty?" he growled. "We would choose another word. Is it your custom to rob travelers?"

Jehane Mor's brows went up. "Do you mean the tolls? They are not theft, but a lawful charge set by agreement between all the cities of the River."

The giant warrior slanted another look from beneath his lowered brows, this time at the visored riders of the Patrol, then back to her. "So how much is this daylight extortion of yours?"

"Extortion is a strong word," Jehane Mor observed, "as is robbery, especially from a newly arrived visitor." She met his sullen stare, her own gaze still tranquil, and he was the first to look away.

"Tell me about these 'tolls' then," he sneered, "since you seem determined to stick your nose—unasked—into our business."

The herald's mouth quirked. "Of course," she replied meditatively, "a man of courtesy would introduce himself before demanding the help that has already been freely offered."

A man laughed and the ranks of the Derai shifted, revealing a bare-headed warrior who had dismounted and was seated on a milestone, apparently at his ease despite the rain and the watching Patrol. "But Orth is not a man of courtesy, Mistress Herald," he said. "He is a warrior of the House of Swords, untiring in his pursuit of war. But courtesy, no."

The warrior Orth muttered under his breath as Jehane Mor studied the new speaker. He was slightly built compared to his hulking companion and far less heavily armed than most of those around him, with only a light mail shirt and a sword beneath his worn jacket. His rain-speckled hair was tawny and cut square across his nape, while the eyes that looked back at her were a warm, bright brown, their expression both humorous and measuring at once.

A dangerous man, she thought, more so even than the other, because this one is clever.

The Derai rose and made a slight, ironic bow before coming to stand at her horse's shoulder. "Allow me to pay the arrears of Orth's discourtesy. I am Tirorn, also of the House of Swords. My companions and I understood that the roads of the River lands were free to all, but now we learn that we must pay money for crossing this bridge. On the Derai Wall we would call that extortion and so we have refused to pay. Yet it seems," with a slight jerk of his head toward the Patrol's impassive riders, "that such a refusal will not be countenanced."

Jehane Mor's brows had crooked together. "Here on the River, we do not consider the tolls extortion. Our cities rule themselves, but the lands between them must be kept safe for travelers and the roads and bridges maintained. Yet if one city were to reach out to control the in-between lands, then that move would be seen as a threat by its neighbors, an expansion." She could see that this, at least, they all understood. "So the Patrol keeps the peace and the Company of Engineers, from Ar, maintains the road. In order to provide for these services, the cities have agreed that all travelers must pay a toll. The charges are gathered at places such as this, where those who use the road and the river come together at one point."

"You didn't pay," Orth muttered, "I saw them wave you through."

"I did pay," Jehane Mor replied calmly. "I bought a herald's pass for my whole journey before I left Terebanth. You could buy similar passes, if you wished," she said to Tirorn.

"So we could," he agreed, "and now that you have explained the matter to us so clearly, Mistress Herald, we will do just that." His face and voice were smooth but she caught another note beneath it, something that might have been mockery, or even a jeer.

"You could have done so before," she said quietly, "if you had wished to understand the clerk. He is a good and patient man and he was trying to help you."

The brown eyes met hers and then he bowed again, more deeply this time. "Forgive our discourtesy, Lady Herald, both to you and this"—he paused, seeming to test the word—"clerk."

"For my part," she said, "there is nothing to forgive. It is the duty of heralds to assist in such matters." She turned to Serivis before the Derai could reply. "If you tell me the charges," she told the clerk, smiling when he blew out his cheeks in relief, "they will pay them now."

All the same, it was sometime later before the process of purchasing passes was satisfactorily completed and the Derai finally clattered off toward Ij. Both heralds watched their departure with thoughtful expressions. "I am certain," Jehane Mor said, "that they speak our River tongue, despite their display of ignorance."

Her companion nodded. "He admitted as much, when he apologized. But why pretend that they didn't?"

"Spying out the way of things, I should think," a cool voice said from behind them. "The Derai are like that, we find."

"Aravenor!" Jehane Mor turned, smiling, as a Patrol horse moved alongside hers. The rider wore a captain's pin on his dark cloak, and the trademark visored helm covered his face. 'The helm of concealment' was what River folk called it, for the Patrol never revealed their faces, or entered a city or town, or stayed in any of the inns along the Main Road. They had their own forts close by the major cities and otherwise camped in the woods and fields, keeping to themselves and maintaining the peace of road and river as they had for centuries. Despite the enigmatic visors, it was still possible to tell Patrolers apart by the personal emblems displayed on their black tunics—below any marks of rank like a captain's bar—and etched onto their helmets.

In this case, Jehane Mor recognized the rider's voice even before she saw the striking hawk device and the captain's pin above it, for they had met many times on the road. The Patrol captain sat relaxed and easy in his saddle, but the focus of his visored helm was on the Derai. "They like to test our resolve," he said, and the closed visor turned toward her. "But you and Tarathan both speak their language—and you were sent to their Wall, five years back. I had forgotten that, until today."

Jehane Mor nodded. "We bore a message to their Earl of Night. But we had no dealings with any other Derai house."

"Night," Aravenor repeated, then shook his head. "Most of the Derai we're seeing are from Swords, like this lot, or the clan they call Blood."

Tarathan frowned. "You make it sound like they're coming here in numbers?"

"They've begun to, especially these past few years." Aravenor glanced around as a wagon wheel clipped the low stone rampart adjoining the bridge and the driver cursed. "There were always some, of course, because of their dealings in specialized armor and weapons. The trade in the metals they mine from their Wall is much larger, but the River merchants have always been the go-betweens for that. Their Derai contacts, if they travel at all, rarely come farther south than Grayharbor."

"But not anymore," Jehane Mor said softly.

"No. Although until today, the Derai who come have still only been in twos and threes—for the weapons trade, they always say, or heading for the southern tourneys, or simply seeing the wider world."

Tarathan's dark gaze studied the hawk visor. "But you don't believe the reasons they give?"

Below the visor, Aravenor's smile was grim. "How many generations has it been? And yet it is only now the Derai are seized by this desire to see the wider world? No, I do not believe it. Besides, there have been too many whispers out of the north in recent years. One is that the Derai have finally tired of their bitter Wall and are doing what we have long feared—turning their warlike eyes to the rich and peaceful River."

"And the others?" asked Jehane Mor.

"Chiefly that their old enemy is stirring again and they seek alliances." It was impossible to tell, from the Patrol captain's level tone, what he made of this. "Perhaps both explanations hold some truth and there are factions within the Derai. But like these Sword warriors today, those we encounter are always pushing to see what they can get away with. So far there's been no real trouble, but it's coming, especially if we have more groups of this size—and attitude." The smile beneath the visor was thin. "Today, though, you drew their teeth, Herald Jehane, and for that I am grateful."

"Only," she said slowly, "because their leader, the one called Tirorn, chose to have them drawn."

"I think you're right," the Patrol captain agreed. "But I am still grateful." He took one long, last look at the Derai band, small now with distance, before turning back to the heralds. "But what of you? What brings you out of Terebanth to Ij so early in the spring, when you haven't been this way for several years?"

"We've been kept busy on the Ephors' business," Jehane Mor agreed, "shuttling between Terebanth, Enkot, and Ar, with the occasional journey up the Wildenrush to keep in touch with the new settlements there." She shook her head, thinking of the miles they had covered. "We've been over into Emer and Aralorn as well. Trade with those lands is growing, particularly in Emer now that the Duke's peace is taking hold. But who would turn down a trip to Ij in time for the Festival of Masks?"

"Who indeed?" Aravenor replied, with a faint smile. "They say it's to be a fine festival this year, the best ever."

"Don't they say that every year?" Tarathan inquired, and the Patrol captain's smile became a grin.

"Look at the crowds—they seem to believe the boasts. We're told the city is overflowing already, so you're lucky you have your Guild House to go to."

Jehane Mor's answering smile was rueful. "Even that may be full, given that the Conclave and festival have fallen together this year. But no doubt we'll find a spare corner. The Guild may not be one of the Three, but we can generally house our own."

"The Three of Ij," Aravenor said, his tone thoughtful. "One should never meddle in their affairs, they say. Then again, the merchant princes, in my experience, are not to be taken lightly either." He raised one gauntleted hand and began to turn his horse. "Safe journeying. I will look for you on the road when the festival is done."

The heralds raised their hands in reply and rode on, weaving their way through the press of travelers that had still not thinned out again after the delay at the bridge. They remained alert for any sign of the Derai, but the Sword warriors were nowhere to be seen. *"They move fast."* Tarathan used mind-speech as he turned in the saddle, his eyes searching the country to either side. *"Or they've left the road, although I see no sign of that."*

Jehane Mor spoke softly to her horse, letting it thread between foot travelers and a well-laden mule train. *"The whole world comes to Ij, indeed."* Her gray extended its stride, clearing the line of mules and overtaking a cart piled high with bales beneath a stained tarpaulin. The carter flicked her a glance from beneath his hat, and the horse pulling the cart shifted slowly to the side of the road. The next cart was some distance ahead, but already the gray horses had begun to narrow the gap. Tarathan caught her eye as his mount drew level with hers.

*"Do you think Aravenor was trying to tell us something at the last?"* he asked. *"Or was he just being cryptic?"*

Jehane Mor grimaced. *"A typical Patroler, do you mean? It would be unusual for the Patrol to comment on the affairs of a city—and who would dare interfere with the business of the Three of Ij?"*

*"Other than at least a half-dozen merchant princes and several Ephors, no one that I can think of."* Tarathan's mindtone was dry. *"It's not unusual for friction to flare up at festival time, and only a fool would ever ride into Ij unwarily."*

*"And we, of course, are not fools."* Jehane Mor's swift, sidelong glance caught the answering gleam of his rare smile.

They let the gray horses increase their pace as the road cleared further—and crested a last, low hill in the early afternoon to see Ij spread out below them, glittering beneath the rainbow arch of a sun shower. Both heralds had seen the jewel of the Ijir before, but they still paused to take in its vastness, which spanned a series of islands between the river and the sea. Three great bridges led into the city on its western, landward side, with a river port to the south that was still clogged with the galleys and barges that plied the Ijir and its navigable tributaries. There was a Patrol fort close by the port, one of the major bases for their fleet of black galleys that patroled the river from Ij up to Enkot in the far west. On the city's seaward side, the islands were hemmed in by the masts of oceangoing ships, the great merchant vessels that traded from Ishnapur to Grayharbor.

The city itself was a sprawling jumble of roofs dominated by three soaring landmarks: the slender spires that marked the Academy of Sages, the great dome of the College of Minstrels, and the single, sheer tower of the Assassins' School. Each dominated one of the city's central islands, with the marble cupolas and copper domes of the old nobility and merchant princes clustered around them. The far greater expanse of tiled roofs that sheltered the lesser citizens of Ij spread away on every side, interspersed by markets and warehouse areas. The heralds' Guild House was located on a large island known as Westgate, where the Main Road officially entered the city.

For the first time since Terebanth, the main road branched at the foot of the hill where the heralds had drawn rein. One branch ran south to the river port and the Great Southern Gate, while the other led north, toward a smaller gate where red-roofed merchant houses sprawled along the city side of the river. The main, western gate was simply known as the Road Gate, and the closer the heralds came to it the busier the road became. Merchants and other long distance travelers were joined by farmers and carters coming and going from the city markets, as well as country families eager for the sights and entertainment of the festival. First hawkers' booths, and then inns and stables, began to crowd along either side of the road—and the clatter of hooves and jingle of harness, the creak of carts and the cries of the hawkers, filled the afternoon air.

The intermittent rain had begun again by the time the heralds arrived at the long bridge into the city, a fine drizzle with the sun shining through it and rainbows dancing in every puddle. A guard post barred the western entrance to the bridge, but Tarathan and Jehane Mor were waved through as soon as they held up their passes. An Emalni merchant was less fortunate and glared at the heralds as the guards threw back the tarpaulins over his wagons.

*"Their feud with Sirith must have flared up again,"* Jehane Mor said.

*"And you know what they say about the spring festival, that the murders and the masks come out together."* The hooves of their horses reverberated on the wide flagstones of the bridge. "I hope they have some spare masks at the Guild House," Tarathan added out loud. "I'd hate to have to try and buy one at this late stage."

"The price would be golden," Jehane Mor said, "if not the mask." She glanced up at the walls and roofs looming ahead. *"At least the city sounds quiet."*

*"For now."* Tarathan moved his horse farther to one side as a wagon approached from the opposite direction. *"It's the middle of the afternoon and the festival has only just begun."*

Bunting fluttered from the city walls, dominated by the heraldic colors of the Three: gold for the sages, the crimson of the minstrels, and assassins' white. The three colors were repeated in the great standard of Ij, quartered by the city's shield-of-arms—the river galley and the scales, the mace and the galleon—which floated above the Road Gate. Both the heralds raised a hand in formal salute as they clattered beneath the gate arch, and the guards on duty there saluted in reply. They seemed more relaxed than their comrades on the far side of the bridge, and the sergeant inquired about the condition of road and river as he stamped their passes.

"Peaceful, eh?" he said, when they had assured him this was the case. "I wish I could say the same, but we've had three assassinations already since the festival began, even though the Conclave won't begin for another three days. It gets worse every year," he added in weary resignation. "It's not just the representatives of the Three jockeying for position, or the vendettas between the great families anymore.

Other folk are bringing their quarrels and feuding here as well."

"What other folk?" Tarathan asked.

The sergeant shrugged. "The quarrels between Emaln and Sirith seem to escalate every year, as well as trade disputes between any number of other cities. But these new folk from the north are the worst."

"Do you mean the Derai?" Jehane Mor asked.

"That's it, your honor." The sergeant nodded, handing back her pass. "They don't seem to like anyone very much, let alone us. Then there's the other northern lot we had for the first time last festival and who're back again this year— the Derai seem to really hate them. Although I must admit, that latest lot give me the creeps." He scratched at his neck. "More than a little bit."

"Who are these other northerners?" Tarathan inquired, his tone carefully casual. "Are they an opposing Derai sect?"

"No," the sergeant replied. "They seem to be a completely different outfit. Envoys, they called the lot that came here last festival—and they certainly spent a lot of time talking with the Masters, although no one seems to know what all their gabbing was about." He spat into the gutter. "Personally, I'd rather not have anything to do with any of that northern lot. Let 'em kill each other off, I say."

"Good riddance, too," agreed another guard, "but just not in our city or on our watch. We've enough going on with the festival and Conclave, without that."

The arrival of the Emalni wagons, rumbling in under the arch, drowned out the muttered agreement from the other guards. Tarathan rode close to Jehane Mor as they emerged into the square beyond the gate, his dark eyes fierce as a hawk's. *"That was interesting news."*

Jehane Mor looked around at the cheerful, festival bustle. *"These new envoys have to be from the Swarm. Very interesting indeed, with Derai here as well."*

Tarathan nodded, but his expression gave nothing away as they navigated the wide cobbled streets that led to the market quarter where the Guild House stood. Ijiri trading houses and embassies from the other River cities adjoined each other, most with trees grown in tubs set to either side of ornate entrances. Tarathan nodded up at the banner above the door to one of the larger trading houses. The blue cloth was so dark and wet with rain that it was almost black, its lone device that of a golden leopard, rampant, with extended claws. *"Unusual for the Ilvaine kin to fly their banner,"* he said

Jehane Mor contemplated the leopard. *"A scion of the house must have come home, but which one?"*

*" 'Ware my claws, lest you wear a glove.' "* Tarathan quoted the Ilvaine motto, then added: *"Perhaps they intend becoming active in the Conclave again? The Ilvaine kin have strong links to both Academy and College—and probably to the School as well."*

*"Yet follow their own road, always."* Jehane Mor's mind-speech was soft.

*"But why get involved again now, after so many years?"* Tarathan's expression was still thoughtful when they clattered into the Guild House yard and found that it was as full as every inn they had passed along the way. The only space left for their accommodation was a landing where some camp beds and screens could be squeezed in.

"And no complaining," the caretaker said, as she brought them towels and soap and blankets. "I've heard there's not a spare corner to be had in the whole city and I hardly expected a contingent from Ishnapur, let alone half the Guild members from Emaln and Sirith."

"Trying to keep the peace, I suppose," said Tarathan. He was already lying on one of the camp beds, his hands clasped behind his head. "Without much success, I gather?"

The caretaker shook her head. She was a slight woman with short, grizzled hair and the trace of an Enkot burr in her voice. "Not noticeably," she said, "although everyone's trying. But an Emalni warehouse burned down the night before last, so of course the stables used by the Sirith consulate went up last night. The fire was put out before it spread, praise be! But with three assassinations already and word on the street that the School is inundated with contracts, it doesn't bode well."

"It doesn't," Jehane Mor agreed. "But what are our Ishnapuri kindred doing here, Naia? We heard no word of their coming."

"They came by sea, with messages from the Shah for the Masters." Naia shrugged. "That's all I know, except that they've been going from Academy to College to School for most of this week. They aren't saying much but I suspect that the desert tribes are growing restless again."

"Even so, it's still a very long way from Ishnapur to Ij." Jehane Mor shook her head, dismissing the matter. "I don't suppose you have any spare masks for us?"

"If you don't mind them old and tatty. Our store has been well picked over with so many in before you—but you won't get anything better for love or money in the city. You appear to have been expected, though," Naia added, pulling some gilt-edged cards out of her pocket and handing them over. "I've already received the usual invitations for you: a banquet at the Conservatory tomorrow night and a debate at the Academy the following noon, with cards for Prince Ath's masque and fireworks that same evening. Heralds are always good for making up numbers," she said slyly, "and for some reason the prince thinks you two have the ear of the Ephors, in Terebanth."

Jehane Mor sat down on her own cot, reading the cards in turn. " 'My vewy dear fwend the Ephor Vhiwinal,' " she murmured, imitating the lisp for which the princely sage was famous. "Will old and tatty masks do for His Illustriousness's masque? I suppose they'll have to. And no one will notice if we stand in a dark enough corner."

"Now that," said Naia firmly, "would not do at all. You know you'll be expected to mingle." She paused. "You will be careful, won't you?"

"We're always careful," said Tarathan. After a moment he raised his head. "Is something in particular bothering you, Naia?"

The caretaker grimaced, her shoulders rising in a half

shrug. "I don't know. The streets are wild this year and there are all sorts of strange folk about. And you two never stay close. You're always off and about, all over the city."

Tarathan smiled at her. "Dear Naia. But we are a little older than the wild youngsters you first knew—and have survived this long, to plague you again now."

"You don't plague me!" Naia protested. "And you were never wild . . ." Her eyes met his and she half smiled before her expression clouded again. "Well, maybe you were, just a little. But all these strangers—what if they don't know that the law forbids violence against heralds? And it's the Festival of Masks, in Ij. Anything could happen."

*Anything could happen.* The words hung, cool as a shiver in the afternoon air, and the heralds exchanged a glance.

"We have to go about the city," Jehane Mor said gently. "We have commissions to discharge. But we promise to be careful, Naia."

## 2

# A Libation for Seruth

Dusk was the festival hour, when everyone who ventured onto the streets went masked. The city was already humming when the heralds left the Guild house, with dancing in the market squares and every street corner boasting a juggler or puppeteer. Lanterns had been strung amongst the trees that lined the wider streets, and flambeaux blazed outside every inn and public house. The festivalgoers laughed as they came and went, yet the heralds detected a nervous edge to the gaiety—as though the Ijiri were tensed for the next fire or random act of violence.

*"But are they random?"* Jehane Mor studied the crowded street from behind her mask.

*"Perhaps we should take a look at the School's register, since it's so full this year?"* Tarathan's mindvoice was dry.

*"The register is not the business of heralds."* Jehane Mor paused, applauding a juggler as he completed a particularly spectacular cascade.

*"Naia was right though,"* Tarathan replied as they strolled on. *"Something's bubbling beneath the surface here. Can't you feel it?"*

Jehane Mor nodded as another performer breathed out fire into the violet dusk. *"Heralds must still stick to their own business and let the Ijiri manage theirs—which they appear to be doing,"* she added as a stronger than usual contingent of the city guard tramped past.

Naia's summary of the overnight news, given at breakfast the next morning, seemed to support Jehane Mor's observation. "No further fires," the caretaker said, "and only one attempted riot, which the guard suppressed before it got under way. Oh, and an assassination attempt on Academy Island, a Conclave representative, but it was thwarted." She placed a square of folded paper on the table. "And here is another invitation, addressed to you both."

Jehane Mor turned the paper over, tapping one finger against the leopard rampant insignia pressed deeply into indigo wax, before passing it to Tarathan. "Ilvaine," she said, as he broke the seal.

"Our attendance is requested at the Inn of the Golden Lute, on the Minstrels' Island," he read out, as Naia brought in more bread with a rounded, yellow cheese.

"Why would an Ilvaine stay there?" Jehane Mor wondered, "rather than in the palace on Academy Island, or the town house by the river port?"

Tarathan folded the invitation again. "Why not? Don't the Ilvaine kin have fingers in every Ijiri pie?"

Naia sniffed, placing a knife by the bread. "So they say, as well as estates in the countryside and ships that trade in every port between Grayharbor and Ishnapur. But not many of the kin actually live here in the city anymore."

"I wonder what this one wants?" murmured Jehane Mor, then looked around as the hall door opened and two heralds in the flowing grays of the Ishnapuri branch of the Guild walked in. They looked alike enough to be brother and sister, and their accents, when they spoke their good mornings, bore the lilt of the far-off southern empire.

Jehane Mor and Tarathan rose and bowed as one, speaking their names and Guild house in the formal style, and the Ishnapuri heralds replied in kind. "I am Ileyra," the young woman said, "and this is Salan, my brother in both blood and the Guild."

" '*It is a very long way from Ij to Ishnapur,*'" Salan quoted gravely, then added, with the ghost of a smile, "but we came by sea, which made the journey swifter. And safer, since I understand the overland route still runs through very wild country." He sat down, reaching for the bread basket. "We have yet more meetings with the Masters today, but fortunately not until this afternoon."

Ileyra smiled. "We stayed out too late with the festival—every night there is more to see and do." She shrugged. "Yet why not, when the Masters of this so-great city are all busy ahead of their Conclave?"

Jehane Mor concealed her surprise. "I would have thought those on the Shah's business would be given priority."

"We have appointments," Ileyra assured her, "but always there are delays. The Masters may be late from earlier meetings, or their advisers cannot get through the press in the streets."

"But at night," said Salan, with a gleam of white teeth, "we get to see something of the famous festival without detracting from our duty. You are also here for business, of course?" His tone made the statement into a question.

"Sadly dull stuff and none of it with the Masters." Jehane Mor set her plate aside. "But we may see you if you are attending the evening revels. The whole world, Naia tells us, is to be at Prince Ath's party. It will be one of the great events of the festival."

Ileyra shrugged and held up her palms. "There are so many invitations. . . . And maybe we shall not see you anyway with all the masks, if it is such a large affair?"

"True, although I am sure that we shall meet again here." Jehane Mor stood up. "But now we must be about that dull business of ours." The sister nodded, smiling, while the brother pulled a sympathetic face. Jehane Mor opened the door into the hall and waited until Tarathan had closed it before mindspeaking: *"Odd, don't you think?"*

*"To come so far and be kept waiting? Yes,"* Tarathan agreed. *"And the Guild is so new in Ishnapur. Why would the Shah commission heralds for his business at all, let alone*

*just one pair? I would have expected an ambassador, or
special envoy at least."*

"Something doesn't add up." Jehane Mor lifted her gray
cloak from a peg beside the door. *"The last rumors I heard
centered around trade treaties or even a maritime alliance.
That* would *require a full ambassador."*

Tarathan tapped the paper with the Ilvaine seal against his
hand. *"I can't imagine the Shah sending heralds for any other
purpose than to announce the ambassador's subsequent arrival. Odd,"* he repeated, and the invitation tapped again.

Naia was sweeping the Guild House porch when they
stepped out into the brightness of the morning. "I'll have
a groom take your horses down to the exercise meadow by
the river port, if you're busy today," she said. "You could
probably leave them there, if you wished, as the Guild keeps
space in the port's livery stable." She straightened, looking
around the small yard. "It will be a pleasanter spot for them
and leave more stable room for newcomers here."

Jehane Mor thanked her, and she and Tarathan spent the
morning delivering the Ephor's dispatches, as well as dropping off sealed reports from business agents in Terebanth to a
series of merchant warehouses. They ate their lunch beneath
an awning in the largest of the Westgate markets, with the
heat of the sun on their backs and the last of the rain puddles
disappearing from the cobbles. A clerk from one of the trading houses found them there, with a request that they call for
more dispatches, and it was mid-afternoon before they turned
toward Minstrels' Island and the Inn of the Golden Lute.

The inn was located close to the great, golden dome of
the College, and was a substantial, three-storey affair, with
the upper levels built around three sides of a large courtyard.
Timber balconies overlooked the central area, and the heralds' boots thudded on the stairs as a servant led them to the
topmost gallery. The afternoon air was heady with the scent
of jasmine growing along the balustrade, and a College bell
rang out the hour. The servant paused before a door of honeyed oak and knocked once before opening it. "Them heralds
are here, your honor," he announced, before slipping away.

Jehane Mor stepped into the room ahead of Tarathan and saw a man lounging in the window seat. "Ah," she said. "I wondered if it might be you."

The man laid aside his lute, rose gracefully to his feet and crossed to a table that was set with glasses, a flask of wine, and a plate of candied fruit. "I was unsure," said Haimyr the Golden, the Earl of Night's minstrel, "whether you knew that I was of the Ilvaine kin—although I suspected that you might." The golden bells on his sleeve tinkled as he raised the wine flask. Both the flask and the goblets set around it were golden, too, wrought from the delicate and costly glass of Ij.

"It has been a long time since the Keep of Winds," the minstrel continued, "but the two of you have remained in my thoughts. Would you care for some wine?"

Jehane Mor came further into the room, Tarathan's shadow stretching alongside hers after he closed the door. "If that is an Emerian white in that flask, then yes," she said. "To whom or what do we drink?"

"We must pour the libation for Seruth," Haimyr the Golden replied, matching his action to the words. "It really is a very fine wine—and from Emer. I salute your perception, Herald Jehane!"

The herald accepted the glass he held out and sipped, regarding him across the rim while he poured a second glass for Tarathan. She noted the faint lines around eyes and mouth that had not been there five years before, but there was no thread of silver in the bright hair or lessening of mockery in the golden eyes. "I *had* forgotten that you were of the Ilvaine kin," she said, after the wine had been duly appreciated. "But once we received the invitation, I reflected further on who might room so close to the College."

"As a minstrel my business is with the College, so it makes sense to stay nearby." Haimyr swirled the wine in his glass. "I could stay in the mausoleum they call our palace, I suppose, but I find all that marble and gloom of family history a little dismal."

"We saw the banner over the Ilvaine trading house yesterday, the one on Westgate. Is that for you, even though you stay here?" Jehane Mor asked. "Or for another of your kin?"

"For me?" Irony glinted in Haimyr's smile. "No, my illustrious great-uncle, the Prince Ilvaine, intends coming in for the festival, and another uncle and several cousins will be with him. Although some other of my cousins," he added lazily, "will be coming by way of Emaln and Sirith."

Jehane Mor felt Tarathan's attention sharpen, but she said nothing, careful to hold her thoughts as still as her face. Haimyr smiled, watching the play of light through the golden glass. "But I did not invite you here to speak of my family. How long has it been, exactly, since we last met? Five years? Six?"

"Over five, since we waited by the Border Mark," Jehane Mor replied quietly.

The minstrel looked at her, his eyes lambent. "And they never came," he said. "I know this because the Earl's agents followed you all the way to Terebanth to be sure you really had returned alone. He was, I regret to say, sadly suspicious of you both. It was not until the following spring that we knew for certain that Malian and her party had turned aside, becoming lost in the winter that fell on Jaransor."

"Jaransor," Jehane Mor repeated, shaking her head. "That information never made its way to the River, or to the Guild. I am grieved to learn it now. Such news makes ill hearing."

The minstrel was still watching her face, but now he shrugged. "It is a long road from the Wall to the River, almost as great a distance, in its way, as the fabled journey from Ij to Ishnapur—which is quite the end of the world, would you not say?"

"Not entirely," Tarathan replied. "But I do not think you invited us here to talk of the distance between lands."

"I suppose it is all in the way one looks at things," Haimyr mused. "Perhaps heralds, who are always traveling the world, think less of distance than those who live more settled lives. But where was I? Ah!" He snapped his long fingers together. "News from the Wall: that was it. But I am forgetting my manners. We have poured the wine and made our libation to

Seruth. Now we must be seated and comfortable in our talk."

Jehane Mor smiled slightly and moved to a high-backed chair, while Tarathan remained standing behind her.

"How many years have you dwelt on the Wall of Night?" she asked.

Haimyr threw up a hand. "Over twenty now, since I first met the young Lord Tasarion and accepted his offer to see the Derai Wall. And there I have remained. Fate is a curious thing, is it not?"

"It is," Jehane Mor agreed. "But I don't think you asked us here to speak of that either. News from the Wall, you said, and that Lady Malian was lost in Jaransor. That seems a very strange road for any Derai to have taken."

Haimyr shrugged. "I think she and her companions were driven there, out of the Gray Lands. Night's trackers found evidence of that before full winter fell across the plain. But the snow came earlier in Jaransor, overtaking Malian and her party—as it overtook us all," he added musingly. "Even on the Wall there had never been a winter so long or so hard. Lannorth and a hundred-squad were bailed up for months in Westwind Hold, waiting for the spring before entering Jaransor."

"The Derai sent numbers into Jaransor?" Jehane Mor could hear the frown in Tarathan's voice.

The minstrel shook his head. "In the end, no. The Commander of Westwind forbade it, so only Lannorth and a handpicked few went in, with the best of the hold's hunters and scouts."

"Wise," Tarathan said shortly.

"As you say," Haimyr agreed. "The shamans of the Winter country believe that the gods walked Jaransor once, in the very dawn of time, and that their memory dwells there still." He took another sip of the wine. "Ijiri lore, too, suggests that it is a place of ancient power, not to be ventured lightly."

"Jaransor-of the-many-legends," said Jehane Mor. She paused before speaking again, conscious of advancing the next pawn across an invisible board. "What did they find, the handpicked few?"

"Dead bodies, mainly." Haimyr's gaze held hers, before shifting to Tarathan. "Lannorth had wyr hounds, accursed beasts in my opinion, even if they can track their quarry across stone and through water. The hounds led them to the guards, Kyr and Lira. Their bodies were still frozen in snow, but they had died from battle wounds, not the cold. The searchers found the bodies of their adversaries as well, all of them Darkswarm. And more Swarm dead later, in a pass further to the south—yet no sign of the Heir; or the boy, Kalan; or Nhairin, the high steward, who were both with Malian when she left the Keep of Winds."

"If no bodies were found," said Jehane Mor slowly, "how can you be certain they are dead?"

Haimyr studied his wine with great interest. "The winter was severe and they had no provisions, even if they could have found shelter. But there are no habitations in Jaransor. The Westwind scouts thought it possible their bodies might never be found, not in that country."

Jehane Mor was silent, recalling snow falling from gray skies above a tall standing stone: the flakes had floated down steadily, soundless as death. Behind her, Tarathan neither moved nor spoke, but she knew his eyes would be intent on the golden minstrel. On the windowseat, Haimyr drained his glass.

"I think something froze in all of us that winter, but with the Earl it is as though the frost has never lifted. For a long time he spoke only to give commands. He wouldn't even talk to Asantir, who has been his right hand these many years." The golden bells chimed as Haimyr shrugged. "Nhairin's defection hit him hard—and what he saw as his daughter's disobedience, even more so. He even spoke of striking Malian's name from the record of their Blood."

"They are a strange people, both rigid and vengeful." Tarathan's tone was dispassionate. "Who else would seek to disinherit one already thought dead?"

"Who indeed?" the minstrel said. "Although I think Tasarion spoke in the anger of the moment. He is not by nature a vindictive man. And he has too much else to occupy him, between reclaiming the Old Keep—vast, benighted place that it is—and rebuilding the Derai Alliance. Asantir, whom you knew as his Honor Captain, is Commander of Night now, and he has sent her to all the keeps along the Wall, strengthening Night's old alliances and seeking to rebuild those broken in the civil war."

"What of allies beyond the Wall?" Jehane Mor asked. "Does Night, too, send envoys to the Masters of Ij?" She paused. "Perhaps that is what brings you here, just in time for the Conclave?"

Haimyr laughed. "The Earl of Night has sent no embassy here—and even if he had, I would not be part of it." He rose and refilled their glasses and his own before returning to the window. "This is certainly a very fine vintage," he said appreciatively, "even for an Emerian white. As it happens, I am aware of the Derai in Ij, but that is not what brought me south." He raised his glass in salute. "The main reason I am here is to speak with you."

Not a pawn this time, thought Jehane Mor: I think the queen just moved down the chess board. Or the Heir, as the Derai would call the same piece. She waited, and felt Tarathan wait with her, their minds an opaque mirror behind expressionless faces.

"I have lost something that is very dear to me," Haimyr continued smoothly. "And dear to friends of mine, also. I believe that you may have the ability to help us find what we seek, however well concealed."

"Lost," Jehane Mor inquired, "or stolen?"

Haimyr considered this point. "Some might say stolen," he conceded, "but really, I prefer 'lost.'" His eyes held hers. "I must have been quite dull-witted all these years, not to have thought of you both sooner. You have found her once before, after all—and under extreme circumstances."

"Her?" Jehane Mor echoed, although she already knew what would come next.

"Her," the minstrel confirmed and set his glass down. "I want you to find Malian, the Heir of Night, and bring her home to the Keep of Winds."

# 3

# *Revelry and Masks*

*T*he silence in the room was so intense that sounds from the yard below were no longer a background murmur, but immediate and distinct. Jehane Mor put her own glass aside. "I am sorry," she said, "but I don't think we can help you."

"Do you not?" Haimyr picked up his lute and began to strum it, a little dissonance of notes. "I was so sure that you could."

"You have told us," she replied, "that Malian perished in Jaransor, five years ago. Even if we found her restless ghost, we could not restore her to this plane of existence."

The long, slender hand swept a flurry of notes from the lute. "But *you* asked *me* how I could be certain she was dead. And in fact I did not say that she was—'lost' was the word I used. I take no responsibility for what the Derai may or may not believe." The lute strummed again. "At first, given the winter, I was inclined to believe the worst. But I was puzzled by Lannorth's report on Kyr and Lira. They had died fighting, yet their bodies were found laid out as though by a comrade."

"By the comrades who were with them, surely?" Jehane Mor shook her head. "All that proves is that Kyr and Lira were not the last to die."

The lute twanged, a mournful eerie sound. "Then, of course, there is Nhairin."

"Who was also lost?" Jehane Mor was careful to keep the question in her tone.

"At first, yes." Haimyr looked up from the lute. "A routine patrol from Westwind found her the following summer, wandering the border between Jaransor and the Gray Lands. Her body was emaciated and covered in terrible sores, all her clothes were rags, and her mind was filled with the madness of Jaransor. Her body has healed since then, but her mind—" He shrugged. "Some thought she should have been executed as a traitor, but the Earl would not have it. He could not, he said, put to death someone who was incapable of speaking in her own defense. Besides, there was the hope that she might recover and we would learn more of what happened in Jaransor." The minstrel played a short sequence of regretful notes on the lute. "But she is too far gone."

"Jaransor," Tarathan observed somberly, "is a dangerous place."

"Especially for the Derai." Haimyr shrugged again. "All we have pieced together from Nhairin's ravings is that Kyr and Lira turned back to fight in hopes that the Heir would escape. So Malian and the others would have been far away by the time the guards fell and could not have laid them out. And their enemies, surely, would have let them lie. So who else, I have asked myself, would—or could—have done it?"

"Even if your belief that the Lady Malian still lives is justified," Jehane Mor replied, "five years ago you wanted her to flee the Wall of Night. Why this sudden urgency to have her back?"

"On the Wall, every boundary patrol of Night sees action now." Haimyr spoke almost to himself. "Asantir says it is the same for all the forward keeps and holds. A great storm is brewing, we all feel it, and this time the ramparts of Night may not hold."

"Not without the Child of Night, is that what you mean?" Jehane Mor asked.

Haimyr smiled. "Ah, the acuity of heralds. That is exactly

it. Malian has not been supplanted or disinherited so she is still Heir of Night. This spring she will turn eighteen and be of age, able to claim her place at the Earl's council table and amongst the Houses of the Derai as of right—if she can be found."

"If she is alive," Tarathan said. "You seem to have as little evidence of her life as you do of her death, and no leads for any seeker to follow."

"Even," said Jehane Mor, "if we were free to help you, which we are not. Our services are contracted well into next year."

The golden eyes narrowed, glittering—and then the minstrel laughed, easy and a little mocking. "I do have a lead," he said. "We have explored all other paths, Commander Asantir and I, which leaves only you, the herald pair who waited a full moon by the Border Mark. Really, it all fits." The voice of the lute sounded, light beneath his hand. "Who else would have the ability or the will to venture Jaransor and survive, then return to the River as though nothing had happened? Who else, I asked myself, had fought beside Kyr and Lira in the Old Keep and would honor their bodies?"

*"Time to bring this to an end,"* Jehane Mor told Tarathan silently. "We mean no discourtesy," she said to Haimyr, "but you are mistaken. Tarathan and I did not conceal Malian of Night, or steal her away, five years ago. We returned alone from the Border Mark to the River."

"Nor," Tarathan continued evenly, "do we know where she may be found. We cannot help you, Haimyr the Golden."

The golden eyes regarded them. "Will not," the minstrel said, very softly, and rose to his feet. He turned his back and looked out the window. "There are some," he mused, "who would consider it unwise to disappoint one of the Ilvaine kin, particularly in our own city."

"There are some," Jehane Mor replied, very cool, "who might hear that as a threat."

"No, how could that be?" Haimyr asked. "I would break the law of every city in the River if I threatened you."

"So you would," Tarathan agreed, "but then you, as you have pointed out, are of the Ilvaine kin."

"Indeed." The minstrel turned back from the window, a smile on his lips. "But would even the Ilvaine kin risk the gates of every city being shut against them, the face of every citizen turned away? We are just one family, after all. I merely expressed the depth of my disappointment; you do wrong to imagine threats." Still smiling, he strolled back to the table. "You are here for the whole of the festival, are you not, as am I. It may be that you will recall something you have forgotten, or think of some way to assist me after all."

"There is nothing we have forgotten and nothing we can do to assist you." Jehane Mor rose to her feet and bowed. "We wish you joy of the festival, Haimyr Ilvaine."

He made no move to detain them, only bowed in return with one hand placed over his heart. "I wish you the same joy," he said. "And we shall speak again. I am sure of it."

*"Now that,"* said Jehane Mor, as they crossed the busy inn yard, *"still felt like a threat."*

*"Because it was one."* Tarathan's mindvoice was flat. *"Let's take the long way,"* he added, when they had cleared the inn gate and turned toward the road that looped around the perimeter of Minstrels' Island. They made their way through the throng of musicians, students, and festival visitors, eventually descending a zigzag path to the Bridge of Boats. The bridge was formed by pontoons of barges that connected the series of islets between Minstrels' Island and Landward, a large island immediately to the north of the river port. The bridge was almost empty when the heralds reached the first pontoon, where the customary statue of the goddess Imulun gazed back toward the College dome. She held the staff of wisdom in her right hand, while a stone lion crouched at her feet.

Jehane Mor stared up at the timeworn plinth, noting the goddess's compassionate gaze and the lion's watchful stare before she bowed her head. The god Seruth, she knew, would stand on the other side of the bridge. In Ij, it was always Imulun who looked toward the city, while Seruth, guardian of journeys, faced the outside world—everywhere, that is, except for the bridges that led to the Assassins' School. The god Kan, the Dancer in Shadow, always kept watch over both those who entered and those who left the Secret Isle.

The heralds walked on until they stood on a pontoon that was well out in the channel. Seabirds perched on the rocky islets or glided lazily overhead, but otherwise, despite a few small craft in the distance, they were alone. Even the water was sluggish here, brown-gray from the flooding but scarcely moving the pontoons. The heralds rested their weight against the roped sides and Jehane Mor looked at Tarathan. *"What do you think?"*

*"The minstrel suspects us, he made that plain."* Tarathan frowned out over the turgid water. *"But suspicion was always going to fall on us. I'm more concerned about doubt being cast on the long-held belief that the Heir of Night perished five years ago."*

*"Malian's enemies would not have taken her death on faith either."* Jehane Mor kept her mindvoice calm.

*"And the least breath of suspicion could stir them onto the trail again."* Tarathan's lips compressed. *"Surely the minstrel can see the advantage of an absolute belief in that death?"*

Jehane Mor watched the languid flight of a gull. *"And why confront us now, when he must have had us watched for some time?"* Her eyes narrowed. *"Unless, having discovered nothing that way, he is trying to surprise us into some ill-considered action."*

Tarathan's lips curved. *"Flush us out, do you mean? Then we had best not jump at any shadows he casts against the wall."*

They continued to lean side by side, watching a curtain of fine rain advance toward them from the sea. *"And the veiled threat?"* Jehane Mor asked eventually.

*"I would never underestimate the Ilvaine kin."* Tarathan's expression became inward looking, then his eyes met hers. His slow smile was like the gleam of a blade being drawn. *"We are the children of the wind, are we not? We shall ride this storm or fall beneath its fury."*

*"Now why,"* she said, as they turned to go, *"isn't that more of a comfort to me?"*

There were no signs of a storm that evening, when a huge crowd shifted and glittered beneath the glass roof of the Conservatory, the main entertainment hall of the College of Minstrels. Glass doors on all four sides opened to the formal garden and the guests had spilled out into the spring night. Wine was flowing as freely as the food and representatives of the city's princely and merchant houses rubbed shoulders with Masters from the three schools and representatives of the Conclave. Almost everyone from the College was there, since this was their grand event marking the beginning of festival. Masters in scarlet robes and silver chains of rank circulated amongst the guests, while minstrels, troubadours, and jongleurs were all vying to outperform each other at different locations around the hall.

*"But no Haimyr the Golden, that I can see,"* Jehane Mor observed, as she and Tarathan drifted with the tide of the evening. *"Despite staying so close to the College."*

Tarathan's eyes moved over the throng. *"Our Ishnapuri colleagues are not in attendance either. And any Swarm or Derai emissaries appear to have bypassed this gathering."* He moved closer to an attendant holding a tray of the crisp pastries stuffed with seafood, for which Ij was famous. "Naia said there was a party at the Academy this evening as well, and that both Ar's ambassador and one of the merchant houses, the Denuli, are giving receptions."

"The mask makers and caterers," Jehane Mor observed, "must be doing a roaring trade."

"No money having been spared on either," Tarathan agreed, going back for more of the pastries. "These are good," he added unnecessarily.

They continued to circulate through the throng, where the masks surrounding them were all miracles of color and fabric, many lavishly adorned with jewels. The mask wearers appeared anxious to be seen and the behavior designed to ensure this grew more frenetic as the evening progressed, although a series of festivalgoers continued to seek the heralds out. Most wanted news of the other River cities, particularly Terebanth and Ar, or information on the current state of road and river travel.

Jehane Mor would murmur a politeness to overtures such as this, but both she and Tarathan paid more attention to the quiet queries about the situation between Emaln and Sirith. "Surely it will not come to war?" was the most frequently voiced sentiment. Or: "Surely the Patrol would not allow armies on the road, or the river either for that matter? Think of the disruption to trade!" Such comments were often followed by an uneasy glance over the shoulder and the mask wearer bending even closer to murmur: "It should never have gotten to this. This is School business; what can the Masters be thinking of?"

"What indeed?" echoed Jehane Mor, when she and Tarathan had sought refuge by a large palm with stiff fronds that kept all but the bravest away. *"It's true that assassins usually settle matters long before any dispute gets to this stage— unless they've been paid even more* not *to become involved. I wonder who would benefit most from that?"*

Tarathan did not reply, for at that moment the crowd in front of them parted and a large figure, resplendent in gold brocade, lace, and a bear mask wrought in silver, swept down upon them. "My vewy dear fwends," he boomed. "How delighted I am to see you—delighted! Have you come from Tewebanth already over these dweadful woads? So valiant of you in all this rain And my vewy dear fwend, the Ephor Vhiwinal, how is he?"

"Prince Ath," said Jehane Mor, without obvious resignation, and proceeded to answer all his queries with patient courtesy. These continued for some time, as the prince was in an affable mood and concluded by pressing them to attend his masque the following evening. "For there will be fireworks, you know, the finest of the festival, I am determined on *that*." Here the booming voice dropped a note to what was obviously intended as a confidential whisper, but in reality carried to half the Conservatory. "Weally, you must allow me to make you a pwesent of new masks. These Guild hand-me-downs may do vewy well for the stweet, but they are sadly shabby. Not at all the thing for events like this—or what such fine hewalds deserve, eh? And then there's the cwedit of my old fwend the Ephor, since you do so much of his hewaldwy these days. Well, well, I will see what I can do!" And he surged away in a manner reminiscent of the river in flood, hailing friends and well-wishers on all sides.

"Not that he will do anything," remarked Tarathan, when they arrived back at the Guild house in the small hours of the morning. "He merely likes to act the fine prince and dig at his dear friend the Ephor in passing, through us."

"*Very* dear friend." Jehane Mor yawned. "*A true prince, such as Erennis of Ar, would never make the whole world privy to his business, even over such great matters as fireworks and festival masks.*"

They were both more than surprised, therefore, to find a large black box, sealed with the bear badge of the Athiri kin, waiting with their breakfasts the next morning. Naia and the other heralds, including the pair from Ishnapur, were all curious to see the box opened, having already met the finely dressed retainer who delivered it. "Very lofty," observed Naia, "even for an Athiri. I did not know they had become so grand!"

Tarathan shrugged, but Jehane Mor obliged by breaking the seal and lifting the lid. "Well," she said, "it appears that our princely friend is true to his word after all." The conversation around the table died away completely when she lifted out the masks, for these were not even good quality market buys, but marvels of the mask maker's art, shaped into the likeness of an owl and a falcon. The owl mask was white and gray, with real feathers tied into it, while the falcon visage was wild and fierce, barred with black and bronze.

"Wonderful," breathed Ileyra, leaning forward, while Naia touched the falcon mask with one reverent fingertip.

"It looks just like the mountain hawks we used to see in the hills around Enkot town," she said. "Whoever made these masks is a master, no question."

"They are certainly a princely gift," Tarathan agreed. "There'll be no avoiding his masque now."

"Or him," Jehane Mor pointed out with a faint smile, "for he at least will know exactly who we are."

As it happened, Prince Ath did not seem to notice them when they arrived in his ballroom, and made no comment on the style and magnificence of their masks. *"Acquiring some manners, finally, to match the magnitude of his gift,"* said Tarathan, as they worked their way around the perimeter of the dance floor. The ballroom of the Athiri palace, like the minstrels' Conservatory, was located adjacent to formal gardens, with a series of marble terraces and clipped lawns surrounding a sparkling fountain. A constant flow of guests moved between ballroom and terraces as the evening progressed, and the hubbub of conversation, combined with the efforts of musicians and dancers, was deafening. Once again, the heralds scanned the masked crowd for any sign of Derai or Swarm emissaries, but found none.

*"Surprising,"* said Jehane Mor. *"You would think events such as these would attract everyone wanting to build alliances with Ij."*

Other guests intervened before Tarathan could reply, sweeping the heralds away from each other. They only came together again at midnight when the whole gathering was marshaled outside for the fireworks display. Afterward, the festivities would continue until dawn, but the heralds slipped away as soon as the fireworks were done, descending the wide marble steps from the terrace to the lawns below. More fireworks were still shooting skyward from other islands across the city, and Jehane Mor paused to watch a particularly brilliant sequence. "Do you think there is a truly quiet spot anywhere in Ij tonight?" she inquired idly.

"I doubt it." She could hear the amusement in Tarathan's voice, masked by the falcon's visage. "They will carouse the night away in the streets and the lesser halls, just as they do in the palaces."

Below them, smoothly mown lawns sloped away, crisscrossed by wide shrubberies and a network of paths that eventually led to a wrought-iron gate and the river. The paths were lined with sentinel poplars that were just coming into leaf, each one casting a black, elongated shadow across the ground. The statue of a lyre player stood poised in the center of the hillside, gleaming between moonlight and the last of the fireworks. The statue's shadow, like those of the poplars, stretched across the lawn. The air already seemed cooler as the heralds started down the hill, and Tarathan pushed his mask up onto his head. "These things get too hot after a while."

Jehane Mor smiled faintly. "It would not have done to take them off, though, not with half the Masters of Ij present, as well as representatives from most of the old nobility and merchant houses."

"It was quite a gathering," agreed Tarathan. "I saw Count Ambard bail you up as soon as Princess Coreil had finished exchanging pleasantries."

"He did. Where the Athiri lead, the Coreil, and now it seems the Ambardi as well, will follow. The Ambardi may be a rising star, and ambitious with it, but neither the count nor the princess had anything particular to say." Jehane Mor shook her head. "I must have pressed at least a hundred palms tonight, most of them hot and sweaty. The Guild should be suitably grateful."

"The Guild is always grateful," Tarathan replied as they turned onto one of the pebbled, tree-lined walks, "even if it cannot house us properly or provide fashionable masks." He removed the falcon mask altogether and spun it by its strings, which snapped, the mask fluttering to the ground. He stooped to retrieve it while Jehane Mor dodged to avoid stepping on either the mask or him—and a crossbow quarrel whined through the space where her head had been a heartbeat before, slapping into an adjacent poplar trunk.

## 4

## *Dance of Shadows*

*B*oth heralds dropped to the ground as a second bolt flew over Tarathan's bent head and into the tree beside him with the same deadly *thwack*. Together they wormed into the adjoining shrubbery, away from the betraying pebbles of the path. The undergrowth was a broad ribbon of low and medium height bushes, with the statue of the lyre player on its far side. The aromatic scent of the shrubs filled the night air, and the babel of voices, laughter, and music from the ballroom was muted by distance. Everything was beautiful and very still. Jehane Mor, lying flat on damp earth a few paces from Tarathan, strained her ears to hear movement, but the assassins, too, had gone to ground.

Carefully, she strengthened and extended the psychic shield that she had snapped into place as soon as they dived for the undergrowth, making sure it covered both of them. Other than at very close quarters, it should foil even sharply attuned senses, making their bodies appear part moonlight and part black, streaming shadow, while their scent blended with the tang of earth and plants and night. Her pulse slowed and deepened, but Jehane Mor knew that those stalking them would be patient, too. It would do them little good, though, for very soon now, Tarathan's seeking sense would have found out both their numbers and their hiding places.

A few moments later, she felt the brief touch of his mind as he began to ease away from her—and knew that now, the hunters had become the hunted.

Long seconds passed into minutes; the moon slipped behind a narrow bank of cloud and the garden darkened. Jehane Mor heard the faintest whisper of a footfall on grass, a hand stirring a leaf—and then a shadow moved on the far side of the shrubbery, holding a crossbow in silhouette. The cloth-wrapped head turned, searching, and she reinforced her shield until it almost acquired form in the darkness.

The moon was still hidden when the assassin moved again, slipping into the shadow cast by the statue. He was almost past the plinth when Tarathan rose up behind him in one soundless, fluid movement, covering the assassin's mouth with his left hand and driving his dagger up through the back of the neck with his right. The body collapsed backward and Tarathan lowered it silently to the ground. Given the distance between them, Jehane Mor had feared that the shield's protection might waver once Tarathan broke cover—but no more quarrels sang. And now Tarathan had the assassin's crossbow.

The moon floated from behind the cloud, flooding the lawn with silver. A shadow shifted beneath nearby trees, away from the light, and then another slid into the darkness cast by a bank of shrubs at the far end of the walk. The first shadow uttered a soft call, the plaintive cry of a nightbird that ended in a sharp coughing moan as Tarathan shot him through the throat. The second assassin disappeared again.

Two down: Jehane Mor wondered how many more there were. Shield or no shield, given the limited size of the shrubbery the remaining assassins must pinpoint their location soon. Although at least the area was large enough that they could not simply pepper the undergrowth with arrows and rely on their job being done—assuming they had enough crossbowmen for that. She continued to lie still, tense with listening, as an owl hooted from further down the hill.

Another bird answered from a grove near the river as a pebble clicked on the adjoining path. The sound was so slight that without her shield in place, Jehane Mor might not have heard it. No other sound came, but she could sense the assassin now: feel rather than hear or see him move closer as his mind brushed against the perimeter of her psychic shield. She felt him hesitate, reacting to the shield's compulsion to turn away—and Tarathan fired his second crossbow quarrel. The assassin cried out, then fell, howling and thrashing on the edge of the path.

*"Run!"* Tarathan was already up and moving toward her. *"Back up the hill to the palace, since the other two are below us still."*

They ran, dodging between trees and shadows to confuse their attackers, and heard a shout and the rush of feet— followed by curses as the partygoers began pouring onto the terraces, calling out to know who was hurt and what was happening. Jehane Mor sprinted after Tarathan, up the grassy slope and into the lee of the palace as a detachment of armed, Athiri retainers pushed their way down the steps and onto the lawn. A quick look back showed two dark-clad figures veering toward deeper shadow. On the terraces, a woman began to scream, a thin, high, shocking sound.

"Assassins!" another voice shouted. "Send for the Guard!" More Athiri retainers shouldered through the throng and onto the lawn, and the assassins fled, racing back down the hill toward the river while the armsmen moved in cautious pursuit.

*"Do we come out now, outraged but unharmed?"* Jehane Mor asked.

Tarathan shook his head, rewinding the crossbow behind a marble buttress. He still had the falcon mask, she noted; he must have shoved it into his belt when they dived into the shrubbery. *"Too dangerous. I don't trust these people. We need to get back to the Guild House as quickly as we can."*

They turned and walked away, keeping to the shadows cast by the palace as they made for the far side of the complex and the main gates. The gates were guarded, but the retainers there were all staring toward the gardens, intent on the clamor concealed by the palace buildings. *"Even with your shielding, we won't get by. We'd have to pass too close to them. If we go farther along,"* Tarathan nodded toward the stables and their adjoining buildings, *"we can scale the wall."*

They angled away from the gate, hugging the shadow of the palace outbuildings until they saw a gnarled tree growing between the stable and the wall. After a last, careful check, first Jehane Mor and then Tarathan climbed the tree and dropped over into the lane that separated the Athiri palace from the neighboring residence. The walls on either side were high, the lane deserted, but the thoroughfare at its far end was crowded. A fresh burst of fireworks split the night over Landward, and most of those in the busy street craned to look, apparently unaware of any disturbance in the Athiri palace.

Tarathan looked at the crossbow with regret, for although small, they did not have their cloaks and the weapon would be impossible to conceal. *"Time to blend with the crowd, unfortunately,"* he said, and pushed the crossbow over the top of the wall and into the grounds of the adjoining residence. Jehane Mor knotted the broken strings of his now-battered mask together, to make sure it stayed on, before they left the lane and moved into the heart of the festival crowd, strolling toward Westgate. The jostling, brightly colored throng made it difficult for Jehane Mor to hold her concealing shield in place, but she knew the sheer number of people around them would also screen their passage. Reluctantly, she let the shield go.

Although outwardly relaxed, she was aware of the crackling tension in Tarathan, mirroring her own. Her training allowed her to walk slowly, applauding the firebreather on the next street corner and exchanging a jest, rather than an insult, when an intoxicated reveler lurched into her. Beneath the apparent calm, her thoughts churned: she had heard of unlicensed assassinations happening before, but never against heralds. And an unlicensed attack should mean one rogue assassin, not five acting together. For assassins to defy the law in such numbers—she bit her lip and thought uneasily about the unprecedented lack of School activity in the dispute between Emaln and Sirith, a dispute that had now come to the brink of war.

*"Enemy. There."* She followed Tarathan's thought and caught the quick dart of movement, ducking below the roofline of a nearby inn. A moment later, a black-clad figure eased into view again and aimed a crossbow down at them. Both heralds leapt for the protection of an overhanging canopy as others in the crowd saw the assassin and yelled, scattering apart.

Jehane Mor caught at the light breeze with her mind and funneled a gust of dust and festival debris up from the street and into the assassin's face. The crossbow wavered and the heralds were at the corner by the time he recovered. They swung into a narrower street that led to one of the many small canals that threaded the city; this one was wide enough to warrant a wooden bridge, the arch garlanded with festival streamers. Tarathan swung over the parapet and beneath the bridge, steadying Jehane Mor as she slid down beside him. Her camouflaging shield was already back in place as they climbed into the deep shadow of the struts that supported the bridge.

They lay there for a long time, listening to the passing and repassing of footsteps overhead and studying the reflections cast across the water. Two black-clad figures hung head down from either side of the bridge to peer into the darkness underneath, but did not detect the heralds flattened against the struts. *"Three more on the bridge overhead."* Tarathan's mindvoice was dark. *"That makes ten altogether. So far."*

The heralds did not move for a long, bone-chilling half hour after the assassins left. *"And this time,"* Tarathan said, as they eased down onto the damp stone of the canal edge, *"we leave the masks."*

Jehane Mor took off the exquisite owl mask, studying it thoughtfully as she recalled how Prince Ath had boomed out his offer of masks last night, yet had not seemed to notice their new masks at all, earlier in the evening. *"Because he did not send them."*

Tarathan nodded, his eyes gleaming through the darkness as he tied the falcon mask around one of the struts. Jehane Mor tied the owl visage beside it, thinking that some river urchin was going to have a fine disguise for next year's festival. She shook her head. *"It's impossible to know who to suspect when so many heard Prince Ath's offer."*

*"That's easy."* Tarathan untied his distinctive knot of braids and let them fall between his tunic and his coat, turning up the collar. *"We suspect everybody."*

But Jehane Mor was frowning as they resumed their indirect course toward Westgate and the Guild House, keeping to canal banks and unlit lanes. *"Could it have been the minstrel who ordered this?"* she asked. *"We've suspected for some time that the Ilvaine have ties to the School of Assassins, as well as to the Sages and the Minstrels."*

*"Close enough to influence ten assassins to break Ijiri and River law for him?"* Tarathan shook his head. *"It doesn't ring true, especially when he has lived on the Derai Wall for so long. But we can take nothing for granted right now, rule no one out."*

It was almost an hour later, having twisted and ducked across the city, that they turned into the long street where the Guild House stood. The noise of the festival fell away, cut off by the large buildings and high walls that lined the thoroughfare. All the trading houses were silent, unlit except for the legally required lantern above their closed gates. The few residences were quiet as well, closed in behind shuttered windows and barred gates. The heralds did not speak, but their footsteps quickened—until Tarathan stopped, placing a hand on Jehane Mor's arm and drawing her against the nearest wall. Startled, she followed his gaze up the long street to the Guild House gate. The lantern set above it was dark, and although the gate stood ajar, as though waiting for festivalgoers to return, no light or sound flowed out into the midnight street. Everything was utterly still.

# 5

# The Guild House

*"I* don't like it," said Tarathan.

Jehane Mor knew what he meant: the gate should either be closed, or if heralds were still coming and going, then why were there no lights inside? In either case, the gate lantern should be lit. *"If you go around the back,"* she said, *"I'll wait until you're inside, then come in through the front."* She paused. *"Then we shall see."*

*"We shall,"* agreed Tarathan grimly, and was up and over the wall of a nearby house before Jehane Mor had taken her first step into deeper shadow, away from the circle of light cast by the nearest gate lantern. Cautiously, she moved along the street, staying out of the light and keeping her psychic shield up, but nothing disturbed its outer edge. She stopped in another pool of shadow ten paces from the Guild House gate, which gaped at her, silent as an unanswered question.

The minutes lengthened, but Jehane Mor remained motionless until she felt the touch of Tarathan's mind, letting her know he was inside the Guild House grounds. The moment she broke cover, slipping out of the shadows and toward the unlit entrance, she caught movement from the corner of her eye. Her head whipped around as a dense inky blot, with long tendrils trailing beneath it, detached from an eave diagonally opposite the gate. The tendrils exploded toward her in a jet of black matter, and she sprang back, gathering her power to counterattack—only to drop to the ground for the second time that night as an arrow sang.

But the unseen archer was not aiming at her and the arrow flew true, piercing the attacker's ink-black core. The creature shrieked, one long, keening whistle, before folding in on itself and collapsing to the street.

Jehane Mor rose to her feet, taking in the stain of black matter oozing across the cobblestones as the archer jumped neatly down from a vine-hung balcony, half a block away. He fitted another arrow to the string, quartering the street and surrounding roofs with his eyes before he walked toward her, but it was not until he drew near that she recognized Tirorn of the Derai.

"Darkspawn," he said matter-of-factly, as if answering a question, and continued to watch the street. His mouth tightened as his gaze flicked to the ooze on the cobblestones. "A particularly nasty little lurker by nature, and aggressive, too, if it catches you unaware. Smotherer is another name we use, because they wrap their tendrils around a victim's face and neck and choke them to death. We get infestations of them around my home keep, from time to time."

Jehane Mor studied him, seeing no sign of the man who had lounged at his ease beside the Farelle bridge. "Is that why you are here?" she asked. "Hunting this creature?"

His sidelong glance was, she thought, careful. "In part," he replied. "We caught some purported Ijiri traders trying to smuggle them out of the Gray Lands, but unfortunately neither the traders nor the lurkers were prepared to be taken alive. Our Earl decided that we had better find out who wanted lurkers that badly and why—and how many they had already obtained. I have been tracking this one for most of today, but there may well be more about."

She continued to watch him closely. "Tracking it back to its base, or away from it?"

"That," he replied dryly, "was what I was trying to find out."

"But now it's dead," she said, "so you have lost the trail. I am in your debt."

Tirorn shrugged. "Perhaps if you had been a warrior and well armed, I might have let you take your chance. But I know these creatures, and you, Mistress Herald, were at a serious disadvantage with only that toy knife of yours." He looked down at her, and the dim light could not hide the glint in his eyes. "You could take this as repayment for your help at the bridge, but if you do not see the assistance rendered as being of equal kind—" He shrugged again. "Well, I understand that others among our Alliance owe you a debt of honor that has never been repaid."

Jehane Mor concealed her surprise that he knew of that. "We do not regard our service to the Earl of Night five years ago as a debt, if that is what you mean." She followed his gaze up and down the shadowed street. "What are you looking for? More lurkers?"

"Or the black-clad friends that accompanied this one here. There were a great many of them," he said when her head turned sharply toward the Guild House gate, "and they were already leaving when I arrived. I assume they posted the lurker to watch for latecomers, such as yourself." He frowned at the gate. "They may also have left other watchers inside—and you and your companion only have knives."

Jehane Mor's heart was thudding with tension and fear and she had to struggle to keep her herald's mask in place. But her tone was calm. "I need to go in," she said.

"You had better let me go with you." Tirorn moved toward the gate. "You'll need someone to guard your back."

She hesitated, aware that Tarathan was inside the house itself now, although he had not signaled any alarm. "I didn't think Derai involved themselves in the affairs of others?"

"I involved myself when I shot the lurker." The look Tirorn shot her was searching. "Are you ready for this?"

Her answer was to step through the gate. At first she thought the yard was empty, with just the usual mix of moonlight and shadow falling across the cobbles. Then she saw that there were darker, more solid shadows sprawled in corners and fallen across doorways. Silently, she knelt by the first body, gazing down into the blank face and unseeing eyes.

"A friend?" asked Tirorn, who had remained standing, intent on the darkened apertures of house and stable.

Jehane Mor shook her head. "Someone I knew slightly, from chance meetings on the road. But a comrade, nonetheless." She looked around at the other bodies, slumped in death, and was aware of a sense of unreality, as though in a moment the corpses would stir back into life again and sit up, laughing at the success of their festival jest. She and Tarathan had known danger many times on the road, had encountered brigands and murderers and been pursued through wild country by those sworn to vengeance, but this—this was the Guild House in Ij, where heralds had been protected by law for centuries.

The ivy that grew across the stable's roof and wall stirred as she rose to her feet. Tirorn's bow came up, then checked as a small owl emerged. "It's an eave owl," Jehane Mor told him. "They're sacred to Imulun, the Mother Goddess."

Slowly, he lowered the bow. "Your patron deity?"

Again she shook her head. "The Guild serves Seruth, the lightbringer, guardian of journeys."

Tirorn nodded, but remained silent. And why, thought Jehane Mor, should the gods of the River mean anything to him, when the Derai had their alien pantheon of Nine? She pushed this thought aside, striving to center herself in the reality of timber and stone and ivy. But the stink of death and blood was everywhere, blunting her senses.

"Where is your friend?" Tirorn asked finally. "What is he doing?"

"Hunting," Jehane Mor said. She walked across the courtyard to the main door of the house, which had been forced open. A knot of bodies lay across the threshold, and this time not all of them wore gray.

"Here," said Tirorn, "the attackers lost their element of surprise."

Jehane Mor said nothing, for the herald dead still bore

no weapons other than their daggers; it was only on journeys outside the River lands that the Guild went armed. She pulled the two black-clad bodies inside the door aside and found Naia's body beneath them. A knife was buried hilt deep in her chest, and Jehane Mor put a hand over the housekeeper's eyes, closing them. "I don't think there's anyone left alive," she said, and kept her tone cool as water, giving nothing away.

"Not that I've been able to find." Tarathan emerged from the darkness at the end of the hall, wiping the blade of his knife clean as he joined them.

The Derai's gaze flicked to the blade, then back to Tarathan's face. "So they did leave watchers behind. Are you sure you got them all?"

"Yes. Two assassins." Tarathan sheathed the knife and asked the question the Derai would expect, although he already knew the answer through the mindlink with Jehane Mor. "What brings you here?"

"Hunting a Darkswarm minion," Tirorn replied. "It was working with the assassins who killed your comrades."

Tarathan frowned. "Swarm minions in alliance with the School of Assassins. That's not good."

"Must it be the School?" Jehane Mor asked, arguing against her own foreboding. The implications, for Ij and the River, of the School and its Masters overturning centuries of precedent and pursuing unlicensed vendetta against anyone, let alone the Guild, were profoundly disturbing. The alternative, that a sizable part of the School had turned rogue and declared their defection so publicly, was almost as worrying. *"How could this have been building,"* she asked silently, *"and no one heard anything, no one have known?"*

Tarathan stared down at Naia. "They don't call it the Secret Isle for no reason." The edge to his voice could have quarried stone. "What if the School no longer wishes to be one amongst Three, and the followers of Kan have decided to come out of the shadows and rule alone? Who would stand in the way of their ambition?"

"All those who have held the River lands together since

the days of the Cataclysm," Jehane Mor answered softly, "including the Guild of Heralds. But if this is the work of the School, and not just rebel elements within it, then we dare not go to the Conclave."

"No," said Tarathan. "We must flee Ij. The rest of the River must be warned."

"If this strike is not already one of many, up and down its length," she said, expressing her deepest fear. *"What of our people who may still be abroad in the city?"* she added silently. *"There were no other mindspeakers here, so we cannot warn them that way."*

*"And the empathy bond is only between pairs."* Tarathan's mindtone was grim. *"Warning the Guild is the priority now, but we cannot do that via mindspeech either. The nearest pair with any mindspeaking strength is in Ar, which is too far for even you or I to reach."*

"We'll need horses," Jehane Mor said, as though the silent exchange had not taken place. "But Naia sent ours to the livery stable near the riverport. We'd have to cross half the city to reach them."

"They're too obvious anyway," said Tarathan. "Who else rides Emerian grays?" His gaze swept the hall and courtyard and his mouth tightened. "But there should be a stableful of mounts here, all of them without riders now."

Tirorn shook his head. "I suspect your enemies cleared the stable. They took a string of horses with them when they left."

They crossed to the stable anyway, but found it completely empty. "Thorough indeed," observed Tarathan dryly.

"You may be less noticeable on foot," Tirorn said, clearly thinking out loud. "Especially if you change your clothes."

"And we have money," Jehane Mor added. "We can hire horses on the other side of the river."

Outside, an owl hooted in alarm and they heard the heavy, startled beat of its wings, crossing the yard. Tarathan jerked his head toward the loft and they fled up the ladder and between the stacked, sweet-smelling bales of hay. Moonlight filtered through a small skylight and there was an opening, partly covered with ivy, that overlooked the yard. It would be used, Jehane Mor knew, for bringing the hay bales in. Tirorn made to pull the ladder up behind them, but Tarathan stopped him. "It's never pulled up," he whispered, and the Derai nodded as the owl called again, mournful, from the house.

Jehane Mor knelt beside the opening, peering down. The gate was still half closed, but she could see sparks of light from the street, and a moment later a flood of black-clad figures poured into the courtyard. There must be at least thirty of them, she calculated, most with crossbows held ready to fire. Moving swiftly, they fanned out toward the house and down the narrow alley that led to the backyard. *"The dancers in shadow hunt in force,"* she observed, as Tarathan eased to the other side of the opening. Tirorn crouched at her shoulder and she held up a hand for his benefit, cautioning silence.

The knot of assassins in the courtyard broke up as another black-clad figure stalked through the now fully open gate. His mask was a blank face of Kan, the eyes dark hollows, and the hilt of his sword jutted forward, gleaming in the torchlight. A taller figure stepped through in his wake and moved to stand against the wall, away from the light that flared across a steel helm fashioned into the likeness of some fantastic bird of prey. He wore armor, too, Jehane Mor noted, and like the helm it was in a style she had seen before.

"Darkswarm." Tirorn breathed the single word into her ear.

Jehane Mor nodded. *"In company with a Master of the School,"* she said to Tarathan.

The Master looked slowly around the courtyard and then moved forward, spurning a body with his boot. One of the assassins who had gone into the house came over to him. "All within are dead, Master." He spoke quietly, but his words carried on the night air. "Even our own, left behind to catch stragglers."

The blank mask turned and the assassin stepped quickly

back. "Who did this?" the Master asked. "How did our own die?"

"They were killed with a knife," the assassin replied, "which suggests another herald. Their bodies are still warm."

"The killer can't have gone far, then. Yet there were to be none left alive, to report on what happened here." The Master swung toward the armed figure in the shadows. "You said that your watcher at the gate would make sure of that—but it, too, we find slain."

The voice that answered was cold and dry as dust. "By a Derai arrow."

"Your ancient enemy." Acid touched the Master's calm tone. "Who now hunt in our Ijiri streets. You also said those Derai who come here have no powers, not even minor ones like those of heralds, so how could they overcome your dark watcher?"

The bird-of-prey visor moved, catching a spark of torch-light. "The watchers are useful, but not intelligent. And one alone may always be surprised."

The waiting assassin cleared his throat. "Could these Derai have slain our people, as well as the watcher? What if they've made an alliance with the Guild?"

"What if, indeed," the Master said softly. "You are sure the house is clear?" The assassin nodded as the Master's masked gaze swept the courtyard. "Search every inch of the grounds as well: unearth every hiding place. Let's make certain the killer is not lurking here before we beat the streets. But be quick—the sands are running out."

*"The roof."* In the loft, Tarathan pointed to the skylight and Jehane Mor nodded, hoping that it was not held down by the mass of ancient, twisted ivy that covered the roof. The Darkswarm warrior, she reflected, as they crept toward the skylight, had to be a danger given the powers she had seen his kind use on the Wall of Night, five years before. No obvious aura surrounded the one in the courtyard, but the ability to detect others' powers often depended on familiarity with their weaves. And that could work either for or against her now, depending on how much the Swarm knew about Haarth magic.

Tarathan was half darkness, half moving shadow ahead of her, and she sensed rather than heard Tirorn following as she strengthened her concealing shield. She focused on making it unobtrusive, part of the natural sounds and movement of the night, and used a weave based on Emerian Oakward lore. Very few in the River, even other heralds, would know of that—or so Jehane Mor hoped as she extended the shield's rim as far out from the stable as she dared.

*"Search around the house first,"* she willed through it. *"Come here last, if at all."* Cold minds, intent on their killing quest, brushed against the perimeter of her awareness and she drew back, letting the edge of the shield dissipate into the rustle of ivy leaves and frayed cobwebs beneath the stable eaves.

Tarathan stopped beneath the skylight and reached up. For a moment Jehane Mor thought the skylight was going to stick, but then it slid soundlessly aside, revealing a narrow cavity beneath the ivy. "You first," Tarathan said to her, and Tirorn knelt, offering his gloved hands as a step. Jehane Mor's brows lifted, but there was no time for hesitation so she put one foot on his locked palms and pulled herself up, slithering beneath the ivy on elbows and stomach. The vines were draped between two gables, with just enough space, close to each gable end, to lie concealed—so long as one hugged the roof. She crabbed sideways, away from the skylight, to make room for the others. The long bow slid through first and then Tirorn followed, reaching down to help Tarathan, who lowered the skylight back into place.

Side by side, they lay between the ivy and the roof. Jehane Mor concentrated her power of concealment on the skylight, covering it with an illusion of the timber planking that formed the stable ceiling. A searcher would have to look very hard to notice any discrepancy, or already know that a skylight was meant to be present.

The scrape of the loft ladder, when it finally came, was startlingly loud. No other sound followed, but Jehane Mor could almost see the assassin's head turning, staring hard into every shadow. The waiting silence lengthened—then snapped as an owl swooped toward the loft opening, before hooting alarm and flapping sharply away. The hoot was answered by a smothered curse as a floorboard creaked, then a voice called down into the courtyard: "Eave owl, Master, but there's probably more than one. Shall we kill them?"

"Why waste time?" The acid was back in the Master's voice. "Or risk being cursed by Imulun's priesthood for our pains?" The unspoken epithet, *fool*, hung on the air. "What else is there, besides the owls?"

The listening silence returned. "Nothing," the assassin said at last. "Just hay, and I've run a sword through that. I'll go through this window and onto the roof, check that, too."

"No need." The Master was crisp. "Lien and Miro have just gone over the roof of the house and can see the stable from there. They say it's clear, too, so we must spread the net wider. I want this quarry found."

"The night is not yet over." The Darkswarm warrior's voice carried clearly to the three beneath the ivy. "We still have time."

"It's not the day I fear." The Master's tone was dispassionate. "Ij is a city of many powers, and our work must be done before the others realize what we are about."

"Together, we are stronger than these others." The cold, dry voice was assured. "Do you doubt us, when we have already delivered those you thought incorruptible into your hands?" Again the small cough that might have been humor. "The Guild House in Ishnapur will wait a long time for the return of its own."

"It is a very long way from Ishnapur to Ij—especially for the unwary." Something in the Master's tone sent a chill down Jehane Mor's spine. "Bringing down the heralds will send a message that no one is beyond our reach. But they must all be dead. No one must escape the net."

"Especially," the dry voice said, "the two from Terebanth. That was our bargain."

A whistle shrilled, piercing with command, and Jehane Mor guessed that the Master was calling the rest of his followers from the house. "Spread out," she heard him order.

"Search the city until you have found and killed every herald, but most particularly the two who wear the masks of owl and falcon. Their bodies you bring to me; any others can go into the canals."

"And the Derai?" the Darkswarm warrior asked.

Jehane Mor could almost hear the shrug in the Master's voice. "We'll kill any who get in our way."

There was a sound that might have been the murmur of voices and the whisper of departing feet, or then again, it could just have been the wind. The night around the Guild House stable grew very quiet after it fell away, troubled only by the soft, even breathing of the three who lay hidden on the roof. They lay so still that eventually an eave owl glided close overhead, as though they had become one with the ivy and the night.

Jehane Mor continued to hold her shield, aware that this was the danger time, when one person or a small group, suspicious or simply cannier than the rest, returned for another look—or perhaps had never left but waited as they did, watching and listening. She felt Tarathan's cautious probing for any such foes and waited for his indication that it was safe to move. Tirorn, too, was patient, but she remembered the Derai Wall from five years before and was not surprised that a warrior who patroled its passes knew how to wait.

All the same, it felt like a very long time before Tarathan raised the skylight slightly and peered through the gap. Again he waited, before lifting the hatch clear and dropping neatly into the loft, his knife ready in his hand as he landed. Nothing moved, and by the time Tirorn and Jehane Mor descended he was at the loft window. "All clear," he said, as they joined him.

"Then let's go," said Tirorn. "They've already come back once. Sooner or later someone is bound to return again."

"First," said Tarathan, "we need to find clothes that are not herald gray, and any money left in the house. We may need more than we have on us just to get out of Ij."

Tirorn looked quizzical. "Bribes?" he inquired, not without irony, and Tarathan shrugged.

"We don't know if this is one Master acting alone or the entire School, or how far the tentacles of this Darkswarm alliance reach into the families and institutions of Ij."

"If it is the School," Jehane Mor said, "then they will go deep. We shall have to travel fast and far." Silently, she added: *"And the Darkswarm warrior asked for our deaths, in particular."*

Tirorn considered her, his expression unreadable through moonlight and shadow, and she wondered how much of the conversation in the courtyard he had understood, how good a grasp of the River speech he really had. "Are you sure there'll be money to find?" he asked finally, as Tarathan started down the ladder and they both moved to follow. "If these assassins are like soldiers, they'll have looted any valuables they find."

"Naia always kept hidden money for emergencies," Jehane Mor replied, descending ahead of him. "The assassins may not have had time to discover it."

They did not speak again as they skirted the courtyard dead or picked their way through the black and gray shadows of the house, with its fallen bodies and the wreckage from the assassins' attack. Tirorn stopped to keep watch at the end of the long upstairs hall, by a window overlooking the courtyard, while the heralds went to Naia's rooms. These were sparsely furnished and largely undisturbed; the assassins must have done all their killing before they penetrated this far into the house. Jehane Mor compressed her lips, trying not to think of the caretaker in the context of the unadorned room: a slight, straightforward woman with an Enkot burr to her speech.

Tarathan knelt and pulled out drawers from a heavy chest, searching in the cavity behind them with careful fingers. *"It's particularly useful, at times like these, to have a keen seeker's sense. Ah."* He drew his hand back, opening a small but bulging leather bag. *"Trust Naia to be thorough. There's a good mix in this—Ijiri gold crowns as well as copper pennies and River marks."*

*"And fortunately for us, she wasn't sworn to the gray. She*

*has plenty of street clothes here.*" Jehane Mor held up a tunic and leggings with a long cloak, their colors indeterminate in the dim light. "*I can wear these, but there isn't much for you. You'll have to make do with just a change of cloak.*" She rummaged further and emerged with a dark cloak and two masks. "*Imulun and Seruth. Not very imaginative, but half the country folk will be wearing them, too.*"

Tarathan swung the dark cloak on and raised the hood. "*My hands ache for my swords and a bow. I have a feeling, a nasty twitch between my shoulder blades, that we'll need them before the night is out.*"

"*We have other ways of defending ourselves,*" Jehane Mor's mind voice was quiet.

Tarathan shook his head. "*I had thought of using the Gate of Dreams to reach those in the Guild with abilities near to ours, but we know too little of what powers the Darkswarm have deployed here. They may well be stronger than us, as some were on the Wall—*" He broke off, shrugging. "*The more we use our power, the greater the risk. Besides, you remember what the Derai were like about their own who had power. We don't want this Tirorn deciding that we need to be filled full of arrows.*"

He took a step toward the door head as they both heard the Derai's swift footstep in the hall. "Lurkers!" Tirorn said crisply. "A pair this time. They're just floating through the gateway now, but may well have allies with them."

# 6

# *Facestealer*

They ran, down the hallway and along another until they reached the steep, winding stair that led to the back door of the house. They fled down as quietly as they could and out through the kitchen garden to the rear wall. Tirorn hauled himself up and over and the heralds followed, dropping down into the backyard of another house and keeping to the darkest shadows as they ran across. After that there was a series of yards and gardens until finally they came out onto another quiet street, with the sound of festival revelry close by. Tarathan adjusted his Seruth mask. "Time to rejoin the crowds."

"And head where?" Tirorn asked. He slipped his bow onto his shoulder, beneath the piled folds of his cloak, which Jehane Mor did not think would fool anyone who looked closely. "You'd be surprised," the Derai said, correctly interpreting her lack of expression as she studied the cloak arrangement, "how little people who are drunk and absorbed in their own celebrations notice about those around them."

"No," said Jehane Mor. "I wouldn't." She looked at Tarathan. "North Gate is less direct. We'd have to double a long way back through the forest on the other side, but for that same reason, they may not watch it as closely as the river port or the Road Gate."

"I'd be surprised if they don't have watchers on the Main Road and further upriver as well, but we'll worry about that once we're safely across." Tarathan looked at the Derai. "And you? I don't know how much you understood of what was said, back at the Guild house, but threats were made against your people here."

Tirorn shrugged. "My people can take care of themselves. Our lodgings are in the northern part of the city anyway, on the island called The Sleeve, so I'll go with you as far as the northern gate. Since," he added, with an ironic glance at Jehane Mor, "I have involved myself in your business."

"Without being asked," she murmured, and he smiled faintly, acknowledging the echo of Orth's words from the Farelle bridge.

They joined with a small group at the end of the street and were gradually drawn into the main current of festivalgoers. There were still singers and dancers going from square to square, but many people were moving more slowly and most were drunk, lurching along the streets and occasionally bursting into song or picking fights. Behind her mask, Jehane Mor wrinkled her nose at the whiff of vomit and urine beneath the smells of sweat, and food, and expensive Ijiri perfume.

Eventually the flow of the crowd split into two streams, one turning east for the Minstrels' Isle while the other carried on toward The Sleeve and the lantern-boat races held on that island's southern side. This second stream thinned as it entered the maze of narrow streets surrounding an old market quarter, and Jehane Mor began to notice furtive movement in side alleys and along overhanging rooftops. Tarathan watched these movements, too, without seeming to, and Tirorn fingered the bow beneath his cloak. "Is this for us?" he asked Tarathan, speaking from the side of his mouth.

The herald shook his head. "I don't think it can be. There are just too many of them, and not everyone on the move is wearing black."

"The guards, too," Jehane Mor said, as six jogged through

the crossroads in front of them. "I've seen more in the last ten minutes than we have the entire night."

Tirorn took another casual survey of their surrounds. "Concentrating their forces," he said, almost below his breath. "But why?"

Tarathan shook his head, his eyes flicking from street, to rooftop, to alley. "I don't know. But staying with the crowd is still our best chance."

They let the throng carry them onto a bridge that crossed another narrow canal, but turned at the thud of running feet and a horn blare from behind them. Along the canal, open shutters slammed closed as a grim-faced detachment of the city guard pounded toward the bridge. It was not clear who or what they were pursuing, but Tarathan nodded casually toward an overhanging rooftop and the shadow that dropped back behind the ridgepole. Tirorn grunted. "Sloppy lot," he said, as they pressed against the side of the bridge to let the guards pass. "Or they're not concerned about being seen."

"Either way," Tarathan replied, "they'll not live to make old assassins."

As if in answer to his comment, there was another rush of footfalls, this time across the tiled rooftops as five, black-clad figures raced toward the bridge. They did not stop or even pause to look down but leapt the gap above the bridge and ran up the roof slope on the other side. The shadow that had ducked behind the ridge sprang up and away and other black-clad figures joined it, fleeing south. The pursuers blew a series of short, sharp whistle blasts and more assassins appeared, racing along another set of roofs to intercept those in flight. Overhead, shutters began to open again.

"Oi! You with the bow! What d'you think you're doing?" Four of the guard contingent had backtracked toward the bridge, their leader glaring at Tirorn. "Weapons are forbidden on the streets during festival!"

The heralds and Tirorn looked at each other. *"But not, apparently, on rooftops,"* Jehane Mor observed.

*"Not his problem,"* Tarathan replied. "Run!"

They took to their heels again amidst a shout from the

guards, followed by the immediate bray of their horn. Soon the streets around them were full of guards, with more horns sounding. On the rooftop, the assassins abandoned their initial pursuit and came streaming after them.

"Not good," muttered Tirorn. "Oh, not good!" He had flung the cloak aside and was unslinging his bow as he ran, but a quick glance back showed Jehane Mor that the assassins were closing and had their crossbows ready. Shielding, she reflected, would be useless here, and she channeled air instead, funneling it beneath the roof tiles. Terra-cotta and slate began to slip and slide so that the assassins' teetered, desperately trying to keep their balance as tiles flew off the roofs like missiles, crashing onto the street and the pursuing guards.

*"Unsubtle, but effective!"* said Tarathan, as they fled around a corner. "Ah!"

A small band of bravos was gathered on the street corner ahead of them, all heavily armed and wearing the livery of the Athiri. "Now what—" began Jehane Mor, breaking off as the men turned their way. Shouting in excitement, they fumbled for their weapons until Tirorn loosed an arrow that flew past the leader's face. The others fell back, their excitement evaporating, but Tarathan continued running toward them. Jehane Mor swirled a wind ahead of him, spiraling dust and rubbish into the Athiri retainers' faces. The bravos batted it aside and shouted again, not at the fugitives this time but at a small band of green-and-black clad soldiery that was advancing along a side street.

*"Katrani colors!"* exclaimed Jehane Mor as they fled past the Athiri unhindered. *"This is street war."*

As if to underline her words, another band of assassins appeared from behind the Katrani soldiery. Completely ignoring the imminent clash between the retainers of Ath and Katran, they swarmed up onto the rooftops and began firing on the pursuing assassins. *"No,"* Tarathan said shortly, *"this is mayhem."* He glanced back over his shoulder to where the city guard was trying to separate the Athiri and Katrani factions. "Time to make ourselves very scarce," he said out loud.

"No one's paying attention to us anymore," replied Jehane Mor, "but getting to the North Gate may be even more of a challenge than we thought."

"It's a running fight," Tirorn said calmly, looking back, "but at least it's moving in the right direction."

Jehane Mor risked another look back herself and saw that he was correct: the Athiri retainers were retreating down one of the side streets, and the roof battle, too, seemed to be moving away. She shook her head. *"Faction war—and division within the School, which answers one question. But Ijiri faction war has never touched the Guild before."*

*"Times change."* Tarathan's mindvoice was flat. *"And not necessarily for the better."*

The clamor fell behind as they progressed northward and into a series of cobbled lanes where houses and shops gave way to granaries and warehouses. They were close to the bridge that led to The Sleeve and were just starting to breathe more easily when Tirorn stopped and spun around, peering intently into the darkness. "Lurker!" he said tersely. "I can always sense the vermin, even at a distance. We need to get off the street."

Jehane Mor's eyes flicked from the silent, shuttered buildings to Tarathan, who hesitated, then nodded at one of the warehouses. "In there," he said.

"Round the back," said Tirorn, and Tarathan nodded. A few yards further on they found an alley that led to the rear of the warehouse, but the narrow back door was locked. Tirorn tested the ground level shutters until he found one loose, prying it open with his knife so they could clamber through. "Upstairs," he said, while Tarathan secured the shutters behind them. "We need to see what's happening out there."

The building was stuffy and the darkness made it difficult to see, but eventually they found the wide wooden stairs that went up three flights, creaking loudly at every other step. "Let's hope no one's here," Jehane Mor said.

*"No one is,"* Tarathan told her, as they reached the topmost floor. Large bales were piled across the wooden floor, and hoists and gantries hung from the ceiling. Very quietly,

Tirorn chinked one of the shutters open, and Jehane Mor and Tarathan went to its other side, all pressed sidelong, peering down into the street.

A clot of blackness, filaments trailing, drifted above the cobblestones, followed closely by a small knot of assassins and the Darkswarm warrior from the Guild House. The assassins seemed edgy, hugging the walls and checking every doorway and entrance before moving past. Several of them kept their eyes and crossbows fixed on the rooftops, but the attention of the watchers, like the warrior's below them, was focused on the lurker.

Tarathan stiffened, leaning forward as if to see more clearly. After a moment he turned to Jehane Mor, his mind-voice terse: *"Look at their faces."*

The small band was directly beneath them now, caught in the light thrown by the lantern above the warehouse door. Most of the faces it illuminated were blackened, or concealed by hoods or wrapped cloth, but one of the hoods had slipped back, framing a face that Jehane Mor recognized. Only that morning, she thought, with a queer sick feeling in the pit of her stomach, the Ishnapuri heralds had sat at breakfast with them and Ileyra had exclaimed over the gift of the owl and falcon masks. Now she stood in company with the Darkswarm warrior and the renegade assassins. Jehane Mor saw Tarathan's hand clench white, and Tirorn looked from one to the other of them, clearly sensing their tension. But he asked no questions, only fingered the string of his bow.

Three storeys below, the Ishnapuri herald turned, looking all around as though their recognition had caught at her attention. Lanternlight and shadow rippled across her face, and both the Darkswarm warrior and the lurker turned as one to watch her. The three in the warehouse stood very still, scarcely daring to breath, and Jehane Mor felt an icy power reach out, sweeping the night. She slipped away from it, letting her mind blend into the musty dark surrounding them, at one with the shadowy mass of piled bales and the outline of hoists overhead—and let that sense of oneness shield them all.

Down on the street, Ileyra's upturned face rippled again before she shrugged and the whole party moved on, the lurker floating ahead of them. The three in the warehouse relaxed, until Tarathan held up an imperative hand. "Wait!" he whispered.

Peering out from a different angle, Jehane Mor saw figures creeping close behind roof eaves and parapet walls. These newcomers, too, were hooded and cloaked, but the bows they carried were long, like Tirorn's. The leader signaled, and the others rose as one and loosed a volley of arrows into the band on the ground. The lurker was hit first and imploded with the same keening whistle that Jehane Mor recalled from earlier in the night. One of the assassins fell to his knees, grasping at the arrow that had pierced his chest, and the Darkswarm warrior shouted. An arrow sprouted in the mail of his upper arm as he spun around, pushing Ileyra back along the street. The Derai continued to shoot as the ambushed party broke and fled. Another two assassins fell, arrows in their backs, but the rest were getting away, Ileyra amongst them.

The Darkswarm warrior was not so fortunate. A second arrow took him in the back of the knee as he ran, and he reeled, lurching across the street. The Derai followed up with a swift, concentrated volley as the warrior stumbled along the wall. Several arrows bounced off his armor, but one buried itself in the back of his neck, punching its way through the fine metal coif.

The warrior fell, sprawling face forward in the street as the ambushers came down from their rooftop. Slowly and deliberately, one of the Derai walked toward the fallen warrior. His build was as massive as the bow he carried, and Jehane Mor and Tarathan exchanged a glance, recognizing Orth from the Farelle bridge. The Derai circled the fallen Darkswarm, slinging his bow over his shoulder and drawing a long, wickedly curved knife. He waited a moment longer then moved forward in one swift movement, wrenching the helmet off the fallen warrior's head, jerking his head up by the hair and cutting his throat.

"Just to be sure," said Tirorn. "Now, being Orth, he'll mutilate the rest of the face and take the ears as a trophy."

The huge Derai did just as Tirorn had predicted before letting the head fall forward again onto the pavement. He looked down at his fallen enemy for a moment longer, kicked the body, then walked back to his comrades.

"Two out of three," said Tirorn softly, then shuddered. "But did you mark the third, the facestealer, who got away? Lurkers are one thing, but a facestealer! The Swarm must have invested a great deal in this alliance with the assassins."

"I saw no facestealer," said Tarathan grimly, "only a turn-coat Ishnapuri herald."

Tirorn shook his head. "You must have seen the way the woman's face rippled. On the Derai Wall, we know that as the mark of a facestealer. They are part of the Darkswarm elite and can shape themselves to the face and form of others, both beasts and people—but they have to kill the victim first. The rippling indicates that a facestealer is no longer holding fast to the change, either because the form has been held too long and the spell is wearing thin, or because the facestealer plans to abandon it anyway."

"Are you sure?" Tarathan asked slowly. "What we saw was the face and form of a herald from Ishnapur, called Ileyra."

"And the Darkswarm warrior did say that they had turned those thought incorruptible," Jehane Mor pointed out.

"No one is incorruptible," Tirorn said shortly, "not once they fall into the power of the Swarm. But in the House of Swords we still learn all the signs that identify Swarm minions, even though we may never encounter them." He paused, frowning. "It's possible that the herald you met was still this Ileyra and that the facestealer only attacked her today. But given the strength of the tremors passing over her face—" He shrugged. "It's more likely that the attack took place days ago, perhaps on the way here, or even in Ishnapur itself."

"'It is a long way from Ishnapur to Ij, especially for the unwary,'" quoted Tarathan.

Inwardly, Jehane Mor reviewed every aspect of their dealings with the Ishnapuri heralds. "We have to assume that Salan, Ileyra's brother, has been compromised as well— which fits with something else." In her memory, she stepped into the Guild house courtyard again, walking between slumped bodies to the front door. "I was surprised there had been little or no resistance to the assassin attack until the killers reached the house itself. I put that down to the advantage of surprise, but now—" She paused. "What if there was no surprise? What if the heralds in the yard knew their murderers and thought them friends?"

"Treachery," Tarathan said heavily. "Or facestealers. Either explanation fits." He stepped away from the window. "But it changes nothing for us. We still need to get out of the city. What about you?" he asked Tirorn. "Will you rejoin your friends now?"

"Not just yet." Tirorn slipped his bow back onto his shoulder. "They seem to be managing well enough without me. Besides, I've never cared much for Orth when the bloodlust is on him."

"Not a gentle enemy," agreed Tarathan, heading back to the stairs.

Tirorn's smile was tight. "No Derai is a gentle enemy, but Orth is in a category all to himself."

"You don't like him," said Jehane Mor.

The Derai had started down the stairs, following Tarathan, but now he glanced back. "Orth excels at killing and that has its uses on the Wall. He is also both blood and sword kin to me, so liking does not come into it. We are bound together, and it is because of that and Orth's excesses, as much as the lurkers, that we are here."

"How so?" she asked.

Tirorn shrugged. "Orth's hatreds are not limited to the Swarm, but extend, amongst others, to our own priestly kind."

"I thought all the warrior Derai were of that mind," Tarathan commented, as they descended another flight.

"Not all," said Tirorn, "and certainly not to the same

extent. We had a civil war long ago, which some see now as warrior against priest, but the House of Swords did not stand with the other warrior Houses at that time. Since then, we have always been far less bitter toward those with old powers. But there are still some whose antagonism is as virulent as anything you would expect from either Night or Blood. Particularly Blood," he added, half under his breath. "Orth is one such, but our Earl is not. He holds to Sword's longtime treaty with the House of Peace, which is the smallest of the priestly Houses and our near neighbor. Peace is an order of healers, followers of the god Meraun, and has no place for warriors, so they get all those born to our House with priestly powers and we get all theirs who have none. Their healers serve us as required, and in return we patrol their boundaries as well as our own and provide armed escorts for their people whenever they travel." He shrugged. "The arrangement preserves the Blood Oath that binds the Derai, and keeps our dealings with each other at arm's length."

Tarathan paused as they reached the ground floor, his eyes checking the shadows. "But that does not sit well with Orth?"

"No," said Tirorn. "He sees this approach to the Oath as lax." His voice turned grim. "Unfortunately, I misread the depth of his hatred and gave him command of a company that was to escort a contingent of healers from Peace's Keep of Bells to the Towers of Morning. I knew his brutality, but had no reason to believe that he could hold the honor of our Earl and House so cheap."

"What happened?" asked Jehane Mor softly. They had reached the door and Tarathan had his hand on the bolt, but despite their own danger, or perhaps because of it, they were both caught in the spell of Tirorn's story.

Tirorn rested one gauntleted hand on the doorjamb, speaking with his face half turned aside. "The priests had a small escort from Bells to the rendezvous with Orth, but were ambushed by darkspawn not far from that point. One of the escort managed to reach Orth, but he refused to move until it was certain he would arrive too late. Everyone in the

Keep of Bells' company died. Naturally, Orth hunted down and slew every one of the ambushers, slowly and painfully in most cases, I'm told. A highly satisfactory outcome for Orth in all respects." Tirorn's fingers moved restlessly against the jamb. "But not for our Earl. He held all our lives forfeit for the stain on his own honor and the integrity of our House."

"But—I thought you weren't even there," Jehane Mor protested.

"No" said Tirorn, "but I gave the command to Orth, a grievous error of judgment. And we are blood and sword kin, as I said, each bound in honor to the actions and deeds of the other. The Earl would have had all our lives, except that the House of Peace intervened. It seems that the Law of Meraun forbids the taking of life, which I suppose explains their arrangement with us. Anyway, their High Priest, who is also their Earl, sent a message saying that enough Derai blood had already been spilt and we should be required to atone for Orth's misdeed instead, cleansing our stained honor by that means. So here we are, on this quest to hunt down the lurkers and flush out whoever is using them." He grinned, with a flash of genuine humor. "Of course, our own Earl made it clear that he would be perfectly happy if none of us ever returned."

"I take it you don't share that view," Tarathan said.

"Not entirely," admitted Tirorn. "I do accept that we have to set right the blight on our honor, but I have always questioned the merit of death, whether by execution or ritual suicide, as a means of setting such misdeeds right. What does it mean in the end but one less Derai to keep the watch? And there are not so many of us now that we can afford to throw lives away."

"So you would like to bring everyone home safely?" Jehane Mor asked. "Even Orth?"

"Even Orth," agreed Tirorn, "although that, in the end, may prove the greatest stain on my own honor."

"I'm surprised you dare let him out of your sight." Tarathan was very dry.

"I have made his limits perfectly plain, both to himself

and the rest of our kin," said Tirorn evenly, "and he has no doubt of the consequence if he exceeds them. That should keep him in check for at least one night without my actual presence." Now he did look at them directly and his expression was sardonic. "But I don't think I'd like to test Orth by reintroducing him to you. He's better than any wyr hound at smelling out the sort of power you've been using." He smiled a little as Jehane Mor's brows went up. "We have been trained from birth to hunt the Darkswarm on the Wall of Night. We may not have power ourselves, but we learn to recognize its taint and stay so still that those who rely on it miss our presence—until it's too late."

Jehane Mor nodded, remembering how neither she nor Tarathan had detected his presence before he shot the first lurker. "We have been careless," she said. And then, lightly, to Tarathan: "But he hasn't shot us full of arrows yet."

Tirorn frowned. "I am not Orth, Jehane Mor. Besides, I already knew that at least one, but probably both of you, had what we would call priestly powers."

"From when we came to the Wall five years ago," she said, recalling that he had alluded to their service to Night previously.

He nodded. "The story's not well known, but the House of Night's new Commander visited the Keep of Swords a year or two back. She brought a veteran called Sarus with her, who had served on joint patrols with our own people in the past. He and his former comrades got to drinking and telling stories as soldiers do, which is how I heard of your venture into the Old Keep of Winds. I'm quite sure," Tirorn added, as dry as Tarathan, "that we only heard a censored account. But I remembered your names, mainly because outsiders rarely figure in any Derai tale."

"And I introduced myself at the Farelle bridge." Jehane Mor was thoughtful.

"Even Sarus's restricted account made it clear that you undertook a great service for the House of Night, which is again our ally. By my reckoning—and that of most Derai—we must recognize a debt."

"Interesting," the heralds said together. Jehane Mor watched Tirorn's hand tighten on the bow when he heard their blended voice with its notes of power.

"We count no debt," she said, as she had earlier in the night.

"But," Tarathan added, opening the door, "we would still be glad of your bow as far as the North Gate."

The night was cool when they stepped outside, but there was a faint stir in the air that spoke of the coming dawn. They walked in silence, crossing the long bridge to The Sleeve without hearing any further disturbance or seeing other people. The revelers, it appeared, had seen wisdom and cleared the streets.

Although long, the island of The Sleeve was also narrow and the walk from the bridge to the North Gate was short. But when they reached the gate, they found it barricaded with wagons and manned by a heavily armed contingent of the city guard. Tarathan folded his arms and sighed, leaning against the wall of the alley that concealed them. "We are going to have to find a boat," he said. "Or swim the river."

"Is that possible?" Tirorn asked.

"Swimming?" replied Tarathan. "Yes, on this northern side, because the floods are already subsiding, and in any case the Ijir delta is little more than a backwater here. The main currents flow to the south, which is why you find all the shipping lanes there. The only craft here will be pleasure barges, moored both up and downstream of the bridge. Most need several banks of rowers to shift them, but we could be lucky and find something smaller."

The first hint, not even of dawn gray but of a lesser darkness, was creeping across the eastern sky when they walked down a little lane onto the riverbank. Soon the true grayness and then the dawn itself would come. "I hope you're right about the currents," Jehane Mor said, as they paused by the deserted pleasure barges. "The far bank looks a very long way from here."

Tirorn grounded his bow, grinning. "It looks cold, too. I

think this is where our ways part, since my duty lies in the city still." He removed a gauntlet and extended his hand to Jehane Mor. "Farewell, Mistress Herald."

She took it in her own. "I will not forget that I owe you a debt for my life."

"I count no debt," he replied, using her own words. "Haven't I told you that already?"

She held his gaze. "Is that because of the Keep of Winds, or because of the debt, through Orth, that you owe to your own priestly kind?"

He smiled a little. "Perhaps it could be a gift between friends?"

"Perhaps it could," she said. "Farewell, Tirorn."

He turned her hand over in his and kissed it, formal as any great lord, then extended his hand to Tarathan. "Safe swimming, my brother of the blade."

Tarathan clasped Tirorn's forearms with his hands. "Light and safety on your road. And our thanks for your aid—but now we must go."

The Derai nodded, stepping back and slipping the bow over his shoulder before retreating to the lane. The heralds made their way out across the moored barges, stepping from one to the other until they were well out in the river. When they stopped on the outermost barge, both the city behind them and the line of the opposite shore seemed very distant. *"No small boats,"* Jehane Mor said ruefully. *"And no time to search further for one. We'll have to swim."*

They pulled off their boots and tossed the masks of Imulun and Seruth into the river. *"It won't matter,"* said Tarathan, when they floated on the surface. *"Masks like that are ten to an Ijiri penny. No one will think anything of seeing them in the water."*

Even as he spoke, they were stripping to their undershirts and hose, and bundling boots, belts, and outer clothes together inside their knotted cloaks. The water was icy cold when they slipped into it, and they gasped and trod water before striking out for the northern bank, drawing their bundles behind them. Tarathan, it turned out, had been right about the currents, although there was still a reasonably strong flow in the middle of the river. *"Go with it but keep moving across at the same time,"* he said. *"We should come to quieter water soon."* He was right about that as well, but the world had grown light by the time they clambered out, dripping and shivering, on the far bank.

The forest came right down to the very edge of the river, with thick undergrowth between the trees, ideal for conceal-ment. Dawn's white mist was just beginning to curl off the water and the domes and spires of Ij rose eerily above it, like a dream of a city. The mist lay more thickly beneath the trees and they made their way cautiously into it, waiting until they were a safe distance from the river before struggling to unknot the waterlogged cloaks and extract their sodden clothes. It was less than pleasant pulling on the cold, heavy fabric, even after they had rung the worst of the water out.

*"What now?"* asked Jehane Mor when they were done. *"Do we squelch our way to Farelle?"*

*"That's the nearest Guild House,"* Tarathan replied. *"But it'll help once we find horses."*

*"And what,"* she said, with rare grimness, *"if our enemies are already ahead of us?"*

He rose to his feet, shaking back the river-darkened braids of his hair. *"That's a risk we just have to take."*

They pushed their way through the undergrowth until they stood on the top of a low bank, overlooking a road swathed in fog. This route was narrow but still reasonably well maintained, and a tall marker stone indicated that it was five miles to the Main Road. The heralds exchanged resigned glances and were about to descend the bank when a sound rang through the fog: the chink of a bridle followed by the clatter of horses' hooves. As one, the heralds dropped into the brush and slithered back into denser cover. And once again, Tarathan's hand was on his knife.

Tirorn waited until the dawn spread grayly along the east-ern sky and the pockets of mist gleamed, thick and pearly above the water. He had found a vantage point beneath an old willow tree, close to the lane and a garden wall. The willow's green veil made a useful screen from prying eyes while still allowing him to see out over the barges to the water. Even his keen archer's sight could not make out anything on the river's far side, which was still shrouded in darkness, but at least there was no sign of pursuit by the heralds' enemies.

They would be all right, Tirorn told himself at last, when he finally began to notice the chill in the morning air. Or they would not. He knew there was nothing more that he could do, but he waited anyway, until the world around him began to wake. A windlass creaked from a nearby yard, followed by the clatter of a bucket, and soon people would begin to come down to the barges.

Tirorn wondered, as he squatted easily on his heels, just why he had gotten involved with the heralds in the first place. He had wanted to track the lurker back to its lair, but that would have meant letting it kill Jehane Mor outside the Guild House—or finding out whether it could. Reading between the lines, someone—or perhaps more than one someone—had thrown around a fair bit of power in Sarus's story of the Old Keep of Winds, even if the veteran had been cagey about details. But Tirorn had recognized the herald from the Farelle bridge as soon as she stepped out into the street's light. His immediate decision to kill the lurker had not even been conscious; his hands had sprung into action of their own accord.

Now, Tirorn shook his head. He did not want to think about Jehane Mor, although he found it almost impossible not to. She was quite possibly the most beautiful woman he had ever seen, and besides, he had liked her from their first encounter—because of her calmness, and the timbre of her voice, and the way she sat on her horse as though born to it. She had seemed so sure of her place in the world, he thought, and yet gave the appearance of not considering it at all.

He shook his head again and gave a short half laugh: undoubtedly, he was a hopeless case. After all, she was an outsider, and priest kind, and there was also Tarathan, her herald partner, in the mix. And the sun would be fully up soon. It was more than time for him to be gone.

Tirorn caught the movement out of the corner of the eye as he began to rise. A shadow lingered where no shadow should have been and the pale light of morning splintered. Tirorn's hand tightened on his bow but there was no time to slip it free and get an arrow to the string. His hand slid to his knife as he turned, but it was far too late. He knew a moment of surprise that he had seen and heard nothing at all—and then a light that was not the sun exploded across his eyes.

### ⊰─═─⊱

# 7

# *Across the River*

*T*he approaching clip of horses' hooves was muffled by the thick fog that looped across the road and into the trees. There was a flat, eerie quality to the half-lit world, as though the forest itself held its breath. The heralds, too, waited, pressed low beneath arching fern. Above their heads a bird called, heralding the day. Another answered it, deeper in the woods, and a moment later a great clamor of birdsong filled the forest, just as the first of the riders emerged through the fog.

The heralds saw the horse's head first, splitting the white air, its ears forward and nostrils flared. A second later, the spiked helmet of its rider appeared, turning slowly in a sweep of road and wood. The visor was lowered, concealing the rider's face, and the horse, too, was armored, its breath curling through the metal chanfron as it walked forward. Together, horse and rider looked like some beast of ancient legend—or something altogether stranger, a shape of night itself emerging from the mist.

The rider stopped on the crown of the road and five others materialized out of the whiteness to join him. The heavy armor of both horses and riders clanked beneath the birdsong, and their breath steamed on the air. The dark, secret visors turned, peering between the trees, but they did not penetrate the heralds' hiding place. After a few minutes the riders moved on, breasting the mist and half-light beneath the canopy. One by one, just as they had first appeared, they disappeared, while the heralds waited, motionless.

*"But what,"* Jehane Mor said finally, *"were Patrol riders doing here, away from the Main Road?"*

*"And can we trust them?"* Tarathan asked.

Jehane Mor considered this. *"Trust is always a risk, more so after last night."* She rose, dusting fern debris off the mud on her clothes. *"Should we take to the hills?"*

Tarathan pushed to his feet as well. *"We need speed—and that means either a swift galley, or horses and a good road, neither of which lies in the hills. And we could waste days hunting out a back way to Farelle or Sirith."*

*"Meanwhile,"* she replied, not without irony, *"we walk."*

Even following the road, their progress was hampered by the need to keep to the shelter of the woods, where the uneven footing was greasy and thick undergrowth clogged their path. The bird chorus died away as they walked, becoming the normal sounds of a woodland day. Even the fog began to lift a little, although it remained thick in every dip and hollow. The sun was too low to penetrate the trees, so the air remained chill and the heralds uncomfortable in their wet clothes. They stayed alert for more riders, as well as watching the side roads that came twisting out of forest and hill. Most of these were little better than rutted tracks, although every intersection, however small, was graced by a shrine to Seruth, the guardian of journeys. The gifts left in the shrines suggested that the side paths led to small villages, or larger farms, but like the main route they were completely empty of traffic.

Shortly after the heralds passed a second milestone, the road broadened and the next crossroad was marked by a larger than usual cairn to Seruth. The side road here was graveled, at least as far back as its first bend, and wider than the others they had passed. Tarathan moved closer to the forest edge, his eyes narrowed on the pitted gravel and verges churned to mud.

"*It took far more than six Patrol riders to mire the road like this.* Cautiously, he moved out of cover, studying the open ground. "*A great many people have passed this way recently, although the Patrol riders were here last. Their horses' hooves are larger, the prints far deeper from the weight of all the armor.*" Tarathan walked back to the crossroad. "*They met up with four more of their kind here, but the larger body passed by earlier.*" He pointed to an indentation in the mud. "*That's the butt of a halberd pole, and someone dropped a crossbow quarrel back there. So—halberdiers and at least one crossbow company, plus a fair contingent of light cavalry. There could be as many as three hundred of them, both foot and horse.*" He indicated the wheel marks across the muddied paving stones. "*With supply carts at the rear. Someone is moving in strength.*"

"But not the Patrol," said Jehane Mor. "*Not coming out of these hills. So who, then? And why?*"

Tarathan shrugged. "*We already saw the beginning of faction war in Ij last night. And a small army on the move is even more reason for keeping to the woods.*"

The ground began to rise as they walked on and the height of the embankment increased, so that the road lay a considerable distance below them. The climb became a scramble around rocks and over fallen logs, and the heralds had to push through scrub that was chest high in places. At last, however, they reached a ridge that provided extensive views of the surrounding countryside. Edging their way to the crest they lay prone, looking out over Ij and the river—but it was the open country surrounding the Main Road that held their attention.

Only a few days before, the plain that lay before them had been a peaceful patchwork of fields and orchards, the Main Road that bisected it thronged with traders and farm carts. The road was busy again this morning, but not with travelers, and the air of peace was gone as well. Column after column of the Patrol, dark and plain in their armor, were marching along the Main Road from Farelle and up the southern route from their fort by the river port. The sun glittered on their spear points like a galaxy of stars, and once they reached the Road Gate crossroad each column moved into the fields and took up a position facing Ij. On the river, too, the Patrol was moving: galleys, sleek, black, and deadly, were strung out across its width, blockading all the navigable channels. From every masthead, the Patrol's plain black ensign fluttered on the morning breeze.

"In Imulun's name!" said Jehane Mor out loud. There was something uncanny, even frightening, about that silent force rolling into place around Ij. *"What are they doing? For a thousand years the Patrol has* never *involved itself in the internal strife of the cities, even when asked to do so."*

Tarathan's eyes were fixed on the plain. *"They are not going into Ij, though, not yet at any rate. Although the threat should definitely deter anyone trying to get out, which helps us."* He pointed toward the crossroad. *"But what have we there?"*

Jehane Mor drew in her breath. A square of black tents, clearly the command post of the Patrol, was pitched close by the intersection. On the opposite side of the road a large pavilion of indigo and gold silk rose high, as opulent as the Patrol tents were plain. A second and smaller tent of pale green stood beside it, and a colorful but well-armed company surrounded both. Pennants curled lazily over each pavilion, although the distance was too great to make out heraldic devices. A series of smaller, but still gaily colored standards was set out in a brave, brilliant row along the road frontage.

*"Our company of three hundred,"* said Tarathan, on a note of satisfaction. *"The banners should tell us who they are, as soon as the wind lifts them."*

*"Indigo and gold are the colors of the Ilvaine kin, but the pale green . . ."* Jehane Mor shook her head.

*"Ay, the green."* Tarathan turned, his dark eyes meeting hers. *"It looks suspiciously like . . . But there's the central pennant now. You're right, that's definitely the Ilvaine leopard. The emerald and black is the Katrani, which is only to be expected if the Ilvaine kin are there. Orange and gold is Teneseti, no surprises there either, but what's the gonfalon*

*beside it? Royal blue and purple—surely that's Ambardi colors? Except that Ambard is an Athiri satellite."*

*"Apparently not."* Jehane Mor's mindtone was dry. *"And see the colors closer to the pavilion entrance: gold, crimson, white—all of the Three, in fact. Someone has been very thorough."*

*"I suppose,"* said Tarathan, with grim appreciation, *"this explains the rooftop war we saw last night."*

*"And the Ambardi presence. That family is known for its links to the School. But that green pavilion . . ."* Jehane Mor hesitated again. *"That does look remarkably like the green of Ishnapur. Yet we are over a thousand leagues from the borders of their empire."*

*"Their heralds were here,"* Tarathan replied, his dark eyes speculative. He studied the plain a moment longer, then stiffened—and Jehane Mor felt the same cold shadow cross her own mind.

*"Demonfinder!"* he hissed as she pushed her shield between their minds and the shadow.

*"We need to leave."* Jehane Mor was cool. *"Who knows how much the demonfinder glimpsed before I shut her out."*

*"Her, is it?"* Tarathan was grim as they slid back down the first steep slope of the ridge. *"But what in Imulun's name is an Ishnapuri demonfinder doing on the River? We'll have to go inland after all,"* he added, stooping through the gap between a fallen tree and the hillside. *"I might have risked the Patrol's lines by night, but not with a demonfinder in their midst."*

They plunged back down the long hill they had climbed so laboriously, keen to put distance between themselves and any pursuit from the plain. Moving as quietly as they could, they remained alert for any noise from the road below, but heard only the normal woodland sounds. Even so, they slowed their pace through the final stretch of forest before the small crossroad and its cairn to Seruth—which this time was not empty. The six riders of the Patrol sat there, still as statues on their armored horses, while another four rode toward them down the side road. The heralds crouched low, watching, then moved away from each other, melting into the thicker brush.

There was a brief, quiet exchange between the two Patrol groups before one of the riders from the side road swung to the ground. Much as Tarathan had done earlier, the rider circled the intersection and then went down on one knee, speaking over his shoulder to the others. One answered briefly and the rider on the ground grunted, studying the tracks again. After a moment the spiked helm came up and its secret gaze pierced undergrowth and mist, looking directly at where Jehane Mor lay. Slowly, the rider stood up, and as he did so the sunlight fell across his visor, outlining the striking hawk device.

High overhead an Ijiri bellbird flitted from one canopy tree to another. A moment later its bubbling song poured out, but Jehane Mor's attention remained fixed on the striking hawk device. *"Aravenor,"* she thought and knew, despite his silence, that Tarathan had also seen the hawk insignia.

The rider took a step forward and then stopped, his visor focused on the concealing wood. He appeared to be listening intently, and Jehane Mor lay utterly still, aware that Tarathan was working himself further away from her position, noiseless as a wood snake beneath the scrub and fern.

"Jehane Mor," the Patrol captain said, very quietly. "Speak to me, if you are here."

What, the herald wondered, had led him to guess that she was there? What had he heard or seen—or was it some sixth sense that guided him? The bellbirds call fluted out again, breaking the long, listening pause that had followed Aravenor's words. The Patrol captain stepped closer to the trees, spreading his hands wide as if to emphasize that he intended no harm. When he spoke again his voice was still low, pitched to carry no further than where she lay. "News comes swiftly to the Patrol, whether on road or river. We know what happened in Ij last night and that you and Tarathan survived it. I guessed you might try crossing the river to escape, and ours is only one of many units out looking for you both."

How could the Patrol have learned what happened in Ij

so soon? she wondered. And why turn out patrols for two stray heralds, especially given the sort of numbers deploying on the plain outside the Road Gate? There was something strange at play, something very odd indeed . . . She continued to lie motionless, waiting.

Aravenor took a third step forward, and his visor seemed to look directly at the place where she lay. "You need not fear our motives." His voice was still quiet, calm. "All know of the Patrol's oath to preserve the peace of road and river, but we swore to another as well, nearly a thousand years ago, when we first took service with the Masters of the River cities. Few remember that pledge now, but it binds us to uphold the law that exempts the Guild from blood feud and vendetta, and to succor and protect its heralds with our lives." He paused, and now even the birds were silent. "Nor," he added, when only silence answered his words, "do we forget the friendships made on road and river—or that friendship, too, has its obligations."

Inwardly, Jehane Mor sighed. Trust is a risk, she reflected, but there are some risks that must be taken. She rose to her feet, brushing more leaf litter and soil detritus from her tunic and meeting the inscrutable hawk visor with an unwavering look of her own. "Aravenor of the Patrol," she said, "do you really expect me to believe that the massive display of military strength marshaled on the plain before Ij has anything at all to do with our chance-met friendship of the road?"

The mouth beneath the visor twitched. "I do not," Aravenor replied. "But it has a great deal to do with the massacre that took place last night."

"I see," she said, and waded her way through fern and bracken until they stood facing each other. "How did you know I was here?"

This time he definitely smiled. "Did you know that your boots leave a distinctive print, the particular style of the Guild's bootmaker in Terebanth? I saw the half-obscured impression of just such a boot in the mud beside the crossroad. As for the rest . . . " He shrugged his armored shoulders. "One develops a certain sense for the watching eye and concealed presence after the length of time I have spent patroling road and river. I didn't know for certain that you were there: it was an intuition, perhaps even a hope, that's all."

Jehane Mor nodded, studying him. It was impossible to read a Patroler through the helm of concealment, but the tone of voice occasionally revealed something, and Aravenor's words seemed plausible enough. "I'm still not entirely clear, though," she said, "how you knew to look for us here."

"I know you both, a little, from the road, and I thought what I would do in your place. I sent searchers south, as well, and there are watchers at the seaport, in case you tried that route instead."

"Very thorough," said Jehane Mor.

His eyes met hers through the slits in the hawk visor. "We have sworn an oath," he replied evenly, "to the Masters of all the River cities, not just to Ij—just as those Masters gave their own undertaking to your Guild."

The herald shook her head, seeing again the long, heavily armed columns on the plain and the galleys blockading the river. She wanted to shiver, thinking of such a long ago oath waking into life beneath the spring sun, but she kept her gaze thoughtful, cool. "I am not ungrateful, Aravenor, but I have come to have a certain . . . regard . . . for the balance of power in the River lands."

"As have I," he replied. "There has been a long equilibrium between city and city, as well as between the cities and ourselves. But the Guild of Heralds is also part of that balance, and we cannot let the murders that took place last night go unanswered."

"No," she said. "I have no intention of doing that. But there are other aspects of these events that I find very troubling."

He nodded. "I agree, which is why I judged that the Patrol's response must be unequivocal. But I don't think that it will come to our investing Ij, if that is what you fear, for even as word of the massacre reached us, the Ilvaine and others among the Masters were moving." His smile was grim now, beneath the visor. "It seems that the threads of kinship were pulled tight last night, even into the School itself."

Jehane Mor remembered the assassins fighting each other across the rooftops while Athiri and Katrani warred in the street below. "Civil strife in Ij does not mean that the situation is resolved," she said quietly. "Also, if the Ilvaine and their allies have moved this swiftly, it begs the question as to how much they already knew of what the renegades intended—and how much they allowed to happen, to suit their own ends."

The same could be said of the Patrol, she reflected, a chill feathering her spine.

"A question," said Aravenor, "that I have not overlooked. But I understand that the city guard now have the streets largely under control and that Prince Ilvaine and the Masters with him have sent word to their fellows in the city, calling for the Conclave to begin at once."

The herald held herself very still. It would not truly be over, she thought, until all those who knew of last night's strike, as well as those who executed it, had been brought to account. "You say that the Patrol has sworn an oath," she said. "Does this mean that you, personally, will stand surety for Tarathan's continued safety, and mine, from now on?"

"Yes," said Aravenor. The hawk visor examined the forest around her. "But given that the two of you hunt as a pair, I would feel a lot more comfortable if Tarathan were somewhere to be seen right now."

Jehane Mor kept her face impassive. "Trust," she said, looking past him to the row of silent, watching horsemen, "is always a risk, is it not?"

Aravenor turned, following her gaze, as Tarathan rose up almost beneath the hooves of the horse nearest the treeline, materializing out of little more than long grass and the last, lingering strands of mist. "So it would seem," the Patrol captain said, very dryly, as the horse snorted and snaked its armored head around. "The world is indeed turned upside down when the Patrol is ambushed by heralds."

Tarathan sheathed his dagger and walked forward, skirting the horsemen. "It wouldn't have been much of an ambush with only a herald's dagger against armored cavalry. Even less so given the numbers we saw outside Ij." He paused when he was a pace away from the Patrol captain, his dark gaze searching. "Numbers, I heard you say, that you judged necessary. Yet I thought only the Lord Captain of the Patrol could authorize deployment on that scale?"

Aravenor nodded. "Your understanding is correct. I am the Lord Captain of the Patrol."

The herald's eyes narrowed. "You?" he said slowly, and Jehane Mor could hear his surprise, echoing her own. "So why," he continued, "would the Lord Captain himself be out scouring the road for two heralds, when you have an army to do such work?"

The hawk visor looked from one to the other. "There are several reasons, but we can speak of them as we ride. If, that is, you are willing to accept my safe conduct?"

The heralds inclined their heads. "We accept," they said as one. "We must go west with all speed, to bear word of events here to both the Guild and the other River cities."

Aravenor nodded. "We can send you on one of our galleys," he said. "That way, no one will outdistance you. But I have already sent word upriver—I did so as soon as I learned of the attack." He paused. "If you were willing to delay, both I and the gathered Masters would greatly value your first-hand account of last night's events. And once we have spoken together you may be able to take a more detailed report to your Guild."

Jehane Mor and Tarathan looked at him without expression, and again the two of them spoke as one: "What more can be added to this account of law breaking and murder?"

The Lord Captain held up one gauntleted hand. "I do not ask you to soften that message. But Prince Ilvaine wishes the Masters to hear first-hand of the attack on yourselves and the Guild House. There may also be pieces of the puzzle that you do not have." Again he looked from one to the other, as though sensing the secret flow of their thoughts. "The pledge of safe conduct remains, whatever you decide to do."

*"He is right,"* Tarathan said. *"We need to learn more of what is happening here. Find out who is playing what part, and why."*

Jehane Mor did not look at him. *"If we can trust the Patrol. And you saw the Ishnapuri banner. Meeting with the Masters will almost certainly bring us into direct contact with the demonfinder."*

She felt his mental shrug. *"I am curious to learn what has brought one of that kind so far from Ishnapur. The trick will be to meet her in the company of others."*

*"And hope Aravenor's safe conduct holds."* Outwardly, Jehane Mor bowed to the Lord Captain. "We will delay," she said, "and meet with the Masters. But after that, we must and shall go upriver."

"I'll make sure you do." Aravenor turned and strode toward his horse. "We have no mounts to spare," he added over his shoulder, "but the distance is short enough for our horses to carry double. If you ride behind me, Herald Jehane, Arin will take Tarathan." He swung into the saddle, then extended a hand for her to mount, while a rider with a coiled serpent on his helm did the same for Tarathan.

The horses stepped forward briskly, leaving the cross-road and the cairn to Seruth behind. For a time the only sound was the clatter of hooves on the road, the creak of leather and clink of metal, and the occasional birdsong from the forest. The last of the mist vanished from between the trees as they rode and the day grew warm. Jehane Mor ran a hand over her wet hair and turned her face to the sun, but her mind flashed again to the memory of pulling aside black-clad bodies while Naia's eyes stared up, unseeing, from beneath them.

The herald deepened her breath, consciously seeking calm, then made herself look at Naia's dead face again—and at all the slain in the Guild house court. At the same time she remained aware of the fall of sun across the forest trees, the movement of the horse beneath her, and the in-termingled smells of steel and leather, sweating horse and sweating human. She felt the touch of Tarathan's mind on her own, half reassuring, half grim. *"How many years has it been?"* she asked him, without turning her head. *"How many dead?"*

*"Too many,"* he replied, but his tone conveyed his acceptance of violence and death as an inevitable consequence of the path they had chosen.

*"That is your strength."* Her mindvoice was grave. *"And my weakness, that I never can."*

*"I do not call it weakness,"* he replied, matter-of-fact.

*"No, you never have."* A bird whistled from a nearby tree, a piping trill of sound, and she listened to it for a moment, her eyes focused on the black wool of Aravenor's cloak, noting every detail of the weave. She waited until the bird fell silent before she spoke. "You haven't told us why you came looking for us in person. Shouldn't the Lord Captain of the Patrol be with his legions, mustered outside Ij?"

Aravenor half turned his head. "I have a very able second outside Ij," he said. "Besides, you and Tarathan are more than just another herald pair."

"Really?" said Jehane Mor. "How is that, Lord Captain?"

She was almost certain that Aravenor smiled. "Firstly, you survived," he said, "when we are not sure that any other herald in the city did. And may tell us, therefore, what no one else can about what happened last night. Also, I know you by sight and speech, which few other of my captains do."

*"True enough,"* Tarathan commented. *"Few other Patrolers on the road ever speak more than necessity demands."*

"The intelligence we've had from the city," Aravenor continued, and now his tone was thoughtful, "also suggests that of all the heralds in Ij, you two alone were singled out by name." The shrill chatter of a jay filled the brief silence. "Do you know why?"

Jehane Mor shook her head. She could hazard several guesses, but none were certainties. "No," she replied, before adding: "I still find it difficult to credit that you are the Lord Captain. One expects more outward show, I suppose."

"It is enough that the Patrol knows who its Lord Captain is." Arin, the rider with the serpent device, spoke with calm assurance. "We don't need to put on a display for the world."

*"Here's pride,"* observed Tarathan, amused.

*"Well, they always have been closed, with their visors and their forts, dwelling apart from the rest of the River."* Jehane Mor was thoughtful, but at that moment their small troop clattered out of the trees and onto the plain, moving past rank on rank of the mustered Patrol. The columns all saluted as Aravenor rode by, dipping their ensigns, but it was clear that every company was on a war footing, their attention focused on Ij. Tarathan, looking around, directed Jehane Mor's attention to sentry posts spaced along the wood shore and back into the hills.

*"A cat at every mouse hole,"* she agreed, then said aloud: "I see we need not fear our attackers' net being cast wider."

Arin nodded. "We stopped heavily armed riders who left the city sometime after midnight, riding down the guards at the Road Gate. Also a river galley, without identification or lights, that tried to slip upriver before dawn."

Aravenor spoke over his shoulder. "A solitary messenger may have left earlier, or taken the long way via forest and hills. But we have the blockade in place here and have raised the boom across the river at Farelle, so numbers will not get through. As yet, though," he added, "we have received no word of disturbance anywhere else."

"Which makes sense," Arin said, "since whoever wishes to control the River must first secure Ij."

"And you think that is what this is about?" Tarathan asked, frowning. "Controlling the River lands?"

The Patrol leader looked around at him. "Or destabilizing," he said quietly. "Don't you?"

Tarathan made no reply, for they had reached the colorful but orderly ranks of the Ilvaine and their allied kindred, with halberdiers, crossbowmen, and plumed and gilded cavalry deployed around the two central pavilions. His gaze lifted to the pennants fluttering on the light breeze, narrowing on the pale green banner as it rippled overhead, revealing a silver lion device beneath a crown of stars. "Not just the green of

Ishnapur," he said, "but the imperial insignia itself. This is a morning for surprises."

"They are an embassy," said Aravenor. He waited for Jehane Mor to dismount then stepped down himself, handing his horse's reins to another rider as Tarathan came to stand beside him. "Apparently they traveled overland in secret, assuming the guise of Ishnapuri merchants seeking new markets, and only revealed their true identity at our southernmost border post, three days ago. The ambassador requested our escort to Ij, but also asked that word be sent to Prince Ilvaine. You may recall," he added, "that the prince journeyed to Ishnapur many years ago and was received by the Lion Throne."

"A signal honor," murmured Jehane Mor.

"So they say." Aravenor's tone was noncommittal. "We will meet with them all soon, but first may I offer some Patrol hospitality in the form of dry clothes and something to eat? Normally I would insist that you be allowed to rest before such a meeting, but I hope you agree that events are too urgent for that?"

Jehane Mor nodded, conscious that Tarathan's braids were frayed rope down his back and her muddied clothes were not even herald gray. Yet whatever their appearance, however weary they felt, they were still representatives of the Guild. "We agree that events cannot wait," she said. "But the dry clothes and a meal will be very welcome."

***

# 8

# The Demonhunter

"We don't have anything gray," Arin said, bringing an armful of clothes to the tent where the heralds were to change. "These are clean and dry, but we only wear black."

*"We'll look like Patrolers ourselves,"* Jehane Mor said to Tarathan as the rider left them. *"Or assassins,"* she added with a grimace.

*"It may be wise to blend in for now."* Tarathan was frowning as he rung out his braids. *"Did you see the horses beside the Ishnapuri tent?"*

Jehane Mor nodded. *"Jhainarians,"* she replied. The only mirror was a steel shield hung from a tent pole, and although it showed little more than a pale blur of face, she could at least repin her hair. She met the reflection of his eyes, dark smudges behind her shoulder. *"Seven of them."*

*"Together with a demonhunter."* His mindvoice was sober. *"But we can't avoid this meeting."*

"No." When they ducked back out into the brightness of the morning, they found a richly dressed youth waiting with Aravenor. The newcomer's appearance, Jehane Mor reflected as he bowed, was quite magnificent. He wore a jupon of apricot velvet over a gilded breastplate, with the Ilvaine leopard device stitched into the velvet with gold thread. Tight, golden-chestnut curls clustered around a classic profile, and the eyes that lifted to meet hers were flecked with amber.

"Honorable heralds," the young man said, straightening. "I am Leto Ilvaine. My grandfather, Prince Ilvaine, invites you to join his other guests in our pavilion. He apologizes," he added, "that you have had no time to rest, but offers refreshment while we talk."

She and Tarathan inclined their heads. "We are tired," they said in their one voice, "but understand that necessity drives the prince—as it does us."

Leto Ilvaine bowed again and walked ahead of them to the Ilvaine pavilion, lifting aside the silken hanging over the entrance. Despite both filtered daylight and the gilded lantern that hung from the central dome, the interior was dim. Jehane Mor's first impression was of an expanse of thick soft carpets and a throng of richly dressed people. When her eyes adjusted, she saw that many of the rich robes reflected the mix of colors displayed on the banners outside. An Ilvaine standard, its golden leopard rampant on an indigo field, formed one wall of the pavilion: the beast's eyes glittered topaz and diamond, its forepaws struck at the air. A second leopard gleamed on the long tunic of the man standing at the center of the gathering, directly in front of the banner. A circlet of gold confined his white hair, and his face was all old parchment and sharply etched bones. Leto Ilvaine stopped a few paces in front of him and sank to one knee.

"My grandfather and my prince," the young man said, "I bring you Aravenor, Lord Captain of the Patrol, and Jehane Mor and Tarathan of Ar, heralds of the Guild from Terebanth."

The old man's gaze found the heralds' faces, where they waited in the shadow of the entrance. "You are welcome," he said. His voice was deep, with no quaver of age. "The more so," he added, turning slightly from one herald to the other, "because of the great injury that has been done to you and to your Guild, contrary to Ijiri honor."

Those who surrounded him stirred, but no one spoke. No one would dare, thought Jehane Mor, looking again at the proud, glittering gaze of the beast above his head. She bowed, mirroring Tarathan at her side, and let her voice speak in unison with his: "We salute you, Prince Ilvaine, and thank you for your welcome. We look forward to hearing your counsel—as well as the message the Masters of Ij wish us to bear to the Guild of Heralds, concerning both redress for our wrongs and restoring the balance of peace within the River lands."

Those around the prince stirred again, but he simply nodded, as if their formal words were no more than he had expected. "All these matters shall be addressed." A gesture drew in the woman to his immediate right, her face humorous and deeply lined above the gold robe of a Master Sage. "May I introduce my kinswoman, Isperia Katran, who is a Master of the Academy. Also my great-nephew, Mykon Ambard." The man standing on the prince's left was powerfully built, with a dark, spade-shaped beard and cold eyes. His black and white garb denoted one the School termed "envoys," assassins assigned to speak in Conclave on its behalf.

*"A dangerous man."* Tarathan was grim.

*"But here,"* said Jehane Mor as they bowed again, outwardly impassive.

The prince raised one hand, a yellow diamond glinting on his finger, and those around him sat while liveried servants set out food and drink on delicate, cross-legged tables. Leto Ilvaine pulled forward chairs for the heralds, and Jehane Mor caught Isperia Katran studying them with shrewd eyes—before the sage's head turned toward a shimmer of bells from the pavilion entrance. "And here," Prince Ilvaine said affably, "is another of my great-nephews."

The hangings were brushed aside and Haimyr the Golden surveyed the assembled company, a smile on his lips. The bow he made the prince was extravagant, and as soon as he straightened he strolled forward and saluted the heralds with equal flourish. "Did I not say that we should meet again? I am glad to see that I spoke true, despite the gloomy forebodings of my cousin here."

"I prefer to call it realism," said Mykon Ambard, without

inflection. "But I concede that my reservations were misplaced in this instance."

The heralds rose and bowed to the minstrel, their heads held at precisely the same, ironic angle, although they, too, kept their voices neutral. "We thank you for your faith in our safe arrival."

The minstrel smiled. "I did have faith—so much so that I brought your horses with me from the city." He switched the smile to Aravenor. "Although I promise the Lord Captain that all other Guild mounts remain safely stabled by the river port."

Jehane Mor and Tarathan kept their one voice soft, looking at and through him at the same time. "We also thank you for our horses, but wonder how you knew to bring them? Just as we have wondered at your part in last night's events, given your words at our last meeting."

"What words were these?" asked Prince Ilvaine.

Haimyr turned to him. "The merest jape, my great-uncle and my prince, a lighthearted jest between friends."

"They do not seem amused," the prince observed. He turned to the heralds. "Do you accuse my great-nephew of designs against your lives?"

"We make no accusation," they replied. "But we require accountability for the heralds murdered in Ij, wherever that may be found to lie."

"Ah." The prince's faded tawny eyes must have been as golden as Haimyr's once. "The Lord Captain has already made it clear that he requires the same accountability."

Mykon Ambard's brows twitched down, a hard line across his nose, but Haimyr's smile remained in place. "Where are our other guests?" he asked. "Surely they shall join our council?"

"They have been sent for," Prince Ilvaine replied. "We shall begin as soon as they arrive." He sat in a wide chair hung with indigo and gold, waving Haimyr to a place beside Mykon Ambard. The minstrel subsided into it with a world-weary air as the heralds resumed their seats.

"Do you truly suspect him of involvement in last night's attack?" Aravenor asked quietly.

Tarathan's answering glance was measuring. "I rule nothing out, at this stage. For that matter, what led you to approach Prince Ilvaine first, once you learned of events in Ij? How did you know the Ilvaine weren't as compromised as the Athiri seem to be?"

"I didn't," said Aravenor. "I sent dispatches to all the Masters of Ij currently residing outside the city. But my rider told me that the Ilvaine hive was already buzzing when he arrived, and they were the first to send men and arms to join us here."

"My grandfather," Leto Ilvaine put in, bringing forward chairs for two more Patrol riders entering the pavilion, "has been saying for some time that something was brewing, although we thought it would unfold at Conclave. So we had been gathering anyway and were able to move quickly when word came. Still," he added, pride clear in his face, "we wouldn't have been here so soon without the old man driving us."

*"Aravenor's word?"* Jehane Mor asked silently, as the young man moved away. *"Or someone else's?"* She did not look at Haimyr, but noted that the focus of Aravenor's visor was in the minstrel's direction. The Lord Captain nodded to Arin and his companion as they took their seats, and introduced the second rider, whose device was a mailed fist, as Sarathion. It was impossible to gauge any of their expressions behind the visors, but when he spoke again, Aravenor's tone was thoughtful.

"Haimyr the Golden has an interesting history—a scion of the Ilvaine kin who is famed throughout the River for his music, but chooses to dwell at the end of the known world, on the Derai Wall."

"So where does his loyalty lie?" Jehane Mor asked softly.

"A question," Aravenor replied, "that has undoubtedly occurred to his princely great-uncle." He paused as a young man who could have been Leto Ilvaine's twin stepped through the entrance. "His Excellency Lord Isrradin, Ambassador of His Imperial Majesty, the Shah of Ishnapur, to the River lands," the newcomer announced in ringing tones. "The Lady Sarifa of Ishnapur. Captain Sorriyith of the Jhainarian Guard."

The prince and all those gathered in the tent rose to their feet as a tall man ducked through the entrance and stepped immediately to one side. He was clad in loose, flowing robes over shimmering mail and wore a spiked silver cap that concealed his hair. His eyes, too, appeared silver in his darkly tanned face and they never ceased watching the assembled company, not even when he bowed to Prince Ilvaine.

"So this is a Jhainarian," Arin murmured, but the ambassador had already entered the pavilion in his captain's wake and was saluting the prince with grave courtesy, as befits one great lord to another. He was a man of late middle years with a flowing beard and dark, thoughtful eyes in an aquiline face. His expression was austere, although his smile was warm as Prince Ilvaine returned the bow, but it was the woman who slipped into the tent in his shadow who caught and held all eyes. She was clad in a full, deep red robe, her hair concealed by a coif of gold mesh worked with garnet and seed pearls. The face within the coif was quartered with crimson and charcoal paint, both eyelids and lips darkened to black. The effect was both rich and a little frightening, and Jehane Mor heard more than one indrawn breath, although no one spoke.

Demonhunter tricks, the herald thought, but did not risk sharing the thought with Tarathan. The Lady Sarifa's painted lids were half lowered, but Jehane Mor knew that she would be sensing the room. The demonhunter looked young, although it was difficult to be sure behind the painted mask. She would undoubtedly be strong, having been sent so far from Ishnapur alone—as much as anyone accompanied by a Jhainarian Seven, Jehane Mor reflected wryly, could be described as being alone.

The demonhunter saluted the assembled company with henna-dyed palms pressed together, before allowing her Ilvaine escort to bow her into a seat on the ambassador's left. The Jhainarian captain moved to stand at the ambassador's right shoulder, his right hand resting close to the hilt of his curved sword.

Prince Ilvaine steepled his fingers—exactly, Jehane Mor

noted, amused, as his kinswoman, Isperia Katran was doing. The prince's gaze searched the assembled faces and his old eyes were slightly hooded. "Kindred, Lord Isrradin, honored guests, we have much to discuss, most concerning last night's events in Ij but some attending on the newly arrived—and very welcome—embassy from Ishnapur." Gravely, he saluted the ambassador again, and Lord Isrradin rose and bowed in his turn. "But what happened last night did not begin when the Lord Captain's dispatch rider arrived at my door, or even when rogue elements within the School attacked the Guild house. It seems likely that it began several years ago, when emissaries from this so-called Swarm made approaches to our factor in Grayharbor. They spoke of trade, yet had little of value to offer the Ilvaine kin. I foresaw, however, that others might see matters differently."

The prince leaned back. "I am old and I do not like to be disturbed from my sitting in the sun, but nonetheless, word was sent along the lines and threads of our kin to remain alert for activity associated with this Swarm." He smiled thinly. "Eventually, the web stirred. First, when my great-nephew, Haimyr, returned from the Derai Wall last autumn and alleged that Swarm emissaries were seeking to foment trouble in Ij. Shortly after that, Mykon Ambard also came to me—in secret, as is the way of his kind."

All eyes turned to the assassin envoy, but he remained impassive. "One is always pleased to see one's kin," the prince continued, "particularly when they have risen high in the Three. And I have always been fond of my niece Cynithia, Mykon's mother. Still, I was perturbed to hear what he had to tell, which was news of a Swarm alliance with the Athiri and approaches, through their prince, to the Assassins' School."

"Ath was always a fool," Isperia Katran said, "even more so than his father."

"Exactly," agreed Prince Ilvaine, "although I had not thought him so lost to honor and the conduct required of a prince of Ij."

Mykon Ambard stirred. "It may be," he said, with every

appearance of reluctance, "that he has gotten in too deep and they have him under some kind of compulsion."

"He is still a fool. A wiser man would have perceived the nature of those he dealt with." The prince waved a hand. "Now *we* must deal with the consequences of his folly."

Aravenor leaned forward. "Why, if you knew this storm was brewing, did you give no warning?"

Haimyr, whose eyes had been closed, opened them. "To see the sky grow clouded is not the same as knowing when or how the storm will break. It may even blow over. There are many who seek alliances with Ij and its Three, for a multitude of reasons." He did not look at the Ishnapuri delegation, but others there did, nodding. "We had a maelstrom of rumors and suspicion, but no sure information. Enough not to be caught completely unprepared, but that is all." Gracefully he concealed a yawn. "It was almost fatiguing, rousing out the kin to do battle with the renegades, once we learned the first blow had been struck."

"Against the Guild of Heralds." Aravenor's tone was even. "Yet not one of your rumors suggested that this might be coming?"

Haimyr shook his head. "There were many whispers, as I said, but no, not one that led me to think that the Guild house might be a target."

"There is no sense to it," Mykon Ambard said abruptly. "No advantage to the School or any of the Three."

"Or to the Darkswarm," murmured Haimyr, "at least that I can see."

"They wished to send a message." Jehane Mor spoke quietly, but every eye swung to her at once—because they are all watching surreptitiously anyway, she thought, to see how Tarathan and I bear ourselves during this discussion of a wrong done to our own. "We heard a Master of the School speak these words to his new ally: 'Bringing down the heralds will send a message that no one is beyond our reach.'"

There was a collective hiss and more than one head turned to look at Mykon Ambard, who stared straight ahead.

"Striking at the integrity of River law and institutions with the same blow," Aravenor said, "while one of the Three is set against the other two, and the School—potentially—divided within itself."

Haimyr shrugged, the bells on his clothes tinkling. "Also setting Ij against the other River cities at the same time. We know, Lord Captain."

"Do we?" Mykon Ambard looked at his kinsman sidelong, a sudden glitter in the cold eyes. "All know, kinsman, how long you have spent on the Derai Wall, tied to one of their dark lords. How can we know that you have not become their mouthpiece? Or that the Swarm are wrong when they say it is the Guild and the Patrol that keep the River divided—easy prey for the Derai, who covet our wealth and fertile lands. Perhaps it *is* only a matter of time before the Derai pour out of the north and overrun us." He let his eyes move around the gathered faces. "The increasing number of northerners 'visiting' our cities suggest that the Athiri may be right in wanting the River unified."

"By the School and by force?" Isperia Katran demanded, as several of the Ilvaine kin leapt to their feet, their hands on their sword hilts at mention of the Athiri. The prince shook his head at them.

"We are here so all may speak freely," the old man said. Slowly, those on their feet sat down again, while continuing to glower at Mykon Ambard. Jehane Mor was watching Haimyr, wondering how he would answer the insult about being a mouthpiece for the Derai. But the minstrel said nothing, just resettled the fall of his golden sleeves.

Prince Ilvaine looked keenly around the pavilion. "It may be true that the Derai covet our River and our wealth. It is certainly true that they have numbers and strength of arms—but this Swarm has sought to destroy us by stealth. That I will not have."

"It is presumptuous, in fact," Isperia Katran said. "Ij is not a puppet, to dance at the whim of others."

Lord Isrradin cleared his throat. "Forgive me, but I am

puzzled." His expression reflected his words. "Surely no one could believe that Ij is weak? The wealth of your city, of the whole River, in fact, is renowned, even in Ishnapur. Today we have seen the vastness of your armies, drawn up on this very plain. Where, then, is the weakness?"

"In the minds of those who were swayed by the blandishments of this Swarm!" Prince Ilvaine said, with a snap that made several of his retainers jump. "Yet not everything is what it seems, as our enemies have now learned to their cost. A very serious miscalculation, do you not agree, Lord Captain?"

Mykon Ambard spoke, frowning, before Aravenor could reply. "Yet who knew, before today, that the Patrol's service to the River lands included defending the Guild? Certainly, I did not."

"Those who needed to know were aware of it, nonetheless." Prince Ilvaine resumed his tranquil manner. "An Ilvaine was amongst those who swore the original oath to protect the Guild, for it was those we now know as heralds who held us together after the world fell. And the Ilvaine do not forget."

Haimyr straightened in his seat. "So . . . an attack on the Guild becomes a direct attack on your personal honor?"

His great-uncle's smile was terrible in its gentleness. "It is. And my honor, as you know, is more dear to me even than my life." His smile deepened and the eyes of the leopard above him glittered in the lanternlight. "The honor of the Ilvaine and all my kin stand second only to my personal honor, and the honor and glory of Ij come very close after that. As for the River, it appears that I have some slight feeling for all our lands. The rest of the world I disregard, unless it intrudes upon my notice—which it has now done."

"Also," said Aravenor, "upon the duty of the Patrol."

Mykon Ambard narrowed his eyes. "You are right, my great-uncle. A serious miscalculation, indeed."

"Yes," said the prince. The day was getting hotter, Jehane Mor thought, just as the atmosphere in the tent was growing close. For all the Ijiri finery, it would stink of sweat before the meeting was done. Prince Ilvaine leaned forward, his eyes meeting hers. "We have reports of last night's attacks, both from the Patrol's sources and our own, but it would assist us to hear your first-hand account."

"It may be painful—" Isperia Katran began, but Mykon Ambard cut her off.

"However painful, they must speak. Given what is at stake, we must know the truth. Or the part of it they are willing to tell."

The last words were hurled down like a gauntlet. It would be easy, Jehane Mor thought, to counter with accusations of School perfidy. Yet that might be exactly what the assassin hoped for. For a moment she saw dead faces, dead bodies again—but this was about doing what needed to be done. She rose to her feet.

"To speak of what happened *is* painful," she said. Out of the corner of her eye she saw the Jhainiarian's head move, almost as though he had jerked it back. "Yet you have a right to hear our story, if what happened last night is to be remedied." A ripple ran through the gathering, like a wind through grass, but Jehane Mor gave no sign of noticing. She kept her voice clear and her manner impersonal as she spoke, first of the gift of masks and then the unlicensed assassination attempt.

Those gathered all leaned forward, intent, when she related the discovery of the Guild House massacre, exchanging glances when she described what she and Tarathan had seen and heard there, before repeating her assertion of an alliance between an assassin Master and the Swarm. Prince Ilvaine listened with his eyes hooded, but raised them when she paused. He signaled a retainer to refill her cup.

Jehane Mor drank, then set the cup back, letting her eyes travel around the gathered faces. "You may find what I have to say next difficult to believe. I could scarcely credit it myself, when events unfolded." Keeping her tone neutral, she recounted how they had seen the Ishnapuri herald, Ileyra, with the assassins, and believed her forsworn, a traitor who had let enemies into the Guild house—until the

Derai, Tirorn, had asserted that she was in fact a Swarm facestealer. She paused again before describing how Ileyra's countenance had rippled and shifted in the light from the warehouse lantern.

A murmur ran around the pavilion. "Can this be possible?" Isperia Katran asked.

Mykon Ambard fingered his beard. "The first explanation sounded more likely."

"Except," said Haimyr, flicking back a sleeve, "that those sworn to the Guild of Heralds have never been known to lie. Or betray a trust. Whereas accounts of facestealers come up time and again in the lore of the Derai."

A woman's voice spoke, husky and compelling. "We have records of them in Ishnapur as well, from the years immediately after what you call the Cataclysm."

Almost every head swiveled toward Lady Sarifa, but Mykon Ambard still looked skeptical. "What is your authority in these matters, madam?"

Isperia Katran clicked her tongue. "Lady Sarifa's robes and visage proclaim her calling. She is a demonhunter, a servant of the Ishnapuri magi."

"I know what she is." Mykon Ambard was curt. "The northerners are not the only ones who presume, it seems, hunting in our city without so much as a by-your-leave."

Sorriyith took a step forward, his hand on his sword hilt, as the gathering disintegrated into a babel of exclamations and questions. The ambassador waved the Jhainarian back at the same time as Prince Ilvaine held up a hand, quelling the gathering. Gradually, silence fell again.

"Lady Sarifa is our guest," the prince said finally. He looked at the ambassador. "But Mykon also has a point. I think we would all like to hear why the Lion Throne has taken the unprecedented step of including a demonhunter as part of its embassy to the River." There were a few scattered nods as Lord Isrradin rose to his feet, his look grave.

"In part," he said, in his accented Ijiri, "Lady Sarifa accompanied us for the same reason that we disguised our journey here. The road is long and fraught with many perils, and her presence offered an extra level of protection." He paused. "She also follows a trail of her own, one that began on our desert borders and has led her to Ij—and may be connected with recent events here."

Prince Ilvaine frowned. "Surely you are not suggesting that a sand demon has made its way from the great deserts to the River? I wouldn't have thought that possible."

"It is *not* possible," Lady Sarifa said, answering the question without looking to the ambassador first. "Both the demons and their masters, the great djinn, are bound to the desert sands. Those I pursue have consorted with them, teaching the desert-bound new sorceries and fouler magics to work against our empire. Our desert border has seen a great increase in blood and terror these past few years, including the torture and murder of several of the magi's adepts." The husky voice was emotionless. "Possession has been reported as well, where the new demon assumes its victim's body. I was sent to hunt these demons down, but also to protect Lord Isrradin against exactly such possession."

Isperia Katran was frowning, her lower lip caught between her teeth. "Possession," she said. "And now, you say, the demons are here, which fits with Jehane Mor's account. This is not good news."

"It would be much worse," Sarifa replied, "if I were not here."

Jehane Mor almost laughed out loud at the demonhunter's arrogance, but the Ijiri were murmuring amongst themselves again. Prince Ilvaine's expression remained bland. "Perhaps so. Nonetheless, to hunt in Ij you will need the permission of the Masters, of whom I am only one."

Sarifa did not shrug openly, but Jehane Mor sensed her indifference to the nuances within the pavilion—and was intrigued that the ambassador appeared willing to let her speak so freely. "The demons are unlikely to stay once they know that I am here, unless their position is well entrenched." Sarifa's eyes, dark within their black paint, rested on Mykon Ambard. "Although I think that is no longer the case."

The assassin looked her up and down. "You are only one. What if your opponents have joined with others of their kind, since the Swarm has numbers here?"

"And if your demons *are* entrenched?" Prince Ilvaine asked, dry as paper. "How will we recognize them?"

This time Sarifa did look at the ambassador, who nodded for her to continue. "Such demons are difficult but not impossible to detect." She held up her left hand, folding down a finger for each point made. "They must kill before they can assume another's appearance, and only a very powerful demon can hold that outward seeming for long. A rash of otherwise unexplained murders, particularly if the bodies are hard to identify, could indicate a facestealer at work. When a stolen face does begin to go, it is the eyes that will slip first. Be alert for cloudiness or the suggestion of color variation in the gaze of those around you. The demons may also have difficulty with minor birthmarks and scars, particularly those that occur on the body rather than the face, so take careful note of such marks on those who are close to you." She folded down her fourth finger. "In some cases, where the demon is a lesser power, or has taken too many faces without respite—we are not yet sure which—the change may send them mad. They become like rabid dogs," she added, then shrugged. "But mad or not, a stake through the heart is the best cure for all their kind."

Lord Isrradin nodded to Prince Ilvaine, as though confirming Sarifa's veracity. "For yourself, Prince, and your Masters, be sure you are always protected by more than one guard, no matter how well you know those around you. And always stay guarded."

The prince's eyes traveled slowly around the circle of troubled faces, stopping at Haimyr. "You are remarkably silent, my other great-nephew. What do you say to this?"

The golden minstrel pressed his fingertips together. "That what has happened in Ij—and now, we learn, in Ishnapur—is just a beginning. The Darkswarm may already be moving to destabilize others who pose a threat, and eradicate all those in their way."

Starting with the Guild, thought Jehane Mor, and felt cold and weary and old.

"And your Derai are different?" Mykon Ambard's gaze was hard, but Haimyr met it, his own unwavering.

"The Derai *are* warlike, with scant regard for others, and may one day threaten the River. But the Swarm will destroy the very fabric of our world if we let them."

The assassin frowned. "Is this assertion based on anything more than Derai superstition and myth?"

"In Ishnapur," said Lord Isrradin, his quiet words carrying to everyone in the pavilion, "we rely on our magi to protect us from the storms of wild magic that come out of the desert. Their fellowship includes those who can peer through the veil that separates present from future. And the seers tell us that a darkness is rising, an all-devouring hunger that presses on their minds and eats at their dreams. Its tide, they assert, will wash over the entire world—and no one who stands alone will stem it. We must unite while we still can, and that—even more than trade—is why I am here."

The quiet in the pavilion deepened. No one looked at anyone else, except for the Jhainarian captain who stared at the heralds with his silver eyes. Eventually Prince Il-vaine sighed. "We have learned of events in Ij from our own sources and now we have heard from the heralds—but the accounts match in every essential. And the wrong done to their Guild, I hope you all agree, must be set right."

Still no one spoke, although several around the tent bowed their heads. In acquiescence, Jehane Mor wondered, or not wanting to meet the prince's eye? His look, beneath the drooped lids, remained keen. "We shall look to this matter of facestealers and other demons, but for now we must focus on our own affairs. We need to move while the recalcitrant and the undecided are still reeling from the Patrol's entry into the game. The rest should fall into place. But right now, we ride for Ij."

He rose to his feet, and Leto Ilvaine and his look-alike sprang to hold the entry open, letting the great walk through. Only the Jhainarian captain took a different path, circling the tent until he reached the heralds. He stared hard into both their faces and said something low and cold in his own language, before turning immediately away. The heralds answered in the same tongue, and Sorriyith hesitated—then kept walking, brushing out through the entrance without speaking again or looking back.

The three Patrol warriors said nothing, although Arin glanced from the heralds to the entrance, clearly puzzled behind his visor. Haimyr the Golden was not so reticent. "What was that about?" he asked, strolling across. "And what exactly are Jhainarians, anyway?"

"They are the Shah's elite auxiliary troops," Jehane Mor replied coolly, "drawn from the clans of Jhaine. Only the Imperial Guard stands closer to the Lion Throne."

"And what he said," Tarathan added, "is that we are lucky to still be alive."

The Patrolers all looked at him. "Your answer obviously gave him pause," Sarathion said finally.

The heralds smiled the same enigmatic smile. "We told him," they said, their voices blending together, "that there is no such thing as luck."

# 9

# *Portside*

*E*arly morning light slanted through the shutters of an upstairs room at the Portside inn, which was located just far enough from the ocean docks to be respectable, without ever becoming fashionable. But the room into which the day crept was respectable enough, with limewashed walls, rag rugs on the floor, and a bowl of potpourri on the table.

"To sweeten the air," the inn-wife said, smoothing her hands on her apron as she showed a new guest to the room shortly after dawn.

She was always up herself by then and thought nothing of a guest arriving so early in the day, for the business of the seaport depended on wind and tide, not the day and night hours that others in the city observed. Still, she didn't think this guest would care much whether the air was sweet or not, despite the rich fabric of his clothes. An odd looking fellow, she decided, descending the outside stair again, ill favored even, although his silver was as good as his cloth. She had dismissed him from her mind by the time she stepped back into the kitchen, which was warm with the smell of baking bread, and noisy with the first clatter of breakfasts being prepared.

The inn-wife's surmise that the new guest was not concerned about the sweetness of the air was correct, although he took a great deal of care in other matters, checking the final flight of stairs as well as both the door and window catches, muttering a few words over each. The mirror on one wall reflected glimpses of a very tall man, thin almost to the point of emaciation, with bone-white hair and deep-set eyes. A fuller view of the face revealed a fine, livid scar from temple to chin. It had the look of a whiplash, or an old burn, and stood out sharply against the guest's pallid skin.

He checked the brightening sky once through the shutters, his thin mouth set in a bitter line, before casting himself down on the bed, his long, narrow hands folded behind his head. Eventually he fell into fitful sleep, his face and body twitching almost continually, and did not wake until several hours later.

For a moment the man lay still—then his hand closed on the rod of carved white jade beneath his palm as he recalled the heavy footstep on the outside stair, which had reached him even in sleep. The rod's familiar chill and the whisper of power at its core were reassuring. He listened intently until the whisper told him who stood on the other side of the door, when a shade of annoyance crossed his face.

"Emuun." He swung his feet onto the floor as the latch was raised gently from the outside, and a much shorter and far more thickset man stepped into the room. The newcomer closed the door behind him and tossed his heavy cloak and traveler's wide-brimmed hat onto a chair.

"Wards on the stairs as well as every door and window! Do you have to be so thrice-cursed cautious, Nirn?" The voice was gravel, echoing eyes that were dark and hard as stone in a square face framed by a multitude of narrow braids, decorated with tiny bones and fetishes. Three ridged scars marched horizontally down his right cheek, echoing the two vertical cicatrices on the left. His mouth was little more than a gash in his hard face, but just now it had a sardonic cast. "They shouted out to me, kinsman, so they'd positively scream your location to anyone capable of tracking power. Although fortunately we're well over a thousand leagues from Ishnapur and their thrice-cursed demonhunters." Emuun pulled out a chair and seated himself astride it, his heavy forearms resting along the back.

"Is that so?" the taller man asked. "Then you will be as concerned as I to learn that an Ishnapuri demonhunter arrived outside Ij in the early hours of this morning."

The other grew very still. "You are sure of this?"

Disdain touched the emaciated face. "I am sure. My uneasiness has been growing for several days, but now there can be no doubt."

"Alone?" The question came with a baring of teeth that could have been a feral smile.

Nirn's thin lips twisted into a sneer. "Apparently not. It seems the magi have grown tired of finding the remains of their adepts staked out over anthills. Their hunter is accompanied by seven others that I can detect, bound into a protective ward."

Emuun spat out a curse. "A Jhainarian Seven! Amaliannarath take them!"

"Ah, so this Seven means something to you?"

Emuun shrugged. "Jhainarians are elite warriors, very hard to kill at the best of times. But from what I understand, when they are bound together as a Seven, in company with a demonhunter to focus their power, they become almost unstoppable."

The pale eyes narrowed. "And of course this Seven, together with a demonfinder, makes an Eight, the number of infinite power. All very interesting . . . But for now, I think we must abandon our Ijiri project. Even facestealing will not fool a demonhunter long."

"This hunter will undoubtedly have a description of mine, anyway. A pity, since I'm comfortable with the look." Emuun frowned at the pale sorcerer. "I note your care to say that you *sense* the demonfinder and the Jhainarians. I thought you would have *seen* them long since."

Nirn shrugged. "The River has been closed to me since the early hours of this morning. My farsight no longer reaches beyond the boundaries of the city." His hand clenched and unclenched on the rod. "Someone, or something, is blocking me."

Emuun whistled. "Have you any idea who, or what?"

"If I knew that," Nirn replied coldly, "then I could begin to deal with it." He studied the jade rod as if seeking answers, a deep frown between his chilly eyes. "And the heralds I most wanted have disappeared behind that wall of blankness."

Emuun yawned. "Eluded our net, eh? I find it hard to see how two couriers could be as important as you make out."

"Well, they are." Nirn's right hand clenched around the rod again. "I cannot foresee precise details yet, but you may trust me in this. They are vital to the influences that oppose us."

The thickset warrior regarded him thoughtfully. "*Can* I trust you, though? Look at what happened last night, after you assured me that you had seen our success down all potential farsight paths. Yet what we have this morning looks more like complete failure."

The whiplash scar whitened and Nirn's voice froze colder than his eyes. "Do you challenge me, Emuun?"

Emuun held up a placatory hand. "I ask the question, kinsman, that is all."

Nirn eyed him narrowly and then shrugged. "No one foresees all potential paths, not even a master. Yet all that I did foresee was entirely in our favor. And you know I was not alone in that seeing. Whatever path we looked down, all saw the River lands given over to anarchy, riven by fire and war."

"And that has changed overnight?" Emuun shook his head. "How can that be?"

The long narrow fingers clenched around the white rod. "I do not know," Nirn said at last, fury licking through the cold voice. "There must be some other power at work that I cannot see. Yet I can detect nothing, just the blankness beyond the river."

"Perhaps," said Emuun, after a short, uneasy silence, "we must put it down to the accursed Two-Faced Goddess. How else can one explain all the potentials turning from favorable to disastrous? Unless . . ." He paused, his hard-as-stone eyes boring into the sorcerer. "You have never been quite the same since you got burned five years ago in the Keep of Winds. Your powers appear . . . less reliable."

The other swung around on him, the pale eyes burning, and Emuun's head drew back a little. "Not *so* unreliable, kinsman, that I could not obliterate you where you sit!" The sorcerer's lips thinned. "Fortunately for you I have already lost one kinsman here and do not have an inexhaustible supply. Not of *useful* kin, anyway."

"I am glad you find me useful," Emuun replied, his hard face sardonic again. "But if blood kin cannot speak the truth to you, kinsman, then who can? So tell me—was your foreseeing ever wrong before you got hit by the Golden Fire?"

The thin mouth tightened still further. "It was not the Golden Fire! It was the Derai whelp, the Heir of Night, who is now dead!"

Emuun shrugged. "So Aranraith maintains, but no one ever saw a body. For myself, I always like to see the body, and better still, have the whole world see it, too." His wide fingers drummed on the back of the chair. "As for the firebolt, I was there when it struck and I still say the flame was golden. Besides, I would have thought there was no Derai spawn living, not these days, who would have a hope of hitting you that hard—and yet you nearly died." The hard eyes studied the sorcerer thoughtfully. "Surely you cannot think this herald pair, these River couriers, were the source of so much power? Or do you? Is that the real reason you have been so avid for their deaths?"

"They are certainly powerful," Nirn conceded, "and their part in the attack on me has not been forgotten. But they were not its source."

"No?" Emuun was silent, his eyes half closed. Then they opened again. "Speaking of dead heralds, I see your adept, Jharin, has abandoned the last face he was wearing."

The chill eyes considered him. "As it happens, the face abandoned him. He could not hold it, even through last night."

Emuun whistled again. "There *must* be more to these couriers than I thought. A power to resist, perhaps, rather than to attack or coerce?" He shrugged. "Although I was surprised—for all the screams and agony that delighted our assassin allies—when even your mindflaying could not break the Ishnapuri pair."

"Which should not have been possible!" Nirn snapped. He took a few hasty steps up and down the room. "There was always a kernel of resistance, no matter the subtlety or sheer brute strength of my work. No one knows the mindflaying better than I, yet still they escaped, slipping into death before I was done with them."

"Most inconsiderate," said Emuun, but he was frowning. "You're right. It should not have happened. And now it seems that not all the assassins were persuaded, in any case. Or did they suspect our facestealing, perhaps?"

Nirn shook his head. "No, not that. Even last night Jharin was able to control the change-back for long enough to escape their company." His expression was sour. "We dared not let them even begin to suspect."

"No," Emuun agreed. "I can't imagine our allies would have been pleased to learn that you failed to break the Ishnapuri heralds, despite the screams—and that Jharin and Amarn assumed their dead faces to conceal the fact."

Nirn's nod was curt. "As you say. But the instability of the change meant that Jharin was unable to help Orn when the thrice-cursed Derai sprang their filthy ambush." Again the long thin hands clenched and unclenched. The emaciated face contorted. "They shot my brother down like a dog in the street, then mutilated him while Jharin could do nothing, *nothing* except flee and hide."

Emuun looked away, fixing his eyes on the sun-splashed wall. "I felt Orn's passing," he said, "and recognized Derai handiwork although I came too late to the place where he fell." The wide, blunt hands flexed on the back of the chair. "It may please you to know that I have killed one of them already, down by the river. I tracked him from Orn's body and caught him unawares with a djinn trick, slipping between light and shadow to hit him with their desert fire before he could draw a weapon. For blood," he concluded softly, "demands blood."

A pale fire burned in Nirn's eyes, but he was composed again. "And death demands death, always. You have made a start, and in time we will have vengeance in full for Orn's death. But not now. We must flee this city before our enemies close in."

"Another debt," Emuun said deliberately. "Who must we pay back in kind for the ruin of our plans? Is it the heralds who escaped your net, or more Derai work?"

Nirn shook his head, and the ensuing silence was filled by a composite of sounds from the world outside: the clatter of dishes and pans from the kitchen, and the rumble of wagon wheels from beyond the inn gate. Someone in the kitchen jibed at an ostler in the yard, and the inn-wife, cleaning a room in the upper storey, called out for more hot water and fresh cleaning rags. "Clearly," Emuun said, when his companion remained silent, "last night's alarms did not reach here."

Nirn did look up then. "What? No—a good reason for choosing this place. That and proximity to the port." His fingertips continued to trace the deeply incised runes on the rod's pale surface, although his eyes remained on Emuun's face. "It was not the heralds," he said, almost reluctantly, "although their thread is in the weave. But this web is strung to another loom."

The warrior held up a warding hand. "No riddles, kinsman. Be plain with me."

The thin mouth twisted. "Plain, is it? Very well. Across the river, all is blank. But here in Ij I now see a host of interlocking threads that were invisible until we began to act—the blood and kinship ties of the Ijiri kindreds." Knuckles gleamed white as his fingers closed. "I was aware of them, of course, but believed them subordinate to the Three. Now it seems, the converse is the case. Someone who knew that has worked very cleverly and silently against us, pulling the threads of kinship tight last night, even in the School that we thought our own."

Emuun's frown was heavy. "Can you name this enemy?"

The sorcerer laughed, a dry hard bark. "Now we come to the Derai taint. I see the hand of a certain Ijiri minstrel who has dwelt long on the Wall of Night."

Emuun's snort was pure disbelief. "That frivolous plucker of strings? I could break him between my hands."

Nirn shrugged. "It was the Ilvaine who formed the nucleus of resistance to our allies in the streets last night and rallied others to support them, most notably the Katrani, the Teneseti, and the thrice-cursed Ambardi. Their kin-lines went right into the School and pulled the assassins away from us, just when we were most sure that they were ours."

"You have *seen* the minstrel's hand in this?" Emuun demanded. The sorcerer nodded, and the warrior shook his head. "So what do we do now? Flee, I know, but after that? You know what Aranraith's like about failure."

The long fingers snapped together. "*That* for Aranraith. We will look to the other irons in our fire, which means I go south. But you—I want you to finish those heralds for good and all. Make sure of it, Emuun."

The warrior grunted. "Just like that, eh? Find them. Kill them. No mistakes."

"Well, you like killing, don't you?" The sorcerer's tone was as impatient as it was cold. "Isn't that why we have a demonhunter on our trail?"

"As you say." Emuun sat back, folding his thickly muscled arms across his chest. "But we may need reinforcements."

"I already have agents in the south, and Arcolin and his coterie are there as well. If you need aid for your hunt then obtain it." The cold eyes held the warrior's stony gaze. "Make no mistake, the heralds' deaths are required. Nindorith, too, has foreseen their part in the pattern that coalesces against us."

Emuun gazed at the ceiling. "Ah. Nindorith."

A brief, mirthless smile flickered on Nirn's face. "I

guessed you'd still hold that grudge. But you'd be a fool to overlook Nindorith's foreseeing just because he stopped your game and took the sea-eyed witch away from you."

The other shrugged. "I never forget who my enemies are. Not that you'll catch me disputing with Nindorith: I'm not a fool. Besides, it's not my eyes that follow her every footstep, or darken whenever they see her safe in Ilkerineth's shadow."

The curl of Nirn's lips became even more pronounced and a sneer flickered across his face. Emuun was still looking at the ceiling, but now he made an imperative, warning gesture. For a moment there were only the inn sounds again, and then Nirn heard it, too: the faintest whisper, as though a leaf had fallen onto the roof—except that spring was not the season of leaf fall. Emuun was already on his feet, drawing a dagger as he rose. Nirn remained where he was, his expression focused, although he spoke idly: "Still harping on that old tune? The only emotion that fills Aranraith's heart is hatred. He's rotten with it."

The pattern of slatted sunlight was broken as a shape moved outside the shutters. Emuun crossed to the window in three swift, silent steps and flattened himself against the wall. Nirn's voice carried on, bored. "And even Aranraith would hesitate to cross Nindorith—or Ilkerineth for that matter."

A narrow blade slid between the shutters, lifting the catch at the same time as a quick tattoo was tapped against the wood. Nirn's face relaxed as the tattoo was repeated, and he nodded at Emuun to hold his hand. A moment later the shutters opened just wide enough to admit the slender, black-clad figure that had hung facedown from the roof to open them. Even the newcomer's face was veiled and wrapped in black; only the eyes, outlined by a dotted blue tattoo, were visible. These widened briefly as the assassin turned to secure the window and saw Emuun, but she showed no other sign of alarm, simply completed what she was doing and turned back to Nirn.

"You're late," the sorcerer said brusquely.

"There have been delays." The assassin was calm. "The

night has gone badly and many of my kin lie dead. Nevertheless, I have done all that my Master bade me."

"It is well," said Nirn. "How soon do we leave?"

"I have had to make alternative arrangements," the assassin replied. "The Patrol is posted at every landward bolthole, their galleys searching any vessel that tries to go upriver. And they have raised the boom at Farelle."

Nirn stared at her, his eyes widening. "The Patrol," he whispered. "The Patrol! Tell me," he added sharply, "why should the Patrol involve itself in this matter?"

The tattooed eyes met his. "Myself, I do not know. But the whisper on the streets says that it is because of the attack on the Guild of Heralds."

Nirn's lips compressed. Emuun watched from beside the window, but said nothing. "So," the sorcerer said at last, as though grudging every word, "what is your alternative arrangement?"

"I have spoken with a sea captain who has done business with us before," the assassin told him. "He hails from Grayharbor and will return there with this evening's tide. There is an islet called Brackwater, which lies a short way past where the harbor pilot will leave the ship. The dunes there are high enough to screen a small vessel that delays to pick up additional cargo—it will not be the first time this particular captain has done so."

"Just where is this Grayharbor?" Emuun demanded. The assassin had been standing so that she could watch him from the corner of her eye, but now she turned her veiled face fully toward him.

"It lies to the north, two days sailing from Ij, and is the last port before you come to wild country. Far enough to be safe, but not so far that it is impossible to return."

"Far enough for all trails to go cold, too," Emuun said to Nirn, "which will not suit our plans." He swung back to the assassin. "This Patrol comprises soldiery, correct? It should be easy enough to slip past their watch."

"So far," the assassin said flatly, "they have caught every

messenger that has tried their cordon, even though we are taught to be masters of stealth. It is uncanny."

"Or you are sloppy," said Emuun, as flat as she, but Nirn's eyes had narrowed.

"Uncanny," he repeated, almost to himself, while the assassin glared at Emuun. The sorcerer shook his head, as though dispelling an unpleasant thought. "We dare not risk this cordon. We must take the ship and pick up old threads from Grayharbor."

"What of clothes, money, equipment?" the warrior demanded. "We are too conspicuous as we are."

"That is arranged," the assassin replied. "If you leave here at dusk and go to the lower harbor where the fishing boats and ferries dock, a boatman will meet you. His name is Nevi and his boat is the *Seamew*—she has eyes painted on her prow. He will take you out to Brackwater, where you will find new clothes and money for your journey. Another of my cadre will bring the adepts you spoke of, if they make the rendezvous you set."

"Good," said Nirn. "Very good." He assumed a pleasant expression. "Extend our thanks to your Master and our best wishes for his continued health."

The tattooed eyes flickered, although the assassin's voice remained steady. "My Master is dead and nearly all our cadre with him. We few who remain seek only to do his final will in this matter."

"Before?" inquired Emuun. The tattooed eyes slid back to him as she shrugged.

"Unlicensed assassination is against the law of Ij. So, too, is any attack on a herald or their Guild. No other Master will speak for us, or their cadre accept us if they did." She turned back to Nirn. "I have done all that I can to keep faith with my Master. I wish you a safe journey."

Nirn nodded as the assassin turned back to the window, although he did not speak. She put her hand to the shutters, but as she did so, Emuun moved, silent as a hunting cat and as deadly. His heavily muscled left arm clamped around her body, pinning both her arms, while his right hand reached around the black-wrapped head in one swift movement and broke her neck. "I take it," he said over his shoulder, lowering the body to the floor, "that you agree?"

Nirn nodded. "She knew too much. But we'll have to dispose of the corpse."

"That's easy," said Emuun. "We put the body in the bed and you pay for another night before we leave. They'll think you've gone out for the festival, and there'll be no reason to come in here before tomorrow morning at the earliest. Maybe even the morning after, if we're lucky." He straightened, flexing his hands. "And the others? The boatman and anyone on the island?"

"The same," Nirn said. "No witnesses. Orn will have shades to keep him company, at least. There is symmetry in that, since his death last night is part of their failure." The long fingers tapped against jade. "But you must do it all. I dare not use my power until we have several leagues of ocean between ourselves and the demonhunter." He paused, studying his kinsman. "You made that quick, not your usual cat-and-mouse."

The hard eyes met his. "This is no time for risks. Besides, she was expecting it—I saw it in her eyes. I liked her courage."

The thin lips sneered. "Aranraith would be worried if he thought you were losing your love for blood and killing." The words *as would I* hung in the air.

The warrior shrugged, the gesture and his expression saying, very clearly, that there was little chance of that. He picked up the assassin's body, the black-wrapped head rolling against his shoulder, and dumped it on the bed.

The sorcerer strode to the window and peered through the slatted shutters. "The assassin has left me much to think about, with this news of the Patrol."

Emuun slouched back to his chair. "Another failure of foreseeing, kinsman? Maybe we should leave well alone for a change."

"Helms of concealment," Nirn muttered, as though his

companion had not spoken. "Yet everyone has a face, a name, however deep it's buried."

Emuun shook his head but said nothing, simply watched while Nirn paced and the day grew warmer. A fly buzzed near the roof, then spiraled lower, settling on the assassin's tattooed, unblinking eye. The droning stopped.

# 10

## A Pebble Falls

"The Derai would disagree, of course," said Haimyr, as they ducked out of the pavilion into spring sunshine and the flurry of the Ilvaine departure. The fife and the drum beat out a brisk tattoo while the armed companies took up their order of march. The pavilions were already being struck as Patrol riders brought up Haimyr's tall bay horse and the heralds' grays. Aravenor joined them as they swung into the saddle, while Arin formed up an honor guard to salute the Ilvaine company.

"They have a Goddess of Luck," the minstrel explained, continuing the earlier conversation. "She has her own temples, and priests to tend them, in every keep."

Jehane Mor regarded him wearily. "Ornorith of the Two Faces; we know. But the context was different, as it happens."

"So I gathered," the minstrel replied. If he noticed the constraint in her manner, he chose not to show it. "He didn't seem particularly friendly."

"He's a Jhainarian," Tarathan said, as though that explained everything. He looked at the journey roll strapped on behind the bay's saddle. "You're not staying here?"

"Someone," said Aravenor, "stirred the Ijiri pot somewhat vigorously last night." The hawk visor studied Haimyr. "I take it that your princely great-uncle is now to deplore your excess of zeal?"

Haimyr smiled. "Let us say that we have agreed that it might be better if I were to absent myself for a time. I had thought," he added casually, "to ride with the heralds and whatever escort you send with them, at least as far as the Farelle bridge. I am assuming that you won't go by galley until upriver of the boom?"

The heralds were silent, but Aravenor nodded. "Although first we must farewell your great-uncle and his guests, and then Tarathan and Jehane Mor may wish to rest before traveling on."

"Time," Haimyr assured him, "is of no consequence to a minstrel of Ij."

Sarathion, on Aravenor's other side, snorted, but Jehane Mor was watching the column. "They're moving," she said. At the same moment a trumpeter lifted a silver cornet to his lips and blew. Halberds and lanceheads glittered in the sun, and the gleam of armor, the tossing of plumes on headstall and helm, and the array of pennants were a brave sight. The sweat of nervous tension gleamed darkly on the flanks and necks of many of the horses, and several danced impatiently beneath their riders' hands. One reared, its hooves striking air, before its rider brought it back under control.

Prince Ilvaine shook his head as he and his immediate companions stopped beside Aravenor, waiting for the forward companies to pass. "They are all impatient to be doing," he observed, matching his tone to the headshake. "It is a failing of the young."

"It's a failing in war, as well," Aravenor observed dryly. "The rash die quickly and too often get others killed at the same time."

"Having confused impatience for boldness and calculated risk taking," added Haimyr, from his other side. "I have heard the keep commander say so many times to Night's younger officers."

"The apostate commander?" inquired Aravenor.

Haimyr's brows rose. "I hadn't expected to hear that epithet used on the River."

"They hear things on road and river," said Tarathan, straight-faced, and Sarathion laughed out loud. Even Aravenor smiled.

"There have been more Derai passing through of recent years," he said.

"Why 'apostate'?" inquired the prince.

Haimyr shrugged. "The Commander of Night seeks to repair a long folly, but in doing so cuts across much that is deep-seated in Derai tradition, skirting an oath that binds them all. And to many Derai, skirting is no different from breaking."

"Hence the 'apostate,'" observed Isperia Katran, with a sage's interest. "And the Earl your commander serves? Is he also apostate?"

"The Earl," said Haimyr, "leaves his commander to manage these matters, since they concern rebuilding the armies of Night, which is the keep commander's business."

"Keeping his distance, then," Prince Ilvaine approved, "so he can disown the commander if need be. A wise man."

Both the heralds and Patrol riders looked sidelong at Haimyr, who shrugged again. "They stand together those two, like Earl and Heir on the playing board."

"Perhaps. But in the final analysis, the Heir piece may still be sacrificed to save the Earl, is it not so?" The expression in the prince's eyes was shrewd. "I suspect your commander knows this as well."

"I expect so," said Haimyr, slightly less easily than before, and Jehane Mor thought she saw the trace of a shadow cross his face. But he was smiling again at once and she could not be certain.

"What does it matter what some commander or other does on the Derai Wall?" Mykon Ambard demanded. "We have more than enough to concern us here in Ij."

"Especially this morning," murmured the prince. "But still—a Master must know something of the world around him."

Mykon Ambrad looked as though he would like to argue, but before he could speak, Leto Ilvaine had dashed up on a fine dun courser. "The column is ready for you to join it, my prince."

"Then we had best not keep it waiting." Prince Ilvaine raised a gloved hand to acknowledge the Patrol's salute, and his party moved onto the road ahead of the Ishnapuri delegation. Both Lord Isrradin and Lady Sarifa bowed in the saddle as the prince passed, then saluted Arin's guard of honor in their turn, but the Jhainarians rode by without looking to either left or right.

"Are they always like that?" Haimyr asked, of no one in particular.

Let him wonder, thought Jehane Mor. She still felt weary and old, but Tarathan's mind touched hers with the same mix of grimness and reassurance as on their ride here.

"Always," he said calmly. "Your great-uncle may regret letting this demonhunter and her Seven into Ij. They serve a purpose, but their worldview is narrow and they would rather kill innocent people in error than let one demon escape."

The hawk visor turned. "I noticed," Aravenor said to Haimyr, "that your assassin kinsman didn't care for the Derai—and that the Swarm's purported objectives were not unpalatable to him. Do you trust him, Haimyr Ilvaine?"

"Mykon?" The golden minstrel smiled. "Implicitly, so long as his interests march with mine. He is ambitious, like all Ambardi, but he is no fool. And like my uncle, he does not wish to see either School or city dance as some other's puppet." The smile widened. "I do not say that he would not bear watching. There is no one in Ij with a mote of ambition and breath still in them who would not bear watching."

"In fact, you probably bear watching yourself," said Aravenor.

Haimyr laughed. "Do I look like a dead man? Or a lackwit? Undoubtedly, I should be watched. So narrowly that I think you should keep me close and feed me as well, while you're offering the heralds here a chance for much-needed sleep."

Aravenor waved them away. "Sarathion will take you to the mess tent. I'll join you later."

\* \* \*

The mess tent was severe compared to the Ilvaine pavilion, and the benches and long trestles had clearly seen many years of hard use. Two sides had been rolled up to let in light, with a couple of Enkot rugs thrown over the benches and floor of the guest area. "A concession to amenity," murmured Jehane Mor, but had no complaints with that, or the cots in the side tent where she and Tarathan were able to snatch a few hours' sleep. When they woke, they found that the Patrol's quartermaster had left saddlebags outside the laced doorflap, bulging with the supplies necessary for those who make long journeys by road.

Jehane Mor stared into the same shield mirror that had been left for them before, a crease between her brows. "*Sorriyith. He knew.*"

"*As soon as you spoke, I suspect. And his bond to the demonhunter would already have told him we had power.*"

"*They will want to come after us.*"

"*He practically promised it, at the end. But the demonhunter will have to conclude her business first.*"

"*So we have some time, before it begins again.*" Jehane Mor let her face grow smooth, clear. "*And the minstrel? Are his hands clean?*"

Tarathan's lip curled back, half wolf's grin, half snarl. "*Almost certainly not, after last night.*"

She caught the thought behind his mindspeech and nodded. "*I agree. He is playing a deep hand between Wall and River. Did you believe him when he said he heard nothing of an attack against the Guild?*"

"*If he didn't, his Ambardi kinsman must have. Someone in the mix chose not to act.*"

"*A house full of dead heralds being a small price to pay for—what? The Swarm exposed? The Patrol activated? The River put on an armed footing and able to serve as a potential Derai ally?*" Jehane Mor considered options. "*Or to resist a Derai invasion? Or both? And the Patrol, for all their vaunted oath, did not press either minstrel or assassin closely.*"

*"Because they know something we don't?"* Tarathan was thoughtful. *"Or want the Ilvaine alliance to set Ij to rights, and so judge it politic to let other matters lie?"*

She felt the crease between her brows return. *"That's a question in itself—what they know. And another: who are they, really? All these years the Patrol have been part of the River landscape but separate at the same time, with their visors and their forts. They serve, all know that, but why? Where did they come from, a thousand years ago?"*

*"Always under our eyes,"* said Tarathan, *"and yet we see them not."*

*"Someone must know, surely."* Jehane Mor wished she felt more certain of that, and smoothed her hands over her hair. *"Well, we won't find answers in here. Who's out there now, besides the minstrel?"*

*"Sarathion, still. Aravenor has just come in, with another Patroler."*

*"We had better join them. Do what needs to be done."* She saw Naia's face again, all the dead faces, and thought: how easily we forget them. The river that is life closes over their heads while the current bears us on to the next journey, the next puzzle that needs unraveling.

She turned as Tarathan stepped close, his dark eyes holding hers—and their memories fused: the swallowtail swords whirled and bodies fell on the bank of a shallow, pebbled river. Afterward she had turned those bodies over and looked down into every empty face, while he stood with both swords hanging down, blood dripping from the blades onto the shingle.

Now she felt his mind, quiet in hers, and for a moment they watched the memory together. *"We had to get across the river,"* he said finally, and she nodded.

*"Yet if my horse had not gone lame, they would never have caught us."*

*"Perhaps."* His hand closed on hers, warm and strong. *"But your horse did go lame. They did catch us."*

*"And now we ride the long road."* Jehane Mor put on her herald's face, serene, untroubled, as she reached to

unlace the tent flap. "*Shall we take the next step, join our hosts?*"

The Patrol riders were sitting with Haimyr when they ducked back into the main tent. All four had battered metal plates in front of them, piled high with food. "I'm sorry about the black clothes," Aravenor said, as though noticing their apparel for the first time.

"I've seen them in black before," Haimyr said cheerfully. "Five years ago on the Derai Wall—when they made their presence felt, in fact."

"So that's how the three of you know each other. I've been wondering about that." Aravenor nodded to the Patroler on his left. "This is Yris. She is one of our river pilots and will take you upriver from Farelle."

Yris bowed, but did not speak. She wore the same long black tunic and visored helm as the riders, but the sword at her side was short, her armor a quilted gambeson rather than a mail shirt. When she bowed, the light reflected off what looked like a stylized wave on her visor. The heralds both bowed in reply before starting to eat, and despite the breakfast in the Ilvaine pavilion, Jehane Mor found that she was ravenous again. She did not argue when a mess orderly brought second helpings.

"What I want to know," said Sarathion, when he had taken another helping himself, "is how you made your presence felt on the Derai Wall. That has the ring of a story."

"If it does," said Tarathan, around a mouthful of stew, "the minstrel can tell it."

"Oh, it's a story," Haimyr said, "although I need my harp to do it justice."

Sarathion shook his head. "No, no, just tell it anyway. Don't worry about the fal-lals of a song."

"Fal-lals!" said Haimyr in mock indignation, then shrugged, the bells on his clothes chiming, when Sarathion persisted. "Oh well, if I must pay for my luncheon, I must, I suppose."

"For a good story," said the Patrol lieutenant, "we'll throw in dinner and supper as well, as many helpings as you like."

Think what you would of Haimyr the Golden, Jehane Mor reflected, listening, but he could tell a good tale. He made their arrival at the Keep of Winds, in the middle of a formal Derai feast, sound full of portent, an opening hung about with the frayed darkness of ancient story—then let that darkness deepen into the blood and horror of the Darkswarm's surprise attack and the disappearance of the Heir of Night. The request for the heralds' assistance with the subsequent search became a flourish out of legend, and every step into the shadows of the Old Keep more fraught, sweeping the listeners through the Darkswarm attacks and into the final, deadly encounter with the Raptor of Darkness.

A profound silence followed his last words, and all three Patrol visors were fixed on the heralds, who concentrated on finishing their meals. Eventually, Sarathion shook his head. "I do call that making an impression, even if only half the story were true. Although I am sure that it is all true," he added immediately.

Haimyr smiled. "I was not present in the Old Keep myself, so must rely on what others have told me of events. For particulars, you will have to ask the heralds here."

It was uncomfortable, Jehane Mor thought, hearing a tale told about you that way—as though you belonged to the legends and the mythic past, rather than the everyday world. She bit into an apple and chewed slowly, grounding herself in the ordinariness of that action. "In terms of the bare facts, it was much as the story related. The glory Haimyr added. As for what we did, it was our heralds' duty, no more or less."

"And any herald pair would have done the same?" Aravenor's tone suggested that he was not convinced of that, reminding her of his words by the river. "I suppose the role you played could explain why the Darkswarm sought your deaths, in particular, last night. But why wait this long?"

The heralds shook their heads. "We don't know," Jehane Mor said, "or even whether the two events are connected at all."

Haimyr stretched, flexing his fingers together. "Perhaps,"

he said, his tone silken, "the Swarm also seeks that which is lost."

Jehane Mor continued to eat the apple while the patrolers looked from her expressionless face to Tarathan's, and then back to the minstrel. "Who or what is lost?" Aravenor asked, when the silence had dragged on too long.

"It's the minstrel's story," Tarathan said, in his darkest voice.

Jehane Mor made a weary gesture. "He refers to the Heir of Night, Malian of the Derai, who disappeared five years ago. Most believe that she died in Jaransor, but Haimyr the Golden has convinced himself that we have her hidden away somewhere."

"Malian of Night," Aravenor said, as though the name were an object he was examining. His voice grew brisker. "As for Jaransor, we know those hills by reputation. It seems highly unlikely that anyone who went into them would survive to come out again."

"And even if the Derai Heir did, why would you have hidden her?" Sarathion sounded puzzled. "Or the Darkswarm want to kill you if they think you know where she is—assuming that the Swarm wants her found. That doesn't make sense."

"We did agree to help her flee the Wall and hide from her enemies." Jehane Mor shook her head. "But we have already told Haimyr that although we waited by the Border Mark, Malian of Night never came there or returned with us to the River lands." She looked across the table at the minstrel. "It may be that you are right, Haimyr, and she is still alive, but we don't know where she is."

The hawk visor looked from one to the other. "She is telling the truth," Aravenor said.

Haimyr shrugged. "What is truth? The whole world knows that many secrets may lie concealed beneath the surface of a herald pair's truth. And if they have nothing to hide, why won't they even try to seek the lost Heir out?"

"You would want that," Sarathion asked, "knowing that Swarm agents are already watching them? If this Heir is alive, wouldn't the heralds lead her enemies straight to her?"

"Besides," said Aravenor, "your own story shows that Tarathan and Jehane Mor have already risked their lives once for your lost Heir. What are the Derai to them, that they should aid you again now? It is not they who owe a debt here, Haimyr the Golden."

Haimyr's brows flew up. "Are you suggesting that I do?"

"Well, don't you?" said Aravenor. He waited while the minstrel's raised brows subsided into a frown, but it was Jehane Mor who spoke first.

"Neither Haimyr the Golden nor the Derai owe us any debt for what we did five years ago. We made that clear at the time."

The hawk visor turned to her. "I suspect the Derai may see it differently."

Tirorn had suggested something very similar, Jehane Mor recalled, but she was watching Haimyr. It was not often that the golden minstrel was put out of countenance, but he looked wrong-footed now.

"It's not about owing or not owing," she said quietly. "But our duty does lie elsewhere. First we must go upriver, and then news of Salan and Ileyra's fate must be carried to their own Guild House—perhaps even to the Lion Throne. We may not be the ones sent, but the Guild may wish to dispatch heralds to the rest of the southern realms as well, to warn them of what happened here—in which case its resources will be stretched." She did not add, *given the tally of our dead in Ij,* knowing the thought would be in all their minds.

"Events are moving," Aravenor agreed somberly. "It may be that what has taken place here is just a single pebble—but every avalanche begins with one stone falling." The hawk visor studied Haimyr. "As for you, Haimyr Ilvaine, I think your great-uncle is right and your part here is played out. You should return to the Derai Wall."

The minstrel leaned back, gracefully casual. "Is that an instruction, Lord Captain?"

Aravenor stood up. "I prefer to think of it as a suggestion,

from one friend to another. A wiser course than following
the heralds upriver."

Haimyr laughed. "Well, we shall see." He, too, stood up,
shaking out his sleeves. "I will consider your—friendly—
advice while we ride to Farelle."

Aravenor nodded, before turning to the heralds. "I must
stay here, but Sarathion and a twenty-squad will escort you
to Farelle. Yris's galley awaits you upriver of the boom and
she will make sure that you arrive safely, wherever you wish
to go."

"And our horses?" Jehane Mor asked.

"Will follow by barge," said Aravenor. "A slower trip than
by galley, but now that the river is going down they should
not be many days behind you."

"Ay, the rains'll be done soon," said Sarathion, "and then
we'll have the true spring. We thought it might be better
if you rode Patrol horses to Farelle anyway, and wore our
helms, so as not to stand out."

There was nothing, thought Jehane Mor, you could say to
that, so she just nodded and followed them out of the tent into
the dazzle of mild afternoon. It must have rained again while
they were sleeping, because there were new puddles and a
sparkling edge to the day. She blinked against the brightness,
then blinked again, wondering if it had been a trick of the
eye that made the light seem to bend around Yris. She looked
again, carefully, but saw nothing more than another Patroler,
of slighter build than many, swirling a black cloak around her
shoulders. Nonetheless, Jehane Mor did not risk mindspeech.
Instead, she let her hand brush against Tarathan's as he took
the helmet Sarathion handed him, her fingers tapping the
herald code that meant: *Beware. Power user.*

Perhaps, the herald added to herself. But it could not hurt
to be careful, until they were sure. She sensed Tarathan's
curiosity, although he gave no outward sign, just studied the
helmet for a moment before sliding it over his head. Jehane
Mor hesitated, then did the same with the one Sarathion
handed her.

The helmet was heavy and there was some loss of peripheral vision through the eye slits, but otherwise the world looked much as it had before. "You'll get used to the weight," Aravenor said beside her, "and the visor. Besides, it's not for long, just until Farelle." He handed her the reins of a Patrol horse. "Ride safely, until we meet again."

"Until we meet again," she said, speaking as in unison with Tarathan. She wondered if she was the only one who questioned whether they ever would.

No one looked back or raised a hand in farewell as their small company clattered through the long ranks of the Patrol and took the Main Road for Farelle. Even Haimyr was unusually silent. It was not until they passed the crest of the first hills and the city dropped from sight that he began to whistle a jaunty tune, half beneath his breath. Soon after that he lifted his golden voice in a slow, sonorous song that the riders seemed to know, for gradually the whole troop joined in. Their singing rose above the road and fields, drawing people in nearby houses to their doors. Some just stood, shading their eyes as the troop rode by, but others waved or called out greetings, and both children and dogs ran out, following the horses.

Traffic on the road was light and they made good time, reaching Farelle and the graceful span of its bridge by late afternoon. The Patrol's boom was still raised on the downstream side of the bridge and their galleys were positioned across the river; another chain barred the bridge. A number of morose and surly river traders, from the first barges and merchant galleys of the season, were stranded on the downstream bank, and a general air of bewilderment characterized both road and river travelers. The toll clerks, clearly bearing the brunt of public dissatisfaction, were the first to besiege Sarathion for reliable information. Jehane Mor, sitting one horselength back from the lieutenant, recognized Serivis, who looked even more harassed than he had several days before.

"There are terrible rumors, your honor, simply terrible," he said, holding onto Sarathion's stirrup. "An attack on the Guild—I can hardly credit it! It explains the Patrol's response, indeed it does, although I hope . . ." He took his hand off the stirrup as though to scrub at his hair, then had to grab for it again as others pressed forward. "But as if that weren't enough, we have another party of those dratted Derai demanding to be let through. A matter of urgency, they say—for at least this lot make an effort to speak the River tongue like civilized folk—but they are well armed, and so we thought . . . Well, we are keeping them on the other side of the bridge, until someone like yourself can speak to them." He cleared his throat, his expression strained and unhappy. "If you would, your honor?"

Sarathion looked toward the far side of the bridge. "Derai, did you say?"

"That's right. And champing at the bit to cross, although they've been polite enough so far. But I don't know how long we'll be able to hold them."

"Black gear and black horses." Tarathan had ridden closer to the riverbank.

Haimyr urged his bay forward. "Black is the color of Night and their messenger horses are black as well. Do they bear a device?" he asked the clerk.

"A winged horse," Serivis replied promptly, "on the left breast."

"Then they are Night," Haimyr said slowly. "Lieutenant Sarathion, I should speak with them."

Sarathion nodded. "We need to find out their business. And Yris's galley is berthed on the Farelle side, so we have to cross over anyway."

Serivis bustled away and a few minutes later the chain was lifted back. "I do hope there won't be any trouble," he cried, as they passed through.

"Cursed Derai are nothing *but* trouble," an anonymous Patroler muttered.

There were eight riders drawn up on the far side of the bridge, and although their black garb was mired from the road, their armor and weaponry looked well kept and the winged horse device glittered on each mailed breast. They had maintained order, despite the delay, and held their formation as the Patrol approached.

"These," said Sarathion, "look like elite troops."

"Honor Guard," said Haimyr, "but riding messenger horses."

Sarathion raised a gauntleted hand, palm outward to signify peaceful intentions, and the foremost Derai mirrored the gesture. Slowly, he and one companion walked their horses forward to meet the Patrol.

"Why," said Jehane Mor, looking past the road mire, "it's Garan and Nerys."

"So it is." Haimyr let his horse range alongside Sarathion's. After a few brief, low-voiced words, it was he who spoke first. "Hail, Garan, Nerys: light and safety on your road. What brings you here, so far from the Keep of Winds?"

"Honor to you and to your House," Garan replied automatically, then exclaimed warmly: "By the Nine, I'm glad to see you, Haimyr the Golden."

"But why are you here?" Haimyr asked again. "This can mean nothing good."

Garan shook his head. "Nothing." He removed his helmet, revealing a dark, mobile face that was drawn with hard travel.

"He comes to announce a death." Yris spoke for the first time, soft as a breath of wind at Jehane Mor's side, and the herald had to prevent herself from jumping—although Garan's expression had already warned her that the pilot spoke true.

"Our orders," the Derai said, "are to find you and bring you back to the Wall, where you are needed." Tiredly, he looked past Haimyr to all the blank Patrol visors, then back to the minstrel. "On the slopes of the mountain," he said, his voice harsh with the weight of his words, "a pebble has fallen. But the one who fell has bidden you stand strong."

# PART II

*The Northern March*

# 11

# The Wolfpack

Carick as cold, tired, and a long time past fear. He had been running and hiding for over two days now, and knew his pursuers would catch him soon. They had forced him to abandon his mule, and most of his gear, and flee into the wild country that bordered the road through the pass. He had been all too aware that this was their territory and that no stranger, however young and fit, would lose the wolfpack in its own terrain. He had known, too, that he could not abandon the road and risk wandering in the wild until he died of exhaustion and exposure—if the outlaws did not hunt him down first.

Unfortunately, his pursuers were also aware of his dependence on the road, and every time he had tried to cut back to it they were there, waiting for him. Now exhaustion and hunger were taking their toll and Carick knew he could not last much longer. He suspected that his pursuers knew it, too, and were already closing in; he could feel their intent, savage presence, ominous as the shadow of a hawk to the rabbit crouching below.

He would not have survived this long if he had not been sleeping a short distance from his campfire and tethered mule. It was this precaution—and the first of the Seruth charms in his pocket—that had gotten him away when the outlaws rushed his camp in the gray, still dawn. He had been dubious of the charms when given them as a parting gift, but the first one had confused his enemies, sending them baying on first one wrong trail and then another while he ran until his lungs were on fire and his heart bursting in his chest. Carick had hoped he might lose them altogether in the confusion, or that they would be satisfied with the mule and his gear, and for a time thought he had won clear. But eventually he had seen the first loping shadow on his back trail and forced himself to run on, and then run further again, even when he felt he could not take another step. And despite having the charms to aid him, the pursuit had never completely lost his trail.

Even so, Carick did not think he had done badly for a River-raised scholar. True, he had lost his bow early on, but he had also crawled through thickets of dense thorny scrub and leapt precariously from rock to rock up streams to eradicate his trail. His pursuers, however, had numbers and the persistence of the wolfpack for which they were named. Now all Carick had left was an almost empty rucksack, a knife, and a dogged determination to die as bravely as he could.

Shafts of early sunshine were finding their way between the trees and onto the narrow ribbon of road. He could see it from where he lay, flat out beneath a thicket of the white-flowering shrub that grew profusely through the understory. It should take the outlaws some time to beat through the brush, although Carick suspected they would smell him out first: they seemed far more wolf than man to him. He listened, but could hear nothing except the cheerful rush of the stream that lay below the road and the occasional call of a woodland bird.

Above him on the hillside a wood pigeon startled up, its heavy wings whirring, and flew to a taller tree. Carick strained to see better without raising his head. There was a rock outcrop near where the bird had flown up; he had passed it earlier and recalled thinking that it would provide a good view of the lower slopes. Now he thought he saw movement in its shadow, just as another bird scolded at something in the brush below him. Silence followed its outburst—and then a man stepped out of the shadow between two trees, onto the road.

The newcomer looked like as much like a wolf as a human being can look, with shaggy brindled hair, a wild beard, and clothes that were layers of indeterminate gray and brown, bound together with strips of hide. He carried a long bow as tall as himself in his right hand and a businesslike sword at his left hip, as well as an assortment of dagger hilts about his person. The man stood very still, with his head up, and Carick could see that he was sniffing the air while his gaze swung from left to right, searching the wooded slopes. Somewhere on the hillside above Carick, a twig snapped.

They'll be onto me as soon as I move, he thought. He lay utterly still, knowing that it was only a matter of time—and not much time, at that.

The man on the road moved to the edge of the trees below Carick's hideout, and the young man's hand tightened on the knife hilt. But the hunter threw up his head again, listening, then faded back into the trees. Carick listened, too, but could hear nothing except the stream and the rustling trees overhead. What felt like several minutes passed before he made out the steady clip of hoofbeats, approaching from the northern end of the pass.

Two horses, or one? Carick wondered. His muscles tensed and he ran his tongue over dry lips, knowing his only chance was to dash for the road and hope that any newcomers were well disposed and well armed—and that the outlaws did not shoot him down as he ran, or shoot the new arrivals instead. Already the hoofbeats had grown louder, and a moment later two horses—one ridden, the other a packhorse—came into view.

The rider did not look much more reputable than the wolf's-head who had been on the road. In fact, he looked decidedly shabby in an old-fashioned ringmail shirt beneath a patched tunic, and the pot helm on his head had clearly seen better days. A hedge knight or a mercenary, Carick thought, probably little better than a brigand himself, and yet . . . He bit his lip, tasting blood, and wondered whether he should call out a warning. But that would give his position away—and what if the rider just spurred on and left him?

The way the rider controlled his horse with his knees and kept both hands free for his bow, which had an arrow ready on the string, was more than businesslike. Carick wondered if the outlaws might let him pass, after all—and then a bow-string sang and the rider ducked as an arrow whirred past. The horses exploded forward as the rider's bow answered, and a man pitched out of the trees, an arrow sprouting from his throat. Carick leapt to his feet, shouting, and crashed down the hill. Behind him, the outlaw pack gave tongue and came baying at his heels. Another arrow thrummed, and he ducked and twisted the last few yards to the road.

The second horse was almost on top of him as he ran out of the trees, but Carick managed to dodge and grab for the cantle of the pack-saddle. He saw the rider's face turn in his direction and hoped the man would realize that he was not an outlaw. He clung to the saddle and a handful of mane, half on, half off the horse, and watched the bow come up—but the rider swung around and shot into the trees again while Carick's horse thundered on. Then he was around the next bend in the road and there were no more arrows as the horse stretched into a flat-out run.

Carick clung on, but the horse swerved to avoid a tree that had fallen half across the road, and his precarious hold was dislodged. He fell into the downed branches and was fighting his way clear when the rider came thundering around the bend behind him. The man did not check, but swept an arm down, hauling him up and across his own saddlebow by main force. Carick gasped like a landed fish as the breath whooshed out of him, but the horse ran on for another jolting, uncomfortable mile before it began to slow.

The first stop was brief, just long enough for Carick to be set roughly on his feet and for the hedge knight to whistle up the packhorse and quickly redistribute gear so Carick could mount again. The man did not say much, other than to inquire whether he could stay on unassisted or would need to be tied in place. He grinned, a somewhat fierce expression, when Carick flushed darkly beneath the grime on his face. "We must travel fast whether you can ride or not." The man glanced back the way they had come. "We'll need to be well clear of this pass by nightfall."

"I can ride," Carick said, and scrambled up. He did not add that he was out of practice—given that an able-bodied student could get most places on foot in the university city of Ar—or that the pack-saddle made for uncomfortable riding. He dared not risk his rescuer abandoning him if he proved a burden, especially when he could see no end to the thick forest and rough country of the Long Pass.

They were good horses though, Carick decided, as the morning lengthened toward noon: sturdy and enduring.

"It's not far now," his rescuer said at their next, brief halt. "The Long Pass doesn't open up until the very end, but we'll be out of it by mid-afternoon." He took a swig from his water bottle before handing it to Carick, wiping his mouth with the back of his hand. "Which is just as well."

"So you think they're still behind us?" Carick took the rabbit and onion pie the man offered him as well. The pastry was stale, but he devoured it in ravenous mouthfuls and wondered if he would ever again, in the life that had been returned to him, eat anything that tasted even half as good.

His companion's smile was grim. "They won't give up easily, not after so long a hunt. And they run like wolves in that band, as well as smell and kill like them, so we'll need to push the horses to stay ahead." He shot Carick a measuring look. "How are you bearing up?"

"I'll hold," Carick said, although in reality every muscle ached bitterly. He bowed awkwardly. "I've just realized—I haven't asked your name, or offered mine, although I owe you my life. I am Carick of Ar."

The rider's sardonic expression twisted into a grin. "An honest River name. You can call me Raven. I answer to it most days."

The name suited the man, Carick thought. He was very dark and there was a sharp edge to his gaze, as though he was used to assessing men and situations at a glance. "Ser Raven?" he said tentatively, not wanting to offend the man. But Raven just shrugged and remounted without replying.

They kept the horses to a brisk, steady pace and soon the pass began to open out. The hills became progressively lower and further apart and the road dropped down in a series of swooping curves that Carick knew would favor the wolf-pack, since they could cut straight down the hillside between each loop. He kept checking back over his shoulder, but saw nothing.

"It doesn't mean they're not there," Raven said eventually, and Carick nodded.

"I know. It just means we can't see them." He had learned that the hard way.

"They're wolves in their nature, too," his companion said. "They'll be with us until civilization drives them off—or what passes for civilization in these parts."

Carick wondered what sort of mercenary or hedge knight would quibble over levels of civilization, especially as the shabbiness of Raven's first appearance did not improve upon closer inspection. The old-fashioned sark had been mended with horn and bone in places, and his cracked leather gaunt-lets, like the helmet, had definitely seen better days. Carick had noted other signs of the disreputable as well: the tattoos glimpsed between the edge of the knight's sleeves and his gloves, the fetishes of bone and feather tied as a crest to his helmet—and horses that answered to a whistle.

The father of one of Carick's university friends, a promi-nent River merchant, held the unshakable opinion that horses that came to a whistle belonged exclusively to smugglers or brigands. In the merchant's world, mercenaries and hedge knights were only one step above brigands.

But, Carick thought, Raven not only fought to cover my escape, he's shared his food with me as well. So does that prove that you can't judge a man by appearances, or does the hedge knight have some other purpose? Finally he shrugged and asked Raven straight out why he had helped him.

His rescuer, who was riding half a horse length in front,

glanced back. "Perhaps you should just be glad that I did."
His voice was not unfriendly, but it was not particularly
friendly either, and Carick flushed again.

"I am grateful," he said quickly. "Very grateful. But from
tales I've heard—" He hesitated again. "Well, not everyone
would, that's all."

"Perhaps," Raven replied, "I hoped you would turn out to
be some fat River merchant's son and that your loving relatives would pay me a rich reward—or ransom."

Carick hoped his alarm wouldn't show in his face, but it
must have because Raven grinned. "Don't worry, boy. I already knew that a rich man's son wouldn't be traveling alone
through the Long Pass."

His accent, thought Carick, was hard to place. It was neither the clip of Ar nor the burr of Terebanth, and certainly
not the drawl of Ij—although he detected a hint of all three
as well as another, more elusive, element.

"The wolfpack would have known it, too," Raven continued. "Lucky for you, then, that they stopped to eat your
mule."

"They ate my mule?" Carick's voice cracked and he bit
his lip again, feeling the pain and trickle of fresh blood
where he had gnawed it before.

"Better the mule than you, which I wouldn't put past them
either. Outlaws live hard in this country, so they wouldn't
pass up a tasty piece of mule meat. That's what saved you.
They assumed it would be easy to catch you later."

"Well," said Carick, not without bitterness, "it was,
wasn't it?"

Raven did not bother to look around this time. "Not as
easy as they thought, for a soft city lad. I'd not have given
you two hours if someone had asked me. Still, having those
Seruthi priests' charms must have evened the odds a bit."

Carick stiffened. "How do you know about those?" he
demanded. "Or about my mule, for that matter?"

The shoulders in the patched tunic and greasy mail
shrugged. "I saw the camp. It wasn't far from the road, and
the wolfpack weren't tidy with the mule or your gear. As for

the charms, I smelt 'em, lad—there, and other places along this road." He glanced back, grinning a little. "You were the one carrying the handful of magic, lad. No need to look so surprised that someone else can smell it." He paused, the grin fading into a considering expression. "Maybe that's what's drawing the wolfpack as well. Something must be, to dog your trail this long. Anyway, it made me curious. I wanted to find out more about someone who was foolish enough to go wandering through the Long Pass alone but had been given charms by a priest of Seruth. For you're no temple get, unless I'm much mistaken."

Carick sighed. "I'm not. I was a scholarship student at the university in Ar and graduated at the end of last summer. I didn't start out alone either. I booked a place on a caravan, leaving from Ar for Emer, but they changed routes after the first pass and went west to Aeris instead." Now Carick recalled the sly look in the guide's eyes as he refunded his caravan fee and wondered if the man had been in league with the wolfpack all along.

Raven shook his head. "You have it too easy in the River lands, with the Patrol to keep road and river safe. But it doesn't explain the charms."

"One of my fellow students was a merchant's son whose father said that you shouldn't travel beyond the River without a few charms of Seruth in your pocket by way of insurance. So my friend purchased them for me, as a farewell gift."

"A generous friend," Raven observed, and Carick nodded.

"I thought they were just an expensive superstition. But supposedly they derive from the old days of the Cataclysm."

"Spoken like a true scholar," his companion said dryly, and Carick stuck out his chin. He *was* a scholar, a graduate of the university, so what did it matter what some hedge knight thought?

"He gave me a Seruthi medal, too," he said, a little sullenly, and fingered the silver medallion at his throat. "They're meant to bring good luck to travelers." He shrugged, refelcting how that belief had now been proven as superstition, and changed the subject. "The caravan guide said that the Castellan of Normarch held the Northern March for the Duke and that his knights patroled the pass. He said I would be safe traveling through alone."

This time Raven slewed right around in the saddle to look at him. "And you believed him?" He shook his head. "The Northern March of Emer is vast and sparsely settled, not like your River lands. The Castellan has his work cut out to uphold the Duke's law." His voice became sardonic. "A solitary traveler foolish enough to venture the Long Pass would have to be someone very important for the Castellan to send a patrol to the rescue. And he would have to know that traveler was coming."

Carick scowled, thinking that the man might as well have called him a fool to his face. Or perhaps he had. In any case, he *had* been a fool and so deserved the epithet. But it irked him, all the same, to find that Raven's opinion of him mattered. It would be so much easier if he could just dismiss his rescuer as an ignorant thug, disreputable and probably illiterate—the popular image of a soldier of fortune in the River lands. Instead the man seemed astute, although as for that remark about smelling magic . . . Carick shook his head. He had never heard of such a thing and wondered how it could possibly be true. But then, he had doubted the Seruthi charms as well, until they saved his life.

Their next stop was at the small, neglected shrine to Seruth—Serrut in the Emerian dialect—that marked the southern end of the Long Pass. The surrounding countryside remained desolate and Carick could see no sign of human occupation beyond the white ribbon of road looping away between dun hills. He ran a hand across his dirt-grimed hair. "Does no one live here?" he asked.

Raven shrugged, winching up a bucket of water for the horses from the well beside the shrine. "Not in any numbers and not for a very long time, if ever. You can see why we're not safe just because we're out of the pass."

"So what do we do?" Carick wished his voice did not sound so thin against the emptiness of the landscape.

The rider cast an eye at the sky. "We have three good

hours until sundown, maybe even four since the days are lengthening. So we'll run the horses from here, medium length runs and short walks, and try and open up a good lead before nightfall. If the best happens, we'll reach human habitation. At worst—" He shrugged. "We'll just have to find somewhere defensible to stop."

"You don't think they'll give up when it gets dark?" Carick asked, without much hope.

"No." Raven's headshake was definite. "They'll know they've lost us if we're still ahead of them tomorrow morning."

Carick wished he felt as calm as this man appeared, as though being hunted by a pack of wild men was just something you dealt with, like drawing up water for the horses. He was worried, too, about whether the horses could last, despite their endurance so far.

"They're hill horses, out of Aralorn," Raven said when he asked the question. "Hardy little brutes—they'll go forever and still have a burst of speed if we need it."

Aralorn, thought Carick, frowning over his mental map, was to the south and east of Emer, a land of sheep, chestnut woods, and quiet hills. He had never heard of its horses before, but these two certainly showed every sign of going forever, and Raven kept to his word about traveling hard. Nonetheless, Carick found himself looking back again as shadow crept out from the western hills. He could almost feel the wolfpack running in their wake, as tireless as the Aralorn horses and eager for the kill. He studied the land ahead of them as well, yet saw no sign of human settlement.

"Why is this country so unprotected?" he demanded at the next short rest. "You'd think the Duke would want to keep the road to the River open." He was deeply tired and could hear the ragged edge in his voice, knowing that in less than an hour it would be twilight.

Raven's eyes were so darkly blue that they looked almost black, his gaze measuring, and Carick wanted to look away before that dark glance plumbed the depth of his weary, frightened soul. But the rider said nothing, simply held out the water bottle. The brackish water was warm in Carick's parched mouth and he held it there a moment before swallowing. When he offered the bottle back, Raven was still watching him.

"Emer isn't like the River," the rider said. His eyes narrowed, as though concentrating on something seen at a distance. "It hasn't had the cities and the Guild to build a peace, or the Patrol to keep it. It wasn't even a united country for a long time, just a host of little kingdoms vying against each other, and what peace there is has inched its way out from Caer Argent. The marches were the very last to be brought under the Duke's law, which is still a chancy thing in remote parts—like here. You're right about the link to the River, but that's also one of the reasons this land has always been fought over."

"You seem to know a lot about it," Carick observed.

Raven shrugged. "I've picked up a little knowledge here and there, is all." His eyes shifted between sky and hills, as he stoppered the bottle. "Time for another run."

# 12

## Nightfall

The horses ran until the tops of the hills were bathed in amber light; and Carick patted his mount's neck as they slowed to a walk again. It had been a gallant effort, he thought—and then jumped as the long, mournful cry of a wolf rose behind them. The sound was distant, but not far enough away for comfort, and Raven nodded. "Ay, that's them. Time to find somewhere defensible, before it gets too dark."

But the land was already shrouded in thick blue shadow by the time he pointed to the remains of a chimney, black in the half-light. Carick could just make out crumbling walls as they turned off the road, and when they rode closer he saw that the low, shingled roof was still intact. An opening in one wall must have been a door once, and the land around the abandoned building was clear, with no outbuildings or sheltering trees. "No cover for attackers," Raven said. He wiped the sweat from his face. "If it was a farmhouse, there'd be an orchard. So it must have been a hunting croft, or a way station for travelers."

Carick thought about the white, soaring walls of Ar, built in the early years of the Cataclysm, but he knew they had to make do with what they had. He tied the horses inside the building as Raven bade him and then helped shore up the doorway, creating a breastwork from blocks of fallen stone. They pushed smaller rocks into the gaps between the crumbling walls and the roof, but Raven was careful to keep openings large enough to shoot through on every side

"I've three bows with me," he said when they were done, "my rider's bow, a foot soldier's long bow, and a crossbow." He flicked a glance at Carick. "I take it you can shoot?"

Carick swallowed, nodding. "Everyone in Ar can. To be a citizen, you have to practice at the butts at least once a week."

"But your focus was on your studies, eh?" Raven seemed to have no trouble reading between the lines. "So long as they're holding back, let me shoot—we'll need to make every arrow count. You rewind the crossbow and keep track of what they're doing, as much as you can."

"And when they rush us?" Carick asked.

"Grab a bow and loose arrows as fast as you can. Don't worry about niceties; once they're bunched, every arrow will hit."

Carick nodded, aware of the sharp hammer stroke that was his pulse, and the dampness in his palms. "And when they reach the walls?"

"Spears first," said Raven, taking an oilcloth bundle from the packhorse and unwrapping four spears. "Don't throw, stab—anything that you can reach." His eyes, black in the twilight, pierced Carick. "The tricky part will be if they get in. You need to get shoulder-to-shoulder with me then, backs to a wall. Failing that, it's back-to-back work, but a wall's better. Hold onto the spear as long as you can, it'll give you reach. Otherwise, you'll just have to use your dagger." Raven's assessing look was grim. "Whatever else you do, don't let them get in between us. And stay close to the horses, that way I can defend you both at the same time." His teeth flashed, very briefly. "Although they'll get a shock if they get too close to the horses."

Carick could not help being impressed by Raven's array of weapons: the man was practically a traveling armory. The observing, scholar's part of his mind also noted that every blade was sharp and well oiled, with the gleam of proven use.

"When you're in my trade," said Raven, interpreting his gaze, "you always buy the best weapons, the best horses, and the best food you can afford, in that order. Everything else is extra."

Carick nodded again. "What are our chances?" he asked, pleased at the steadiness of his voice.

Raven's eyes searched the dusk that was deepening into night around them. "Better than you might think. They have numbers, but no discipline."

The wolf's howl rang out again, closer this time, but Carick was aware that Raven had stiffened a half second before, as though hearing something else. He strained his ears, listening, and then heard it, too—the distant clatter of a large company of riders, coming up the road from the south. Carick's heart leapt. "Could it be the Castellan's men after all?"

"I'd better take a look," said Raven, and handed him the crossbow. "Shoot anyone except me who tries to get in." He peered into the dusk again, then vaulted over their hurried breastwork—remarkably lightly for a man in a ringmail shirt—and disappeared into the darkness beyond the croft.

Carick waited, listening intently as the clatter of hooves became a thunder and trying to make out what was happening from the mix of sounds. First there was the trampling and snorting of what sounded like a great many horses, then a voice barked a command. Raven's horses were listening, too, their heads up and their ears well forward, although they made no sound that would betray their presence.

O Sagacious Horses, thought Carick, and remembered how they would come to a whistle. The sharp voice was still speaking, apparently asking questions, but there seemed to be more than one person replying. The wait seemed interminable, until finally Carick heard another barked command and horses moving—and grasped the crossbow more tightly as a heavily armed company of twenty or more horsemen swept into the open area around the croft. He wondered whether Raven really expected him to shoot at these newcomers, then relaxed as he saw his shabby companion standing beside the foremost horseman.

So it is rescue, Carick thought. He studied the stamping, shifting melee and knew that the riders must be the Castellan's men. In this remote part of Emer, no one else could field so large a company.

"Give me some light here!" Carick recognized the voice that had rasped out commands and questions. The speaker was peering into the blackness cast by the croft, and Carick realized that Raven must have told the riders he was there. No more hiding then, he thought, putting down the crossbow, and began to pull away the stone of their makeshift barrier.

"Don't just gawp—someone help with that stone!" A couple of riders sprang down and started dismantling the barrier from the other side, while others lit pine-pitch torches that caused some of the horses to snort and sidle. Beyond the torch glow, Carick could now see the silhouette of more riders drawn up along the road. One of the young men on the other side pulled out the largest block of stone and tossed it aside, before reaching out a hand to him. "Are you all right? D'you need help to get out?"

"I'm fine," said Carick, with a quick shake of his head. "Just tired," he added, clambering over the last of the rubble.

"But it does sound as though you've been having a tremendous time," said the second young man. "Playing hide-and-seek with the wolf's-heads through the pass!"

Carick looked at him with barely concealed amazement, wondering what the hedge knight could have told them. But he knew where his duty lay, so walked over and held out his hand. "Thank you," he said. "I'd be dead now if you hadn't helped me."

His words rang out as the riders fell silent, and Carick saw that their leader was watching with frowning interest from beneath his raised visor. After a moment, the man tugged off his gauntlet and leaned down from the saddle, extending a hand to Carick. "Ser Bartrand Ar-Griffon," he said, "Captain of Normarch. And you, I think, are the new ducal cartographer from the River lands. Luckily for you, the Castellan decided you were well overdue."

"I am," said Carick. He was careful not to look at Raven. "Maister Carick of Ar at your service, Ser Bartrand."

The Normarch captain nodded, without much interest now that the courtesies had been traversed. He raised his voice again. "I want pickets out in force along the road to the north and more sentries around the croft. See to it, Girvase. Hamar, make sure that the horses here are fed and watered; Raher, you go with him. The rest of us can have something to eat while we talk. Audin, with me, if you please, and Erron, too. We must hear what these two have to tell us about the wolfpack."

Carick watched curiously as the horsemen sprang to do their captain's bidding. The two who had helped clear the door must be Hamar and Raher respectively, since they both moved to organize the horses. Ser Bartrand addressed the older man who came to stand beside him as Erron, so the brown-haired youth with them must be Audin. Those who were not helping Raher and Hamar with the horses were sharing out food, or holding the torches so there was light for the others to work by. They seemed remarkably well organized, competent, and cheerful, and Carick's spirits sank as he thought about his flight through the pass. These young men were going to despise him as soon as they heard the tale.

Ser Bartrand studied Raven, a slight, cynical curve lifting his hard mouth. "I take it that it is *Ser* Raven?"

"It is," Raven agreed, not shrugging the title aside as he had with Carick. "I shall take knight's service in Emer, if I can find it. Otherwise I'll follow the tourney circuit over the summer and move on to Lathayra in the autumn."

"The circuit, ay," said Ser Bartrand. His fingers drummed against the leather of his tall, horseman's boots, but then he nodded. "You start, then. Tell us your story."

"It's the maister here's story," Raven replied. "I came into it late. I'd seen his tracks on the road, of course, traveling alone through the pass with a mule, but I only got interested when I saw the first of the outlaws' marks cut across his.

Later, I found the destroyed camp and the mule's carcass. They'd have had him, most likely, if they hadn't stayed to eat first." The look he flicked at Carick was dispassionate as he repeated this observation from earlier in the day. But he did not, Carick noted, mention the Seruthi charms or anything about smelling magic. "I guessed he'd have to try to get back on the road sooner or later—assuming he could stay alive. So I was expecting the warning my horses gave, early this morning, when we drew close to the wolfpack."

Ser Bartrand glanced at the horses, which had been brought out into the yard. "Hill horses, out of Aralorn. They'd know all right. Hamar," he called, "see those Hill horses get some grain, too, while you're about things."

"I have feed for them," Raven said. His tone was neutral, but the horsemen around him stirred, studying him sidelong.

The captain shrugged. "Keeps the lads out of mischief. And we can spare the grain. What happened when you encountered the wolfpack?"

Raven described his charge along the road to meet Carick's dash down the hillside. He shrugged. "And then it was just a matter of pressing on hard and hoping to survive the night—which we might not have done, if your company had not turned up."

"We wouldn't have been patrolling this way, except that the Castellan felt the Duke might want to receive his new cartographer in one piece." Ser Bartrand's heavy gaze swung to Carick, measuring him. "But what in Karn's name were you thinking, traveling alone through the Long Pass?"

So Carick told him about the caravan that had turned aside and the guide who told him it was safe to proceed alone. He felt foolish, repeating that story, and the two days flight through the wild country adjoining the pass did not make for much better telling. He had survived long enough to meet Raven, but that was all.

Ser Bartrand shook his head. "You've had nothing short of Imuln's own luck, it seems, although I'll warrant you didn't think so at the time." He turned to the lean, grave man at his side. "What do you say, Erron?"

The older man's voice was slow, thoughtful. "The outlaws cannot have known who Maister Carick was, else they would have tried for a ransom."

Raven had been studying the ground, but now he looked up. "They were hunting for the kill, not for capture and ransom."

Carick cleared his throat. "I don't think anyone in the caravan knew who I was. And I have no great wealth or position in Ar. I was on a prince's scholarship at the university."

"Ah, well." Ser Bartrand began to draw on his gauntlets. "We must escort you both to Normarch and see what the Lord Castellan says."

"He will send word to the Duke, too, Maister Carick," Audin put in, speaking for the first time, "so he knows why you are delayed."

"Of course," agreed Ser Bartrand, with a short laugh. "Lord Audin here will keep you right with the court, Maister Cartographer."

Carick thought a slight color might have risen in Audin's cheeks, but that could have been the torchlight, for the young man's tone remained calm. "What are your orders, ser? Do we camp here overnight and drive the wolfpack back into the hills tomorrow?"

"I and the rest of the company, yes," Ser Bartrand replied. "I want you to take eight riders and escort our guests back to Normarch tonight. Maister Carick will be safest there." The hard, assessing stare found Carick again. "I won't ask if the Hill horses are up to a night march, but what about you, Maister Cartographer? Can you stand it?"

Carick stiffened, meeting the stare. "Yes," he said, "although it would be easier if I could use something other than a pack saddle for the ride."

Audin laughed, and even Ser Bartrand smiled. "I think we could probably manage a spare horse. Erron?"

The quiet man nodded. "One of the dispatch mounts, I think, rather than a warhorse. Mallow, perhaps," he said to Audin.

"Mallow it is," agreed Audin. "And you, Erron? Do you ride with us or stay with Ser Bartrand?"

Erron and the captain exchanged a glance. "I need you here," Ser Bartrand said. "Audin can manage the escort." He sketched a nod between Carick and Raven. "Maister; Ser Raven. I will see you both in Normarch soon, Imuln willing."

Audin looked from one to the other as the captain strode away. His smile was pleasant, although his gaze, too, was measuring. "We had best be on our way if we are to reach Normarch before midnight. Although we should have good light once the moon rises, since it's near full. Come with me, Maister Carick, and we'll get you that horse."

"Just Carick will do," said Carick, limping after him. He had stiffened badly while they talked.

"Carick, then," said Audin, with another quick smile. "Oi, Hamar! Bring out Mallow for Carick here. And bring your own horse with her. You, too, Raher. We are to escort our friends here back to Normarch."

"I knew this would happen!" exclaimed Raher. His scowl was intimidating. "Mollycoddling us again!"

"You know why," Hamar said calmly, but Audin had not stayed to hear Raher's outburst. He was rounding up the rest of his eight, and one of them, Carick saw with surprise, was a young woman. Her helmet was tucked under one arm, revealing a dark braid wrapped around her head. She seemed shy, Carick thought, watching her stare at the ground while Audin spoke, nodding in response to his words.

"Don't mind Raher," said Hamar, bringing two horses out from the line. "He's always longing to hack or skewer something, and is equally convinced that Ser Bartrand is determined to hold him back."

"Well, he is!" insisted Raher, but with a grin this time. "And don't pretend that you're not as keen to get in amongst the wolfpack as I am!"

"No one," said Hamar with great firmness, "could possibly be as keen as you, Raher. Poor Maister Carro here has been convinced you're mad, ever since you told him what a splendid time he must have had being hunted through the pass."

Raher opened his mouth to protest, but Audin, returning, quelled him with a shake of his head. "Utterly mad," he said, and passed the reins of one of Hamar's horses, a golden-bay mare, to Carick. "This is Mallow, who will treat you well, I think. She is a great lady and wiser than the rest of us together."

"Except perhaps Erron," said Hamar.

"True enough," agreed Audin, while the mare looked at Carick out of dark, calm eyes and blew softly against his hands. He could see, looking at the tall, spirited chargers his escorts were riding, that he had been given a safe mount, but not a sluggish one. He stroked Mallow's velvet nose gently.

"I think we'll do," he said, and Hamar gave him a cheerful thumbs-up.

They all seemed friendly enough, Carick decided, as Audin's riders assembled around him. Even Raher's ire seemed to be directed at Ser Bartrand, rather than him, and the only person who was silent while they waited for Raven was the young woman. She had led out a great, red roan warhorse and patted its neck while she listened to the cut and thrust of conversation between the other six, who obviously knew each other well. The youth swapping jokes with Hamar was called Arn, while Tibalt, who had a moth-shaped birthmark on his cheek, held a torch steady so that another young man, whose name seemed to be Guyon, could adjust his stirrup leathers.

Carick noticed that they all became more circumspect once Raven joined them. War was what they trained for, he supposed, looking around at their flame-touched faces and recalling what he knew of Emer. The hedge knight might be an unknown quantity in many other ways, but it was clear that however shabby his appearance, war was his stock in trade. And even Ser Bartrand, Carick suspected, had been impressed that Raven snatched him from the wolfpack single-handed.

The eighth rider, and the last to join their company, was the young man called Girvase, who met them at the road and exchanged a resigned glance with Raher. "*Curse* Ser Bartrand!" he said. The others all laughed.

"Never fear," said Audin, "our time will come."

"True," agreed Raher promptly. "Even Ser Bartrand can't live forever!"

Everyone laughed again, but Carick saw more than a few make Imulun's sign against ill luck—or Imuln, as they called the Great Goddess here. He shivered, and Audin at least seemed to catch his mood for he said sharply: "Never wish anyone dead, even in jest! Now let's move, for it's a long ride to Normarch. We'll use the torches until moonrise and then douse them. Raher and Girvase, I want you riding point on either side—and stay alert. Hamar, you and Jarna are rear guard. The rest of you behind me."

The escort wheeled their horses as directed, and Mallow fell into a smooth stride behind Audin's destrier. Carick glanced at Raven once, but the hedge knight's face was expressionless beneath his battered helm. No doubt I'll learn to understand this new world in time, he thought. I'll have to, if I want to live here and see other lands beyond the River. But for now, I just have to hope that I can stay awake and in the saddle—and still be able to walk in the morning.

It had, he reflected, been a very long three days, but he would not complain if his body punished him for the next three—or even three weeks. He was glad simply to be alive and amongst those who seemed disposed to keep him that way. Carick gave thanks to Imulun for that, and to Seruth, the guardian of journeys, as the horses' hooves drummed around and beneath him, bearing him on into the darkness that was Emer.

# 13

## Normarch

Carick woke to pain cramping his right leg. He cried out, trying to massage the spasm away, and for a moment was completely disorientated. Then the cramp eased as he remembered the long night ride to the castle called Normarch, and reeling with exhaustion when they finally clattered into a cobbled yard. He recalled the squire called Hamar bracing him as he half fell off his horse and the jumbled impression of torches, voices, and confusion that followed—but that was all. "I'm still alive," he whispered, feeling the wonder of it again after his flight through the pass.

"Yes." A grave voice spoke from beside the bed. "But your lip is bleeding again. You will have to remember not to bite it for the next few days." The owner of the voice moved so he could see her more easily, holding back a heavy, russet curtain that fell from a wooden rail overhead. He blinked, trying to focus, and this time saw a young woman with a cloud of dark hair framing a delicate face. "Drink this," she said, lifting a cup to his lips. "It will help you recover."

The drink was as cool as her voice, but with an edge of bitterness, and Carick fell asleep again as soon as he had drunk it down. When he woke next, the sun was warm on his face. The russet curtains had been hooked back and the casement shutters opened, letting in the smell of bread baking and a murmur of voices from outside. Carick felt deeply re-laxed and it was several moments before he realized that his whole body was still a dull ache of bruises, chafed skin, and overworked muscles. But he remembered the cramp and the girl with the dark hair, and suspected that he might feel far worse if she had not given him the drink with the bitter edge to it.

The room, he supposed, turning his head, must be somewhere in Normarch castle and appeared to be accom-modation reserved for guests—although it was plain by River standards. The bed was comfortable, but the only other furnishings were a painted cabinet, a couple of sheepskins on the floor, and a small, metal-framed mirror on the white-washed wall. Although perhaps, Carick reflected, even such simple furnishings counted as luxury on Emer's Northern March.

He wondered where Raven was and how he was housed, but suspected that the hedge knight would make himself comfortable anywhere. He turned his head toward the sound of a horse's hooves, clopping over cobbles, and heard a smith's hammer ring out. The baking bread smelled as warm as the sunshine, and his stomach gave a sharp, imperative rumble, punctuating a tap on the door.

"Aha, so you are awake at last!" said a voice so smooth and rich it made Carick think of cream. The door opened wider, admitting one of the largest women he had ever seen. She must have been at least six feet tall, with a mass of curl-ing, dark brown hair piled up haphazardly and kept in place by combs. The body between shoulder and ankle billowed generously and was arrayed in layers of blouse, kirtle, and a lavishly embroidered cote that made her seem larger still. There were some, Carick knew, who would have called her blowsy, but he thought she was beautiful, with skin as creamy as her voice and the largest, merriest, velvet-brown eyes he had ever seen. It was only when she came to stand by the bed and smiled down at him that he saw the deeply etched crow's-feet at the corners of her eyes, and threads of silver in her dark hair. "Well, well," the woman said, smiling still, "we were starting to think your sleep was going to last forty years, like the young man in the fable."

Carick sat up, wincing as every muscle in his body protested.

"Yes, you'll feel it for some time," the woman said, sitting on the end of the bed and regarding him with sympathy. "Your friend, the Raven, told us about your run and that you were out of the habit of riding."

"Ser Raven," Carick said. "He saved my life yesterday."

The woman's smile deepened. "So I hear. Although from what he told us, you must have done at least some of the saving yourself. But it was not yesterday, young man. This is the second morning since your arrival here."

"Second?" Carick echoed, startled. "How could I possibly have slept so long?"

She shook her head. "Dear lad, you were mentally and physically exhausted. To have slept like that is not at all surprising."

"You must not call him 'lad,' Manan." A new voice spoke lightly from the door. "You heard what Audin said. This is Maister Carick of Ar, the Duke's new cartographer."

"I know who he is, Damosel Impertinence," Manan replied. "Now bring in that breakfast tray before the poor lad starves to death."

The young woman with the dark hair came carefully into the room. Despite balancing a tray of dishes that looked too heavy for her delicate build, her step was as light as her voice.

"Don't worry about Malisande," said Manan, correctly reading his expression. "She's stronger than she looks." The dark-haired girl smiled and set the tray down on the bedside cabinet, before straightening again and meeting Carick's gaze.

"Was it you I saw when I first woke?" he asked. He studied her curiously, because her speech and direct gaze did not fit with what he knew of servants. "You gave me something to drink."

"I did," Malisande replied. "I am helping Manan this

week and gave you the draught under her instructions."

Carick looked at Manan, guessing that she must be some sort of healer. "Best eat your breakfast," the big woman said with her warm smile. "Then you may get out of bed, if you wish." She surged to her feet, and Carick realized that she wore no shoes, a fact he found vaguely astonishing. "They'll want to see you in the castle as soon as you're able to walk up the hill."

Carick blinked. "Isn't this Normarch, then?"

"Yes and no. You're in the inn, which lies at the foot of the castle's hill, on the path to the village. They left you with me since I am Normarch's healer as well as the inn-wife." Manan nodded a farewell, and Malisande left as well, smiling back at him as she closed the door.

After the meal was done, Carick looked around for his tunic, flushing as he realized that someone must have removed his outer clothes before putting him into the bed. Or maybe he had undressed himself but forgotten doing so? He almost bit his lip, before remembering and shrugging instead: whatever had happened was done now and must be accepted. And the clothes were there, sitting in a clean, neatly folded pile on top of his rucksack, which was propped against one wall.

He dressed himself slowly, wincing when his clothes touched chafed skin, before making his way to the window. The inn appeared to be a large one, with a buttery and brewery on one side of a cobbled yard. A stable was built along the other, opening onto a smithy, which explained the ringing of hammer on anvil. Looking the other way, Carick could see the boughs of an orchard above the buttery roof, and wooded hills rising, blue in the distance. He had to lean right out the window to catch a glimpse of the castle, which was built of the same gray stone as the inn. Its walls were considerably lower than those of either Ar or Terebanth, and the central stronghold was little more than a single donjon with a series of roofs stretching away on either side. Halls, Carick supposed, cudgeling his memory for details of Emerian castle architecture, and there would be armories and more stables as well. Kitchens, too, he thought, as fresh baking aromas drifted up to the window. He felt hungry again already.

Craning further out again, Carick saw figures wheeling and maneuvering on horseback beneath the castle walls. He spotted archery butts as well, and guessed that these must be the garrison's training fields. A working stronghold, he thought, and remembered what had been written in a cramped hand on one of the few maps of Emer to be found in Ar. *Normarch*, the notation had said, and then, in even smaller letters: *the Duke's bridgehead in the north.*

"Do you like what you see?" Malisande had entered so quietly that Carick was taken by surprise and hit his head on the window arch. She laughed and then apologized as she came to stand beside him.

Carick rubbed his head. "I'm glad you weren't with the outlaws or they'd have caught me on the first day."

She shrugged a little, as if to say she doubted that. "So what do you think of Normarch, after your River cities?"

He hesitated, then decided it was best to be honest. "It does seem a little small."

"All River visitors think that," Malisande said, but without rancor. "Not that we have many of them. And even our own people, those who have been to Caer Argent, say that Normarch is nothing by comparison." She smiled. "We had some Ishnapuri travelers through a while back, and you could see they thought it was like nothing on earth."

"They would, of course," Carick agreed. "River merchants who travel there say that the Perfumed City is larger than Ij, Ar, and Terebanth put together."

"All the same," the dark-haired girl replied, "it is Normarch that holds the north of Emer for the Duke. Most of the outlying settlements would be lost inside a year without the garrison here to protect them from renegades." Carick tried to keep his expression neutral, but she shook her head. "You are thinking that you didn't see much of that protection as you came through the pass, aren't you?"

"Well, yes," he said. "Or in the adjoining lands, for that matter."

Malisande sighed. "Audin says you are a cartographer?" She paused as Carick nodded. "You must look, then, at the Castellan's maps of the Northern March and see how vast it is. Normarch is stretched protecting even the established settlements, so we rely on travelers and merchants going through the pass in large, well-armed companies. Even those Ishnapuri merchants had Jhainarian mercenaries with them."

Young women in Ar, thought Carick, never talked about things like this—or the young men either, he reflected after a moment. "Surely, you must be safe here, though?"

She shrugged again. "You only have to see the aftermath of one raid to know how fragile our security is. But you have already learned that for yourself."

Carick shivered. "Yes. It's not at all like the River, where it's quite safe to travel the Main Road, even on your own, because of the Patrol."

"Ah. Yes. Your Patrol. I've heard of them." Malisande was thoughtful. "Sadly, there's nothing like that in Emer, perhaps because we are not so rich as your River."

Carick had not thought of it in terms of wealth before, but he supposed that someone must pay the Patrol and that their hire would not come cheap.

"Is it true though," Malisande went on, "that the Patrol are really demons bound to the River's service and that is why they never show their faces to anyone?"

"What?" Carick stared. "Is that what people say here?"

"Some do," she replied. "Is it not true, then? Have you seen their faces?"

"Well, not exactly. They do always keep their visors lowered and no one is allowed inside their forts, but—" Carick shook his head. "You can see their mouths and chins below the visors, and they speak just like everyone else. You look disappointed," he finished, starting to grin.

"The demon story *has* always sounded exciting," Malisande admitted. "Still, I suppose the thousand or so years the Patrol has served in the River lands would be a long time to suppress their demon natures. And it's probably just as well they aren't demons, since I think Raher and Girvase are planning to go over there one day and find out. Challenge them, if need be."

Carick rolled his eyes, because it sounded exactly like what he could remember of Raher and Girvase from his night ride.

Malisande laughed. "They're true Emerians, always wanting to challenge someone—and terribly disappointed to miss the chance of action against the outlaws pursuing you." She sobered quickly. "Mind you, normally we wouldn't send out a party that was all squires and newer recruits. But Ser Rannart's dealing with a major renegade insurgency further west, and the Castellan was just about to lead a routine patrol south *and* escort our new maister back from Bonamark on his return, so he had no choice. Not once he decided that you were overdue."

Carick was frowning. "How did the Castellan know that, though?" he asked.

Malisande looked surprised. "The Duke sent him word to expect you, of course. We've had a lot of heralds coming through lately, too, not just going to Caer Argent, but on into Aralorn, Lathayra, maybe even as far as Ishnapur. One pair bore a message from your university in Ar, saying that you were about to set out."

She seemed to know a great deal about it, Carick thought, for a girl who worked in an inn. Although—and here he took in details such as her smooth hands and confident manner—he was suddenly less sure that was her role, even when she picked up his breakfast tray. "Do you live here at the inn?" he asked, testing the waters.

Malisande shook her head. "I am one of the Countess Ghiselaine's companions, from the Girls' Dorter. But we are all here to learn, and Manan has the greatest knowledge of herbs and healing north of Caer Argent, maybe even in all Emer—as well as being the finest cook. So we all take our turn working with her."

"I'm surprised she doesn't live in the castle itself, then," Carick said. In Ar, someone that learned would almost certainly be at the university or living in the palace.

"Oh, she's much too independent for that. They all are, Erron and Herun and the others." Malisande moved toward the door, her smile sly. "The rumor is that she was the Castellan's lover once, when they were young, and that's why he lets her do pretty much as she pleases." She paused before letting herself out. "You should come down now."

I suppose I should, Carick thought. By the time he made his slow, stiff way down the stairs, Malisande and the tray had disappeared, so he walked out into the sunlit yard. The cobbled area was still empty, although he could hear voices from both kitchen and buttery. He hesitated, then moved toward the stable and the sound of hammer blows from the smithy beyond. It took a moment for his eyes to adjust to the dim interior and make out a heavily muscled man in a sleeveless jerkin shoeing a horse, while a lad held the animal's head. When the man put the horse's hoof down, Carick recognized the squire called Hamar. He understood, too, seeing the strength in those arms and shoulders, why the young man had been able to clear the stone barrier from the croft doorway so easily.

Hamar came forward when he saw Carick standing in the entrance, while the lad stroked the horse's nose and whispered in its ear. "So you're awake at last," the squire said. "Even knowing what you'd been through, we were all starting to worry."

Carick smiled ruefully. "We're not used, on the River, to dodging outlaws through wild country."

"You did well," Hamar said. He made a gesture toward the horse. "I don't suppose you have to shoe your own horses either, on the River?"

"Not if you're a scholar," Carick admitted. "A knight in such wild country would have to, though. I can see that."

"And make and mend armor as well," Hamar agreed. "But I enjoy the work and the inn forge is less busy than the castle's, which is why I come down here."

Carick nodded, looking around the forge and then back to the horse, which was a tall, red roan destrier, bred to carry the weight of its own armor, as well as that of a knight, into battle. "Is this a great horse? The breed for which Emer is famous?"

"The finest in all Emer," said Hamar. "But that's because Jarna trained him." He grinned at the lad holding the horse, and Carick, looking more closely, realized that the boy was in fact the girl squire who had formed part of his escort to Normarch.

"Hello," he said, and the girl nodded back. "Did you really train him? What's his name?"

For a long moment, Carick thought Jarna was not going to answer, but then she met his eyes, a quick shy look. "Madder," she said finally. "It's another way of saying 'red.'" Her voice was low-pitched, almost husky, and with a cap over her thick plait, she was broad shouldered and flat chested enough to pass as a boy. She smiled now and stroked the horse's nose again. "We all have a gift for horses, in my family. That's what my grandfather says. Although Hamar has the gift, too," she added.

Hamar shook his head. "No. I'm good with horses, but you are something more, Jarn."

This time Jarna did just shrug and look away, but Carick noticed that she flushed as well. "Ser Bartrand and the others," he said. "Did they return safely?"

"Ay," Hamar nodded. "The wolfpack tried to slip away but there was no chance of that with Erron on their trail. Outlaws never stand and fight against numbers," he added, "not if they can avoid it."

"A true wolfpack, then," Carick said, "going after the straggler."

Hamar hesitated. "It was not wise of you, venturing the Long Pass alone." Then he grinned. "But we're all keen to hear your story in detail, especially what happened before you met Ser Raven."

For the adventure of it? Carick wondered, remembering Raher. Or to learn more about those who preyed on this wild country, or perhaps both? He returned a noncommittal answer, but accepted Hamar's invitation to visit the squires' practice yards once Madder was shod.

The yards turned out to be the training field he had seen from the inn, broken up into distinct areas by brushwood and stiles. Squires using swords and shields were training by the castle gates, while others practiced archery at the butts. Beyond the butts lay the horse field where squires in full armor—Carick saw, amazed—were practicing vaulting onto and off their horses. Other riders were charging up and down long rows of brush hedges, ditches, and hurdles, clearing the obstacles and hacking at straw-bale and wooden targets set up on poles. The targets were constructed to swing around and buffet any rider who missed a stroke, unhorsing more than one.

Carick soon realized that the skill of the horse was as crucial as that of the rider—and that some horses stood out from the rest. Audin's black was one, and Hamar's bay another, but the big roan called Madder was outstanding. He said as much to Raven, when the hedge knight came to stand beside him.

Raven nodded, still studying the riders. "You've a good eye," he said finally. "In two days, I haven't seen the roan put a foot wrong. Long, long hours have been put into training him and this is where it shows."

"Jarna rides well, too," said Carick, "as though she and the horse were one."

"Ay," said Raven. He continued to follow Jarna's progress along the field. "She's no sluggard with her weapons either, but there are others who're better. Hamar and Girvase, in particular."

They continued to watch for some time, and Carick wondered what it would be like to grow up in a world where every man lived by the sword and the rule of law was uncertain. "I take it," he said eventually, "that the Lord Castellan is still not back?"

Raven shook his head. "And Ser Bartrand says that we are both to remain at Normarch until he returns—although I get a bunk in the barracks, rather than a fine room at the inn." He grinned when Carick opened his mouth to disclaim. "I've had far worse quarters, including bivouacs in the wild."

They both moved aside as more riders clattered past,

before Raven left to watch the ground fighting. Carick, fascinated, stayed to watch the squires gallop along the field and shoot at targets with recurved bows, their chargers' hooves a drum roll across the hard-packed earth. Heavy cavalry, he reflected, was the essence of what the River meant when it spoke of Emerian knights—as well as contributing much of the glamor inherent in their fame.

Over the following days, Carick found that many aspects of the life were far from glamorous. The squires were always well up before he opened his shutters, and spent their mornings on the training ground. The training was hard and relentless, with most squires always sporting bruises, and several at any one time asking Manan to treat cuts or sprains. When they were not training, or making or mending armor and weapons, the squires had what they called "book lessons." These sounded fairly rudimentary to Carick, but many of the squires seemed baffled as to why the Duke should consider it necessary for them to read, write, and figure numbers at all. The damosels, he learned, joined the squires for these lessons, but practiced their own weaponry in separate classes.

He was surprised, the first afternoon he climbed the hill to watch the girls ride up and down the long field, shooting and hacking at the dummies, to find Raven there before him. Occasionally the hedge knight would point out some finer technical point for his benefit, but he said little until half the young women dismounted to train on foot. "Now," said Raven, "you will see something unknown on the River, the Emerian lady's pike—although most people just say ladyspike."

Carick had to admit that the weapon, a wickedly curved blade on a long staff, was impressive. He watched, fascinated, as the girls attacked and counterattacked under the instruction of a short, dark woman with a spiral of blue tattoos across chin and cheeks. The instructor's name, Carick learned, was Solaan, and she was as cool and businesslike as Raven, although considerably older. Her cropped hair was gray as iron, and there were deep tracks around both eyes and mouth in her weather-beaten face.

"The tattooing?" Carick murmured to Raven. "Is that usual here?"

"She is of the Hills," Raven replied, as though that explained everything. "More importantly, she is a master of this weapon."

"Yes," agreed Carick. He could see that both blade and staff were equally a part of the weapon, and guessed that the length would give considerable advantage against a sword, whether wielded from the ground or horseback.

"It will gut a horse as easily as a man," said Raven, when he voiced this thought. "Numbers will always tell in the end, but skilled users can hold a defensible position for some time. We've attracted attention," he added, and Carick saw that several damosels had broken off and were riding over. The young women rode as lightly as the squires, most with long braids trailing from beneath caps of leather or steel. Only the central rider was bare headed, sitting straight and slender in the saddle while the bell of her red-gold hair lifted in the breeze.

"Ghiselaine, Countess of Ormond," Raven murmured, although Carick had already guessed: she sat amongst the other riders like a queen among her knights. He also knew that the youthful countess was famous for her beauty—and this girl was undoubtedly beautiful, with clear, apricot-tinted skin, a perfect oval face, and fine gold-brown eyes beneath arched brows. Like a painting of beauty, Carick thought, as he sketched a bow. He felt out of his element, awkward as a boy rather than a graduate of the university in Ar, and was amazed and a little resentful at the grace of Raven's bow. "Countess," the hedge knight said.

"Ser Raven," the countess replied. She leaned down, holding out a gloved hand to each of them in turn. "Maister Carick. I am Ghiselaine of Ormond. Welcome, both of you, to Normarch." She straightened, smiling. "We are honored, sers, that you watch our training."

"It never pays to overlook any potential opponent." Raven

glanced at Carick. "As the outlaws found when they under-estimated the maister here."

"So we hear," said the young woman on Ghiselaine's right. At first, seeing her slight build and the black hair below her cap, Carick had thought she was Malisande, but realized his mistake when she drew near. This girl had smoke-gray eyes in a dark face and spoke with a lilt to every word. "Girvase says that you did remarkably well, to outwit the wolfpack for so long." The smoky eyes studied him, as though trying to assess the substance behind his story.

"Well, if Girvase says it," murmured the young woman beside her, then held up a hand as if to ward off a blow. "A jest, that is all, Alianor." Her speech was languorous, almost a drawl, and her gaze a little sleepy. Carick thought she looked a lot like Ghiselaine, although her hair was fairer and the sleepy eyes blue. "We are all longing to hear the tale firsthand, both your part, Maister Carick, and Ser Raven's, too, of course." She glanced at them from beneath downcast lashes, smiling when Carick flushed. He thought Raven looked amused, but his rescue came from another quarter.

"No games, Linnet," said Ghiselaine, and a yellow-haired damosel giggled. "It was I who wished to introduce myself, Maister Carick, because we have heard so much of the great university in Ar. I am honored to meet one of its scholars." Her smile included Ser Raven. "Knights are not so rare in Emer, alas, but I am grateful that you were able to help the maister reach us safely."

"It was not the easiest welcome to our country," Alianor said, her gaze still measuring Carick.

"No," said Carick. He was wondering why Malisande was not there, since she had said that she was one of Ghiselaine's companions. "Although," he added boldly, "it may have been an accurate one."

Alianor nodded. "Perhaps, for these border lands. Things are different in Caer Argent and the inner wards, and even the Marks are more settled these days."

Solaan shouted, calling the damosels back to their training, and they wheeled away, waving their farewells. "So now you've seen her," Raven said. "The Lily of Ormond."

"She's betrothed to the Duke's son, isn't she?" Carick asked. "Lord Hirluin?"

Raven nodded. "To be married as soon as she turns eighteen—sealing wax on the Ormondian peace. But she'll still be Duchess in Caer Argent, which is why some already call her the Fair Maid of Emer."

"The other girls were pretty, too," Carick said, weathering Raven's sardonic look.

"Candle flames," the hedge knight replied, "beside the sun."

True enough, Carick thought. He was still thinking about the countess and her companions that evening, eating his dinner in the inn kitchen and watching the play of shadows across the wall. The door banged open and Malisande blew in on a gust of wind, her arms full of herbs. "I hear you watched our training this afternoon," she said, putting the herbs down on a bench and reaching for scissors and string. "And Ser Raven did, too. The boys watch sometimes, but not many of the knights ever do."

"No?" Carick shook his head. "They should. That lady-spike is a wicked weapon."

"All weapons are wicked," Malisande said. "Or that's what Audin says. But this is Emer and we must be able to defend ourselves at need. I wouldn't have been let off, except that Manan said she needed help with these herbs."

Carick nodded, but she had reminded him of something else. "The first night, before I came here, I was sure I heard Ser Bartrand call Audin 'Lord'?"

"Yes." Malisande tied a bunch of herbs together and hung them from a rafter. "Audin Sondargent. He's the Duke's nephew, and the others—Raher and Girvase and Hamar— were sent here as his companions, just as Linnet and Alianor and I are companions to Ghiselaine." She hooked up another bunch of herbs, then stopped, frowning at her handiwork, although Carick was sure that she was seeing something else. "Ormond was the largest of the old, independent kingdoms," she said slowly, "and the last to come into Emer after many years of war. It is important for the peace that this marriage happens."

Carick pulled a face. "Does it matter what Countess Ghiselaine wants?"

Malisande shrugged. "She knows her duty. We all do. That's why we are here."

Carick had wondered about that, too: why remote Normarch would foster so many of the young nobility of Emer, including the Duke's nephew and the Countess of Ormond. But apparently it was the way of Emer for children of both the great and lesser nobility to be sent away as young as six or seven, to grow up in another household.

"So we get to know each other, I suppose," Malisande said now, "which helps bind Emer together. Though some, like Ser Bartrand, say it is so we are not spoiled by our families, but learn the discipline and manners required to survive in the world."

That idea, too, Carick knew, would seem very strange in the River lands. He glanced at the smoke-blue dusk, pressing against the small panes of the windows, while Malisande tied away the last of the herbs. A voice called from outside and he heard the stable doors being pushed closed. Malisande wiped the bench clean with a damp cloth.

"Lord Falk, the Castellan, says that we shall all go to Caer Argent for Midsummer this year. There's always a tournament as part of the festival and the squires will compete—unless they fail in their vigil, of course. It's likely that Ghis will remain there, although the wedding won't be until next spring. Audin will stay, too. So you see, you will already know people at the court, just because you came here first."

Carick nodded, but asked another question that had been niggling at him. "Why is it that Jarna alone trains with the squires, and not with you and the other damosels?"

Malisande looked surprised. "Because she is a squire, of course," she said, as though that were obvious.

"I think," said Hamar, opening the inn door, "that Maister

Carick is asking why Jarna is a squire at all." He scraped his boots on the mat. "It's a longstanding tradition here, one that evolved out of the Cataclysm years. When families have no son to pay the knight's service owed to their lord, the old custom says that the eldest daughter must be both son and daughter to her house and undertake the duty." He moved to lean against the end of Malisande's bench. "Jarna is the eldest of six daughters, and both her father and uncle died in the fever, seven years back. Now there is only her grandfather to hold their demesne from the Duke, so he has sent Jarn to do a son's service here."

"Although these days," said Malisande, "most families would adopt a son into their house instead, marrying him to a daughter. Or pay the Duke gold in lieu of service."

"You have to have the gold first," Hamar replied. "And Jarn says that her grandfather is too proud to adopt a boy who is not of their blood." He shrugged. "The old man sounds half mad to me, but that's why Jarna's here."

"She looked so forlorn the day she arrived, sitting up on that huge horse." Malisande shook her head. "I didn't think the Castellan would agree to it. And do you remember Ser Bartrand?"

"Spitting daggers." Hamar grinned, then sobered again. "The Castellan had no choice though. He *had* to agree, or shame Jarna and insult her grandfather. Even these days that could end in a declared feud. And Jarna's family have ties into the Hills. Lord Falk wouldn't want to risk ill feeling there."

"Still," Carick said, recalling how quiet Jarna was amongst the other squires, "it must be hard on her, especially if Ser Bartrand is against her being here."

Hamar just shrugged again. Malisande looked as though she would like to say more, but refrained, and Hamar began to rummage through the cupboards, looking for jam tarts.

Carick yawned and excused himself shortly after that, yet despite his tiredness he found he could not sleep. He got up again and opened the shutters, gazing out at the sprinkle of lights that was Normarch. The moon, worn almost to a half disc now, was just lifting above the eastern hills. Its light seemed muted against the misty brilliance of the spring stars, so much larger and closer here than in brightly lit Ar.

Carick stretched and moved to pull the shutters closed, then paused, sure there was someone standing against the stable wall. Watching, he thought with a shiver. The shadow was little more than an outline of deeper black within the night's darkness, and he tried to make out more details without leaning forward. Light cut across the yard as the kitchen door opened and Hamar stepped out, Malisande's voice floating after him—and when Carick looked back at the stable, the watching shadow had gone.

But there had definitely been someone there. He fastened the shutters with greater care than usual and got slowly into bed. Probably it had just been a villager, wanting herbs from Manan but too shy to ask while castle folk were in the kitchen. All the same, Carick kept his face turned to the window, and sleep eluded him for quite some time.

❉

# 14

# *Maister Gervon*

*A* clangor shattered the morning's peace, followed by voices shouting. Still half asleep, Carick fumbled the shutters open, shading his eyes against the early sun. Girvase and Hamar were circling each other in the center of the yard, swords in hand, while their comrades yelled from the perimeter. Carick recognized Malisande and Alianor, looking down from the loft, while Raher, Audin, and Jarna stood just inside the gate. The two combatants continued to cut and thrust, their faces intense with concentration. When Carick leaned further out, he could see Ser Bartrand striding down the hill, with Col, the Master Archer, beside him.

Ducking back inside, Carick raced to pull on his clothes and comb his hair into a semblance of order. When he looked again the two combatants were still hammering away at each other, but their adherents had fallen silent, easing away from a chestnut destrier that had appeared in the gate. The chestnut's rider was bareheaded; the early breeze riffled thinning sandy hair as he surveyed the yard, and the voice that spoke was light, but with an edge beneath the even tone. "What," the newcomer asked, "is going on here?"

The rider had not seemed to raise his voice, but it cut across the clash of swords all the same. The two combatants sprang back, lowering their blades; their faces wore matching expressions of chagrin and apprehension as they turned toward the gate. "Lord Falk," Girvase said, gasping for breath. "Ser, we didn't realize . . ."

So this, thought Carick, taking in the mix of dismay and apprehension around the yard, is the Castellan of Normarch, the Duke's foster brother and strong right arm in Emer's wild north. Curious, he leaned further out.

"That I was back?" Falk of Normarch inquired. "So I apprehend." The light eyes continued to survey both combatants a moment longer before traveling around the inn yard. "Now have I, or have I not, forbidden private contests such as this?" He turned as Ser Bartrand strode through the gate. "Ah, Bartrand, good morning. Col." He nodded to the Master Archer.

"My lord." Audin stepped forward before either of the newcomers could speak, his expression respectful. "You have forbidden such contests in Normarch, but we took that to mean the castle and training grounds, not the inn yard."

The Castellan's brows rose. "Indeed?" he said. "I have always understood Normarch to include the castle and its demesne. And the demesne includes not only this inn and the village below it, but the whole Northern March of Emer, where my word, as I also understand it, is meant to be law." He shook his head, checking Audin as he began to speak. "No, Lord Audin. The Duke has sent you all here to be trained in the knightly skills that will defend Emer, not to kill yourselves in private contests. In due course, no doubt, you will all attend tourneys and can amuse yourself in this manner to your hearts' content. But you will not have that opportunity until Ser Bartrand and I say that you are worthy—and this morning's episode does nothing to convince me of that."

"But my lord," protested Raher, "it wasn't serious. It was just in fun."

The silence that followed filled the inn yard, and Carick found that he was holding his breath as Lord Falk studied

Raher. "Now, does that make it better," the Castellan mused, "or worse? So, what brought about this particular piece of fun? Audin?"

Audin looked uncomfortable. "Er, Hamar held that Countess Ghiselaine would be crowned queen of this year's Midsummer tourney in Caer Argent, but Girvase expressed doubt on that point, ser."

"He did?" The Castellan looked at Girvase. "Why was that?"

Girvase said nothing, just stared stolidly in front of him until Audin answered again. "Girvase thought that the crown should go to Alianor, ser."

Lord Falk shook his head. "You should never let either loyalty or admiration cloud the evidence of your eyes, Girvase. But hear me, all of you! I'll have no more of this nonsense anywhere in the Northern March. Do I make myself clear?" Heads dipped around the courtyard, and he nodded. "Well and good. Ser Bartrand, I'll let you decide on suitable chastisement for these miscreants—not excluding the young ladies, whose presence might be construed as encouragement for the squires' willful disobedience." Lord Falk began to back the chestnut destrier out the gate, then paused, looking up at Carick in the window. "You must be Maister Carick. I will see you in the castle as soon as I've had my breakfast."

The castle's outer yard, when Carick reached it, was filled with the men and horses that had returned with Lord Falk. He had to weave his way through to Raven, who was standing in the hall door. "We are to see Lord Falk together," the hedge knight told him. "But he is closeted with Ser Bartrand and Erron at present."

And that is Emer, thought Carick, inwardly amused, where a Castellan's horsemaster is as important as the captain of his guard. A pennant fluttered by the stable door and he jumped, his amusement evaporating as he remembered the previous night's shadow. He had almost forgotten it in the aftermath of Lord Falk's arrival, but now that the memory had revived, found he could not shake off a sense of something out of place. Eventually he asked Raven for his opinion. "I'm not used to this country," he explained. "In my place, what would you do?"

"In your place?" Raven shrugged. "I would speak to the Castellan or Erron. This isn't the kind of country where you take chances."

Carick hesitated. "Would the wolfpack trail me here?"

Raven's gaze sharpened. "Is that who you think it was?"

I must sound like a nervous fool, Carick thought, aware that he had no reason other than his lurking uneasiness for suspecting the wolfpack. Yet a short time later, after they had been called into his presence, Lord Falk repeated Raven's question. The Castellan's eyes were the color of barley ale, their expression thoughtful as Carick shook his head.

"I'm not sure." He could not bring himself to admit that it was just a feeling that had dogged him from the moment he remembered the shadow.

Ser Bartrand scratched at his chin. "They certainly pursued you for longer than I'd have expected, once they had your mule and goods. But for an outlaw, even a scout, to come all the way here . . ." His expression said he thought it unlikely.

"There are those," Erron put in quietly, from the deep window embrasure, "who refuse to turn aside from a chase once they have begun it. But those who run in the wolfpack are not usually of that kind."

They do think I'm a nervous fool, Carick reflected, and wished he had never said anything.

Lord Falk switched his attention to Raven. "Ser Bartrand tells me that you are looking to take service in Emer?"

"For a time," Raven replied. "If there is a place to be had."

"I always need men," the Castellan said, "both for garrison duty and to train the squires. But you would find easier service if you went farther south, into the Mark country or the six Wards around Caer Argent."

Raven smiled, a wry twist of the lips. "They might not

look past my rough exterior. I will take your service, my lord, if it pleases you."

Lord Falk nodded. "Well enough, Ser Raven." He turned back to Carick. "And you, Maister Cartographer, I must get safely to Caer Argent. We will be going there for the Midsummer festival, but I will send a messenger to find out whether the Duke needs you before that. Meanwhile, I have some maps here that could use your attention, if you're willing?" He waited for Carick's nod, then added: "I take it that Manan has been looking after you well?"

"Very well," said Carick.

Lord Falk smiled. "I would ask you to try and pass on your scholarship to our young dunderheads, except that we have brought back a priest for that purpose: Maister Gervon from Serrut's monastery in Bonamark. Best not to tread on his toes, perhaps."

"No," said Carick, although he wondered why they could not both teach, if they had separate skills to offer. Ser Bartrand, he saw, was looking amused.

"How many maisters can they need," the captain asked, "to learn how to write their name and cipher out a letter? They have enough to do on the training ground—although I suppose there could be room for a little more heraldry, if they're going to court."

"The arts of war, eh," said Lord Falk, "softened by a few courtly graces? But the Duke does not agree that what was good enough for our generation will do for the next. He thinks we must knock some book learning into their heads— and I am inclined to agree with him, hence the Maister of Serrut." His smile, as he glanced at Ser Bartrand, was sly. "I heard, recently, that the Duke plans to endow a university in Caer Argent."

Ser Bartrand's expression made it plain what he thought of that, but he merely shrugged and bore Raven away to induct him into the garrison while Carick returned to the inn. He wondered what study Maister Gervon had specialized in and looked forward to meeting him, but soon found that the priest of Serrut was not disposed to be friendly. The man inclined his head when Lord Falk introduced them, but made it plain, through his manner rather than his words, that he preferred to keep Carick at a distance.

He thinks I'm a threat, Carick thought, and shrugged inwardly, concentrating on the Castellan's maps instead. These were in sad condition, but Carick thought they could be rebacked, with care, and the faded lines re-inked. He was more concerned, given their age, that the detail being redone might be highly inaccurate, and that there were too may blank areas on every chart.

"Do what you can, Maister Carick, and I will be grateful," Lord Falk said, when Carick approached him with his concerns. "There's no coin to spare for new surveys, not when we have the entire north to garrison." He was standing by his dayroom window, gazing down at the village, and he beckoned Carick to join him. "It looks peaceful, does it not? But each year is a constant struggle to get the harvest sown and gathered, both for the folk in those fields and all those like them throughout northern Emer. Yet without the harvest, we all starve." He shot a glance at Carick. "Starvation is not a thing you experience often on the River, from what I hear, but it's as great an evil as anything a knight might slay with arrow or sword. And there is only so much I can wring out of these folk, even for the necessities to defend them."

Carick nodded, resolving to do the best he could with the resources and time available, which quickly stretched from two weeks into three. The days became warmer as Normarch began to focus on the festival of Summer's Eve and the accompanying vigils for those squires and damosels who were coming of age.

"What exactly is the festival about?" he asked Malisande, one fine evening when she was down at the inn again, helping Manan sort and bag herbs. The damosel looked up in surprise.

"Don't you celebrate Summer's Eve on the River? The festival honors Imuln in her aspect of Maiden and is always held on the first new moon of summer. Those coming of age keep their sacred vigils and lovers make binding vows to each other." She smiled. "That is the serious side, at any rate. But we also celebrate the beginning of the really fine weather by lighting bonfires, and use up the last of winter's stores baking special cakes and breads. The fires are lit on the actual eve, but the next day there is dancing and feasting through into the night. And because Manan is the most famous cook in the entire Northern March, people come from all over to buy her spice bread and sweet pastries." She wrinkled her nose. "So we won't have the inn to ourselves anymore."

"It sounds like fun, though," Carick said.

"It is," Malisande agreed. "And this year most of us will be keeping our vigil. Dame Nelys says that if the weather is fine we can ride up to the old Temple in the Rock, which lies an easy day's ride into the hills. The weather should be fine, don't you think, Manan?" she asked.

Manan smiled. "I am no weather prophet. And a temple is a temple. I don't see why you're all so mad for the Temple in the Rock."

Malisande threw out her hands. "It would be an adventure! And the Temple in the Rock is one of the oldest Imulni precincts in Emer. A vigil there would *mean* something."

Carick had already gathered from the squires' conversation that keeping a good vigil, which was the final step in becoming a knight of Emer, was tremendously important. Apparently it was the same for the damosels as well, so he hoped they would get their fair weather and the prestige they wanted, since it was almost as important as family standing in Emerian society. He had quickly worked out that Raher and Girvase, as well as Audin, had been born into the greatest houses of Emer, but whereas both Audin and Raher bore the prefix Sond before their surnames, Girvase was known as Ar-Allerion. The Sond or Ar denoted legitimate or illegitimate birth, and Manan had explained the distinction further when he asked, her arms in flour up to the elbows as she kneaded bread.

"Children born to the Ar, as we say it, can never inherit land or titles, not while any Sond of their blood remains alive. Although they frequently marry both, especially if they have distinguished themselves in war or the service of Duke or Duchess." She had sighed, knocking the dough back. "Where would the armies of Emer—or the priesthood either, for that matter—be without the Ar's and the younger sons?"

Both Hamar and Jarna, like Malisande, were of less elevated lineage, so prestige would be doubly important to them. Impoverishment, Carick gathered, was an old story for many knightly families who had poured out both resources and blood supporting the great lords through centuries of war. "I am sure," he said now, "that the weather will be settled by the first of summer. It usually is on the River."

The only cloud on the surface of his Normarch life was Maister Gervon, whose initial distance had quickly become outright hostility. Carick tried to stay out of the man's way, but their paths kept crossing. He would turn a corner and find Gervon there, the man's pale blue stare turning to ice when he recognized him—although the maister only spoke if there was no one else present to hear his sneers or acid-etched derision.

Carick ventured a casual comment about this one rainy afternoon when Ghiselaine, Alianor, and Malisande had come to kick their heels in the map room. The countess pulled a face. "Priests of Serrut can be like that, unfortunately."

"I think the real problem," Alianor said slowly, "is that so many are bound to the life against their will, because they're Ar-born or younger sons." Her opinions, Carick was coming to realize, reflected a thoughtful nature. "The isolation," she added, "only compounds the bitterness for those whose temperaments are not suited to it. And there is a great deal of bitterness in Maister Gervon."

"He must have thought it a great thing, becoming Maister to the Castellan of Normarch," Malisande added, "only to find you here. Not only another maister, but one from the famous university in Ar—*and* appointed to the service of the Duke. You have cast him into the shade, Maister Carick."

Ghiselaine nodded. "He will not forgive you for it. But he

will stay and you will go soon, so you mustn't let one warped priest spoil your time with us."

Sound advice, thought Carick—but he found it hard to put into practice when he met Gervon later that evening. It was still raining and the dusk was thick as he returned to the inn, which was not a place he expected to meet the Serrut maister. So he was taken by surprise when he ducked through the gate, head down against the weather, and bumped straight into the man. They both drew back, Carick apologizing and the maister hissing like an angry cat. Then Gervon drew himself up, his glance flicking right and left across the empty yard. When he looked back, his pupils had narrowed almost to pinpricks and there was so much malice in the man's face and manner that Carick automatically took a step back. The priest's lips twitched and Carick saw foam appear at the corners of his mouth.

"Are you well, Maister Gervon?" he asked, striving for a normal tone. The corner of the man's right eye twitched and Carick tried not to stare at the jerking flutter.

"I?" Gervon wiped at the foam with a hand that shook. "Look to your own health, interloper!" His voice hissed again as he stepped forward. "You think yourself so fine, with your learning and your River ways, but you know nothing—*nothing* of what really matters in this world." Gervon drew closer still, so that Carick caught the stink of his breath and could count the red veins across the priest's narrowed eyes. The man was whispering now, but this only increased the venom in his tone. "You will scream and I shall laugh to hear you. Soon, oh soon, my fine River maister."

"Maister Gervon." Hamar had appeared in the stable doorway, a needle stuck into the torn saddlebag in his hand. His voice was friendly as always, but he was frowning as he surveyed the priest. "And Maister Carick. I thought I heard voices."

Maister Gervon's head swiveled. Carick half expected him to hiss again, but when he spoke it was in his normal, chilly tone. "Ah, Hamar. I was just leaving when Maister Carick and I, hmmm, bumped into each other—a consequence of the ill weather!" He did not wait for a reply, but pulled his hood well forward and strode toward the castle, while Carick stared after him, heedless of the rain.

"Are you all right, Maister Carro? You look like you've seen a ghost." Hamar propelled Carick into the shelter of the stable. "Manan would say you might end up one, standing outside in this weather."

Carick inhaled the mingled smell of horses, leather, and fresh straw, and tried to avoid the memory of Gervon's venom—as well as the question in Hamar's eyes. Shaken, he brushed at his damp cloak.

"That must have been quite a collision," the squire said, "and I suppose old Gervon said it was your fault, even though he had his head down, too. I saw him go past and then I heard that hiss, the way he does when he's having a go at someone."

"He certainly seems to dislike me." Carick drew another deep breath, remembering the man's eyes glittering at him and the spittle at the corner of his mouth.

"He gives me the creeps," said Hamar. "None of us like him. But Lord Falk thinks we need a maister, and men of learning are few and far between on the Northern March."

Carick nodded. "Unfortunately, when someone behaves like Maister Gervon it makes one doubt his scholarship as well."

Hamar grinned. "That's what Ghiselaine says, too. I think she prefers what we have seen of the scholarship of Ar. But it's those gray, pebble-like eyes of his that I don't like—and the glazed stare! Jarna says it makes her skin crawl."

"I thought his eyes were blue." Carick shook himself like a dog, trying to get rid of the damp, then grinned. "But I'm not sure I want to look more closely. Or discuss matters of scholarship either, given the man's attitude." He peered out into the dusk. "I'll be sorry if I miss Manan's dinner, though. I can smell it from here." He looked at Hamar. "Are you eating with us?"

"No, I'm wanted back on the hill as soon as I've finished this." The squire cast a quick, doubtful look at Carick. "Do you think I should have a word with Lord Falk? I don't think he'd be impressed by Maister Gervon's notions of courtesy."

Carick shook his head, knowing that everyone would think less of him if he did not fight his own battles. Gervon was bitter, as Alianor had said, perhaps even to the extent of being unhinged, but there was not much the man could do to harm him.

Yet Carick's dreams that night were uneasy, coalescing into a vision of Maister Gervon coming toward him through a wall of white mist. A sickly green light hung about the man, and in the dream his eyes were indeed gray as pebbles and burned with pale fire. Flame wreathed his hands as well, shifting from leprous white to the sickly green, then back again. *"Soon,"* the apparition whispered. *"Oh, soon!"*

Carick jerked awake, his heart thundering. A nightmare, he told himself—and not surprising given his latest encounter with Maister Gervon. Just a bad dream, that was all. But he knew he would not sleep again, and lit a candle instead, watching its comforting flicker until dawn crept through the shutters.

He found it hard to work at all that morning and sat motionless in the map room, staring blankly down at the charts. When he did eventually look up, Raven was standing in the doorway, but the hedge knight made no comment, just spread out a roll of maps from Lord Falk and began going through the Castellan's notations. Carick forced himself to concentrate, but his hand shook a little at one point as the dream flashed through his mind again, and he knew that Raven noticed.

Maister Gervon was in his usual place when Carick went down to the midday meal in the castle hall, and did not look like a man who suffered from nightmares. "Indigestion," Malisande murmured. "That expression would sour any food." The young people around her laughed, and it was clear that what Hamar had said was true: none of them liked the maister. Carick felt unreasonably cheered by this and stepped out more briskly when he returned to the inn that evening. All the same, he delayed extinguishing the candle after finally going to bed.

The dream came more swiftly this time and the apparition did not speak, just closed in on him. Pale, glowing hands reached out, murder in the burning eyes as Carick remained frozen, unable to move or speak. He smelled the foulness of the priest's breath, rank as decaying flesh, and even in the dream he felt nausea rise, followed by a dizziness that sapped his will to resist.

The scrape of metal rasped through the mist and the apparition whipped around, peering into the brume. Carick was finally able to pull away, and when the mist cleared he found himself standing on a high place. A rampart, he thought, then realized that it was one of the castle's inner walls, immediately above the small chapel to Serrut that stood in an enclosed garden. The mist was thick, but he could still make out a circle of hooded figures, motionless within its whiteness.

In the dream a cock crowed, fraying both the mist and surrounding darkness and pulling Carick awake. His body felt as chill and clammy as though he really had been standing on that predawn wall, and his heartbeat was a staccato tattoo. He could not deny the vividness of his dream, which had seemed real. The cock crowed again, imperative from its village dunghill, and was answered by a rival within the castle. Carick stumbled to the window, pushing back the shutters and drawing in a great draught of cool air.

A drift of mist hung over the orchard, but otherwise the world was clear and pale: the day was going to be beautiful. He rubbed the heels of his hands against his eyes, lifting them at the sound of running feet. Two dark shapes appeared in the inn gateway, and a moment later he recognized Hamar and Malisande as they pounded on the door. "Manan!" Malisande cried. "Maistress Manan, wake up!" Neither she nor Hamar appeared to have noticed Carick, gazing down at them.

"What is it?" he called softly. "What's wrong?"

Their faces turned upward. They were both pale and Malisande's eyes were huge as she shook her head.

"What is it?" Carick repeated, more urgently this time. He could hear someone moving in the house as Hamar answered, his voice harsh.

"They've just found Maister Gervon in the chapel of Serrut." He stopped, his face twisting, and Carick's breath caught. The blood pounded in his temples, and Malisande's voice, speaking again, sounded thin and distant.

"Erron insists that Manan come at once." She paused. "The maister is dead, Carick, quite dead, with a stake through his heart."

## 15

## The Chapel of Serrut

**M**anan strode from the inn with surprising speed, despite her bulk, while Malisande clutched a bulging herb satchel and hurried to keep pace. Why the satchel, Carick wondered, if Maister Gervon is already dead? But Hamar shook his head when he said as much.

"Manan is the lay-priestess of Imuln in Normarch, and the sisterhood uses salves and linens for laying out the dead." His eyes were still dark with whatever he had seen in the chapel. "Serrut is lord of life's journeys, but eventually they all bring us to Imuln."

So they do, Carick thought, and shivered. On the River, the temples taught that even Kan, the dancer in shadows, must bow to Imulun in the end—which was perhaps not surprising given that Seruth and Kan were both her sons. Light and dark, the giver of life and its taker, the healer and the slayer: the divine twins, one the mirror image of the other, forever opposite and conjoined.

Carick shivered again and thrust his arms into his jacket, glad that Hamar had waited for him. The Emerian squire seemed made for the everyday world of sunshine and fresh air, with his open expression, broad shoulders, and square, powerful hands. Yet he was still white about the mouth and the shadow in his eyes remained. Carick turned away from the kitchen door and helped himself to a generous slice of bread and cheese. "We might as well eat first," he said "Did you see the body?"

"We all did." Hamar followed his example, his eyes narrowed as he munched. "The squires, that is. We were getting ready for predawn training with Ser Bartrand when a maid ran screaming out of the garden." Half reluctantly, he grinned. "You should have heard her screech! It was enough to wake the dead, let alone the entire castle."

"Which she did, I gather," Carick replied. "But what was she doing there?"

Hamar's eyes rolled. "Her sweetheart is campaigning with Ser Rannart, off in the West, and she wanted to leave a wreath for his safe return. The usual kitchen maid stuff. Dawn is a good time, being sacred to both Imuln and Serrut—except the poor girl found rather more than she was expecting."

"It was bad, I take it?" Carick began to pull on his boots.

"Very bad." Hamar's expression turned grim again. He was still wearing his sleeveless practice shirt, but did not seem to feel the nip in the dawn air as they started for the castle. "We all piled in, of course." Hamar's breath misted as he spoke. "But what we saw—well, you couldn't blame the girl for screaming. None of us liked the man, but still . . . He didn't even look like Maister Gervon anymore. And the stake through the heart!" The squire shook his head. "That's folktale stuff: Oakward lore. Not what you expect when you get up in the morning."

Carick shrugged deeper into his jacket, uncomfortably aware of the similarity between his dream and Maister Gervon's death. I will not think of it, he told himself. Yet when he looked around at the new day, the little feathers of mist across the training field reminded him of the white fog in his nightmare. "Does one ever expect such things?" he asked, speaking more to himself than Hamar, but the squire shrugged.

"Probably not. Erron and Ser Bartrand kicked us all out as soon as they saw the body, but that won't stop the rumors, not with half the castle in the yard by then and the kitchen girl still having hysterics. Everyone'll be imagining demons under bed and brushpile. I've seen it before here, after a bad harvest or an outbreak of disease." Hamar grimaced as they stepped into the castle's outer yard and saw the gathered knots of castle folk, muttering amongst themselves. "See?" But he slowed rather than pushing his way through, calling out a greeting here and a light jest there, and forcing the mutterers to meet his open gaze.

Deliberately easing the tense atmosphere, Carick thought, impressed—then jumped as Raven tapped him on the shoulder.

"What's happening?" Hamar asked.

"The Castellan wants you and the other squires back at your lessons," Raven replied. "Setting a good example, I believe he said." He switched his gaze to Carick. "But you're to go to the chapel. Lord Falk wants you to map what's in there for him."

Carick swallowed. "I'll need my pens. And paper. I won't be long."

Or wouldn't have been, he realized a few minutes later, except that everyone between the courtyard and the map room wanted to ask him questions. Raher, of course, was openly envious when he learned that Carick was being allowed into the chapel itself. "How come you have all the luck?" he demanded, detaining Carick with a hand on his arm. "Maybe I should take up this scholar business as well."

This drew a derisive shout from every squire within earshot as Carick removed the hand. "You are holding me up," he pointed out, and the other squires fell back as well, letting him move toward the stairs. A quick glance around showed only somber faces, with Audin and the Countess Ghiselaine's heads bent close in conversation.

Well, they are the leaders here, Carick thought—before nearly stumbling over Girvase and Alianor on the first landing. They were standing by the window, but although Alianor nodded a greeting, Carick sensed tension beneath their studied calm. Girvase moved aside, his eyes flicking to meet Carick's—and the maister almost drew back, because it was like looking down a length of drawn blade. Yet the look was gone almost before Carick had registered it, so he returned Alianor's nod and hurried on.

Did I imagine it? he wondered, as he snatched up his drawing tools—but had forgotten the incident by the time he returned to the garden. Raven was standing guard at the narrow gate and let him through with a look that might almost have been sympathy, which made Carick's stomach muscles clench. And he vomited, even before he saw the body, because of the smell. Ser Bartrand, he thought miserably, seeing the knight waiting outside the chapel, would despise his weakness, but the knight only shrugged. "It's bad, but still not the worst I've encountered. Wait until you come upon an entire village that's been slaughtered by outlaws several days before."

Lord Falk, standing just inside the chapel door, stopped his captain with a gesture. Erron and Manan were waiting at the far end of the nave, by the desecrated altar, while the tracker, Herun, knelt to one side of the corpse. Carick tried not to look at the body too closely, or the stake and the blood splashed everywhere. Pushing aside the smell was harder, but he swallowed back another lurch of nausea and made himself focus on Lord Falk.

The Castellan's pale eyes were remote, but the hand he placed on Carick's shoulder was firm. "The body must be removed and the chapel cleansed," he said, "but first I want you to map this room for me. Mark down everything you see: the position of the body and every bloodstain. Can you do that?"

Carick nodded, not trusting himself to speak. And he did do it, with care and meticulous attention to detail. Gradually, the concentration required for the work took over and he was able to hold his awareness of the body at a distance, at least for the time needed to complete his task. He knew when Ser Bartrand left, his retreating footsteps heavy, and was equally conscious of the four who remained, watching him. They had each retreated to a separate corner of the chapel, and he was surprised, afterward, at their ability to remain unmoving for so long. But at the time his attention remained fixed on his work, until it was done.

"The stench," he said, as he placed his drawings in Lord Falk's hand. "Surely that isn't right, for a body so newly killed? It smells like the flesh has putrefied." He hesitated. "And the stake. It looks like a cut-down ladyspike."

The Castellan shook his head. "There are many things we have to consider, Maister Carick. So in the meantime, please don't speak of what you have seen here."

Carick nodded again, but his legs were unsteady as he stepped out into the garden, and he sat for a long time on a bench by the gate, his eyes closed. The sun crept around and when he opened his eyes again, Raven was watching him.

"So now you know what battle is," the hedge knight said. "There is no field of glory, only the charnel house."

Carick shook his head, remembering his dream and how Maister Gervon had advanced on him before the rasp of metal frightened him off. "I saw no evidence of battle," he said. "But it was certainly a charnel house." He wondered whether the Castellan's prohibition on discussing what he had seen included Raven, and decided to err on the side of caution. Besides, he didn't want to talk the scene over, like a gore-crow picking at bones. "I am beginning to understand," he added, "how lucky the River is."

" 'The peace of road and river,' " Raven quoted. "Scant pickings for my kind."

Carick pushed to his feet. "I think I'll go back to the inn. Will you let Lord Falk know where I am, if he wants me again?"

Raven nodded, then spoke again, his voice harsh as that of his namesake. "One more thing. A warning, if you will." Carick blinked at him, then his thoughts flew to the dream and he fought to keep his expression calm.

"A warning?" he repeated.

"You are a stranger here," the hedge knight said, "marked out by both dress and speech. Now we have a killing with all the hallmarks of a demon slaying, and Maister Gervon's dislike for you is also well known."

"But . . ." Carick's voice trailed off. *I am the Castellan's guest,* he wanted to protest, *and appointed to the ducal court.* A spurt of anger pushed his tiredness away. "So the foreigner with an accent will do to point the finger at? Is that what you mean?"

"Don't be a fool," said Raven. "It's the nature of the pack to turn on the outsider, as well as on the vulnerable and the weak—the more so when the pack grows afraid." He turned back toward the garden. "I advise you to have a care for yourself, that's all."

Carick drew in his breath, unable to think of an assertive answer. Besides, there was something peculiarly daunting about Raven's turned back. *The man's just a blade for hire,* he told himself as he trudged down the hill. *What can he know about honest folk and their ways?* But Carick remembered what Hamar had said, and the whispering amongst the people gathered in the courtyard, and thought that perhaps Raven was right, after all, and he was a fool.

The rest of the day passed slowly, but he was not sent for again. Manan only returned to the inn during the late afternoon, and it was evening before she found time to sit opposite him at the scrubbed table. She looked tired, with shadows beneath her normally merry eyes and a frown creasing her brows. "Who do you think killed him?" Carick asked.

Manan shook her head. "Even if I knew," she said, "I would not be allowed to say. But truly, I do not know." The frown deepened, and the tisane between her hands cooled as she stared into its depths.

Carick hesitated, but Manan, he reflected, had been in the chapel and no one else was present to overhear them. "Ser Raven said that it looked like a demon slaying."

"Did he, indeed?" The frown disappeared as Manan's brows rose. "What else did he say?"

"Not much," Carick admitted. "Except that I should be careful, because people will be fearful and I am a stranger here." He watched her closely and saw that he had her full attention now. After a moment the inn-wife nodded, sighing.

"He may be right to advise caution. We do what we can, but too many of our people are fearful and ignorant."

Carick swallowed, wishing she had said that Raven was wrong and there was nothing for him to be concerned about. Tiredness weighed on him, and for the first time since the pass he was sharply aware of how far he had stepped beyond the safe bounds of the River world.

His thoughts must have shown in his face because Manan stretched out a hand to cover his. "Caution is prudence, Maister Carick, but Normarch does not give in to superstition and fear. We will not let anyone harm you."

We? Carick wondered, and was not surprised when Lord Falk himself came in a little later, Erron a shadow at his back. The horsemaster went to stand by the fire, while Lord Falk seated himself across the table from Carick, his eyes yellow as a fox's in the lamplight. He smiled at Manan as she set a tankard down, and Carick remembered the tale that they had been lovers, and wondered whether it could have been true, after all. Manan caught his eye and he flushed, looking away, only to be snared by Lord Falk's stare.

"It seems, young man," the Castellan said, "that I cannot do without you. I will try and get a replacement maister when we go to Caer Argent, but in the meantime, we have no one but you to knock some learning into those hotheads on the hill."

"That isn't the method I would contemplate using," Carick murmured, and the Castellan smiled with an irony similar to Raven's.

"From what I've heard," Lord Falk observed, "any method you choose could hardly be worse than those employed by the late Maister Gervon. I suspect he knew that, since he made no effort to hide his dislike for you."

Carick felt the full weight of the day settle on him again. "I didn't kill him," he said.

"I did not say that you had." Lord Falk considered him across the tankard. "We cannot discount any possibility, but you are an unlikely suspect. Neither Ser Bartrand nor Ser Raven is flattering on the subject of your weapon skills, whatever hopes I may have of your scholarship. And whoever wielded that ladyspike knew what they were about."

Carick said nothing. He was still uneasy about the similarity between his dream and the circumstances of Maister Gervon's death, but felt he had made himself into enough of a fool reporting the shadow outside the stable. While he hesitated, Manan told Lord Falk of Ser Raven's caution.

The Castellan's expression was hard to read. "So the Raven croaked out a warning, did he? Well you know what they say of ravens: they are the bird of ill omen, the harbinger of battle and blood. But what do you say, Manan?"

Her firelit gaze rested on his, her tone thoughtful. "In matters of blood and war, one should heed the harbinger."

Lord Falk nodded. "Well, you are better placed than anyone to know, being halfway between castle and village. And close to both as lay priestess of Imuln." He leaned back, his shadow leaping as he stretched out his legs. "Well, that's settled then, Maister Carick. You will teach our charges as best you can and we shall have a care for you while you do. Unless there is something more that you wish to discuss with me?"

Carick shook his head, pushing back any qualms about his dream. "No, nothing," he said.

Lord Falk smiled. "In that case, we must all drink more ale, to seal our bargain and wash away the day."

"All the same," the Castellan said conversationally, when Carick had made his escape after only one handle of the light Normarch ale, "there's definitely something bothering our guest. We shall have to find out what it is."

Manan frowned at the closed door. "Surely you don't suspect him of this killing?"

"Of the killing, no." Falk's reply was calm. "It is highly unlikely he could have done it. But of being ill at ease about something—yes, I do suspect him of that."

Erron spoke from his place by the fire. "It's Maister Gervon who is the key, or what appeared to be Maister

Gervon. Whoever he was, we know that he hated and feared Maister Carick. Everyone noticed it."

"But why?" Manan asked softly. Her eyes met Falk's. "You are quite right, my heart, we must keep him here. Perhaps," she added, "as much for his own sake as for ours."

The fox eyes gleamed. "That consideration, too, had not escaped me. And my foster brother would not be at all pleased if we were to lose his precious cartographer."

# 16

# Summer's Eve

Normarch buzzed following Maister Gervon's death: first with speculation, then unease when no ladyspikes were found to be missing from the castle armory. No one besides the maid had been seen either going into or out of the garden, and rumors multiplied, widening to include the Oakward, the legendary protectors of Emer.

It was not entirely clear to Carick, listening to these tales, whether the Oakward were spellcasters, or a dedicated order of priests, or simply demonhunters, although often they sounded like a mix of all three. He was not sure why he was so fascinated by the stories, since folklore was not his study, but listened avidly whenever the subject came up. Perhaps, he reflected uneasily, it was another aftermath of his last nightmare about Maister Gervon, which he could not quite shake off.

The whispers, which had started to die down after the first few days, built again when reports of bolder raids by outlaw bands, this time accompanied by demons that were half man, half beast, began to filter in from outlying settlements. Lord Falk doubled the Normarch patrols in an effort to counteract the growing fear with bright steel and a show of strength, but the disquiet persisted.

"Werewolves, evil spirits, and blood-drinking ghouls," Raher said with relish, one evening in the inn kitchen.

Arn shrugged. "Everyone in the inner wards says that even the Oakward is just superstition, a hangover from the bitter years that followed the Cataclysm. They don't believe in a secret circle that pushed back evil anymore."

Girvase raised one eyebrow, but Audin interposed a comment about the Summer's Eve vigils, and the conversation turned to the subsequent Midsummer tourney in Caer Argent and whether they should ride in it as a company. "My cousin, Ser Ombrose, says they're looking for companies on the southern border with Lathayra." Audin stretched. "And that way, some of us could stay together."

But not all, Carick thought. He had learned, since Malisande first mentioned the Midsummer tourney, that not everyone would go to Caer Argent. Many of the new-made knights would return to their family homes after Summer's Eve, and if they did proceed on to the tourney would ride in the companies of their clans or close kin.

Gradually, Summer's Eve became the main topic of Normarch conversation again and Carick found it difficult to keep his students' minds on their lessons. Most made no secret of the fact that they found scholarship dull, despite both Audin and Ghiselaine showing genuine interest. Or was it more, Carick asked himself, that Ghiselaine was interested and Audin wanted the excuse to be in her company?

Girvase began to show application once he realized that mathematics could be applied to siege engines and tunneling, while Alianor, Malisande, and Hamar usually made a decent appearance of attention. But watching Hamar and Girvase practice with swords, or Malisande working with Manan—well, Carick knew that they were being polite about their lessons, but that was all. He had some hopes for Alianor, though, when she took an interest in the maps. "They're practical," she said, "not just another thing Lord Falk wishes us to learn."

Unlike the other girls, Alianor rarely smiled, but next to Malisande, Carick knew her best of all the damosels. She was Sond, from one of the great families, but spent as much time at the inn and in the stable as she did at the castle.

Carick suspected that was partly to spend time with Gir-vase, who was openly her sworn man—far more openly than Audin was Ghiselaine's. "I feel sorry for them," he said to Malisande, one rainy, wild evening shortly before Summer's Eve.

"Alianor and Girvase?" Malisande looked surprised. "You need not be. Ar may always marry Sond, even if it cannot inherit the titles."

"And Audin and Ghiselaine?" Carick asked.

Malisande shrugged. "She'll be Duchess of Emer. She will have to be content with that."

Carick was surprised by her coolness, but the door opened before he could reply and Ghiselaine and the other damosels trooped in. To help Manan make sugared sweets for the festival, they said—but really, he decided, retreating to a settle by the fire with his book, to complain about the weather.

"We'll never get to the Temple in the Rock if it's like this!" exclaimed Selia, who had recently returned from a visit to the south. Her silvery-blond hair fell almost to her knees, and now she tossed it back in exasperation—or to make everyone notice it? Carick wondered, looking up.

"I'm sure it'll clear." Alianor shook sugar from a cluster of sweets. "What do you say, Herun?" she asked, looking over to where the castle tracker sat with Raven and Col, sharing a jug of ale.

"Rain'll pass." If possible, the tracker was even quieter than Erron. "Likely this is the last spring squall."

Linnet spread out her skirts before the fire, trying to get rid of the damp. "It can't pass soon enough for me. I'll never get used to this wet."

"The weather's always best in Ormond," said a damosel called Brania, smoothing back coppery curls. Her expression was guileless, but there was an edge to her voice and Carick remembered Alianor telling him that Brania's grandfather, lord of the Murreward, had died in the last great battle with Ormond. She was distant kin to Lord Falk, on her mother's side, and had always seemed friendly with both Ormondians. Linnet just shrugged and looked at her sideways beneath sleepy lids, more than a little like a cat.

"We'll be in Caer Argent from Midsummer, and the weather's drier there—" Alianor began, but stopped as footsteps drummed across the yard and Jarna came in with a rush, rain thick on her dark hair.

"Maistress Manan!" the squire called, then checked perceptibly, seeing the gathered damosels. Linnet's brows rose in delicate question, while Selia looked Jarna up and down.

"Do you smell something?" she asked, a general query of the room. "I thought I caught a whiff of stable dung."

Several of the damosels giggled, including the yellow-haired girl that Carick had first met at the practice ground and now knew was called Ilaise. "Horses and sweat," another girl said. Alianor made a movement as if she intended intervening, but Linnet forestalled her.

"What would one expect," she murmured, with the slightest lift and fall of one shoulder, "of one whose skills are more fitted to the stable than the training ground?"

Jarna turned a dull red from neck to brow, groping behind her for the door latch. Carick set the book down and rose to his feet. "Is this the famed courtesy of the ladies of Emer?" he asked. From the corner of his eye he saw Raven, Herun, and Col watching, their ale jug forgotten. The damosels looked startled, and several, including Ilaise, glanced down or away. Selia's eyes were narrowed on him, but it was Linnet who spoke.

"But I, Maister Carick, am of Ormond. What care I for either the tradition,s or"—with a brief, contemptuous glance at Jarna—"the sweaty, commonplace squires of Emer?"

Now everyone was tense, recognizing a challenge to the fragile unity of Emer. The colorful, illuminated page of a book Carick had read shortly before leaving Ar flashed into his mind. " '*Fair Ormondie,*'" he quoted, " '*high home of courage and of courtesie, the very pattern and mirror for the valor of Emer.*' Or do I have that wrong, Damosel Linnet?"

"No," said a new voice, and every eye flew to Ghiselaine, standing in the stillroom door with Malisande at her shoulder. The young countess moved into the room, the lamplight shining on the red-gold bell of her hair. "You have it exactly, Maister Carick. We stand rebuked, and rightly so."

Selia turned white, but Linnet was frowning. "Who is he to rebuke us?" she demanded. "He is of the River, nothing more than a common clerk for hire."

"Common is as common does," said Ghiselaine, her clear gaze fixed on her cousin, although Carick knew she spoke to the whole room. "And speaks. A lady owes a duty of courtesy to all, whether of high or low degree. We must strive to see past appearances to true worth, whether in scholar or squire." She looked from Linnet to Selia. "I believe squire Jarna is owed an apology—and Maister Carick also."

Linnet bit her lip, but she would not, Carick guessed, go against Ghiselaine. "I apologize," she said tightly, addressing Jarna. Her gray eyes did not quite meet Carick's as she dipped her head. "To you also, Maister."

She looked as though the last words would choke her, and Carick thought that Selia might not get them out at all, her lips were pressed together so tightly. "I apologize," the blond damosel muttered finally, echoed a moment later by Ilaise and the rest of the gigglers, who all kept their eyes down. Jarna looked wretchedly ill-at-ease and made her escape upstairs, looking for Manan, while Carick bowed to Ghiselaine and resumed his seat and his book. On the far side of the room, Raven and his companions went back to their ale. Alianor placed the last of the sweets in a covered crock and handed it to Malisande, for the stillroom. "I think we should all go, Ghis," she said.

It was very quiet after they left, with just the drip, drip, drip from the eaves and the rattle of rainwater in the guttering. Raven and his companions finished their ale and left, too, without saying anything about the incident. Carick pretended to read his book.

"Why did you intervene?" He had forgotten that Malisande was in the stillroom and jumped when she spoke. She tilted her dark head as she stepped back into the kitchen, studying his small shrug. "Because Jarna already gets a hard enough time from Ser Bartrand, is that it?"

Because I hate bullies, Carick thought, and all those who
see vulnerability as an invitation to attack. "He doesn't teach
her the same way he does the other squires," he said. "I've
seen that—and the way Hamar and Audin try to make up
for it." He did not add that he had noticed how close Hamar
and Jarna were as well, because he was not sure anyone else
had yet.

Malisande sat down on the opposite settle and drew up her
feet, wrapping her arms around her knees. "You're right. It'll
get her killed, one day. Or her friends," she added, matter-of-
fact, "trying to keep her alive."

They were both silent, staring at the flames. Malisande
rested her chin on her knees. "You were clever, though. Not
just taking the sting out of Linnet's declaration for Ormond,
but opening the way for Ghis to reinforce it." Her eyes narrowed. "What Linnet said about Ormond and Emer was
close to treason. And not wise either, in front of Brania and
the Castellan's men."

Carick thought about Audin's head bent close to Ghiselaine's, on the morning Maister Gervon's body was found.
"Does Ghiselaine support the peace?"

"Who knows?" The damosel's smile was as narrow as
her eyes. "Both she and Ormond are bound to it through the
treaty made with Caer Argent, but Emerian history is full of
broken compacts. And more still that were made simply to
be kept until the time was right."

"You're a cynic," Carick said, but Malisande shook her
head.

"No. A realist. But now, thanks to you, the whole matter
will blow over and be forgotten, although it could so easily
have been otherwise." The dark brows crooked. "I did
wonder, though, how you knew about that old saying—the
one about Ormond and the valor of Emer?"

Carick grinned. "I read it in a book, an old one from the
library in Ar. I wanted to know more about Emer before I
came here."

Malisande shook her head. "And that's what you found?
Still, it was useful tonight." She straightened, stretching. "I

think the rain may have slackened off. I had better get back to the castle."

A draft crept through the room and touched the back of Carick's neck. "I'll see you up the hill," he said.

"I'll escort her." Jarna appeared through the half-open door that led to the upper floor—almost, Carick thought, as though she had been waiting just out of sight on the stairs. The squire's jaw was set, her eyes the slate-blue of storm clouds, and he wondered how much of their conversation she had overheard. "That is," she said to Malisande, "if you don't mind the smell of the stables."

"Jarna—" Carick began, but she cut him off.

"I don't need your kindness—or anyone's pity." The stormy eyes flashed at him, then back to Malisande. "You should be safe if I walk downwind of you."

"I'm sure I'll be safe." Malisande nodded to Carick. "Good night, Maister Carick."

By the time Carick went to bed the rain had definitely eased, and when he looked out the moon was showing its face through broken cloud. The same moon sailed through his dreams, silvering the droplets that fell in a steady drip from tree and hedge. A ground mist rose in pallid tendrils, and even in his dream Carick could smell damp earth and rain-misted wool as a cloak brushed against wet leaves. A hand, white as bone in the moonlight, grasped a mailed arm.

*"Fool!"* a voice hissed, although all Carick could see was what looked like two cloaked shadows against the blackness of a wall. There might have been trees rising above the wall, but he could not be sure. *"Why did you allow the River boy to interfere? I had primed the girl perfectly—but all for nothing now. Nothing!"*

*"I am not one of your coterie."* Carick moved uneasily in his sleep, for the voice's timbre was elusively familiar, despite the shadows woven through and around it. *"Besides,"* Carick could almost hear the speaker's shrug, *"stepping in once the scholar spoke up would have struck a false note,*

*drawn the wrong kind of attention. And those present will remember what the girl said anyway."*

*"It could have been so much more—was intended to be!"* The bone-white hand drew back and the voice hissed again. *"I had heard you were unreliable. But don't think that Aranraith won't hear of it, if you upset what we do here again."*

The shadowed voice remained indifferent. *"Think well, spellbinder, before you make threats. You would not be the first to regret having crossed me."*

The answering silence was strained as a cloud drifted across the dream moon. After a moment the hissing voice spoke again, but Carick could not hear what it said, or even decide whether it was male or female. When the cloud cleared, both the cloaked figures were gone and the only sound was the steady *drip, drip*—but when Carick forced himself awake, he realized that the water was coming from the inn's eaves. Already his recollection of the dream was blurring, and he wondered if he had been mistaken in thinking the shadowed voice sounded familiar. And even if it had, could that not just have been the dream fitting a known voice to its twists and turns?

Carick scowled and pummeled his pillow, trying to get comfortable. He slept poorly and woke half expecting more bad news, but the day that followed was uneventful. He yawned his way through it, and the strangeness of the dream faded. Over the next few days the roads grew busier, with the first merchant train arriving through the Long Pass. As soon as it departed another came up from the south, with news from Caer Argent, Aralorn, and sun-dry Lathayra. The inn's rooms filled up, both with traders and Marcher folk coming to keep the festival with Lord Falk.

"'Keeping festival' is what they call it," Hamar told Carick with a grin. "What they mean is: judge my dispute, apprentice my child, formalize my betrothal."

"'Betrothed on Summer's Eve, wed at Midsummer'," said Manan cheerfully, turning out yet another batch of the saffron buns that Carick found irresistible. "If we get any busier, Lord Falk may have to let the maister bunk down in his map room."

The castle itself was starting to be full to overflowing, but Carick thought a cot in the map room might be pleasant enough if it got him away from the constant coming and going. He had already had enough of stifled laughter from behind closed doors as everyone plotted over coming-of-age gifts, or the festival tokens to be given to lover or sweetheart. It was the last straw, he decided, one stiflingly warm afternoon, when he opened the map room door and found Girvase and Alianor standing close together, as though whispering secrets.

"Haven't you anything better to do?" he asked, exasperated. Yet although they jumped apart and apologized, then as quickly left, Carick found he could not concentrate on the fine detail of repairing maps. He didn't want to watch whoever was on the training field either, pursuing the endless Emerian business of practicing war. Hamar might be in the forge, though, and need someone to hold a horse or pump the bellows—honest work, Carick told himself, and it will get me out of the castle.

The inn forge was empty when he arrived, and the stable quiet as well, except for a small gray cat sitting on top of a grain bin. Carick paused, watching the dust motes in a bar of sunlight, and thought he heard voices from the orchard. He crossed the yard and entered the scrubbed coolness of the buttery, which was empty, too, although the voices were clearer and interspersed with a dull, repetitive *thwack*. Cautiously, Carick peered through the buttery's outer door into the orchard.

The *thwack* was Jarna, laying into one of the straw and timber dummies usually set up on the practice field, while Raven watched and Hamar sat on a nearby stump, his sheathed sword across his knees. Occasionally, the knight gave an instruction, his dark face impassive, but he seemed aware of Carick's arrival and looked around, nodding for him to join them. Hamar nodded, too, but said nothing. As for Jarna, Carick doubted she knew he was there as she continued to attack the dummy. Sweat ran down her face, although she had knotted a rag around her forehead to keep it out of her eyes, and her shirt stuck to her back in dark patches. "One hundred," she finally gasped out.

"Take a few minutes, then we'll go through the same pattern with Hamar." Raven looked at Carick. "Unless Maister Carick would like to try his hand?"

"Me?" Carick said. Hamar grinned, and even Jarna smiled.

"Why not?" said Hamar. "Surely even scholars learn the sword, on the River?"

"I've had a few lessons," Carick admitted, "but they're expensive. Only archery is compulsory for everyone—and the training's provided free by the prince's guard."

Hamar stood up. "You should take advantage of Ser Raven's offer, then. He's going to teach Jarn to counter opponents who are stronger and have a longer reach."

"I wondered why you were here." Carick gestured at the orchard. "Is it a secret?"

"No." Raven nodded to Hamar, who unsheathed his sword and came to stand opposite Jarna. "But it's good to be private when you learn something new." He turned to the girl. "In the field, your horses will always be an advantage, given your ability to train them, but any knight can be unhorsed. So try what I have shown you. Hamar, don't hold back."

Hamar came in like a storm, but instead of trying to meet the blows head-on, Jarna shifted her ground, parrying and feinting until she could slip a real blow through. The approach would work, Carick thought, watching critically, so long as she had room to maneuver and did not tire before her opponent. But then, anyone could tire in the chaos of battle, or trip, or be knocked down by a riderless horse. "I suppose," he said, when Raven finally let the squires rest, "that no matter how strong or skilled you are, in many cases survival is still a matter of luck?"

"Strength and skill help make luck," Raven replied, "even in battle."

"Battles can go on for a long time," Hamar said, recovering his breath. "But a duel's over quickly. A matter of minutes, usually, even for skilled adversaries."

"Given the Duke's new edict forbidding dueling amongst his knights," Raven said dryly, "neither you nor Jarna will be fighting any." He ignored Hamar's rebellious expression, studying Jarna with a dispassionate eye. "Your stance could be stronger. We need to work on that."

Carick watched the knight adjust the girl's placement of her feet and her grip on the sword. "How long has this been going on?" he asked Hamar.

The squire shrugged again. "The best part of a week. He's very good," he added, almost grudgingly. "Adept with the sword and every other weapon I've seen him use."

"War is his trade," Carick said. "You'd expect him to be good at it."

"True enough. But still—" Hamar hesitated, running a hand through his sweat darkened hair. "It does seem unusual that someone who's that skilled should be a hedge knight. Things may be different on the River, but in Emer or Lathayra men like that stand at the right hand of the greatest lords."

Carick thought about that. "There must be some," he said finally, "who prefer the open road to civilization and city walls, however much gold they may command within them. Maybe Ser Raven is of that kind."

"Maybe." Hamar sounded doubtful, and Carick supposed it did sound unlikely in the context of the Emerian world. "Still," the squire said again, "I'm grateful he's putting the time into Jarn. She deserves it."

Ghiselaine, too, Carick noticed, was speaking with Jarna more often—making a point of it although the squire remained wary. But the Countess of Ormond was difficult to rebuff, especially when Alianor seconded her friendliness, although Linnet and Selia continued to stand aloof. Yet even their mood picked up as the weather stayed fair and everyone agreed that it would almost certainly be fine for Summer's Eve. More travelers arrived at the inn, and Carick was certain that he would have to relocate to the map room soon—until one fine bright morning when a band of Hill people rode in to speak with Lord Falk.

# 17

# Oak and Hill

Carick came running with everyone else and stared at the spirals of blue tattooing that covered the Hill people's faces—and he gathered, listening to the murmurs around him, their entire bodies as well, beneath their leather and scale mail. The new arrivals formed themselves into two loose groups in the castle's main hall: the first around a grizzled, powerful, middle-aged man standing beneath a white, horsetail banner; the second in a half circle about a weather-beaten woman of similar years, below a standard crowned with antlers. The two leaders bowed deeply to Lord Falk, who stood in greeting and called for the guest cup, a wide bowl of antique bronze with silver along the rim. He poured wine and then lifted the cup to each of the Hill chieftains in turn. "Hirn of Hillholt. Hawk of Barrowdun. What brings you to Normarch this spring?"

The chieftain called Hirn took the cup and drank, before passing it to the woman. Both chieftains placed their lips on the same place where Falk had drunk, and after Hawk, the cup was passed around to each of their followers in turn. "We seek Normarch's aid, Lord Castellan." Hirn waited until the cup was handed back to Lord Falk before speaking again. "We call on the bond sworn between Oak and Hill, when your foster brother, the Duke, first came into his power."

Lord Falk was silent for a long moment, the morning sun glinting in his fox eyes. "A matter of importance, then," he said at last, "especially since it brings Barrowdun and Hillholt together on the same errand."

The woman smiled thinly. "It's true that Barrowdun and Hillholt are as likely to raid each other as stand together. But what preys on our farmsteads and hunting runs now is not of the Hills, even though the incursions against Barrowdun have been made to look like Hillholt work—and the attacks on Hillholt like ours."

"The brown bull of Barrowdun driven off and harried to its death in Dunmuir Slough," Hirn said, his eyes fixed on the Castellan. "Hillholt's swiftest horses found hamstrung and gutted by the Standing Stones, first having run mad with terror."

Lord Falk looked from one to the other. "But you both say that appearances lie?"

Hirn shrugged. "If it were just those two incidents we might have believed it of the other. But steads and hunting camps have been razed and their inhabitants put to the blade: young and old, man, woman, and child. That is war, Lord Falk, not Hill raiding."

"And those few who have survived report uncanny things." Carick caught the flicker of something that could have been fear in Hawk's fierce eyes. "They speak of creatures who are half man and half beast, demons whose shapes change and shift beneath the moon."

"On every raid," Hirn concluded harshly, "they have left something behind—a weapon of Barrowdun in the Hillholt camp, a token of Hillholt in the ruins of a Barrowdun farmstead. Someone, my lord, wants war in our Hills."

"And on my March," said Lord Falk softly. He considered them from beneath his brows. "Someone who knows enough about Barrowdun and Hillholt to provide what should have been sufficient provocation for traditional enemies. I am curious, my friends, as to why you are here together with your clanfolk still in check?"

The chieftains exchanged a sidewise glance; Hirn stroked

his tattooed chin. "We pledged to your foster brother that there would be no more war in the Hills. But the long rivalry between our two clans is well known. What was unknown is that a youth of Hillholt went astray in his hunting, many years ago, and met a young woman out of Barrowdun who had turned her ankle in the ruins at High Tor." He shrugged, half dour, half smiling. "What would you? It was Imuln's festival of Summer's Eve, then as it is now, and we became each other's springtime love, Hawk of Barrowdun and I. There was no future in it, we both knew that, and we have seen each other rarely since, but still—"

"Still," said Hawk, "we both remembered the person we had met that spring, and neither could believe these slayings were the other's work. Or at least had sufficient doubt, taken together with our oath to your Duke, to pace out the truce-moot before we turned our clans loose, one against the other."

"And now," Lord Falk said gravely, "you bring this matter to me."

The two chieftains inclined their heads, a gesture that was respectful yet without servility. "Our scouts," said Hawk, "tell us that raider bands are gathering on the borders of our hunting runs. We fear they will strike soon and strike hard, and our numbers are few. So we invoke the bond sworn between us. Let the shade of Emer's oak be cast over our hills, as was promised, against those who seek our destruction."

Carick felt a queer thrill, as though a current had rippled down some old line of power, touching everyone in that watchful hall. He guessed that the Castellan could not refuse the request, for he was the Duke's warden in the north and these stocky, tattooed folk were keeping faith with the Oak-tree of Emer in their own, half-wild way. He saw that same knowledge in all the faces present, together with the reckoning of what force they could muster. "It could be a ploy," Ser Bartrand said heavily, "to draw our strength away from Normarch, knowing that Ser Rannart is still tied up in the west."

"Either way," said Raven, speaking up unexpectedly from

his place off to one side, "the timing bodes ill, given the advent of Summer's Eve."

Lord Falk turned to him with a lifted brow, but Carick thought he detected understanding in the faces of the Hill chieftains as they, too, looked at the hedge knight. Ser Bartrand simply looked blank. "In all the lands between the River and Ishnapur," Erron put in quietly, "Summer's Eve is sacred to Imuln as Maiden, but it is not just the festival of the first new moon. It also marks the last of the old, the dark of the moon, and that is sacred to another god altogether."

"Karn," whispered Hawk, and all the Hill folk openly made the sign that averts ill luck. "The Dancer in Shadows, the slayer and avenger, the drinker of blood."

Erron nodded. "It was not unheard of in the dark times for Karn to be offered his sacrifice of blood at Summer's Eve: the giving up of life in exchange for the coming of summer and the rising of the new moon."

"Old superstitions!" Ser Bartrand said harshly. "All such practices were outlawed long ago."

Erron said nothing, but Lord Falk nodded, as though agreeing with what was left unsaid. "Those who raid the Hill clans do not observe the Duke's laws. It may well serve their purposes to use the old rites of Karn for their own ends."

"It would be an ill omen indeed," Manan spoke for the first time, frowning, "if the promise of Imuln's moon were to be drowned in blood."

"And so both need and honor call us to the Hills," Lord Falk agreed. "Ser Bartrand, you will muster our troops for departure at first light the day after tomorrow. Erron will command here in my absence."

"But surely," Ser Bartrand protested, "we will need Erron with us?"

The Castellan shook his head. "With you and I gone, Bartrand, Erron is the one the people will look to and follow. He will have Ser Raven to call on for experience of war."

Ser Bartrand shot a frowning look at the hedge knight. "I thought he would ride with us, given that experience."

"I would prefer it," Sir Falk said, "but with Ser Rannart

away we must leave one knight here." He stood up. "Hirn, Hawk, sers. We will meet again later to break bread as friends and discuss strategy. But for now, we have a great deal to do if we are to prepare an expedition—and no time to waste."

They left two mornings later, a strong company of horse and one of archers marching out behind the black oak banner of Emer on its green ground, with Lord Falk's red fox ensign flying bravely beside it. Carick watched from the castle wall as the early sun caught on speartip and helm, shading his eyes until the strange, spike-backed serpent finally disappeared through a gap between forest and hills. "And we," said Raher, standing beside him, "are left behind. As always."

"With the maidens," said Hamar, his tone an echo of Raher's but with a sly grin at the damosels, who had also come up to see the column depart.

"Exactly," said Raher. "I've had enough of lessons. It's time they took us seriously."

"We've got garrison duty," Audin pointed out, "which makes us part of the castle's strength."

As if to underline that responsibility, Raven worked them harder than ever on the training field and spared none of the squires who came against him, whether on foot or horseback. "You pay for every mistake," said Hamar, after a hard-fought melee that seemed to Carick, watching, to be all dust, swiftly turning horses, and hard blows.

"But," said Jarna unexpectedly, dabbing at a puffed and bleeding lip, "you don't make that mistake again." Her face was shining through its mask of grime, her usually downcast eyes a-blaze.

"There's no second chance in battle," Audin agreed, and Jarna's abused mouth twisted.

"That's why I don't mind how often or how hard he hits me, so long as I'm learning."

She must mean it, Carick thought, because Raven worked her harder than anyone, so that she always had more than her share of scrapes and bruises. "Yet she thrives," Malisande pointed out that evening, grinding up herbs with a pestle and mortar. "And I overheard Erron saying that Ser Raven would make knights of them all, even Jarna."

"She will deserve her vigil," Carick agreed. "And you have the good weather you wanted for the Temple in the Rock."

Malisande shook her head, her smile tight. "Haven't you heard? With Lord Falk away and unrest in the Hills, Erron has forbidden us to go."

The damosels' outcry over this decision echoed throughout Normarch, and Carick entered the hall the next morning to find a deputation arguing their case to Erron. "The Hills are *leagues* away from here!" Ilaise wailed. "And the Temple in the Rock is *completely* in the other direction! We'd be in absolutely *no* danger."

"There has been unrest in the west as well," Erron replied. "That is why Ser Rannart is there."

"He's campaigning a lot farther westward," Selia said quickly. "The Temple in the Rock is less than a day's ride from here."

"And," Alianor put in, "there's been no incursion within Normarch's demesne for at least quarter of a century."

"We'll have numbers, too," Brania added, "and weapons, which we know how to use."

Erron shook his head. "We can't send an escort with you, not with the garrison depleted. And we dare not risk Countess Ghiselaine."

"Why does everything always come down to *her*?" Selia snapped.

Linnet's foot tapped. "Ghis is just their excuse for making us all little better than prisoners. Alli's right—there's been no incursion anywhere near here for years."

"You are forgetting Maister Gervon's death," Raven pointed out. He had been standing back from the confrontation, but now came forward to join Erron.

The damosels hesitated, before Linnet waved the observation aside. "A single murder is not an incursion, *Ser* Raven."

"Nonetheless," said Erron, "my decision stands."

"The *effrontery* of it," declared Selia as they swept out, clearly meaning to be overheard. "A horsemaster and a sword-for-hire daring to tell *us* what we may and may not do!"

But Erron had already left, and when Carick glanced at Raven the knight just shrugged, his expression more sardonic than ever.

Carick shook his head. "I don't understand their obsession with the Temple in the Rock. Do you?"

"A little. Emerian tradition claims that it was the center of Imuln's worship throughout what we now call the Southern Realms, back in the days of the Old Empire—more important even than Jhaine, although that seems hard to believe now." Raven shrugged again. "It may be true though, because there's a line of ruined fortifications along these hills, which suggest the Empire wanted to protect something in the area."

It wouldn't have been Normarch, Carick reflected. He had learned enough about Old Empire ruins to know that the Castellan's stronghold in the north, if it existed at all in those days, would have been little more than some minor lord's folly. As for the thwarted expedition to the Temple in the Rock, Carick felt sure it was a minor storm that would soon blow over. Still, he grinned when he recalled how fierce the damosels had been in the hall—and how the squires were going to have to rise well before dawn for their vigil. The castle's chapel to Serrut had not yet been reconsecrated after Maister Gervon's death, so the squires would be riding to the one in Crosshills village, four miles away.

When Carick walked down the hill at midday, he saw that the wood for the Summer's Eve bonfire had been stacked beside the training grounds, with another pile on the common outside the village. On impulse, he turned aside, thinking he might find Hamar in the forge, or perhaps the orchard—although the sessions there had ended now that Raven was training all the squires. The stable interior was dim, but peaceful with the mingled scents of straw and leather and horses. Carick heard a rattle, as though someone were shifting harness, followed by a murmured word as the gray cat whisked out of the tack room. He stooped to stroke it before looking around the door—and instantly drew back, heat flooding into his face.

The tack room was darker than the stable, but still light enough to make out the two figures locked together against one wall: one standing, the other seated on a storage barrel. A chink in the roof illuminated Jarna's face, tipped back with her eyes closed, and revealed the slight, half-moon curve of her breast where her shirt was unlaced. The young man with her had his back to the door and his shirt still on, but there was no mistaking the broad back or gleam of russet hair.

Hamar and Jarna. Carick drew in a deep breath and stepped silently away from the door. They had not seen him—and would not have heard him either, absorbed as they were in each other. Carick flushed again, recalling the pale curve of Jarna's breast, and wondered why it bothered him. He had already guessed anyway, given the amount of time the two spent together. But guessing, he found now, was not the same thing as knowing, and he took a deep breath as he emerged into the yard. He had seen what he should not, no question of that. Not just because of the intimacy of the moment, but because he strongly suspected that Lord Falk would frown on the liaison.

Yet none of that, thought Carick, sitting down on the edge of the well, explained why he felt as though he had been punched in the stomach.

"Maister Carick." He looked up to find Ser Raven regarding him. "Are you well?"

"Er, yes. Fine." Carick tried to pull himself together, but instantly saw Jarna's breast again, with Hamar's arms wrapped around her and the girl's legs twined around Hamar's waist. He felt the color creep up into his face. "Were you looking for me?"

"No." The knight studied him curiously before glancing toward the kitchen. "I heard Manan was making a fresh batch of saffron buns. Although I would like to go over those maps with you again, if you have time."

They were sitting on the kitchen step, eating the buns and some jam pastries that Manan had given them, when Hamar and Jarna emerged from the stable. The pair looked happy, Carick thought, a little sourly until he realized that Raven was watching him. Once the two squires joined them, it was hard to believe that the scene in the tack room had actually happened. Jarna was her usual self, shy and withdrawn, while Hamar disappeared to wheedle more buns out of Manan.

Shouldn't they seem different, Carick wondered, if they're in love? And *did* Raven have to give off quite such a strong aura of secret amusement?

"More night training again tonight, ser?" Hamar asked, returning with the buns. A few extra pastries had been tucked into the corners of the basket.

Raven shook his head. "Not with the vigils starting the day after tomorrow. You'll need your sleep for that."

"True enough." Hamar looked solemn, but then a grin broke through. "And after that, Caer Argent. Jarn and I have been talking about the tourney. We thought I'd win the sword competition, but leave the horsemanship trials to her."

"Those events would suit your strengths." Raven rose to his feet. "Could we look at those maps now, Maister Carick?"

So Carick had no choice but to follow him back to the castle and focus his mind on cartography for the rest of the afternoon.

# 18

# *Vigil*

*T*he following night, Carick woke in the dark hours to the muffled sound of horses walking along the road verge and the occasional clink of bridle or stirrup. He raised his head, realized it must be the squires leaving for Seruth's chapel, and went back to sleep. When he woke again it was full day but remarkably quiet, with no clatter in the yard or distant clangor of training. He was dressing, taking his time and thinking it was going to be a long day, when he heard a horse gallop down the hill and away through the village. By the time he opened the shutters, the rider was long gone. Manan, too, was nowhere to be seen when he went downstairs.

Of course, Carick thought, helping himself to breakfast. She's the lay priestess of Imuln, so she'll be at the village shrine with the damosels.

The peace lasted until he walked through the castle gate and noticed visible tension in the guards on duty. By the time he reached the hall, he could hear a woman's flurried, anxious voice. Dame Nelys, he thought, stepping inside, and saw the chaperone from the Girls' Dorter standing with Erron and Raven. She looked as though she might faint at any moment, while the handful of younger damosels in the background appeared frightened and excited at the same time. "I can't understand it," the dame said, twisting her hands together. "I had no idea of this, none at all."

"They are not in the village," Raven said. "And their horses are gone from the stables, together with supplies for an overnight journey. They have gone to the Temple in the Rock."

Erron frowned, his expression deeply troubled. "Who urged them to this madness? Do you know, Dame Nelys?"

Nelys shook her head. "I knew nothing. Heard nothing, not even a whisper."

"Linnet was wild for the venture." One of the younger damosels spoke up nervously. "And Selia, too. She kept saying that all the most famous daughters of the Old Empire, those whose lives and leadership made a difference, were consecrated at that shrine in its great days. And the way she spoke—" The girl shook her head. "All I wanted was to go along with whatever she said."

"She had a scroll," a second girl said. The scattering of freckles across her nose stood out sharply against a pale face. "I was there when she showed it to Ghis—the Countess. It recorded a prophecy that Emer would only rise to true glory when its Duchess had kept her vigil at the Temple in the Rock."

Erron's frown deepened. "I've never heard of such a prophecy," he said.

"They all wanted to go anyway," another girl whispered. "For the adventure of it. And they swore us to secrecy."

"Surely they'll be all right." Dame Nelys gripped her hands together. "They will be all right, won't they?"

Raven and Erron's eyes met. "We must ride after them," the knight said. "At once."

The dame's hands twisted again. "But—that would destroy their vigil."

"Better that than dead." The knight was brusque. "I'll have to take the squires," he said to Erron. "We can't do this otherwise, and still keep a realistic garrison here. And we dare not strip this place of its last strength, even for the Countess of Ormond."

"But their vigils," Dame Nelys moaned. "Think of the ill luck!"

"I am thinking," Raven said, "of the ill luck to Emer if Ghiselaine of Ormond dies while in the Lord Castellan's care."

"You fear treachery," Erron said, his words a statement, not a question.

"I smell it," Raven replied. "This comes too pat with the Castellan's departure. It may be a two-pronged attack, both against the Countess and this castle if we leave it undermanned."

"Vigils or no vigils," said Erron, "we will not do that."

Raven nodded and his dark stare flicked to Carick, standing just inside the door. "I will need your maps, Maister. We need to see if this shrine is marked anywhere and what paths lead there, especially from the border crossings we looked at yesterday."

He cursed, a soldier's pungent epithet, when Carick returned and unrolled the maps. "Two routes in," he said grimly, "besides the road we'll take. One from the western foothills, true as a leyline down this ridge, and the other from the east, up this riverbed. What's it called, the Rindle? And the shrine placed squarely between the two, as neat a trap as one could wish for."

"They are not trapped yet," Erron said quietly. "We will get them back."

Raven slanted a quick, bleak look at him. "If it were not for the Countess, I would say they must take their chance. We do not have the numbers for this folly, and we risk losing the squires as well, going after them."

Erron shook his head. "The squires are about to become knights, in any case. And this is what they were trained for. Risks of this kind will come to them sooner or later."

Carick hesitated, unsure whether his opinion would be welcome. "The girls are their friends," he said finally. "They'll want to go."

"Friendship may also cloud judgment," Raven said, not dismissively but as one stating a fact. "Another risk they will have to overcome if they are to be effective as knights."

"You had better take Herun," said Erron. "He's our most experienced tracker. Darin and Aymil, from the guards, are both good in the woods—and Solaan goes, too. The damosels may listen to her once you catch them." He turned at a sudden rush of hooves outside. "They are back. Let's hope that Manan has managed to calm them a little."

It must have been Manan galloping that horse earlier, Carick realized—and it made sense that she would have missed the young women first, when they never arrived at the village temple.

Erron had been right about the squires being unsettled. Keyed for their vigil and then pulled away from it, the young men crowding into the courtyard were bewildered and furious. Carick glanced at Manan, walking her horse up and down to one side, and thought it said a great deal that she had not only gotten the squires to the castle, but maintained some semblance of order. Only a semblance, though: one look at their white, angry faces made it clear that whoever had called them back would have to provide a very good explanation.

A second look told Carick something more. Beneath their anger the squires were afraid, because they knew that a vigil would only be broken in exceptional circumstances. Raher had his hand on his sword and his horse moved restlessly, tossing up its head. By contrast Girvase sat very still, but his hand, too, rested on his sword hilt, and his eyes were hooded as Erron and Raven came down the steps. Audin moved his horse forward to meet them. He was pale, but holding himself in check. "Erron?" he asked. "I know a priestess of Imuln may break a vigil once it's started, but Manan said that Ghis and the other girls were missing?"

"They are," Erron said. "We believe they have ridden to the Temple in the Rock, against Lord Falk's express order."

Raher's brows snapped together. "You break our vigil for *that*?" he demanded. "Isn't it their right to keep vigil for the Goddess where they will?"

"Ser Raven suspects treachery," Erron told them quietly, and their attention swung to the knight.

"That's why Manan went after you," Raven said. He seemed so ordinary in his worn hauberk, the shadow of the rowan tree beside the steps stippling his face like old scars, but Carick saw some of the tension go out of the squires. He is used to leading men, he thought, watching Audin's eyes meet the knight's with almost painful intensity.

"Tell us," the Duke's nephew said. And then they were all dismounting, tramping into the hall and crowding around to look at the map, while Raven related what facts they knew. In the background, servants began to set up trestles and bring out food. "We understand," Audin said finally, spokesman for the rest, "both what we must do and why. But what does this mean for our vigils, if Summer's Eve has passed by the time we return?"

Raven looked at Manan. "A quest may be substituted for a vigil," the lay priestess said, "although that does not happen often in these more peaceful times. And it is just custom to sit one's vigil at Summer's Eve, not necessity."

Raher fidgeted. "Summer's Eve is the most auspicious time. Everyone says so."

"A quest is also auspicious," Manan said gently.

"If we survive it," Raher muttered. "Otherwise we die unknighted."

"In Serrut's name, Raher!" Audin was terse. "Ghis, Alli, and the others may be riding into an ambush. Let's not waste time!"

"Besides," said Hamar, "we could all have died unknighted anytime these past eighteen years." For the first time, a few grins flickered amongst the squires, and even Girvase, who had been staring at the maps with a white, set expression, looked up.

"Audin is right," Raven said, before he could speak. "Given the damosels' start, there's no time to waste."

The next hour was all activity as the squires armed and provisioned themselves, not just with food and water and weapons, but also with tarpaulins and ropes, pitch torches, tinder boxes, and entrenching tools. "More like a campaign than a search party," Raher muttered, and no one disagreed.

Carick frowned, but focused on going over the most uncertain details of the maps with Raven and Herun.

"Although I can't guarantee that any of these are accurate," he told them. "Seruth knows when they were last checked against the terrain."

"Better than nothing, though," said Hamar, when the others had gone again and he was helping Audin into his armor. The young lord was very pale, his brows a single, frowning line as he waited for Hamar to finish. For the first time, Carick saw the black oak of Emer on his jupon, set within the oak-leaf circlet of the ducal house. From outside, he could hear the edge to Girvase's voice as he organized the horses.

Those two know what's at stake without needing to be told, he thought. Carefully, he rolled up the scrolls and lashed them into sturdy, watertight coverings: they would need to be well protected if Raven wanted them with him.

"In the yard," Audin told him, when the job was finally done and Carick looked around for the knight. When he reached the door, Raven was already on horseback. The knight was wearing full armor and had abandoned the light Aralorn horses for one of the castle chargers. The beast rolled a restless eye at Carick, but he scarcely noticed because a groom was leading Mallow out, with a journey roll strapped behind her saddle.

"Best get whatever other gear you need, and swiftly, Maister Carick," Raven said. "You're coming with us."

"Me?" Carick thought about his inglorious flight from the wolfpack. "Why?"

"Because I need someone to interpret those maps against the terrain," Raven said curtly. "I'll have other things to worry about."

"Perhaps he can't read," Raher whispered, adjusting a stirrup leather alongside Mallow. "Lots of my father's knights can't." An odd expression flitted across the squire's face. "In fact," he added slowly, "m'father can't either!" He laughed, a reluctant bark of humor, before springing into the saddle. Carick shrugged, because regardless of whether Raven was lettered or not, he already knew that the knight could read a map.

"Hamar says you'll need help to arm." Jarna appeared beside him, holding up a brigandine. "He said this would be best, since you're not used to mail, and that you'd better have a sword as well. You did say you'd had some lessons," she added.

"Yes." Carick hesitated. "But war was not our business in Ar, as it is here."

Jarna looked away. "Hamar said to find you one. And a helmet, too."

"I have—" Carick began, but Jarna had already disappeared. He looked around to meet Girvase's measuring stare.

"A short sword would be better for you," the squire said. "It'll be easier to manage since you're not used to fighting from horseback."

"What he means," Raher put in helpfully, "is that you'll be less likely to cut Mallow's head off."

The look Girvase turned on his friend was level. "I meant what I said. If Jarna can't find anything suitable, he can have the sword I used when I first came here."

But the sword Jarna brought back was serviceable, and the weight and balance seemed right—although Carick still felt like a fraud when he finally rode from the castle with the others. Villagers came out to watch them pass, and children ran beside the horses for a few hundred yards before dropping away. Hamar waved a hand to the last of them before turning his face to the wooded hills rising beyond the village fields. "What can have possessed the girls to ride out like this?" he demanded, of no one in particular. "I would have thought Mal, at least, would know better. And Ghis is always so level-headed. It doesn't make sense."

"I can't imagine Alianor agreeing to such madness either," Girvase said, from his other side.

"Well, they certainly organized well—and kept it secret, too." Audin's tone was light, but Carick saw the bitter worry in his eyes and caught the shared unease of all those around him. Even Raher was momentarily subdued.

The road narrowed once they reached the woods, and they were forced to ride no more than two abreast, knee brushing knee. Their company was thirty strong and chiefly made up of squires, although Raven had included four experienced guards as well as Herun, Solaan, and Carick. The knight sent Herun and the guard called Darin ahead to scout, while Solaan rode beside him, the tattoos on her face blending into the pattern of light and shadows beneath the trees.

The damosels had traveled by the known road, and Hamar pointed out the pitch torches, burnt out and discarded, that they must have used to light their way once the village was left behind. "Did they need to reach the temple by dawn?" Carick asked.

The squire shook his head. "Only dusk to dawn is absolutely required, although dawn to dawn has become traditional for those wishing to be knights. So they only need to reach the Rock before dusk. And," he added, "the dark of the moon."

That part of Summer's Eve sworn to Kan, thought Carick, remembering the conversation before Lord Falk left for the Hills. The sun was well overhead now, and he wondered if they would catch the damosels before nightfall or would have to journey back through that moonless dark. "We won't catch them," Hamar said flatly, when Carick asked the question. "They're too far ahead for that. I imagine Ser Raven will wait until we get there before deciding whether to return by night or stay at the Rock."

"Depending," added Girvase, who was riding behind them now, "on the level of threat and defensibility of the shrine."

They found Herun and Darin waiting for them at the first crossroads, which was little more than a glade in the woods with a lichen-covered standing stone at its center. The Normarch road ran on east to join the main road, while a bridle path snaked north and west toward the old temple. The damosels' hoofmarks followed the second route—but something else, Herun said, had turned off with them. "Something that lay concealed in the undergrowth and followed once all had passed. But the tracks are confused. At first I thought it was a man, but then the prints changed, suggesting a beast."

"It only followed them for a short distance," said Darin, "then cut away across country. Getting ahead of them, maybe, or joining up with allies."

"Or both," said Raven. "Is there any way we can do the same—try and get ahead of the damosels from here?"

"Not with armed men on horseback." Herun's face remained calm, but there was no mistaking the worry in his eyes. "Not in this trackless country."

Raven nodded. "We carry on as we are, then—but I want scouts out on all sides. We need to know everything that moves out here. Take no action on your own, though, just observe and report back."

"Darin and I will scout ahead again," Herun said. "Girvase is woodcrafty, he can circle back with Aymil. Hamar and Solaan, you take either side."

Of course, Carick thought, as Girvase and Hamar dismounted and began shedding the bulk of their armor—it must be impossible to scout effectively in knight's gear. And then all six scouts had mounted again and vanished into the woods.

The main party rode deeper into the hills, following the hoof-churned track. From time to time Herun or Darin would reappear to report that the way ahead was still clear, and Carick began to hope that everything might turn out all right. The scouts could have been mistaken, after all, in thinking there had been a watcher by the crossroads. His hope strengthened as they progressed without incident—until they rounded a bend in the track and found Herun holding the reins of a black courser.

Audin drew in his breath and Raher whistled. "That's Sable," he said unnecessarily, "Alianor's horse." When they drew closer, they saw that the horse's neck and shoulder were covered in blood.

"Not his own," said Herun, answering Raven's question. The tracker's eyes slid to Solaan as she slipped from between the trees.

"If there had been an accident," the Hill woman said, "one of the other girls would have caught the horse."

Raven nodded. "So now we ride hard. But keep scouting. This could be a trap set for us, as well as the damosels."

They pressed on as fast as the terrain allowed. Carick concentrated on staying in the saddle and keeping up, aware of the heightened tension all around him. Raher's eyes held a hard gleam, and even Audin's quiet manner had an edge to it, now that the danger was real. Yet despite their speed, it was mid-afternoon before they came down the last, tight curve of track to reach the ford on the Rindle. Across the river, Carick could make out a vast rock outcrop through the trees and what looked like ruins above it, but there was no sign of human activity.

Darin was waiting for them, just within the edge of the trees. "No bodies," he said, "but there's been a melee on both sides of the ford."

Raven leaned out of his saddle, peering at the trampled ground. "What more have the tracks told you?"

Darin rubbed at his forehead. "There are too many prints on top of each other to make real sense of what happened. But the main party of damosels stopped here, while three went on ahead." He pointed to the other side of the river. "Their tracks climb past the bank. There's no sign they came back, but I haven't been up to the ruins yet. The main party was attacked from behind, from these woods here. The signs suggest the attacking party was small, maybe no more than an advance guard set to watch the ford." He shrugged. "From the looks, there was a skirmish here before most of our girls fled across the river. Then they separated, some going up-river and some down."

Solaan had joined them with Hamar and was frowning at the empty riverbed. "Yet there're no dead or wounded?"

Darin shook his head. "There's plenty of evidence of a struggle, but no bodies. Herun's already gone upstream, but we agreed I should wait for you before starting down."

"We need to check the ruins as well," said Raven. "Work out which way the Countess fled."

Selia was right, Carick thought. It does always come back to Ghiselaine. Beside him, Jarna was staring at her gauntleted hands, clasped around the saddle horn, and he wondered what she was thinking, knowing her life could well be at risk for the very damosels who had mocked her.

"Maister Carick," Raven said, and Carick's gaze swung back to him. "Let's see what more your maps can tell us about this country while the scouts are gone."

By the time Carick had retrieved the maps and unlaced their weatherproof wrappings, the scouting parties had left. Raven had sent the guards Marten and Sark after Herun, while Ado and Gille went downriver with Darin, and Solaan took Hamar and Raher across to the temple ruins. Jarna dismounted to help Carick, spreading her cloak out on the driest part of the riverbank and weighting the edges of the maps with stones.

"They're hard to read, aren't they?" she said, frowning at his carefully re-inked lines.

And already, Carick thought, the shadows are lengthening. In only a few more hours it will be dark—but he refused to continue that line of thought. Audin and Raven squatted on their heels, watching as his finger traced the line of the Rindle. "Downriver, the Rindle bends east until it joins the Swift. Upstream—" Carick pointed. "One tributary comes out of the hills that separate Emer from Aeris. The other seems to start here, in the mountains."

"But surely," Audin said, "whichever way they've gone, they'll try and head back toward Normarch?"

"If they can," said Raven. He did not need to add that the pursuers would aim to prevent that. "If the way downriver is clear, they'll come to the main road eventually, although close to the Long Pass. Still, we might be able to intercept them by striking through these hills. But upstream." He shook his head. "North toward Aeris is very rough country, almost impassable on horseback."

Carick pointed again. "The second tributary flows from the high terrain to the southwest, but the contours ease here, around this village."

"The Leas," said Solaan. She had come up quietly behind them, still accompanied by Raher and Hamar. "Your contours are right, Maister. The land there is open meadow, although any village is long gone."

Raven studied her face. "What did you find?" he asked.

"Three dead on the path to the ruins," the Hill woman replied. "Shot with arrows, all of them. The horses had their throats cut."

Not Alianor, then, Carick thought.

"Not Alli," Hamar said, as if he had read Carick's mind. Both he and Raher were very pale. "Avice," the squire added after a moment, and Carick recalled a thin girl with brown hair, not one of Ghiselaine's immediate circle.

"And Annot," said Raher. "You know, Brania's cousin. And her friend, the one with the mousy hair."

"Isolt," Tibalt said. "Her family—" He paused, swallowing hard as they all looked at him. "Her family's demesne, it's not far from ours. In Wymark," he added, as though it was important they understood that. No one said anything. There was nothing to be said that would make one bit of difference for the three dead girls.

Solaan squatted beside Raven, her expression hard beneath the spiraled tattoos. "War and plague cleared out The Leas long ago. But there's still a cart track that goes there, branching off the old northern road. That's mostly gone back to the wild, too," she added, glancing at Raven, "but there's enough of it left to be useful for us, if we get that far."

The knight leaned forward. "This dotted line, here. What's that?"

Carick peered at it. "Probably a foot-track used by shepherds or hunters. But this map is very old. Any path could be like The Leas village and have disappeared long ago."

"See where it runs," said Raven, "up over this ridge— cutting almost directly from the ford, here, to The Leas."

Carick looked at the map contour, which was very steep, and then at the sheer rise of hillside that contour represented. But potentially, if the damosels who went upriver had taken the southwest tributary, Raven's company could use the dotted path to cross the ridge and reach The Leas ahead of them. No, he corrected himself silently, if Ghiselaine has gone that way—and if the route's still there and passable for armed men and horses. He looked again at the steepness of the ridge and shook his head.

"Whatever the scouts find," Raven said, "the damosels are still too far ahead of us. A straightforward pursuit will never catch them in time." He stood up. "So let's find this track."

Easier said than done, Carick thought, but he joined the search as soon as the maps had been stowed away. He found Solaan first, walking along the base of the ridge and studying the forested slope for places where a route might follow the natural contour. A hopeless task, in Carick's opinion, but he followed her example anyway, and eventually felt himself being drawn into the green murmur of the trees and the warm scent of earth underfoot. He could feel wind and sunlight filtering through leaves—and almost hear the path calling to him as it curved beneath fern and bracken, climbing away from the ford toward the rugged heights.

Carick followed that call, scrambling through scrub and beneath bushes to find what was little more than a rut, twisting up the first, steep thrust of ridge. A squirrel bounded down from the tree behind him, chittering, as he turned back to where Solaan stood, her gray eyes unfocused. He saw her blink, registering his approach, and the look she gave him was long and considering. But all she said when he showed her what he had found was: "It's very narrow, true, but you may tell Ser Raven that you have found his track."

Yet Carick could not shake the feeling that the Hill woman had already seen it, even before he led her to the path's beginning.

# 19

# Dark of the Moon

$F$inding the track had taken longer than Carick realized, and both the up- and downstream scouting parties had returned when he reached the ford. He stopped, registering that Aymil and Girvase had still not caught them up—but the scouts' faces already told him they had nothing good to report.

"Seven dead, a couple of miles downstream," Darin was saying. "They must have run into the attackers head on—but they took some with them. Outlaws," he added, before Raven could ask the question. "And Linnet Ar-Ormond, riding the Countess's horse and wearing her cloak."

"They must have swapped," Audin said. His fists were clenched hard, his mouth a grim line. "To confuse the pursuit. So if Linnet went downriver—"

Raven nodded. "Then the Countess went up. Herun?"

"The larger party fled that way," the tracker agreed, "and they're being pursued. I trailed them to where a northern tributary joins the Rindle, and both groups were still keeping to the riverbed at that point. The banks are high, farther up," he explained, "and the country to either side steep and very rough, so the shingle wash between the river braids makes for easier going."

"But they followed the main stem of the Rindle west?" Raven asked, and Herun nodded.

"We have to try this hill path," Audin said. His face twisted suddenly. "I'm the Duke's nephew, but my life is as nothing against the Ormondian peace."

No one spoke, but Carick saw the same bitterness and frustration in every face. Jarna shifted a little closer to Hamar, so their shoulders were almost—but not quite—touching. Carick looked away, narrowing his eyes at the sky. The sun was already low and he was not sure how far they could get before night fell. But if they waited until the morning . . . He began to understand the bitterness in the squires' faces.

Raven, too, had been studying the sky, but now he nodded. "Getting ahead of them is the only way." Following his lead, the party began to mount up, but stopped as Arn, on lookout, signaled that someone was coming. A moment later the squire held up two fingers.

"Aymil and Girvase," Raher muttered, but every hand stayed on a weapon until the two emerged from the trees, looking hot, sweaty, and tired.

"There's nothing behind us, ser," Aymil reported to Raven. "Not unless you count flies and clouds of midges at every little seep that passes as a stream." A few squires grinned at that, but everyone was remarkably quiet. They were all watching Girvase, Carick realized—and saw the squire notice Sable. A dangerous light flared in the young man's eyes and his mouth tightened, but he said nothing, just walked his own black horse forward until he could lean down and touch the blood matted into Sable's shoulder. "Who found him?" Girvase straightened. "Where? What sign was there of Alianor?" Even as he spoke, he was turning his horse toward the river.

Carick had not seen Raven move, but the knight's mount was between the squire and the river all the same, forcing the black horse to stop. Raven's stare crossed Girvase's as the young man tried to go around him.

"Get out of my way!" Danger blazed out of Girvase's face. "Alianor's hurt out there. She may die if I don't find her."

Raven's horse blocked Girvase again, and this time the shiver that crept along Carick's spine had nothing to do with lengthening shadows. "She may already be dead," the knight said. His voice was even, his eyes pitiless as stone. "She may be alone and hurt—or she may be safe with those who went upriver. But what *we* are going to do now is stay together and find the Countess of Ormond, not scatter across country looking for individual damosels. Do you understand me, Girvase Ar-Allerion?"

Girvase's hand slid to his sword hilt. Beside Carick, Hamar's breath hissed. Only Raven seemed relaxed, almost lounging in the saddle, although his eyes did not leave Girvase's face. "Even now, enemies are pressing upriver," he said, "eager to catch and kill those damosels who still live. So you will obey orders or I will kill you myself."

He means it, thought Carick, and could see that everyone else there knew it, too—but that none of them would take Girvase's part, despite their bleak expressions. His own fingers clenched on Mallow's reins as Girvase's sword hand tightened. Then the squire gave a queer little jerk of his head, and his hand fell away from the sword hilt. "I will follow your orders," he said sullenly.

Raven's cold gaze continued to measure him, then he nodded. "See that you do."

They had to push through chest-high scrub past the beginning of Carick's track and then ride single file in a slow steady climb that traversed the first ridge above the Rindle. Herun went ahead and always managed to find the path, even when it seemed to peter out in patches of yellow gorse or the aromatic, white-starred brush of Emer. At the first clearing, Carick was surprised to see the river already far below them.

"We're making good time," said Audin, who was riding immediately ahead of him. "At this rate, we'll reach the main ridge before full dark."

"There'll be no moon," Raher said abruptly, from behind Carick.

Audin turned in the saddle as a ripple of disquiet ran along the line. "Well, you wanted adventure," he said, and several of the squires chuckled.

The track was very steep from that point and often became more of a scramble than a climb, forcing them to dismount and lead the horses. They reached the ridgetop just as the sun was slipping redly beneath the horizon and rested in the woods below the crest, chewing on food from their saddlebags.

"It's another hour, no more, before full dark," said Herun. "Do we carry on?"

"Those pursuing your damosels will not halt by night," Raven said. "We must reach The Leas before tomorrow or risk losing any advantage this route may give us."

"Yet this," Ado muttered, "is the night when the power of the Dancer, the drinker of blood, is at its height."

Raven's expression did not change. "He has already had his offerings of blood and death today. We ride on."

"We have torches," Solaan said, her tattooed face a shadowed mask in the dusk. "We can use them as soon as this ridge lies between us and the pursuers' route along the Rindle."

Ado and those around him looked far from convinced, but said nothing. Hill people were renowned for their superstition, so if Solaan was prepared to go on, anyone who held back would look unduly fearful. Yet Carick felt the tension as their line fell in behind Raven's signal, and saw the uneasy glances to either side as they rode. He suspected that every noise, however natural, was going to sound doubly strange once night fell.

The first owl called, mournful through the gloom, and Solaan moved ahead of Herun. She must have keen eyes, Carick thought, as the Hillwoman led them unerringly on into full dark.

The night grew cold as the stars changed position above them and the track alternately climbed and plunged down. Carick stumbled more than once when he had to lead Mallow, and tried not to think of Malisande and Alianor, or the other damosels, lost somewhere in the moonless hills—or already lying dead in the deep channels or shingle wash of the Rindle. He stumbled again and wished he was a cat, or one of the Patrol, since River legend claimed they could see in the dark. Yet despite his poor night vision, he was still not sure how he and Mallow came to be at the end of the line after their next stop, the path behind them lost in darkness.

A short distance further on the path began to drop so steeply that Carick, leading Mallow again, had to concentrate on every footstep. The mare slithered and eased her way down behind him and it was some time before he realized that he had lost sight of the horse in front. The last glow from the torches had also disappeared, and he slid a few more yards before halting, unable to see the path ahead.

Carick listened intently, but heard no chink of metal or creak of leather, no huff of breath from a horse. He wondered if he could have taken a wrong turn—and became intensely aware of the night, pressing in, and the immensity of wild country all around. Mallow whickered and threw up her head against his restraining grip, the whites of her eyes showing. Tales whispered on the River flooded into his mind: about pockets of ancient darkness that lingered amongst Emer's empty hills, feeding on fear and the blood of travelers gone astray. Kan, those whispers suggested, might not be the only power that stalked Emer during the dark of the moon.

Fear seized Carick, high and cold in his throat, and his heart pounded out the pattern of Raven's words about the dark god: *blood and death, death and blood.* Compulsion followed the spiral of fear: a wild desire to run, crashing down the hillside until he plummeted from some rocky height or fell, breaking his neck—or his leg, so that he died slowly, starved, thirsty, and alone.

Breathe, you fool, Carick told himself. He gritted his teeth and made himself count the sharp, painful thuds of his heart until it steadied. Horror stories, he thought, taking a deep breath into his stomach and relaxing his shoulders: that's all those tales are. I need to keep going and find the others, not give in to irrational fears. But another part of his mind, detached and cool as water, held him motionless, staring into the blackness ahead.

A horse snorted on the hillside above him and Mallow whinnied a reply. Carick remained frozen in place, unable to turn—then stifled a yell as someone brushed past his shoulder. Girvase, he realized a split second later. The squire stopped a pace in front of Carick, his head turning to search the night as Hamar, leading both their horses, slid the last few feet to join them.

"Here you are!" He clapped a hand on Carick's shoulder, then shifted it to rest on Mallow's neck, stroking the mare gently. "Look at you, girl. You're covered in sweat."

Carick shuddered and found that he could move again, although he felt dazed, blinking from Hamar beside him to the dark silhouette that was Girvase. "I'm not sure what happened." He took another deep breath in, then released it. "I must have dozed, I suppose. And then—" He paused, unwilling to mention the panic that had seized him. "I couldn't see the torches or which way the path went."

"Something was here," Girvase said. His voice held an odd note that Carick could not quite place. "I felt a sense of darkness pressing in as I stepped past Maister Carro. But I didn't see anything." He paused as Hamar stepped forward to join him. "And it's gone now."

*Yes,* said that cool, detached voice inside Carick. He shivered, feeling how cold the night had grown.

Hamar, by comparison, was brisk, almost cheerful. "We need to go, too, if we don't want to lose the others completely. You lead, Gir, and I'll take the rear, just in case whatever-it-was comes after us." He sounded untroubled by this prospect, and Carick felt his spirits lift—until a fresh realization struck him. He hesitated, frowning from one dark silhouette to the other.

"You're not carrying torches. Either of you."

"Your eyes adjust soon enough." Girvase turned back to pick up his horse's reins and Carick almost felt his shrug. "And we've both got good night sight."

"That's why we were the ones sent back," Hamar explained. "But you'll definitely travel faster with a torch, so we'll use one now we've found you."

Girvase nodded. "But keep close, all the same," he told Carick. "And stay awake."

# 20

## The Leas

*E*ven with the torch their descent was slow and weary. The path dropped steeply for a long time, only to rise into a second, brief climb before dropping down again. Despite Girvase's admonition, Carick was nodding on Mallow's back when they finally reached more level ground and the path widened. He jumped awake as two shadows rose from the fern on either side, arrows on the string, then relaxed as he recognized Raher and Aymil. A few seconds later and he was dropping from Mallow's back into the middle of a fireless camp, with sleeping bodies curled amongst the tree roots.

Carick leaned against the mare's shoulder while his companions sought out Raven to make their report. "Is this The Leas?" he whispered to Audin, when the Duke's nephew appeared at his side.

"Herun thinks we've come out just above it," Audin murmured back. "We'll go on at first light." He glanced up through the canopy. "Which can't be far off now."

Not what I needed to hear, thought Carick, but he forced himself to look after Mallow and shake out his blanket before rolling into sleep. He felt as though he had barely closed his eyes when Hamar was saying his name again, shaking him awake. "It's still dark," Carick protested.

"Not for long," Hamar said. "We'll hear the first birds any moment now and then it'll be dawn. Ser Raven wants us moving before that."

Carick groaned, wondering if there was a bone or muscle in his body that didn't ache. All around him a quiet bustle through the half-dark confirmed that the company was checking gear and preparing to ride. Jarna handed him a hunk of bread with cold meat, which he devoured, and then they were all up and in the saddle.

By the time they reached the thinning trees on the forest edge it was light and a cacophony of birds masked their passage. Everyone seemed calm, but a tautness was there all the same, discernible as the current of cooler air from the meadow. Only Raven was bareheaded still, mist droplets beading his hair. He looked alert and not at all like someone who had just completed a grueling night march, snatching a few brief hours sleep on hard ground.

The company halted just inside the treeline, studying the open land. Banks of mist rolled out from either side of the Rindle, which had dwindled to a small stream here as it purled from wooded hills. More ranges rose behind them, blue and wild, until they reached the jagged heights of the Western Mountains. The peaks were tipped with dawn as Carick turned to look back the way they had come. The ridge they had crossed swept up and away, still drowned in shadow that was broken only by jagged outcrops and sheer cliffs of pale stone. He found it hard to believe that they had made their way down in darkness and remained unscathed.

Raher followed his gaze. "It'll make a fine tale when we get back," he said cheerfully, "the night march of Ser Raven and the squires of Normarch—even if you were just about to walk over one of those cliffs when Hamar and Girvase found you."

"Shut up, Raher," said Hamar, but without heat. Girvase said nothing, simply turned and looked at Raher, who became absorbed in adjusting his shield strap.

Carick wondered if his expression looked as hollow as his stomach felt. He was remembering how Girvase had stared into the darkness ahead of him when they first met—and how the squires made sure there was always one of them ahead and one behind him, for the rest of the descent. "Don't worry about it, Carro," Hamar said now. "The main thing is that it didn't happen."

Out in the meadow a skylark rose from the mist and arrowed heavenward, its song pouring into the new day. Slowly at first, then with startling speed, the line of foothills turned from gray, to gold, to burning copper along their tops. Beneath the forest eave the company sat like statues, waiting.

"They're coming," Solaan said. Her eyes were fixed on the skylark and she spoke so quietly that only those immediately around her heard. "Pursued and pursuers, both," she added, "following the far bank of the Rindle."

How does she know? Carick wondered. He tried not to stare at the Hill woman, but he was remembering how she had taken the lead last night, as soon as it became dark. And she had known before he told her, when he found the beginning of the path across the ridge. Yet neither Raven nor Herun questioned Solaan's statement, and those within earshot remained intent on the riverbed and wooded slopes beyond.

"Do we ride out to meet them?" Audin asked.

"No," said Raven. "We wait and keep the advantage of surprise."

"But what," Girvase demanded, his hand tight on his sword hilt, "if they all die before reaching The Leas?"

"They won't," said Raven.

Hamar's horse moved, shaking out its mane. "Not all of them." The squire's eyes were fixed on Raven, his voice level. "But some may. You are relying on the rest being willing to sacrifice themselves to let Ghiselaine escape."

The knight's stare raked them all. "Should I throw away your lives because the damosels of Normarch went willfully into danger? For now, they must take their chance."

Audin grimaced at Hamar, briefly, once Raven turned back to the meadow, but no one spoke. Carick shifted in the saddle and wondered how long they would have to wait.

"The gap is closing fast." Solaan's eyes remained fixed on the skylark, a tiny speck against the growing blue. "Soon the hunters will snap at their heels."

Girvase's hand clenched and unclenched on his sword. Raven turned to Herun and the guards. "Take your longbows and the five best archers from amongst the squires and get as close to the stream as you can without breaking cover. As soon as the damosels cross, shoot at will into any pursuit." He paused, his eyes quartering the meadow again. "Once we show ourselves, remount but stay in the woods as reserve. A single wind of the horn from the main melee and you charge. Hit them as hard as you can in the flank. Two horn blasts will mean retreat. Then you must cover us while we get ourselves and as many damosels as we can clear."

The skylark plummeted earthward, its song done. Herun and the guards disappeared along the curve of the wood with five of the squires, Gille and Ado amongst them. Carick could feel the grimness in the air as the remaining squires checked and rechecked their weapons, holding to the reassurance of habit. Raven broke in on his thoughts. "You, Maister Carick, will remain here with Solaan. In the last resort, the two of you must try and get the Countess away."

The color washed up into Carick's face, then ebbed as quickly. "I can shoot a bow," he said.

He thought Raven might turn away without replying, but the knight shook his head. "So can Solaan—and use other weapons well. But her first responsibility is Ghiselaine and the damosels. Yours, now that you've gotten us here, is to help her at need. And stay alive if you can, Duke's cartographer." This time he did move away, leaving no opening for further protest.

"Well, you are no fighter, Carro, we all know that," Raher pointed out, bringing his horse up on Audin's left side. "In a melee, you'd just be in the way."

"Shut up, Raher," said Audin and Hamar in unison.

"Here they come," said Girvase. He was staring at the steeply wooded shoulder that formed the first bend in the Rindle, below the The Leas. A moment later a small knot of horses appeared around it, galloping for the river. A ripple ran through the waiting horsemen, but Raven's hand held them in check as the oncoming riders pounded across the flat land and splashed through the ford.

Only three riders, Carick thought, chewing his lip, with two more horses running loose beside them. But he thought he glimpsed red hair beneath a blown-back hood.

Hamar leaned forward. "That's not Ghiselaine," he said, as the five horses came out of the river and galloped on. "That's Brania." Girvase nodded, agreeing.

"Riding decoy." Raven sounded grimly approving. "Let them go," he added, at Audin's question. "If there are enemy foragers out, they're ignoring the dangled bait."

"So where's the main group?" Raher asked, when the far side of the Rindle remained quiet. Carick tried not to gnaw his lip again.

"There," said Girvase, pointing to another thickly wooded slope. "Through the trees on the river terrace."

Carick stared, but it was several seconds before he made out the first flicker of movement. A few moments later the flicker became riders, weaving between tree trunks and creeping down the last plunge of hillside to emerge on open ground. They were keeping close together, moving steadily rather than at the decoy riders' wild gallop. Carick counted ten horses, with seven ridden, but one mount carried a double burden—the figure in front was collapsed forward over the horse's neck, black hair mingling with the horse's mane. Further back, a body was tied over a led horse, a long, silver-blond braid spilling from beneath the covering cloak.

He could see no sign of pursuers but the riders kept glancing back, so they could not be far behind. Foam swirled around the horses' knees as the eight reached the ford—and a long, bestial cry emanated from the trees. All along the squires' line the chargers plunged, and the eerie ululation made Carick's skin crawl. The damosels' horses scrambled to get clear of the water, their ears flat to their skulls as the first pursuers burst from the trees and streamed toward the

Rindle. Carick looked at Raven, but the knight's expression remained closed, his raised hand commanding the hold.

The damosels were through the ford now and galloping across the meadow, still in a tight group as they followed the line of the previous riders. Behind them, the pursuit howled and swept down on the river in a confusion of men and beasts—and creatures that were neither man nor beast, but seemed to blur and shift between the two shapes, even as they ran. And they ran astonishingly fast. As if realizing that not all could escape, two of the damosels peeled off from the main group, wheeling their horses on a line parallel to the ford. As they rode, they dropped what looked like small bundles onto the ground.

Twigs, Carick wondered, staring. Or rags?

"What are they doing?" Jarna asked, her voice strained.

"Delaying the pursuit," Hamar said grimly. Carick, glancing at their faces, thought that both he and Girvase understood whatever was happening. The damosel closest to the river was riding toward the ford now and a shortened ladyspike gleamed in her hand as the first of the hunters came leaping through. The horse snorted and sidled, fighting its rider, and Audin groaned.

"They'll simply overrun her," he said. "Hamstring the horse and pull her down."

"If her mount doesn't throw her first." Girvase was terse, but Carick was watching the other horse, a tall gray carrying the slumped damosel and her companion. The gray was moving at an easy pace, still on a line parallel with the river, but before Carick could ask a question, the slumped rider pushed herself upright. Behind her, her companion stood up in the stirrups and drew the string of her bow back to her ear, then loosed several arrows in swift succession. The wounded rider watched each arrow with immense concentration—and every shaft ignited as it flew, curving down into one of the bundles dropped along the line of the ford.

"Oh, well done!" cried Audin, as the bundles exploded in the face of the pursuing vanguard and continued to burn fiercely, each conflagration far larger than its source. The first rush of pursuers fell back while others rolled smoldering on the ground.

Girvase shook his head. "It will not save them. They will still be overrun."

Carick's mouth was open as he stared at the squires on either side, wondering if he was the only person present unable to believe what his eyes had just seen. But there was no time to wonder what he *had* seen because Girvase was right. Another wave of beast-men was sweeping past their vanguard and through the fire barrier; at any moment they would be on top of both horses. Carick could not bear to watch, but could not look away either. All the squires were fidgeting, barely held in check by Raven's raised arm.

"Cavalry still holds," Raven ordered, his voice carrying the length of their line as the first flight of arrows arced from the wood, curving down to where the rider with the lady-spike was striking at the first of the beast-men. Her horse reared, screaming: a cry of terror, not the fighting scream of a knight's warhorse. The other rider was still shooting, but at the beast-men this time, while her companion had slumped back onto the gray's neck.

Carick threw a prayer to whatever god might hear him, then realized that the first assailants were down, spiked with arrows. A second volley flew from the wood and Raven's arm finally came down. At the knight's signal, Arn lifted his horn and wound the advance.

Raher's horse reared, trumpeting a challenge that echoed the horn, but the rest of the line held steady, emerging from the woods at a rolling walk before advancing to a trot. The early morning light flashed on helmet and breastplate, and off the edge of drawn swords. Carick wondered how it must feel to be part of that advancing line. Were the squires' mouths as dry as his, or did the impetus of the charge bring its own exhilaration—or were they experiencing both at once, the exhilaration and the dread?

The archers loosed a third and then a fourth volley, allowing the damosels by the river to break away. The main body of the pursuit, a mix of outlaws with knots of beast-men loping at the center and to either side of an uneven bunch, continued to advance. There were more pursuers than squires, perhaps as many as fifty, Carick thought, his hands clenching on Mallow's reins—although all were on foot and the outlaws poorly armed. He had learned enough at Normarch to know this still gave the horsemen the advantage. The beast-men, hunting in tight packs of five or six and with their savage jaws and claws, appeared to be the real danger. The air around them wavered as they came on, and now every arrow aimed their way fell harmlessly aside. Beside Carick, Solaan began to mutter words in a dialect he could not understand.

The meadow was like a chess game, at the stage when there are pieces all over the board—except all these pieces were moving, their relative positions constantly changing. The damosels' rearguard had almost reached the line of the squires' charge now, but the gray with the double burden was laboring. Carick's fists clenched, willing it on.

The squires' trot extended into a gallop, and for the first time Carick heard the thunder of Emerian warhorses as they charged. Unable to stop himself, he whooped aloud, his voice cracking in exultation. Further around the wood, Herun and the reserve were mounting, while the damosel with the ladyspike circled to join the squires' charge. A wave of energy rippled out from the beast-men toward the advancing riders—and Solaan raised her right hand, the palm turned out, and spoke more of the strange words in a clear hard voice. But beneath the tattoos, her face was strained.

Carick bit his lip, frowning from her to the meadow. A series of small whirlwinds were building ahead of the charging destriers, swirling up dust and debris and gaining speed as they went. Energy wave and whirlwinds met, rearing up against each other—then both collapsed, disintegrating as the line of the squires' charge crashed into the pursuers, turning the center of The Leas into a cutting, slashing confrontation. Then the squires were through the pack and turning to come back, closing up the gaps in their line where several had gone down. The beast-men were regrouping as well and leaping for the squires' line while the outlaws fought more raggedly, some in larger groups, others in isolated twos and threes.

"They will break soon and run," a cool voice said. Carick jumped, slewing around as the gray horse with its two riders approached along the edge of the wood. A moment later he recognized the filthy, bedraggled rider as Malisande, although her companion remained a mass of black hair across the horse's neck. "But the beast-men—" The damosel broke off, her eyes hollowed darkness as she studied them. "They are savage and have uncanny powers."

Carick thought of her burning arrows and the fires, larger than the material that fed them, which had erupted where they fell. "You checked them," he said quietly.

Malisande shrugged. "That was Alli, not me." So then he knew who the slumped figure was. Carick glanced at Solaan, still focused on the fighting.

"Twice," he said, thinking it through. "With the dust-devils as well, before the squires' charge struck."

"Girvase or Hamar most likely, with Solaan or Herun's help." Malisande was completely matter-of-fact. "Don't look so shocked, Maister Carick. Surely you didn't think the Oakward was really a myth?" She turned back to the meadow, where fresh ripples of power had become a surge as beast-men closed in, pulling a horse and rider down. The horse shrilled terror—and then the surrounding earth erupted, clods and stones exploding outward and flinging the beast-men with it. The horse came to its feet in a wild scrabble, the squire streaming blood but clinging grimly to the saddle.

Girvase, thought Carick, recognizing the black horse as the squire swung back into the fray. The two remaining knots of beast-men had converged on Raven, their power blasting toward him like flame. Yet the knight appeared unaffected by the energy storm as his charger half reared, striking with its front hooves while his sword cut against snarling fangs and ripping talons. The foremost beast-man bayed defiance, a note that changed to something very like alarm in mid-attack—an instant before Raven's blade sliced head from body.

Malisande, Carick saw, was watching the knight with narrowed eyes, but half smiling, too, as the other beast-men echoed their comrade's howl and fell away from him. The howl rose again, mournful across The Leas—and then all the beast-men broke off, racing for the Rindle while the outlaws followed in a retreating straggle.

"Behold the raven of battle." Solaan was somber.

"At least some of our dead are avenged," Malisande said.

Not, Carick thought, that it does them any good. But he kept his opinion to himself, watching as Raven called the squires away from any pursuit. They reformed around the knight, then began picking up their dead and wounded, dispatching any enemies still living. Carick's face must have shown his shock, because Solaan shook her head. "We cannot take them with us, and most would die anyway. Would you have them linger on, alive, while the carrion eaters picked at their flesh? And if they did survive, what then? They would only return to slay another hill farmer, or the lone traveler on the road, as is their way."

"A clean death is more mercy than they would have shown us." Malisande, bent over Alianor, looked up. "We may have to tie her on. That effort with the arrows took the last of her strength."

"We found Sable with blood on him," Carick said, as he dismounted to help. "Between Normarch and the Rindle."

"She turned a strike meant for Ghiselaine." A brief tremor disturbed the damosel's coolness. "It would have succeeded, too, if Alli hadn't caught the movement. But that story will keep. The others are coming."

For a moment Carick thought she meant the other damosels, except that they had kept riding, following the same route as Brania and her companions. A necessity, he supposed with an inward grimace, given the paramount importance of Ghiselaine's life. But Malisande was referring to the return of Herun's reserve, and Raven and the squires were also moving their way. Carick could see Jarna, apparently unscathed, riding knee-to-knee with Hamar, a battered and bloodied Girvase on her other side.

Audin was there, too, and Raher, and the damosel with the cut-down ladyspike. If anything, she looked even more haggard and dirty than Malisande. A trickle of blood smeared across her face when she tried to wipe it away, but it was not until she took off her metal cap and a yellow braid tumbled down that Carick finally recognized Ilaise. He could not believe it, could not reconcile the giggling Normarch girl with the rider who had turned to face the beast-men alone and then joined the squires' charge. He stared openly, and Ilaise's expression pinched, but she did not speak, just looked away.

Herun stopped beside Malisande. "You did well, with the fires. Or was that all Alianor?"

"Not quite all. But most. And now—" Malisande indicated Alianor's condition.

The tracker nodded. "We need to get her down so I can look at the wound."

Alianor roused when they reached up, and then she tried to help herself, half sliding, half falling out of the saddle. Herun bent over the wound and his expression did not change, but Carick thought his mouth tightened. Eventually, however, he nodded and glanced sideways at Girvase, who had come to kneel beside him. "She should live, so long as she does not use her power again and we keep the hurt clean."

The squire was studying the wound, his mouth thin. "She's been stabbed by a knife at close quarters. How did that happen, Mal?"

"Not now, Girvase." Malisande kept her voice low. "Let's catch up with the others first."

Girvase stared at her, then gave the same queer little jerk of his head that had ended his confrontation with Raven. "All right, since *you* ask. But this stinks of betrayal."

"And dark arts," Solaan said from behind him.

Carick glanced up, remembering her raised hand and the strange words she had spoken during the battle, and how the earth had exploded outward around Girvase and thrown off the beast-men's attack. And what exactly had Malisande said, with that little edge in her voice: *Surely you didn't think the Oakward was really a myth?* Soberly, he looked around the faces that had grown so familiar: Herun and Solaan, Girvase, Hamar, and Malisande—and began to understand why Erron, a horsemaster, had been left in charge at Normarch while Lord Falk was away.

# 21

# The Old Road

The skylark was singing again when they left The Leas. Or perhaps, thought Carick, it was another bird pouring its song into the morning, unperturbed by battle and death. Mist still feathered the meadow and it was hard to believe that barely an hour had passed since the sun rose. And harder still to accept that young men who had been alive and eager in the gray predawn, like Guyon and Arn, were now corpses trussed across a horse's back. They were leaving horses behind as well, some slain in the battle and others put down afterward.

Carick swallowed against the dryness of his mouth and wondered why hero stories never mentioned the wounds and mess, or the finality of death. He glanced across at Alianor and Malisande, together on Sable now, while Ilaise led the gray horse. They were all silent, Alianor no more than semi-conscious at best.

Darin and Herun had gone ahead, but Raven held the main group to a steady pace, so it was mid-morning before they finally caught up with Ghiselaine's company. The young women had heard them coming and were drawn up in the road, the young Countess out in front with her hood thrown back. Her red-gold hair gleamed in the sun but her expression was set. Carick could only speculate on what her thoughts must be—

how they must all feel, knowing that the tally of Normarch dead and wounded was a direct consequence of their folly.

Raven walked his charger forward until he was abreast of Ghiselaine, but neither knight nor Countess spoke until Ilaise kicked her horse forward, too, with Malisande following. "We belong here," the yellow-haired girl said, falling in with the rest of the damosels. "Not with the squires."

Raven's eyes remained on Ghiselaine. "Punishment is Lord Falk's province—but if you were a squire, Countess, Ormondian peace or not, I would knock you off your horse."

Ghiselaine bowed her head, as though a weight had been placed on it, but Alianor's face wavered up, her eyes fixed on the knight with painful intensity. "Betrayal," she whispered, repeating Girvase's word from The Leas, then echoed Solaan: "And dark arts."

"We will hear it all," Raven said quietly. "But not now, unless there is need?"

Alianor stared at him, but did not reply; gradually, her head drooped forward again. Worry touched Ghiselaine's expression. "We have not seen Brania and the others yet. We hope they are not far ahead . . ." Her voice trailed away.

"We'll catch them," Raven said. "Herun, Darin, see what you can find ahead. Solaan, Girvase, Hamar—I want you watching our back trail. But be careful, all of you. Those we routed this morning may not be the only enemies out here."

The two companies formed into one and rode on, although the atmosphere between squires and damosels was strained. Yet after a few miles, Jarna took the gray's reins from Ilaise, and Audin dropped back to ride beside Ghiselaine. At first they did not look at each other, until Audin reached across and covered Ghiselaine's hand with his own. She did turn her head, then, and Carick looked away from what he saw in her expression, focusing instead on the yellow flowers growing beside the road. But what he was seeing was the fighting across The Leas, and the dead tied facedown across their horses, and Alianor slumped over Sable's neck while her black hair mingled with his mane. The whole tale had been there, written in that brief glimpse of Ghiselaine's face turning toward Audin. Raven had said that punishment lay with Lord Falk, but Carick did not think Ghiselaine was waiting, she was carrying it all on her shoulders already.

Even a remnant cart track made for easy riding after the night climb across the hills. Between that and Mallow's smooth gait, Carick half dozed, half listened to snippets of conversation: "It's hard to believe that today is Summer's Eve" . . . "Do you think Lord Falk will punish us very harshly?" . . . "Surely they would not dare attack Normarch itself?" . . . "Did you see—those beast-men were terrified of him!" . . . "What about Girvase throwing off the ones that pulled him down? That's the old ward at work" . . . "Alli, too" . . .

Mallow stepped down into a rut and out again, jerking Carick fully awake, to find Malisande reaching for his rein. "Falling asleep," he admitted. "How's Alianor?"

"Holding up. But I'll be glad when she's under Manan's care." Malisande shook her head. "We wouldn't have made it without her, you know. She was the one who knew we could follow the Rindle, from studying your maps." The dark-haired girl was silent for a moment. "And took the blow that was meant for Ghiselaine."

"So it was treachery," Carick said softly.

Malisande checked to see whether Girvase was close. "It was Selia. She drew steel when it looked like Ghis would get clear. Linnet was horrified—but guilty at the same time, as though she had known something was going to happen."

Alianor pushed herself upright again and spoke thickly, her eyes still closed. "Glamored," she said.

Who? Carick wondered: Linnet? Or Selia? But Alianor had subsided again.

Malisande was frowning. "I think we must all have been glamored, to even consider embarking on the expedition in the first place."

"You weren't." Ilaise spoke for the first time since rejoining the damosel company. "You were against it from the beginning."

"I didn't persuade anyone, though, did I?" Malisande's

expression was weary. "But I think it was the guilt," she added to Carick, "as much as duty, that made Linnet swap with Ghis to confuse the pursuit."

"And Selia?" Carick asked, although he had already seen the silver-blond braid, trailing beneath the cloak-covered body on the damosels' led horse.

"Dead." Malisande looked as though she had chewed on something bitter.

"Mal killed her," Ilaise said. "And kept Alli conscious so she could put her own glamors on our backtrail and hold the pursuers up." She looked across at Malisande. "*And* you warned us before the beast-men attacked last night."

Audin looked around, frowning. "So they did catch you before The Leas?"

"We had to stop," Ilaise said, when Malisande remained silent. "The horses needed rest, and we didn't dare use the few torches we had left, anyway. Mal was on watch—and you heard something, didn't you?"

"It was more just that way your skin prickles." Malisande sounded reluctant. "When you know something's out there even though you haven't actually seen or heard anything."

"So what happened?" Several voices spoke, and Carick saw that Jarna, Raher, and Ado were all listening closely.

"Mal woke us," Ilaise said, "and we had just grabbed our weapons when a pack of beast-men came leaping in. The confusion was terrible, all snarling and struggle and the horses trying to stampede. None of us knew what was happening except that *we* weren't the ones fighting. It was—" She broke off, throwing a helpless look at Malisande, who still looked as though she would prefer not to be talking about it at all.

"I don't know either," she said. "There was a tremendous blackness, dense as pitch, and the sound of forces contending—and then it was all over. Just like that. But when we finally risked lighting a torch, after everything grew quiet again, we found two of the beast-men dead in the brush."

Raher was shaking his head. "How is that possible?"

"We can't explain it," Malisande said simply. "We can only tell you what we experienced."

Ado rubbed at his chin. "Last night was the dark of the moon," he said finally. The others looked at each other—uneasily, Carick thought—but no one spoke. As they rode on, his mind kept returning to the darkness he had met on the mountain and the stories whispered on the River, as well as the outlawed sacrifices once made to Kan.

Shortly before noon they finally caught up with Brania and her companions, waiting with Herun and Darin where the cart track joined the old northern road. "How old is it?" Carick asked as they joined them, thinking that it looked like a decayed version of the River's Main Road.

"They say the road dates from the Old Empire," the guard called Marten replied, when Raher and Ado both shrugged. "This was all settled country then, before the war and plagues that followed the Cataclysm."

"Well," Darin said dryly, "folk're here again now. Outlaws mostly, from the looks of the old campsites, but fresher tracks, too, plenty of 'em, all through these woods."

A murmur of consternation ran through the company and Raven looked grim. "Are there other routes to Normarch," he asked, "besides this road?"

The Normarch guards looked at Herun. "Innumerable small tracks and deer paths," the tracker said finally, "some of which may take a hunter on foot there more quickly. But not a large party like this, with wounded as well."

Raven frowned at the surrounding sweep of hills, then looked from Herun to Solaan. "We need to get word to Erron, so he knows what's happened even if he has no one to send to our aid. And whoever goes must be woodcrafty, someone who knows the hill routes well."

Herun rubbed at his upper lip. "I'll go." He paused. "But you'll need more scouts out, from now on."

The ghost of a smile touched Raven's lips. "I know." He looked at Darin. "You and Aymil, with Girvase and Hamar—I want both sides of the road ahead covered." His gaze switched to Solaan. "Choose whoever you need to replace them and maintain the watch to our rear."

Herun and the forward scouts disappeared into the woods

as the remainder of the company continued along the road. Tension had clenched tight in Carick's stomach when he heard Darin's news, but eased as Mallow's stride extended and he began to feel sleepy again. The old road, he decided drowsily, was like a slow, strong river curving between the wooded hills. He let his mind climb away from it, along gullies thick with leaves and over fallen trees, the dampness of moss and cool gray lichen filling his nostrils.

The scent drew him in, just he had felt attuned to the land by the Rindle the previous day. Carick could hear individual leaves stir and sense the slow creep of tree roots through earth—in much the same way Solaan, he thought drowsily, must follow the movement of beasts and birds. He recalled yesterday's squirrel, chattering down a tree toward him, and how the Hill woman had taken the lead last night once the first owl flew. Using their eyes to see through, he realized finally, just as she used the skylark's eyes this morning. Through the medium of his half dream, Carick could even tell which mind *was* Solaan, picking out the nearby spark that was both at one and separate from the surrounding world.

He could sense others, too, although at a greater distance. A dark malevolence hunted through the wild country, pursuing a quarry that ran and dodged and doubled back—but still the pursuers were closing in. Dreamily, Carick began to see how he could thwart the hunt by encouraging trees and brush to shift, concealing old tracks or creating new ones, and changing the path of tiny streams so that they washed out the trail and scent of the hunted. He felt his influence spread through the forest—and knew, too, the instant the dark will changed focus, snapping its attention onto him.

The malevolence rushed toward Carick like a torrent, and although he fled at once the nightmare tide swept through the dream forest behind him, flooding every pathway he had forged and surging after him. He ran faster, bounding up rocky slopes like a thar, burrowing beneath tree roots, dissipating himself into the whispering of myriad leaves . . . And felt the moment when the malevolence lost him and stopped, questing after his scent like a baffled hound.

A hand grabbed Carick's arm with iron fingers, jerking him from the dream realm. Fighting vertigo, he clutched at Mallow's mane. Alianor must have roused herself because he could see her face, a pale blur staring at him, and someone was saying his name. "Carick! Carick, are you all right?"

He straightened, still shaken, and saw that the iron fingers were a gauntlet grasping his forearm. Raven, he realized, and Solaan was there, too, her eyes flint. Jarna was holding Mallow's rein, but the voice belonged to Malisande. "Carick," she said again. "What happened? Was it some kind of fit?" Yet she seemed to be speaking to the others as much as to him.

I don't know, Carick thought dizzily. Not exactly, anyway. But he remembered the malevolent will and his compelling need to escape drowning in its darkness.

"The maister has power." Solaan spoke so quietly from Carick's other side that Raven had to lean forward to hear her. The knight's scent, of sweat and blood, leather and armor and dirt, was sharp in Carick's nostrils, and he wanted to draw away from it—and from the hard edge in Solaan's voice, her measuring stare. "He is attuned to the natural world, as am I. But he needs to learn its caution."

"Did he attract attention?" Raven released Carick's arm, but his scrutiny remained intent. "Was he attacked?"

Solaan's eyes were still narrowed on Carick. "Both, I think. But it all happened so fast. I cannot be sure whether they tracked him back to us or not."

They didn't, Carick wanted to say. He licked at dry lips, summoning his voice. "They're hunting someone else," he said.

"Our scouts?" Raven asked. The knight did not mention Herun, but Carick knew the tracker would be in all their minds. He shook his head, because instinct told him the hunt had been further away.

"No. Although I think there's more than one person being pursued. And they're heading this way."

Raven did not demand how he knew, just studied the surrounding terrain before turning to Solaan. "Do you know anywhere along this road that's defensible?"

Marten cleared his throat. "I've hunted through here and there's a line of ruined forts along these hills—Old Empire ruins mostly, but the old lords maintained a few until the last round of wars. There's one such close to where this road crosses the pass into the upper Normarch vale. The outer walls and donjon still stood, the last time I came this way: enough to be defensible. And it has a well. Deep, with good water."

"What about our scouts?" Audin asked.

"They know to look for us along the road," Raven said. "And if the maister has seen a real danger, then we may need this fort." The knight studied Carick, his expression impossible to read. "If he hasn't, we'll still be riding in the right direction."

Carick wanted to ask what exactly had happened to him, what the others had seen, but Solaan's expression, as she turned her horse to ride beside him, did not encourage questions. The pace Raven set was faster now, the company focused on both the road ahead and the surrounding slopes, alert for the least sign of danger. And the day had grown hot. The air stank of horse and human sweat as the road began to climb, and Carick's mouth filled with dust.

"Too cold last night, too hot today," Raher muttered.

"Cold and shadow," Alianor gasped out, "will come again soon enough." Her face was clammy, her hands twisted tightly into Sable's mane as she struggled to lift her head.

"What does that mean?" Raher demanded, but Solaan quelled him with a look.

"She's barely conscious," the Hill woman said, "and may have wound fever starting. Don't overreact to what she says."

I'm surprised she's conscious at all, Carick thought. He caught Malisande watching him, her dark gaze assessing, and looked away.

A mile further on, they almost rode Aymil down as he emerged from a dense thicket of willow and alder. "Where's Darin?" Raven asked.

The guard wiped sweat from his face. "He sent me back. The woods are full of tracks, mostly small bands but all moving in the same direction we are. Toward Normarch," he clarified, and the company shifted in their saddles, exchanging worried looks. "You're bound to run into 'em, probably sooner rather than later on this road. Darin said he'd scout a bit further, see if he could get a look at whoever's making the tracks and meet up with the two lads. But he wanted you warned."

Raven nodded, short and grim. "We suspected, but knowing's better. Marten says there's an old fort near here that's defensible, so we'll make for that."

Audin glanced at Ghiselaine. "Maybe we should still try running for Normarch while we have the chance. Or turn back." But Aymil shook his head.

"It's too far to run, Lord Audin, without a change of horses. And the tracks we've seen—together, we reckon they number hundreds. And they're all over these hills. Forward or back, we'd just end scattered across country ahead of the hunt."

Carick licked at his dusty lips and found that he was watching Raven; they all were, their expressions intent. "We have to assume," the knight said, as calmly as though they were standing in the Normarch training yard and not out in wild country with danger pressing close, "that they've been infiltrating this country since Lord Falk left Normarch."

And Alianor, Carick thought, had suggested that the damosels had been somehow lured—he was still unclear quite how this had happened—into the ill-fated expedition that had drawn off more defenders from Normarch. Insects buzzed, loud against the surrounding heat and the company's silence.

"But discipline," Raven continued, "can hold a defensible position, even against numbers. Once we reach Marten's fort safely we can reassess our situation, but for now we should assume that we're riding into trouble."

# 22

# The Hill Fort

*T*he road began to climb more steeply, toward a cleft in the skyline that marked the pass, but bend followed bend with no sign of the fort. Despite the heat, the afternoon shadows were already lengthening and soon the sun would be striking into their eyes as they climbed. And what, thought Carick, if Marten was mistaken and there was no fort? What if they just kept riding until the jaws of the trap closed around them?

"There." Solaan pointed, and Carick caught a glimpse of gray stone through distant trees, followed a moment later by a line of solid wall. They rounded another long, climbing bend and this time saw the whole site, weathered and crumbling on a small hill rising from a treeless plateau. The road, which divided the plateau from the wooded hills to the north, continued on toward the pass, while a causeway branched off it to reach the fort. The small hill, Carick saw, ended in limestone bluffs on at least two sides, limiting the scope of an attacking force.

"The open ground's boggy," Marten told Raven, "especially after rain. That's why they built the causeway."

A crow flapped out of the trees beside the road, startling Raher's horse, which shied. High up on the slope beside the road, a scream split the quiet air.

Malisande's head whipped toward the sound. "Time to run!"

"Hold together!" Raven's voice cut across the tension. "Audin, you lead: keep the Countess close. Jarna, make sure those spare horses stay with us. Raher, Tibalt, Ado, you stick with Solaan as rearguard for the main company. Guards—with me. Go!" he said, as a second scream tore the afternoon apart. A ululating wail followed, terrible in its triumph.

They went, a thunder of horses toward the causeway. Carick twisted to look behind and saw Raven and the guards turning, weapons out, as something came leaping and bounding down the wooded slope toward them. The ground dipped, pulling his focus back onto Mallow as more wailing cries resounded amongst the hills. The mare stretched further into her gallop, her ears flat against her skull.

"Keep together!" That was Solaan, shouting above the storm of hooves as they turned onto the causeway. The fort's hill rose above them, higher than it had seemed from a distance, with the tower and walls frowning down and a gate arch yawning wide. Carick snatched another look back and saw figures breaking from the woods, but could not make out Raven or the guards. His fists clenched hard on the reins, and Mallow snorted, foam splashing from her mouth—but they were almost at the fort now. Ahead, Audin had begun the gallop up the hill to the gate.

A wild outcry sounded behind them, but this time Carick did not look back. Mallow was already slowing as they thundered beneath the gate arch, and Carick tumbled from her back as she stopped. "Walk the horses," Solaan commanded, and the damosels leapt to obey while the squires grabbed bows and rushed up the narrow stairs to the walls. Raher and Tibalt were last through and flung themselves out of the saddle, racing to the wooden gates pushed back against either wall—but the gates were sunk into years of weeds and dirt. The squires cursed and went to hands and knees, trying to dig them out with knife blades and their hands.

"Carro, here!" Malisande was struggling to help Alianor

off Sable's back, while Ilaise held the black horse steady. "We need to get Alli under cover."

Carick sprang to help, glancing toward the crumbling donjon with its low, tile-roofed outbuildings. "We should check inside," he said. "Make sure none of the wolfpack got here first."

"I'll go." Ilaise passed Sable's reins to Carick, but Ghiselaine, approaching from the other side, shook her head. Her eyes still looked haunted, but her expression was resolute.

"Not alone," she said firmly.

"I'll go, too." Jarna had been tethering the spare horses, but already had her bow on her shoulder. She slapped the last horse aside and jogged toward the donjon as Ilaise hesitated, then ran to catch up. Ghiselaine frowned at the gates.

"They must've been stuck like this for years," Tibalt panted. "And the hinges are rusted. But I think this one's coming clear."

"We'd better hurry." Raher spoke shortly, but he kept flicking rapid glances toward the wooded hillside and the road. "Someone find those entrenching tools."

"I'll get them." Brania turned toward the squires' horses, her companions from The Leas following.

"Look for material to barricade the gates as well," Ghiselaine called after them, and Brania nodded, lifting a hand to show she understood.

"What of Ser Raven and the guards?" Malisande was down on one knee, supporting Alianor on the ground. "What's happening out there?"

Carick stared through the gateway at the horde of wild-looking men spilling out of the woods and onto the road. A wave of dizziness made him put out a hand, steadying himself against the gate. "There's hundreds of them—at least six or seven times as many as at The Leas. And I can't see Ser Raven and the guards at all."

Beside him, Raher grunted and the gate shifted but failed to come clear. "Down already maybe. As we'll be if we can't *move* these."

Tibalt said something about the tools, but Carick barely

heard him as his eyes searched the edge of the wood. He could not believe that Raven and the others had fallen— would not believe it until he saw bodies.

*There*, he thought, catching a glimpse of horses between thinning trees, further along the hillside—at least two riders, making their way toward the fort. Raven, Carick wondered, or our scouts? He jumped as Brania handed a short-handled shovel to Tibalt, tossing another to Raher, then was gone again.

Carick wondered why the horde hadn't spotted the horses in the brush yet. The riders were being very careful—trying, he guessed, to reach a point from which they might win a sprint to the fort. He squinted against the sun and thought that one of the horses creeping closer might be carrying double—and now they were finally in the open, two great gray chargers of Emer bursting from the wood in an all-out run for the gate. A yammer went up from the horde and several packs of beast-men loped out of the trees, moving to intercept the riders.

The boggy, rough terrain was far easier for the beast-men to negotiate than the horses, one of which *was* carrying double. Already, it had begun to fall behind and the gap between the fugitives and their pursuers was closing fast. Raher threw down his shovel. "We have to sally!" he cried, and ran for the wall.

Yet even a sally, Carick knew, might not break the numbers and momentum of the beast-men—and could leave the squires caught in the open. He picked up Raher's shovel and began to dig, but remained focused on the drama of pursuit and flight playing out before him for the second time that day.

The leading rider had turned in the saddle now, notching an arrow to his recurved bow. "Shot!" exclaimed Tibalt as the first arrow took out the closest of the beast-men. The rider shot again, and a second beast-man collapsed and lay still. But there were still too many of the hunters, too wide a stretch of ground between the riders and the gate. Carick groaned as boots clattered on the stone stairs behind him, sure that even if a sally could be pulled off, it was going to be too late.

"Sacred Imuln!" Tibalt shouted. Carick blinked, trying to take in what was happening as Raven and the guards came up out of a hollow close by the causeway, which had been invisible amongst the low scrub and rock. They must have been holding their horses down: it was a trick he had heard spoken of, one used by the light cavalry of Lathayra and Jhaine. Now the five erupted from cover with a yell and charged across the open ground in a close, heavily armed line that would hit the beast-men in the flank—and hit them hard.

"Mount up!" Audin called, and a quick glance back showed nearly half the remaining squires swinging into the saddle. Raher was at Audin's right hand, Gille and Ado close on his left.

"That fourth rider with Ser Raven—" Malisande said. She and Ghiselaine had dragged Alianor clear of the horses' path, propping her against the wall. "That's Girvase!"

It *was* Girvase, his black charger stretching into a gallop alongside Raven and the three guards—although their pace ended as more of a lumber, given the puggy ground. The nearest of the hunters were turning to meet them, forming a loose line of their own, and the bestial faces snarled bloodlust. Yet for some reason they seemed reluctant to engage the five—and Carick recalled how the beast-men at The Leas had also backed away from Raven.

The five's charge looked set to meet the hunters full on until at the last possible moment all five sheered away, cutting back toward the fort on a line that would intersect the gray horses. The beast-men howled and turned as well, racing to stay between the two groups. The archers with the horde loosed a volley at the five, and although the arrows fell short, they would find the range soon enough—and the whole ragged army was beginning to move, flowing across the plateau toward the fort.

"Now," said Audin, from immediately behind Carick, "we sally." And he pulled his visor down.

The squires left the gate at a walk, keeping shoulder-to-shoulder down the hill, but gaining momentum as they went. Soon the vanguard of the horde would be surging up to meet them, but it looked as though the gray horses would just get there first. The beast-men put on a final surge of speed as Raven's five and the gray riders finally came together, and the archers on the fort wall began to shoot. Audin's sortie swept down, using the impetus of the hill to brush aside the first rush of outlaws.

Blades flashed and warhorses plunged, striking with their shod hooves as the three groups of riders coalesced into a single, retreating unit. The beast-men leapt forward to rend and tear, but Carick noted that they still kept away from Raven. The archers on the wall loosed another volley, the arrows arching high before dropping down amongst the attackers. But the air around the beast-men shimmered as it had that morning, and too many of the arrows splintered in midair or fell harmlessly aside.

"We mustn't waste them," Tibalt said. Carick pulled his attention back to the fort and the gates. "And we need to get these closed and barricaded as soon as everyone's back inside." The squire had finally dug his gate clear, but it would only move stiffly. Carick's gate, when they tested it, also resisted moving.

"We need more people," Ghiselaine said to Malisande. "To lift or push."

The dark girl nodded, turning on her heel with only a brief glance at the fighting retreat outside. There were gaps in saddles now, and Carick could see a horse down at the foot of the hill. Beyond the dead horse, the horde's main mass was swirling to encircle the fort.

"We won't have much time once the sortie's in," Tibalt said. His expression was tense and grim, his hands closing and unclosing against the edge of the gate. Running footsteps heralded Malisande's return with Jarna, Ilaise, and a tall girl called Ro.

"The buildings were clear," Ilaise said. "And Brania and Enna are bringing everything we've found for the barricade." But her eyes, like everyone else's, were fixed on the retreating riders, who were now very close.

They'll make it, Carick thought. But *can* we get these gates closed and secured before the main rush hits?

*"Help me!"* Carick jumped, but no one else seemed to have heard the whisper. He glanced uneasily around and saw that Alianor had pushed herself up from the wall while Ghiselaine tried to support her weight. *"Maister . . ."*

Malisande turned. "Alli, what are you doing?" She took a step toward her friend, then hesitated, her attention drawn back to what was happening outside.

"Help me—up," Alianor's voice was strained, but her gaze was fixed on Carick, compelling him. "The gate."

"It might kill you." Malisande turned back to her again. "You *heard* Herun."

But it was Ghiselaine who replied. "We'll all be dead, Mal, if we can't close the gates. Help me with her, Maister Carick." Her tone did not allow refusal, and Carick lifted Alianor from the other side, half carrying, half dragging her to the gate. The first of the horsemen passed them in a flurry of flanks, saddle leathers, and voices shouting orders. And then everyone was through, and Tibalt and the damosels were straining to push the gates together.

"Help," Alianor whispered again. She seized Carick's hand with surprising strength and slammed it hard against the nearest gate. He yelled as fire burned through his hand— but the gates snapped closed. Voices howled outside as Alianor slumped and Carick dragged her aside to let Brania and Enna through with their materials to reinforce the gate. A cart with one warped wheel was jammed into place, together with half a rain barrel and an array of planking that looked like it had been pried from a wall. And maybe it had been, because Jarna had a hammer and a handful of long, round-headed nails in her hand. Jarna leapt onto the cart and began nailing the planks across the gate, while many hands held them in place. Carefully, Carick eased Alianor to the ground.

"To the walls!" That was Raven, Carick thought, although he couldn't see because Girvase was shouldering him aside to take his place beside Alianor.

"We need to get her to the donjon," Ghiselaine said, pale and worried from Alianor's other side.

"I'll take her," said Girvase, and picked Alianor up before anyone else could move to help.

"Help us with this," Jarna called to Carick. She was struggling to wedge the iron barrel between the cart and a heavy feed chest that had been dragged from the old stables. Voices shouted from the walls, answering a swelling roar from outside and a series of thuds, dull against the gates. Carick gave the barrel a final shove and rested his still burning palm against the gate timber, feeling it vibrate.

It would hold for now, he thought, because of the barricading—and what Alianor had done.

"At least we won't have to use horses," Brania said, and Carick knew he must have looked as startled as he felt, because she shrugged. "It's what we do, Maister, when there's nothing else available. Kill our horses or farm beasts and pile the bodies into a barrier."

"We may come to that yet," Tibalt added, "if they use a ram." He turned to Ghiselaine. "Jarn and I should be on the wall. Can you hold here?"

The gate shuddered again beneath Carick's hand, but for the first time he really took in the significance of the half circle of young women around Ghiselaine, several with bows but the rest holding the wicked-headed ladyspikes in a businesslike fashion. Jarna gave him a shy grin as she jumped down from the cart. "The gate'll hold for now, Maister. You don't need to prop it up."

Carick took his hand away. "I can shoot, too," he said, "if there's a spare bow."

"We would prefer, Maister, if you helped us." The voice that spoke was dark in tone as a bronze bell, and Carick jumped, because he had not noticed the gray-clad rider approach. A herald, he corrected himself automatically, finally recognizing the garb and the shield badge that pinned the rider's cloak. The gray clothes were stained, as though the herald had been traveling hard, and the multiple braids of his hair, clubbed into a knot, were coated with dust. The eyes that looked out of the travel-mired face were dark and a little fierce, yet there was something else there, a flicker of amusement that was gone almost before Carick detected it. He blinked and shook his head against another bout of dizziness.

I need to eat something, he thought. "How?" he asked, puzzled.

"With the wounded damosel," the herald replied. He turned to Ghiselaine. "If she is to live, we must tend to her at once."

Ghiselaine's eyes met Carick's, and he read her fear and guilt. "If there is anything, Maister Carick, that you can do . . ."

He swallowed again, still feeling disorientated. "Of course. Whatever I can. Although healing is not my training."

"I know it's not." Ghiselaine kept her voice low. "But Alianor sought your help with the gate. And there's what happened earlier, in the hills."

Carick wanted to protest that the gate had been all Alianor, but he needed to do something other than listen to the clamor from outside and wait for the fighting to begin. So he nodded instead and followed the herald. Bodies were being laid out in a lean-to beside the crumbling stable as they passed, and he made himself look at the dead faces. The guard, Sark, was there, and fair-haired Gille, who had ridden out beside Audin. Carick licked at the trickle of blood on his lip, and re-membered the screams from the hill and the wail of triumph that had followed—and that one of the heralds' horses had been carrying double. He hurried to catch the man.

"Who—" he began, and the dark gaze flicked back to him.

"I am Tarathan of Ar, from the Guild House in Terebanth."

Carick glanced away, disorientated again, and thought that the herald did not have the look of someone from Ar. But Tara-than was already turning onto a short flight of stairs outside the main donjon door, which led to what must once have been a private chamber, with a steeply pitched ceiling and windows that faced both east and west. Both were half shuttered still, half open to the elements, and Girvase was standing beside the embrasure overlooking the yard. Alianor had been placed on a stone settle built into the south wall and her eyes were closed, her face colorless within the black cloud of her hair. The second of the herald pair, a woman with dark blond hair braided around her head, knelt beside her.

"She has expended a great deal of power," the woman said. "That, on top of her wound, which went deep, and the flight across country, has drained nearly all her strength."

"If only Manan were here," Girvase said, turning. "But you are heralds. You can save her." His hands closed tight. "Can't you?"

"Perhaps," the fair herald said gently. "But we are not Manan, or physicians of Ishnapur either, although we will do what we can: clean the wound and hope infection has not already set in. And give her some of our own strength. Then, if Serrut is kind, the body may heal of its own accord."

Carick wondered if he had missed something. "How can we possibly give her strength?" he asked.

"You have already done it once," the herald said. She had beautiful eyes, he noticed, gray-green and luminous. "At the gate. But this time, rather than facilitating the flow of power out of Alianor, we must all give her a little of ours—to help bring her back from where she walks, on the borderland of death."

Carick's hand tingled with the memory of power blazing through it like fire as the gates slammed closed, and Malisande's words echoed again in his head: *Surely you didn't think the Oakward was really a myth?* "That's what Normarch is about, isn't it?" he said to Girvase. "A stronghold of those with the hidden power of Emer?"

Girvase nodded. "That's why we get sent there—either as apprentice to the Oakward, or for others, like Audin and Ghiselaine, to learn to know the power that protects Emer from hidden evils." He shrugged. "The Oakward is always based where Emer's need is greatest. That, too, is part of what we learn."

All the same, Carick thought, I doubt the Duke would have sent Ghiselaine to Normarch if he had not thought the

Oakward would keep her as safe there as within the walls of Caer Argent. A decision the ruler of Emer might soon come to regret.

Erron, Manan, Solaan: he listed the names to himself. Herun and the smith, Welun—and then, understanding— Lord Falk himself. Disorientation seized Carick again, but he shook himself clear of it, aware of the heralds' continued scrutiny.

"And you," Girvase said roughly, "are more than just a River scholar. We always glimpsed a spark of power there, hidden deep, but now you're alive with it." He looked down at Alianor's pale, drained face. "And we need you to use it, to help us save Alli."

It was like being in the white mists again, the morning Maister Gervon had died, and in the vibrant green of the forest at the same time. Carick could sense Alianor somewhere in the mist ahead, but hidden from him. He wanted to search for her, but the heralds held him back.

*"You will only lose yourself and you will not save her."* He could not be sure whether it was one or both who spoke, their voices calm inside his head. *"We must strengthen her on the plane of the living."*

The mist lifted as they spoke and Carick found himself looking down at Alianor's body. She was lying on the stone settle like an Emerian knight upon a tomb, while he felt as though he were floating near the ceiling. *"Closer,"* the heralds said—and now he was standing beside the damosel's carven figure. Her hand, when he reached for it with his left, was chill as marble. Girvase was there, too, and the heralds, like spreading oaks. Yet River lore held that heralds' abilities were small, misdirection and illusion, seeking and concealing, not this deep magic, tied to the fabric of the world.

*"Now."* At the heralds' instruction, Carick placed his right hand on Alianor's clammy brow. Girvase's left hand was set down on his while the heralds placed their hands above the damosel's heart. Carick felt a gentle wash of power, very different from Alianor's wildfire at the gate, flowing through

their hands and into the girl—like water from a spring, only this time it was seeping down rather than bubbling up. He thought the pulse in Alianor's temple might have strengthened, but could not be sure. *"Step back."*

Both the mist and the green vanished. The heralds were impassive, calm, and Girvase, too, gave nothing away as the fair herald leaned forward. "She feels warmer. And her heartbeat is strong."

Alianor's breathing seemed easier as well, Carick thought. He stretched, yawning—then tensed as a clamor rose from the walls. "It's the attack," Girvase said, and was already at the door as Jarna pounded to the top of the outside stair. But she did not look at him as he slipped by, nor at Carick, watching her. Her eyes were fixed on the heralds.

"Ser Raven says you're needed. Both of you, for the defense."

# 23

## New Moon

The attackers came in a wild rush, baying like wolves as they poured across the ditch and shoved ladders of hastily lashed-together branches against the wall. The fighting was brief but furious, with the defenders pushing the ladders back and shooting down into the horde—but more kept coming and soon it was hand-to-hand fighting along the parapet. Defenders and attackers snarled into each other's faces, hacking at one another with sword and dagger, and bodies were tumbled into the courtyard to keep the parapet clear. Carick and Malisande dashed back and forward, picking up spent arrows or pulling them from the bodies they dragged aside. They kept their weapons close so they could rush to the gate if it were breached, but the yard, too, needed to be kept clear and as many arrows as possible returned to the wall.

One attacker turned out to have been only stunned and leapt to his feet with blade and teeth bared when Carick grabbed his shoulders. It was Malisande who killed him, knocking aside the knife with the flat of her snatched-up ladyspike, then thrusting the point through the attacker's chest. "That felt good, after the Rindle," was all she said, as they threw the body onto the pile of attacker dead. The corpses all looked human beneath the hides and unkempt hair, Carick noted, with no sign of beast-men yet. He snatched another look at the struggling line along the parapet and wondered why, since the hunters' uncanny powers might well tip the balance against the defenders.

Malisande hesitated when he said so, the shoulders of the next body propped against her knees. "Some powers are stronger at different times of the day—or night. It may be that." But she did not sound certain, and Carick wondered if she, too, had noticed the way the beast-men held back from attacking Raven. He turned another attacker over, feeling the emaciation beneath the rags—and reflected that the beast-men might simply be relying on numbers prevailing in the end, and so not placing themselves at risk.

"Or," Malisande said, "they may fear *us*. They know we have power, too, after this morning—and those heralds are something more than I'd expected." She resumed dragging the body clear, but he caught her considering look, one that said, as clearly as if she had spoken out loud: *And then there's you* . . . Before he could reply, she straightened, gazing up at the wall. "It's over."

She was right. The wrestling, shoving combat was done, all the defenders crouched below the parapet again.

"Repulsed," Brania said from the gate. The fair-haired herald, too, had been posted there—the reason, Carick was almost sure, that the gate had held. His eyes searched both wall and yard, looking for faces he knew. The squires' dead were relatively few, compared to the attackers, but Tibalt was among them, the moth-shaped birthmark livid on his cheek. Carick swallowed hard, because he could still see the dirt on the squire's gloves from trying to shift the gate such a short time before. Yet now Tibalt would never return to Normarch, or take his rightful place as a knight of Emer.

Emer was not the River, with its long tradition of peace. Carick had known that before he accepted the Duke's invitation, but now, experiencing the reality for himself— "War and death," he whispered, shaking his head.

"Is what the Northern March still is," Ghiselaine said simply. Raven had ordered her well back, away from the fighting, but now she was helping with the wounded and the dead. Her expression, as she surveyed Tibalt, was set. "Once it was the same throughout Emer. And now we are fighting for the peace of the north again."

"Of all Emer," Audin said, walking down the steps from the wall. Raher and Girvase were with him—and Carick finally saw Hamar, half a pace behind with Jarna in his shadow. But the squire's normally open, cheerful expression was stone, his arms and torso caked in dried blood beneath fresh splashes from the recent fighting. Carick felt his own expression tighten. He was not sure he wanted to know who or what that old blood belonged to, and made himself focus on what Audin was saying. "If we lose you, Ghis, it will mean civil war again, as like as not."

"And the north could well be lost." Hamar's tone matched his expression, each word bitten off.

Audin nodded. "Emer would be cut off from the River and lose the overland trade to Ishnapur that has grown again with the peace."

"Or looked at another way," the herald Tarathan said, descending from the wall behind them, "the River would then be isolated, cut off from the lands to the south." His dark voice compelled attention, and this time it was Hamar who nodded.

"That may well be what our enemies are trying to achieve with all these attacks."

No one said anything. They all knew that without Normarch, the north would fall. Carick frowned, because most people on the River—if they thought about Emer at all— would consider it only in terms of a remote backwater. Few would dream that events here could harm them or put the River at risk.

Ghiselaine's expression hardened, and for the first time Carick saw the shadow of the rulers who had held Ormond against the rest of Emer for centuries. "Then I had better stay alive."

"You had." Audin looked as though he wanted to draw her close, although he did not move. "And we must hold here."

Raher gave a short bark of laughter. "Despite limited supplies and no knowing when relief will come."

"If it comes at all," Malisande muttered, glancing toward the sunset sky, and Carick remembered her speculation that the beast-men's power might be stronger at night.

"We hold," Hamar said harshly, "or we die."

"Another night for Karn," Girvase muttered, but the fair-haired herald, who had come to join them, shook her head.

"No," she said. "Throughout Haarth, tonight belongs to Imuln."

They ate a scanty meal in what would once have been the fort's main hall, all aware that another attack could come at any moment. Ser Raven expected it, in fact, Audin told them: it was why the knight wanted everyone to eat and rest in shifts.

"He wants us to dig out the latrine—and a pit for the bodies as well," Raher said gloomily. "Says we can't have them rotting in the yard. But digging's no work for a knight."

A few of the squires grinned at that, but the atmosphere was subdued. The fair-haired herald's name—Carick finally learned, as Audin turned to speak with her—was Jehane Mor. She and Tarathan had been returning from a long journey through Aralorn, then around into Lathayra, when their path crossed that of the were-hunters. Since then they had been running and dodging through the hills, trying to reach Normarch and safety.

Much as I did, Carick reflected—except that I was not pursued by beast-men. Or were-hunters, as the heralds had called them. His memory stirred at the name, as though he had heard it before. Perhaps there had been a reference in some book he had read at the university, or someone had told a story with were-hunters in it, the summers he worked on the River barges—but Carick could not place the recollection. He looked up to find Hamar watching him. "Not quite what you expected, I imagine, when you left the River?"

Carick shook his head. "I don't think anyone expects

beast-men. Were-hunters," he amended, with a quick glance at the heralds.

"Beast-men, were-hunters." Girvase's voice was hard. "What does it matter what you call them? They still did for Darin."

The screams, Carick thought. Audin leaned forward. "You were together?" he asked. But it was Hamar who answered.

"Girvase and I met up with Darin after he'd sent Aymil back." He ran a hand through his hair. "We agreed to separate again and scout further ahead, then rendezvous at the road. But a wind gust must have brought the beast-men Gir's and my scent. We fled, but they're faster than a horse in the woods and caught us, pulling my mount down. We fought free, but more beast-men were coming." He shrugged. "They would have done for us if the heralds had not arrived."

Carick glanced at the blood on Hamar again, then away, but could not shut out the series of vivid images that flooded across his mind: *the dead horse, and Hamar and Girvase with their backs against a rock; the heavy musk of the beast-men as they came in with raking claws and bloodied canines; the shimmer of power in the air. One beast-man circled, leaping onto the rock above them—and Tarathan of Ar rode out of the trees, shooting it in mid-leap.*

Girvase had been frowning down at the stone floor they were all sitting on, but now he looked up. "I agreed to ride and warn the rest of you while the others tried to draw off the hunt. I met Darin again just before we both reached the road, but his horse had gone lame—and the beast-men came at us just as we saw your cavalcade." His face twisted. "Darin yelled at me to ride on, to warn you."

"You had to ride straight down that hillside," Jarna said softly. "Even with a sound horse, Darin could never have done that."

"Not many of us could." Hamar's grimness eased, into a quick smile for Jarna before he looked across at Girvase. "But Darin would have known you had a chance."

"He was riding Onyx," Raher protested. "That would give anyone a chance."

"Not you," Hamar retorted, "even on Onyx the Sure-Footed."

But Girvase, Carick thought, still looked haunted. He wondered if the squire would always hear the screams from the hill—assuming any of them survived this siege.

Girvase stood up. "I'm going to check on Alli," he said, then glanced at Jehane Mor. "I won't disturb her."

The herald nodded, but said nothing. Audin cleared his throat. "We should get back to the wall, relieve the others. Hamar—"

Hamar nodded. "I know. The pit for the bodies."

"I'll help," Carick said, beginning to rise. A horn sounded, blowing the alarm, and he was almost knocked over as both the squires and heralds rushed for the door. The damosels, too, were grabbing their weapons as Malisande steadied him.

"I fear what's coming in the dark hours," she muttered as they emerged into the dusk-filled yard.

We all do, Carick thought—before plunging into another nightmare round of clearing away bodies and dodging arrows as they hailed down, only to gather them up again. And this time, the second attack was followed almost immediately by a third, including an assault on the gate.

"Fire!" Aymil yelled from the wall. "They've gotten brushwood against the gate and set it alight." Soon there was a chain of damosels with any vessel that would hold water, including dead men's helmets, while Brania and Ilaise came staggering with the other half of the rain barrel.

"Dirt," Malisande said, grabbing up the shovels. She and Carick dug furiously, piling earth onto cloaks and hauling them to the rampart, where they tipped their contents onto the smoking brushwood below. The torches across the plateau were like a galaxy of baleful stars in the gathering night, and dark shapes swarmed beneath them, pressing toward the walls. Inside the fort, Jehane Mor knelt on the makeshift barricade, her gloved palms flat against the braced gate. Her face was expressionless—but even as Carick turned to fetch more dirt, the brushwood fire collapsed and the herald's eyes opened, meeting his.

Carick reeled, dizzy again, and had to clutch at the wall

beside the stairs to stay upright. Keep going, he told himself, hoping no one else had noticed and thought him weak or afraid. Later, when the assault finally fell back, he picked up one of the spades and began digging the pit Raven had asked for. Ghiselaine called Malisande to help with the wounded, and although Brania brought one of the pitch torches to light his work, she wedged it into a gap between the lean-to and the stable and did not stay.

The torch's light was sullen, but steady enough, and once it was clear that the next attack would not come soon, both Hamar and Tarathan arrived to spell him. "You've done enough," Hamar said. "You need to rest."

What about you? Carick wanted to ask, knowing they were setting a different standard for him. But when he looked at the blisters on his palms, he decided to just be thankful for the respite—and once he sat down on the mounting block by the stable door, the weariness that hit him was so great he thought he might never stand up again.

Hamar and Tarathan worked in a steady rhythm and the digging went more quickly, but although the night was growing cool, both were soon sweating and stripped to the waist. Hamar, Carick could not help noticing, still had skin unblemished by wounds, while the herald carried old scars. Blade cuts, in fact—and here Carick sat up a little, despite his exhaustion, as he recalled how Tarathan had always been in the thick of the fighting on the wall. Not, he reflected, what the River expected of a herald at all.

Although what sort of life did heralds lead, really? Were they born to the gray, or could someone like Tarathan of Ar have had another life before joining the Guild? Carick sighed, stretching out his legs—and nearly tripped Malisande as she walked past. Her eyes flashed at him, gold in the torchlight, but Marten joined them before Carick could apologize.

"Ser Raven says you're wanted," the guard said. "All of you, up on the wall."

An all-out attack must be coming, Carick thought, groaning inwardly as he pushed himself to his feet and crossed the yard. Raven and Solaan were waiting at the top of the gate stair, their faces masks of sweat and grime and blood, with Girvase close by on Solaan's left. The remaining defenders were scattered around the wall and their numbers looked pitifully thin. Soon they would be too few to hold the perimeter, even with the limestone bluffs to protect much of it. Carick shook his head to push such dark thoughts away, then jumped as Jehane Mor came quietly up the stairs behind him. "What's happening?" she asked.

"They pulled back into the woods after the last attack," Solaan said, "but now they're massing again."

"Ay, they're something more than an outlaw rabble." Carick followed Raven's gaze out to the dark bulk of hill and forest, with the horde's torches massed along what he guessed must be the road. "They may look wild, but the way they've pushed those attacks there has to be at least a stiffening of trained fighters amongst them."

"That would better explain their numbers as well," Girvase said. "Even if they have recruited every outlaw band between here and Aeris."

"Any sign of a ram yet?" Hamar asked. He had pulled his shirt back on as they crossed the yard and was buckling on his armor.

Raven shook his head. "They'll have to cut down a tree and will want daylight for that. Solaan thinks something else is stirring out there."

The Hill woman, Carick saw, was watching the heralds, who both had their heads turned, studying the horde. "The were-hunts?" Tarathan asked.

Solaan nodded. "I fear so.

Carick glanced at Malisande, who had also feared what would come during the darkest hours. But Solaan's gaze remained fixed on the heralds—or more correctly, Carick realized, on Jehane Mor. "Tonight belongs to Imuln," the Hill woman said, repeating the herald's exact words from after the first attack. "I do not ask lightly," she added, and Jehane Mor nodded without looking around.

Ask what? Carick wondered. He shot a glance at Raven,

but the knight was as impassive as the heralds behind his grime. Hamar finished strapping on his sword. "Solaan's right," he said. "Something bad is brewing. I can feel it, too."

Carick stared toward the road again and saw that bonfires had been spaced at intervals amongst the army of torches, with dark shapes bulked around them. A gout of flame leapt up from the central fire, silhouetting bestial heads and grotesque helms—or were the two one and the same?

"They're stronger at night," Malisande said, half under her breath. "We may need Alli . . ." Her voice trailed off again, but her arm brushed Carick's and he felt her tension. Solaan's focus remained on Jehane Mor. *As though she's waiting for something,* Carick thought, and despite fear and danger he remained aware of the detached observer within himself—*waiting,* too.

Beyond the wall, a howl rose and fell away, followed by a series of yammering shouts from the horde. A second howl came, wilder and more ferocious than the first, and Jehane Mor finally turned to Solaan. "I fear you are right about what's coming," she said calmly. "And that only a great working will prevent the worst."

Solaan hesitated, and Carick could not shake the sense of a second layer of meaning to the communication between herald and Hill woman. But Jehane Mor was already studying the surrounding wall. "The gate is the weakest point so I will need to remain here, with the rest of the Seven spaced evenly around the perimeter—and Tarathan farthest from me. Hamar, you stand with him." Hamar nodded. "Solaan and Carick will take the positions on either side of me."

*I don't belong in this,* Carick thought. *I'm a River scholar, a student of logic and reason, not an Oakward adept with powers born from Emer's dark past. All I've really done is help Alianor; she's the one with the power.* He wanted to protest—but looked around at the others' grim faces and remained silent.

"Malisande." Jehane Mor's eyes rested on the dark-haired damosel. "I need you on Tarathan's other side. Girvase, you take the place one along from her."

The howling across the plateau had risen to a crescendo as the herald spoke, and showed no sign of abating. The bonfires were flinging out vermilion flame, and a pack of five or six beast-men paced around each conflagration. Carick stared, puzzled, then rubbed at his eyes before looking again. One of the beast-men padded away from the central fire toward the fort—then howled and circled the blaze again. This time Carick was sure of what he had seen: the monster's silhouette had expanded as it moved around the flames. *All* the beast-men, he realized, were growing larger with each circuit.

And when they were large enough—Carick's skin crawled, knowing that the fort's low walls would prove no barrier to the giant were-hunters. The horde surrounding the bonfires swayed and growled, foreseeing the same moment. Jehane Mor, however, turned her back on them completely.

"This working is called Seven," she said, "and is sacred to Imuln, which means that it is also an invocation and those performing it must stand upright. So we will need a psychic shield to fool the eyes that watch us." She looked from Girvase to Hamar. "Normally concealment would be my role, but tonight I must be the summoner. So you two will have to do it." The squires nodded, their expressions serious.

And me? Carick wondered. His throat was dry and his palms sweating, but he kept his voice steady. "Are you sure I can play the part you want?"

Jehane Mor considered him. "There is power in you," she said finally, "although it has only begun to unlock. Keep your mind focused, but open to mine, and the rest will happen of its own accord."

Carick was not sure he liked the sound of that, as though he would be giving up control over himself. But there was no time for argument. The beast-men were still growing, and the shouting from the massed attackers had built into a dull roar. The others moved to their places, crouching low beneath the ramparts as they waited for Jehane Mor's signal. Carick fought to keep his mind clear and his breathing steady, blocking out the sound of the horde. He wiped his sweating palms and noticed that a fine mist had begun to rise above the open ground. The horde surged forward and then back again as black figures, antlike beside the growing bulk of the were-hunters, threw more fuel onto the bonfires. The flames leapt redly up and the were-hunters howled in unison.

Soon now, Carick thought: soon the attack will come.

Jehane Mor stood up—and Carick and the rest of the Seven rose with her, as though drawn upward by strings. The herald extended her arms wide, invoking the dark sky, and Carick's arms lifted in unison. His mind was detached now, cool—aware of the small figure that was himself, and of the six others disposed in mirror image around the walls, while Raven crouched a few paces away on the stair. He was conscious, too, of the distant pounding of his heart, waiting for the rain of arrows to come. But no rain fell.

The mist thickened, wreathing level with the parapet so that Carick breathed its dampness into his lungs. He felt a touch in his mind, light as a hand extended on either side to join with his: Jehane Mor, cool as the mist, from the left, and Girvase on his right. Carick's fingertips tingled as though stretching to meet theirs, although none of the upraised arms around the battlement moved.

A voice was speaking, like the rushing of wind through trees, and Carick knew it belonged to Jehane Mor although he could not understand the language. A line of light was building, linking the outstretched hands of the Seven: pale and slender as a new moon, the line curved into the same sickle shape. And now, at last, the were-hunters turned fully toward the fort, their deep-throated growls shaking the earth.

The wind-voice swelled, growing stronger. The detached, watching Carick saw Jehane Mor's eyes turn pale as moonstones—and then all the Seven's eyes were glowing silver. Mist poured from the herald's throat, mingling with the brume that had risen from the ground. *"Imuln!"* soughed the voice of the night wind: invoking, summoning, as another sickle moon flowered into life on the herald's brow. Like a diadem, Carick thought, his hands on fire. He felt the connection between the Seven strengthen again, and the light surrounding them began to float outward, toward the attackers.

The were-hunters roared, a thunderclap across the night, and the bonfires exploded. The horde shouted and rolled forward, the giant beast-men striding ahead. The wall had become a puny thing beside their vastness, able to be stepped across at will, while the bestial maws were large enough to swallow a defender whole. Even Carick's detached self shuddered at the sight.

*"Hold to me."* The voice in his mind was the night wind and the mist and the sickle moon. *"For this is Summer's Eve."*

Carick's whole being was on fire now and his skin felt like a seed pod waiting to split. He could smell damp earth underfoot and last year's leaf mold on the forest floor; he could feel the spring sap rising, a sweet green fire in his veins. The Seven's light was moving faster now, growing and brightening as though the new moon had risen on the plateau instead of in the sky—and now sailed to meet the were-beasts' advance. Carick felt the rush of its force in his head, careering toward the moment of impact.

"Imuln! Great Imuln!" The rest of the fort's defenders were pointing at the sky. "Imuln's moon rises to our aid!"

Carick steadied himself—and saw the horned sliver, pale and new, lifting above the black rim of the hills. The crescent on Jehane Mor's brow blazed in answer and a cry of dismay ran through the horde. But the beast-men forged on, their jaws stretched wide to rip first the ground-moon, and then the fort, apart. The moon overhead floated higher, casting a pale silver track to Carick's feet.

The were-beasts' power gained momentum, rearing up ahead of their advance like a great wave; the frail barque that was the Seven's ground-moon turned prow first into the onslaught and began to climb. Vertigo seized Carick as the abyss beneath both wave crest and moon barque yawned at his own feet. He wavered, trying to step away from it, but misjudged—and plummeted into the void.

# 24

## Shadows in the Mist

C arick raced through a mist-bound oak forest with gray shapes in pursuit. Pursued and pursuers ran in silence, but he could hear the rustle of undergrowth and rough breath behind him. He tripped over a root, sprawling full-length as a bowstring twanged.

A second arrow thrummed overhead, but he could not see the archer and the sound could have come from any direction, distorted by the mist. An animal shriek split the whiteness, followed by a furious mixture of snarls and growls. Using the noise as cover, Carick scrambled to his feet and ran on, and this time no shadows ran nose-to-ground at his heels. Side-stepping another knotted root, he stopped as the oak bark before him twisted into a fox's mask. *"Well, well,"* said the fox. *"What have we here?"*

Carick wanted to reply but no words came. The fox continued to watch him, its expression quizzical, until the mist thickened and rolled between them. I've been in this fog before, Carick thought—and remembered his dream from the night that Maister Gervon died. There had been another dream, too, where hooded figures exchanged hard words, and he recalled a hand, white as bone, gripping a heavily muscled forearm. Now he crept forward until he saw a cloak-wrapped figure beyond the wall of mist, standing on an open hillside.

A second figure came walking out of the wood and up the hill, long robes trailing and the hood pushed back to reveal a pale, high-boned face and shadowed eyes. The newcomer's head was completely shaven except for one long hank of hair that was plaited from the crown and curved down the right side of the face.

A woman, Carick thought, although he could not have said why, since the bones of the face, the body beneath the long robes, and the hissing voice were all androgynous.

*"Wielding your blade against our own goes beyond interference, Emuun. Shall we tell Aranraith you have turned traitor?"*

*"Do what you will, Adept."* The sinewy, shadowed voice was familiar from Carick's earlier dream. *"I told your spellsister what would happen if you got in my way."*

The pale face contorted, then smoothed out as the mist crept around the woman and her shape began to fade. *"And now she and others of our coterie are dead. We have held back out of respect for what you were and the one you serve. But the next time you thwart our work we* will *bring you down."*

The cloaked man did not reply and the silence around the hillside deepened—until the man turned back toward mist and wood as though sensing another presence. Carick heard the chink of armor, concealed beneath the cloak, and glimpsed tattoos between vambrace and sleeve as the hooded man's hand went to his sword hilt. But the mist swept between them, shutting out the secret figure.

Close by in the whiteness, a twig snapped. Carick froze, his heart pounding as he caught the musty stink of damp fur. The rankness grew more powerful as a shadow ghosted closer through the gloom. A second twig snapped and a beast snarled immediately behind him. Carick turned slowly, maneuvering to keep both the shadows stalking him in sight.

*"Did you think your deceiver's mists would save you?"* a beast's voice growled into his mind.

*"One at a time we will bring you down,"* the second beast snarled. *"And your puling moon with you."*

Hot, fetid breath gusted over Carick as the beasts crouched, preparing to spring, and he raised his arms in a futile warding gesture. Air whispered, cool past his ear—and an arrow buried itself in the first beast's eye. The second beast howled and leapt for Carick, only to drop like a stone with another arrow through its chest. The body disappeared as it hit the ground, and Carick saw that the first beast, too, was gone.

"We thought they would try for you first," said Tarathan of Ar, materializing from between tangled saplings and a bank of mist.

"Because I'm the weak link," Carick replied, not without bitterness.

"Because that's what they think," the herald said. "As they are meant to, I suspect." The dark eyes regarded him, as though reckoning odds. "Let us say that I chose not to let them discover otherwise."

Carick stared back at him, bewildered. "Ah well," Tarathan murmured, his expression now that of a man confronted by a riddle that was more intricate than he had first thought. The herald looked around at the secret wood. "I think our work here may be done, in any case."

Killing the beasts? Carick wondered. He shivered, remembering the way Maister Gervon had come at him through a similar white mist. "This is real in some way, isn't it? Not just a dream. And if it's not a dream . . ." He hesitated.

The herald watched him, a question in his eyes. The man was an enigma, Carick thought, a member of the heralds' Guild yet clearly a warrior as well. And although Tarathan had killed the beasts, that did not necessarily make the herald trustworthy. Yet Carick found that he did trust him. "I've been here before," he said abruptly. "At least twice, in what I thought were dreams. After one of those dreams, Maister Gervon, the maister of Serrut at Normarch, was found murdered. And the way he died—"

Carick broke off, shivering again, then made himself relate what he had seen in the blood-spattered chapel. "And I can't help thinking . . ." He paused, then continued in a rush: "What happened was so much like the dream. And if the mist is real and I can move through it, what if *I* murdered Maister Gervon, only can't remember?"

The herald's brows had drawn together, but now he shook his head. "I doubt it," he said, cool as his partner. "The death you've described does not have your stamp."

*An intervention. But why?*

Carick jumped—then realized that a third person had not spoken, after all. What he had overheard, through some trick of this strange place, was the herald's inner reflection. He shivered, but no further thoughts slipped into his mind. When he glanced around, he saw that the trees had begun to fade. No, not fade, he amended: *they're drifting away from us.*

"Time to go back," said Tarathan of Ar. He stretched out a hand and Carick hesitated, thinking that he was a grown man, or should be, not a child. The herald's eyes gleamed, as if guessing his thought—but as soon as Carick, nettled, took that gauntleted clasp, the strange dreamlike realm began to rush away from him, like fog blown apart by the wind. It was only at the end, before the mist and trees finally fragmented, that he glimpsed the hooded, secret figure again, watching from a fog-wrapped hill. The very last thing Carick saw was the tattoos on the watcher's forearms unfold into a flock of dark wings that rose above the cloaked head, blotting out the new moon.

His eyes opened to find that he was not in the abyss after all, or being hunted through a mist-filled forest. Stiffly, he turned his head and saw the moon, framed within a stone-edged window. The slender curve looked paler than he remembered; a moment later he realized that the window must look west and so the moon was sinking, its night's course run. He turned his head the other way and saw Jehane Mor lying beside him, her face white and still above a bundling of cloaks. Abruptly, Carick sat up.

"Easy." He had expected Malisande, but it was Hamar who came forward, his face drawn into tired lines. The squire squatted on his heels and studied Carick, a curiously assessing stare. Carick felt a ripple of the same disorientation he had experienced with the heralds and blinked, letting his gaze slip sideways to Jehane Mor. "Is she—?"

"She's alive. But there's a price to be paid for the kind of power she called on last night." Almost absently, Hamar tucked a fold of cloak closer around the herald. He shook his head. "A great working, and only possible on two nights of the year. And she did it with a makeshift Seven."

Carick remembered the two sickle moons: one sailing to meet the beast-men's onslaught, and the other called into the sky when it should not have risen for another night at least, perhaps even two. There had been a third moon, as well, crowning the herald's brow. "Summer's Eve," he whispered. "And Midsummer." Both great festivals were sacred to Imulun, while Autumn's Night belonged to Kan, and Midwinter was sacred to Seruth, the Risen God. "It must have worked, then, what we did?"

Hamar nodded. "Although for a while I thought the earth itself might break, with the wind roaring, trees being tossed down, and the bonfires exploding into wildfire. But then the fires just collapsed—*pfft,* like that, as though the wind had sucked the air right out of them. All that's left now is huge black rings on the ground."

"And the beast-men?" Carick asked.

Hamar's expression deepened into grimness. "All dead, from what we can see, fallen in the place where their power and ours collided. But the horde must have other captains, because we can still see campfires along the forest fringe."

Carick hesitated. "They may be afraid to come against us now," he said finally, "because of what we wrought."

"If whoever's leading them knows anything about power at all," Hamar said slowly, "then they'll know that a great working leaves all the participants exhausted." He glanced at Jehane Mor, then back to Carick. "We think they'll hold off from attacking again so long as our moon's in the sky, but once the sun's up—" Hamar shrugged. "We're still outnumbered, and with all those trees down they'll have their ram at last."

So it wasn't over. Carick sighed, feeling unutterably

weary, then frowned. "Why are you the one here? Shouldn't you be on the walls or at the gate?"

Hamar's smile was crooked. "We can't assume that the were-beasts were the only enemies out there with magic to bring against us. So long as you remained unconscious, we had to assume that you were vulnerable—and still may be, in Jehane Mor's case. And Gir and I are the best at watching for that kind of incursion."

Just as it was you and Girvase, thought Carick, who came after me when I was lost on the mountain. But all he said was, "So Girvase is safe? And the others?"

"Mal was knocked around a bit, but it was Jehane Mor who bore the brunt. And you." Hamar paused, studying Carick again with that assessing look. "Tarathan's fine. And Solaan, too. All the Hill people are tough as old tree roots."

"I wish I was," Carick said ruefully. He glanced at the setting moon again. "I'd better get up. Get ready for whatever's coming next." He pushed the covering cloaks aside—and realized that between Jehane Mor and himself, a great many of the defenders must have volunteered to spend a chilly night. Or the cloaks might have belonged to the dead. Carick gritted his teeth and forced himself to his feet.

"You'll do," Hamar said. "They must breed them tougher on the River than Ser Bartrand thinks."

Carick nodded, unready to deal with Ser Bartrand's view of the world just yet. "I'm not sure I'm up to more digging, though."

The squire grinned. "No need to worry about that. Tarathan's just finished the job." He sobered. "I think it took his mind off Jehane Mor, especially since our sort of watching's not his aptitude." Carick nodded again, but it was not until he moved to the door that he finally noticed Alianor, asleep on the stone settle. They must, he supposed, be keeping those hurt by magic apart from the physically wounded in the hall below; that would make it easier for Hamar and Girvase to keep their watch. But unwounded or not, he felt stiff and tired as an old man as he made his way down the outside stair.

The night was already beginning to lighten, with a faint

graywash along the eastern horizon. Carick could see the black outline of sentries, although most of the defenders were asleep on the packed earth floor of the stable. The pitch torch—or a fresh one—was still burning by the lean-to, illuminating both the stable entrance and the freshly cast dirt where the pit had been dug. He frowned, guessing that the soil covering was shallow and would be scraped away again after the next attack. But better that than having the flies hanging in clouds as soon as the day grew warm. Better, also, than having to dig a fresh pit.

The well chain clattered, sharp in the still air. Carick started, but quickly identified Tarathan pouring a bucket of water over his head. Washing away the dirt, Carick supposed, and then blinked as he realized the herald was completely naked. He seemed indifferent to the possibility that anyone might see him—although only the sentries on the wall or someone coming or going from the donjon would, given the well's location. Carick looked away, but the image was still there, limned against his eyes: the heavy fall of chestnut braids and the water sluicing across strongly defined muscles and golden skin, smooth except for the pale cicatrice of old scars.

"Pretty, isn't he?" Carick started again, because he had not seen Raven at all, standing in deep shadow by the corner of the outside stair. He wished it was darker, in case his expression gave him away—and so he could not see Raven's grin as the knight stepped away from the wall. "And dangerous, too. I've heard there's more than one has found that, to his cost."

The knight stopped by the hall door, one foot on the threshold and his eyes on Carick's face. "A word to the wise." Raven's voice was even, casual, as if it were any spring morning and they had stopped to discuss the weather. "Here in Emer, it would be dangerous for a boy, even the Duke's cartographer, to be seen looking at another man like that, no matter what's permissible in the courtly houses of Ar."

"I wasn't looking 'like that,'" Carick said, flushing.

Raven quirked an eyebrow. "No?"

"No!" Carick bit back sharper words. "I was *thinking* that

he doesn't look much like a native of Ar." And he doesn't, Carick thought defiantly: those multiple braids of hair and golden skin just aren't seen amongst the people there.

"Heralds travel throughout the southern lands and many adopt the fashions of those countries." Raven was matter-of-fact. "And Ar does grant citizenship to people from other places."

"I suppose so." Best, thought Carick, to change the subject. "Jehane Mor's still unconscious. Or she was when I left the room."

Raven straightened his gauntlets. "What she did last night came at a cost. But you did well, too, you and the others."

Carick flushed a second time, this time for the praise. He wanted to say something graceful in reply, but no words came to mind and Raven did not seem to expect any, just nodded and passed into the hall. The sky was definitely turning light now, and when Carick dared look again he saw that Tarathan was dressed and knotting the chestnut braids out of the way. The herald buckled on his quiver and the harness for the swallowtail swords, before picking up his bow and crossing to where Carick stood.

"You look better than you did last night." He spoke with the clipped consonants that were all Ar, overlain by the trace of a Terebanth burr. Carick felt embarrassed by his suspicions, especially given his recollection of events in the white mist, and made himself meet the herald's eyes.

"I remember you shooting the beast-men that were hunting me. I . . ." He paused, the right words eluding him again. "Thank you."

Tarathan inclined his head, as though it was something that had needed doing, like digging the pit, and so he had done it, no more or less than that. Carick had assumed that he would continue on up the stairs to check on Jehane Mor, but instead the herald lingered. "When the attack comes," he said, "Hamar will be needed at the gate, in Jehane's place. Will you keep watch over her then?"

Carick hesitated. "I cannot watch in the way that Hamar does."

"You can take care of the fire, at least, to ensure she stays warm." There *had* been a fire, Carick recalled now, although he had barely noticed it when talking with Hamar.

"I'll do what I can," he murmured, then looked away, still ill at ease.

In the hall, Aymil was sitting opposite the door, cloth wadded around his thigh but with a crossbow, a ladyspike, and a dagger laid out on the floor beside him. On the wall, Audin was making his way from one sentry to the other, while at the gate Brania and Ilaise stamped their feet against the morning chill. In the stable, the first of the sleepers stirred.

The sentry by the gate shouted, then blew the alarm. Raven came out the hall door, chewing as he ran, and Tarathan was already halfway across the yard when Hamar sprinted down the stairs. The sleepers in the stable stumbled to their feet, grabbing their weapons and running for either gate or wall. Outside, the horde yelled battlecries and Carick heard Raven's voice above the din, sending archers to either side of the gate. So Hamar was right, he thought—the attackers must be using one of the fallen trees as a ram.

The squire was already at the gate, with Girvase beside him, as Carick mounted the stairs. The damosels stood in a loose half circle around them, holding their ladyspikes, and Carick wished he could make out individual girls from amongst the turned backs and metal or leather caps. Another horn brayed in answer to theirs, echoing off the hillsides, and he fingered the hilt of his sword, guessing that he might finally get to use it. Despite the fire with its play of jewel-bright flames, he felt chill and gray as the morning when he stepped into the upstairs room.

"Maister," Alianor said, and Carick turned quickly toward her. For the first time since The Leas, the damosel's eyes were clear, but she spoke so quietly that Carick had to lean close to hear her. At the same time, he was straining to interpret the clamor from the wall and waiting for the first ominous boom of a battering ram.

"I . . . remember," Alianor whispered. "Selia . . ."

Perhaps, Carick thought, she has forgotten until now that Selia died at the Rindle. Alianor's hand clutched at his. "Mal killed her. But that's—not it." Her eyes held his, their expression bruised.

"You said she was glamored." Carick remembered how Alianor had struggled to communicate that fact before, first to Raven when they caught up with Ghiselaine, and later on the old northern road.

"Linnet was glamored. Perhaps we all were." Alianor's fingers tightened on his hand. "But Selia—her face *was* the glamor. When she drew steel on Ghis, first her eyes and then her whole face changed: she became someone else. And when Mal killed her . . ." The damosel gnawed at her lip, but her eyes remained clear despite their stricken expression. "I saw another," she began again, and it was as though she had to force every word out. "Always there in my dreams . . . dark dreams . . ."

She's not fevered, Carick thought, sitting back on his heels, even if she is finding it difficult to speak. He was recalling Maister Gervon, his face curiously featureless in death, and the way his corpse smelled—as if it had been decaying for some time, rather than newly killed. "So an attacker could look like anyone," he said. "*Be* anyone." As he spoke, he felt the line of fire run between their joined hands again, just as it had at the gate. The sense of the watcher within grew clearer: focused and intent.

Another horn blew, sounding very near the gate now. Still no sound of a ram, though, so the archers must be doing their work. Alianor pushed herself up onto her elbow, strained and pale from the effort. "*Not* anyone—" she began, then broke off, collapsing back against the settle.

" 'Ware. Someone comes." Carick almost jumped, because he could have sworn the voice came from the fire. And it sounded like Jehane Mor, although that was impossible. He heard footsteps on the stair and then there was no time left to wonder or ask questions as the voice from the fire spoke again: "*Conceal yourself.*"

# 25

# Dancer of Kan

"Maister Carro." Malisande stopped just inside the door, her dark head turning as she surveyed the room. "Oh. I thought he was up here."

Alianor said nothing as Malisande moved further into the room and stooped to gather up the cloaks where Carick had lain. The newcomer smiled at her friend. "You've done surprisingly well, all things considered." Briefly, she studied Jehane Mor's unconscious face before turning back to Alianor. "I regret the necessity, but I really cannot allow you to speak of what you've seen." And gliding across the floor, she clamped the bundled cloaks across the wounded damosel's nose and mouth.

Alianor's hands clawed at Malisande's as the jewel-bright fire exploded, hurling a fireball across the room—and Carick dropped from where he had been pressed into the ceiling above the door. But Malisande was already moving, too, flinging up a hand to ward off the fireball. She muttered a word that caused it to disintegrate a split second before Carick knocked her sideways. He paused to pull the cloaks away and in that moment Malisande came at him, her eyes shifting from dark, to topaz, to carnelian. And then they were both down, grappling across the floor.

"You!" Malisande snarled. "I should have known there

was something more than luck at play, for the soft River maister to have survived the Long Pass."

Carick kicked free and somersaulted to his feet, grinning as she sprang upright in the same moment, a knife appearing in her right hand. "It is a wise person who knows the face of her enemies," he said. "Especially when she wears a mask herself, damosel Malisande."

The face before him still looked like Malisande, but grown older and grown hard. "Malisande! A sad nonentity with her herbs and healing cantrips. At least *that* one"—her chin jerked at Alianor, who was struggling upright again on the settle—"has enough power to be a nuisance. But you— perhaps I should have fed Gervon's madness and let him take your face after all." She leapt forward as she spoke, the knife flashing, but Carick slid clear of the blow and struck back, the heel of his hand glancing off her chin as she sprang away. Crouching, she drew a second knife with her left hand.

Carick shifted to keep between her and Jehane Mor, as well as Alianor. "So it was you who murdered him." He was remembering the cut-down ladyspike and the blood every- where, the chapel of Serrut polluted by violent death.

Her expression, fixed on him, was half chill smile, half snarl. "I did. He was so far gone he could barely hold onto the face he had stolen—and his hatred was drawing unwelcome attention." She feinted, baring her teeth as he evaded the strike. "Then again, perhaps his madness sensed the decep- tion in you. So what are you, River spider? Hiding in ceilings and sleight of eye—that's an assassin's trick." She attacked again, the left-hand blade darting out while she held the right reversed along her forearm.

Carick evaded, blocking simultaneously into her wrist and throat. She swayed away from the blow to the windpipe, the right-hand dagger coming into play—but he already had a lock on her left arm and snapped it into a throw, twisting the knife free. A shock of pain contorted her features as she fell back, the left arm held at an odd angle while her dark eyes turned carnelian again, flaring to topaz when he spoke.

"The River is diverse, demon. Not all those who dance for Kan serve the Assassins' School."

"Demon, is it?" Calculation replaced pain in what had once been Malisande's face. "What, then, does that make you?"

More horns blew before Carick could reply, one on a deep somber note, the other sharp and clear. Malisande's face stretched—then widened again as she flowed forward, changing shape as she came. Her teeth extended into incisors, her hands into claws as her body became a sinuous panther leaping for Carick's face. If he dodged, the beast would land on the herald's body: except that Jehane Mor was no longer prone but rolling to her feet. Her hands came up, the air between them twisting—and the creature that had been Malisande hurtled backward, sliding hard into the foot of Alianor's settle.

Carick sprang forward, intending to finish her before she could recover, but Malisande was already moving. So, too, was Alianor, raising herself up enough to catch the shapechanger by her mix of hair and fur and draw a knife across her throat.

"That for *our* Malisande," the damosel said, but the changeling's eyes were on Carick, cloud shadows chasing across them even as her face stilled for the last time. He had the uncanny feeling that someone other than the shapechanger was looking out at him, perhaps more than one someone. And then the eyes glazed over and the face was not Malisande's anymore.

Alianor fell back against the wall as Jehane Mor joined Carick. "How did you come awake so quickly?" he asked her. "Was it the fire?"

The herald sank onto her heels beside the corpse. "It was a trap," she said, studying the body more closely. "When we performed the healing on Alianor, we realized that someone had placed a compulsion on her—that was part of what was sapping her strength. Girvase and Malisande were the most likely suspects, being closest to her, but it could have been anyone." Jehane Mor paused. "If we had removed the compulsion entirely, the culprit would have fled or gone to ground. And we didn't want to frighten whoever it was into precipitate action."

"Hence the trap." Alianor's voice sounded strained, but her eyes did not waver from the herald's face, even at a renewed outburst of yelling from the walls.

Jehane Mor nodded. "We countered the compulsion sufficiently for your returning strength to begin to fight free naturally—and for the one compelling you to realize the coercion was weakening, but still believe there was time to remedy the situation."

"I *saw* her at the Rindle," Alianor said, "when she killed Selia. I knew then that she wasn't Malisande. But I lost consciousness, and too much blood from the knife wound, and she always stayed close to me after that. I tried, but I couldn't shake off her hold. I could only do what she allowed me to."

"And yet—" Carick turned his head, because the horns had fallen silent and the yelling sounded more like cheering now. "She could have joined with Selia and killed Ghiselaine," he continued. "Yet Ilaise said that she argued against the expedition from the onset. And then she helped you to escape the beast-men."

"In the mists last night," Jehane Mor said, rising to her feet again, "the were-beasts were trying for her as much as they were for you, Maister Carick. She eluded them quite easily, but the situation did make us wonder."

"Whether she was with another hunt?" Carick said slowly. "One with a goal other than slaying Ghiselaine . . ." He studied the herald. "Given your suspicions, you took quite a risk having both Girvase and Malisande in the Seven."

"Life is a risk," Jehane Mor murmured. "The fact that both Ghiselaine and Alianor were still alive, despite the compulsion, suggested interests at least temporarily aligned with ours. And the situation was desperate."

What, Carick wondered, would set facestealers at odds? And this one had expressed regret over the need to kill Alianor. Yet he felt empty, almost bitter, as he recalled the shadow he had seen lurking outside the Normarch inn so soon after his arrival there. Was that the evening when it happened? Had the facestealer lain in wait for Malisande and killed her between inn and castle? Whatever the circumstance, a girl he liked had been murdered, possibly while he stood by and did nothing. Although, Carick thought wearily, *I will probably never know exactly when the facestealer struck. And self-recrimination won't change anything.*

The uproar outside, he noted, was dying away—and Alianor was staring at him, her brows drawn together. "Maister Carick," she said, as though testing the name. "Yet *she* called you a dancer of Kan, a River assassin. Is that really true?"

Ah, thought Carick: truth. "I have been trained by the Shadow Band," he said, "which follows Kan, but in service to the princes of Ar. To protect them from our fellow dancers who serve the School and others of ill intent. I am also," he added, "a cartographer, trained at the university in Ar."

Alianor's eyes had widened as he spoke and now she leaned forward. "I do believe—" she began. She paused. "You're not even a man. Are you?"

Jehane Mor's eyes met Carick's, her smile wry. "Your illusions have been deep spun, my dear. But I fear they're slipping."

The damosel looked from one to the other, with an expression that said she was beginning to fit all sorts of pieces together. "Who—" she began, but footsteps thudded outside and Hamar burst into the room.

"Mal—" he began, then broke off, staring at the body on the floor.

"She's dead," Alianor told him, then sobbed, a single harsh wrench of breath. "But she wasn't our Malisande."

"No," said Hamar. He reached out and clasped Alianor's shoulder, a brief reassuring gesture. "But I didn't mean Malisande, Alli." He released her shoulder and took a step forward. "I was talking to Maister Carick."

Alianor's expression became a mix of concentration and puzzlement, but she said nothing. The herald, too, was silent as Hamar lifted off his helmet, shifting it into the crook of his left arm. His eyes did not leave Carick.

"Or rather, the person behind the cartographer's mask," he said in Derai. "If we are done with this masquerade— *Malian*." He finished in the tone of an adept speaking a word of power, one that could be either invocation or closure. And the last of the self-imposed illusions that had concealed Malian even from herself, hidden behind the impenetrable mask that was Carick, burned clear. All her memories snapped back into place, integrating with everything the youthful maister had observed, and she allowed an echo of Haimyr's slight, mocking smile to touch her lips.

"Whose masquerade, *Kalan*?" she replied, also in Derai. "But what happened at the gate?" she continued immediately, reverting to the language of Emer, which was so similar to that of the River. "I never heard the ram."

Kalan scrubbed a hand across his hair, a gesture that was still all Hamar, the Emerian squire on the verge of knighthood. "Did you hear the horns? They were ours—Lord Falk and the force that went to the Hills." A smile broke through the grief and weariness of his expression. "Herun didn't go to Normarch. He knew there was no one there to come to our aid, or the castle's if the horde got through. So he set off to reach Lord Falk instead, but found he was already on his way back." He scrubbed at his hair again. "They found the tracks you see, all heading away from the Hills, and guessed what must have happened. And Lord Falk and Manan have a form of empathy link, enough for him to know when the Summer's Eve trouble broke. Once they met Herun, well—" He shrugged. "Obviously they were already close and force-marched last night to reach us."

With Lord Falk scouting through the Gate of Dreams, Malian thought, remembering the fox mask.

"Lord Falk's troops attacked as soon as they arrived," Kalan said. "The ram bearers were caught in the open, making their way to the gate, and the rest just broke and ran when they heard the horns. So no more losses here, thank Serrut."

Serrut, Malian noted, aware of Jehane Mor watching them both. No doubt the herald was wondering how much of the old Derai bond still endured after so many years apart. Malian wished she felt more certain on that point herself as she studied the young man before her and tried to decide whether she was imagining the hint of reserve in his expression. The squire Hamar had been quick to befriend Maister Carro, but he might well feel differently now that the Heir of Night had resurfaced. Or perhaps he was simply searching for signs of the girl she had been, just as she sought signs of the novice called Kalan behind Hamar's Emerian exterior.

"And then," Kalan said slowly, "I saw Malisande go up the stairs."

The puzzlement in Alianor's face deepened. "So did you suspect her, too?" she asked.

Kalan shook his head. "Tarathan and Jehane Mor already knew from our first meeting on the hill that I was no enemy agent and took me into their confidence. And Lord Falk and Herun joining Solaan meant three full Oakward here, as well as the heralds." He shrugged. "I guessed that might spur the culprit to tie off loose ends and was sticking as close as possible to Gir when I saw Malisande move." The weariness settling back into his face made him look older, Malian thought. "I feared the worst then."

*"And hoped,"* his mindvoice added, *"that whatever disguise you had woven was not so deep-layered that you would be unable to protect yourself."*

Mindful of Alianor, Malian just shook her head, swallowing bitterness as she thought about the real Malisande again.

"Alli—" Kalan met the damosel's frown. "No one outside this room must know anything of this, not until we've spoken with Lord Falk." He looked at Jehane Mor. "I take it we can rely on your silence?"

The herald inclined her head, but Malian saw the doubt in Alianor. "It's Oakward business," the damosel said slowly, "but—how do *you* know a dancer of Kan from the River, Hamar? I think that has to be Oakward business as well."

"Lord Falk knows the answer to that question, Alli." Kalan's eyes remained steady on hers. "Will you trust me long enough for us all to speak with him?"

She was silent, still frowning, but finally nodded. "So long as I'm there, too." She made a face as she looked from Malian to Jehane Mor, then back to the squire she knew as Hamar. "I think I deserve that, as the bait in your trap."

Kalan looked as though he wanted to protest that it hadn't been his trap, then he grinned, just a little. "Fair enough." His eyes, gray with the flecks of gold Malian had first noticed in the Old Keep, five years before, found hers. "So Maister Carick remains in place, I take it?"

"Until we've spoken with Lord Falk, at least," Malian replied. The moment stretched, a little awkwardly, until Jehane Mor went to the window overlooking the yard and Alianor closed her eyes. Her bloodied knife lay beside her on the settle, and after a moment Kalan picked it up and wiped the blade clean on his already bloodstained tunic. Alianor opened her eyes briefly, then closed them again. She looked exhausted, and momentarily, as he replaced the knife by her hand, Kalan did, too.

Over five years, Malian reflected, since we said good-bye in the Winter Country and began our separate journeys south—and now we have nothing to say to each other. Yet she was the Heir of Night, born to the Blood that had led the Derai Alliance from the beginning. On the Derai Wall, it would be up to her to bridge whatever gap time had opened up between them.

*Although we are not on the Wall now.* But Malian pushed that coward's thought away. "Before we left the Winter Country," she said, speaking in Derai again, "we agreed that we must never change to each other. Five years is a long time and the circumstances difficult, I know, but even so . . . I am glad to see you again. My friend."

For one hollow instant she thought Kalan might refuse to take the hand she held out, but then the hint of reserve eased and he clasped her hand between both of his. *"Malian,"* he said into her mind, and this time her name was recognition and greeting rather than an invocation of power. His lips parted, as though he meant to say something more aloud, but Jehane Mor spoke from the window, breaking the moment.

"The others are coming," she said quietly. So when Girvase appeared in the doorway a moment later, Kalan was standing beside Alianor, and Maister Carick was back in place.

# 26

# Fires for Imuln

The rest of the day was wearily long. Lord Falk dispatched strong patrols to scour the nearby woods and another to secure the Normarch route. Once there, they had orders to join up with Ser Bartrand, who had ridden hard for the castle the day before with an advance guard, and return as soon as possible with carts and horse litters to transport the wounded. Those left behind disinterred the pit beside the stable: the bodies of the outlaws went into another, much larger trench dug close to the edge of the wood, while the Normarch dead were reburied in a long grave outside the fort.

Too many dead, Malian thought, as she listened to Lord Falk speak the committal: Darin, his remains retrieved from the hill; Gille and Guyon, Arn, Tibalt, and Sark. Malian studied Ghiselaine's face, pale as skimmed milk against the bright bell of her hair, and guessed that she would be feeling the weight of every name, dead because of her careless folly as much as her place in Emer's fragile peace. Audin stood close on the young Countess's right, with Ilaise on her left, as though between them they would shore her up. Knight and battle maid, Malian thought—and look though she might, she could find no sign of the spoilt, feckless Normarch damosel in Ilaise's expression.

Both Kalan and Girvase turned their faces away as Lord Falk spoke the final invocation, first to Serrut, the guardian of journeys, and then to Imuln. Jarna shifted closer on Kalan's other side, and Malian saw his hand reach out and take hers; he did not release it until a dark mound of freshly turned earth was raised above the grave.

"We'll come back," Raher said, his voice ragged, "and build a cairn here, with all their names etched into the stone."

Kalan shook his head. "No, a plaque—cast in bronze. I'll make it, with Welun's help."

But who, Malian wondered, will pass by to see the cairn and read the names? She did not speak the thought aloud, though, just followed the rest as they trudged across the plateau to where a pyre had been raised, close by the pit for the outlaw dead. The bodies of the were-hunters—half human, half beast even in death, but returned to natural size with the failure of their magic—had been piled onto it, while the corpses of the two who had assumed Malisande and Selia's faces lay together at one end. In Emer, as on the Wall, the bodies of demons and those who had been possessed by them were always burned in order to prevent any trace of the evil lingering.

Fires for Imuln, Malian thought, as Herun thrust a torch into one end of the pyre and Solaan lit the other—though this was no Summer's Eve celebration, despite the orange flames licking swiftly through the dry wood. She bit her lip and glanced aside, only to find Raven watching her, the flames coloring his face where he stood behind Lord Falk. She held his gaze for a moment, as though puzzled, and then looked away, because that was what Carick would do.

The rough-edged knight had slipped into the background now that Lord Falk was here, with little outward sign of the man who had led them safely through the hills in the dark, then into battle at The Leas—and held them together through the night of siege. None of the damosels or squires would still be alive without him, Malian was reasonably sure of that. Normarch itself might not have survived if the horde had not been kept at bay here, but instead swept down on the under-garrisoned castle before Lord Falk could return.

The Darkswarm, Malian thought, her unseeing eyes fixed on the pyres, had made a bold play. If it had worked as intended, Audin and Kalan's analysis could well have proven true: the north lost and civil war in Emer over Ghiselaine's death, cutting the River off from the lands further south. Although it had been Tarathan, in fact, who had drawn the implication for the River. Malian glanced around at the heralds, who were almost as self-effacing as Raven in their travel-stained grays. Not that anyone caught in the siege would be convinced by their quiet demeanor again, having seen Tarathan fight and watched Jehane Mor summon Imuln's moon early, into the Summer's Eve sky.

Something about that niggled as Malian watched the pyre flames roar higher. She could not shake the feeling that she was missing part of a puzzle—and perhaps more than one piece, given her suspicion that Darkswarm agents might have been working against each other on the Northern March.

Everyone was turning away from the pyres now, all except Herun, Solaan, and a squad of guards who would stand watch until every corpse had burned to gray ash. Lord Falk crossed to where Carick was standing. "You and I," the Castellan said quietly, "must talk, Maister Carick. We will use the upstairs room, since Alianor wishes to be present." His gaze found Kalan. "You, too, Hamar. And bring the heralds, if you please."

Now, Malian thought ruefully, I have some explaining to do. She glanced at Kalan, but he was already turning toward the heralds and his mindvoice remained silent.

Five years, Malian reflected again. Maybe he is more a squire of Emer now than he is Derai. She wondered why that possibility had never occurred to her before, even when the distance between Emer and Ar had challenged their few snatched conversations through Nhenir—communication that had eventually stopped altogether as they both became absorbed in their new lives.

She had thought Lord Falk's summons might provoke curiosity from the rest of the company, but most of the squires and damosels were still gathered close together, intent on their own somber conversations. Only Raven glanced around as she started up the stairs, but the knight's glance was casual as he continued on into the old stable. Malian shrugged inwardly and stepped through the chamber door to find Alianor sitting upright on the stone bench, her hands gripped together, while Lord Falk stood by the eastern window. She inclined her head to the Castellan, who studied her with the same considering stare as the fox mask beyond the Gate of Dreams.

"Alianor says you're an assassin," Lord Falk said, as soon as Kalan and the heralds had entered the room behind her. "Although you have not harmed us yet, she fears the reasons behind your coming here."

And you? thought Malian. What do you fear?

"And I," Lord Falk continued, as though catching the echo of her thought, "wonder why you felt the need to deceive us with the mask of a River scholar?"

"Lord Falk—" Kalan began, but the Castellan shook his head.

"Not yet. I want to hear what Maister Carick has to say."

Malian continued to meet Lord Falk's gaze. "The River scholar is not a deceit," she replied. "I am an adept of the Shadow Band, but I also trained as a cartographer at the university. I've worked the Ijir as a barge hand during the River summers as well." She paused, deliberately not looking the heralds' way. "I take it you know what happened in Ij, earlier this spring?"

Lord Falk did look at the heralds, with a slight nod of acknowledgment. "Yes. The Guild itself sent word via another herald pair that was traveling south. We also spoke with the envoy from Ishnapur when he and his company broke their journey here, on their way to the River. I assume you are familiar with that business, too?"

Malian nodded, because she had seen the Shadow Band's reports on the Ishnapuri ambassador and the demonhunter he had brought with him. Cairon, an Elite of the Band, had had eyes-and-ears at their meeting with Prince Ilavine as well, and she had read the account of what was said in the pavilion outside Ij. "The Guild sent out many messengers after Ij," she said, "including to the prince and council of Ar, who brought in the Shadow Band. We wanted to know how many more such webs had been spun, further afield than Ij, or even the River—and to flush out other facestealers abroad in Haarth."

"And at the same time," Lord Falk said, "my foster brother—conveniently it would seem—sent to Ar for a cartographer."

"Yes." Malian paused again, but no one spoke, although she could almost feel their close attention. "Of all the River cities, Ar has the closest ties to Emer, including those of family since a princess of Ar married the grandfather of your current Duke."

Lord Falk's fox eyes gleamed. "So for reasons of family feeling the Prince of Ar has sent a Shadow Band adept, disguised as a cartographer, as envoy to our Duke?"

Put like that, Malian thought wryly, it did not sound good. "I am charged with a warning to Duke Caril, yes," she replied. "But the Elite also thought my journey here, if talked about openly, would offer an apparently easy victim to any facestealer seeking access to the Duke."

"So you were bait?" Lord Falk was thoughtful. "That could explain why the wolfpack pursued you so tenaciously through the pass—as well as why the city-reared maister eluded them for so long. And Ser Raven? Is he your accomplice in this business?"

Malian thought it prudent to let her surprise show. "No. His arrival on the scene was pure chance."

The heralds had been listening quietly, but now they spoke as one. "We do not believe in luck. And we feel much the same way about chance."

Malian met their eyes. "It was chance for me," she said. "I had never met him before."

Lord Falk was still regarding her closely. "So the bait was taken up, although the attempt on you in the Long Pass failed. Which brings us to Maister Gervon, Selia, and Malisande—a viper's nest of facestealers, it would seem, with Gervon the only one we already suspected."

Malian nodded, remembering what Malisande had said at the last, which tallied with the Band's report on Sarifa of Ishnapur's advice to the Ilvaine kin. "I think the facestealing had driven him mad," she said. Gervon might also, she guessed, have been reacting to some taint of the Derai about her, even if he had not been aware of it.

"I don't see how he could have had anything to do with the Long Pass, though," Kalan put in, "since he was traveling to Normarch with Lord Falk while you were fleeing the wolfpack. But I do think he saw an opening and intended to assume your identity."

Malian looked around at their intent faces, Alianor frowning a little but the rest impossible to read. "The Malisande facestealer thought so as well," she told them. "That's why she killed him. She said as much before she died."

Lord Falk looked more thoughtful than ever. "So Alianor told me earlier. And that this one facestealer, at least, did not want the Countess of Ormond dead. Interesting, don't you agree?" Malian saw her nod echoed by the heralds, and then by Kalan, before the Castellan continued: "I am not ungrateful to you, Maister Adept, for the part you have played—although I do wish that you had been more open in your dealings with me."

Malian bowed, a gesture that mingled apology and regret. "The thing about facestealers, my lord, is that they may assume anyone's appearance."

"Even mine, eh?" After a moment, Lord Falk nodded. "A fair point. Although I think the trap sprung here on the Northern March has turned out to be larger than any of us would have believed."

"Yet may only be one part of what is at play in Emer." The heralds still spoke as one, and Lord Falk nodded again.

"You're right. So much hangs on the single thread that is Countess Ghiselaine's life. We cannot assume that our enemies will stop simply because this attempt failed. I am also intrigued," Lord Falk added softly, "that these facestealers knew where in Emer to find and infiltrate the Oakward."

*"Allies in high places."* Kalan's mindvoice was grim,

and she saw the same understanding reflected in the others' faces. But Lord Falk was watching her again, his expression speculative.

"Alianor also claims that you're a young woman, not the man we thought you."

"And somehow, Hamar knows her," Alianor put in, "even though he came to us as your ward, my lord. A Sondsangre," she added, shooting a defiant glance between Kalan and Lord Falk, "from your liege-hold by Aldermere."

Kalan shifted his weight, but said nothing. Sondsangre, Malian thought, amused in spite of herself at the play on Kalan's House of Blood lineage. Lord Falk smiled at the uneasy damosel. "He is my ward, Alianor, and I gifted the Aldermere manor to him"

*"Since to be a knight of Emer either the knight or his family must hold land,"* Kalan explained silently

Malian had to fight to keep her face impassive. Lord Falk, she realized, had made Hamar Sondsangre real, not just a cover story—and bound Kalan to Emer at the same time. Clever fox, she thought, reluctantly appreciative.

"But he came to us from beyond Emer," the Castellan continued. He did not, Malian noted, say "from the River," although Alianor would probably interpret his words that way. Lord Falk's gaze met Malian's again, guileless. "I can see what Alianor means about you, though, now she has pointed it out. Here in Emer we're taught that magic has largely fled the River, but your illusions are both profound and very well woven."

*"I almost didn't recognize you when we first met,"* Kalan agreed. She could hear his inward grin through the mind-voice. *"But I made sure I was the one who got Maister Carick to bed that first night at the inn. I don't think even your deep illusions would have fooled Manan long if she'd seen you without clothes."*

Malian recalled waking that first morning at the inn and wondering how she had gotten where she was—but because of the depth of illusion cloaking her, any concern had never been more than a nebulous unease. She also remembered the amusement that had flickered in Tarathan's eyes when they first met, and her disorientation around both heralds— ripples across the illusion weave because she had known them before and her hidden identity was beginning to rouse.

"There's more power in the River than many realize," she told Lord Falk, before the moment stretched for too long. She glanced at the heralds again. "But for a long time there's been little need to use it."

"And now there is, not just on the River but here as well." Lord Falk nodded, as though reaching a decision. "A time for alliances perhaps. I, for example, see benefit in continuing the fiction of Maister Carick, who can remain close to Countess Ghiselaine once she journeys to Caer Argent for Midsummer. Or has the Band charged you with other orders, Maister Adept?"

"No," said Malian.

The speculation in Lord Falk's eyes had become measuring. "But I spoke of alliance, and you will wish for something in return. Something," he added, switching to recognizable but awkwardly accented Derai, "to meet the personal objectives that brought you into Emer? For you, unless I am mistaken, must be Kalan's liege, the Heir of the Derai?"

This time the silence did stretch. Alianor, excluded by Lord Falk's use of Derai, was frowning, while the heralds remained impassive and gave the appearance of waiting. For what? Malian wondered. What do they truly seek in all this? Kalan had moved to the window opposite Lord Falk, the one that overlooked the courtyard. Checking for listeners, Malian supposed, remembering how keenly he could both hear and see. Although this long deferred meeting between his old and new lives must be difficult for him, so perhaps he just needed to move away.

*"When he took me in as his ward, five years ago,"* Kalan said, into her mind, *"one condition was that I must tell him my full story. The other was that I teach him Derai."*

Lord Falk was still watching her, waiting for an answer. "You are right," she replied finally, also in Derai. "I am Malian of Night and I am here about my own business as well as the Shadow Band's." Her eyes shifted from his shrewd fox's stare to meet Kalan's troubled gaze—and this time she spoke only to him.

"I have come to announce a death," she said, using the formal words. "On the slopes of the mountain a pebble has fallen, but the one who fell has bidden us stand strong. Death and honor, Kalan of the House of Blood, call us both back to the Wall of Night."

~·≈·~

# 27

# Rumor and Doubt

"**I** don't want to go," Kalan said, resting his elbows on the parapet as though absorbed by the prospect of wood and hills, diminishing into blue distance. By tacit consent they had climbed to the wall after the interview with Lord Falk was over, standing in plain view but where they could see anyone who came near. Malian stared at the mound of dark earth below the wall and then across to the pyre. Herun and Solaan were still there, watching it burn, while the guards waited at a little distance.

She felt no deep surprise at Kalan's words: she had seen over the past weeks how the Emerian life suited him like a handcrafted gauntlet. Here, he had the life she knew he had always longed for—and Lord Falk, it appeared, had given him a foothold within the Emerian world. Malian pulled an inward face, because the most likely prospect that a return to the Wall of Night offered either of them was being shut away in some Keep's temple quarter for the rest of their lives. Not, Malian reflected, a happy outcome, unless—the old unless— she could muster sufficient power to make her own terms within the Derai Alliance.

She turned away from the pyre and leaned her weight back against the parapet. Below her, Jarna was walking Madder around the yard while Girvase crossed to the outside stair:

going to see Alianor, no doubt. Raher lounged into the stable entrance as Kalan looked around, his eyes hard.

"But I must. We owe her a debt for saving us from Jaransor." He paused, the hard expression softening. "How much do you know about how she died?"

"Not much." Malian narrowed her eyes at the flock of starlings swirling across the sky behind his head, a sure sign that evening was drawing in. "The Band has eyes-and-ears amongst the caravans that journey to the Border Mark, and also in the Grayharbor warehouses that specialize in the Wall trade. Yet all they have gleaned so far is a furor of whispers: that she was slain by Honor Guard arrows; that my father has gone mad with grief and shut himself away in the Earls' quarter; and that Asantir executed the murderers herself. Plus the entire Alliance watching like vultures, hoping for advantage."

Kalan was frowning. *"Or wondering whether this is the beginning of the prophesied Fall of Night. Perhaps that's what the murderers—and whoever set them to it—hoped to achieve?"*

Malian compressed her lips, conscious of the old, enduring frustration that the mindlink between them was only one way. "A great many of our people always believed that she ensorceled my father," she replied, keeping her voice low. "They may have seen that as the reason he has not put her aside all these years and gotten a new heir for Night." And *why* didn't he? she wondered. I thought he would have seen it as his duty.

*"As he should have, for her sake."* Kalan's mindtone was as hard as his eyes had been. "The Derai Wall is no place for outsiders."

"No." That knowledge must eat at my father now, Malian thought. She was thinking, too, about honor guards being implicated and how that must have shaken the Wall world, even if the slain woman was an outsider. No Derai would doubt why Asantir, the former Honor Captain and now Commander of Night, had hunted them down herself. "Rowan Birchmoon was a shaman of the Winter people," Malian continued softly, "and a seer, yet she could not save herself."

*"Tarathan thinks she foresaw her own death but chose not to avoid it. And she herself told us that her power lay in winter. It takes time to call that into the world, especially out of season."* Kalan looked back at the wooded hills, watching them darken into evening. *"What about the Gate of Dreams? Have you learned anything that way?"*

Malian shook her head, thinking how often she had stood before the Keep of Winds in her dreams, watching it rise through the white mists. Yet Nhenir had been right, that night in the Winter Country. So long as she dwelt within Haarth, assuming its fabric and texture as her disguise, the realm of the Derai would remain largely inaccessible to her—unless she forced a way through the ancient barriers that protected it.

I may have to at some stage, Malian thought, but now is not the time for large risks. She glanced at Kalan, wondering if his Oakward experience of the overlapping realms was any different, but decided not to ask. One of the first lessons one learned in the Shadow Band was when to keep silent, which was more often than not. She did not ask about Yorindesarinen's gift of the black pearl ring for the same reason, although she was aware that Kalan had never worn it in all the time since she arrived at Normarch.

"A debt is a debt," he said, so low she almost did not hear him. "Death does not cancel such things out."

Malian nodded. "We must find those behind the suborned guards, if no one else gets there before us. But I think the true debt we owe Rowan Birchmoon is to save Haarth. That is what she asked of us, five years ago. And events are moving everywhere: on the River, and now here. In Ishnapur, too, from the sound of things. But it's still the Wall that will bear the brunt of this storm."

Kalan shot her an abrupt, frowning look. "So regardless of Rowan Birchmoon's murder, you think it's time to go back anyway?" In the yard below, Raher shifted out of the stable door to let Jarna lead Madder inside. The girl's glance back over her shoulder seemed wistful, even if her expression was obscured by the stable's shadow. Another complication, Malian thought, but stopped herself from sighing.

"Not regardless," she said. "But through my father and Night, her death has triggered uncertainty on the Wall, an opportunity that we need to seize before anyone else does. And given Swarm activity—" Malian shrugged. "I don't think we have much time."

*"And now Lord Falk says that he will help you find the Derai Lost if you can keep Ghis alive through the formal rebetrothal ceremony at Midsummer."*

Malian found it impossible to tell, from his expression, what Kalan thought about Lord Falk's offer. She was remembering her long summers working up and down the River, when she had always listened for any rumor of other fugitives from the Wall. The Shadow Band's sources indicated that some did escape the Derai temples and enter the River lands, both via the overland route and by sea from Grayharbor. They also knew that the fugitives did not remain on the River, but Malian had been unable to find out who was hiding them, or where the Lost went once they left the Ijir.

There were so many players on the River, that was the problem: the Three of Ij, the great princely and merchant houses of the cities, the Guild, the Patrol, the Shadow Band—as well as the priesthoods of Imulun, Seruth, and Kan. She had followed various trails over the years but they had always petered out: at a farmhouse, a wayside inn, a brothel—even an Ephor of Terebanth's hunting lodge. Malian checked a gesture of frustration.

"The Lost *are* another reason behind my journey here," she told Kalan. "At the end of last summer, the Band received a report of strange doings in Aeris. Lightning and thunder out of a clear sky one day; on the next a stone barn caught fire and couldn't be put out. I investigated and the Lost weren't there—but they had been." She watched his eyes widen.

"The Little Pass from Aeris to Emer," he said. "They must be using that. It's hardly more than a goat track, but passable in summer. And once in the wilds of northern Emer they could go anywhere if they had the right guides."

Malian nodded. "Central and southern Emer, Lathayra, even Jhaine, although that's so closed off from other realms . . ." Her tone conveyed a shrug.

*"Xenophobic, you mean. I doubt they'd harbor refugees from the Derai temples, even if they are ruled by priestess-queens."* Kalan's mindtone was tart, but his voice grew thoughtful as he continued aloud: "Lathayra's always in upheaval over something or other. It'd be easy to escape detection there. And if they're coming through Emer, I'd expect the Oakward to know about it—although in all the time I've been here, I haven't heard anything." He paused, his frown deepening, and Malian guessed that he was reflecting that Lord Falk might well have kept the knowledge from him.

"Looking back, does anything at all make you wonder?" she prompted.

"Small things," he said slowly. "Like Girvase being able to see in the dark, almost as well as I can. Being Ar-Allerion, not Sond, doesn't mean anything in itself, but his mother did die when he was born without ever revealing who his father was. That's unusual here."

Half Derai, thought Malian, a little disconcerted by the possibility. But if Derai Lost were passing through Emer, then such liaisons might well happen. She would find the Lost anyway now that she was on the right trail, but in light of events on the Wall she would much prefer not to have to trawl the length and breadth of the southern lands to do so. "Will Lord Falk keep his word?" she asked.

*"Yes."* Kalan hesitated, the frown still in place. "The Lost may not wish to return, you know, even if you do find them." His eyes met hers and he did not have to restate his own reluctance to see the Derai Wall again

"We need them," she said simply. "In all these years, I've not heard so much as a whisper of Yorindesarinen's lost arms, either the sword or shield, being in Haarth. I still hope to restore the full strength of the ancient bond with Hylcarion, and through one Fire reactivate the others, but without the weapons of power—" She shrugged. "It's an uncertain business at best."

*"Like Hylcarion."* Malian did not need a mindlink to know that he was reflecting on how diminished the Golden Fire in the Old Keep had seemed, five years before, compared with the great powers of Derai legend. *"And without a Golden Fire at full strength in every Keep . . ."* He shook his head. "You don't need the Lost, you need an army."

Always *you*, thought Malian, never *we*. She felt hollow again, as though the Heir of Night was still a fragile identity beneath the masks of both scholar and Shadow Band adept. Girvase reappeared in the door of Alianor's room, and Kalan, turning in time to see him, raised one hand in casual salute. Is he lost to me? Malian wondered. Has he become too much a part of Emer?

In the cook shelter that had been set up beside the donjon, a guard began to bang a metal spoon against a shield. "Hot food!" Kalan exclaimed, heading toward the stairs at once. Malian followed more slowly as squires, damosels, and guards streamed toward the makeshift servery. The heralds emerged from the stable, their gray cloaks drifting into the lengthening shadows, and Malian stopped, the mosquito niggle that had persisted since the committal service finally resolving. Kalan paused, too, looking back. *"What?"*

"The Seven." Malian hesitated, ordering her thoughts. "When we summoned Imuln's moon, Solaan *insisted* that Jehane Mor lead the working—not shield the rest of us as I would have expected. And you said that such a working was only possible on Summer's Eve or at Midsummer, the two great days dedicated to Imuln." Kalan threw a longing glance toward the cook shelter, but waited anyway. "So surely such a working could only be led by one dedicated to the Goddess?"

Kalan whistled softly. "Yet heralds, their entire Guild, are sworn to Serrut. And the language she spoke, I didn't recognize that either." He frowned. "But you're right, it was

Solaan who insisted, and she's Oakward, so it may not mean anything amiss."

"Not amiss, no." Malian began to descend the steps again. "But it is a puzzle, one to be mindful of."

"Agreed." Kalan's pace quickened as they reached the yard, where there were too many people around them to continue the conversation. A water tub had been set to one side of the servery, and everyone queuing for food was stopping to wash their hands. Raven, Marten, and several of the guards who had been out on patrol were ahead of them, and Malian stood back while they pulled off gauntlets and vambraces, plunging their forearms into the water. A cook threw fat onto a gridiron and flames roared, stretching in a crossdraught. The glow illuminated Raven as he reached for the patched cloth that was serving as a towel. Malian moved, intending to hand it to him, then stopped, transfixed by the tattoos that rippled blue along his forearms.

Some kind of bird, she thought, seeing the winged pattern repeated on either arm: a raptor, perhaps, with that fierce beak. She blinked—and the cobblestones beneath her feet and the day around her shifted. In that instant she was back in the mists beyond the Gate of Dreams, hearing a voice that seemed eerily familiar beneath the shadowing of power. Once again, she saw the tattoos on the cloaked watcher's forearms unfold into dark wings, blotting out the young moon.

Malian blinked a second time, her hand frozen in midair, before the world shifted back into place. Raven wiped his hands and forearms dry. But as he did so he looked over his shoulder and his eyes met hers, as hard and full of hidden knowledge as the corvid for which he was named—or had named himself.

# PART III

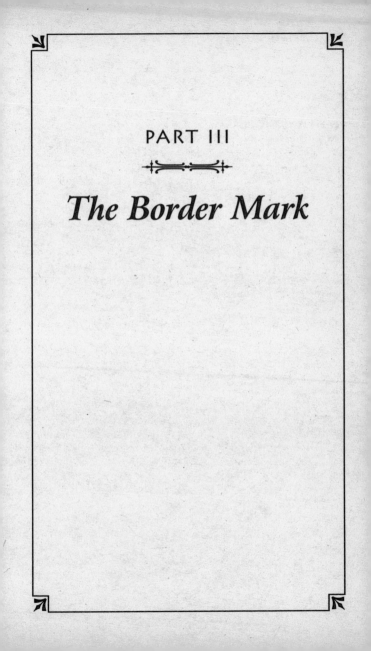

# *The Border Mark*

# 28

## *Border Crossing*

"Just what we need," said Garan. "A coterie of Stone priests." He had led his company out of the Barren Hills just on dusk, intending to camp overnight by the Border Mark, only to find another group of travelers already settled in by the standing stone. And not just any travelers, Garan thought with an inward groan. Stone priests were the nearest thing to a warrior class within the three priestly Houses, and as rigid as the House of Blood in their adherence to the divisions that had arisen out of the Derai's civil war.

He rubbed at his chin, aware of the quality of Nerys's silence beside him and mutters amongst the other Honor Guards. The minstrel they were escorting said nothing, his expression untroubled. Nothing in his appearance reflected the grueling weeks they had spent on the road north, contending with the wildest of spring and early summer weather as they traversed the Barren Hills. As though road dust doesn't even stick to him, Garan thought—and although Haimyr had put aside his usual golden garb for the wool and leather of the road, there was no denying that he did not look Derai. But then again, if the Stone priests wanted to pick a quarrel, they would find a reason, whether it was because the newcomers were retainers of Night, or because they rode with an outsider.

Garan shrugged, reaching his decision. "We ride in slowly and make our camp away from theirs. And we don't fight them, no matter what provocation they offer."

"Do we need to camp here at all?" Eanar was a newcomer to the Honor Guard, a slim dark recruit from Westwind hold. "We've crossed the Gray Lands by night before."

"Not if we can avoid it," Garan said. The more experienced guards nodded, all too familiar with the deteriorating boundary situation. As fast as they cleared out one infestation of low-level darkspawn, another would take its place, all wearing away at the Derai patrols. Even the Gray Lands were increasingly hazardous.

"There are Morning priests with the Stoners," Keron said. He was another new recruit to the guard, but he had keen eyes. "I count six, maybe seven in House of Morning colors."

Garan rubbed at his chin again; he needed to shave. "If the Stone priests are doing escort duty, they may be less inclined to pick fights." He wasn't going to rely on it, though, not given what he knew of Keep of Stone priests and their ways. The Morning priests were more of an unknown quantity. All he knew about their House was that they followed the goddess Mayanne and were given to studying the patterns of the stars and the weather, or grubbing over history buried in the ground. "We have to camp," Garan said finally. "So let's go in." He caught Haimyr's eye. "Try to stay in the background if you can. Stone priests don't like outsiders much."

The minstrel raised golden brows. "From what I've heard," he replied, "that is considerably understating the case."

Nerys's mouth twitched and Garan grinned, only half reluctantly. "You're right. But all the more reason to be careful, especially as they outnumber us—by what, two to one?" he asked Keron.

The younger guard nodded as their horses headed down the last stretch of road. "If you don't count the House of Morning priests."

Innor, one of the veterans, snorted. "I don't think anyone

*ever* counts Morning priests. Or the House of Peace lot. That's probably what turned the Stone priests so sour."

The rest of the honor guards chuckled and Garan grinned again, although he had heard the joke before. The grin faded as they drew closer to the Border Mark and saw the Stone priests drawn up to meet them. They had the shaven heads that marked the House of Adamant and were all built like barracks' brawlers, with long knives at their belts. Those facing the small Night contingent carried long staves or pikes as though they knew how to use them, which they undoubtedly did. Garan drew up far enough away to be unthreatening and raised his right hand in formal salute. "Light and safety on your road."

"Night!" The Stone priest spat out the name as he stepped forward, ignoring the traditional response. He wore a burgundy tabard over his robe of grayed indigo and his expression was as flat and hard as his voice. "And coming from the outside lands, I see." He did not look at Haimyr, the avoidance more particular than an open stare.

"Night's business," Garan replied evenly. "We'll make our camp on the far side of the standing stone from you." The site would be more exposed to the constant wind off the Gray Lands, but better, he judged, than being close to hostile company.

The Stone priest continued to stare, studying all of them as they sat quietly on their weary horses. "Suit yourself," he said finally. "Make it downwind, though. We don't want to breathe the outside taint you bring with you."

The Morning priests nearby exchanged uneasy glances, but Garan simply nodded, as though the man had spoken courtesy rather than its opposite. He let his horse move off and the rest of the Night riders followed, although they were careful not to turn their backs on the Stone contingent.

"So the rumors are true," Ter murmured, when they were far enough away. "They *are* worse then Blood warriors." Nerys snorted, but no one else spoke. The risk of their words carrying back to the Stone priests was too great.

They pitched camp quickly, getting the horses fed and

watered and their campfire built up before twilight became full night. Keron and Eanar were on cooking duty, while Ter and Innor, both experienced boundary campaigners, wove together a brushwood screen against the wind. "It's easier than the loose stones we have to use on most border patrols," Ter said, when Haimyr came to see how they did it.

Innor made a face. "Not that we'd need it, if we'd found more civil company here and could camp in the lee of the hills."

Haimyr glanced at the outline of the surrounding hills, low and rounded in the dusk. "Ay, that would be pleasanter— although your screen does keep off the worst of the wind." He pulled his cloak more tightly around him and settled into the shelter of the brushwood, unwrapping his harp and beginning to test the strings.

"It's always like this in the Gray Lands," Eanar said, looking up from the vegetables he was peeling, although the small knife continued to move deftly. "The wind never stops blowing. It's always a sly wind, too. The only place it eases off is close to Jaransor, although it doesn't pay to get too close to those hills."

As the High Steward Nhairin found out, Garan thought. He repressed a shudder, remembering the physical and mental wreck of the former steward, whom Westwind scouts had found on the borders of Jaransor the summer after the Heir was lost. Even now, Garan wished that he had not been one of those chosen to escort the Earl to Westwind, and so seen what the scouts had brought back. Many on the Earl's council had called for Nhairin's death as a traitor, but the Earl had invoked the old tradition that said the mad were sacred to the Nine and could not be held accountable for their crimes. The council had decried his decision as unwarranted mercy, but Garan had seen the Earl's face as they left the Westwind tower room where Nhairin was being held. Privately, he still had his doubts about the mercy.

"Dark thoughts," Haimyr said. His tone was light, but Garan heard the question beneath it.

"Old ones," he replied shortly, because it was not something he wanted to talk about. Besides, the minstrel was as close to a friend as the Earl had, which was why the commander had sent them to fetch him back from the River. But who really knew how much it was safe to say either to or around him? Although, Garan reminded himself, Haimyr had also been Nhairin's friend once. "Best not play any of our Night songs with that Stone lot so close," he said, changing the subject. "Who knows how they'd take it?"

Haimyr just shrugged, but when he did begin to play later, after they had eaten and night closed in, he chose a wordless melody that Garan had never heard before. The notes were delicate and pure, curving beneath the occasional snap of the flames and out into the surrounding dark. The tune was simple, both sweet and sad at the same time, and Garan could see the heads of the Morning priests silhouetted against their own campfire as they turned to listen. The Stone priests kept their faces turned away.

The minstrel's hands fell quiet on the strings, and Garan wondered if everyone listening felt the same way he did: like a prince in one of the old stories, waking out of a trance. "What song was that?" Innor asked finally, and the golden head lifted.

"It was composed by a minstrel of Ij who served a great lord, but fell in love with the lord's wife. The melody was written for her and has endured beyond many works that were grander and more imposing."

Simple tunes often did, Garan reflected, like the marching airs of Night that were still sung by the guards, while the sagas and song-cycles of the great Derai heroes were only heard on special occasions.

"It would be pleasant to be loved like that," Asha said softly, and the others grinned, because Asha was renowned in the barracks for always wanting stories about romantic vows and doomed love. She had been promoted from the Keep garrison after the Swarm attack five years before, one of the few guards who had managed to survive the ambush that killed the former Keep Commander and most of his troop. Her shield comrade, Lawr, another survivor of that disaster, was on watch with Ter in the darkness beyond their camp perimeter.

"Well, the minstrel's love did the lady no good," Haimyr said, "as is so often the way in these cases."

"What other River songs do you have?" Eanar asked, and Garan realized that he had never heard that question asked before, either on their journey here or in all the years the minstrel had been playing for them in the Keep of Winds. Always, they asked him for the old Derai songs or the new ones he had made for them.

Haimyr played a stern sonorous chord. "The Patrol refrain, from the River Merchant cycle." A ripple of notes followed. "A rowing song, from the River galleys. And this"—the tune became eerie, with a thread of darkness through it—"is the opening sequence from the ballad that tells of the founding of the Shadow Band to ensure that Kelmé, the child prince of Ar, lived to grow up."

"Play us that one," Innor said. She stretched her hands toward the fire as a thin bark coughed out, somewhere in the darkness. A moment later the coughing bark repeated and the Stone priests were on their feet, staves bristling.

Garan stood more slowly, in case one of them had a bow. "Rat-fox," he said, pitching his voice so they could hear. "They live in burrows beneath the plain and come out at night." He did not add that Night's patrols into the Gray Lands used the coughing bark as a signal. "They call like that if they've been disturbed. Someone's coming."

The Stone priests did have bows. Garan caught the movement as arrows were fitted onto strings. "They may be friends," he cautioned.

"And they may not!" the leader of the Stone priests retorted.

He's right there, Garan thought. He himself would not be happy to see more Stone priests right now.

The rat-fox bark came again, followed by the brief twitter of a disturbed bird: Ter or Lawr letting them know that a small company of riders was approaching. Garan looked to Nerys and saw that she already had her bow ready. "Take Asha and Eanar out with you—and stay there even when these others come in. We leave nothing to chance until we're sure." He saw that the Stone priests had formed a square, two rows deep, around the Morning priests they were escorting— useful for a close quarters attack, Garan thought grimly, but not if someone else has archers out there in the night.

Nerys and her companions melted away, joining Ter and Lawr in the brush, while the rest of the Night guards looked to their weapons. Haimyr seemed absorbed by the need to pack his harp away. Garan could not see his expression, but the minstrel was a cool one: he would keep his head and his nerve. The rat-fox barked again, twice in quick succession, and was answered from further out on the plain. "Night riders," Innor said softly. "*They'll* not like that," she added, without looking at the Stone priests.

A few minutes later shod hooves rang against stone and a voice called out, confirming the newcomers as Night. Ter answered, pitching his voice to carry to the camp as he named the Houses present at the Standing Stone. You could always rely on Ter, Garan thought—he had warned whoever was out there what awaited them, while keeping his tone matter-of-fact. Garan hoped it might persuade the Stone priests to relax a little, but he saw no evidence of that in the brief seconds before the newcomers rode in. The Morning priests, in the center of their escort's square, looked strained and nervous, and Garan felt a brief flash of sympathy. Morning was not a warlike House and yet here they were, out in wild country and likely to be caught—or so they must fear—by the bitter enmity that lay between their escort and their unwelcome fellow travelers.

"Keep an eye on those Stone priests," Garan muttered to Innor. He moved as close to the camp edge as seemed prudent—and then the riders were there, emerging out of the darkness almost on top of him. Mainly black horses and black gear, but not messenger horses: Garan recognized Aeln, Sergeant Sarus's second in the Honor Guard, with young Morin carrying the pennant, and then the Commander of Night, Asantir herself, rode into the light of their campfire.

Garan snapped to the salute, thinking how grand his former captain had grown. Asantir's clothes and armor might still be plain black, but Night's winged horse insignia on her breastplate gleamed with gold, ruby, and diamond. Even the cuffs of her gauntlets were worked with gold thread— necessary, Garan knew, for the prestige of Night, but out of keeping with the Keep Commander's austere expression and keen dark eyes. "Commander!" he said.

"Garan." Asantir acknowledged the rest of the guards' salutes as well, her gaze taking in the hostile company of Stone priests before finally resting on Haimyr. "Well met, my friend," she said to the minstrel. "Light and safety on your road."

Haimyr bowed, all grace. "Honor to you and to your House," he replied, his use of the formal response instantly putting the Stone priest's earlier ill manners to shame. Garan thought someone in their ranks cursed, but could not be sure above the movement of the horses. Asantir was already swinging down from the saddle to embrace the minstrel, the formal gesture of a guest friendship that had lasted for more than twenty years.

"Why are you out here?" Haimyr asked. "Surely you've not come to meet me?"

Asantir stepped back. "I have. Eria told us that her half of the talisman she gave Garan for the journey had begun to glow, so we knew you were close. There have been several incursions along the passes already this season, so I decided we should strengthen your escort through them, back to the Keep—and at the same time give Var and Vern added protection on the most dangerous stage of their journey to the Sea Keep."

Garan, looking past her, saw the two young priests toward the rear of the company. They still wore the silver-gray robes of initiates, although with the black trim and winged-horse emblem that denoted those who kept the new five-year-old watch on the portals between the New Keep of

Winds and the Old. Vern was studying the Stone priests, his expression serious, but Var smiled slightly when he caught Garan's eye.

"Asantir the Apostate—so called." The head of the Stone contingent had left his defensive square and moved forward, flanked on either side by two of his fellow priests. The priest to his immediate right had a knot of burgundy on his tabard: the second-in-command, Garan guessed. "The great Commander of Night nursemaids a River catamite while her Earl locks himself away, mad with bitterness and grief for his outsider whore."

Something's not right here, Garan thought, as Asantir turned to face the newcomer. The House of Adamant's hostility toward the warrior Houses was one of the major divisions that had defined the Derai Alliance for centuries, but assassination and blades in the back was their style, not open confrontation. Unless—and here Garan swallowed, his throat suddenly dry—Adamant had finally decided to break the treaty that had ended the civil war five hundred years ago: the one that bound all Nine Houses to never again use the old powers against other Derai.

Before Asantir could reply, three of the Morning priests had left their place within the Stone priests' square and hurried forward. The central figure was elderly and obviously stiff, using a stick for aid. A woman, Garan realized as she stopped beside Torlun. It had been difficult to tell at first glance, because just as the Stone priests all shaved their heads, those from Morning wore theirs cropped very short. A middle-aged man and younger woman accompanied their elder, and although they kept their faces calm, Garan saw the rapid pulsing of a vein in the man's temple, and the tremor in the young woman's hands before she thrust them into the folds of her robe.

"Torlun, no," the old woman said. "This is no time or place to pick over old quarrels."

"Isn't it?' Torlun looked down his nose, his eyes still fixed on Asantir. "I say differently. In any case, this is Stone Keep business, old woman, not yours."

"You are contracted as our escort," she protested.

His answering laugh was short. "You are under my orders for this journey to your House of Peace kin—that's in the contract, too, if your old eyes are capable of reading the print. Just as Stone Keep business must always take precedence."

"And what," Asantir put in calmly, "is the Stone Keep's business with me?"

"You're here, aren't you? The Keep Commander of our greatest enemy." Torlun widened his stance a little. "A meddling, interfering Keep Commander, always riding here and riding there, seeking to erode our power base with new alliances for Night. Don't think we don't see what you're about."

Asantir's expression was thoughtful. "*Is* the House of Night your greatest enemy?" she asked. "What of the Swarm of cursed name?"

Torlun sneered. "Yes, we know how hard you're peddling that story along the Wall. *'If Night falls, all fall'*: that's worked in your favor for a long time, but some of us just don't believe in it, or your failing House, anymore. Time for Night to fall, we say, so a more fitting House can lead the Derai."

"And that would be you?" Asantir asked, so mildly that the three Morning priests relaxed a little.

"Why not?" Torlun demanded. His expression grew predatory. "Night used to be powerful in the magics that define the Derai, but now Stars, ourselves, even your Sea House lackeys, are stronger. You've abrogated your right to lead the Nine Houses."

"Unless," his second said, "you can prove otherwise." His smile was unpleasant. "Of course, if you can't, you'll be dead."

"Boras!" the old Morning priestess said again. "Torlun, this is unacceptable—"

Without looking around, Torlun backhanded her across the face. He did not wear a mailed gauntlet as a warrior would have done, but he was a big man and the old woman was knocked sprawling, blood welling from her mouth. The younger priestess sprang to support her, while her male companion stared at the Stone priests, anger, shock, and fear warring in his face.

"We have waited for this opportunity," Torlun said. "We won't let it pass us by." His lip curled. "And you needn't think those bedtime stories the warrior Houses are peddling—the ones about your tampering with the Oath— are going to save you."

"I tamper with nothing," Asantir said. Garan recognized her dangerous edge, like the sheen of a blade before battle, but wondered if the Stone priests did. They had evicted the remaining Morning priests from their armed square, which now formed a compact knot behind Torlun and his escort. The Morning priests were huddled around their elderly leader, looking as if they had woken to find a nightmare real.

"The bedtime stories are true," Var said, urging his horse forward while Vern followed more slowly, his dark face set.

"Bootlickers," Boras said contemptuously. "It's as we've always thought, you've abandoned your birthright to grovel at the warrior kind's feet."

Var went white. "That's not true—" he began, but Asantir checked him with a gesture.

"They're baiting you, Var," she said quietly. "Don't let them." The young priest nodded, pressing his lips together tightly, but Vern was frowning at the Stone priests.

"Commander," he said, the rough burr in his voice pronounced, "they're building power against us within their square. I can feel it."

"They are," Torlun mocked. His grin was sharklike. "And what can you do about it, just the pair of you? As for the rest—" His gaze flicked across the assembled Night guards, contemptuous. "You've actively disarmed yourselves all these years. Now you pay the price."

Garan had to force himself not to show his unease, because he could feel something now, a sensation as though the air itself was pushing at him. He knew the other guards would be feeling it, too, although Asantir still seemed very calm, almost . . . indifferent, Garan decided, puzzled. Var and Vern were both sweating, their expressions set. Trying to block whatever the Stone priests were doing, no doubt— but as Torlun had said, there were only two of them to oppose sixteen, and Garan could feel the pushing sensation building. Stay steady, he told himself: follow the captain's lead.

Asantir was still watching Torlun, and Garan thought there might be an assessing quality to her stare now. He could not be sure without moving to get a clear view of her face—and movement, he reflected, might well trigger the Stone priests into all-out violence: *not* a winning strategy right now. Torlun's stance remained assured as he met Asantir's gaze, but the line of his mouth had tightened. He frowned sideways at his second-in-command. "Boras, this is taking too long."

"Someone is helping them," Boras said tightly. "Deflecting our force." He swung around to glare at the Morning priests. "If it's you—"

The young woman raised a protective arm. "We're not!" she said. "You know we are forbidden to fight."

The old Morning priestess had propped herself into a sitting position, and her gaze darted between the Stone priests and the Night company. Her male companion's eyes were narrowed on Asantir. "She must be immune to power," he said slowly. "It would explain that story—how she could have slain a siren worm."

Everyone stared then, even the Stone priests. Asantir's brows went up. "Even if I were," she said, "I doubt the effect would stretch to cover all my companions." Which was undoubtedly true: Garan saw the recognition of that in all the priests' faces. "Perhaps," Asantir went on, addressing Torlun, "your powers are not so great as you thought. But although your companions of Morning may be forbidden to fight, we are not." Deliberately, she shifted her hands to the hilts of the two blades—one long, one short—at her belt.

"Commander, I beg of you—" The old Morning priestess threw out an imploring hand. "Do not draw those swords."

Boras's gaze darted from Asantir to the blades, while Torlun's lip curled. "Another crawler," he said. "Do you think we don't know how to deal with swords?"

"Fool!" The old woman spoke with asperity despite her cut and bruised mouth. "She's carrying black blades—*that's* how she defeated the siren worm five years ago. That's where all your power is going now, too, unless I much mistake the matter."

"Black blades—fables for children!" Boras said, but Garan noticed they had all taken a step back.

Torlun looked openly doubtful now, his eyes shifting to the sword hilts beneath Asantir's hands. Slowly, he took another step back. "You know this isn't over."

"No?" said Asantir. "I think that it is. Quite over."

✦━━✦━━✦

# 29

# The Commander of Night

Torlun hesitated. Trying to think of a comeback, Garan guessed, although everyone knew the confrontation had ended once he took that first step away. Everyone, that is, except Boras. Torlun's second snarled something, whether threat or curse, Garan would never afterward be sure, and drew the knife at his belt. The young Morning priestess cried out as Boras sprang, the knife hand rising—and an arrow flew out of the darkness and pierced the Stone priest through the throat.

Nerys, thought Garan, as Boras collapsed to his knees, his hands clawing for the arrow and blood spurting from his mouth. Or perhaps Lawr, but most likely Nerys with so sure a shot. Boras looked surprised, and then blank, before collapsing forward. The other Stone priests brought their staves up, but—"I really wouldn't," said Asantir.

Garan wondered how the Stone priests could possibly have forgotten about the Night guards on watch beyond the camp perimeter. But perhaps they had counted on being able to use their power quickly, before anyone else realized what was going on.

Torlun's hands clenched into fists as his companions picked up Boras's body. "I claim blood debt for this," he grated out.

No one said anything. Boras had been party to provoking the encounter and he had drawn a weapon first, so there were no grounds for blood feud under Derai law—but that had not prevented blood feud being called in the past, particularly since the civil war. Torlun and his followers retreated, pausing only long enough for their leader to spit at the huddle of Morning priests. The gobbet landed wetly on the edge of the old priestess's robe. "Cowards and fools," Torlun said. "Why should we risk ourselves protecting weaklings? Consider our contract at an end." He stalked away, snapping out a command to the Stone contingent, who immediately began breaking camp.

"Do we let them go, Commander?" Aeln asked. "He meant it about the blood feud."

"Murdering them instead won't help matters," Asantir said, very dry.

Aeln fiddled with his sword hilt and shifted his feet. Thinking things through, Garan reflected, was not the guard's strongest point. "What about the Morning priests, Commander?" he asked quietly. "They'll never survive out here on their own."

"I know. We'll have to offer them an escort." The commander began walking toward the Morning contingent, her boots crunching on the stony ground.

"They're still Derai," Garan explained to Aeln, who was looking indignant and perplexed at the same time. "We might as well kill them outright as leave them to make their own way." He started after Asantir, then turned back. "And get some guards between the commander and that Stone lot. We're not the only ones with bows."

Too slow on the uptake, Garan thought, exasperated. Typical of one of Lannorth's recruits, although at least if you pointed Aeln in the right direction he could usually see his way—like now, as he ordered a cordon of guards forward.

Asantir had sunk onto her heels beside the old priestess. "That mouth looks bad, Mother." It must be the polite way to address Morning priests, Garan supposed; as Commander of

Night, Asantir would know such things. "I have a medic who can look at it, if you wish."

The Morning priests drew closer together. "We look after our own," the male priest said curtly.

Not very well, Garan thought, then glanced away, abashed, as the old woman looked straight at him. Could Morning priests read thoughts? he wondered uneasily. Had anyone ever been able to, for that matter, in the long history of the Derai?

The old woman rested a hand on her companion's wrist. "The commander means no disrespect, my son. Commander, I thank you, but my own people can provide the help I need."

"That's right!" a voice jeered from the Stone priest contingent. "Crawl to the Night bitch, you weaklings!"

Some of the Morning priests hunched their shoulders as though this jibe cut, but their leader shook her head. "They only see the stone wall in front of their noses," she said to Asantir. "But they are right, whether we go on to the Keep of Bells or turn back for our own Towers, we are not equipped to cross these lands."

Asantir looked from the old woman's battered face to those of the priests surrounding her. "I will give you an escort, if that is what you wish, Mother." Her smile glinted. "After all, I think I may owe you. Or did I misread events?"

The other priests exchanged puzzled glances, but the old priestess looked almost mischievous.

"I've heard you are a clever one, Commander. My son here thought you were immune, but how could that be, when only the Darksworn, in all our long history, have ever had that power?"

It must have been her broken mouth, Garan thought, that made it sound as though she said Darksworn, rather than Darkswarm. The middle-aged male priest had flushed, but Asantir was shaking her head.

"I am afraid that such matters have not been my study, but I am sure, given your learning, that you are right."

"Courteous, too," the priestess said. "Cut from the old cloth, indeed." Despite her years, her eyes were still sharp.

"Well, I'm glad to have met you, after all the stories we've been hearing."

"And I, you," Asantir replied. "Both for the help and your quick wits, thinking of black blades."

All the surrounding priests were frowning now. "What does she mean, Grandmother?" the young priestess asked. "What help?"

The old lady made a brief, irritated gesture, but the male priest said, as though requiring an answer: "Mother?"

She looked suddenly tired. "Blocking is not fighting," she pointed out.

Haimyr had come quietly up beside Garan and was listening, too, despite adverse looks from some of the Morning priests. Most of them, though, were staring at the old woman, their expressions deeply shocked.

"Mother—" the priest began.

She glared at him. "Should I have allowed what that Stone thug did to pass unanswered? Or stood by and let him injure the right hand of the only leader in five hundred years who is actively trying to reunite our people?" Her voice wavered suddenly, cracked and a little querulous.

Asantir rested a gauntleted hand on hers. "Do not fret, old Mother. Or doubt that I am grateful for what you did."

The old eyes swiveled to her face, their expression shrewd again. "Oh, don't think you can fool me, young woman, with those ways of yours. I know I did not *save* you—and that it is Torlun who owes me gratitude!" She peered more closely at Asantir. "What I heard in our Towers was that they really *were* black blades that you used against the siren worm."

The Commander of Night smiled. "You know what rumor is, Mother. And stories are little better, for all our hearts beat faster when we hear the great ones told." Pointedly, she looked at the other Morning priests. "I will let your people look after you now. Tomorrow you shall have your escort to wherever you decide to go." She stood up, inclining her head to the old woman and those with her, then gazing across to where the Stone priests were finally departing. Amusement glinted again as she met Garan's eyes. "You look disappointed, Garan. You didn't really believe I was carrying black blades?"

Garan grinned, following her toward Aeln's cordon. "The old lady was very convincing, Commander. As were you." His eyes shifted toward the Stone priests *"They* believed it, after all."

As well they did, he added silently—and I have always wondered about that siren worm, especially after the spear you brought into the Old Keep. Curiously, he glanced back at the old priestess. "She must be very strong, to block out all those Stone priests. And why didn't *her* people know she was doing it?"

"Perhaps you should make it your business to find out, Garan," Asantir suggested. "An Honor Guard, after all, should learn everything he can about his enemies—which for Night, officially includes the House of Morning."

"Everyone in fact," Haimyr put in lightly, "who is not an ally." He appeared to reflect. "And perhaps all that are as well. One can never be too careful, after all."

"One never knows what face an enemy may wear," Asantir agreed, and Garan glanced from commander to minstrel, sensing undercurrents of meaning although their outward demeanor gave nothing away. He twitched his shoulders, listening to the slight ring of his mail shirt as the Stone contingent began to ride out. The Night riders had positioned their horses so they could not be overrun by a sudden charge, and Var and Vern watched intently, alert for power use.

Torlun stopped by the standing stone's shadowed face and turned his own toward Asantir.

"Blood feud," he said, "between your kin and mine, your House and mine, until this is done." His gaze shifted to Var and Vern and he spat onto the ground. "Do not call yourself priest-kind. We do not recognize anyone who has traffic with warriors as priest-kind. Not anymore. We do not see you, we do not hear you: you are dead to us." He leaned forward. "Expect no mercy if you come beneath our hand. Just as we showed no mercy to the Sea House whore you sent us, twenty years back."

He leaned back again, smiling, as a stir ran along the Night line. "Did you think we would welcome her? She was already tainted beyond redemption: married to a warrior before he cast her off; contaminated, through him, by association with outsiders." He did not look at Haimyr but everyone else did, a sideways dart of the eyes. The minstrel's gaze was hooded, but Garan thought his expression looked unusually rigid. Torlun's smile widened. "No, we beat her like any other cur and chained her in the kennels with the dogs, to be used like the bitch she was whenever it pleased us."

Haimyr stepped forward, but Asantir gripped his arm. "I will respect the truce of the road, despite your words," she said to Torlun, "but you had best leave now."

The Stone priest threw up his head, half snarling, half laughing—but Innor trained her crossbow full on him and he kicked his horse forward without daring another word. Surprised by the sudden rake of spurs, the horse bounded forward into the darkness and the rest of the Stone priests followed in a rush, as though they had the sense to fear remaining behind.

"Commander, are you sure?" Aeln demanded. "You heard how they insulted Night! Surely only blood can answer such words?"

"You know," Haimyr said, his voice silk, "I am inclined to agree." The commander, Garan noted, still had not removed her hand from his arm.

"Technically," Asantir said, "they did not insult Night—much as they sought to do so—since the Old Earl formally expelled Lady Nerion from our ranks. And the Earl, in case any of you have forgotten, has explicitly forbidden us to duel or skirmish with retainers from other Houses, no matter what the provocation."

Innor frowned. "They will say that we are weak, Commander."

"They are already saying it," Morin added gloomily.

"But you know it is not true," Asantir said. "As I know it. The Earl of Night has set a cause and a purpose on us: which of you would be the first to let him down?" She lifted her hand clear of Haimyr's arm—and Garan was startled by the golden blaze of the minstrel's eyes, although his familiar mocking smile was back in place.

"You are wise as always, Commander of Night," Haimyr said, and his tone, too, was lightly mocking. "We will play the adults here and show restraint."

"What do you mean 'play'?" Garan demanded. He shook his head. "Nine knows, the Derai Alliance needs someone to be adult!"

Innor and Aeln immediately demanded to know what he meant by that as Nerys and the other guards came in out of the darkness, arrows still ready on their bows. They had not heard Torlun's parting words, so had to be told. Then more hot words were spoken until Asantir cut them off by ordering the Night camp relocated into the lee of the hills, with fresh watches set around the perimeter of the Border Mark. She and her company had to eat as well, and by the time their meal was done the edge had gone from the honor guards' anger.

The Morning priests had moved back to their former place, but there was little conversation between the two groups. Haimyr did not play again, but stood for a long time with his face turned in the direction the Stone priests had taken. Almost, Garan reflected, as though Torlun's taunts had stung the minstrel's honor as the Earl's friend—an unsettlingly Derai response for an outsider, even one who had lived amongst the Derai for over twenty years.

It was not until those who were not on watch had settled down to sleep that the minstrel came back into the circle of their camp, and even then he sat staring into the fire, his eyes hooded. Asantir materialized out of the darkness and sank onto her heels beside him, holding out her hands to the flames. The two heads, one dark, one golden, were limned with copper as they gazed into the fire. When the minstrel spoke, his tone was thoughtful.

"So is there any truth in what the Stone priest said? That Tasarion has run mad? Is that why you called me back?"

"He's not mad." Asantir was matter-of-fact. "This blow

has hit him very hard, though. And there have been so many others." She met the minstrel's eyes. "You are the only one of us who does not serve him, who can be just a friend."

The minstrel's golden brows drew together. "Even so, there's something more, isn't there—more than the Winter woman's loss?" The angle of his head was a question, and Asantir nodded, her expression a mix of regret and distaste.

"The loss was sufficient reason. You'll see when you meet him. But—with impeccable timing—we've been offered a marriage contract at last. A Daughter of Blood, so not the alliance we'd hoped for—and very young with it." Abruptly, the Commander of Night stood up. She tossed the dregs from her cup onto the flames, which hissed then leapt up again, baleful against the darkness of the plain. "Given everything else, I wanted you back before I presented him with that."

# PART IV

*Midsummer*

# 30

# The Welcome Cup

*A* fist banged on the outside of the wagon where Malian was sleeping. "Wake up, Maister Carro," Ado called. "We're starting at sunup today whether everyone's breakfasted or not."

Malian burrowed deeper into her hollow between sacks of grain for the horses, armor and weapons stitched into oiled cloth and wrapped inside quilted sacking, and bales of brightly colored tourney pennants. She had been dreaming deeply, reliving the rain-spattered evening five years before when she and Linden, the Spring singer of the Winter people, had walked into the River's northernmost trading post on the Wildenrush and found Cairon of Ar sitting by the autumn fire.

Even now, Malian wondered by what diverse means a message had gone out from the Winter Country and brought an Elite of the Shadow Band so far into the wilderness. But information, she had learned since, ran through Haarth like a river, often following its own secret, underground path and reemerging far from where it had disappeared. The years following that first, fireside meeting with Elite Cairon had been like shooting rapids on the Wildenrush, learning to follow the flow of that secret river and become one with the shadow world of the Band—while establishing the persona of Carick the scholar at the same time. Living in the sunshine, Malian thought drowsily, remembering Carick's summers working the River barges. But whether shadow or sunshine, she understood Kalan's reluctance to return to the Wall.

She had left him the freedom to choose, five years ago in the Old Keep, when she refused to let him swear a blood oath of loyalty to her. Because I wanted a friend, Malian thought now, not just another Blood-sworn retainer. She made a face, mocking herself.

*"A decision that did more credit to your heart than your head."* The voice of Nhenir, the moon-bright helm, was as cool as its name. *"And being swayed by the heart is a luxury that the Heir of Night and Chosen of Mhaelanar cannot afford."*

Malian grimaced again and sat up, fully awake now, as a fist banged on the outside of the wagon again. "Last call, Maister Carro," Raher sang out, sounding cheerful at the prospect of her missing breakfast.

"Coming!" she shouted back and stood up, smoothing the worst of the wrinkles out of her clothes and combing at her hair with her fingers. *"Lord Falk has promised me the whereabouts of the Lost if I get Ghiselaine safely through Midsummer."* She paused, halfway through dragging on a boot. *"Now if you were able to hunt out even a whiff of your comrades-in-arms, Yorindesarinen's sword or shield, at the same time . . ."*

Nhenir remained silent as Malian pulled on her second boot. Her adept's weapons were already concealed about her person, but she eyed the helm sourly as she settled Maister Carick's belt dagger into place. *"To claim my birthright,"* she said silently, *"I will need power at my command. More than what you bring me on your own."*

Again, the helm did not reply, and Malian wondered, not for the first time, whether Nhenir simply did not want to concede any blindness to portents or events. She studied its current disguise—as one of the winged silver caps newly fashionable amongst the young men of Ar—for a moment longer, before stooping to unlace the wagon flap. But the decorative wings had made her think of the pattern tattooed onto Raven's forearms, and the hair on her nape prickled.

*"Ay, he is dangerous."* Nhenir spoke at last. *"As dangerous, if not more so, than the herald he warned you against. "*

Malian paused, one hand on the flap. *"What else have you discerned about him?"*

*"Very little."* The helm's mindvoice was soft. *"Except that he was interested in the heralds—and even more so in Maister Carick. Have a care, Heir of Night."*

*"Vague as always,"* Malian said, a little tartly, although she was grinning wryly as she jumped down from the wagon.

"You look cheerful," Audin said.

"Of course he's cheerful," said Raher. "We're finally going to see the towers of Caer Argent today."

Malian joined the circle of newly made Normarch knights and took the bowl that Girvase handed her, blowing on the porridge to cool it. It was six weeks now since they had left the old fort, with the dark earth of the grave mounds scarring the green ground, and ridden back to Normarch—and three weeks since those going to Caer Argent had begun their journey south. The Summer's Eve survivors had ridden close together throughout, as the Northern March gave way to the Land Marks and then the inner Wards that surrounded Caer Argent.

They were all, Malian knew, keenly aware of the invisible gaps in their company, the places where Arn and Guyon, Gille and Tibalt, should have ridden, or sprawled beside them on the grass. Everyone was beginning to laugh more readily now, and the silence that had lain beneath even mundane conversations—about each day's route, or finding better feed for their horses—had begun to fill up with the anticipation of Midsummer and the tourney. Yet still, the underlying reserve was there.

They will get over it in time, Malian thought, drawing on her childhood in a fighting keep. Or get used to it anyway, if they are set to keeping the peace along Emer's fractious borders and more of their fellowship are lost—but she did not like the darkness of that thought and pushed it away as she took her first mouthful of porridge. She had been pleased to find Maister Carick still included as one of their number, even if Kalan remained guarded behind Hamar's open, cheerful manner.

"You forget," he said now, grinning at Raher, "that Maister Carro's no raw Marcher lad like you. He's from the great River city of Ar, which must be two or three times Caer Argent's size."

"I'm always glad to see any new place, though," Malian replied, keeping the peace. She looked around with a cartographer's eye. "And this is pretty country, much gentler than the Northern March."

"The inner Wards have been peaceful for a long time," Audin said, "even compared to the Land Marks. But only the Marches are true wild country now."

The silence that had been with them since Summer's Eve flowed in again, and Malian guessed that all their thoughts, like hers, had flown back to The Leas and their defense of the crumbling fort. Because of those events, Lord Falk had decided that he could not leave with the March so full of fear and unrest, and so the Normarch company had been escorted south to Bonamark, then traveled on with the Marklord's retinue. Ghiselaine and her companions had been swept into Lady Bonamark's orbit, riding at the front of the cavalcade and sleeping in a large, richly furnished pavilion at the center of the camp. And since neither Ser Bartrand nor Ser Rannart could be spared from the Northern March either, Raven had been sent along as captain of the tourney company.

At the time, Malian had thought that might be as much because he was the only Summer's Eve survivor amongst the experienced Normarch knights—and wondered how he would manage the more formal etiquette of inner Emer. But she had to admit that he had done a faultless job so far. She could see him now, making his way back from the predawn briefing with Lord Bonamark's captain, in which the day's route and the cavalcade's order of march would have been laid out.

"The main Bonamark company will push to reach the

city tonight," Raven told them when he reached the fire. "But after events in the north, Lord Falk asked that Countess Ghiselaine's safety not be risked in the press of Caer Argent's streets—and Lord Bonamark agrees that's wise. So those competing in the tourney will turn aside at Argenthithe and escort Lady Bonamark and Countess Ghiselaine to Lord Tenneward's lodge. The ladies will spend the night there and complete the journey to the city by barge tomorrow, while the rest of us cross the Argenthithe bridge to the tourney ground."

The young knights exchanged glances, and Malian saw their realization that now the old Normarch company was truly breaking up. In reality, the process had begun before they left, with many of the new-made knights, as well as damosels such as Brania and her friends, choosing to return to their family homes instead of venturing Caer Argent. Another effect of Summer's Eve—but this parting had a greater sense of finality.

"The journey by river will be pleasanter anyway," Audin said at last.

"I believe that consideration weighed with Lady Bonamark," Raven replied, with a flicker of humor.

"Besides," Raher put in, "to most in Caer Argent, Ghiselaine's still Ormondian—a traditional enemy. Her first appearance needs to be a grand one, not covered in sweat and dust."

Which just went to show, Malian thought, that even Raher could see to the heart of a matter sometimes. "And then," he continued cheerfully, "they'll fall in love with her beauty, just like we all did, and she'll be *their* Fair Maid of Emer in no time at all."

But still, Malian reflected, carefully not looking at Audin, blind to what lay beneath his nose.

*"Raher is a brute,"* Kalan's mindvoice observed, and she had to prevent herself from giving the tiniest of nods, aware that Raven was looking her way. She scraped the last of the porridge from her bowl and stood up with the rest of their small company, moving to smother the fire and gather

equipment together. Throughout the camp the Bonamark retainers were doing the same, as they had every morning of the journey south, so that the cavalcade was on the road with the sun.

The countryside they rode through was a far cry from the emptiness of the Northern March. Whitewashed homes, some roofed with deep thatch and others with lichened tiles, were dotted amongst fields divided by neat hedgerows. Each house had its garden and orchard, and Malian frequently saw the curved sails of a windmill in the distance. Every other crossroads boasted a smithy or an inn, sure signs of prosperity, and the whole great valley of the Tenne, from the Bonamark border to the river Argent, was as fertile and peaceful as the River lands.

Despite their early start, the roads quickly filled up with country people going to market, as well as merchant caravans and the retinues of Emerian nobility, all on their way to the capital for Midsummer. The ragged folk, tramps and tinkers and beggars with their bowls held out, were pushed to the sides of the road, and the dust rose in clouds as the day warmed. Malian tied a dampened cloth over her mouth and nose and pitied those who must go on foot or eat the dust of the larger cavalcades.

"It's always like this at Midsummer." Audin had his hat brim pulled low to protect his eyes. "The sun is fierce and the roads dry—but you can't keep people away from Caer Argent, not with the Duke's fair and the tourney happening together, plus Imuln's festival falling on Midsummer itself. Every inn in the city will be overflowing, so we're lucky Lord Falk buys a campsite in the tourney ground every year. And after the tournament's over we can go to his town house, which is close by the court."

Malian blotted at the sweat and dust on her face. "I hear that people come from all over the southern lands for the fair."

"And the tournament. That's why so many new-made knights want to ride in *this* competition. To do well here can make a knight's future."

She nodded. "Although you will serve your uncle, as a matter of course?"

"So it doesn't matter as much for me as for the others, is that what you mean?" Audin grimaced. "Except that *because* I'm the Duke's nephew it's important that I show I can stand on my own. Not to win a place, but to be respected in the one I'll hold."

It would be the same on the Wall, Malian knew. The Earldoms might be hereditary, but the Nine Houses still needed to have confidence in those who led them. More than one Earl and Heir in the Derai's long history had been put aside, either bloodily or quietly, when their House would no longer follow them.

"We've all talked about it," Audin continued, "and agreed that we'll ride as a company in the melee. That's our best chance of staying together afterward, rather than having to accept individual places with either the Duke or other lords."

Malian wondered what part Kalan had played in these discussions, but Audin was shading his eyes to study a jostle of riders up ahead. "Lathayrans," he said, gazing along the western arm of the crossroads they were approaching. "And Allerion knights behind them. All heading for the tourney, no doubt."

Malian shaded her eyes as well, keen to catch her first glimpse of riders from the turbulent country to the south and west of Emer. The Lathayrans were said to be distant kin to the Hill people of northern Emer—and equally prone to feuding amongst themselves. Unlike the Hill people, they tended to serve as mercenaries beyond their own lands. Their light cavalry and horse archers, according to Shadow Band intelligence, were found throughout the southern realms.

"Except Jhaine," Audin said, when she asked. "The Jhainarians are horsemen beyond compare and say they have no need of Lathayrans to swell their ranks."

"What you really mean," Kalan drawled from behind them, "is that Jhainarians are xenophobes with little love for those beyond their borders. Besides, they're mercenaries themselves: Jhainarian auxiliaries are among the Shah of Ishnapur's elite."

"One in seven," Audin agreed. "Or that's the story—that every seventh Jhainarian child is given to the legions that serve the Shah."

"That sounds like a tribute," Malian said. The others looked surprised, but then most of them nodded.

Raven, a few horse lengths ahead, turned in his saddle. "Think about it from Jhaine's point of view," he suggested. "The country is mostly plains and they've borders with Ishnapur, Lathayra, southern Aralorn, *and* Emer. A tribute could be worthwhile to buy peace with their largest neighbor and a strong military alliance to deter the others from war." He shrugged his mailed shoulders. "Besides, although it may have been a straight-out tribute once, back in the dark years, now I think Ishnapur obtains equal benefit from having a stable northern border."

Malian let her horse move up alongside his as their cavalcade halted to let the two smaller companies pass through the crossroads first. The Lathayrans' faces were dour beneath conical, fur-trimmed helmets and they all sported long moustaches trailing down to clean-shaven chins. Malian supposed they must have armor in their packs, just as the Normarch party did in the wagons, but for now the visitors wore loose coats of leather and wool, and trousers tucked into knee-high boots. All bore swords, some with straight blades but others curved; white most carried bows and long, slender lances.

"They hunt wild beasts with those lances," Raven said, "always from horseback."

"You've been there?" Malian asked. "To Lathayra?"

Raven nodded. "It's a wild, bloody realm, just as Emer used to be before the Sondargent dukes began to impose their peace. I've also soldiered with Lathayran companies-for-hire in other places."

The Allerion company, a strong showing of heavy cavalry and longbowmen, was passing now, and two knights turned off to speak with Lord Bonamark and his captain. "The truce of Midsummer prevails," Raven said, "but Lord Allerion will have waited until the Lathyarans came though before dispatching his own people."

"To make *sure* it prevails," Girvase murmured. Unlike Raher, he did not grin, and Malian remembered that he was Ar-Allerion and so kin to the Marklord.

Lord Bonamark let the Allerion knights' dust die down before giving the word to proceed, but there was still too much traffic and Malian had to dampen and retie her face covering every other hour. "Mud in winter, dust in summer," Ado said, shrugging, but Malian sighed for the paved Main Road that ran the length of the River, and envied Ghiselaine and her companions who would complete the rest of the journey by water.

They first glimpsed Caer Argent in the late afternoon, sunshine flashing off the city's famous spires as they emerged from an avenue of oak trees that spanned the road. The river flashed, too, a broad ribbon that bent across the Argent vale, bisecting a tapestry of orchards and fields, villages and great houses, that merged gradually into the haze of city roofs. "The ducal palace and Imuln's temple are on an island that was the original Caer Argent," Audin explained, "although the city's expanded to either side now. Mostly to this side, because of Maraval forest to the west, but the tourney and fair grounds are on the Maraval side. That's why it makes sense for us to cross at Argenthithe, rather than going through the city."

The day was beginning to cool before the ladies left the main cavalcade, accompanied by a small escort of knights-at-arms and the Bonamark and Normarch tourney companies. Malian could see Ghiselaine up ahead now, her back spear straight, as it had been all the way south from Normarch, with Alianor and Ilaise riding to either side. Ilaise turned to wave as they entered the poplar-lined avenue that led to the river, but Alianor was drooping, and Malian guessed that with a recently healed wound she was finding the riding hard.

Cicadas whirred and the poplar leaves rustled together although there was almost no breeze. Across the fields, Malian could see workers making their way home and towers of mellow stone rising above a low hill. She wondered what Lord Tenneward's lodge would be like—and almost laughed out loud, a few minutes later, as the avenue ended in gates with stone lions, the entrance framing a house that looked larger than Normarch castle. The lodge was built of pale yellow stone, with tall windows and a creeper twining across its face. Stables and mews and kennels, all in the same yellow stone, were set on the far side of a wide graveled courtyard to the right of the house.

"The Tenneward pier and the barges are on the far side of the lodge," Audin said. He brushed at the layered dust on his jacket. "I take it we're expected, although I don't think Lord Tenneward's here, since there's no standard flying."

In the end it was Lord Tenneward's steward, a graying, slightly built man of middle height, who greeted them. He bowed low to both Lady Bonamark and Ghiselaine, and pointed out the stables and storage barns to the captains, together with a guardhouse set off to one side. Jarna rubbed her sleeve across her forehead. "Rich," she whispered.

Ado nodded, looking around as though he expected the whole place to vanish in the shift between light and shadow. "And this is just a lodge."

"Welcome to Caer Argent," Raven said dryly, before taking Ado, Jarna, and Kalan with him to stable the horses and secure the baggage wagons. The steward sent pages in Tenneward buff and russet to hold the ladies' horses as they dismounted, then lift down the bags from behind their saddles. Grooms led the horses away afterward, following Raven and the others, but a great many retainers remained gathered in both hall and yard. Malian was puzzled by their numbers until Lady Bonamark began to mount the lodge steps, her hand resting on the arm of her escort captain. Audin stepped forward and extended his hand to Ghiselaine, who placed her fingers on his—and a low murmur ran through the gathered servants as they shifted forward like a wave, falling back again as Audin and Ghiselaine followed Lady Bonamark to the lodge door. The steward and the servants with him all bowed very low.

Of course, Malian thought, waiting at the foot of the steps with the rest of the company: they all want to see their future duchess. She wondered what they would make of the reserved, almost stern young woman who had returned to Normarch after the ill-fated Summer's Eve expedition—but if the Tennewarders saw anything amiss, they did not show it in face or gesture. Ilaise shifted slightly, and Malian saw that Alianor was leaning against her friend's shoulder, her eyes closed.

The steward smiled as he rose from his bow. "Countess," he said. "Lord Hirluin has sent a gift for you—a welcome to Caer Argent."

Lady Bonamark's dark, strongly marked brows lifted. "He did not come himself?"

"No, my lady, although he is expected back from the Eastern March for the tourney. But he sends this welcome cup, as his pledge to the Countess of Ormond."

"A pretty gesture," Lady Bonamark said approvingly. Audin's smile looked a little stiff—but he was the Duke's nephew and born to this game; no question that he knew how to play. Malian studied the young girl who was walking to meet Ghiselaine, a great cup held carefully in front of her. She looked a little like the steward and her dark hair was bound back by a silver ribbon. Her face was pale—with excitement, Malian guessed—and she kept her eyes lowered. The cup she bore was smooth yellow gold with a white-gold rim, the surface engraved with lilies and oak leaves twined together. A nice detail, Malian thought: he knows how to make a gesture anyway, this Hirluin.

The girl sank down in the curtsey one makes to royalty, her lashes cast down against pale cheeks and her hands shaking a little as she extended the great chalice above her head. Ghiselaine was smiling as she drew off her travel-stained gloves, and a long ray from the sinking sun reached out and touched the cup. The gold shimmered in the burnished light, and Malian blinked against a dark afterdazzle as she caught the aroma of spiced wine: the heavy tang snatched at the back of her throat. Ghiselaine's hands reached out, white and slender, to take their place on either side of the girl's and lift the cup—and Malian hurtled up the lodge steps, knocking the vessel aside.

"The cup is poisoned," she said, as the Tenneward retainers cried out, and Girvase and Raher raced up the steps behind her. "And the wine," she added, although those close enough could already see the spilled liquid eating into the stone steps. Even the glancing blow to the cup had eaten through Malian's coat and shirtsleeve and into the leather armguard below. The girl remained kneeling, her dark head bowed forward.

"What in—" Lady Bonamark began, then broke off as a servant began to wail.

"The girl," Ghiselaine said, and knelt, but Malian was ahead of her, putting out an arm to hold the countess back—because she did not see how the girl's bare, unmarked hands could have held that cup. The girl's head was still bowed to her chest and she had not moved or spoken since the cup was knocked aside. Malian hesitated, then slipped off her coat and wrapped it around her hand, before lifting the girl's chin—but the young body slumped sideways as soon as the cloaked hand touched her.

Mindburned, Malian thought, tilting the girl's head to stare into the seared, empty eyes: someone must have kept the girl animated until she delivered the cup.

In the background, she was aware of Raven and Kalan arriving at a run. "She's dead," she said, spreading her coat to cover the girl's face while her eyes darted from yard to rooftop, alert for concealed archers. "We need to get Ghis into cover and secure the lodge," she added sharply. "And send word to the Duke."

# 31

# Tenneward Lodge

"**Y**ou don't think Lord Hirluin really sent it, do you?" Audin asked. Kalan thought that he had never seen him look so haggard, not even during the hill fort siege.

Lady Bonamark shook her head. "Highly unlikely, I should think. I can see nothing for your cousin to gain by it, Lord Audin, and a great deal for him to lose."

They were in the lodge's library, a room that looked as though it saw little use. But it had heavy wooden doors that could be closed against the uproar in the rest of the house, where the steward and servants were all under guard. Kalan himself had pulled the velvet curtains against the dusk and prying eyes, before returning to the table where Ser Amain, Lady Bonamark's captain, was seated at his Marklady's right. Audin sat opposite him, with Kalan around the table to his left, and Malian and Ser Raven on his right.

Kalan sighed inwardly, wishing it could have been Alianor or Girvase at the table instead of him. But Alianor was too tired for this sort of conference, and Girvase wanted to stay close to Alli, so it had been logical to leave them with Ghiselane. Covertly, Kalan glanced at Malian, almost certain that she had managed to conceal Nhenir in the rooms given over to Ghiselaine and her companions. He hadn't noticed anything obvious, but knew that it would take considerable focus to detect the Helm of Secrecy when it did not choose to be seen. And its presence would give Malian ears into Ghiselaine's rooms, if ears were needed.

This time, Kalan frowned to himself rather than sighing. He had always disliked the idea that the Shadow Band of Ar, created to fight the fire of poison and daggers in the dark with matching fire, was the best training ground for Malian's power. But he had to admit that she had served both Emer and Ghiselaine well today.

*"The cup must have been warded against Oakward detection."* Kalan shared the thought with Malian. His bond to her was strong enough for him to know that she had heard, although she gave no sign, maintaining Maister Carick's grave outward demeanor.

"I agree," Audin was saying, but Kalan, who knew him, could tell how deeply unhappy he was. "Not that I know Hirluin well . . . Yet whoever sent the cup must be close to my uncle's inner circle, enough to know that we would be stopping here."

"What I'm wondering," Ser Amain said, his gaze fixed on Malian, "is why a River scholar could perceive what no one else here did?"

The inevitable question, Kalan thought, seeing the echo of the knight's query in Audin's face and Lady Bonamark's scrutiny. Knowledge of poisons and their antidotes was one of Karn's arts, of course, but Malian couldn't tell them that—or what she had already told him, which was that she had seen the dark afterdazzle of the warding spell when the cup caught the light. Right now, though, her expression was all Maister Carick, a mix of diffidence and apology.

"On the River," she said, "poison is widely used by assassins sworn to the Ijiri School. So detecting their use is taught as well, and was part of my study in Ar—and the wine in the cup was heavily spiced, a favorite disguise of River poisoners."

"Is that who you suspect here?" Lady Bonamark asked. "River assassins?"

Malian shook her head. "It's not a River poison. It was

only the heavy spice that alerted me. From my brief study of the cup I would guess Ishnapuri—or possibly something originating from the great deserts. But I will have to test it to be sure."

She's so calm, Kalan thought—maintaining that diffident exterior with everyone.

Ser Amain pursed his lips. "Ishnapur, you say? A group of their merchants traveled through Emer, early in the spring."

"An Ishnapuri poison does not mean that citizens of Ishnapur brought it here." Malian's tone remained that of the River scholar who has some knowledge, but does not wish to instruct. "One only needs access to those who trade in such things."

"But whoever it is," Audin said slowly, "will almost certainly have had watchers here, waiting to report back."

*"Who will have seen you act,"* Kalan observed to Malian, letting his unhappiness on that score color his mindtone.

"Yes," Malian said, and he knew that she was answering both observations.

"And may well strike again before anyone can reach us from Caer Argent." Lady Bonamark looked from Ser Amain to Raven. "Are we prepared for that?"

Both knights nodded, and the next few moments were a discussion of resources and their disposition—keeping the Tenneward servants under guard in one area, and restricting their own use of the lodge to its most defensible wing. Watches, it was agreed, would be kept throughout the night, with one of the two knights always awake and in command at all times.

"Although there's still that business of the girl," Ser Amain said finally. "Looking alive, but really being dead or the next best thing to it—that's the stuff of Oakward fables."

"Not what we expect to encounter in our everyday world," Lady Bonamark agreed, standing up. "We shall have to hope that keen eyes and sharp steel are enough to get us through." But there was no mistaking the uneasiness in her voice.

"I've got a psychic ward up around this part of the lodge,"

Girvase told Kalan, when he reached the landing of the wing they had decided was most defensible. Malian was still in the library, studying the cup; Lady Bonamark had retired to her rooms with her own ladies; and Ser Amain and Ser Raven were discussing watch details in the hall below. "Nothing's touched it yet."

Kalan peered out the lead-paned window to where the lingering dusk had finally become fully dark, with a fine mist drifting off the river. He let his mind touch Girvase's shield, but could only make out night sounds: the scampering of mice beneath a hedgerow and the stealthy passage of a fox. "Nothing may happen," he said finally. "But we should plan otherwise."

Girvase nodded. "I wish Lord Falk had come, or Erron."

I wonder why they didn't? Kalan asked himself. The Northern March was fragile, and the Oakward was always located at the point of greatest danger from the use or abuse of magic, but still . . . Are we bait? Kalan wondered. Or is this a test, either for us or for Malian? He shivered, thinking that if it was, then the Oakward was gambling high, with Ghiselaine and the peace of Emer at stake.

"Audin's gone in to see Ghis," Girvase told him, "but Ado's outside the door. Jarna and Raher are watching the entrance to the adjoining wing."

"Ser Raven wants someone on both the inside and outside of the girls' door," Kalan replied, "so we're going to be stretched." He turned back to the stairwell as the library door opened, and a moment later Ser Raven and Malian came up the stairs together, while Ser Amain's footsteps retreated across the hall. Kalan nodded to Girvase and followed Malian and Ser Raven into the main chamber set aside for Ghiselaine's use. Audin was by the window, looking drawn, while Ghiselaine sat by the fire, the fall of her hair shielding her face. Ilaise stood behind her chair, and Alianor sat on a stool opposite, her chin propped on her hands. Both damosels looked around as the door opened, an identical wariness in their expressions.

Ghiselaine turned as well, then straightened and stood up.

"Maister Carick," she said, extending both hands to Malian, "You saved my life, I believe. But not just my life. If what was done to that poor child is any indication, my death, once I took the cup, would have been painful—but not slow."

Kalan wondered if anyone else in the room caught Malian's slight hesitation before she spoke. "There was a compulsion on it," she said then, as if understanding that Ghiselaine needed to hear the truth. "You could not have put the chalice down, and once you held it you would have *wanted* to drink, despite whatever warning others cried out."

"And the liquid?" Audin asked harshly.

Malian met his eyes. "We all saw it on the stones."

"From now on, all your food must be checked before you eat." Alianor sounded as exhausted as she looked. "We must suspect everyone, Ghis."

"How long will it go on?" Ghiselaine whispered. "Will it end with the formal betrothal ceremony? Or the marriage? Or only with my death?" She pressed her hands to her face and spoke through them, her voice muffled. "And there's no way back. Renouncing the marriage would tear Emer as far apart as my death by murder, or even misadventure." She took her hands away and looked from Alianor to Audin. "Can we assume that division *is* the purpose, rather than simply my death—that this is not just some long held grudge against Ormond?"

"Not when it would do such damage to Emer," the Duke's nephew replied grimly.

"You reason as a sane man," Raven pointed out, from where he had remained by the door. "Someone consumed by the desire for revenge may not see anything beyond the purpose that eats away until it is fulfilled."

They were all silent, and the crackle of flames from the hearth grew loud in the pause. "Still," Kalan said finally, "division seems most likely." He wondered if Malian, too, was thinking of the Swarm and what the heralds had told them of events in Ij during the early spring. And there were plenty of old enmities for Darkswarm agents to draw on, lying just below the surface of a newly unified Emer. "We don't know what alliances have been made or what drives them. But if we lose you, Ghis, we lose the game." He narrowed his eyes, calculating odds. "I'm picking, though, that every step you can get through—the formal betrothal, the marriage—will see you safer."

"When you have a child that is heir equally to Caer Argent and Ormond," Audin said, sounding as though every word cost him considerable effort, "the threat may fade completely."

Ghiselaine frowned at him, her lower lip caught between her teeth. "But pass to my child?"

No one said anything—because, Kalan thought, that risk could not be ruled out, depending on who had been behind the cup. In the end, it was Alianor who spoke. "The risk will never completely fade, but the longer you and Lord Hirluin are together, and once you have children . . ." The damosel shrugged. "I believe many more people will see the Duke's hope of a lasting peace and want it for themselves."

Ghiselaine continued to frown, then shook her head as if to clear it. "Alli, look at you. You need to rest."

The dark-haired damosel nodded. "We all do. You, too, Ghis. But I think we should have two people awake at all times—the guard and one other." Someone to watch the watcher, Kalan guessed, as Alianor's gaze shifted to Malian. "Maister Carick, would you stay here in the outer room and share the watch with Ilaise?"

Ser Raven's gaze went to Malian as well, but he did not dispute Alianor's plan. "Hamar, you take first guard here," was all he said. "Lord Audin will relieve you, and Girvase can take the final watch."

So we all know who should be in here and when, Kalan thought, although it won't help much if there's another face-stealer in our midst. He recalled Malisande's dead face again, and Maister Gervon's mad eyes, and felt repulsion twist his gut. But he nodded with the rest, and Ser Raven left, taking Audin with him.

Kalan watched with a certain degree of amusement as Ilaise bought out quilts from the adjoining room for herself

and Malian, before entering the second chamber himself—
ostensibly to check the window catches, but really to set
additional wards over both the casement and the room. Once
he returned to the main chamber, careful to leave the adjoining door half open, Kalan took up Ser Raven's former station
by the door. Malian was lying on the window seat with her
hands behind her head, while Ilaise snuffed out the candles
one by one.

When she was done, the damosel settled down in front of
the fire and wrapped herself in a quilt. She lay quite still for
a short time then sat up, looking at Kalan with an expression
that he could see quite clearly through the shadows but found
difficult to read. "D'you think Lord Hirluin really sent the
cup and someone took advantage of that?" she asked him.
"Or was it all just a ploy?"

Kalan shook his head. "I don't know."

Ilaise sighed. "It seemed such a pretty gesture, like Lady
Bonamark said. And I saw Lord Hirluin once, before I
went to Normarch. He's young, still, and handsome. Good-
natured, too, my mother said." Ilaise sighed again. "Like
Audin. Not that it would matter if he wasn't. Even if he had
a bad temper or a mouth full of rotten teeth, still Ghiselaine
must make this marriage and smile for the world."

Malian spoke from the window seat. "I thought, when I
first came to Normarch, that you didn't like her."

Ilaise shifted under the blanket. "I thought I didn't. My
family's holdings are in Lyonmark, on Ormond's western
border, so there's the traditional enmity. And Ghis is so beautiful and everyone likes her—I told myself it was because she
was going to be Duchess and they were just currying favor.
I knew it wasn't true, but I still thought it."

"Until the ambush and flight to The Leas," Malian said.

The yellow head nodded. "And now this. They'll make
her into little better than a prisoner, just to keep her alive."

Perhaps she is anyway, Kalan thought: a hostage for Ormond's good behavior, even though the warfare ended before
she was born. A log snapped in the grate, sending up sparks,
and Ilaise shrugged.

"Mind you, if my family requires it I may have to make the same sort of marriage—one where it won't really matter what I want. Love is just for songs and the courtly tales, although we all like to pretend."

Kalan's thoughts went instantly to Audin—and then to Jarna, remembering the first time he had seen her, a rawboned girl trying to look brave, perched on top of one great horse and leading another. He had felt sorry for her then, with Ser Bartrand determined to make her pay in sweat and bruises, broken bones, even, for her grandfather's decision to send her to Normarch. A rush of fellow feeling for anyone thrust into an unwelcome life had followed—together with his conscious decision to befriend her, knowing that Audin would agree and that the rest of the squires would follow their lead. Kalan found it more difficult to pinpoint when the nature of his friendship with Jarna had changed, but sometime over this past winter camaraderie had flowered from the usual storytelling and jokes around the squires' fire, into something more.

A springtime love, Kalan thought now. It was one of the oldest traditions in the knightly history of Emer, with a cycle of songs composed around both the tradition and some of the more famous lovers. He tried to imagine either the tradition or the songs transported to the Derai Wall, and failed. He could not help grinning, though, just thinking about it—although his grin faded when he reflected how much *he* did not want to return to the Derai world. I don't belong there either, Kalan thought restlessly, any more than an Emerian lament for springtime love dues.

He must have moved, because he felt the cool, smoky touch of Malian's eyes through the firelit dark, although she did not speak. It will be the same for her as for Ghiselaine, he thought, once she returns to the Wall and reclaims her place as Heir of Night. With so few of Night's Blood left, she will have to marry to strengthen her House's position in the Derai Alliance—and the choice of bridegroom will come down to bloodlines, as well as who can bring the most spears to the battlefront, or votes to the council table.

Assuming, he reflected grimly, that she *can* reclaim her

position as Heir: without followers at her back, or the arms of Yorindesarinen, her chances are not particularly good. And even if the Lost *will* follow her . . . Kalan had to stop himself from shaking his head, because they would still be priest-kind in a world that had cast them out. As I will be, too, he added grimly.

Ilaise, he saw, was still watching him through the gloom. "Springtime love," she said softly, as though her thoughts had marched with his. "But already it's Midsummer."

Kalan felt the tug of her uncharacteristic melancholy—the feeling that the good times had already slipped away. Maybe they have, he thought, still grim, but not if I can help it. "Go to sleep, Illy," he said gently. "I can't keep watch if you're talking to me."

The Ilaise from before The Leas would have tossed her head and pouted, but now she simply nodded and lay back down, pulling the quilt almost over her head. Kalan tested the edge of his psychic shield again, extending it beyond the walls of the lodge. The mist was growing thicker as the night cooled, lying in thick banks across the grounds and surrounding fields. Inside the house, all was dark and quiet as well, although Kalan's keen ears caught suppressed sobbing from the hall where the Tenneward retainers were being held. A woman, he thought, concentrating briefly: a relative of the dead girl, he supposed—and wanted to curse those who would use an innocent so ruthlessly.

He focused on Malian instead, her face turned to look out the window. *"Has your seeking found anything?"* he asked, and saw the slightest shake of her head: no.

Maybe, Kalan thought, we'll be all right after all. Almost immediately, he felt sleepy from the long day's ride on top of three weeks steady travel, followed by the tension and fear surrounding the poisoned cup. He concentrated on keeping his eyes open, as wary of the waking visions of the Gate of Dreams as he was of falling asleep while on guard. To keep himself alert, he checked the bounds of his shield again—and thought he heard a hound bay, somewhere beyond the banks of mist.

*No.* Kalan forced his eyelids wider apart, conscious of Yorindesarinen's gift ring, with its black pearl caught amidst strands of plaited metal, lying like a weight against his heart. It was too fine a jewel for Hamar Sondsangre, from the modest manor of Aldermere, to wear—or so he had told himself, keeping it sewn into the breast of his coat all these years.

And right now, he thought grimly, is not the time to step beyond those mists: not without other Oakward here to anchor me to the oak forest that is the Emerian route through the Gate of Dreams.

"There's something there," Malian said, so quietly that even Kalan almost did not hear her as she rose to her feet. Automatically, he glanced at Iliase, but the rise and fall of her breath was even and she did not stir. A floorboard creaked, loud in the silence, as he joined Malian at the window and looked out. The scene below reflected the world that his psychic shield had conveyed: banks of mist lying above the grounds of Tenneward lodge and extending into the avenue they had ridden along that afternoon. The mist was thickest on the lawn beyond the perimeter of his shield, and as Kalan watched, the heart of the whiteness began to drift apart. He narrowed his eyes.

*"Is it a cairn?"* he asked uncertainly.

"Yes. But it's not really here." Malian's voice was still very soft.

No, Kalan thought, his keen eyes peering through the mist to what looked like a shingle plain, with a stone cairn rising out of it. He knew it was not anywhere in Emer. A dog lay before the cairn, the line of its body expressing weary resignation. At first Kalan thought it was a stone beast, carved to lie before the memorial, but then he saw its fur riffle in whatever wind blew there.

"I think it's the Gray Lands," Malian continued slowly, "and this is Rowan Birchmoon's grave, with one of her hounds keeping vigil."

Was that a catch in her voice? Kalan wondered. She had seemed so emotionless about the Winter woman's death up until now, both when she first spoke of it in the hill fort, and the few times they had discussed it since. As though the honor and duty she had invoked in relation to the death really belonged to someone else, some Malian other than the one who spoke and breathed in the everyday world.

Kalan stared at the cairn, recalling the first and only time he had seen the Winter woman: a rider cloaked in white and seated on a white horse amidst falling snow, with a hawk resting still as stone on her forearm. In Jaransor, he thought—and was seized by the loss, pain, and terror, mixed with exhilaration, that had accompanied their flight through those hills. He clenched his hand hard around his sword hilt to stop himself crying out against the memories' sharpness. The metal of pommel and guard pressed into flesh, cold as the snowflakes that had fallen from an iron sky, five years before. He had thought they might die in that snow, but instead Rowan Birchmoon had opened the door into winter that saved them.

From the Swarm as well as the blizzard, Kalan thought now—and without her strange power, and her sponsorship amongst the Winter people, I might never have come into Emer. His anger licked, bright as a flame in thatch, because what he remembered most from their one brief meeting was not Rowan Birchmoon's power, but her gentleness.

I acknowledge my debt, he said silently, staring at the cairn: I will not forget. He allowed the flame to lick again, then as deliberately let it cool, like water tempering a blade. *"An opening from Emer into the Gray Lands?"* he queried Malian. *"I thought that was impossible without resorting to force?"*

"Nothing is impossible," Malian said, although her tone suggested a frown. "The Gray Lands are not the full Wall, and she was of Haarth, but still . . ."

Still, thought Kalan, watching the mist begin to draw together again—and felt a darkness touch the rim of his shield. He closed a warning hand on Malian's shoulder, but she nodded, indicating that her seeker's sense had picked up the same presence.

Of course, he thought. She has lived as a Dancer of Kan. How better to hone a seeker's sense to danger wrapped in night's shadows? *"There,"* he said, catching the faintest hint of movement beneath a mist-wreathed tree. A moment later a tall, cloak-wrapped figure stepped from beneath it and stared toward the lodge.

"There's more." Malian spoke on a half breath, and a split second later Kalan sensed them, too: four more cloak-shrouded figures emerging to watch the house. "I have seen their kind before, I think," Malian added. "Within the Gate of Dreams on Summer's Eve . . . But perhaps before that as well, at Normarch."

Darkswarm, then. Kalan's heartbeat drummed as the figures began to glide toward the lodge. In just a few more paces they would encounter the psychic barrier of his shield—and they already knew about the Oakward. He had to assume that they had come prepared.

A greater darkness brushed across his mind, like cloud across the moon—and both mist and night billowed apart, a formless darkness pressing through. It reminded Kalan, just a little, of the inchoate darkness they had encountered on the mountainside during the dark of the moon, the one that had tried to lure Malian—in her guise as Maister Carick—to her death over a cliff.

*"Do you see it?"* Even Kalan's mindvoice was a whisper, but he felt the dark mind regard him—as though my shield isn't even there, he thought, his heart lurching. Except that this new power did not appear more than momentarily interested in either him or his shield. Its focus was on the cloaked figures, and Kalan felt their fear, but also their rage. A wild, sharp-edged bolt of power surged out of them toward the lodge, but the formless dark rolled along the edge of his shield like a black fog, absorbing the blast. He sensed cloaked figures dismay as they stepped raggedly back, then began to melt away into the trees. The darkness followed, blending with the deep shadows between the fog drifts until the whiteness roiled, rising up around the cloaked figures. When it settled again, the night was empty.

"They're gone." Kalan could hear the confusion in Malian's voice. "An intervention," she added, as though repeating something heard elsewhere. Or perhaps she was just responding to Nhenir, speaking for her mind alone. "But why?"

Kalan shook his head, reflecting that they already suspected the Swarm of divergent purposes. But as to why—he shook his head again, then stiffened. *"Look."*

Malian peered out, and this time Kalan saw her frown. A tall figure had emerged from the shadows of the lodge entrance, to the left of the window where they stood. Kalan could hear gravel crunch as he walked to the edge of the lawn and stopped, looking toward where the cloaked figures and the dark power had disappeared. "Raven," Malian said.

She never called him Ser, Kalan noted, when she spoke of the knight away from the others. *"He must have been there all along."*

"He can smell magic." Malian spoke almost absently. "That's what he said when we first met. So he would have picked up on the Swarm minions' arrival."

Kalan frowned, trying to think who amongst the powers of Haarth had that ability, but couldn't recall anything from the Oakward's lore. In much the same way as the formless darkness had done, the knight below seemed to feel their attention, for he turned and looked up, his shadowed regard meeting theirs where they stood, shoulder-to-shoulder, gazing down at him.

# 32

## *Cockcrow*

"*What* was *that darkness?*" Malian asked Nhenir, when Raven had walked back into the house and Kalan resumed his post by the door.

"*A power,*" the helm replied, at its most uncommunicative, its voice a chime of ice through the midnight room.

"*A Darkswarm power?*" she persisted, and received the mental equivalent of a nod in reply. Of course, she thought: those others would not have gone without a fight otherwise. But why would a Darkswarm power intervene against its own?

She fretted at that thought, and the puzzling window that had opened onto what she guessed was Rowan Birchmoon's tomb, until her eyelids grew heavy. Her slumber, too, was uneasy and her dreams restless. She glimpsed a solitary tower, squat against a green wood. A storm of wings rose on the wind's back, blotting out the sky as the dream changed into dust, swirling above an empty road.

The landscape surrounding the road was drear, with a thin, unhappy wind whistling across a stony plain and prying at Malian's clothes. The cairn she had seen through the mist stood directly in front of her now, with the same hound lying before it. The beast lifted its head as she drew near—as though it, too, *is in the dream*, Malian thought, *or can see me through it.*

"Falath," she said, and the hound whined, deep in his throat. "You must be an old hound now." In the dream, she rubbed his head as she had when they were both younger and dwelt in the Keep of Winds. Falath thumped his feathery tail.

You saved me five years ago, Malian said to the silent tomb, but could not save yourself from the hostility of the Derai. Or chose not to, she added, drawing Falath's ears gently through her dream fingers. She was almost surprised at the ache in her throat

*A pebble has fallen.* Malian repeated the traditional phrase to herself. But why this pebble? And why now, after so long?

"*Why?*" A voice echoed her thought, speaking from behind the wind. "*What did they hope to achieve?*" Malian recognized Haimyr's intonation, even though her dreamscape remained empty of anything except the cairn and the hound.

"*What they have, perhaps.*" Asantir, thought Malian. Falath, too, lifted his head. "*The marriage alliance Night needs, which would not happen while he kept her with him. 'Polluting keep and hold' was the way one of the Sons of Blood put it. Forthright perhaps—but none of our allies liked her presence here.*"

"*And so she was murdered.*" Malian could almost see Haimyr's remote, dreamy expression. "*Three arrows in the back and one in the throat, Garan said.*"

"*I did not say it was right,*" Asantir replied, in the quiet, even tone that Malian remembered so well. "*But you asked why.*"

The wind gusted, stirring up grit. When it died away Haimyr was still speaking. "*. . . and the killers?*" Did he hesitate? Malian wondered. "*Garan said you hunted them down yourself?*"

"*Blood demands blood.*" Asantir's voice bore echoes of the stone plain and the unceasing wind that blew across it. "*And they were Honor Guard yet betrayed Earl and oaths. Justice needed to be seen to be done, and done swiftly.*"

"*And those who set them on to the deed?*" Haimyr asked.

*"I have not found them,"* Asantir replied. *"Yet."* The wind gusted again, mournful, and Asantir spoke softly beneath its plaint. *"He loved her. I would kill them for that reason, even if I had not called her friend myself."*

*"We cannot get the dog to leave."* Malian did not recognize the new speaker. *"But Teron's people, out of Cloud Hold, have been bringing it food."*

*"Teron's people?"* Malian could hear Haimyr's astonishment. *"He despises outsiders."*

*"Yet wept when the Winter woman fell."* Asantir's tone was impossible to read. *"Although perhaps only for the Earl's sake. But his clan honors loyalty above all else."*

The wind blew more strongly, swirling grit in clouds, and Falath's head sank back onto his paws. "Farewell my braveheart," Malian said, knowing that the dream was either changing again, or ending.

She turned away, but another voice spoke out of the heart of the cairn, ominous as distant thunder: *"There is always a price . . . And now Winter's heart lies buried in these gray lands, Winter's blood soaked into barren ground."*

Malian found it impossible to sleep again after that. She lay silent, watching the darkness beyond the window while Audin replaced Kalan on watch, and then Girvase, bleary eyed from only a few hours' sleep, took Audin's place. Eventually she got up and went to the small table, lighting a candle and opening up her wallet to search for the handful of Imulni amulets she had bought from Ar, companion to those crafted by the priests of Seruth. She drew out the little tangle and began to unravel the threads, aware that Girvase was watching her. "What are you doing?" he asked finally.

He was in service to the Oakward, Malian thought—and he had seen what happened with the cup. She knew he would work it out soon, if he had not done so already. "I am working on amulets for the damosels," she said. "Ones that will resemble favors of Imuln, the sort that priestesses give out."

"Like the ones you used against the wolfpack?" Girvase

asked. "I always thought," he added slowly, "that they were remarkably effective for Serruti charms."

"Adepts of the Shadow Band learn these things," Alianor said, from the doorway of the adjoining room. She was wrapped in a quilt, with her dark hair loose down her back.

Girvase's eyes rested on her, their expression softening, and Alianor smiled back at him. Briefly, Malian felt—What, she wondered. Envy? Regret? She shook her head at herself as Alianor moved to the window.

"Lord Falk said that we could tell Gir if it became necessary," the damosel said. A little belatedly, she glanced at Ilaise by the fire.

"Don't worry she's still asleep," she said. "But I imagine a lot of people will begin to speculate, if the business with the cup gets about." She shrugged and held up one of the amulets. "If you wear these, the charm I'm working should be strong enough to warn you of another poisoned cup, or the dagger in a hand that seems well-disposed. You can tell the world that the three of you wear them as friendship tokens."

Alianor looked over her shoulder, her gray eyes serious. "Thank you." Her fingers drummed briefly on the sill as she returned her attention to the shadowed pane, her reflected expression a mix of doubt and resolution.

Somewhere in the lodge grounds a cock crowed, to be answered almost immediately by another nearby. Malian let her seeker's sense follow it, extending her awareness as a third bird called from a greater distance. Lords on their dunghills, she thought, smiling to herself—and then her hands stilled as she sensed the reverberation of horses' hooves, drumming on the earth. A great many horses, she decided, approaching from the direction of Caer Argent.

Malian kept her mind tuned to them while she finished the bindings on the amulets. The lodge cock crowed again and Ilaise sat up, stretching and yawning, as Ghiselaine came to the connecting door. Unlike Alianor, she was already fully dressed and her fingers were busy, binding her hair into a long braid. She studied Malian, the smudges beneath her eyes pronounced. "Have you slept at all, Maister Carick?"

"Not a great deal," Malian replied, and the young Countess nodded.

"Nor I," she replied softly, going to stand beside Alianor at the casement. "I can't get that child from yesterday out of my head. And as soon as I closed my eyes I saw the others, all the dead from our ill-fated expedition."

"The glamor," Alianor began, but Ghiselaine shook her head sharply.

"No. I'm sure there was a glamor, working on us all, but I *wanted* to go. I longed for an adventure—just once, before we came here and the door closed on the gilded cage. So I persuaded myself that Erron was being overly cautious and denying the others their opportunity because of me. But really, I wanted the adventure for myself—and closed my mind to the truth that if there was a threat, I would be the last to pay the price."

"Oh, Ghis," Alianor said, and rested one arm across her friend's shoulder, her dark head pressed close to Ghiselaine's bright one. "We were all part of it. We all wanted to go just as much as you did. It would be arrogant, you know," she added gravely, "to take it all on yourself."

Ghiselaine nodded, her smile crooked. "All the same, it might have been easier if Ser Raven *had* knocked me off my horse, after The Leas."

Alianor squeezed her shoulders. "Sent the Countess of Ormond and future Duchess of Emer sprawling in the dust? I think he is too wise for that."

"Besides," said Ilaise, sitting up and stretching, "from what the boys say of his blows when training, I don't think that would have helped at all."

Girvase grinned and looked as though he was going to speak, but Malian got up abruptly and went to the window, peering at the graying world. "Did you hear something?" she asked, although she already knew that the approaching riders had turned off the main road and into the poplar avenue. The others shook their heads as she unlatched the casement, but then they all heard the rumble of hooves, moving at a smart pace. Girvase crossed the room in two swift paces and leaned out, before striding back to the hall door. "Riders coming!" he shouted, flinging it open, and the next minute the sleeping lodge was an uproar of shouting voices and running feet.

"Let's hope it's friends," Ghiselaine said, half under breath, and Malian guessed that could have a double meaning, given that she was Countess of Ormond, the longstanding enemy of Caer Argent.

The damosels disappeared into the bedchamber to dress, while Malian descended to the landing window in time to see a lancer unit in green and black clatter into the yard. All wore the oak of Emer displayed on the front and back of their doublets, and the black plumes on their captain's helmet riffled in the breeze. "Those are ducal colors," Audin said, pausing on his way down the stairs. "Maybe my uncle's come himself."

A few moments later the yard was full of a trampling, colorful mass of riders—as many as fifty of them, Malian thought, and mostly men, although the few women in their rich riding habits and ornate headdresses stood out. They were all laughing and talking together and looked far more like a hunting or picnic party than an escort into Caer Argent: The throng began to settle as Ser Amain and Raven emerged from the lodge, and a space opened up around a central group of riders.

The foremost horseman was bareheaded, with a coronal around closely cropped hair, and Malian caught the glitter of gilded mail beneath a black jupon that bore an oak tree in gold across its breast. Caril Sondargent, Duke of Emer, Malian guessed, noting the authoritative lift of the iron-gray head. The body beneath the black jupon had thickened with age, but he looked powerful still, although well worn—as you would expect of the man who had ruled Emer since he was seventeen, cementing the peace that was the last long battle of his father's and grandfather's wars.

The woman on the Duke's right wore the deep blue robe and veiled headdress of a priestess of Imuln, while the man to his left was younger and richly dressed in a wide-sleeved tunic of mulberry silk. The sleeves were turned back to show their embroidered black lining, and the full tunic was slit from thigh to ankle, revealing the fashionable hose beneath, with one leg mulberry like the robe, the other black.

A peacock, Malian thought, amused to find a style favored by the great nobility and merchant princes of the River here. She wondered if this was Lord Hirluin—although the Tenneward steward had said that he was still on the Eastern March. The mulberry-clad rider looked taller than the Duke and was fairer of face. More like Audin, Malian decided, with the same mouse-brown hair and clean-cut features, although she could see that one cheekbone was curiously flattened. By a blow, she supposed. Unusually, though, for an Emerian, this man wore his hair long, and flowing loose down his back.

"Ombrose Sondargent," said Kalan. "It has to be."

"With that hair," Girvase agreed. He and Kalan had come down the stairs together, and despite having washed and tidied, both still looked like young men who had spent three weeks on a dusty road.

*"He's the Duke's champion, as well as his nephew,"* Kalan told Malian privately. "He's won the tourney crown for the past three years," he added aloud, "ever since he returned from campaigning in Lathayra."

*"The Sondargent wolf."* Malian heard Elite Cairon's voice in memory, as he handed her the Shadow Band's reports on Emer. *"He gained the epithet in the border confrontation with Lathayra six years ago, where he rose to command the Emerian troops. Although the wolf is also the symbol of his mother's house, the Sondcendre."*

"Somehow, though," Malian said, as Ser Amain spoke to the Duke, "I don't think they're here because of us. We may even be in the nature of an unwelcome surprise."

If they were unwelcome, you would not have thought so from the Duke's manner when he came into the house to greet Ghiselaine and Lady Bonamark. Both he and Ser Ombrose embraced Audin, calling him kinsman, and the Duke listened to the account of the welcome cup incident with a heavy frown. "No messenger reached me," he said. "Who did you send?"

"Two of my knights-at-arms, Your Grace," Lady Bonamark replied. The morning sunlight highlighted her harried expression. "Both reliable men."

The Duke looked at Ser Ombrose. "You had better set an investigation in train. And send for Lord Tenneward so he can put his house to rights." He turned back to Ghiselaine as his champion saluted and went outside. "I am very glad to find you well, Countess, even if we did not know of your situation before arriving here."

Ghiselaine bowed, acknowledging the courtesy. "I am well," she replied formally, "and we shall all be glad to complete our journey. But if I may ask, Duke Caril, what has brought you and so large a company into the Tenneward, so early in the day?"

Just for a moment, Malian—who was watching from the side of the hall with all the Normarch knights except Audin— thought the Duke looked as harassed as Lady Bonamark. But the expression, if she had read it correctly, was gone in an instant and Caril of Emer smiled, apparently completely at his ease. "We ride to meet an embassy," he said, "guests who have come to enjoy our Midsummer fair and the tourney."

"An embassy, sire?" Audin asked. Malian wondered if they were all thinking the same thing: that it must be a great embassy indeed for the Duke to ride out and meet it himself. And why, she wondered, include a high ranking priestess of Imuln in the party, when it was more customary for the priests of Serrut to participate in affairs of the world?

The Duke nodded. "Emer has been greatly honored," he replied smoothly. "For the first time, a queen of Jhaine is attending our Midsummer festival."

"Jhaine!" exclaimed Audin. Lady Bonamark and Ghiselaine looked equally startled. "But why, sire? And surely they'd come from the south, not via the Tenneward?"

The Duke's expression, resting on his nephew, was affectionate. "They *are* coming from the south, but using quiet routes: first north through the southern March, then east across Wymark and Vert. Because the main roads are choked at this season, Ombrose suggested that they detour through Maraval wood and enter the city by river barge—the same route as the Lady Countess." He nodded to Ghiselaine. "As for why—" The powerful shoulders shrugged. "The world is changing, even in Jhaine it seems. Lathayra's a morass of warring entities, and Jhaine's relationship with Aralorn has always been uneasy, so it's not surprising they'd look to us. They seem as interested in expanding trade as anyone else, and say they want to strengthen the bloodlines amongst their horse herds. And with Imuln's worship so strong in Jhaine, Midsummer's the logical time to send their embassy."

"A queen of Jhaine." Audin still looked bemused, but visibly pulled himself together. "I do see why you're riding to greet her yourself, sire."

The Duke nodded. "Under the circumstances, it may be best if you join us. The queen has rested a day at Highvert, but we're to meet her on the far side of Maraval wood at noon. If we ride together, those of us entering Caer Argent by water will form one party—while the contestants can swell our escort and still make their way to the tourney camp later today."

Lady Bonamark looked as though she would much prefer to bypass the honor of another long ride to welcome the Queen of Jhaine, although she did not say so. Ghiselaine glanced quickly at Alianor. "I would gladly join Your Grace," she said, "but Alianor Sondazur has been ill and needs to rest."

"Sondazur, eh? Well, we'll see what Ombrose can contrive." The Duke's gaze switched from Alianor to the rest of the company. "Who else is in your Normarch party?"

Audin glanced at Lady Bonamark, but she gave him a little nod, so he made the introductions: this was Lady Ilaise Sondlyon; this Ser Raven, Lord Falk's captain. The Duke's gaze lingered on Raven, his scrutiny keen, before he moved on to speak briefly with each of the new-made Normarch knights in turn. "And this," Audin said finally, "is Maister Carick, the cartographer from Ar."

Malian bowed, managing scholarly competence but no more than that, and the Duke surveyed her, the keenness back in his expression, before extending his hand. "Maister Carick. I am very glad to have you with us here in Caer Argent at last—and hope there will be no more of the adventures we have been throwing at you."

"From what Ser Amain tells me," Ser Ombrose said, reentering the hall, "it was more a case of the maister throwing himself into the thick of yesterday's events." He looked brutally strong beneath the mulberry silk, Malian thought, with a barrel chest and powerful breadth of shoulder. His cool, blue-gray gaze rested on her briefly before he turned to the Duke. "A serious business, sir, which warrants my staying here—if you can spare me?" He nodded when the Duke agreed, and then a second time when the plan to merge the two companies was set out.

"That would make things easier to manage, at least until Tenneward and more of our own arrive from Caer. But if Lady Bonamark were prepared to stay and lend her knights to my own handpicked few, there's no reason why the damosel Sondazur could not rest here. Not the Countess, though." The champion did not so much as glance at Ghiselaine. "Best if she rides with you."

"In which case," the Duke said briskly, "if we're going to make the Maraval rendezvous and avoid insulting our royal guest, we had better get on the road."

They did not leave straight away, of course. The Duke's retinue was still eating breakfast, while the Normarch company had to saddle their horses and change into apparel suitable for riding to meet a visiting sovereign. Malian clambered into the Normarch wagon and rummaged amongst her gear, pulling on a clean linen shirt and the cartographer's best black coat and short, River-style cape. The coat was fine wool and the cape black velvet. Both would be hot once the early morning coolness burned away, and Malian could almost feel the sweat trickling in anticipation. She thought

briefly about wearing Nhenir, which she had retrieved from
Ghiselaine's rooms, but chose a wide, flat-crowned hat to
keep off the sun.

"Besides," she told the helm, "*I need you to keep an eye
on things here.*"

"*I don't think any enemies will return now,*" Nhenir replied. "*Not after last night.*"

"*Maybe, but I don't want anything happening to Alli.
And,*" Malian added, closing the wagon flap behind her,
"*think on to this and listen for any whisper: what* is *one of
the nine priestess-queens of Jhaine doing in Emer at all?
Because every record the Band has, few as such reports are,
indicates that the priestess-queens are not only forbidden to
leave Jhaine, but also their own temple complexes, under
penalty of death.*"

# 33

# *Maraval*

"*E*xcept in a Great Year," Raher put in, surprising everybody. "Or to make a Great Marriage, whatever that is."

He and the rest of the Normarch company were waiting in the shade of the lodge as Malian crossed the stable yard to rejoin them, dodging the groups of chattering, strolling courtiers and tall horses being walked up and down. Audin, his brows knitted into a frown, had just echoed Malian's observation to Nhenir—that he hadn't thought the priestess-queens *could* leave Jhaine.

Now the others all stared at Raher, while Jarna handed Mallow's rein to Malian.

"Raher—" Kalan broke off, shaking his head. "How do you know anything at all about Jhaine?"

Raher shrugged. "M'father's Lord Castellan of Westermarch."

"Which is not," Audin pointed out, "located anywhere near Jhaine."

"But it's got a border with Lathayra," Raher said. He finished the last of his breakfast bread and cheese and wiped his sleeve across his mouth. "And the Lathayrans have a long border with Jhaine. They like to raid across it, too, although the horsemen of Jhaine make that a risky proposition.

Anyway, that's what the Lathayrans say about Jhaine: it has to be either a Great Year or a Great Marriage—otherwise no one leaves, from the queens down to the commoners."

"Except for the Jhainairian auxiliaries we spoke of yesterday," Girvase said

"So what in Serrut's name," Ado asked plaintively, "is a Great Year? Or a Great Marriage either, for that matter?"

A series of shrugs was his only answer. Malian patted Mallow's neck as the Duke emerged onto the lodge steps, with Ser Ombrose flanking him on one side and Ghiselaine on the other. "Ghiselaine looks beautiful," Jarna said softly.

Both Kalan and Audin glanced around as though surprised by her comment, or perhaps they were just surprised that Jarna had made it. Although it was clearly true: Ghiselaine looked every inch the hereditary ruler of Ormond and the future Duchess of Emer. Her traveling dress was a plain dark blue, but the color set off the red-gold sheen of her hair and brilliance of her complexion. Behind her, Ilaise was carrying a folded silk mantle, its sapphire ground worked with flowers in silver and gold and green, which Malian guessed would only be donned for the actual meeting with the Queen of Jhaine.

"Daisies for Imuln," Audin said, almost as softly as Jarna, but was summoned forward to join the Duke as the cavalcade bustled to mount. A trumpeter blew a merry note and the lancer vanguard moved off down the drive. Duke Caril saluted Ser Ombrose, who remained behind on the steps, then followed the lancers, with the whole colorful, richly clad gathering falling in behind him. Once out the gate, a holiday mood took over and everyone was talking and laughing as they clattered onto the Argenthithe bridge. The horses' hooves rumbled on the timber span while the waters of the Argent flashed and glittered a long way below—and then they were across and weaving their way through narrow country lanes, with Maraval wood a distant smudge along the horizon.

Vertward proper lay on the far side of that wood, Malian knew, with Wymark and the Southern March beyond. And beyond that again, Lathayra and the plains of Jhaine—and finally, Ishnapur. She felt the old magic of the names, luring her, and wondered if she would go there yet, on her quest for the Derai Lost. But no flicker of foreknowledge answered the thought, not like the flare that had burned through her when the Shadow Band received word of the strange conflagration in Aeris.

Mostly, Malian let the others talk as the miles fell behind them and Maraval forest rose up ahead like a green cloud. The Normarchers conversation was much the same as on the road south, discussing the tournament and the events they should all enter. The Caer Argent courtiers spoke of the tourney, too, although their speculation was centered around whether there would be any serious challengers to Ombrose Sondargent for the champion's crown, and who the champion might crown as tourney queen. The formal betrothal of Lord Hirluin and Countess Ghiselaine at Midsummer was touched on briefly—or rebetrothal since the original vows had been made for them as children—but every conversation soon returned to the state visit by the Jhainarian queen.

No one, Malian decided, appeared willing to accept the embassy at face value. Almost all the courtiers seemed convinced that Jhaine was opening up some diplomatic game, although none expressed any clear idea as to what the game might be. On the fringe of the woods, bored with their chatter, Malian began to whistle a bargee's song from the River beneath her breath. Raven, who was riding beside her at that point, glanced sideways, and Malian shrugged, answering the look. "I used to work on the River during the summer. Lots of students do. It's a fine way to see the other cities—and you get paid for the work."

"Hard work," was all Raven said, and she nodded, pushing back her hat as the road took them deeper into the woods. Gradually the cavalcade fell silent, and the only sound was the clip of their horses' hooves, the song of birds, and the deep susurration of the myriad leaves overhead. The canopy was more open here than in the forest surrounding the Rindle and the hill fort, with sunlight slanting across the road.

Malian turned her head from side to side, aware of the same stirring of power that Maister Carick had encountered on the Northern March.

Here the sensation was light-edged, like the leaves over-head, but Malian could feel the dark peace of roots reaching deep beneath the sun-warmed earth. As though Emer itself is aware, she thought, trying to catch the elusive music that comprised light, and shifting leaves, and earth, all woven together. A magpie screeched, startled by their passage, and the sound scraped across her awareness, splintering the green murmur. Sunlight lanced down between two trees and she blinked, seeing a figure outlined against the afterdazzle: a tall figure in supple white leather with a bow across one shoulder.

But you're dead, Malian thought, staring: they told me you were dead—and the same ache that had closed her throat when she knelt beside Falath in her dream made it difficult to swallow. She closed her eyes, and when she opened them again the image had become a woman in battle-rent armor, with a crown of stars in her dark hair.

You're definitely dead, Malian told the apparition, at least on this plane of existence. Yet the armring of Yorindesarinen burned, cold beneath her sleeve. And this time Malian was sure it was the trees that shifted, shutting out both the apparition and the shaft of sun. The magpie jabbered again and her head swam as memories flooded in, not just of the Oakward and the Northern March, but of Jaransor five years before, and Rowan Birchmoon calling winter into its power.

What if it isn't just Jaransor? Malian asked herself, fighting to stay upright in the saddle. What if it's all of it—if the whole of Haarth is aware at some level, in a way the Derai have never encountered before?

She wanted to remain stock-still, listening for the turning of the world that she had first heard clearly on a long-ago night in Jaransor. But Mallow kept moving forward and she could see the flank of Raven's horse, keeping pace. Slowly, the sounds of the road intruded again: the clip of hooves, the jingle of metal, and the murmur as one courtier said something to another about lunch. Behind her, Ado made a joke, and Malian smiled automatically as the others laughed. Even Raven smiled slightly, although he shrugged at the same time. "An old joke," he said, "but a Midsummer favorite."

*And everything is new at Midsummer.* Malian knew both the saying and the joke from the River. Except here in Emer the saying was *made* new, although she supposed it meant the same thing. A time of making—which was why so many marriages were celebrated as part of the festival, as well as treaties signed, binding lordly houses, and contracts made between merchants. She glanced around and saw that Kalan, riding beside Ado, was watching her with a slight frown. "Are you all right?" he asked.

Does he know about this possible aspect of Emer and of Haarth? she wondered. How much of their lore *have* the Oakward revealed to him? Or is the land's awareness—*if* it is aware—so fundamental that they would no more speak of it than they do of breathing? Malian shook her head, resolving to put her questions to him later. "It's very warm now," she said, as if answering his query, "even here beneath the trees." She used her hat to fan her face, emphasizing the warmth, and guessed that Kalan would sense her evasion but not press further.

In the end, they rode for nearly three hours before the road finally ran out of Maraval wood into blazing sunshine, on the crest of the Vertward down country. The landscape ahead was a patchwork of wheat and barley fields, interspersed with orchards, hop gardens, and neat rows of vines. The late morning air was languid, almost sleepy with heat, and dust rose in a long plume above the road to the south.

"It must be time for lunch," Ado said, and Malian felt her own stomach grumble in agreement as she thought longingly of shaded inn yards and cool beer. The Duke, though, had drawn rein and shaded his eyes, watching the approaching dust plume. After a moment he pointed to a knoll several hundred yards ahead, lying just clear of the road, and the horses started down the hill.

The knoll, Malian thought, would allow their whole company to be drawn up in formal array without blocking the road—while the rising ground, with the sweep of the hill behind, would give them the advantage over those approaching. She allowed herself a small, inward smile as their cavalcade circled onto the knoll, but noted that the Duke was frowning as he oversaw the disposition of their company. Audin was smiling at something the priestess had said to him, but Malian knew him well enough now to register a faint tightness to his expression and tension in the set of his shoulders. Ghiselaine remained as remotely grave as she had been since the hill fort, although she smiled her thanks when Ilaise brought out the embroidered mantle and helped place it about her shoulders.

Like everyone else, though, Ghiselaine must be wondering what this embassy really meant—especially given the forthcoming renewal of her betrothal vows that had sealed the Ormondian peace. A Great Year: Malian repeated the phrase that Raher had used, feeling its resonance. If what the Marcher youth had said was correct, then it must have something to do with this visit. She kept her expression neutral, but wished the Band's information on Jhaine had not been so scanty. Then again, it was a long, weary road from Ar to Jhaine, almost as far as the proverbial route from Ij to Ishnapur, so why should the Band concern itself?

Except, she reflected wryly, that the Shadow Band concerns itself with everything that happens in Haarth, at some level. And likes to keep its secrets, even from those taken within the Shadow fold.

The lancer vanguard was drawn up on either side of the road now, in guard-of-honor format, while the rest of the armed escort grouped itself in crescent formation around the Duke and his retinue. The priestess of Imuln remained at the Duke's right hand, but now Ghiselaine had taken Ser Ombrose's place to his left, while Audin was on her left again. The Normarch company was placed on the far right of the Duke's retinue, immediately adjoining the guards, where they had a good view of the Highvert road. The trumpeter unslung his silver instrument as the Duke moved his horse a few paces forward of the main group, his attention fixed on the dust plume ahead.

The noon sun was intense in the open, and sweat prick-led down Malian's back and beneath her arms as the plume crept closer and became a cloud, spreading across the fields to either side of the road. When she glanced around, she saw that both Kalan and Girvase had their eyes shaded, staring into the glare.

"I can see wagons," Kalan told her, "all richly painted, mainly in burgundy and wheat, and drawn by horse teams, not mules. Plenty of guards," he added after a moment. "And there's seven riders out in front. No, eight. They've seen us now and are heading this way." Another pause: "They can ride, too, as though they and their horses are one."

Soon they could all see them, eight riders galloping out of the dust raised by the caravan behind them. The mounts at either end of the approaching line were a dun and a gray respectively, with two blacks, two bays, and a chestnut in between—and one milk-white steed in the central position. The horses seemed to float above the ground, their manes lifting on the wind of their speed; the riders' hair, too, flowed out like banners. Sunlight flashed off the armor worn by seven of their number, while the central rider wore crimson beneath a pale mantle that curved against the sky.

"Seven warriors, all men," Kalan said, confirming what Malian had not yet been sure of, because of their long hair. "The central rider is a damosel."

The priestess-queen, Malian thought. The warriors' armor, as they drew closer, looked similar to that of the Lathayrans, although she could see the hilts of the swallow-tail swords that the Jhainarian auxiliaries in Ishnapur had made popular throughout the southern lands. The hooves of the approaching horses were a thunder on the Midsummer earth, the rush of their speed unchecked.

"Surely, they'll stop?" Jarna's frown matched the Duke's. "I mean, the horses . . ."

Malian thought the guard of lancers had more cause for worry, although they remained stolidly in place. Audin's horse tossed its head restlessly, but the Duke continued to sit like a statue. Malian could make out every detail of the oncoming riders now: the slight, graceful girl in the crimson gown, her hair, golden as wheat, streaming back above the mantle; the mail-clad riders, three to one side and four to the other of the milk-white steed, their armor flashing with semiprecious stones and gold inlay. The warriors all wore their hair as long as their queen's, some in braids woven with jewels, the rest flowing free. Their faces were all young, and clear-eyed, and fierce.

No more than sixteen at most, Malian thought, the queen included. She glanced at the Duke, but his expression gave nothing away, not even when the oncoming wave-crest of horses slammed from full gallop to a sliding, mane-tossing halt immediately in front of the lancers' honor line. A magnificent display of horsemanship—and they know it, too, Malian thought, taking in the Jhainarians' carefully expressionless faces. The white horse took a step forward, ahead of the rest, shaking out the length of its silken mane while the young queen remained unmoving on its back.

She wore no crown; needed none, in fact, although a narrow gold fillet circled her brow. A border of goldwork edged the pale mantle, and the broad, linked belt around the queen's waist was also gold. Like Ser Ombrose's tunic, her crimson gown was slit for ease of riding, so that everyone could see the tanned legs extending into boots of honey leather, rolled to above the knee. Malian could sense the men around her, all trying not to stare. She would have smiled openly except for the proud lift of that wheat-gold head and the austere young stare—although the queen's eyes, the shadowed gray of dawn skies, were fixed on the Duke.

The escort warrior on the chestnut horse moved forward, close on his queen's right. His voice, when he spoke, was clear as the ring of sword on sword. "You are the Duke's Grace, Caril Sondargent of Emer?"

"I am." The Duke, too, was unmoving, his manner calm, although Malian thought his eyes had narrowed—but that might just have been the sun's glare.

"I am Rastem, First of the Seven sworn to Queen Zhineve-

An of Jhaine. I greet you, in the name of Jhaine and the Nine Queens."

The Duke inclined his head. "Welcome, First Rastem," he said. "I salute you and your brethren." All seven warriors bowed from their saddles, although none lowered their eyes. "Through you, I salute the Nine Queens and the land of Jhaine." This time, the young queen also bowed her head.

Slowly, the Duke walked his horse between the line of lancers, until he drew abreast of Zhineve-An on her white horse. His expression was hidden from those behind him as he looked into her face, but for an instant Malian thought the young queen's austere mask wavered, like the riffle of wind across summer grass. But then she was pulling off her gold-worked glove and extending her hand; the Duke raised it to his lips, and the moment—if moment there had been—was in the past.

The Duke straightened and spoke formally, his hand still clasping the young queen's: "I welcome you, Queen Zhineve-An, so long awaited, to Emer."

# 34

# *The Tourney Camp*

"What did he mean, 'so long awaited'?" Audin demanded, sounding more savage than Kalan had ever heard him. Sparks snapped from their cooking fire as the young lord poked at it hard with a branch of green wood. Audin might have played his part in the formalities that surrounded Queen Zhineve-An's arrival, including the picnic lunch beneath the eave of Maraval wood—but he had barely spoken since they left the Duke's party for the tourney ground, remaining withdrawn as they set up camp and ate their evening meal.

Raher grinned. "So that's what you're brooding about. You heard the same palaver the rest of us did—probably better, since you were at your uncle's elbow when he talked about the invitation his grandfather extended to the Nine Queens."

"It doesn't make sense," Audin said impatiently. "Duke Caril's grandfather was my great-grandfather, and every family story agrees that he was hard as nails. He wouldn't have cared two clipped pennies for it being a Great Year or whatever the pretext for this visit is."

"The Imulni priestess did say that a Great Year's auspicious," Ado put in, "and even more so having a priestess-queen of Jhaine here for the Midsummer ceremony."

"My great-grandfather wouldn't have cared for that either." Audin's mouth thinned into a disparaging line—and then he grinned for the first time since they had farewelled the damosels at Argenthithe; an unusually sour expression for him, but a grin nonetheless. "I was close enough to see the queen's eyes when our priestess called her 'sister.'"

Kalan raised an eyebrow. "You don't think she sees it that way?"

Audin snorted. "Not her. More like 'scullery maid' than 'sister.' I'm not sure the priestess picked up on it, though."

Girvase, who had been reclining on one elbow, staring into the flames, sat up. "If you look at a map, you can see why an alliance with Jhaine would have seemed like a sound, long-term strategy in your great-grandfather's time."

"Because Jhaine borders Ormond as well as our Southern March?" Audin replied. "But what does it mean, if my uncle's still pursuing it now that we have the Ormondian peace? And how convenient," he added, savage again, "for the Jhainarian queen to arrive now, just in time to overshadow the formal ceremony for Ghiselaine and Hirluin."

The others stirred, glancing at each other uneasily. Kalan shook his head. "Three generations of Emerian dukes have dedicated their lives to ending the war with Ormond. Your uncle would never throw that over for a chancy alliance with Jhaine."

Ser Raven looked up from the tear he was mending in his saddlecloth. "The Ormondian peace need not preclude an alliance with Jhaine," he pointed out. "Both countries have a border with Lathayra, which is always turbulent, so it makes sense to talk closer ties. They would have done so long before now, I'm sure, if Jhaine were not so closed."

"And if Jhaine's queens can only travel in a Great Year," Girvase suggested, "maybe this is just their way of doing things?"

Audin continued to frown, before shaking his head. "Maybe," he said reluctantly.

"Although why send so young a queen," Kalan said, thinking out loud, "if it's a serious embassy?"

"Maybe the rest are even younger," Raher replied impatiently. He jumped to his feet. "I've had enough of this queen business anyway. Let's look around the camp and see who else is here."

Jarna surprised Kalan by springing up first, although the others were all getting to their feet as well. Only Ser Raven remained by the fire. "I've seen tourney camps before," he said, so they left him there.

The horizon was primrose, the long Midsummer evening deepening to velvet overhead, as they strolled through the gathering of fighting men from throughout the southern realms. The tents varied from the patched to the sumptuous, but otherwise each campsite was much the same, with a fire pit at the front and men sitting or lying around it. Most of the knights were Emerian, with the colors of Ward, Mark, or march fluttering above the central tent. The knights' personal arms were painted on their shields, which were either hung around the tents or stacked to either side of the entrance.

As well as knights and their squires, the Normarchers passed long- and crossbow archers, staff- and pikemen, all come to test their skill and compete for the rich prizes put up by the Duke and magnates of Emer. Not all the knights they saw were finely dressed, though. Many reminded Kalan of Ser Raven, their clothes and appearance shabby, although what he could see of their weapons looked keen and well oiled. The drunken disorder of tourney camps was a byword, but so far the contestants appeared to be mostly sober—and probably the true wildness would only begin once competitors began to be eliminated.

Most of the Emerians nodded as the Normarchers passed by, but few spoke. The Lathayrans were all camped close to each other, any homeland rivalries temporarily set aside, and they did not even look up, let alone nod. Kalan could feel their watchfulness, though, a twitch between his shoulder blades as he walked by.

"It's very big," Jarna said finally. They had worked their way along one arm of the camp and were standing in the shadow of the tourney stands, one of the boxes used by the high nobility soaring above them. The base had been painted crimson, Kalan noted idly, and wondered if the color choice was to honor Queen Zhineve-An.

"Still, we should go all the way around," Ado said. "See everything at least once."

But Jarna was staring away from the camp, toward a box on the opposite side of the ground. "That must be where the queen of the tourney sits," she said. Kalan watched her brow pucker. "Serinna Sondcendre," she said finally, "Ser Ombrose's cousin. That's who was crowned last year, so she'll be this year's queen."

"Ombrose has chosen a different cousin each of the past three years," Audin said. He paused. "But if he wins this year, it'll have to be Ghiselaine."

Because Ser Ombrose was the Duke's champion and Ghiselaine was marrying the Duke's heir. After five years, Kalan knew how these things worked in Emer.

"Although," Jarna said to him, very quietly as the others began to move off, "did you see the way Ser Ombrose looked at Queen Zhineve-An, when they met at Argenthithe?"

Kalan shook his head, because he had not been paying much attention to all the formal exchanges by that stage.

"If he is champion again this year," Jarna said slowly, "and if he feels he can choose, then I think he'll offer the tourney crown to her."

But there's no point, Kalan thought, since she won't be coming back here again if all they say of Jhaine is true. And Ser Ombrose isn't free to choose—not unless he wants to direly offend his uncle and his cousin. Both his cousins, Kalan corrected himself, glancing at Audin, a few paces ahead. "It won't happen," he said out loud, and grinned at Jarna. "We all know Gir's going to win and offer the crown to Alli."

Girvase shook his head. "You could win just as easily as me."

"Ser Raven says anyone over a certain skill level can win." Ado flexed his fingers together, cracking the knuckles. "He says that tourneys are like battles and there's always an element of luck involved. Even a top knight's horse can go lame, or a sound weapon break under too much pressure."

" 'Ser Raven says'," Raher mocked him, then his eyes narrowed. "I wonder if *he* intends to compete?"

"I don't think so," Kalan said. The opening rounds in the tournament would begin the day after tomorrow, and unlike Ser Ombrose—who as last year's champion would not have to begin competing until the quarterfinals—the Normarchers would have to fight all the elimination rounds. Kalan had heard that was as much a trial by exhaustion as skill. He glanced at Jarna, hoping that she would do all right in the sword ring. Horse archery and the horsemanship trials were her preferred events, but every knight had to enter at least one of the hand-to-hand weapon contests. And like all of them, she had chosen the sword.

Preoccupied with his thoughts, Kalan had to sidestep as Girvase stopped to study another series of tents. "I've never seen that style of armor before," his friend said. "And where's their insignia?"

The campsite immediately ahead was larger than most they had passed, with close to fifteen men gathered around the fire. Both their armor and faces shouted "Derai" to Kalan, although he didn't think they were from either the House of Night or of Blood. Swords, then, he told himself: they have to be.

"What are you looking at, boy?" The man who addressed him was a hulking brute, almost as broad as he was tall, and used a heavily accented version of the River dialect. The other warriors said nothing, just watched, their eyes cool on Kalan and Girvase. But it was Audin who answered, shifting so that light from the fire illuminated the oak tree on his breast.

"We have just ridden in, sers, and are seeing the camp. We mean no offense."

"Careful, Orth." Another of the warriors, an older man with gray in his thick hair and a snarl of scarring around one eye, spoke quietly in Derai. He must have been lucky, Kalan thought, not to have lost the eye to whatever attack left him with the scars. "This one's of their Blood, here in Emer. Kill him in the contests if you must, but right now you would be breaking the tourney truce we all swore to."

"Always best to let Blood slay Blood," another warrior put in, then switched to the River dialect. "No offense taken, young sers."

"They're all babes in any case," the older man said, still in Derai, and the warriors around him grinned, not entirely pleasantly, as the Normarch group moved on. The warrior called Orth snorted.

"If they carry weapons and enter the contest then they must stand as the warriors they claim to be." His laugh was harsh. "Even the wench if she faces me."

The older man's answering tone was indifferent. "I didn't know they had women warriors here. But she's not like one of our own. She'll die quickly."

"Quicker if she meets Orth," the other man said, and all the Derai laughed. Kalan's lips tightened, but hot words would only show that he understood Derai—and if violence followed, he would be just as much in breach of the truce as these Sword thugs.

"Even Ser Ombrose may have his work cut out against that giant," Girvase observed quietly.

Kalan nodded, knowing Orth would have the advantage of height, reach, and the force he could put behind each blow. "Let's hope he's slow on his feet," he replied. "Many bigger men are."

"I wouldn't underestimate my cousin either," Audin said.

Raher nodded. "M'father fought with your cousin during the Lathayran incursions. He always calls him Ombrose Wolf and says that he was brutal in battle."

"Ombrose Wolf?" Jarna echoed.

"Another nickname," Audin explained. "Like the wolf of Sondargent."

"He got both nicknames," Girvase said, "because of the way he waged the Lathayran campaign. And they say he's killed more than one man in tourney melees."

Audin looked as though he would have liked to argue,

but could not. Raher and Ado exchanged glances as they turned into a cross-lane leading back to the Normarch site, but Jarna was looking toward an adjoining square of black tents. Kalan followed her gaze and saw a white banner flying above the central pavilion. Even in the darkness his eyes were keen enough to make out its unknown black unicorn device. He could also see fire-glow from between the tents, and guessed they must surround an enclosed central space. Unlike the other sites they had seen, this one had turned its back on the rest of the tourney camp. No voices carried from either the central area or from inside the tents, and Kalan wondered if the campsite might be empty—until the night breeze billowed the nearest tent, drawing his attention to the tall presence standing in its shadow.

Kalan took in details without seeming to: blue-black armor beneath a long black surcote, and gauntleted hands resting on the pommel of a tall, two-handed sword. The guard's visor was open, but he wore his mail coif in the Ish- napuri fashion, veiling the lower part of the face, so that Kalan could detect little of his features. He did not think that the man was Ishnapuri, though, despite the coif.

The guard did not speak or move, simply watched as they walked past, and now Kalan saw another posted near the end of the encampment. Like the first guard, he stood very still within the shadow of the tents and it was difficult to see his face. Kalan glanced across at Girvase, whose night vision was almost as good as his. "That armor," he said, "and the black unicorn device? They're not from the southern realms."

"Nor were the giant and his friends," Girvase replied. "The reputation of the tournament must have grown."

Raher slid a glance toward Ado, grinning slyly. "Ser Raven says that the Midsummer prizes here are richer now than any given on the River."

I suppose we value the tourney more, Kalan thought. Still, it was strange to think of knights coming to compete beneath coats-of-arms that Emerians did not even recognize. And he had never expected to encounter Derai this far south. Fortu- nately he looked northern or central Emerian anyway, with his House of Blood coloring, so there was little risk of being recognized. And even if the Sword warriors did recognize him as Derai, what could they do? This is Emer, Kalan told himself grimly: the Derai have no power here.

"You look serious," Jarna said.

"Do I?" He had to stop himself from reaching out and giving her braid a light tug. "I was thinking about what Gir said—how great the tourney has grown."

He watched her consider that, her expression as serious as any he might have worn. "Audin says the prize for each individual contest is to be a bag of gold coin. If I could win one . . ." Her tone was wistful. "That would mean a good dowry for Aenide."

Kalan nodded, because he knew that Aenide was the eldest of Jarna's younger sisters—and about the importance of dowry to making a good marriage in Emer. "You'll have a fair chance in the horsemanship trials," he told her. "The horse archery, too."

She made a face. "The Lathayrans always win that."

"Do you think the Jhainarians will compete?" Raher asked abruptly. "We all saw the way they rode today. They'd definitely give the Lathayrans some competition. You, too, Jarna," he added, by way of an afterthought.

Kalan reached out and shoved him, hard enough to send the Marcher youth sprawling in the dust. Raher sprang up in an instant and hurled himself at Kalan, and the next moment they were grappling on the ground in a flurry of arms and legs while the others shouted encouragement. Kalan was half laughing, half serious, and could see the same snarling grin on Raher's face. For a brief space the contest between them was even—and then Kalan had Raher facedown in the dust with his arm shoved up his back.

"Enough," said Audin, their usual arbiter. He was grinning, too, though. "We should save our energy for tomorrow."

Raher was still half laughing as he got to his feet. "Wrestling against you, Hamar, is always like fighting stone. And saying the Jhainarians would give Jarna competition isn't the same as saying she'd lose."

"I can do it again," Kalan warned. Looking past Raher, he saw someone else grinning at their scuffle. A very young knight, he noted, barely more than a boy, wearing the same blue-black mail and dark surcote as the guards between the black tents. Something about the planes of the youth's face looked familiar to him, although Kalan could not place the resemblance. The young knight looked as though he wanted to speak, or even join them, and Kalan raised his hand, prepared to be friendly. But someone moved in the shadows behind the youth, speaking in a language Kalan did not recognize. The warning tone was clear, though, and the young knight nodded, his expression regretful as he turned away.

Kalan shrugged and turned away himself. They were almost back at their own campsite and he felt all the weariness of the past two days' events settling into his shoulders. He rotated them, loosening tension, as someone added wood to a fire up ahead. A gout of flame shot up and he realized it was their campfire, but the person feeding it was not Ser Raven. Kalan tensed again, and both Jarna and Girvase glanced his way—but the fire sent up another explosion of sparks and this time he recognized the herald, Tarathan of Ar, sitting back down beside Jehane Mor.

The heralds looked up as if his stare had caught their attention, the firelight refracting across their eyes. Raven nodded, his own gaze inscrutable as they all trooped in, greeting the heralds and settling noisily around the fire. Audin and Ado both brought out ale, and everyone rummaged through their gear for mugs as the flagons went around. Kalan concentrated on filling his cup, then looked across its rim at the heralds. "We didn't expect to see you here so soon."

"We met another herald pair just past the turnoff for Aeris," Jehane Mor replied. "They took our dispatches back to the River while we have brought theirs on here. We called in to Normarch again," she added, "and all was quiet there. Lord Falk said he might come south if it stays that way, but for Autumn's Night, not Midsummer."

All the young knights, with the possible exception of Audin, would have moved on from Caer Argent by then, either hiring out as a company or serving individually as knights-at-arms to some great lord. Kalan and blew ale froth off the top of his cup, not wanting to think about where he might be on Autumn's Night, and studied Jehane Mor instead. She looked just as she always had, no more or less than a Guild herald in travel-stained grays. But Kalan could not shake off his memory of the new moon's slender curve rising into a sky that should have remained dark.

So much power, he thought. He had thought so then as well, and tried to discuss it with Solaan after their return to Normarch. The Hill woman had just looked at him, apparently surprised. "Heralds *have* power," she had said. "The whole world knows that."

Malian, though, had spent the past five years on the River and disagreed. "Not that much power," she had commented shortly. Yet perhaps she's wrong, Kalan thought now. Tarathan and Jehane Mor have always had a lot of power; we saw that on the Wall, five years ago. And they had been eluding the beast-men for days when they helped Gir and me in the woods above the hill fort.

"Meanwhile," Jehane Mor was saying, "Lord Falk gave us more money for Ser Raven, since tournaments and festivals, as he put it, are an expensive business. Most of the River dispatches are for merchants at the fair, so we'll ride that way tomorrow and then on to Caer Argent." The herald paused, her gray-green eyes reflective. "Tourney camps always breed rumors, but the camp is full of talk tonight—mostly of a queen of Jhaine arriving here, but there were also mutterings of an attack on Countess Ghiselaine?"

"Both true." Audin kept his voice low. "We think the attack involved sorcery as well as poison. As for the queen—" He shrugged. "We rode with my uncle the Duke when he met her today."

"She has a Seven with her," Ser Raven said idly, "all young and wild as hawks."

Jehane Mor nodded. "If the queen is young then her Seven will be also. They are always bound together from their cradles. Why is she here, do you know?"

"What do the rumors say?" Audin countered bitterly. "I'm sure there are as many variants as there are people to tell them. And don't heralds hear them all?"

The herald regarded him thoughtfully. "Not always. The main theory we heard is that the queen is here to marry Duke Caril in some special ceremony at Midsummer."

They all glanced quickly at Audin, but he just shrugged, as if this sort of tale was no more than he expected to hear. Tarathan of Ar lifted his eyes from contemplation of the flames. "The second rumor," he said, "was only spoken by those who whispered of an attack on the Countess of Ormond. It also mentioned marriage, but not to the Duke."

Jehane Mor nodded, her voice joining with his. "The real plan, these whispers claim, is for Lord Hirluin to marry the queen and dispense with the need for either Countess Ghiselaine or the peace." The heralds paused, the firelight turning their faces to masks before they spoke again as one. "So Emer can finish with Ormond once and for all."

# 35

# Caer Argent

*T*he rooms set aside for the ducal cartographer turned out to be two small chambers crammed under the eaves of one of the older towers, on the far side of the palace complex from either the main Black Tower or the new guest wing adjoining it. The sleeping room was barely more than a closet, although the day room was larger, with a view out over the city's rooftops. Malian had been shown to the rooms close on midnight, and the first thing she did then was persuade the lead-paned casement to open, initially to let in cool air and secondly to swing herself out and climb to the tower roof.

Even when her eyes adjusted to the dark she had not seen much of the palace, just a surrounding patchwork of roofs and towers. An early morning climb to the same vantage point revealed a great deal more. "'The island of Emer'," Malian murmured, knowing that this foothold in the Argent had *been* the dukedom once, during the troubled centuries that followed the Cataclysm, when war had surged back and forward across what was now Emer. Control of the island with its command over the river and surrounding countryside had been one of the great prizes, but the Black Tower was an Old Empire structure and it had never fallen, in part because of foundations dug too deep into rock to be undermined.

At least by Haarth technology, Malian reflected, although

she had to admit that the tower was impressive, rising sheer from the northern end of the island. The great dome of Imuln graced the skyline to the south, with a small, enclosed wood on its river side. The rest of the ducal palace was a series of halls and wings sprawling out from the Black Tower: a warren, she thought dispassionately.

The much smaller tower she crouched on was built into a palace wall, which backed onto the mews that formed the first circle of the old city. Another wall extended beyond the southern bounds of the palace, with more towers spaced evenly along its length as it followed the river toward the temple complex. The towers must have been guard posts, she guessed, although they looked abandoned now. On their landward side, a ribbon of green curved between the wall and the mews, while beyond the mews she could see more rooftops crowded together. Narrow towers rose everywhere, tapering into steep spires, until finally the old city leaped its walls and spilled across the river.

Malian shaded her eyes against the morning sun, noticing what appeared to be a relatively large area of open space on the river's eastern bank, located close to the water. The distance was too great for her to guess what she was actually seeing, so she pulled her focus back to the palace's jumbled sprawl. "An *insecure* warren," she said aloud—and her best proof that the Ijiri School of Assassins was not yet active in Caer Argent.

She stretched, aware that it was time to find Ghiselaine and go over the apartments assigned to the Countess of Ormond, which she hoped would be considerably better than those given to the ducal cartographer.

And the supposed Maister Carick, Malian reflected, as she climbed back down and in through the small casement, would probably be summoned soon to present his credentials to the Duke.

Her good clothes were still stained with dust and sweat from yesterday's travel, but Maister Carick did not have many, so Malian had to brush off the cape and jacket, settling for a clean tunic and wearing Nhenir in its guise as a

fashionable silver cap. *"So what impression did you gain of
Ser Ombrose yesterday?"* she asked the helm, descending
the tower's narrow twist of stairs.

*"Competence, efficiency, indifference to others. Lord
Tenneward,"* the helm continued, *"was all noise and bluster, fearing that he might be seen as the hand behind the
poisoned cup."*

*"But he wasn't?"*

*"Neither he nor any of the lodge servants knew any-
thing of it. It turned out that supposed female relatives had
brought the girl from town earlier in the day and then left
again—or appeared to do so. The bodies of the Bonamark
messengers were found in a ditch, close to the main road."*

*"So someone watched and waited?"*

*"And would have seen Maister Carick act,"* the helm
agreed.

Malian shrugged at the note of reproof. *"To have let Ghiselaine take the cup would have been worse. I can dispense
with Maister Carick if need be."* She would prefer not to,
though, at this stage.

At ground level, a skein of corridors reinforced Malian's
first impression of the palace as a warren. She was certain
she could find her own way, but it was useful to know what
routes the palace dwellers took, so she snared a passing page
and asked him to guide her to the Countess of Ormond's
suite in the guest wing.

The page's eyes widened, before comprehension stamped
itself across his narrow features. "She's not in the guest wing,
that's where the foreign queen is staying. The Ormondian
lady's housed in what we call the Gallery wing—it's older,
but it's been kept up because of being right next door to the
Black Tower, where the Dukes always live." He darted away
down a narrow corridor thronged with people and said back
over his shoulder, "Not that she'll be there. She'll already
have gone to the reception hall—you know, where the Duke
grants audiences." The boy grimaced. "He does a lot of that
at Midsummer, which makes more work for us."

He dashed ahead again, and Malian quickened her pace to

keep him in sight as he switched from one corridor to another and led her up and down between levels. Buildings layering onto each other, she guessed—and then they were passing through a wide hall with a floor of checkered red-and-yellow tiles, darkly paneled walls, and considerably fewer people. The double doors at the far end were also painted red and yellow and opened onto a long gallery with sunshine flooding in through tall windows.

Malian blinked at the brightness, taking in the few, brightly clad courtiers strolling on a lawn outside, and the halberdiers in ducal uniform at the far end of the gallery. The latter studied Malian as she approached, but barely spared a glance for the page. Emer is *not* the River, she told herself—because in Ar not even a page boy, however well known, would ever be taken at face value. Her companion stopped and threw out his chest. "Maister Carick of Ar," he said, "the new ducal cartographer, here to pay his respects to the Duke's Grace and the Countess of Ormond."

The halberdiers looked Malian over again, not quite hiding their doubt, but eventually one of them nodded and opened the door. Malian fished in her wallet for a coin and handed it to the page. "What's your name?" she asked, pausing on the threshold while the halberdiers looked on, expressionless.

"Hirluin," he said, slipping the coin inside his tunic rather than the wallet at his belt. "Because I was born on Lord Hirluin's birthday—but everyone calls me Luin."

"Or trouble," a halberdier muttered, but Luin had already started back down the red-and-yellow hall, waving a cheerful farewell.

The room on the other side of the doors was as large and light as the gallery, with sunshine spilling through more tall windows to dapple the polished floor. Sepia tapestries hung facing the windows, while a golden oak tree with leaves of beaten silver decorated the wall opposite the entrance. The intervening space was crowded with courtiers, and although a few looked around as Malian entered, most returned to their prior conversations immediately.

She shrugged inwardly and began looking for Ghiselaine, but it was only when a knot of courtiers separated that she saw the three tall chairs set in front of the golden oak tree. Ghiselaine sat in the chair to the left of the tree, with Ilaise standing beside her; the chair to the right was occupied by Queen Zhineve-An. The queen's Seven had formed a loose semicircle around her, and Malian caught the glint of mail beneath their flowing tunics. Zhineve-An's expression was as closed as it had been on the Vertward road, and her only ornament, in a gathering bright with jewels, was a necklace with a crescent moon superimposed onto a disc of dark, antique gold.

"She's like a gilded doll," Alianor said softly, slipping between two groups of courtiers to stand at Malian's elbow. "I don't think she spoke two words together on the trip downriver yesterday."

Malian turned, taking the cup of wine that the damosel held out. "While you look like a great lady of the court," she murmured, her nod encompassing silk and jewels.

Alianor shrugged. "I am Ghiselaine's friend and a Sondazur. I must play my part." She studied Malian's silver cap. "Is that a River fashion? It's very distinctive."

*"The cap disguise may have to go,"* Malian said to Nhenir, *"since it seems the fashion has not yet reached Emer. Unlike,"* she added dryly, seeing the crowd make way for Ser Ombrose, *"the parti-colored hose and lined tunic favored by the Duke's champion."* She watched his progress down the room and had to concede that the man had presence, both in the way he held himself aloof from the courtiers' effusions, and in his clothes, which outpeacocked them all. He has even chosen peacock colors, she thought, secretly amused as she took in the full robe of royal blue, lined with emerald, and the matching emerald and blue hose. And yet, Malian reminded herself, you need to look past appearances: this is the man Lathayrans call the Sondargent wolf.

"So what's the occasion?" she asked Alianor.

"An audience for envoys from some northern place. Not Aeris or the River," Alianor clarified, and Malian's heartbeat quickened, her thoughts flying to the Wall. "They've been treating with Ser Ombrose up until now, and today they meet the Duke. It's just a formality, but we're all interested in seeing who these people are."

Yes, thought Malian. She was wondering who on the Wall would send out envoys beyond its bounds at all, let alone as far as Emer.

"And then," Alianor went on, "there's to be yet another grand luncheon, although this afternoon should be a little quieter. But we should join Ghis now Ser Ombrose is here, since he's the one sponsoring the envoys today."

"And the Duke?" Malian asked, threading between the gathered courtiers.

"Oh, he's here already, talking to the group by the window." Alianor nodded in that direction. "He was with Queen Zhineve-An until just before you arrived."

Was there a tightness in her voice as she said that? Malian wondered. But there was no time to speculate, as she had barely straightened from her bow to Ghiselaine—feeling the eyes of Zhineve-An's Seven on her throughout this maneuver—when the Duke crossed to the central of the three chairs. Zhineve-An and Ghiselaine both rose as courtesy required, and he bowed to each of them in turn, but without undue formality. He was dressed very much as a plain man, in another of the black jupons over a mail corselet, but without yesterday's goldwork and jewels. The Duke had set aside the coronal as well, going bareheaded—so whoever these envoys are, Malian reflected, he doesn't think they're as important as a queen of Jhaine. She hoped Zhineve-An was duly flattered, but then again, perhaps the young queen would simply see it as her due.

Malian eased back, standing behind both Ilaise and Alianor as Duke Caril seated himself. If this was a Derai embassy, impossible though that seemed, then it was vital that she observe without being seen herself. Already the courtiers were withdrawing to either side of the room, opening up a clear path between the three tall chairs and the doors that the halberdiers had now pushed open. Two more halberdiers stepped into the room, standing to attention on either side of the door as Ser Ombrose moved to the Duke's right hand. Malian could see no mail beneath the champion's royal blue silk, but he was the only man in the room, besides the Duke, permitted to carry a sword. She was almost certain the Seven would have hideout weapons, though, as she did herself—and Lord Falk's commission to use them if required, although she certainly hoped that would not be necessary today.

She craned forward with everyone else, trying to catch a first glimpse of the envoys as one of the Duke's stewards stepped forward to formally announce them. "Lord Arcolin," the man said in ringing tones as the noise in the room died away, "and Lord Nherenor, envoys of the Many-As-One to Duke Caril of Emer."

Malian's heart lurched and darkness wavered around her eyes. For one disorientated moment she thought she had even forgotten how to breathe—and then the armring concealed beneath her sleeve burned her forearm with cold fire and her vision cleared. Nhenir remained utterly silent, and Malian's hands closed, the close-trimmed fingernails biting into her palms as she stared at the two men pacing to meet the Duke. Both were tall, but the envoy farthest from Malian had the appearance of a man in his thirties, while his companion looked very young—younger even than me, Malian thought with a slight shock. If asked to guess, she would have put his age at no more than sixteen.

The disparity in age—or in the appearance of age, she reflected grimly—was not the only difference between the two. Both had long black hair bound back from their brows by a narrow silver band, but the older envoy was dressed in a full, floor-length robe of indigo silk, while the youth wore a white surcote over a shirt of blue-black mail. A rayed sun, worked in yellow gold with a wash of red across it, covered the breast of the indigo robe, while the device on the white surcote was smaller—a black lightning strike above the left breast, with a unicorn superimposed above it.

Together they presented every appearance of great and

powerful lords, similar to those of Emer. They had even brought the correct small retinue of servants, drawn up formally by the door. And both envoys were handsome by the standards of the southern realms, Arcolin almost floridly so with darkly blue eyes above high cheekbones and a full, sensuous mouth. The youth's face was high-boned, too, but narrower, his almond-shaped eyes as black as his hair. His coloring was exotic here in Emer—and Ilaise by no means the only lady in the room studying him with interest. But his appearance would not, Malian thought, her mouth very dry, be unusual amongst some of the Derai houses on the Wall of Night.

He's Swarm, she reminded herself sharply. He can use their sorcery to give himself any appearance he chooses.

Ilaise leaned close to whisper something to Alianor, and when she shifted back the emissaries were straightening out of the correct formal bow to the Duke. Someone has briefed them well, Malian thought, and her eyes went to Ser Ombrose as he turned to address the Duke. The champion's right hand gestured to the older of the two men first. "Your Grace, may I present Lord Arcolin and his fellow envoy, Lord Nherenor. Lord Arcolin, Lord Nherenor: His Grace Caril Sondargent, Duke of Emer."

The next quarter of an hour were taken up by formalities: the Duke's speech of welcome, followed by Lord Arcolin's thanks and assurance of the Many-As-One's great desire for friendship with Emer. Introductions to Queen Zhineve-An and Ghiselaine followed, with further expressions of goodwill toward Jhaine.

Is *this* why the queen is here, Malian wondered: to be part of meeting this embassy, since only Ishnapuri envoys are allowed into Jhaine? Or *part* of why she is here at any rate? Except if that were so, she did not think either the young queen or her Seven looked at all happy about it. The queen's face was a blank mask, her eyes remote, but the Seven's half circle had drawn in close around her chair. Why? Malian wondered. What do they know that the Emerians don't?

*"The queen and her Seven are bound together."* Nhe-

nir's thought slid into her mind. *"They sense the Darkswarm taint, although they may not know what it is."*

Arcolin's attention was focused on the Duke, but Malian, watching closely, thought his eyelids flickered—as though he had sensed some other power in the room when Nhenir used mindspeech.

"Kinsman." Nherenor spoke in a clear voice, his accented Emerian attractive rather than heavy. "Do not forget that we have brought gifts."

"I have not forgotten." Arcolin was smiling, easy, as he turned to Ser Ombrose. "With your permission, Lord Champion?"

Ser Ombrose looked to the Duke, who nodded, and now everyone was craning forward again as the waiting servants carried in caskets of plain black wood, each one inlaid with silver and white jade. "Ishnapuri work?" a courtier beside Malian whispered, but his companion shook her head.

"I have made a study of Ishnapuri designs for my jewel box collection. This is similar, but not one of their styles."

Someone else shushed her as Nherenor opened the first chest and lifted out a silver birdcage with a jeweled golden bird inside. Every detail of feather and beak was perfectly rendered—and Malian was as amazed as everyone else when the young man turned a key at the base of the cage and the bird opened and closed its wings and began to sing. She did not recognize the tune but it was clear the Emerians did. "The spring song of Rolan and Lyinor," the woman courtier whispered again. "How wonderful!"

As soon as the song stopped, Arcolin took the birdcage from Nherenor and presented it to Ghiselaine with a sweeping bow. "For the Countess of Ormond," he said.

A bird in a cage, Malian thought—and a song of doomed springtime love. It could be pure coincidence, but these envoys were Darkswarm, so she suspected the concealed barb. Clearly, they had good intelligence as well, although with two facestealers infiltrated into the ranks of the Normarch damosels, that was not surprising. No one else appeared to have noticed anything, though, and Ghiselaine was smiling as she inclined her head and Ilaise received the gift. Arcolin's intense stare took in the damosel and dismissed her, before turning back to his fellow envoy.

"And for the Queen of Jhaine." Arcolin bowed to Zhineve-An as Nherenor took a slender book, wrapped in black silk, from the second box. "We offer a work by J'mair of Ishnapur, his rare *Seasonal Analects*."

"Not rare," the Duke said slowly, before any of the Jhainarians could speak. "I understood that there were no copies of the *Seasonal Analects* left in existence."

Arcolin smiled. "Your Grace, the Many-As-One have always included those with a gift for finding that which others have abandoned seeking. It is only one of many skills that we would willingly share with our friends."

So is it the real book, Malian wondered, or a clever simulacrum—a little Darkswarm sleight-of-hand to draw the Emerians into their orbit? Rare gift or not, Zhineve-An did not look at all pleased. Two fiery spots of color burned in her pale cheeks, but she nodded stiffly and one of the Seven—Zorem, Malian thought, recalling the Maraval introductions—stepped forward and took possession of the book.

If Arcolin was aware that he might have caused offense, it did not seem to trouble him, although Malian noticed that Nherenor's smile had vanished. Ser Ombrose was frowning slightly, but the Duke simply waited. And clearly, Malian thought, his gift must come next—and outshine the other two.

"For the Duke's Grace," Arcolin said, on cue, "we offer not one but two presents, a mark of the great esteem we hold for his person and the depth of our affection toward Emer."

Malian was almost certain the Jhainarian First's lip curled, but everyone else appeared focused on what Arcolin was passing to Ser Ombrose. Another book, she saw, this one larger than the gift made to Zhineve-An. She thought the silver-and-gold design embossed onto the black cover looked familiar, but Ser Ombrose had handed the book on to the Duke before she realized that it showed the same depiction of Haarth that had graced a map table in her Derai home, the Keep of Winds. As though, Malian thought—and although the day was warm she felt chilled—the map had been drawn by the same hand, or hands that knew the same skills.

Duke Caril was turning the pages slowly, his attention caught, and Malian guessed that the book must hold a series of maps, either of Haarth or of Emer. "The detail and precision," the Duke said finally, "are outstanding."

"Ser Ombrose told us how you value learning," Arcolin replied, "and that you hope to found a university here, to rival the one in Ar. We felt this gift might be of practical benefit as well, given you have a new cartographer from the River."

Malian really held her breath this time, the blood beginning to pound as she wondered whether the Duke would request Maister Carick to step forward, bringing her to the personal notice of the Swarm envoys. But the Duke just nodded, closing the book. "I will certainly let him see it," he said, "once I have studied it in more detail myself."

Arcolin inclined his head, his expression impossible to read, and presented the second gift. It looked like a flat-bottomed spirit lamp, of the kind said to originate in Ishnapur but found throughout the southern realms—except that this lamp appeared to have been cut from crystal. The facets flashed in the sun as Arcolin turned it, but when he passed his palm over the lamp's surface, the crystal lit up from within. The courtiers gasped and even the Duke leaned forward as the initial spark steadied to a soft glow. Arcolin passed his hand across the lamp's surface again and the glow faded.

It's like the lamps set into the wall in the heart of the Old Keep, Malian thought; and a little like the cone lamps that our priests used there, too. She was aware that her pulse was pounding again, and she had to force herself into the Shadow Band discipline for achieving calmness, so that she could hear past the roaring in her ears. But Swarm agents giving Derai lamps as gifts, while a Derai map graced the cover of their book—Malian swallowed back bile, even as she kept a courtier's smile starched onto her face.

*"Why do you fight against the truth that you already*

*know?"* Nhenir inquired, but she pushed the helm's mind-voice away, concentrating on what Arcolin was saying as Ser Ombrose brought the lamp to the Duke.

"These gifts are a token, not just of our esteem, but of the knowledge and skill that we shall continue to gift to all those who join with us in friendship."

Malian was remembering how the lamps in the Old Keep had activated at her touch yet not Kalan's—but the Swarm had made sure that this lamp worked for the Duke. She watched him pass his hand across its surface, his expression thoughtful as the white light flowered, before he passed the same hand back, letting the glow fade. "You are generous with your gifts, Lord Arcolin," he said at last.

Arcolin bowed. "The Many-As-One *are* generous, Your Grace—but also humbly pleased that our gifts find favor."

"And in return for such generosity?" Duke Caril asked. "What, besides our reciprocal esteem and friendship, do the Many-As-One seek?"

Nherenor made a slight gesture; surely not of dissent? Malian thought. Does he really expect the Emerians to believe that such extravagance is offered without any thought of recompense? Arcolin turned slightly, catching his fellow envoy's movement, and Nherenor stilled at once.

"The Many-As-One greatly esteem the friendship of Emer," Arcolin said, smooth as cream. "So much so that we offer formal alliance."

"So my champion tells me." The Duke's nod was crisp. "Nor do we discount the benefits such an alliance could bring. We are willing to hear you further, and Ser Ombrose will arrange the necessary meetings. But for now, I hope that you will stay and join our luncheon?"

Malian could see the rigidity in Alianor's back—and remembering Summer's Eve and the were-hunts ravening on the Northern March, she dared not look at Ghiselaine. Surely, though, the Duke must know that the Many-As-One whose envoys he was entertaining were the same Swarm who had been behind those attacks, as well as the poisoned cup that had been sent to Ghiselaine in his son's name?

*"Yet we have already accepted,"* Nhenir interposed coolly, *"that Swarm actions in the north suggest their agents may be working at cross-purposes. As does the intervention at Tenneward lodge."* Again, Malian caught the surreptitious movement of Arcolin's eyes, as though he sensed the breath of another's power in the room: a clear indication that he was a sorcerer or adept of some kind himself.

The Duke stood up and joined Nherenor, signaling the end of the formal audience. "Ombrose tells me that you're competing in the tourney?" the Duke said, and the young envoy nodded, his expression growing animated. The servants began to withdraw with the empty caskets, and both Ghiselaine and Zhineve-An rose to their feet. Ghiselaine's smile had not reached her eyes, which looked strained. Zhineve-An was still very white, her gray gaze shadowed as she stared at Arcolin, and the Seven remained in their tight, protective formation.

"She looks as though she's seen a ghost," Alianor murmured. "But I'm not sure whether she is frightened or just angry."

Malian was fairly certain that the young queen was both. "Let me take the birdcage back to your apartments," she replied, just as quietly. "I will go over it while you're at this luncheon and make sure it's safe."

Alianor's eyes widened slightly and then she nodded. "I wish Lord Falk were here," she said.

Inwardly, Malian agreed. I have Lord Falk's commission, she thought—but what if that turns out to be contrary to the will of a Duke who has a queen of Jhaine sitting at his right hand and has just received Swarm emissaries with favor? Mind you, she reflected, if the Duke doesn't know about Lord Falk's commission, then he can't countermand it.

She found that thought cheering, despite her fear for Ghiselaine and foreboding at what the Swarm's presence here, bearing gifts and honeyed words, meant for the Derai Alliance. And I don't know the Duke's mind, she reminded herself; I can't be sure that he's been taken in.

"Do you think Ghiselaine could ask to see the J'mair

book?" she asked quietly. "I need the chance to look at every one of these gifts."

What better place to plant a fallback trap, after all, should the alliance talks fail—unless access to the palace and those about the Duke was the real fallback option. Malian folded her lips together, feeling as somber as Alianor had looked a few moments before. "I wish Lord Falk were here, too," she said, watching as the Duke bowed to Zhineve-An, offering her his arm. "Or any of the others, for that matter. But they aren't and we are." She relieved Ilaise of the birdcage as Ghiselaine accepted Ser Ombrose's escort from the room. "So," she added, her vision narrowing on the Swarm envoys being mobbed by smiling courtiers, "we'll just have to do the best we can."

# 36

# The Sword Ring

*T*he heralds, Kalan decided, had been right about tourney camps breeding rumor—and now, by the third day of elimination rounds, speculation was rife. It was hardly surprising, he supposed, given that Queen Zhineve-An had accompanied the Duke during the opening ceremonies, then spent the second afternoon with Ser Ombrose beside her in the ducal stand, while Ghiselaine had not yet made an appearance. The Normarch company might know that was because of the incident at Tenneward lodge, but all most people saw was the presence of the Queen of Jhaine and the absence of the Countess of Ormond. It did not help that Lord Hirluin had not yet arrived back from the Eastern March either, although he had been expected to attend the tournament prior to the ceremony officially reconfirming his betrothal to Ghiselaine.

No wonder people believe these rumors that he's going to marry Queen Zhineve-An instead, Kalan thought. Personally, he was starting to wonder what the Duke's heir was about, while Audin's habitual expression had become a frown. One Choughmark knight had been unfortunate enough to repeat the Lord Hirluin marriage rumor just before he was matched against Audin in the joust trials, and Kalan had never seen anyone go backside over crupper so fast.

"You know that story about Lord Hirluin can't be true," he had said, very quietly, while checking Audin's armor after the bout. "Not when your family have worked toward the Ormondian peace for so long."

Audin had looked down at Kalan, his mouth pinched. "My uncle could have some long-term strategy in mind."

Kalan had snorted. "Very long-term if it involves Jhaine." But he had bouts of his own after that, so there was no more time, then, for talk. They were in the final knockout rounds of both sword and joust now, which would continue throughout the day and determine who would proceed to the tourney proper. Jarna was still in the running to go forward in both the horse archery and the horsemanship trials, although the Lathayrans were proving as tough as she had expected in the archery.

"And horsemanship alone won't get me a place in a lord's household," she said to Kalan, with a small worried frown. The Normarch knights had retired to a low hill behind the ducal stand, where three oak trees spread welcome shade.

Kalan was keeping his eye on the sun, aware that he had more sword bouts in the early afternoon, but now he forced himself to concentrate on Jarna. He wanted to reach out and smooth away that frown with his fingertips, but he knew they had to remain careful, even amongst the inner circle of their friends. For her sake, even more than for his. He smiled at her reassuringly instead. "You'll be fine. And I'll come and cheer for you once my sword bouts are done."

Raher, who was sitting opposite them on a gnarled oak root, grinned at Jarna. "Of course you'll be fine," he said. "Even if you don't make any finals we're still going to ride as a company in the melee, and m'father says that you need knights who can do that well, rather than always charging down individual glory. Although," he continued after a moment's reflection, "I'm all for personal renown myself."

Girvase made a rude sound and they all chuckled. As always over recent days, Audin's grin faded first, replaced by a grim inward look. Kalan suspected that they all noticed, although no one said anything. He yawned to hide his sigh and stretched, knowing that he must not let himself stiffen up ahead of the afternoon contests. Girvase shaded his eyes, looking down the hill. "Here's Ilaise," he said.

It *was* Ilaise, Kalan saw, riding a tall cream mare and accompanied by two of the Bonamark pages. "She looks very fine," Raher said, standing up, and Kalan had to agree. He could not have said why, precisely, except that her dress looked very fashionable and her hair was caught up in a gold-and-silver net. But she waved as soon as she saw them and her smile was still the Ilaise he knew. Only Audin was frowning still.

"What are you doing here?" he asked, going to stand at the mare's head.

"Getting out of the palace," Iliase replied. "Ghis can't and Alli's still tired after the journey south, coming so soon after being wounded. So I said I would find out how the tournament was going. Also, I have an invitation for you all."

"A page could have brought that," Audin said. "This is a rough place, Illy."

She widened her eyes at him. "I know. I watched some of the bouts earlier. There was one knight—*if* he was a knight," she added, sniffing. "Anyway, apparently he comes from some savage northern country and he *looks* savage, more like a bear than a man. He fought like a savage, too." Her tone and expression grew reflective. "Like the kind of man who would maim an opponent deliberately."

Kalan flicked a look at Girvase and knew they were both thinking of the Derai, Orth, from their encounter the other night. "Besides, I have these pages," Ilaise continued, "and Lady Bonamark sent four guards as well. Once I saw you, I said they could wait and eat their lunch at the foot of the hill."

She undoubtedly had a knife somewhere about her, too, Kalan thought, remembering The Leas. "She'll be all right, Audin," he said. "What's the invitation, Illy?"

Ilaise smiled at him. "There's to be a grand fireworks display this evening, to honor the Queen of Jhaine. Ghis would like you to watch the fireworks with us, from the gallery of the ducal wing, and Lady Bonamark said she thought that would be unexceptional. Un-ex-cep-tion-al," Iliase repeated, with a wink that the pages behind her would not see.

"We'll be there," Audin said, and Girvase nodded.

Of course they would be, Kalan thought, amused. "But right now," he said, "Gir and I should both be back at the sword ground."

"I'm for the lists," Raher said, but he was still grinning at Ilaise. "You can come and watch if you like."

"You falling off?" she inquired, but she turned the cream mare and accompanied their clanking progress down the hill. The ducal palace, Kalan gathered from her remarks, was not the exciting place she had hoped it would be, despite the Midsummer festivities. "It's as crowded as the tourney camp," she said, wrinkling her nose. "And because Lord Hirluin's still not back from the Eastern March, Ghis's troth-pledge might not be until after Midsummer."

Kalan did not need Audin's quick frown to tell him that would be unfortunate, since the most auspicious time for both marriage and formal betrothals was Midsummer itself. He pulled an inward face and wondered what *was* keeping the Duke's heir. The deepening of Audin's frown suggested that he was wondering the same thing—but right now the trumpets were braying the resumption of competition and they all needed to focus on the bouts ahead. Killing an opponent might automatically disqualify a contestant, but accidents happened anyway, and injuries that crippled or maimed were also far from uncommon. Kalan had no intention of attracting ill fortune through lack of concentration.

"Who're you fighting?" Audin asked him, when he and Girvase had fully rearmed and they were all studying the board where the tourney marshals chalked in the competitors' coats-of-arms. It had amused Kalan to adopt the House of Blood's crimson, with a black horse head—all he dared use of Night's insignia—when he first came to Normarch. The colors opposite his were blue and orange, with a badger holding an oak branch.

"That's Vast," said Girvase, who always knew such things, "from Wymark." But he frowned at his own opponent's device, which was a black unicorn superimposed over a lightning bolt, both on a white ground. "Do you recognize it?" he asked.

"Only from the black tents," Kalan said, "the ones we saw the other night. I don't know the device, though."

Audin shook his head. "Or this sheaf of swords either," he said, studying the arms shown opposite his. "But we had better get to our places. You're both second round, and I'm fourth up." Bouts, as they all knew, rarely lasted long, even with opponents who knew each other's skill and were equally matched.

Girvase was right, and Kalan's opponent was Ser Alric of Vast, a tall, broad-shouldered man with receding hair and a discolored front tooth. An exponent of the swing-and-hew style of swordsmanship, Kalan thought, dodging the initial sweep of the Wymark knight's broadsword, which if it had connected would have cut him in two. But he was quicker on his feet than the taller knight, and despite one rough buffet when his dodge was not quite quick enough, was able to deflect the initial whirlwind assault and counterattack. Superior skill told, as well as speed, and once on the back foot Ser Alric had no answer to Kalan's attack. Within a few minutes it was all over, Kalan's boot resting on the blade of Ser Alric's sword and the tip of his own weapon at the disarmed knight's throat.

"You're good," the Wymarker said, as they shook hands under the bout marshal's eye. He accepted his sword back, his grin rueful. "Strong, as well, when I thought I at least had that advantage."

Kalan grinned, too, since Ser Alric seemed disposed to take his defeat in good part, but he was keen to see how Girvase was faring and ducked away as soon as courtesy allowed. Knowing his friend's ability, he was surprised to see that the round was still in progress—but then that, he supposed, was what tournaments were all about: testing your skill and aptitude against a wider field. The watching crowd was absorbed, and a few noisy bets were starting to be made.

Girvase and his opponent were a match for height and build, and the stranger knight looked lithe and compact in the blue-black armor Kalan recalled from beside the black tents. The helm was closed so it was impossible to see anything of the knight's face, but his speed and supple grace suggested that he was young. As soon as the combatants locked swords, Kalan could see that there was no advantage between them in terms of strength. They broke quickly and circled again, both light-footed as cats despite their armor, looking for an opening. The black knight sprang forward and Girvase moved back, his blade blurring in a flurry of counter and riposte. Locked together again, the swords rolled—and then it was Girvase who was attacking.

"I wonder how long they can keep this up," said a knight in Murreward colors.

"They're fit," one of his comrades replied. "This may go to points."

Those around him disclaimed immediately, because it was almost unheard of for bouts at this level to be decided on points, but Kalan noticed how closely the marshals were watching. Clearly, they thought they might be called upon to rule against one knight or the other. He could see the black knight's seconds now, two tall knights on the far side of the ring wearing the same blue-black armor, the lightning and unicorn device stark on their white surcotes. But he did not look long, because Girvase and his antagonist were raining blows on each other in a display of skill and power that made Kalan purse his lips in a silent whistle.

The black knight's style was fluid, almost seamless, he thought critically, while Girvase's was crisper. And although they must both be tiring now, he still could not fault either combatant's footwork or stance. He watched Girvase beat the black knight's sword aside and thrust forward, while his opponent leapt nimbly back, diverting the attack with a circular riposte—and wondered how much longer the marshals would let the bout continue. A great many trials still needed to be completed that afternoon, if the tourney finals were to start tomorrow.

As if heeding Kalan's thought, the senior marshal raised a whistle to his lips and blew a series of shrill blasts. Two of his fellows, both carrying heavily padded staves, moved forward to thrust the combatants aside—but Girvase and the black knight must have registered the whistle, for both were falling warily back. The marshals said something and both helmeted heads nodded, then raised their swords in salute before withdrawing to their corners. Kalan pushed through to reach Girvase and saw that two Allerion knights were ahead of him. "One of ours," the foremost said, as though warning Kalan off, but Girvase shook his head.

"My sword brother," he told them, and the Allerion knights nodded, stepping back. Girvase was breathing deeply but steadily and had pushed his visor aside. He was wearing the cool, intent look Kalan knew well. *"The sword and the warrior are one,"* he thought. It was a Blood axiom, one his father had been fond of quoting, but Girvase, Kalan thought, understood it in his soul. He grinned—and after a moment Girvase grinned back, the sword's-blade look receding. "I was enjoying that," he said. "But I suppose the marshals had to stop us."

"Given the time," Kalan agreed. "And no sign of any advantage developing either." On the far side of the ring the black knight had his visor open as well, and despite the veiling coif Kalan could see that he was the same young man who had grinned at his scuffle with Raher, on that first night in the camp. But the marshals had finished conferring now and their leader beckoned the contestants back to the center of the ring.

"We need a fighter like that back in our own Mark," one of the Allerion knights murmured to the other, so low that no one but Kalan could have overheard. Which boded well for Girvase, he supposed, before realizing that he had missed the senior marshal restating the black knight's name. Now the marshal was reminding everyone that Girvase Ar-Allerion was the second contestant—and then he raised both knights' arms high, signaling a draw, and the watchers erupted into cheers. The black knight leaned around to shake Girvase's hand and both young men were smiling.

"They're both unbeaten so far." The taller of the Allerion

knights craned to see the board. "So they'll definitely go forward."

His companion grunted. "A good decision, then. Although normally I don't like an inconclusive result."

And that, Kalan thought, seemed to be the mood of the crowd, with most of those he overheard just wanting to see both combatants fight again in the higher rounds of competition. The Allerion knights drifted off before Girvase returned, and the black knight and his seconds were walking away as Kalan removed his friend's casque. "Where was your opponent from?" he asked.

Girvase shook his head. "I didn't recognize his accent. Fire something, or somewhere, I thought the marshal said." He used a rag to towel the worst of the sweat from his hair, then narrowed his eyes at the board. "We're both done, for now. If you check on Audin's bout, I'll see how Raher's doing in the joust."

The crowd was deep around the ring where Audin was fighting, but very quiet, which meant that the clang of sword on sword was louder than usual. Kalan zigzagged his way between the onlookers until he had a clear view of the ring. Ado was in Audin's corner, his expression strained. A knot of men in well-worn armor faced him from the opposing corner of the ring, but it was what was happening within the ropes that held everyone's attention. Audin was taller than Kalan and almost as strongly built, but he looked slight, almost fine, beside the man who hulked opposite him. Orth, Kalan realized—with a sinking feeling in his stomach as he joined Ado, because in full armor the Derai looked as though he had been hewn from the rock of the Wall itself.

Kalan could not see the warrior's face behind his lowered visor, but the savagery Ilaise had spoken of was evident in every movement of his body and hammer blow of his sword. Bloodlust rolled off the man, and Kalan's fists clenched. Ilaise was right, he thought, this is someone who will deliberately maim an opponent, or even kill, uncaring of tourney rules. So far Audin was holding his own, but only just. It was clear to Kalan that the Derai warrior was overpowering him every time their blades met—and that Audin dared not let the swords lock lest his wrist be broken outright.

The question, Kalan thought, was not whether Audin could win, but how long he could hold out—and how much damage Orth would inflict before the marshals stopped him. The Derai seconds' faces were impassive as they watched their comrade pounding into Audin. They must have seen it all before, Kalan supposed, his anger sparking.

Audin was visibly tiring now, unsurprisingly given the onslaught he was facing. He was still using his shield, but holding his arm in a way that suggested he had taken damage. The Sword warrior's blade hammered down again, beating Audin's sword aside as though it wasn't there. Audin interposed his shield, and this time it took the full weight of the downstroke; he kept his arm and shield up but went down onto his knee. Ado groaned as the Sword warrior came in like a battering ram, raining blows onto the shield as Audin tried to swivel sideways and regain his feet. Across the crowd of silent watchers Kalan saw the knights in blue-black armor, disinterested behind their screening coifs and the spark of his anger quickened.

The Sword warrior's blade pounded down again and Audin rolled, a maneuver designed to bring him back onto his feet before his opponent caught up. He almost managed it, but the Sword giant covered the ground between them in a single stride and swung his blade like a club, catching Audin a tremendous wallop in the side. The young knight staggered sideways, fighting to regain his balance and turn—to get his shield in place.

"Serrut!" whispered Ado. "I think he's going to kill him."

Kalan thought so, too. The intention was written in every line of the Sword warrior's body, and Kalan could hear the blood thirst in the giant's roar as he raised his weapon again. Now everything was in slow motion: the sword coming up and Audin starting to straighten, to turn, bringing his shield up but not in time. It could never be in time, and given that last strike he might not be able to hold it anyway . . . Kalan was vaguely aware of riders watching from behind the heads of those crowded around the ring and hoped that one of them was not Ilaise, returned from watching the joust. Orth's sword had reached its apex now and was starting to descend: it was sweeping down, a mountain of force behind it—and Kalan pulled raw power out of the Emerian earth and willed it into Audin, infusing strength into his friend's shield arm and his legs.

The shield came into play in time and—impossibly—held. A sigh that was half a groan rippled through the crowd as Audin managed to stagger up, retreating from the Sword warrior's renewed assault. Kalan could gauge the blows himself now, through his bulwark of earth, and could not imagine how Audin had managed to last even this long. The Derai warriors were murmuring to each other, and from what Kalan's acute hearing could catch, they were equally amazed that Audin was still standing.

Kalan gritted his teeth, trying to shield his power use as best he could, but he dared not withdraw it. Audin might be on his feet and doggedly evading, but even with the infusion of additional strength he looked as though he might fall at any moment. Kalan bit his lip, aware of how much Audin wanted to make his own way, rather than rely on the Sondargent name and his standing as the Duke's nephew. Yet in battle none of them would have qualms about using Oakward power to thwart an enemy, especially if confronted by a squadron of Orths.

The tourney ground is not battle, Kalan thought—but this bout has turned into life and death.

The Sword warrior had stopped roaring now and was pursuing Audin in silence, intent as a stalking wolf. In a distant corner of his mind, Kalan wondered why the marshals were letting the situation play to its bitter end, when the bout was effectively already over. He didn't think he could afford to wait until they finally decided to take action, in any case: Audin was too near done. And even warrior Derai like Orth and his Sword comrades were bound to sense that he was supporting Audin sooner or later.

So if I am going to intervene further, Kalan thought grimly, it has to be now.

On the opposite side of the ring the young, black-armored knight took a step forward, ignoring the restraining hand of one of his companions. Almost, Kalan thought, still with that distant, observational part of his mind, as if he's thinking exactly the same thing I am. The coif concealed the young knight's expression, but his body stance and the angle of his head suggested a total focus on the endgame now being played out.

In the ring, Orth's sword thrust forward and the point would have driven between Audin's pauldron and gorget, piercing the vulnerable armpit area, if he had not twisted clear at the last moment.

More than time, Kalan thought, to finish this.

He drew a deep breath and concentrated power within himself, intense as the summer lightning that flickers above acrid earth. Orth pivoted, drawing his sword back for another hammer blow—and Kalan sent a flare of invisible energy leaping along the giant's sword blade and up his forearm.

For the first time, Orth was the one to leap back, yelling, although he did not drop his weapon. Audin lurched after him, although it looked as though even lifting his sword took everything he had. The two weapons rang together, sparks flying from the clash of metal—and Kalan released the molten flicker again, unseen beneath the blue Midsummer sky, and shattered Orth's blade.

Everything degenerated into confusion after that. The marshals leapt forward to hold Audin back while Orth kept yelling, a roar of inchoate rage that increased in volume as he focused on the two mounted watchers on the edge of the crowd. The riders were heralds of the Guild—Tarathan and Jehane Mor, in fact, Kalan registered, in a quick glance around as Orth bellowed out something about murder, revenge, and blood debt.

The yelling was in Derai, but Kalan was fairly certain that everyone present got the gist of thwarted rage and bloody mayhem. Eventually, when the marshals' poles were barely keeping Orth in his corner, the other Sword warriors mobbed their comrade and dragged him away. Only one of their number remained behind—to hear the outcome of the bout, Kalan supposed, although it was slow in coming.

"He'll win on points," Audin said, speaking indistinctly even after they had pulled his helmet off, because his mouth was full of blood. They had half carried, half led him into the shade of a pavilion awning, sitting him down on a wooden barrel that Ado dragged forward. He seemed to be finding it hard to keep his head up, and held the cloth that Kalan had given him clamped against his mouth.

"We thought he was going to kill you." Ado's voice was ragged.

Audin lifted his head sufficiently to meet their eyes. "The tourney life," he replied thickly.

Kalan shook his head. "Ado's right," he said. "This went beyond that." There was the business with the marshals as well, he thought grimly: the way they held back for so long. He hesitated, watching the heralds moving toward them around the edge of the crowd, and wondered how much more he should say.

"Is he all right?" The knight in blue-black armor was standing within a few paces of the awning, but not close enough to intrude. Seen up close, there was no question that he was very young, his dark eyes concerned beneath finely marked brows. Kalan kept his expression noncommittal as Ado went to speak with the newcomer, aware of the intent gaze of the young knight's companions, standing at a watchful distance.

"I'm fine," Audin mumbled into the bloody rag, and Kalan caught something else that sounded like: "Not a damosel."

"You're not," he agreed, grinning although his face still felt stiff. "But we should get you back to camp and out of that armor. Count your ribs to make sure they're all still intact."

"Be wary of the Derai," the young man was saying to Ado. "They are murderous and vengeful, even more so outside the ring."

"I'm not sure I can walk back," Audin said at the same time.

"Can you ride?" Tarathan asked, overhearing, as he swung out of the saddle. "If we can get you onto one of our horses?"

The black knight was looking at the heralds curiously—almost as though he had never seen one before, although Kalan thought everyone between Ij and Ishnapur would at least have heard of the gray-clad Guild. The marshals, were finally making their way through the crowd, and the young knight must have seen them, too, because he spoke a few more correct words to Ado and left with his companions.

The marshals, as expected, declared Orth a clear winner on points. Audin just nodded when they told him: beyond caring, Kalan suspected. And he was right, winning and losing were just part of the tourney life. As if feeling this, the last of the crowd had melted away to watch other bouts by the time they got Audin up onto Tarathan's horse. Kalan walked beside the tall gray as they started out for the Normarch camp, putting up a hand to support Audin when he swayed in the saddle.

"Good horse," Audin muttered. "Like one of Jarn's."

And Kalan realized that he had forgotten all about Jarna and his promise to watch her in the final elimination rounds of the horse trials.

# 37

## Adept

*O*utside the narrow windows of the Duke of Emer's study, fireworks were still bursting against a deep blue dusk, and Malian kept her eyes turned away from the exploding dazzle so as not to lose her night vision. She had entered through the deep window embrasure on the opposite side of the tower room and was crouched in the shadow of the floor-to-ceiling tapestries that served as its curtains. Shadow Band fashion, she kept her body angled to watch both windows and the door into the room while she studied the Darkswarm's gifts.

As far as she could tell, with a mental reservation around the subtleties of Swarm sorcery, the lamp and map book, like the gifts made to both Ghiselaine and Zhineve-An, were free of either magical or physical traps. Did that mean, she wondered, that the Swarm's embassy was genuine, or simply that the gifts would have been too obvious a ploy? They already knew about the existence of the Oakward, enough to bespell the welcome cup against detection, so would know that the gifts might be inspected.

*"Can you sense anything?"* she asked Nhenir, now in the guise of a flat, black felt cap fitting close around her head. *"Some passive magic I may have missed?"*

*"No,"* the helm replied. *"The gifts are as they seem and fit for their intended purpose."*

*"To impress."* Malian pursed her lips thoughtfully, although they had already discussed the gifts' subtle display of artifice and acumen. A more obvious present, for the Duke at least, might have been fine armor or weapons. Instead, what had been given complimented his known thirst for learning, on which he might well pride himself. The covert implication was clear enough as well: if we have the skill to create these objects, what might we not offer in the way of weapons and the crafts of war?

What indeed? Malian thought. She had not missed another implication either: that a Swarm alliance offering arms and the skill to make them, might well undermine the Derai's five-centuries-long trade with the River in metal ores, and the finest armor and weapons to be bought in Haarth. A trade, she reflected, that secured much of the food and other supplies that enabled the Derai Alliance to continue garrisoning the otherwise unlivable Wall of Night.

*"And,"* Nhenir added, *"by giving gifts of artifice and learning, the Swarm underlines its own culture and civilization."*

*"Compared to those who offer only raw materials or arms—although the hint that these, too, may be forthcoming is still there. Clever,"* Malian added, forced to admire the cunning of it.

*"The Duke comes,"* the helm said. *"With his champion."*

Malian was on her feet in an instant, restoring the lamp and the map to their places before concealing herself in the window embrasure, behind the tapestry curtains, as the door began to open. Someone with a light tread—a page, she guessed—lit the lamps, but withdrew as two heavier sets of footsteps entered the room. "You should use your gift lamp," Ser Ombrose said.

"The others are lit now," the Duke replied, his tone implying a shrug. A chair creaked, and Malian guessed that he had sat down. "I hear some northern thug came close to killing Audin today."

"The boy was outmatched." Ser Ombrose was matter-of-fact. "A herald pair attended his injuries afterward and I'm told he'll recover, with rest."

He did not, Malian noticed, mention Kalan's view—which Ilaise had brought back from the tourney ground—that the marshals let the bout continue far past the point where it was clear that Audin's opponent intended to kill him. She heard fingers drum against a wooden surface. "No more tourney, eh?" the Duke said. "The lad won't like that. I take it he's still at the camp?"

No, Malian thought, because Ilaise had told her about helping organize both the litter and the Bonamark escort that had brought Audin to the Normarch town house, close by the palace.

"I can find out," Ser Ombrose replied. More fireworks exploded and an outburst of applause followed. Malian heard the chair creak twice after the applause died away, as though the Duke had moved his weight forward and then almost immediately back again.

"And Hirluin?" he asked. "There's still no word?"

"None," Ser Ombrose answered. "I've sent a company east and I expect word soon, but delays on the road are not impossible, even at the height of summer. Is the Ormondian making demands?"

Caril of Emer's laugh was a short harsh bark. "No, that's Queen Zhineve-An's domain at present."

"Ah, the business of the Great Marriage." Was that humor in Ser Ombrose's voice? Malian wondered. Until now it was not a quality she had associated with the man. "I don't know where she gets the idea that it was implicit in the invitation your grandfather extended. Our clerks can find no word of it."

"And tact," the Duke observed dryly, "is clearly not taught in the temple precincts of Jhaine. Today she conceded that my heir may do just as well if I do not care for the idea."

"Pack her home," his champion replied.

"Don't tempt me." The Duke's chair creaked sharply, followed by the sound of pacing footsteps. "But a Jhainarian alliance will benefit Emer, and the last thing we want is the Nine Queens going to Lathayra instead. So I need to find a way to deal with her—and offer something attractive to Jhaine by way of a treaty."

"You could just meet her demands," Ser Ombrose said.

The pacing stopped. "I could," the Duke replied finally. "But I need to know more about this Great Marriage first: whether it is a true marriage or just a rite, and what the implications of either would be for the balance of power within Emer." The fireworks had stopped now although there was still plenty of noise, the talk and laughter rising above the music that had started up. "And there's the other business."

His tone had not changed, but Malian was instantly aware of the seer's stillness within herself, the recognition that he was saying something that had the potential to profoundly influence the pattern of unfolding events. Concealed behind the heavy curtains, she narrowed her eyes, waiting.

"The endless questions about the River and Guild of Heralds you mean?" Ser Ombrose's tone was indifferent. "I've told them to speak with the River maister, your new cartographer."

"I believe they've already spoken once, when Countess Ghiselaine asked to see the *Seasonal Analects*." The Duke resumed pacing, and Malian could almost hear the headshake in his voice as he spoke again. "Clearly, they are looking for someone and their suspicion has fallen on the Guild. The queen is not particularly subtle—and you've seen the Seven. They're wild as half-trained hawks, and with a similar notion of consequences, I imagine. But I don't want any trouble, Ombrose, not right now, so we need to keep them away from any herald pairs in the city."

"Or throw them together," the champion drawled. "See what transpires."

The Duke laughed again, the same short hard bark. "Not right now, Ombrose. First we need to get through Midsummer."

"Yes." Ser Ombrose paused and the Duke's pacing stopped—caught, Malian guessed, by the edge to his nephew's voice. When the champion did speak, he sounded as though he was choosing every word with care. "It might be easier to do that, sire, if you did not intend relinquishing the Sondargent name as part of the rebetrothal ceremony. *That* was never part of the peace treaty—and many gathered here will dislike it."

"As you do," the Duke replied quietly. "But sometimes in order to have peace we need to *make* peace—to give something, as well as demand concessions. And Midsummer is the time for making the world new."

"Sondargent is the history of Emer." Ser Ombrose's voice was tight. "You can't just give that up."

Malian heard the Duke move and guessed that he had stepped closer to his nephew, perhaps even clasped his arm. "So is Sondormond, Ombrose. And Ghiselaine is the last of that line. My hope is that if she and Hirluin both take Sondemer as their name, and their children are born to it, that will help create the peace we want."

But does Ser Ombrose want peace? Malian wondered, mindful of his reputation from the Lathayran wars. The Duke moved again, his step brisk. "Speaking of Countess Ghiselaine," he said, "have you made any progress on the business with the cup?"

"Nothing but dead ends—" Ser Ombrose began, but broke off as someone rapped on the door. A moment later a boy's voice spoke.

"Your Grace, you asked me to call you when supper was about to be served, so you could escort the queen."

"Ah yes. We'll talk again later, Ombrose—although I suppose you'll be retiring early, since you're to compete in the tourney yourself from tomorrow." Malian thought the Duke sounded almost regretful, as though wishing he could be the one taking part.

The champion murmured assent, and the page snuffed out the lamps as the men left the room. Their voices receded, cutting off altogether as the page, too, departed, closing the door behind him. Malian waited, just to be sure she was completely alone, before opening the window. The night air was cool, and this side of the tower dark, as she eased onto the ledge.

*"I suppose I should join what's left of the festivities,"* she said to Nhenir, *"although I gather most of the courtiers will go roistering in the city afterward."* It had been the same in Ar whenever the prince entertained at the palace, with some of the courtiers always ending up fighting with students or the watch before the night was over.

Malian made her way around the ledge to another window embrasure, then down the finger- and toeholds on the buttress that supported it. She was aware of the jumbled roofs and small courtyards below her, but had never been afraid of heights—and despite its sheer appearance the Black Tower was not a difficult climb in these lower reaches. Still, it was not until she finally dropped into one of the courtyards that she allowed herself to review the overheard conversation.

*A dead end in respect of the cup was perhaps not surprising with the Swarm in the city as guests. But,* she resolved, *I need to find out more about this Great Marriage as well, especially if it could affect the balance of power in Emer.*

The terraces facing onto the river were thronged with people, and Malian mingled with the crowd, pretending to drink from the goblet she took from a servant's tray. Queen Zhineve-An was seated amongst a cluster of Emerian nobles, with the Duke talking to others nearby. Malian thought the young queen looked more like Alianor's gilded doll than ever, her smile fixed in place, and noted how the Seven hovered close, nervous and restive. Ser Ombrose was watching them, too, from his place on the edge of the group, a place Malian thought at odds with both his position and his flamboyant clothes.

The champion's gaze drifted across the crowd and she felt his regard linger briefly on Maister Carick before shifting on. Malian waited for the tune to end before moving further along the terrace, but could see no sign of Ghiselaine or any of the Normarch knights, and guessed they had already returned to the Gallery wing.

The way there involved crossing the wide paved court-yard by the main gates, which was as crowded as the rest of the palace. A dancer of Kan's boon, Malian thought, negotiating the fringes of the bustle. The moon was rising, yellow and not quite round above the palace wall: it would be full tomorrow evening, for the first of the three nights that marked the Midsummer rite.

The door into the Gallery wing banged back and the Nor-march company surged down a flight of stone steps and into the yard. Malian watched the torchlight cast fire across Kalan's tawny hair—except that he was all Hamar here, seen amidst the circle of his friends. They milled at the foot of the steps, waiting for their horses, and Malian thought that all the young knights seemed subdued. Because of Audin, she wondered, or did all the day's contests go badly? She was about to make her way over to them when grooms brought up the horses with a clatter. One horse shook its head, whinnying shrilly—and a darkness slid along the top of the courtyard wall.

Malian stood very still as the darkness changed form, blending into light as it crept above a lantern bracket, then dropping back into shadow again, but always keeping pace with the riders as they moved toward the gates. The breeze gusted, and an unmistakable Darkswarm taint licked at the edge of her Band-honed seeker's sense.

*"Conceal me,"* she said to Nhenir, calling on the helm's fabled ability to pass by others unnoticed. She was already seeking for additional enemies as she followed the darkness toward the palace gates, careful to let her use of power fray into the nighttime life of the city: the swirl of people around inns and food vendors' stalls, the stealthy movement of cats and rats in back alleys, and the gossip from one house to another as neighbors prepared to pull their shutters closed. Where there was one darkspawn, there could easily be more—and the spring's events in Ij made it clear that the Swarm had found assassin allies.

A group of courtiers strolled past and Malian moved with

them, assisting Nhenir by adjusting her pace and the rhythm of her walk to theirs. The guards waved them through, their expressions half bored, half envious. A short distance from the gate, the street opened out into a square, with a statue of some long dead Emerian hero at its center and plane trees around the periphery.

Malian caught a stronger whiff of the Darkswarm taint at the corner, as though the shadow she followed had lingered there. She paused herself, searching for any evidence of assassin activity, but could detect none. The Normarch company had dismounted outside a town house of creamy stone on the far side of the square, with Lord Falk's fox banner above the gate, while Girvase watered his horse at the trough outside a nearby inn. Malian waited, letting the courtier band move on without her.

She was not surprised, a few moments later, when the heralds appeared in the gateway to the Normarch house, because Ilaise had said they intended accompanying Audin into the city. But she did blink at the little rush of gladness she felt as the torchlight cast a halo across Jehane Mor's familiar, calm expression, and Tarathan's clubbed braids.

Malian began to work her way toward the house, easing from group to group with every shift and sway of the evening crowd. She would occasionally pause, as though listening to gossip or watching children play draughts beneath a tree. Once, she tossed a coin to a girl strumming a lute; a few paces further on she bought a skewer of grilled fish from a vendor's stall.

Odd, Malian reflected, enjoying the sweet-sour mix of the sauce, to be feeling momentary nostalgia for the small gray world of Normarch, when Caer Argent and the rivers of information that flowed through the Midsummer festival had always been her goal. Perhaps it was simply that the Normarch life had seemed so certain, the issues of survival on the edge of Emer clear-cut. She licked her fingers, letting her gaze move across the square—and saw a blot of darkness stir in the entrance to an unlit alley.

Her seeker's sense told her that the watcher's attention was focused on the group outside the Normarch house. She shifted position so she could still see the alley while also taking in the town house entrance, where Raher was talking to the heralds. Kalan and Jarna had crossed to a booth selling Midsummer fruit, and Malian saw Jarna smile as Kalan hung long-stemmed cherries over her ears. They swung when the girl moved her head, glowing richer in the lanternlit dusk than any jewels worn by the great ladies of the Emerian court.

Kalan leaned close, saying something, and Jarna ducked her head shyly, but she was still smiling. Malian, watching, was conscious of a pang that she had not felt before. Of something lost? she wondered. Or the confirmation, if she had needed it, that Kalan more than half belonged to Emer now? She bit her lip as Jarna glanced up again, the young knight's feelings written all over her face for anyone who happened to be looking.

Girvase led his horse back to the Normarch gate and the company mounted up. The heralds must have advised them not to disturb Audin, Malian supposed—but now the dark shadow was moving, too, following the Normarchers again although it kept well back. Malian sauntered in the same direction, keeping to the densest part of the crowd. A group of young men passed her, laughing as they headed toward the inn, and again she adjusted her pace, using their movement as a shield to reach the far side of the square. She found the watcher more quickly this time, pressed into a door arch halfway down the road the Normarch company had taken. Malian waited, ostensibly watching a noisy game of dice at the boundary of street and square, until the company disappeared around a corner and the shadow left the sheltering arch.

Now it moved more swiftly, but no one in the evening crowd appeared to notice anything amiss. Malian moved quickly as well, slipping into a side lane and scaling the nearest house wall. From the wall, it was easy to reach the dwelling's chimney and swarm up the roughly stacked stone.

A cat looked down at her, surprised, then sprang away as she raced along the edge of the parapet, jumping the narrow gaps between the close-built houses until she could peer down onto the street the Normarchers had taken. They were just turning off it into another thoroughfare, but the shadow was still with them. Keeping to the rooftops, Malian ghosted after them all.

The city's Maraval gate was open and the watchmen there barely looked around as the Normarch company rode through. This time, though, the dark watcher turned away, finding another narrow alley and flowing up the walls and onto the rooftops. Malian pressed herself flat against tile and stone, only following when the shadow began to move away from her, eastward across the city. It gained speed as it went, billowing out like a cape, and she wondered exactly what kind of Swarm minion it was.

The silent journey over the rooftops of Caer Argent ended in an area dominated by the homes of prosperous merchants, with the houses rising three and four levels to meet the sky. The garden into which the shadow descended was warded by sorcery. Malian could feel the grid of power from her rooftop on the far side of the street, and her lip curled at the unmistakable Darkswarm taint. Delicately, she let her awareness trace the rim of the wards, searching for any hint of weakness.

The garden below the wall was cloaked in darkness, but stone steps rose out of it to join a small terrace, with lamplight gleaming through the floor-to-eave shutters beyond. Malian waited, patient, until the shadow glided up the steps and tapped on the shutter, a precise tattoo that carried clearly in the quiet night. She committed the pattern to memory, her fingers repeating it against the roof parapet as she counted silently, timing the seconds until the shadow watcher knocked again. The second sequence replicated the first exactly, she noted, as one panel of the shutters folded back.

Malian recognized the figure that stepped put onto the terrace to search the night with a seeker's mindsweep, although the last time she had seen its like had been in a dream. She remembered the long trailing robes and the head that was completely shaven except for the hank of plaited hair that curved down the right side of the androgynous face. Yet she was as sure, now, that the seeker was a woman as she had been in the white mists on Summer's Eve.

The seeker's voice hissed and the shadowy figure replied. Malian noticed a hint of impatience in the low tone, just as she registered that the seeker's sweep did not extend much beyond the line of established wards. Another voice spoke from inside, a man's deep tone, and the hissing voice replied. The mindsweep probed the night again before the robed figure stepped aside, allowing the newcomer to enter.

The air around the dark watcher bent, the shadows billowing outward again—and a human form emerged, stepping away from the smoky swirl of darkness and folding what looked like a cloak across his arm. Nherenor, Malian thought, recognizing him from the audience with the Duke—and could have laughed out loud for the sheer surprise of the shadow cloak. They were in all the stories, but until you saw the transformation take place . . . And it explained how Nherenor had blended into the light as he passed the torch above the castle courtyard.

The mail corselet the young man wore over his otherwise plain black clothes rippled like the scales of a living fish as he stepped into the lighted room, lifting a hand to push his long hair back. He doesn't look like a Swarm minion at all, Malian thought—which I suppose makes it certain he's another facestealer.

*"Darksworn."* Nhenir's mindvoice was sure, and Malian's lips thinned. Another figure moved into the narrow frame of the open shutter before she could respond and she recognized Arcolin, wearing similar robes to the woman. He was holding what looked like an Ishnapuri calligraphy brush between gloved hands, and Nherenor looked away from it, his expression one of distaste as he moved to close the shutter.

*"Time to get closer,"* Malian said to Nhenir, deciding that it should be possible. The wards were strong, but bound to the perimeter of the property—and a great elm formed the whole of the neighboring garden. *"I may need your help to listen in, as well,"* she added, and began the descent from the roof.

# 38

## Hide and Seek

$A$ few minutes later, Malian was concealed amongst the elm's branches and could see more of the house where the Swarm envoys were staying. A graveled walk ran the length of the building, linking the rear garden to a formal courtyard at the front, and a feature window of colorful Ijiri glass was set into the wall of the shuttered room. The colored panes made it difficult to see clearly, but she could make out the three Darkswarm, their shapes clearly distinguishable whenever they stood between the lanternlight and the glass. One of the elm's lower branches extended over the boundary and would bear her weight; she should be able creep along it as far as the wall without triggering the protective wards.

Carefully, Malian eased forward, almost to the wall, then reached up to touch the helm. Whatever form Nhenir presented to the world, her fingertips always felt its true shape: the visor wrought in the shape of Terennin the Farseeing's dawn eyes, and the inlaid wings that swept up and wrapped around the back of the casque. *"Ready?"* she queried, and lowered the visor.

" . . . I don't know why you waste time watching the Normarchers." Arcolin's voice was amused, and as clear as though Malian were standing beside him, which she might as well have been. "They must be the most uncouth of all this land of savages."

"Savages that thwarted Rhike and the were-hunts in the north." Nherenor was cool, and Malian heard the woman hiss. "And someone used power today in the sword ring, to stop the Derai before he killed the Duke's nephew."

"I thought that might have been you." Arcolin sounded idle, but Malian did not miss the note of steel. "I am glad that it was not. Bad enough that you feel you must compete in their petty games of war." Malian watched his hand rise in a checking gesture. "Oh, I know that it is politic. I even agree that it may serve our cause—but these Emerians are nothing more than short-lived insects. Never forget that, or who you are: who *we* are."

"Insects with some power," Nherenor returned, although he sounded stung.

"Atavistic animism," Arcolin replied, and Malian saw his shrug. "We have slain their Oakward before, in the past, and will again at need."

*"Emuun,"* the woman hissed, with considerable venom, and Arcolin nodded.

"He likes to play his games, and at the moment Nirn's hand remains over him. But he will undoubtedly pay, sooner or later, for the wreck of your work in the north."

"Work," Nherenor pointed out, "that went against what we try to do here."

Arcolin shrugged again. "We play for high stakes and need more than one strategy for the game. I am willing to try Nindorith and your father's way here, although both Aranraith and Nirn oppose it." He turned away from the window. "Yet I confess to being puzzled at why Nirn believes this one herald pair are important enough to let Emuun run amok."

"I saw them today at the tourney ground." Nherenor was hesitant. "They have some power, of the kind our people on the River report of their Guild, but nothing out of the ordinary. Not that I could detect, anyway."

"Nirn *sees*," the woman hissed again.

"And may also be quite mad," Arcolin answered, deep

and dispassionate. "Still, I concede that this pair evaded our hunters for a long time in the north. And I understand *your* anger, Rhike, because driving them into Emuun's hand should have been enough. But the fist refused to close." The envoy's voice grew contemplative. "Even so, it was not herald magic that stopped our agents on the Northern March. The Oakward had a hand in it, but there was at least one other power in the mix that we cannot place. And the hint of a Derai taint."

"Derai?" Nherenor sounded as though he was frowning. "How is that possible?"

"It's not *im*possible," Arcolin replied. "Not many of their power users escape that cursed Wall, but there's a suggestion some do—and that they're harbored by interests within Haarth." Rhike hissed again. "Ay, *if* we come across them, we'll stamp them out like rats. But finding them is not our priority. Not yet."

"But that moon . . ." Nherenor dropped his voice. "Nindorith says it may have been of Haarth itself."

"Then let Nindorith deal with it," Arcolin said, almost with a snap. "For now, we have other business."

*"Nindorith."* Nhenir's voice was a sliver of ice across Malian's mind and she nodded, taking the warning. Emuun, she guessed, must be the warrior she had seen beyond the Gate of Dreams. What she could recall from Summer's Eve fitted with the implication that he was playing a deep game. But what game, and why: the same questions that could be asked about Arcolin, in particular, but also Nherenor.

*"Who* is *Nindorith?"* she asked Nhenir.

*"A great power."* The helm's mindvoice was a chime of ice and darkness again, but Malian's head turned, her enhanced hearing catching the clip-clop of hooves. Four horses entering the street, she thought, calculating, or was it five? The hooves fell silent and a sharp knock sounded from the gate.

The three Swarm silhouetted against the window paused as though listening, and then Nherenor moved out of Malian's sight. No one spoke, but she heard an internal door open and close. A moment later, wood scraped across stone from the direction of the main entrance. The front door was concealed, but Malian could make out the gate onto the street if she craned forward. A tall warrior in blue-black mail and a white surcoat crossed from the house and drew the bolts, letting in four dark, cloaked figures. As soon as the gate closed again, the hooves clipped away.

The newcomers had deep hoods pulled well forward and their cloaks were long, almost touching the ground as they walked toward the house. The foremost visitor must have moved too close to the paving's edge, for he cursed when his left foot slipped, his cloak snagging on a shrub as he regained his balance. He paused to unhook it and Malian saw that one leg was clad in emerald green, the other peacock blue. Many men in Caer Argent were wearing the fashionable, parti-colored hose, but still . . . sapphire blue and emerald green were expensive dyes, the sort only the richest men could readily afford. It might be coincidence that Ser Ombrose had been wearing those exact colors during the Swarm's audience, and again today, but Malian doubted it.

Admittedly, it was no secret that the Duke's champion was the official liaison to the Swarm delegation—but to visit so secretly and late at night, when he had let the Duke believe he would be retiring early because of the next day's tournament . . . Malian shook her head, thinking that it did not look good.

"At last," Arcolin said. "But you had better leave, Rhike, before Nherenor brings them in. We don't want to scare our guests off."

Rhike bowed her head to him, then stiffened. "Nindorith comes," she hissed.

The portal tore open almost directly in front of the elm branch where Malian lay. She recognized the power that surged through from the grounds of Tenneward Lodge—and that what she had encountered was only the shadow of the entity that was arriving now. For a split second it reminded her of Hylcarian, but the flames that ignited around the edges of the portal were black, and the force behind it was greater than anything she had ever felt before, even in the heart of the Old Keep.

Unfettered power, she thought dizzily, as darkness swept over her; the backwash of energy nearly knocked her from the branch. An outline danced in the heart of the black fire, shifting like the shadow cloak—as though whatever being had just stepped through into the Caer Argent night could adopt whatever shape it chose. Malian let her own mind grow clear and still, her awareness flowing into *seeing* the true form that lay at the heart of this unknown darkness.

*"No! He will percieve you, even through me!"* Nhenir's denial blocked her as the flames roared, twisting serpentlike around the portal. For a moment the shape at its core looked like a giant horse with a sweep of fire instead of a mane, and blazing meteors where Malian expected eyes. Sparks flew from igneous hooves, and the great head turned: the long, razor-sharp horn extending out of its forehead pointed directly toward her heart.

He does see me, she realized, frozen in place. Even wearing Nhenir, he still sees me.

Her body began to shake with the effort of holding the dark regard at bay. The power that buffeted at her was immense, snatching away both her breath and her grip on the tree. She fell, tumbling through twigs and leaves, and only just managed to catch at her strength and training in the last moments, landing in a crouch on her feet.

Power gusted again and a jagged line ran through the wall that separated her from the house used by the Swarm. The next moment, the wall came tumbling down in a thunder of bricks and clouds of mortar dust. It was the touch of the horn that had done it, Malian knew that without needing to be told. She could see that the portal was closing, too, but not before more warriors in blue-black armor swarmed through behind Nindorith, silver-white lightning bolts striking down on either side of their closed helms. The Swarm demon had grown formless again, but she could feel his will, grasping for control of her mind. Grimly, Malian threw him off—and felt Nindorith's ripple of surprise.

*"Who are you? What?"* The voice of power cracked around her, crashing into her head like storm waves so that she almost fell again. She gritted her teeth, forcing herself to stay upright. Her hand and mind moved instinctively toward the sustaining cold of Yorindesarinen's armring, because right now all that mattered was escape and Nhenir had gone completely silent, inert as any base metal. Hiding, she realized, recalling how Nindorith had looked through illusion and shadow and *seen* her.

Malian's lips moved, mouthing an incantation that thickened the cloud of mortar dust as she slipped sideways into the elm's shadow. The lightning warriors were spreading out across the wall's fallen bricks as Nindorith grasped for her mind again. The shutters along the terrace had been pushed back and someone inside the house was yelling. Malian caught the words "intruders" and "enemy attack" as she flung off Nindorith a second time. But she knew she could not fend him off for long.

A bowstring thrummed from the terrace, and she pushed back hard at Nindorith, diving into what was left of the shrubbery beside the fallen wall and worming her way through it like a snake. The dark mind darted after her, quick as a serpent itself, and the warriors shouted, running to close off physical escape. Malian knew Nindorith would direct them straight to her unless she could conceal both mind and body—but the garden was too small. Wherever she hid, they would hunt her out soon.

She hesitated, the scent of earth and rotting leaves and the mustiness of mice—there must be a nest nearby—strong in her nostrils. The green power that had stirred in Maraval wood welled through her as she breathed in, intensely aware of the elm's deep roots and the shallower fibers of the shrubbery—as well as the numerous insects and minute night creatures that inhabited this small world. A beetle crawled out of leaf mulch and over her hand as another tendril of dark power slithered across her mind.

This time Malian did not throw it off, but instead let her energy dissipate amongst the myriad small lives of the night garden. A man's voice cursed, very close to her, and across the street a shutter banged open, a querulous voice demanding to know what was going on. Malian's lips moved again, not gathering illusion and shadow this time—the stock-in-trade of the Shadow Band—but drawing the tiny pulse beats and formless thoughts around her into a loose weave before tapping deeper still, into the memory of the trees in Maraval wood shifting to banish Yorindesarinen's apparition.

The elm creaked, although the night breeze had died away—and Malian cast her net of small energies and diffuse minds outward, spreading to catch the Swarm hunter. The elm creaked again, dangerously, its great trunk bending and its branches whipping to the ground. The warriors cried out, jumping back, and Malian felt her patchwork net close over Nindorith's power. She sensed the dark mind recoil, then almost immediately recover, flowing along the cobwebbed weave to find its source. But she was already springing for the outer wall, pulling a flurry of shadows along with her to confuse the hunters.

Behind her, the net disintegrated, and Malian bit her lip, hoping the weave had been loose enough for the small night creatures to flee through the gaps—but she was over the wall now and away, sprinting past the nearest alley and down a side street. Her eyes raked its length for a quick route to the roofs as Nindorith's mindsweep blasted: she staggered, knowing it would have wiped her mind clear had she not been steeled for it. She wanted to throw up but kept her feet, the nausea persisting as she ran on. Behind her, a gate thudded open and boots pounded on cobbles. Her temples pounded, too, as she felt the tremor that heralded a second mindsweep building.

A psychic shield slammed around her like rock, and Malian heard the half sob of relief that was her breath as the mindsweep was shut out. *"Here!"* She caught the mental image in the same moment as the mindcall—a coal hatch at the end of the alley where the buildings stepped lower, with an easy climb from there to the top of the wall, and then the roof. Behind her, the pursuing voices had grown confused. Having lost their guiding intelligence, she guessed they would now be checking every alley and peering through gates into shadowed gardens. She sprang onto the hatch and leapt for the arms that came down and grasped hers, hauling her bodily to the roof.

*"Let's go!"* said Kalan, as he and Tarathan released her arms. Malian nodded, sucking in a great lungful of air, then racing after them along the roof. She could still feel Nindorith's power, shockingly strong on the far side of the shield's buffer. A quick glance back showed the rooftop still empty as they ducked around the gable end of the next house. They ran along the eaves then up the adjoining roof toward a cluster of chimneys, dropping into the deep shadow at their base and slithering to the far side of the brick stacks. All around them, Caer Argent stretched away, a sea of tiles interspersed by slender spires, with the basilica of Imuln a great island in the distance.

Another mindsweep shook the night, but passed harmlessly away as Kalan swung the crossbow off his back. The sword at his side was short, with a long dagger on the opposite side, and the haft of another just showing above his boot. He was wearing an archer's leather cap and quilted gambeson—to avoid the betraying rattle of metal, Malian guessed. On his far side, Tarathan still wore his herald's gray, but carried a short, recurved bow and had the swallowtail swords strapped to his back.

"How did you know where I was?" she asked, keeping her voice very low but avoiding the betraying hiss of a whisper.

Kalan shrugged. "Because of our bond, I knew you were there when we left the palace yard. But then in the square I realized that you were tracking someone else." He glanced sideways at the herald. "Tarathan knew you were close, too."

"That's been easier since the Seven and Summer's Eve," Tarathan said, and she nodded, accepting that. "I was able to follow you at some distance until Kalan joined me and could shield us both."

"Where's Jehane Mor?" Malian asked.

"Somewhere they won't find her easily," Tarathan replied. "But we remain linked to each other."

"Which is helping with the shielding." Kalan sounded almost breathless, as though he was running again. "Nine-cursed darkspawn is strong though," he added, as another mindsweep blasted across the night. "My shield may not hold, not against this."

"They want to know who I am," Malian replied, "and then see me dead. We need to lose them."

Kalan grunted. "I vote for opening a portal and disappearing."

*"No."* Nhenir's interjection was incisive. *"The boy's shield is not sufficient to prevent Nindorith sensing a gate opening—and tracking through the Gate of Dreams is one of his specialities."*

Wonderful, thought Malian. She extended her seeker sense beneath the cover of Kalan's shield and detected a patch of darkness, then several more, drifting up toward the rooftops. "No time now," she said conversationally. "We've got company."

A half second later several blots of inky blackness appeared above the eaves, long filaments trailing beneath them. A line of warriors in grotesque helms rose up beside them, their bestial heads turning left and right. Tarathan strung his bow.

"The tendriled creatures are lurkers," he told them. "They sense heat and movement, so the shield won't protect us once we move or they get close enough. We can take out one, perhaps two, but then we'll have to run regardless."

"But if you have any Shadow Band sleight-of-eye to play . . ." Kalan added.

*"Or if you were willing to make yourself useful,"* Malian said to Nhenir. She was remembering what the crow had told her, long ago: that the moon-dark helm had a will of its own and should be treated with circumspection. Not to be relied upon, Malian thought, surprised at her own lack of bitterness. Her eyes narrowed as she watched the Swarm

warriors fan out across the roof, with the lurkers floating ahead.

Soon, she thought—and Tarathan drew back his arm, the loosed arrow striking dead center amidst a lurker's inky blackness. The creature collapsed, not unlike a deflated balloon, but the second arrow was already flying, followed rapidly by a third, bringing the lurkers down in quick succession. They shrieked as they collapsed, but the warriors in the grotesque helms remained completely silent, retreating out of range and unslinging their own bows. They would almost certainly have some sort of link to either Arcolin or Nindorith, Malian thought. "Time to go," she said.

"We need to separate," Tarathan said briefly. "Split the pursuit."

Malian nodded, knowing that made sense. She did not have to like it, though, as the herald went in one direction and she eased down the roof behind Kalan, then ran, bent low, along the eaves. She probed with her mind as she went, loosening tiles on several of the adjoining roofs and catching at a wreath of smoke from a kitchen chimney on the other side of the street. She sent the tiles sliding and clattering down at the same time as the smoke separated into two figures, each racing in a different direction along midnight ridgepoles. Voices shouted at last and Malian grinned, following Kalan down to the next, lean-to level.

Another mindsweep powered across the night as she landed, crouching as close to Kalan as possible. She hoped that the strength of each sweep would begin to dissipate soon, as Nindorith was forced to cast a wider net. "We need more distance," Kalan said, already back on his feet. "Are you sure you can't just open a portal—get us out of this?"

With Tarathan gone it was safer to speak of Nhenir, but Kalan shook his head when she relayed what the helm had told her. "So much for heroic weapons!" He was moving as he spoke, and Malian sprang to catch up, feeling a rush of exhilaration, so darkly fierce it was almost joy, as they cleared the first narrow street, cobbles flashing beneath them. To fall would be to die—but they were not going to fall. Her blood sang as they ran on, keeping to the narrow lanes and close-packed houses of the poorer quarters where there were plenty of sharp angles and deep shadows to hide in.

Soon they were running as one, each knowing intuitively how the other would move, racing up roof slopes without hesitation and plunging down the far side, floating effortlessly across the gaps between buildings until Malian felt as though she were flying above Caer Argent. The pale gold moon kept pace alongside, so close it seemed she might touch it, or gather the white stars for a crown like the one worn by Yorindesarinen—if only she stretched out her hand at the right moment.

They dropped down to street level again several times, but the old parts of the city were a maze, the streets little more than alleys with many dead ends. The roofs offered a clearer path, and they could orient themselves by the towers of the palace complex and the basilica's dark crown. Malian was unsure when the mindsweeps stopped, but it was a long time after that when she noticed the stars growing pale, a reminder that the Midsummer dawn came early. She knew they must have crossed half the city and by rights she should feel tired, but instead she felt wonderfully and gloriously alive.

They were circling what appeared to be a ruin now, even though it lay within the city boundaries. The wall that backed onto the neighboring houses was crumbling, and Malian could make out dark foundations beneath fallen beams, and a jagged curtain wall rising into a solitary tower. "This must be the old Cendreward mansion," Kalan said. "Audin said it caught fire in his great-grandfather's time and has never been rebuilt." He paused. "One of the stories is that the Cendreward lord of that time set the fire himself, out of madness and grief for his sons who all died in the Ormondian wars."

Perhaps he was a little mad to start with, Malian reflected—although it was exactly the sort of thing a Derai would do and not be thought mad at all. I'm starting to see things with Haarth eyes, she thought, and shivered, shaken out of the exultant, rooftop rush. She noticed the brooding quiet at once, and extended her seeker's awareness into the thinning dark. Kalan's head turned, too, listening—and he wound a quarrel onto the crossbow as Malian slid throwing stars out of her sleeve.

A line of warriors wearing blue-black armor, with lightning flashes on their helms, appeared above the roof ridge ahead. The nearest warrior laughed, and although he wore the same closed helm as the rest, Malian recognized Nherenor before he spoke, his voice holding the same thread of laughter. "Did you think to escape so easily, assassins or Derai pawns or whatever you are? You may be clever, but we have one who can see through time to where our enemies will be—and open doors in the air to bring us there."

"Enough talk," said another warrior, drawing back his javelin to throw.

Kalan shot him, the crossbow quarrel punching through the eye slit in the warrior's helm as Malian cast the throwing stars in quick succession. She aimed for eye slits as well, and any gaps between pauldron, gorget, and helm closure, making the warriors duck and swerve as she jumped for the edge of the wall. Kalan swung the crossbow as a warrior leapt for him, knocking the man's sword aside then battering the heavy bow into his face before he followed Malian. A bowstring twanged above them as they hung side by side, full length from the edge of a buttress.

*"You lie low,"* Kalan mindspoke as the arrow whined past. *"I'll draw them off."*

Malian dropped, mortar rattling around her. The ruined house was a tangle of shadows, with what had once been a garden grown wild on every side. She could hear Kalan, making just enough sound to seem inadvertent as he moved away, with the Swarm warriors in pursuit. Not all of them would follow him, though—or she would not, in their place, and she had no reason to think they were fools. Silently, she moved deeper into the ruins, alert for the sounds of pursuit as well as cellars or stairwells opening beneath her feet. She wondered how close or far Nindorith might be, and whether Nherenor or one of those with him was also a seeker.

She assumed it was Nindorith that had used prescience to predict their route, even if the Swarm power had not yet *seen* who they were: Nherenor had still been guessing at that when he taunted them. Malian stopped, frowning, because Nhenir had always told her that peering through time and space was a chancy business—one in which seers might not always see actions and outcomes as clearly as they believed. And a powerful enough seer, knowing what was happening, could counteract another's sight.

Her frown deepened, her fingers clasping Yorindesarinen's armring. The touch reassured her, although the bracelet's full power had not flared into life since she found the moonbright helm in Jaransor, five years before. *"And a fine help you've turned out to be,"* she said to Nhenir, *"as soon as I meet an enemy with real power. But now,"* she added, her mindtone level, *"I need you to exert yourself if we're to get out of this situation intact."*

# 39

# *Darksworn*

*O*n the far side of the ruin someone shouted—followed immediately by a cry, abruptly cut off. More shouting answered, and Malian thought she detected confusion and rage beneath the yells. She paused, already half turned back toward where Kalan must be, when his mindvoice came at her like an arrow: *"Keep going!"*

She hesitated a moment longer then went, gliding from shadow to shadow toward the tower. The sky was definitely paling now and she could smell the dawn, lying in wait.

The shouting had died away by the time she slipped into the tower and found a stone stair that wound upward, following the curve of the wall. Memory flashed, taking her back to the hidden tower in Jaransor and a crow sitting on her shoulder—but this donjon was solidly physical and a great deal lower in height. She reached the upper level in a few short flights and paused in the shadow of a crumbling door, studying the derelict hall beyond. The roof was half intact, half fallen in, although the wall that separated the hall from the adjoining street looked solid enough. Beyond it she could see the stark silhouette of Imuln's dome, closer than she had thought, and banks of fog above the river. The air was hushed and Malian inhaled deeply, feeling the mist's chill in her lungs as she stepped out, onto the tower roof.

"Nindorith said you would come here." Excitement and triumph mingled in Nherenor's voice. "Now, spy, we shall find out exactly who and what you are."

He jumped down from the high point of the bastion, cutting off any retreat through the door. Malian moved to the edge of the tower, where it joined the ruined hall. A streamer of mist hung along the street on the other side of the wall, the cobblestones dark beneath it. "You are confident," she said. And, she added to herself, bound to Nindorith in some way.

He laughed. "I am Nherenor, Ilkerineth's son." His tone changed, and she guessed he was frowning behind his visor. "You have no sword. But it doesn't matter. I have two daggers. We will use those, so no one can say that you fought at a disadvantage."

Malian raised her eyebrows. "I have a dagger," she said, although in fact she had several, concealed about her person. She drew the hunting blade from its scabbard at her back and Nherenor laughed again, sheathing his sword and drawing a dagger himself as he came forward. Malian stepped back onto the wall that separated the ruined hall from the street. She thought he hesitated before advancing, and stepped back again, her feet feeling every indentation of the stone through the leather of her adept's boots. Now she smiled, too, for this was Shadow Band territory: the high narrow place, the dim light that facilitated illusion shift, and the slender blade.

Nherenor sprang forward, the lunge of someone who wanted to disarm, rather than an eviscerating thrust to the stomach or slash across the throat. Malian moved with his movement, curving her body away from the blow while her blade locked his at the wrist. She pushed the dagger away, forcing it down as she advanced into the space that had been his a split second before. Neat as a cat, he jumped back, throwing off the lock on his wrist. Malian waited, poised on the balls of her feet as he came forward more cautiously, before retreating further along the wall. Her adversary, she noticed, was not laughing anymore.

Mist curled around her ankles as she slip-stepped back—and a lurker rose out of the ruined hall, its trailing tendrils reaching to engulf her. Malian slashed with her knife as Nherenor yelled, racing forward. The lurker shrieked and used its unsevered tendrils to push away from her, while spitting a jet of inky blackness toward her face. Malian somersaulted backward, hearing two simultaneous cries as her feet found the narrow stone again. She landed with one palm flat to the wall for balance, the other holding the knife ready to cut or throw.

The lurker was falling, with an arrow protruding from its central core—but Nherenor was teetering, too, his knife falling from nerveless fingers as he dragged at his helmet with the other hand. Malian saw the wet slick across the visor and realized that the lurker's poison must have caught him full across it and penetrated the eyeslit. The young warrior wavered again, the helm forgotten as he struggled to keep his balance on the narrow wall. Malian sprang forward without thinking, sheathing her knife and grabbing for his arm. But even as she moved, Nherenor's body jerked, his back arching—and then he fell, crashing from the wall toward the cobbled street below. The loosened helmet fell clear, clanging and rolling along the cobbles, and the youth's long black hair streamed out around him.

I have *seen* this before, Malian thought, when I looked into Yorindesarinen's fire. The vision, she recalled, had snatched her away before she could lift the black hair and see the face that lay beneath, but now she felt compelled to complete that final step. A quick survey of the wall showed sufficient cracks and unevenness to provide a route down to the nearest buttress, and from there it was an easy descent to the street.

The ground mist was thicker than it had appeared from the wall—more as she recalled it from her five-year-old vision—and there was a lot of blood, both on Nherenor's blue-black mail and pooling across the cobbles. A curious smell, half sweet, half acrid, hung over the body, and Malian guessed that this must be residue from the lurker poison. She pulled out the same kerchief she had used against road dust and wrapped it around her nose and mouth, careful to maintain her distance as she unthreaded the hunting knife's sheath from her belt. Squatting on her heels, she extended the thick leather scabbard to lift back the curtain of black hair, using her free hand to shield her eyes.

She had half thought that Nherenor's face might have been smashed when his body hit the cobbles, but the head was turned sideways, rather than being facedown as she had always believed. His neck was broken, she realized, but the side of his face that was turned up was relatively unscathed. Her first thought was that in death he looked a little like Alianor. The second, with realization sick in her stomach, was that he looked like her.

The fall of black hair was common enough in both Emer and the River lands to pass unremarked, but the finely sculpted cast of his features could have looked back at her from a mirror. Even the name he had spoken so proudly, Nherenor, Ilkerineth's son, had a Derai ring—but that did not explain why the face beneath the blood-matted hair could also have been hers. Or why, Malian thought, I am kneeling here with my throat aching for a Swarm adherent, even if he wouldn't fight me while I was at a disadvantage.

"Darksworn." She whispered the word that Nhenir had used when they watched Nherenor remove the shadow cloak. She had pushed the word aside then, just as she had tried, over the past five years, to forget her conversation with Kalan in the heart of the Old Keep—the one where he first told her of the Darksworn, the Derai who had been with the Swarm from the beginning. She had not wanted to believe that ancient secret could be true, so much so that she had striven to suppress the knowledge ever since, even within herself. Yet now the bitter truth stared up at her, etched into Nherenor's lifeless face. His appearance had not altered in death, so she knew he was no facestealer—and she found it impossible to deny that he looked as Derai as she did.

"He looks like me." She could barely speak the words, her lips were so stiff. Nausea churned in her stomach, and the hand holding the scabbard shook.

Feet thumped to the ground a few paces away and Malian

spun around, letting the long hair fall and palming another hideout dagger—then relaxed as she recognized Kalan. Blood was splashed across his wrist guards and one sleeve was soaked red, but he did not move as if he were wounded. He looked weary, though, and a little white around the mouth as he crouched at her side. Silently, he took the hunting scabbard and did as she had, lifting the fall of Nherenor's hair. She watched his brows twitch together and the set of his mouth twist. "I know him," he said finally. "Knew him. I saw him yesterday, in the sword ring. He could really fight. Even Girvase couldn't beat him outright."

"He's Darksworn," Malian said, forcing the word out. She watched for Kalan's reaction, but he just nodded. "His name was Nherenor," she added, feeling that it mattered, although she was not sure why. "Ilkerineth's son."

*"An enemy."* Kalan's expression remained a mix of grimness and regret, but she could hear his frown reflected in his mindvoice. *"But . . . I think he may have wanted to be a friend."*

He certainly had notions of honor, Malian thought, like defeating me in single combat rather than letting the lurker intervene. "We have to get out of here," she said. "Before the demon comes." She did not want to invoke Nindorith by speaking the Swarm power's name aloud. "They had an empathy bond, I think, and if it's two way . . ."

*"Too late."* Kalan's head came up in the same moment that she, too, felt the first fracture across his psychic shield, heralding Nindorith's approach.

"Run!" She heard Tarathan's warning a split second before she saw him, a gray-clad figure emerging through mist and half-light along the parapet that led to the far side of the derelict hall. He had his bow in his hand, and she guessed, even as he slung it over his shoulder and followed her route down the wall, that he must have loosed the arrow that killed the lurker. Energy surged as the herald reached the ground and they all ran, recognizing the bow wave of power that signaled a portal opening.

A quick glance back showed the air boiling, and Malian's

fingers worked into her wallet, extracting an amulet as they pounded toward the corner. Her lips moved, triggering a cantrip for confusion as she cast it behind her, into the center of the lane. The ground mist swirled around it, gathering up dust and rubbish, and began a slow rotating whirl toward Nherenor's body.

*"It won't stop that dark demon long. He's too powerful."* Kalan skidded around the corner beside her. *"I don't know how we'll lose him if we can't open a portal of our own."*

"This way!" said Tarathan, as fragments of mist, dust, and rubbish blasted out of the lane entrance. A tremendous howl of grief and rage split the growing dawn—and Malian cast a second amulet down as she followed Tarathan around another corner, this time into a wider street with small trees marching along its length.

"Deception," she mouthed, and set a flock of shadow images flying: north, south, east, and west along other streets, similar to her trick on the rooftop. It might not fool Nindorith for long—would not—but even a little time could make a difference now.

"Head for Imuln's temple," Tarathan said tersely. "We can hide ourselves in its greater power."

Is that where Jehane Mor is? Malian wondered—then flinched as Nindorith's mindsweep blasted across them like a storm wind, flattening Kalan against the nearest wall. He clung there, his fingers pressed into stone as he held his shield intact. When he lifted his face, his eyes were dark with strain. "I don't think I can take much more of that," he gasped.

Last one, thought Malian, extracting a third amulet. "You go on," she said, and Tarathan nodded, propelling Kalan toward the main avenue that led to the temple bridge and great square beyond. The world was definitely gray now, and soon the first people would be about—those who had not already sprung from their beds as Nindorith's howl rose above Caer Argent. The amulet between her fingers was lead, with a name rune scratched into the back. It looked like any other sigil made to give away to travelers in Seruth's name—

except his was not the power that Malian had bound into it before leaving Ar.

Now she crouched down and slid a fine wire out of her cuff, her fingers flying as she bound it around the amulet. As her fingers worked the pattern, her mind recalled every detail of the entity that had tried to lure her to her death during the dark of the moon, on a mountain ridge between the Rindle and The Leas. That night had been dedicated to Kan, but she had walked in the Shadow Band's temple and knew that the entity she had encountered was not the god. Yet it was a power nonetheless, part of the ancient, forgotten legacy of Haarth.

Another mindsweep battered across her, but Malian dared not break her concentration, although this time, further away from Kalan, she felt its pain, like daggers piercing mind and flesh. She clenched her jaw and forced the pain away. Her lips formed the invocation to the god whose name she had carved into the amulet, followed by a binding as she summoned the inchoate power encountered on the mountain. Lastly, she spoke a word of opening, creating a narrow door into the forest of Emerian oak that lay beyond the Gate of Dreams. The white mist there lifted as her lips closed on the final word—and she saw the Haarth entity, summoned by a power greater than its own, flowing toward her.

"Misdirection," Malian breathed, and tossed the amulet through the portal she had opened. The dark shape before her stretched, and she could see the reflection of her own form reflected on its surface as she directed it deep into the Emerian oak forest. *"Go!"* she commanded—and closed the gate into the mists between worlds.

She dared not wait, though, to see whether her ploy would work. Already she was back on her feet and running for the temple square and whatever protection the great dome of Imuln would provide.

# 40

# The Dome of Imuln

The temple of Imuln took up one side of Caer Agent's oldest market square. Soon the wide expanse would fill up with vendors and festivalgoers, but for now the square was empty. The only movement was the glitter of spray from a central fountain, rising into the air, then falling back. Power rippled across the square as well, spreading out from the temple complex: Malian could feel its low hum through the soles of her boots.

Expanding circles, she thought, skirting the open plaza. And layers of power within each concentric ring, with the high priestess occupying the inmost of the nine levels of temple power. Malian knew, from her years on the River, that each circle had prescribed rites and rituals that continued through every day and night of the year, creating the steady hum of power—but that the temple would be particularly active now, for Imuln's great festival of Midsummer.

Tarathan's right, she thought, the collective power will disguise our individual sparks.

"Here," the herald called softly, and she finally saw them both, standing in the shadow of the temple steps, where a narrow alley ran between two arms of the complex. Kalan still looked drawn, but he was no longer leaning on the herald. At first Malian thought the blood from his sleeve must have soaked through onto Tarathan's tunic, then realized that the red splashes continued across the gray fabric. "We go down first," the herald said, before she could ask about the blood. "Then up."

Down, Malian found, meant prying up a grilled hatch at the end of the lane and dropping through one by one. As soon as they were within the temple's walls, the sense of the world outside was dulled, as though the buildup of power focused on Imuln created a different kind of shielding. Kalan trailed a hand along the wall, and Malian saw that he was frowning as Tarathan led them up a narrow stair. "So much power," he murmured, following them both up the first of a series of ladders nailed int the walls. "I wonder if that's why the Oakward has never been centered here in Caer Argent since the inner wards became more peaceful?" He paused, the frown deepening. "I still wish Lord Falk were here now, though."

Tarathan looked down. "You could reach through to him," he said. "If you were willing to open yourself to the Gate of Dreams rather than walling it out."

Malian glanced down herself, in time to catch Kalan's grimace. She kept hter own expression neutral, but she was shaken by Tarathan's revelation. Kalan's love of the Emerian life must be even stronger than she had realized—a great deal stronger if he was walling out the dreams that are part of his Derai heritage.

Her seer's prescience brushed at her awareness, a feathering of raised hairs along her nape, and she knew that the life of an Emerian knight was not for Kalan no matter how greatly his heart might desire it. She shivered, recognizing the echo of Tarathan's phrase from Jaransor, five years before. But it felt apt—unless of course she was allowing her own wishes to color her seeing. Malian pulled an inward face at this thought and craned to see further up the ladder. "We must be climbing into the dome," she said, and caught Tarathan's brief smile.

"Jehane Mor is already there," he replied. "It's a fine vantage point from which to stay in mind contact with others, especially when unprotected yourself."

"She could draw on a great deal of power here," Kalan agreed, as they stepped onto a stone walkway between the basilica's two layers of wall. Small metal grills were spaced every few yards along it, and Malian stooped to peer through the nearest one. The nave, far below, was just a flicker of lantern-light and shadow—Tarathan had already begun to climb the next ladder. She stood up, staring at his ascending back.

"The Swarm envoys spoke of you and Jehane Mor tonight," she said. "Apparently one of their sorcerers, called Nirn, perceives you as a particular threat." Perhaps, she thought, because he was one of the Swarm—or Darksworn, she corrected herself, although the word was still bile in her mouth—who invaded the Old Keep: it may be as simple as that. But she wanted to hear what Tarathan would say, what explanation he might offer.

The herald had paused with his hands on a hatch above his head. "Did they say why?"

Malian shook her head, her eyes meeting his as he looked down at her. "No. And Nherenor, the envoy who died, thought you were just heralds."

"No such thing," Kalan said from below her, a grin in his voice—and then Tarathan had lifted the hatch aside and they all climbed through into the loft of Imuln's dome.

The interior, Malian thought, was disappointingly plain. A network of wooden beams crisscrossed the copper dome above a bare expanse of floorboards, liberally spattered with bird droppings,. Four unshuttered openings were set around the low walls, each one deep enough to prevent any but the worst weather penetrating the interior. But not, Malian thought, the birds—in fact she could see two owls right now, roosting high up in the dome. Jehane Mor was standing at the east facing window, but she turned as they appeared, the first light haloing her fair head.

"The demon's gone," she said, and her faint, approving smile rested on Malian. "That was clever, what you did with the Gate of Dreams. But the power storm has brought others out."

"Who?" Kalan asked, crossing to the window.

"Look to your left," the herald said as Malian joined Kalan at the opening. They had to pull themselves half into the embrasure to see the defensive wall that extended from the palace complex, along the riverbank to the temple perimeter. The first light was just striking the series of old watchtowers that Malian had observed on her first morning in the palace. It also illuminated the catwalk where seven figures stood, the dawn breeze riffling their long hair as they faced toward the city.

"The Jhainarians," Kalan said. "I thought they never left their queen."

"She is a priestess of Imuln as well as a queen," Jehane Mor said, "and will have felt the blasts of power. As will the Seven, through her if they have no individual power of their own."

Malian peered in the direction of the Seven's gaze but could only see a jumble of tiled roofs. "The Duke thinks they're pursuing some purpose of their own," she said thoughtfully. "Aside from this Great Marriage they seem to think was implied in the invitation given by his grandfather."

Kalan looked around at her, clearly surprised. "The Duke *said* that to you?"

"I, um, *overheard*." Malian grinned at him, just a little, and he looked shocked and amused at the same time.

"Shadow Band," he said, half under his breath as he switched his gaze back to the Jhainarians. "Well, they're leaving the wall now. They must have realized that whatever caused the power storm has departed—for the moment." He slid out of the window embrasure, back into the dome. "And since it has, I need to get back to the tourney camp. Before anyone sees me," he added, indicating the blood on his wrist guards and sleeve.

"Of course, you still have to fight today," Malian said. She had quite forgotten that in the events of the night. Kalan just shrugged, as if saying that he would have to manage.

"Take the vambraces off," Jehane Mor advised, "and the shirt as well. You can go sleeveless, the way so many of the Aralorn men do."

Kalan's expression cleared, and a moment later he had stripped the wristguards and was pulling the gambeson over his head. His sleeveless jerkin followed and then the shirt, his muscles rippling as he pulled the jerkin back on again. He really did look very strong, Malian thought critically, as heavily muscled as Ombrose Sondargent across the shoulders. And he looked far more Emerian than Derai as he replaced the gambeson and pulled his hair clear of his face with a leather tie.

His gold-flecked eyes met hers as the short sword back on. "Gir return to the palace to make sure one of us stayed close to Ghis last night, and if all goes well today we'll try and get in again tonight. You said Nherenor was one of the Swarm's envoys, so I can't imagine them just letting his death pass."

No, Malian thought. And Nindorith may have followed the portal I opened into the Gate of Dreams, but he won't be fooled for long. She remembered the Swarm power's tremendous howl of loss and grief on discovering Nherenor's body, and was sure that she would be dealing with blood feud now, not just the desire to root out a spy.

Wood scraped, and she blinked, realizing that Tarathan was lifting the hatch. She wanted to tell Kalan to be careful, competing in the tourney while he was already tired, and not get maimed or killed through a foolish mistake. But you could not say such things, either to a Derai warrior or an Emerian knight. "Take care," she said finally, temporizing.

Surprisingly, he grinned. "A day of contests after night watch and drills was part of our Normarch training. I'll be all right." *Or I won't.*

Had she heard the ghost of a thought? Malian wondered— but Kalan was already descending through the hatch. The last she saw of him was a raised hand, and she closed her eyes, hit by a deep unexpected weariness as Tarathan lowered the hatch again. Even behind her lids she remained aware of the heralds' presence: Tarathan's fire, and Jehane Mor, cool as deep water. "You've got blood on your tunic, too," she said, addressing Tarathan without opening her eyes.

"It's not mine," he replied, answering her unspoken question. "And Jehane has my cloak. I can wear that back to the Guild House." He paused, but she kept her eyes closed, letting their heralds' silence flow around her. "It was clever," Tarathan said finally, "what you did in the ruin, manipulating the paths of prescience. I, too, am a seer," he added when Malian opened her eyes, meeting his. "I am beginning to know you as well, so I felt it when you touched the strands of seeing."

It was as much Nhenir as me, Malian thought—although she had not, she supposed, allowed the helm the choice of refusal. "Nindorith, the Swarm power that pursued us, is also prescient," she told them wearily. "The envoy, Nherenor, said as much when he intercepted us. I knew I had to counter that so I worked an illusion through the Gate of Dreams, a smoke dream"—she used the Winter Country term—"so that anyone using prescience would see whatever they wanted to happen, actually happening."

"A Haarth trick," Jehane Mor said, "not Derai. That may have been wise."

Malian closed her eyes again. "Wise too late. Nindorith saw me clearly when he first arrived here tonight." And may have seen Nhenir as well, she thought, although the helm was being coy about that. "I had to use all my power to escape, and although the demon may not have worked out the *who* and *what* yet, he will. And then he will track me." Her lips thinned. "I still have Lord Falk's commission to protect Countess Ghiselaine to discharge. But once this Nindorith starts searching in earnest—" She shrugged. "Even here, I might not be safe for long."

She was not sure why she kept her eyes closed, her head tilted back against the stone of the window frame. "Swarm activity is Derai business," she said softly, although she suspected many in Emer, from the Duke down, might hold a contrary view. "So I have to find a way to disappear again while still remaining Maister Carick, right here in plain sight." She straightened, finally opening her lids, and the heralds' eyes pierced her, just as they had on the night she first met them in her father's High Hall.

"There is a way," they said. Their voices wove in and out of each other, and Malian felt the stirring of power: not just theirs, but the deep magic layered into the dome beneath them, with a taproot into the green heart of Emer. She could sense that heart now, even more clearly than when she had ridden through Maraval wood. But it was not the power that made her eyes widen.

The heralds had moved together while her eyes were closed and now stood shoulder-to-shoulder, watching her. The light of the new day was behind them in the eastern window, outlining Tarathan's chestnut braids and the fair coronal around Jehane Mor's head. Hair like a crown, Malian thought. In her mind's eye she saw the herald's arms raised in invocation, summoning Imuln's new moon to rise early on Summer's Eve—which only a high priestess sworn to the Goddess should be able to do.

"They look like you," she whispered, her eyes shifting to Tarathan. "Or *you* look like them. The Jhainarians."

Tarathan and Jehane Mor said nothing, just continued to watch her, their eyes full of secrets.

"And it's you they're looking for, with all their questions." She ran both hands over her hair. "So are you going to tell me why? And what exactly this way of yours is, that even mentioning it creates such a current of power?"

# 41

# *Passage of Arms*

*K*alan twisted sideways, out from beneath his opponent's overhand strike, and brought his own sword around in a blow that sent his adversary jumping back. His morning had blurred into a succession of antagonists, into the jar through wrist and arms as sword met sword, and the feel of sweat soaking through wool and leather beneath his armor. The challengers he dispatched with ruthless precision, shutting out the sun's glare and the blaze of color from the stands, where the rich and great of Emer were gathered. He shut out the ocean roar of the crowd as well, that swelled whenever a blow struck home. His own weariness and the aftermath of last night's events lay beyond the roar and the color—as well as the knowledge that the black unicorn device had been withdrawn from the tourney.

But these matters were all for later: now was the time for muscle and sinew and sword, and the hard earth of the sword ring below his booted feet.

His opponent attacked again, more slowly this time, but he was not, Kalan judged, a defensive fighter—and a moment later the leaping assault came. Kalan beat it aside and slid forward, rolling the other knight's blade around and beneath his own, before delivering the final flick of both wrists and blade that jerked the sword hilt from his adversary's grasp.

The crowd swayed, roaring as he stepped back, and the list marshal seized his arm, dragging it skyward. The defeated knight picked up his sword and they both made the salute, but this opponent was no Ser Alric. He ducked quickly through the ropes and back to his seconds, disappearing into the crowd of knights and squires.

It was, Kalan supposed, raising his visor and wiping the sweat from his face, all more serious now, with the Duke's purse of gold for each individual contest winner and the tourney championship at stake. Ser Ombrose Sondargent was here somewhere, too, defending that championship against the cream of Emer and the southern realms, and had led the contestants' salute to the Duke at the beginning of the day.

Kalan stared at the surrounding crowd, taking in merchants, minor landholders, and artisans on the cross benches, while servant girls, apprentices, and men-at-arms packed the embankments. A girl caught his eye and leaned over one of the hurdles that separated the spectators from the competitors, tossing a flower at his feet. He blinked, then picked it up as the girl ducked back, giggling. The bloom was of a kind that grew wild along every roadside and was already starting to wilt, but he worked it into the knot of ribbon around his arm—Ghiselaine's colors, which reminded him to turn and raise his sword to her, where she sat at the Duke's right hand.

"Audin wants us all to wear Ghis's favor," Girvase had said, after they rode back into camp that morning. "Queen Zhineve-An is the Duke's guest and sovereign of a neighboring state, so he's sure that Ser Ombrose will be wearing her colors and not Ghiselaine's. Audin," Girvase had added slowly, "thinks that the champion will be glad to, given the old enmity between his mother's family, the Sondcendres, and Ormond."

They had all known that would lessen Ghiselaine's standing in the eyes of the Emerian world, however much the Queen of Jhaine was the Duke's guest. "But if *we* all compete for Ghiselaine," Girvase had continued, "that will send a strong message to everyone watching—because Lord Falk is the Duke's foster brother, and also because Normarch has always held to Caer Argent."

And Audin is Sondargent himself, Kalan had thought, so this company, with Alianor and Ilaise added in, represents half the great families of Emer.

They had all agreed, and Jarna found and bargained with a peddler for enough white and yellow ribbons to knot into Ormondian favors for them all. Audin had sent a pennant bearing Ghiselaine's guerdon as well, and the lily of Emer on its gold ground fluttered below their Normarch standard as Kalan offered his victory to Ghiselaine. She bowed, smiling, and the crowd cheered—and cheered again when Ilaise leaned forward and blew him a kiss.

"Next bout," the list marshal said, and Kalan ran a quick eye along the heraldic shields that lined the hurdle barriers. Ado's shield was gone, he saw—and frowned, his stomach muscles tightening, as a shield displaying a sheaf of swords was put up beside his. But the Derai who ducked into the ring to face him was the older warrior, whose name turned out to be Gol. He proved a canny fighter, their bout intense and fierce, but the marshals held Kalan the clear winner on points. He fought one of the Allerion knights after that, defeating him in short order, and this time when he returned to his corner he found Ombrose Sondargent watching, his handsome face impassive.

He must be between bouts, Kalan thought. He hesitated, then raised his sword in a brief salute to the champion. Ser Ombrose nodded, but his gaze was cool as he turned away, moving to the next ring, where Girvase was fighting. Checking out his opposition, Kalan thought: he would do the same himself, given sufficient time between bouts.

And Audin had been right about the Duke's champion riding for Queen Zhineve-An. Ser Ombrose had a scarf of burgundy and wheat, beaded with gold, bound around his mailed arm, even though the young queen was notably absent.

Kalan wondered about that briefly, until one of the tourney pages handed him up a water bag. The water was warm and tasted of leather and sweat—or perhaps that was just the inside of his mouth. He rotated his shoulders in turn, working against his fatigue and the muscle ache that would come as soon as he stopped moving for any period of time. A shield with a black crow carrying a spray of green oak leaves went up beside his, and he handed the water bag back, turning to face the knight climbing into the ring.

In the end Kalan defeated all his opponents before the sun reached its zenith. He studied the shield wall as the trumpets shrilled out the midday break in competition, and saw that there were only eight coats-of-arms remaining. Both he and Girvase had made it through into tomorrow's final round. Ser Ombrose's oak tree and wolf was there, too, beside a sheaf of swords that had, Kalan thought with an inward groan, to be Orth. The next three shields were all Emerian, displaying arms he did not know, while the fourth belonged to a Lathayran knight.

"A good fighter," Raher said, as they walked back to the competitors' pavilion. "He made short work of me. Fortunately I'm stronger in the joust."

"I wish I was." Ado was gloomy because he had lost in his first bout. At least, Kalan thought, he has a family estate to return to eventually. He doesn't have to make his way in the world through his skill at war or on the tourney circuit. "Still, Ser Rannart said he'd have me back as a knight-at-arms, so even if I don't do well in the joust, or we don't get to hire on somewhere as a company, it won't be the end of the world."

"You'll be all right," Raher said, "you've got a good horse. What?" he demanded, when they all grinned, shaking their heads. "What's so funny?"

Kalan gave him a shove. "You are." But the mention of horses made him think of Jarna, competing in the trial field outside the main tourney ground, and he shaded his eyes in that direction. "I should have time to get there and back before the jousting starts," he decided.

"Ser Raven's over there," Ado said. "We don't need to go." But Girvase, who had sat down and begun to eat a pie bought from one of the many vendors circulating through the grounds, got to his feet again. "Hamar's right. We should see how Jarn's going, since she's the only one of us in those events."

Raher shook his head. "I'm going to look at the ground for the joust again. And check on my horse."

In the end, Kalan, Ado, and Girvase all clanked their way over to the field, where the horsemanship contests were continuing. Jarna was riding when they arrived: they could see Madder weaving his way neatly through of a line of pikes. But a quick survey of the shield display showed that she had not made it into the final six for the horse archery. "Still," Kalan said, keeping his tone cheerful, "this competition is her real strength."

"There's Ser Raven." Girvase nodded to the gate where competitors entered and left the field. But the crowd between them was packed close and the view from the knoll where the shields were displayed was better, so they stayed where they were, evaluating Jarna's progress up the long field. She looked good, Kalan thought, and handled herself well in the one-on-one encounter with a Lathayran horseman. Madder's superior training showed up well in the small melee, too, where Jarna had to get past three other contestants riding as a company.

"She's a fine rider." Kalan had been aware of someone joining them, but only took in that it was Ser Alric of Vast when the knight spoke. "And obviously has a gift for horses. Anyone who can train destriers to that standard could walk into a horsemaster's job from here to the Southern March." Even a girl: the words hung unspoken on the air.

Ado and Girvase both turned their heads, and Kalan knew their expressions would mirror his own cool, level look. "She's Ser Jarna," he said flatly, "not a horsemaster."

"One of you, eh?" The knight's look was shrewd. "I heard she won her spurs in the recent troubles on the Northern March, that you all did, but all the same—" He pursed his lips. "Whoever thrust her into this life did her no kindness."

Kalan frowned, although he had often thought the same thing himself. But Jarna was one of their Summer's Eve company, as the knight had said, and Ser Alric little better than a stranger. From the corner of his eye, Kalan could see that Girvase's stare remained cool, while Ado's frown matched his.

Ser Alric shook his head. "Ay, I'm a presumptuous clod from the Wyvernmark. But look at those lasses over there." He indicated a group of damosels in their holiday best, perched on hay bales on the back of a wagon for a better view. "She'll never be one of them, will she? And there's precious few lords who'll want her among their men—or knights who will accept her outside your small group. I wouldn't have her amongst my own men," he added, matter-of-fact.

Kalan thought of Yorindesarinen and all the Derai heroes who had been women—and Captain Asantir, in the depths of the Old Keep, casting a black spear against the Raptor of Darkness. He remembered the guard Lira as well, on the last morning he had seen her alive, and felt a savage spurt of anger on Jarna's behalf.

"Hamar." Girvase put a warning hand on his arm. "Ser Alric means no offense."

Kalan gritted his teeth and bit back the obvious retort. The Wymark knight eyed him warily. "I don't think there's many knights here who would wish to cause any of you offense." He rubbed at his jaw. "But have you spared a thought for why your captain's been at all her events these past days, rather than yours?"

It was true, Kalan thought, even though he had noticed the fact without fully taking it in until now. A quick glance to either side showed the same realization on Ado and Girvase's faces. If he had thought about it at all, he would have assumed Ser Raven's presence was the natural extension of the extra training the knight had given Jarna at Normarch.

Ser Alric nodded, reading their expressions. "I didn't think so." He rubbed at his chin again. "Tourney grounds are rough places, full of rougher men whose business is war. As many brutes and thugs as upholders of chivalry, if not more." The knight's tone remained matter-of-fact. "Not a safe place to be the one that's different from the crowd, or a woman alone, even one who knows how to use the weapons she carries. And she's the only one of you spending time at these fields. The way I see it, your Ser Raven's sending a message."

Kalan looked toward Ser Raven again and thought that he did not look like he was paying much attention to what was happening on the field. But much as it galled him, he knew Ser Alric was right. Just by being there Ser Raven was saying that he took Jarna's being one of his company seriously—and *I wouldn't want to get on his bad side,* Kalan thought, *not if I didn't have to.* Yet his anger still burned against Ser Alric, all the same.

"And any commander here," the Wymark knight said, "will know there'll always be the possibility for that kind of trouble."

*But Jarna can't be a horsemaster,* Kalan thought bitterly. He had suggested that to her once himself, idly, when they were working together in the Normarch forge, but she had shaken her head. "Knightly families employ horsemasters," she had told him, "they don't become them, that's what my grandfather says. He would die of the shame, and it would ruin my sisters' chances of making good marriages."

Yet what Ser Alric was saying, without actually speaking the words, was that if they included Jarna in their company in the melee—the usual indication that knights were seeking service as a unit—their chances of finding it might be over before they rode onto the field.

Ser Alric cleared his throat. "Something else to be mindful of, given it's your first tourney, is that the melee's sometimes been used to deliberately maim or even kill a fellow contestant, by those who're ill-disposed."

The anger Kalan had been holding back flared into red life, sweeping away the weariness of a sleepless night and a morning of back-to-back sword bouts. "Is that a threat?" he asked, all steel.

The knight from Vast stepped back, raising both of his

hands, the palms wide. "Nay, lad, it's a warning—a *friendly* warning from one who's campaigned a few more years than your Normarch crew, no matter how fearsome you and your friend here may be with a sword."

"Hamar." Giryase's hand tightened on his forearm, his coolness countering Kalan's rage. "You know we were talking about such stories the other night."

Kalan shook off his friend's restraining hand, but clamped down on his anger at the same time. "I accept," he ground out, "that it was not a threat."

"Ay, well." Ser Alric eyed him warily, then shook his head. "You're right, I've overstepped the mark. Ser Raven's your captain here. I should leave such matters to him."

Ado murmured something, smoothing matters over, but Kalan didn't catch the words because he was watching Jarna canter off the field to a few ragged cheers. She had done well, he thought, the aftermath of his fury like bile in his mouth. He could see her patting Madder's neck as she walked the roan over to Ser Raven, but there was no time to try and make their way through the crowd: they needed to get back for the joust. Ado shook his head as they walked away.

"What got into you, Hamar? Normally you're so easy going. But just now—well, you frightened me."

I frightened myself, Kalan thought, still feeling that sour aftermath of anger. While he was in it, though, the emotion had felt right, satisfying even. "I've been friends with Jarna a long time," he said finally. "I didn't like him talking about her like that."

"Even though it was truth?" Girvase asked coolly.

*Because* it was truth, Kalan thought.

On his other side, Ado started to grin. "You know, I think Ser Alric only spoke up because he liked you, Hamar. He was betting on your bouts this morning. But the way you looked at him—" He shook his head again, still grinning. "I think he thought he'd woken one of the ice bears they say live in the Winter Country."

Kalan had seen one of those bears once, from a safe distance. "You're right," he said ruefully. "Ser Alric was an unworthy target." They did not discuss what the Wymark knight had said, but Kalan knew it would come up again. *Don't tell Raher,* he wanted to say, but knew he couldn't. If they were going to ride as a company, any matter than affected the group had to be agreed upon by all of them.

The muscles along his jaw tightened as the anger flared again, although he was not quite sure who he was angry with: Girvase, for articulating that what Ser Alric said was true; or Jarna's grandfather for sacrificing her to satisfy his own skewed notions of honor and how the world should be— not, Kalan thought savagely, how it *is,* at all. He was angry at himself as well, for closing his eyes to the reality that Ser Alric had just outlined so clearly. And, if he was honest, with Jarna, for presenting another complication to throw into a mix that held Derai and Darkswarm and the Heir of Night, awake now behind the layered masks of cartographer and adept, and measuring them all with her cool, smoky gaze.

Easier by far just to get on a horse, clap a lance into place, and thunder full tilt toward another heavily armored opponent, and—Kalan thought, baring his teeth as he did just that—knock him out of the saddle. The anger had burned away his weariness and he rode its wave through the blaze of afternoon, his eyes narrowed on finding the precise spot that would send a succession of opponents crashing to the ground. Raher was doing well, too, he saw, when he had time to take in the shield array, and Ado was holding his own. He could not see Girvase's shield, which was farther along the wall from the marshaling area.

"Ser Ombrose is still here, of course," Raher said, in a snatched conversation, "and a few of those northerners, although they don't seem to be very good at jousting."

Well, they wouldn't be, Kalan thought. The use of a lance, tourney style, was not a skill much called for on the Wall of Night. The Derai had to compete, though, if they wanted to be seen as serious contenders in the tournament—even, he reflected grimly, if they were really here on other business. He scowled, suppressing his concern about what that business might be, given the Swarm presence in Caer Argent.

Instead he urged his horse back to the end of the lists, concentrating on the heft of another lance before clamping it
beneath his arm and bearing down on another opponent.

One of the Sword warriors, he saw, once his lance had
done its work and the man was on the ground. His next opponent was a Lathayran, who lost his lance but only came
half off his horse, clinging to the saddle bow until he reached
the end of the lists. After that it was Raher, who kept his
lance and just rocked backward in the saddle. The bout still
went to Kalan, who had maintained both balance and lance,
but he realized that his opponents were getting stronger. It
was almost with a sense of inevitability, in the final bout of
the day, that he looked down the lists and saw Ser Ombrose
facing him at last.

Kalan supposed he should feel nervous, afraid even, but
instead he was cool, almost detached, as he selected a lance
and closed his visor. Ser Ombrose might be tourney champion, but in the end he was just another knight with strengths
and weaknesses, no different from himself or any other com-
petitor here.

I have met the hero Yorindesarinen, who slew the Chaos
Worm, he thought. I will not be overawed by anyone's reputation, next to that, not even the champion of Emer. "Ready?"
a list marshal asked, and he nodded, settling the lance into
place.

The baton came down and his horse exploded forward
with a powerful thrust of its hindquarters, hooves drumming against the hard ground. Kalan's eyes narrowed on
what was no longer a person but a fast-approaching gleam
of steel beneath green and black. He looked past the lance
tip, crouching low behind his buckler as he automatically
assessed Ser Ombrose's body position and balance, all his
attention focused on the point that would displace the other's
weight while maintaining his own.

The shock of the lance against his buckler jarred through
Kalan's whole body, but he kept his weight forward and
stayed grounded in the saddle. Ser Ombrose had taken the
impact on his shield, too, and also kept his seat, which meant

another round. The contest would go to three before the marshals made a declaration.

"You held him off!" Raher was practically howling with excitement. Girvase was there, too, and Ado, plus other competitors whose faces blurred into the background. Kalan had no time for anything beyond a quick check of horse and harness before his friends lifted up the next lance and he was thundering down the lists again. His world contracted into the roar of his blood, which might also have been the roar of the crowd, and the oncoming rush of armored horse and armored rider, and brightly colored lance.

The second impact, coming immediately on top of the first, was sickening, and this time both lances splintered from the force driven along their lengths. Kalan had bitten the inside of his mouth and tasted blood, but he managed to throw the lance away so the splintered shaft did not catch in his opponent's armor, or the eye slit of his helmet. He was still in the saddle, but so, too, was Ser Ombrose, and the champion had also tossed his lance clear, so there was no advantage there.

"Hamar! You champion!" Raher ran to meet him as he cantered back, and this time Jarna was at his destrier's head when he stopped, her face white with fear and excitement as her sure hands checked his horse's legs for strain or injury.

"Not champion yet," Kalan said, taking the water bag Ado gave him and squirting water into his mouth.

"Armor's good here," Girvase said, as Kalan spat out blood and water before taking another swallow.

Raher nodded agreement from the other side. "And here."

"He's clear," Jarna said, stepping away from his horse. She did not say "take care," as Malian had that morning, but he could read the words in her expression. He took time over his lance selection, careful over weight and balance, before turning to face Ser Ombrose again.

The baton dropped for the last time, and again his destrier leapt forward. Lists and stands whipped past in a blur as Kalan crouched low and kept his shield centered. Ser Ombrose was a crouched mirror image pounding toward him, his lance rock steady. Kalan's vision narrowed until only knight and lance filled it, alert for any nuance that would reveal an opening. The champion swept closer, and Kalan kept his own lance locked in, all his weight behind it as he drove square and true at his opponent—but at the last instant Ser Ombrose's lance tip rose and thrust for his helmet.

Kalan's head snapped back as the blow connected, and his torso followed. He rocked in the saddle before catching the movement and throwing his weight forward, fighting to retain his seat and hold onto his lance at the same time. His horse thundered on, but he had the reins still and was able to check its speed before they reached the end of the ground. "You rocked him," one of the knights there said, "but not enough."

And striking the helmet, Kalan thought, fatigue washing back in on the tide of his disappointment, is a more difficult maneuver. The senior list marshal must have agreed, for a moment later he directed his baton toward Ser Ombrose Sondargent, who raised his lance to the Duke and then the surrounding stands, accepting the victory.

# 42

# *Rites of Honor*

"It was close though," Raher said, when Kalan had dismounted and they were helping him out of his armor. "No one expected that, Sondargent included, I imagine." Raher grinned. "He rocked me as far back as my horse's rump in the first exchange."

"Everyone's saying that he's never had to go to three lances before," Ado agreed.

Kalan nodded, although his whole body felt like it had been pounded by a smith's hammer and his head was aching from the helmet blow. The inside of his mouth stung where he had bitten it, but at least it had stopped bleeding. He caught Girvase's eye. "Did you joust against Ser Ombrose, too?"

"No, but I did go up against the northerner who fought Audin yesterday." Everyone stopped, and Girvase's rare grin dawned. "He's big, but he can't joust. I beat him on the first lance."

"I don't think any of the northerners are in the joust final," Ado said. "But you and Hamar both are."

"And Ser Ombrose, of course," said Raher cheerfully. "So now you have it all to look forward to again." Kalan groaned.

"You've drawn a crowd, too," Girvase murmured, and Kalan, looking beyond their small circle, saw that it was true. The bulk of the tourneygoers might be dispersing, but there was still a mix of nobility, merchants, and common people pressed as close to the list barrier as the marshals would allow. Ser Raven was nearby, talking with one of the marshals, and Kalan saw Ser Alric—holding back, but still there—and the two Allerion knights who had watched Girvase fight yesterday. He nodded to Ser Alric, a little stiffly but a nod nonetheless, before his eyes slid to Jarna, who was walking her horse. She caught his gaze and smiled, her face bright, and he guessed she must have done well in the horse trials. When he looked back, Ser Raven had turned away from the marshal. The knight smiled, too, an expression as rare on his face as it was on Girvase's.

"You made Sondargent work for his victory," he said. "Well done."

Kalan grinned, feeling as though he had just received his accolade from the Duke himself, and a little of his disappointment lifted. Trumpets rang out, bright and silvery, and everyone looked around. "The Duke's leaving the lists," Ser Raven said, and Kalan took the hand Girvase held out and heaved himself to his feet.

The cavalcade rode close by them, the Duke lifting a hand in acknowledgment as he passed. Ghiselaine, too, raised a gloved hand and bowed from the saddle, fair and graceful as the lily of her guerdon. Alianor and Ilaise rode behind her, together with a mix of other guests who included clerics in the robes of Serrut and Imuln. Both damosels waved, and once the last riders had passed a pair of heralds crossed from the shadow of the ducal stand, making for the list barrier. The gathered watchers fell back on either side to let the great gray horses through.

You would not guess, Kalan thought, studying the heralds' impassive calm, that Tarathan of Ar had spent half the night contending with Swarm agents across the rooftops of Caer Argent. He was conscious of relief, too, as they made their way toward him, because their presence here must mean that Malian was safe, pursuing whatever business Maister Carick was meant to be about in the ducal palace.

"We have a commission," the heralds said, drawing rein

by the barrier and speaking in formal unison. "We are sent by Ghiselaine, Countess of Ormond, to salute all those who wore her colors today."

A murmur sounded as the tourneygoers craned forward, anticipating one of the chivalric gestures that were part of the magic of all tournaments, but especially that of Midsummer, which was sponsored by the Duke.

*"I, Ghiselaine of Ormond, greet you,"* the heralds intoned, still speaking in their one voice, *"on my own behalf as Countess of Ormond and on behalf of my betrothed, Lord Hirluin Sondargent. In both our names, I salute your achievements today and also the spirit of friendship and honor in which you have made gift of them to me, as individuals and as the Normarch company. In return, I offer each of you these tokens of my friendship and esteem."*

The crowd murmured again as Jehane Mor unwrapped a square of folded cloth, revealing seven yellow scarves with the lily of Emer brocaded into the silk. We need Audin for this, Kalan thought, but Girvase gave him a little shove forward and he lifted both hands to accept the scarves. "We salute Countess Ghiselaine," he said, projecting his voice so the crowd could hear, "and accept her gift—in the name of Falk, Castellan of the Northern March, and our liege, Caril, Duke of Emer."

Cheers erupted from the crowd as he turned and held the scarves out to the others. Even the knights and marshals were cheering, Kalan saw, because their small company had been successful today and this was Emer, where everyone loved tourneys and the grand courtly gesture. Clever Ghis, he thought with an inward smile, knowing how to play to that. He looked up from tying the scarf over the peddler's ribbon—to fresh cheers from the onlookers—and nodded to Ser Raven. "There's one there for you," he said.

Just for a moment, he thought the knight might refuse— but then Ser Raven picked up the cloth and knotted it around his arm. "My honor," he said, as if he meant it, although he must have known that it would be unwise to say anything else given the sentiment of the crowd. A sentiment, Kalan reflected, that might all change tomorrow if another knight or company won their fancy. For now, though, they were all for Ghiselaine and the Normarch contingent.

"Which," Girvase said, as they made their way back to the tourney camp, "was what Audin and Alli hoped for when they spoke with me this morning." His fingers touched the scarf around his arm. "Not all service," he added softly, "is with the sword."

No, Kalan thought, although excelling at the tourney and in war brought glory, which carried as much weight as either birth or gold in Emer. He turned his face to the sun, which was descending slowly toward the western horizon, and thought that this life, of a warrior amongst warrior comrades, had always been his dream—even when cruelly relegated to the unwanted life of a temple novice. He knew that he could be Midsummer tourney champion if he stayed in Emer, perhaps not this year but the next, and win not just glory but wealth as well, and a place in the councils of the dukedom.

But you are not Emerian, his inner self reminded him coolly, just as those early dreams of glory were never of Emerian tourneys and border wars. And the reason you are here at all is not because of your own cleverness and strength in breaking free, but through the grace of others, not least Captain Asantir and Rowan Birchmoon. The heralds, too, he reminded himself, conscious of where they rode a few paces behind him. For that was another part of the courtly rituals loved by the Emerians—that Ghiselaine's emissaries must be invited to eat with them before returning to report on the outcome of their commission.

Rites of hospitality and honor, thought Kalan—really, when all was said and done, the Emerians were very like the Derai. He felt contented, absurdly so, to be walking back to camp with his friends around him, knowing that Ser Raven was with the marshals and other captains, going over the order of tomorrow's events on their behalf. Even, he thought wryly, if all that I am and have here is only by the grace of others. Giving in to impulse, he reached over and tugged Jarna's braid. "You did well today, too," he said, "making the finals."

She smiled back, fingering the scarf around her arm. "And Countess Ghiselaine sent me her colors. This is much finer than my peddler's ribbons—but then, they all look so fine and grand now, don't they, the damosels? And did you see Serinna Sondcendre this morning, wearing the tourney crown, how beautiful she was? One of the Lathayrans said that she was fairer than the dawn."

"Poetic, for a Lathayran." Girvase sounded amused.

Jarna patted the roan's neck. "My sisters used to talk about it all the time, what it would be like to be crowned queen of the Midsummer tourney."

Had she dreamed about it, too, Kalan wondered, until her grandfather decreed a different fate? Raher laughed. "My sisters were the same until m'father brought a mirror." The others looked at each other, not quite sure what to say, although Girvase rolled his eyes and even Ado looked taken aback.

"Well, there are no mirrors in my grandfather's house," Jarna said finally.

Raher opened his mouth as if to say something more, but caught Kalan's warning look and closed it again as they dismounted to lead their horses into the camp. There were already gaps along the tent rows where contestants who had not made it through to the final rounds had left. Many had stayed, though, to visit the fair and see the champion acclaimed. Most of these had also begun drinking the moment they knew they no longer had to fight. The camp was raucous with their singing and jeers, and several times the Normarchers had to detour around men on their knees vomiting, or passed out in the lanes between the tents.

The black tents were still there, Kalan saw, although there was no sign of activity amongst them, not even the silent guards he had seen on the first night in camp. Darksworn, he thought, and felt the familiar insect crawl along his spine, although he had never resisted the knowledge that there might be Derai amongst the Swarm in the same way Malian had. Perhaps because Brother Belan had told him the story when he first arrived in the temple of Night, and the crazy old man seemed like his only friend at that time. Or perhaps, Kalan thought, because my experience of the Derai Alliance meant I saw our people with less idealistic eyes than one raised to be Heir of Night.

But if the lightning warriors were Darksworn, then they wouldn't just be mourning Nherenor, they would be out hunting for blood.

"Tarathan of Ar and Jehane Mor." Orth stepped out from a line of Sword warriors, all heavily armed, who blocked the lane to Normarch campsite. His voice was a growl. "High time, I say, to find out what you did with our captain."

Tarathan and Jehane's expressions remained unchanged, even as Kalan and Jarna moved automatically to shield their left, while Girvase, Ado, and Raher fanned out to the right. Kalan could see other knights stirring around their campfires or lifting bleary heads from ale kegs, but none of them spoke.

"We last saw your captain in Ij," Jehane Mor said quietly. "He was well then."

"I say you lie!" Orth snarled. "You're weirdlings, some kind of priest-kind, and I say you bewitched and betrayed him!"

Now the camp around them grew very still. Even the drinking songs from more distant campsites seemed muted in the hush that followed Orth's accusation.

Jehane Mor and Tarathan looked at him remotely. "We are heralds of the Guild," they said, their voices weaving in and out of each other, "and we do not lie."

The Derai behind Orth stirred, and Kalan could almost smell their uneasiness. Some of them, at least, had the sense to know they were out of their own world and must tread carefully. But Orth's head lowered, glaring at Jehane Mor. "Don't think I didn't see it, that day at the bridge. You put your evil eye on him—you and your cursed familiar, that pretends to be a man but can't even talk for himself!"

Tarathan of Ar sighed. He will fight, if he has to, Kalan thought, reading that small, weary sound. He has done it before, and not just from rooftops in the dark.

"I can speak for myself," the herald said, in his dark voice.

"If I choose to. When last we saw Tirorn he was alive and well, as Jehane Mor has already told you."

A gust of wind set the nearby tent flaps fluttering, but Kalan kept his eyes on the Sword line. The older warrior, Gol, stepped closer to Orth. "Perhaps," he said, speaking in Derai, "we should wait until after this tourney truce is done. It will not help our work if we are banished from this realm. Or dead."

"Do you take their part, Gol?" Orth growled back. "Tirorn was my kinsman as well as our captain. I claim right of blood to slay these vermin."

Kalan could see the man was poised to explode into violence—and once a one-to-one challenge was issued in a language the watching camp could understand, there would be no going back. The Emerians were like the Derai in that respect as well: herald or not, Duke's law or not, Tarathan would have to fight.

Facing the Sword warriors, Raher already had a fighting glint in his face, and Kalan knew without looking that Girvase would be wearing the cool, sword's-blade look that said he was ready to finish whatever business the Derai started. He could feel his own blood rising as he recalled Audin and the sword ring yesterday, and contemplated the pleasure of doing his level best to pound Orth's face into the dirt. Yet his head, cooler than the surge of adrenaline along his veins, reminded him that if he gave in to that impulse, then he, Girvase, and Jarna would all be disqualified from the tourney finals.

I can't do that to Jarn, he thought, gritting his teeth—and it would be disastrous for Ghiselaine as well, after her very public salute to our company. He did not even want to imagine how heavily the Duke's wrath might fall on those who broke the tourney truce as well as their knightly word. So *think*, Kalan told himself, choking back the desire for violence. And stay calm. Try not to seem either aggressive or afraid.

"What happened to your captain?" he asked, pitching his voice across the tension and making eye contact with Gol.

Orth twitched his shoulders as if a fly had stung him, but did not reply. Gol cleared his throat and spoke in the River tongue. "The last time we saw Tirorn he was going to their Guild house in Ij. He never came back. We went there ourselves, looking for him, but everyone in the house was dead and the city a hornet's nest." His eyes flicked from Kalan to the heralds. "But now these heralds turn up here, alive and well."

Kalan nodded, seeing how to them that would not look good. "We know about that massacre," he replied, keeping his voice steady although his heart was hammering. "Tarathan and Jehane Mor escaped because they were elsewhere in the city at the time."

"Our captain was seen with them that night," Gol persisted.

"But no one saw him killed? And you have not found a body?" Kalan was aware that the focus of their tableau had shifted away from Orth now to center on him. He kept his eyes on Gol. "Did anyone see these heralds vanish him?"

Gol frowned. "No," he said, and a tiny ripple ran through his companions.

Thinking at last, Kalan hoped—although Orth was still the danger point. "So," he said, very carefully, "you have no actual evidence, no reports from others, that these heralds harmed your captain?"

Orth roared. "They're priest-kind! That's evidence enough!"

The rest of the Derai looked considerably less certain. "Orth—" Gol began, but the giant warrior shook his head.

"What do we care for their pathetic laws and truces? We are Derai." He switched back to his rough version of the River dialect. "I swore by kin and blood that I would kill these two when I saw them next." Deliberately, he drew his sword and took a step forward, his gaze raking the small Normarch line. "Who amongst you will prevent me?"

Tarathan dismounted. "They will not have to," he said. "I will fight you, if I must."

A cold voice spoke from behind Kalan. "If it's blood they want, we will give it to them." Tall figures in blue-black mail, with lightning bolts on their closed helmets, moved past the Normarch knights. Some carried spears, while the rest had their hands on their sword hilts. The Sword warriors snarled and snatched for their weapons, apparently recognizing their adversaries as Swarm despite the closed helms.

"No," said Ser Raven, stepping from between two tents. "You won't." His expression, as he looked from the Derai to the Darksworn, was similar to the one he had shown Girvase during their confrontation at the Rindle. "All competitors have sworn to the truce, so if you force a fight here you will be oath-breakers *and* guests who have abused the hospitality of Emer. For that, any sworn knight present can have you shot down like the curs such actions make you."

"We are not competitors," the lightning knight returned, "and our envoy, who did swear your oath, is dead. Do not think," he added to the Sword warriors, "that we missed the cursed Derai stink about that business."

"Does your envoy's death make his word valueless?" Ser Raven asked. "And if he was an envoy, as you say, then you should take your claim for retribution to the Duke. But there will be no disputes here while the truce stands."

Ser Raven gave no obvious signal, but at his last words a circle of archers emerged from between the tents. Ser Alric was with them, an arrow notched to the longbow he carried, with more bowmen from Wymark on either side—but Kalan could see the badges of Bonamark, Allerion, and Tenneward as well, and several of the tall, quiet men from Aralorn. He could not see the Darksworn's faces, but a look at Orth convinced him that it was only the archers that had stopped him. The Sword warrior did not look like he cared a clipped coin for any truce, even the Derai's, if it did not suit his purpose.

"This isn't over," Orth grated out, his stare fixed on the heralds.

"No," they said, in their joint voice. "We didn't think it was."

"Now that," Ser Raven told Orth, "inclines me to just shoot you and have done."

Orth's glare swung toward the knight, and Kalan could

almost feel the torrent of his hatred, switching course. Slowly, the giant ran his tongue over his lips, studying their Normarch line. He looked poised to utter more threats, but his companions surrounded him, much as they had at the sword ring the day before, and forced him away.

The Darksworn leader's attention was fixed on Ser Raven. "You play a very dangerous game," he said, and if his voice had been cold before, now it was wintry. He jerked his head toward the Derai. "And keep poor company."

"I am not of their company," Ser Raven returned. "I took service with Falk of Normarch this spring, and through him, the Duke of Emer. And I hold to my oaths."

"As do we all." The Darksworn's voice was level. *Until the times comes to break them.*

Kalan almost jumped, but no one else appeared to have heard the chill thought. He found that he was shaking, both from the unexpectedness of the situation, coming at the end of a grueling day, and the coiled tension. But the Sword warriors were retreating, keeping Orth pinned between them, and the Darksworn, too, had stepped back.

"We will respect your tourney camp truce," their leader said to Ser Raven, "not because of your arrows, but for the boy's sake." He must mean Nherenor, Kalan thought. "But we will still have blood—including yours, if you get in our way."

"You dare threaten—" Ser Alric began, but Ser Raven stopped him.

"Words mean nothing," he said. "Let them go."

Kalan let his breath out again in an almost silent huff, but Ser Raven was right, the Darksworn were withdrawing. The knight watched them go, his expression impossible to read, while the heralds were still looking in the direction the Derai had taken. "They are unworthy of their former captain," Jehane Mor said, and despite her cool tone, Kalan thought she sounded sad. The inclination of her head toward Ser Raven managed to include all the archers. "For your timely intervention, we thank you."

Ser Raven's answering smile was grim. "For sparing Tarathan the trouble of killing him?" he inquired.

Jehane Mor shook her head. "One can never tell how these matters will turn out," she murmured. "And there was the truce to be considered as well." She turned to the rest of the Normarch company. "Under the circumstances, it's probably best if we return to the city now. We would like to be there before moonrise in any case, since tonight is the beginning of Midsummer and Countess Ghiselaine is to keep the First Night watch with Queen Zhineve-An." She smiled at Jarna. "That was our second commission from the Countess. She asks if you will share guard duty over the vigil with Alianor and Ilaise, since no man may enter the temple's inner precint, not even the queen's Seven."

Jarna had to try twice before words came out. "I would . . . I would be honored," she said finally. "Let the Countess know that I will join her before moonrise."

They all watched as the heralds rode away, the gray horses joining the steady stream of people returning to the city. "That was clever, to think of archers," Girvase said to Ser Raven. "But how did you know what was happening?"

"One of Ser Alric's men brought word of trouble brewing." Ser Raven nodded at the other knight. "He did the rest."

"Half my company are archers," the knight of Vast said. "I didn't have 'em all with me, but they rounded up a few more easily enough. Archers never mind bending their bows against the knightly kind, given opportunity," he added with a wink, and everyone laughed, even Raher, who could be tenacious over knightly dignity.

"You'll share our dinner, of course," Ser Raven said, "as thanks for your help."

The meal was a mess of bacon and onions, quickly fried up with reheated stew from yesterday's dinner, and followed by a Wymark cheese that Ser Alric and his archers brought out. Most of the other archers had stayed as well, and the talk quickly became cheerful as everyone discussed how the tourney had gone so far and what might happen in the final events. Some of them glanced sideways at Jarna, but no one said anything amiss—had better not, Kalan thought, since she was one of the handful present who had made it into any of the finals.

Several of the bowmen wanted to know whether they would get to see the Jhainarian queen the next day, given Ser Ombrose was wearing her colors, which brought a burst of speculation as to why she had not been there today. "Lord Hirluin, too," a Bonamark archer added. "Isn't the formal rebetrothal on the last day of the festival?"

Ser Alric cleared his throat in the suddenly awkward silence. "Those northerners'll cause you Normarch lot trouble in the melee. That's my pick."

Kalan and Girvase exchanged looks. "First we have to survive the sword contest." Kalan tried not to answer shortly. "One of us is bound to have to fight Orth there." If we haven't expired from exhaustion first, he added silently.

"Oaf Orth!" Jarna said, with unexpected venom.

Raher plucked moodily at a clump of grass. "I don't care for these northerners at all."

"No one does," said Ser Raven. "They are brutal and bigoted and care only for their own." His expression was dark, and Kalan glanced at him curiously.

"Have they been to a tourney here before?" he asked.

"Never, that I've heard of." Ser Alric's tone said that they could stay away in future, too. Kalan made a face at his plate, because he was still Derai, no matter how much he would prefer not to be. Yet he found it hard to deny that Nherenor had seemed worth ten of Orth and his companions. A Darksworn, Kalan reminded himself quickly, wincing as the tart cheese stung his bitten mouth.

Ser Alric and his archers left soon after that, and the other bowmen, too, gradually drifted away. "We need to get you to the temple before it gets dark," Kalan said to Jarna, stretching against the single dull ache that was his body. His muscles were already stiff, but he forced himself to his feet, and Jarna joined him without a word.

"We should all go." Girvase got to his feet as well. "We can see Audin—and the way the camp's going, we should probably take most of our gear to the town house anyway."

Kalan suspected that he did not want to leave the outer watch over the temple sanctuary to the Jhainarian Seven, and with Darksworn present he felt much the same himself. They both glanced at Ser Raven, but he nodded rather than objecting.

"I can ask Ser Alric's men to watch this site. And you'll probably get more sleep in the town house, even if it means an early start." As if to underline Ser Raven's point, a nearby gathering roared out a drinking song, one famous for its innumerable verses.

"Let's get the horses," Kalan said to Jarna, as the others began collecting up saddlebags and armor. He had not really expected the horselines to be more private, but there were already knights drinking along the poplar row that separated the field from the camp. No chance to even snatch a kiss, Kalan thought regretfully, and could not help remembering stolen moments at Normarch and the sweetness of Jarna's lips on his, unexpectedly soft in her sun-browned face.

"Say hello to Audin for me," she said, as they finished saddling up. "And keep on Raher in line."

Kalan grinned. "Impossible," he replied. He fought back the impulse to kiss her anyway, joking with her instead as they led the horses back to the camp and helped the others with their gear. The western sky was vermilion as they mounted up, and Ado whistled a tune as the camp fell behind.

"Not long now until Midsummer's moon rises," he said, letting the whistle die. "But we'll reach the temple first," he added hastily to Jarna.

"Imuln's moon," she said softly, and Kalan wondered if all their thoughts had flown to Summer's Eve and the horned moon rising.

"Imuln's luck," Girvase replied, and everyone except Ser Raven nodded.

"Luck's what Lathayrans say a Great Marriage is about," Raher said abruptly. "Though in their dialects it could just as well mean well-being, or even survival."

And Kalan, listening to the steady clip of their horses' hooves and the first hoot of an owl through the gathering dusk, thought that perhaps all survival was luck.

# 43

✦━◆━✦

# *Moonrise*

*T*he scent of night earth and rotting leaves filled Malian's dream, sifting through the green canopy of Maraval wood and tree trunks shifting to hide a vision of Yorinde-sarinen. The formless thoughts and tiny pulse beats of small night creatures formed a web around her—only to be torn apart, their minute energies fragmented by an explosion of dark power that blasted her into a forest of fog and Emerian oaks.

Now she had become a hunted creature, darting and dodging between black-barked trunks and along deer paths with the dark power in pursuit. She had power of her own, tied to old, hidden corners of the land, but if the pursuing terror caught her it would extinguish her with a thought. Desperate, the fleeing creature plunged into a deep fog bank, flowing beneath a long-fallen tree and out the other side.

The trees here were taller, their vast trunks soaring skyward around a narrow glade with a small fire burning at its heart. A woman with stars in her hair sat beside the fire, the hood of her cloak thrown back as she played cat's cradle with the flames. The creature hesitated, but the pursuing darkness was close behind, crackling out power like a lightning storm. Terrified, the creature darted toward the fire, cowering low as the woman rose to her feet. Her expression was grim as she surveyed the being crouched at her feet. *"Someone,"* she said, *"has used you hard."*

The woman looked through the fog toward the approaching storm and raised her right hand, still with the fire in it. The flame roared, leaping skyward, then twisted into a ribbon that circled them both. In the distance, hounds yowled, and the fire blazed hotter, becoming a conflagration. The star-crowned woman's smile was thin. *"Even Nindorith,"* she said, *"will not like to meet that hunt."* She turned the other way and the flames parted, opening onto a rugged mountainside in northern Emer. *"Go,"* she bade the creature at her feet. *"And stay away from the Derai in future, for we are not kind to those who cross either our will or our path."*

The creature slipped away, disappearing into the Emerian dusk. The fire roared again, reforming into a mirror through which Yorindesarinen's scarred face studied Malian, who gazed back at her through the medium of the dream. *"You have grown hard, child,"* the hero said, *"to sacrifice others so ruthlessly for your need."* Her expression changed, becoming weary instead of grim. *"Is this the person you want to be? Or the leadership the Derai needs?"*

I was desperate, Malian wanted to cry out. I had to elude Nindorith, or be captured or killed outright. But the flames twisted again, sweeping across the mirror and shutting out her vision of Yorindesarinen. The hounds bayed for blood and death as wakefulness tugged at her, yet the fiery mirror still burned. And this was the first time Yorindesarinen had spoken with her in five years.

If only to rebuke me, thought Malian, grieved. A fresh wash of fire crossed the mirror and the flames cleared again, but it was no longer the dead hero that looked out. Instead, Tarathan of Ar and Jehane Mor gazed at her with light-filled eyes. *"There is a way,"* they said, their voices blending together in the way that spoke to Malian of truth and power. *"If you are willing to walk the path, Heir of the Derai."*

A bell called from Imuln's temple, heralding the first night of festival. The sweet clear tone pulled Malian awake to find sunset a splash of amber across her wall—and realize that she had slept through most of the afternoon. She had not thought she would sleep at all when she lay down, with her mind still full of Nindorith, the Darksworn, and Nherenor lying broken in the cobbled lane.

Unsurprising really, she thought, that my dreams were dark as well. She shivered, still feeling the night creature's terror as Nindorith hunted it through the Gate of Dreams. However ancient and formless on its mountainside above the Rindle, it had been unable to slip the binding that she had made with her amulet and escape the Swarm demon. And she had known that was possible when she used the spell.

Malian covered her face with an arm to shut out the sad weariness she had seen in Yorindesarinen's face: *Is this the person you want to be? Or the leadership the Derai needs?*

I was desperate, she whispered to herself again. I have grown in strength since I left the Wall, but I dared not stand against this Nindorith.

Yet she remembered her fear, when thrown through the Gate of Dreams on Summer's Eve, that it might have been she who murdered Maister Gervon, only not remembered doing so when in the waking world. Tarathan had said that the killing did not have her stamp, but maybe he would say differently now if he knew about the night garden and the detail of what she had wrought with that final amulet. And on the mountainside above the Rindle, she was the one of all their party that the primitive darkness had been drawn to. To its subsequent rue, she thought, if the dream told true—in which case Yorindesarinen had saved it despite its innate dark nature.

"So the Gate gives me paradox," Malian said aloud—when what she had undoubtedly merited, after the previous night and a morning spent dealing with Zhineve-An, was the sleep of exhaustion. She smiled wryly, recalling how she had barely slipped back into her room, shortly after dawn, before the page, Luin was knocking on her door with an urgent summons to join the Duke in the guest wing of the palace.

A few minutes in the young queen's company had made

it clear that Zhineve-An understood the significance of the power storm that had raged across Caer Argent during the night. "These envoys, the Many-As-One," she said to the Duke, her hands closing around the arms of her chair as she leaned forward. "We suspected before, but now we know. They are in league with the demons the Ishnapuri seek—the same demons that slew successive generations of queens in Jhaine, during the Dark Years. We will have no more dealings with them."

"The Dark Years." The Duke had looked taken aback. "That was a very long time ago."

"We do not forget," the queen retorted, drawing herself up. "The demons believed that a priestess-queen of Jhaine would be instrumental in their final fall and so sought to exterminate us all. We did not know," she added, "that their kind were active in the world again."

Is that why the queens closed Jhaine, Malian wondered now, and bound themselves to their centers of power—because the Swarm was exterminating them?

"And the Abjured as well," Zhineve-An had continued fiercely, her hands opening and closing again, "the Forsworn. I felt *their* power, too. I could not mistake it, despite all here that is foreign and strange."

"A Queen threat," Rastem put in, with his hand on his sword. "We cannot protect her against such dangers in the midst of your tournament crowd. The situation is too open, the risk too great."

"So you don't wish to attend, is that it?" The Duke had shaken his head. "I will have my guards there—but you are our guest and must do as you wish. I will send more guards to protect these rooms, as many as First Rastem wishes. And Maister Carick here will be happy to answer all your questions about the River lands."

Happy is not the word I would have used, Malian thought now. The queen had sat for some time, her brows drawn together and her lower lip caught between her teeth, staring at the door through which the Duke had left. When she finally roused herself, it was to spend the next few hours grilling

Malian with questions about the River and the Guild, particularly how the herald pairs were selected. When done, Zhineve-An had again just sat and stared through her, to the extent that Malian wondered if the queen had penetrated the illusion spells around Maister Carick.

"The outside world is more complex than we thought," Zhineve-An had said at last, looking beyond Malian to Rastem. "But today is still the First Night of Midsummer, and the High Priestess has asked me to keep vigil in the original sanctuary. Lore claims," she continued, her gaze switching back to Malian, "that it was ancient even before the world fell, like our sanctuaries in Jhaine. I have already asked your Countess Ghiselaine to keep the watch with me," she added, before finally dismissing Malian from her presence.

*My Countess Ghiselaine,* Malian repeated to herself now, with another wry smile—although, in fact, she would accompany the Countess as far as the temple complex, even though she had business of her own to pursue that night.

*There is a way,* the heralds' voices said again in her memory, *if you are willing to walk the path, Heir of the Derai.* The last phrase, Heir of the Derai had never been spoken in Imuln's dome—so Malian took the dream's message to mean that the heralds' way must be significant, but possibly dangerous for an alien Derai.

She knew she should move but lay still anyway, watching the sunset light on the wall and listening to the distant shrieks of children, playing through the palace's courtyards and halls. She was lying on top of the bed's coverlet, beneath her cloak, which smelled of road dust and wood smoke and horses—but right now she found that comforting. A certainty, she thought, in a world that is far from certain. She saw the long road from Ar to Caer Argent in her mind's eye: the dangers of the Northern March, and last night's wild rush across the city's roofs, which had ended in Nherenor's death—a death first seen in Yorindesarinen's fire, five years before.

*I still don't know why it was significant enough for me to foresee, though,* Malian reflected. *Or perhaps it isn't signifi-*

cant at all, perhaps it's just one of many things that *might* be, some of which come to pass while others don't. She sat up, touching the heavy medallion around her neck. And some, she added silently, that are unforeseen—at least by me. Yet the series of visions seen in Yorindesarinen's fire so powerful that she almost lost herself in them. It was Tarathan who had rescued her, grasping her hands and stepping out of the fire's heart in order to show her the path back.

Tarathan of Ar, Malian repeated to herself, and slipped the fine silver chain over her head in order to study the medallion. The face depicted the round disc of the full moon, with a horned crescent in bas-relief against its base. It was the same ornament that Zhineve-An had worn on the morning of the Swarm audience. "The insignia," Jehane Mor had said, as she placed the disc between Malian's hands that morning, "of the priestess-queens of Jhaine."

A gift and a challenge, Malian thought now, her hand closing around it—one she wanted to take up, even while apprehension tightened the muscles in her gut. One I dare not refuse either, she added grimly, since Nindorith may already be hunting me down. And the heralds' way offers me the chance to alter the essence of who I am, and so disappear while remaining in plain sight.

She traced the face of the moon disc with a thoughtful fingertip and wondered if she had already journeyed too far from the Wall, not in physical miles but in herself. She was Malian of Night—but what would that mean once she took the first step along the path this medallion offered?

*"No going back."* Nhenir's voice was cool as moonlight across her mind.

Malian nodded. *"You're right, although that's been true ever since I left the Keep of Winds."* My choice, she reminded herself, even if Asantir, Haimyr, and Yorindesarinen all encouraged it.

*"I will take you with me to the temple and hide you, so there's an additional watch over Ghiselaine."* she told the helm. *"I'm not sure I entirely trust Queen Zhineve-An."* She was not certain that she could trust Nhenir either if the helm

decided that Ghiselaine's well-being was not important. But given Lord Falk's promise with respect to the Lost, it was difficult to see even Nhenir reaching that conclusion.

She slipped the medallion back over her head and stood up, pulling her last clean shirt and hose from her rucksack, and washing with water from the ewer in the corner of the room. The shirt and hose, as well as the sleeveless tunic she pulled on over the top, were black, but of everyday fabric, not the fine clothes she had worn to meet the Jhainarian queen for the first time. She was careful to conceal both the moon disc and its chain beneath her clothes before braiding her hair into the queue favored by River sailors, slipping her hideout weapons into place, and setting Nhenir, in its flat, black cap form, onto her head.

The children had vanished by the time Malian descended the narrow stair from her room, although the courtyard outside the Gallery wing was full of revelers celebrating the first night of Midsummer. She could hear a clamor rising from the city as well, louder than the night before, as Ghiselaine's party joined with Queen Zhineve-An and four of her Seven to walk to the temple. Rastem and his companions walked to either side of them, with six ducal guards clearing the way ahead and six marching.

Malian had assumed they would go via the ribbon of park that stretched between the palace and the temple grounds, where the rest of Zhineve-An's Seven were already keeping watch. But Ghiselaine explained that they had to enter by way of a formal gate, so the guards took the route along the mews. Automatically, Malian scanned the rooftops, which remained clear, although the festival clamor was growing. There was even a mixed party of Lathayran and Emerian knights drinking by the fountain in the temple square. "It'll be the same everywhere," Alianor said, following the direction of her gaze. "The knights who are no longer competing will drink through to the end of the festival. Although some do keep vigil at Midsummer as well."

"Not many, though," Ilaise murmured, and Alianor nodded, her expression wry.

They met the company of Normarch knights by the temple gate closest to the mews and found Audin there as well, with his arm in a sling. He was moving stiffly, but managed a creditable courtier's bow for Ghiselaine and Zhineve-An. Jarna was fingering the yellow and white scarf around her arm, her expression nervous but excited as she, too, scraped a bow to the Jhainarian queen. A temple priestess, robed in the midnight blue of Midsummer and anonymous beneath a deep cowl, indicated that they should all follow her into a private courtyard, before ushering the vigil keepers toward another, smaller gate. Malian could see tall trees beyond the inner wall and guessed that this must be the enclosed wood she had seen on her first morning in the palace.

"The moon will rise soon," the priestess intoned, as though speaking the words of ritual. "You must be inducted within the ancient sanctuary before it does."

Ilaise, the last to pass through the second gate, made a face back over her shoulder, as if to indicate that she had had enough of vigils. Yet Ghiselaine could not have declined Zhineve-An's invitation without causing offense—something it seemed easy enough to do.

"Luck," Audin wished them softly as the priestess closed the grilled gate from within. The ducal guards began to file out, their part done, while Rastem and Zorem took up position facing the temple square; their two companions looked toward the inner gate.

"We are the Countess Ghiselaine's company," the Duke's nephew said to Rastem, "so will share the watch with you."

Their official escort duty had ended when Ghiselaine reached Caer Argent, but the Seven probably would not know that, especially as the Normarchers were all wearing the countess's colors. Even Raven, Malian thought, surprised. Her eyes had flicked to his face when Audin spoke, but the knight said nothing, and although Rastem did not seem pleased, he did not argue either.

"I can stand two watches," Ado said, "since I'm not competing tomorrow." So he and Girvase stayed, while the others walked back to the Normarch town house—since as Audin pointed out, they might as well be comfortable. Malian murmured agreement to this, but excused herself when they reached the mews, saying she must return to the palace. Only Raven did not call out a farewell, although he nodded as she turned away.

She had to wait a few minutes until the narrow street was clear in either direction, before climbing to the roof of the row houses and making her way to the rear wall. Once there, she crouched below the parapet and surveyed the greensward below. The old watchtowers along the river were dark silhouettes, the palace to her right a blaze of lights. On her left she could see the postern into the temple grounds and the remaining three of Zhineve-An's Seven on watch there. Keeping low, she crept along the guttering between roofs and wall, glad of Nhenir's ability to help her pass unseen.

The moon was beginning to rise, turning the eastern sky to amethyst as Malian reached the temple grounds. She paused as one of the Seven did a careful survey of the nearby walls and towers, and only slid over the temple wall once she was sure that all three guards were looking away. From there, she hung full length by her hands before dropping the final few feet into the enclosed woodland below. She caught the scent of jasmine, dizzyingly sweet, as she landed, and saw gravel walks twisting between stands of trees. The cupola of the old temple, dwarfed by the bulk of the main precinct, was visible between two of the copses, and Malian made her way toward it, walking on grass to avoid the betraying crunch of gravel.

The entrance to the chapel was on the building's woodland side, below the cupola. Two dark yew trees guarded a small portico, built to shelter a heavy wooden door. Malian glided from shadow to shadow along the edge of the trees until she reached the far side of the building, but was unable to find any other entrance. Only the cupola rose above one level, but although the narrow windows could be easily broken, the panes were small and the lead between them would take a little longer to force. Secure enough then, she decided, especially with the main temple close by. She placed Nhenir on one of the flat stone sills and was impressed at how her eye slid over its presence. Even when she forced herself to focus, she only saw a lichened stone urn set within the window embrasure.

*"Take care, Heir of Night."* The helm's voice was a chime of ice as she turned away, and Malian almost shivered. She nodded acknowledgment and moved deeper into the enclosed woodland, following the most overgrown paths. The grounds became wilder, until a tangle of elder and may trees opened up, revealing a deep, still pool. The rising moon's reflection was just beginning to creep across the water, and she could feel the same power that filled Imuln's dome humming beneath her feet. The power would build, Jehane Mor had told her, as the moon filled the pool—an event that only happened on the three high days of Midsummer.

At first Malian thought that she had arrived too soon and was alone, until a deeper shadow moved beneath an elder tree. She tensed, remembering the dark figure that had watched the inn door in Normarch, but the figure took another step out of shadow and into moonlight, and she saw that it was Tarathan. He, too, was wearing black, rather than herald's gray, and although he still bore the swallowtail swords, his braids hung loose down his back. As they had when he rinsed off dirt and sweat and blood in the hill fort, she thought, feeling the shiver of that dawn memory run through her.

Tarathan stopped, facing her, but even in the moonlight Malian found it impossible to read his expression. He was carrying a cup between his lean strong hands, and now he held it out to her, neither of them speaking a word. Their fingertips touched as she took it, and she felt the fire that was at the core of both their power spark.

Seeker's fire, she thought, with a trace of the dizziness she recalled from Summer's Eve. A warrior's, too, she added silently, for that was why he was here, to stand as First to her proxy queen in a ritual that was as old as the worship of Imuln in Haarth.

"Although only in Jhaine," Jehane Mor had told her beneath Imuln's dome, "are the oldest ways still remembered. And even there, the true rite that brings together the power of the Goddess and the power of Haarth at the zenith of a Great Year, for the weal of all, is rarely performed."

The true rite, Malian thought now, that will transform my essence, blending it with that of Haarth so that Nindorith will be unable to seek me out. If I can perform the ritual successfully.

"I will hold a shield from here," Jehane Mor had told her, "to deflect outside attention—not just Zhineve-An or the dark seeker, but the priestesses in the temple as well. Tara- than will be with you as First and to speak the words of the ritual, the chant that will enable you to walk the Midsummer path of moon and earth."

Malian glanced back at Imuln's great dome, dark and unrevealing against the sky, then lifted the cup, scanning its contents with her Shadow Band-trained senses to detect the presence of poison or drugs. Tarathan placed his hands over hers. "It is water drawn from the sacred pool, which enhances the ritual, that is all."

A ritual of Haarth, Malian thought, which may not accept me—but the touch of Tarathan's hands was warm, his eyes steady on hers. She placed the rim of the cup against her lips and drank.

# 44

# *The Path of Earth and Moon*

The moon was a glowing, aqueous shield reflected in the heart of the pool as Malian stepped barefoot onto the moon track that stretched across its surface. The water from the cup had been cool fire, traveling down her throat, and now moonlight shimmered along her veins. The weight of Tarathan's chant wove around her like a cloak, and she could see the threads of power spinning out ahead of her. It reminded her of Yorindesarinen's silver path through the Gate of Dreams, which Jehane Mor had called a ropewalk across vast deeps. Now Malian felt the rough strands beneath each footstep, even though her eyes told her that she was walking down into the water, descending to the heart of the reflected moon.

It's a portal, she thought, another pathway beyond the Gate of Dreams. The medallion beneath her shirt glowed, answering the moon and creating a golden nimbus with Malian at its center. The border realm between moonglow and dark water flickered, and her breath quickened as visions spun into being around her.

The first images were easily recognizable: a unicorn with flaming eyes materialized out of half night and mist to bell out grief and rage over the body of a black-haired youth; a slender youth in the garb of a River scholar stared into darkness on a Normarch mountainside; the same youth lay concealed in brush, listening to the clip of horses' hooves, approaching through the Long Pass.

Water rippled and the images reformed into children, playing across sunlit courts: seven small boys and a girl with fair hair who had been bound together from their cradles. The children grew a little taller, and now their games were weapons practice, and sleight of eye and hand and mind. They practiced the powers of Imuln, too: healing and scrying through water and fire, as well as prophecy and foreseeing. Always, when it came to *seeing*, it was one of the seven, a boy with chestnut hair, who excelled—when lore and instruction taught that it should have been the girl who held those gifts. Already the eight knew enough to conceal this truth, for any reversals of the Goddess-ordained order were called abominations in Jhaine, and fire, hot irons, and the headsman's axe were how the hierarchy dealt with such offenses to Imuln.

Malian's vision sped on and the children became young adults. The boy's gift grew stronger and he began to foresee through dreams as well as in smoke, fire, and water. The fair girl walked with him in the world of dreams, shielding him from those who might have found him out, and seeing, through the link between them, much of what he foresaw. His visions revealed a great darkness poised to overthrow their world—and the face of one who might have the power to turn that tide, if they played their part in events unfolding beyond the closed boundaries of Jhaine.

The fair-haired girl, who had been consecrated at birth as Zhehaamor, both priestess and queen, spoke mind-to-mind with her fellow sovereigns in their temple strongholds, sharing the dark threat and arguing that Jhaine must play its part against it. But the other priestess-queens ranged themselves against her like an iron wall. The ways of Jhaine, they said, were the will of the Goddess made manifest, and what had saved them from the Cataclysm when the rest of the world was riven. The realm of the Goddess must remain inviolate—and a priestess-queen whose visions undermined that sacred duty should be examined for unholy influence and, if necessary, exorcised by the unified hierarchy.

Water and moonlight swirled around Malian . . . and Zhehaamor and her Seven fled for Jhaine's border with southern Aralorn, the pursuit hard on their heels. The flight became a series of skirmishes and ambuscades, and one by one her Seven fell. Only three remained when a patrol threatened to cut them off, just hours from the border. One of the three turned to delay the pursuit while the others fled on—but Zhehaamor's horse went lame and the vanguard of those following, the Seven of another queen, caught them on the Jhainarian bank of the border river. The vision disintegrated into a whirl of swords on the shingle flats and blood staining the shallow water. When it was done, the First with the chestnut hair stood with his head bowed, blood dripping from his swallowtail swords, and all of the vanguard Seven were dead.

The second of Zhehaamor's remaining Seven also lay on the shingle, more bleeding wounds than sound body. Somehow, his companions got him onto a horse and limped across the river, heading for the nearby woodland as the main body of their pursuers thundered toward the Jhainarian bank. The pursuers' horses milled around the bodies of the fallen Seven in a cloud of dust and curses—and the call went up, closed realm or not, to cross the river and finish the last of the Forsworn. The first riders began to move that way, until a line of cloaked and hooded figures emerged from the trees and fanned out along the Aralorn bank. The newcomers bore no obvious arms and stood unmoving, but the advance toward the river stopped. After a long silent wait on both sides, the Jhainarian pursuers turned their horses back.

Again the pool swirled, the vision shifting to the gates of the Guild House in Terebanth and the two who waited outside, their clothes and boots worn thin. They stood side by side, their young faces somber but resolute: priestess-queen and First, enduring friends and sometime lovers, comrades-in-arms, soon to become heralds of the Guild with their secret faces turned to the world. The gates of the Guild house closed behind them and did not open again—or not for Malian's seeing.

The medallion on her breast blazed brighter, and she began to hear the song of Emer through Tarathan's chant. The tune, like the chant, was a weft and warp of threads: the light-edged lilt of Maraval wood danced through and around the creep of tree roots along the old northern road; the path that had called to Maister Carick above the Rindle sang its siren song again, bright notes of bracken and fern beneath the scolding chitter of a squirrel. As the tug of the water grew stronger, Malian heard deeper notes: the drum of hooves across Emer and Jhaine; the sonorous, swift-moving River currents; and the slow relentless grinding of rocks within earth that was Jaransor.

Alive, Malian thought, her heart answering the strong, sure beat of the song. I was right, it's not just Jaransor: the whole of Haarth is aware.

Water funneled and rolled, pressing in on her eyes, nostrils, mouth. A roaring in her ears drowned out Tarathan's chant, and the light from the moon disc flickered, then strengthened again. Through it, Malian saw the entire world of Haarth—as though she were looking down on the tabletop map in the Keep of Winds, except that what she saw was real, and riven by earthquake and fire. The strong, sure song was lost as rivers changed course, drowning towns and farmland, and the ocean swept inland behind huge waves, smashing everything in its path. In Jaransor, the towers that had stood beyond time and memory shook—and fell.

The nine temple sanctuaries of Jhaine survived, but the land around them was torn apart by quake after enormous quake, its cities and strongholds thrown down. In desperation, the high priestesses joined together as one and the voice of the Goddess answered, speaking like stone out of earth and darkness. Nine men of Jhaine stepped forward, as the temples began to crumble around them, and the high priestesses, their faces painted black for the moon's darkness, raised bare arms in invocation. The sun set in fire and the moon rose in blood as the nine performed the oldest and darkest of all Imuln's rites—and blood flowed, down into earth, binding the world into stillness again.

Blood sacrifice, Malian thought, understanding at last: the oldest, darkest union of earth and moon—and made willingly, the vision around her sang that, too, in order to generate the level of power needed to bind a disintegrating realm back into wholeness again. She shook her head, tasting blood where she had bitten her lip, as famine and disease followed the widespread devastation—the Cataclysm that had been wrought by the Derai's arrival on Haarth.

*Sacrifice offered willingly,* sang the voice of stone and moon and water—*but what happens when the earth lies quiet and yet the blood is spilled again every Great Year, by force rather than being offered freely? What then?*

"Desecration," Malian whispered. And wondered: does the Duke know this, that the Great Marriage in its oldest form requires blood for the binding to work?

The moon vanished, the pool becoming a lightless well through which she dived until she felt made of darkness. *"You must learn to eat the dark lest it eat you."* Malian recognized Nhenir's voice, cool across another memory, and knew, then, when she had made this dark, unending dive before. Until now, though, she would have said that this vision was not of Haarth and should have lain outside the ritual's path of earth and moon. The darkness splintered into crystal, a cavern ringed with blazing torches and filled with endless rows of stone biers—but the sleepers were gone.

The guardian was gone, too, or had hidden itself from her Midsummer vision. The sleepers had been waiting, the guardian had told her, for an hour and time appointed—although Malian was not the one who would wake them. So who had? she wondered. And where had they gone?

For the first time in five years, she felt Yorindesarinen's armring burn on her forearm. *"I seek out the hidden, the lost I find."* Malian murmured to herself. Is that why I have been shown this now? Are the sleepers more lost that I must find?

Her brows drew together, her vision shifting to the three great standards at the heart of the cavern. They were blank, both the fiery colors and insignia from her previous visit here erased. All three biers below them were empty now, too— but she remembered the face of the commander, his stern expression full of weariness and grief. The sword upon his breast had been unadorned, but she recalled the way it had called to her, a blade asking to be taken up and used.

Yet now the sword, too, was gone.

*"Beware!"* The whisper seared the air, although Malian was not sure who had spoken, whether Yorindesarinen through the armring, or the power that had haunted this place last time she was here. *"They come."*

*"Accursed!"* The interwoven voice was a serpent's hiss, but the shapes that unfolded from the cavern floor were those of seven women, veiled in black. A dark moon rose behind them, a tide of old blood rippling across its face, and the discs upon their breasts were blood-washed black as well. *"Forsworn!"*

The voice reminded Malian of heralds, with the distinct strands twisting together to make one voice. Seven, she noted, not eight—and was surprised she cared that Zhineve-An was not part of this; that the young queen had either never been part of it, or Jehane Mor's shield had been effective in walling her out. But why not these others, then? Malian wondered.

*"They have used blood to bind themselves to the ritual itself."* She felt the flare of Tarathan's fire as his mind touched hers. *"As soon as the rite began, the bond would have pulled them in."*

And there are seven of them, Malian thought, seven high priestesses of the Goddess, each one drawing on the power of her own sanctuary. And seven, although considerably less than nine, was still a number of power in Jhaine. She knew that she should have been afraid, but instead she laughed.

*"Forsworn!"* The serpent voice spat out the word. *"Did you think you were the only one in the sanctuaries of Jhaine who could part the mists of time and see? We knew you would come here in the Great Year—that your unholy visions would require your interference in our great ritual. So*

*we bound ourselves to wait and now you will die: death by strangulation as prescribed for the Abjured, since we cannot cleanse either the queenship or Jhaine of your pollution by burning you alive."*

The dark moon fragmented in a torrent of black water that swept the empty cavern away, roiling the veiled queens into a serpent's form that whipped itself around Malian, drawing the coils closed. Death by strangulation: she could feel the dry slither of the serpent's scales, even though she knew its essence was water, as she darted upward like a fish. The serpent's teeth sank into her ankle, dragging her back down. Each tooth was a red-hot dagger, sinking in—and then retracting with a hiss as the serpent's head drew back, regarding her sidelong.

A net of power spun out to engulf her, but Tarathan, still linked to her mind, showed her how the Jhainarian magic could be severed. The serpent's head reared up, spitting out a curse like cobra's poison, but she channeled fire and turned it aside.

The serpent twisted, and for the first time Malian heard the rustle of separate strands within the interwoven voice. *"He is here with her, the doubly accursed, the slayer . . . defilement . . . all these years she concealed . . . perversion of the sacred order . . . the abomination . . ."*

*"Slayer!"* The conjoined voice clanged, harsh as iron, and Malian smelled the acrid whiff of blood, saw the whirl of swords again and the Seven dead on the shingle. *"Abjured!"* She sensed Tarathan through the ritual's link, his fire banked down—waiting for them to act, she realized. Even through her, he would not strike the first blow. Power thrummed, deep within her, not just her own strength and his, but the fire of Yorindesarinen's armring and the song of Haarth.

"Even Imuln's moon," she told them, her voice shadow and stone, "changes its face. Water flows deep underground and wells up again wearing a different form. Do you presume to dictate the path Imuln's power will take in the world, which face it will wear? Fire, torture, blood: you are the serpent that is strangling Jhaine in its coils."

The serpent hissed, its head whipping around to regard

Malian again from a pupil-less eye. *"You are not her—not the Forsworn. You are* other: *a greater abomination. Yet she* has given you the sacred insignia. Not just to meddle, then . . ."* The sibilant voice sank to a whisper, then explored into a roar: *" . . . but* destroy! *She has sent you to undo all that we are!"* And the serpent's mouth gaped wide, rushing forward to devour.

Churned-up water buffeted Malian, sweeping her this way and that as the giant maw drew closer. The disc around her neck became a rock, pulling her down, but instead of fighting, she went with it and the serpent overshot. Her foot touched the ropewalk path again and she raised her arms as Jehane Mor once had, in Jaransor, funneling the water of the pool between her open palms.

The serpent whipped back toward her, but Malian set the funnel spinning along its length. Any sense of pool or moon or cavern disappeared: now there was only the water funnel and the serpent being engulfed within it. Voices cried out, and Malian guessed that the power that bound the priestess-queens together was fraying apart within the sanctuaries of Jhaine. The ropewalk swayed as she spun the whirlpool tighter, intent on banishing the conjoined queens from the Gate of Dreams.

Tighter still the waters spun, and the serpent thrashed, but kept slipping deeper into the vortex until the mouth of the funnel finally began to close. Malian raised her hands to shut it—and the serpent's tail flicked up, striking her legs and pitching her head first into the maelstrom: *"The price of the path you walk is always blood."* The serpent voice hissed at her as she fell. *"Are you willing to pay it, interloper? Or will you condemn another to pay in your stead?"*

Malian turned the pitch into a dive, but the darkness around her was absolute: she could not see or hear anything. Water pressed into her nose and mouth as she tried to work out which way was down, which up, pushing outward with her hands—and another's hands reached down and grasped hers, hauling her upward.

This, too, had happened before—except then she had been

caught in fire and not water. Malian drew deep on the core of her strength and a spar of light answered, distant through the blackness. She tightened her grip and kicked toward it. The light brightened, growing stronger as the maelstrom fell away and she rose through impenetrable white mist. Unexpectedly, she smelled jasmine, as dizzyingly sweet as when she first stepped into the temple grounds. The mist thinned and trees appeared, their trunks a smooth dappling of light and shade. Somewhere in the distance, a nightingale was singing its moonlit song.

The nightingale, Malian knew, was one of the enduring motifs of Emerian springtime love. She wanted to smile, but already her bare feet were touching grass and the mist had grown fine as a veil, with only a single drift, like smoke, crossing the crescent of the blue moon overhead. A second moon, three-quarters full and green as winter twilight, shone lower toward the horizon. Twin moons: Malian knew she had heard a tale of that, too, somewhere in her years on the River, although she could not recall what it signified.

*"The Goddess's isle of the blessed,"* Tarathan said. *"J'mair of Ishnapur used the motif often in his poetry. You have brought us both here in our physical bodies, something I could not have done on my own."*

He was still holding her hands, and Malian did not withdraw them. The moonfire sang in her veins, and this, she knew now, lay at the heart of the true rite—the priestess-queen for Imuln, and the hero or king for the land, coming together in the Great Marriage that was Midsummer. And the First of a Seven was the closest thing to a king that there was in Jhaine.

Tarathan lifted her hands to his lips and kissed them, the touch of his lips warm against her skin. And then his arms were around her, drawing her close. She could feel his heart beating: sure and strong, she thought, listening to its rhythm, strong and sure. *Beautiful,* the moonfire sang, and dangerous, Raven's word from the hill fort—but she was remembering how Tarathan had kept the fire of his power banked, unwilling to attack the seven queens in their serpent form.

*"I am still of Jhaine,"* he said. She nodded, understanding that, and leaned back a little, so she could study the stark planes of his face and the dark, fierce eyes. He smiled, austerity softening into something warmer as one hand loosened the queue at her nape, his fingers threading through the fan of her hair. *"I have wanted to see what you would look like, without the illusions of Maister Carick to cloud the face of the moon."*

Malian shivered, half from the moonfire and the touch of his fingers, half with the fear that Yorindesarinen's dream rebuke had raised: that hers might be the moon's dark face—like the seven queens, their black moon stained with blood. Ruthless, she thought, even while Tarathan's fingers traced a line of fire along her collarbone and throat: a dancer of Kan.

*"Darkness is one of the moon's faces,"* he said. Both hands slid beneath her hair, and when she leaned her head back against them she could see the blue moon, hanging above them like a pendant jewel. *"But it is never the only one turned to the world. And it was light that drew me here—the light that is the heart of what you are."*

"They said there must always be blood," she whispered. "At the end, just before the vortex closed. They asked if I was willing to pay that price—and if I were not, who I would condemn to pay in my stead."

Tarathan shook his head, and she snared one of his many braids between her fingers, slipping the binding free. His eyes, dark and steady, held hers. "Blood freely given," he said, and turned his forearm so she could see the red line where a dagger point had parted the skin. "I have already paid, Malian of Night. Blood has been shed; the earth's hunger has been fed. "

She could tell by the way he spoke that the last words must be part of the rite. Her fingers freed another braid, unraveling its full length as he had unbound her queue. She had loosened enough of the braids now that his chestnut hair was a fall of silk, heavy down his back. Malian smiled, thinking how it would sway as he moved, following the line of his spine—and swing around them both, shutting out the world, as their bodies came together. He was smiling, too, as she leaned forward and kissed the hollow of his throat.

"Malian of Night," he said again, in the tone that was dark as wild honey.

She lifted her head and kissed him on the lips, silencing speech as his eyes met hers and body answered body, sinking to the grass. And far off in the shadowed woods the nightingale was singing again, sweet and sad beneath the twin moons, blue and twilit green, of Imuln's blessed isle.

# 45

# First Night

*K*alan was so tired that sleep eluded him. The thick walls of the Normarch town house muted the noise of roisterers in the square outside, but every muscle in his body ached and his mind refused to be still. And dwelling on his need for sleep, only kept him wider awake. Eventually he got up and went to the window, where the full moon overhead seemed larger than usual. The silvery face was almost liquid, as though it were swimming in the sky.

"Imuln's moon." He repeated Jarna's words from their ride into the city and hoped that her first true knight's service outside their company was going well. The roisterers' latest song ended and the ring of shod hooves on cobbles sounded in the lull. A large number of hooves, Kalan decided, and coming from the direction of the palace. He crossed to a window that provided a clearer view of the town house gate, with the square beyond, and a few moments later a company of armed horsemen passed.

Ducal guards, Kalan thought, his night sight picking out the green and black in their livery. They seemed purposeful, and he listened until the hoofbeats faded eastward. Even the noisy occupants of the square seemed subdued by the guards' passage, for a few minutes went by before they began another song.

Kalan recognized the spring song of Rolan and Lyinor, and guessed the singers would grow maudlin over the last sad verses. For some reason he felt melancholy himself, listening to the refrain with its promise of parting and loss—and he was still wide-awake. He sighed and decided to check over his arms again, ahead of the morning's finals. Rather than relying on the bedside candle, he went to fetch the hallway lantern and saw a gleam of light beneath Audin's door. The town house steward had given the Duke's nephew the largest of the guest rooms, and when Kalan knocked, then peered around the door, he saw Audin sitting at a table scattered with scrolls, the lamp beside him turned up high.

"I've turned scholar," Audin told him. "Maister Carro would be proud of me." Despite his light tone he was pale beneath his outdoor tan, with dark smudges under his eyes. Kalan guessed that the injured arm was causing him considerable pain, even if Jehane Mor had been sure it was not broken—and his friend's shoulders and ribs were heavily bruised as well.

"Why?" Kalan asked, shutting the door behind him then crossing to the window seat. He bit back a groan as he sat, and Audin grinned.

"Ombrose looked in on me last night," he said, the grin fading, "to tell me I had done well against the northerner. He also mentioned the queen's visit because he thought it would amuse me, especially her expectations in terms of my uncle and this so-called Great Marriage." Audin did grin again, briefly. "Apparently Hirluin will do just as well as my uncle—if he ever gets here. Alli spoke of the Great Marriage, too, when she and Ilaise visited today, because Queen Zhineve-An asked Ghiselaine if it was still practiced here. But when Ghis asked her what it was, exactly, the queen clammed up."

Audin eased back in his chair, frowning at Kalan across the disordered tabletop. "I had nothing better to do, so I asked Ilaise to go to the temple of Serrut for me and ask for any information about Jhaine and the Great Marriage in their records. Not that the temple here is anything like the university in Ar, but still—" His voice implied a shrug. "I gave Illy my signet ring, in case the priests proved difficult, and one of them turned up late this afternoon with these." He gestured at the scrolls. "Mostly they just contain snippets, the odd reference here and there to the backwardness and oddities of Jhaine, but there's more in some of the older records."

Kalan found that he was interested, despite it being the middle of the night. "So is it a true marriage," he asked, "or just a ceremony?"

"Both, I think." Audin was thoughtful. "But what gets invoked depends on the circumstances. The most auspicious time for the ceremony, the one when it bestows the greatest benefit, is at Midsummer during a Great Year—which is why we have Queen Zhineve-An here now, I suppose."

"To what end, though?" Kalan asked.

Audin leaned forward. "That's where it gets interesting. Everything I've found alludes to the rite being one of binding. I think its oldest form bound rulers to the health of the land, because the mysteries of Imuln here in Emer derive from that, too. But the big legend out of the dark years is that the priestess-queens of Jhaine used the rite to bind the world back into calm when the Cataclysm threatened to tear it apart."

The Cataclysm that we caused, Kalan thought bitterly, when our Derai Alliance arrived on Haarth. "That would be a very powerful magic," he said slowly.

"Goddess wrought, is what the story claims. And paid for in human blood." Audin made a face. "From what I can gather, the rite almost always involves blood being shed."

"Human sacrifice?" Kalan asked, shocked.

Audin nodded. "I think that's exactly what the Cataclysm story refers to. I don't know how prevalent the blood aspect is now—although if it is still part of their rites, it might explain why the priestess-queens keep Jhaine so closed. In terms of the bindings made, there's a passage in this scroll here"—Audin picked up an age-spotted parchment—"that suggests the Great Marriage ritual can be perverted to bind one participant's will to that of the other partner."

"Enslavement?" Kalan asked, with a quick flash of loathing as he remembered his own forced confinement in the Temple of Night. The Jhainarians and their rite, he thought, still tasting that loathing, were sounding more unpleasant by the moment.

"A puppet," Audin agreed. He tapped the scroll against the tabletop, his expression grim. "I think my uncle needs to read this passage as well."

Kalan straightened, his pulse quickening. "Do you think that's why the Jhainarians are really here? Trying to create a puppet Duke of Emer?" The idea almost defied belief. Yet, he admitted to himself a moment later, I would never doubt the potential for such a plot if we were talking about the Swarm.

Audin spread his hands wide. "I know. It sounds impossible when you say the words out loud, the stuff of Oakward tales from the dark years. Not many people believe in those old magics now . . ."

But we know they are real, Kalan finished silently, at least in terms of the Oakward and our experience of the Swarm on Summer's Eve. So if real in Emer, why not also in Jhaine? He glanced out the window at the Midsummer moon. "Queen Zhineve-An seemed very keen to keep her vigil tonight," he said finally.

Audin's eyes held his with painful intensity as he set the scroll aside. "Do you think she would harm Ghis? Especially if she saw the Ormondian treaty standing in the way of whatever her ambitions may be?"

Kalan shook his head. "This vigil has been too public." Yet now that doubt had been sown, he could not quite shake it off.

"We're standing guard as well, I suppose. And I can talk with my uncle tomorrow, before he leaves for the tourney finals." Audin still sounded unhappy, though, as he knuckled his eyes. "You need to sleep," he added abruptly, frowning at Kalan. "You're going up against Ombrose tomorrow and he never gives any quarter."

"I think it might be today," Kalan replied, then paused as his keen hearing caught an almost silent step from the main hall below, then the tiny click of the front door opening. He turned, peering down from the window, and saw a cloaked figure carrying a ladyspike cross to the open gate. "Ser Raven," he said. The knight stopped within the shadow of the gate and remained motionless, looking out across the square where the revelers had stopped singing altogether after their spring song. Probably still weeping on each others' shoulders, Kalan thought wryly, given the influence of the drink.

"I suppose he's going to the temple." Audin had crossed to the window as well. "Although I thought I heard Raher leave a while back, to relieve Girvase."

Someone *had* gone out, Kalan remembered then, although he had been too busy trying to fall asleep to pay attention. "Maybe Ser Raven can't sleep either and has decided to spell Ado anyway." He surprised himself with a yawn as the knight left the gate. "You're right," he told Audin. "I should sleep before my turn on watch."

This time his eyes grew heavy as soon as he lay down and sleep claimed him swiftly, pulling him into a sea of white fog in which hoofbeats drummed, reverberating through the Emerian earth. The fog billowed, melting into long fingers of mist between the black oaks that marked the Emerian portal into the Gate of Dreams. Kalan swallowed, feeling sweat prickle along his palms, and then as quickly chill as he wondered what power could have reached through his careful barriers and brought him here against his will.

He could still hear the hoofbeats drumming out their steady, imperative tattoo, but could detect no hint of any power he recognized: not the Oakward, or the Hunt—or even Malian, despite the empathic link that had existed between them since the Old Keep. Kalan was no seeker, but he extended his psychic awareness as far through the mist as he could, pushing down fear at the same time. For throughout the years that he had been in Normarch and Malian on the River, the link between them had always endured, a faint but tangible part of his world.

Perhaps there *is* something there after all, Kalan thought—but it was almost an echo of what he was used to. As though—and here fear rose up again—Malian was somewhere much further away than the River. And this was the Gate of Dreams, with its profound uncharted deeps, that both he and Malian could enter in their physical bodies as well as through dreams.

So if she's done that, he reflected grimly, she could have gone anywhere at all, either through her own volition or because she's encountered an enemy like Nindorith again.

She's strong, Kalan tried to reassure himself. She just needs someone reliable to guard her back. *Someone like you?* the cool little voice from the tourney ground jeered. *When you have already let her know that you're only returning to the Wall because of the debt you owe Rowan Birchmoon? And now she's learned that you're shutting out dreams as well. So why would she confide in you, if she had plans that involved going deep within the Gate?*

Kalan could not think of a satisfactory answer to that question, so he settled onto his heels and waited, as the Oakward had taught him, for the Gate—or whatever power had brought him here—to reveal its purpose. The fingers of mist deepened, flowing around him so that even the nearest oaks faded into ghostly silhouette.

" . . . *trust me in this. They are vital to the influences that oppose us.*" The whisper through the blankness was so faint that even Kalan had to strain to hear it. It's like overhearing a wisp out of memory, he thought, concentrating, rather than actual mindspeech. A pause followed. "*Make no mistake, the heralds' deaths are required.*"

Kalan held very still, letting his thoughts assume the same chill whiteness as the fog surrounding him. The weight of the black pearl ring around his neck grew lighter, but he clamped his mind around it, refusing to let it glow. He was remembering something the Huntmaster had said, the first time they met in a brume very like this one: *There are too many who walk here heedlessly, sure of their own power. They never think to ask who may ghost through the mist beside them, or overhear when their words or thoughts plummet like stones into the deep places.*

After a moment another voice spoke, hissing out a single word. *"Emuun!"*

A man answered, deep and dispassionate. *" . . . this pair evaded our hunters for a long time in the north . . . driving them into Emuun's hand should have been enough. But the fist refused to close."* The deep voice strengthened, no longer memory's echo but the clear tone of someone standing just beyond the bank of mist. Kalan waited, careful to keep his breathing soft. *"Of course, with Nindorith out of the game for the moment—"*

*"Because of Ilkerineth's whelp."* Kalan heard satisfaction in the hissing voice.

*"As you say."* The man's voice was indifferent. *"But we are now free to pursue our own course and deal with Emuun at the same time."*

The voices faded, but Kalan could not see the oak trees at all now and suspected that the world of dreams had shifted around him, away from paths frequented by the Oakward. The herald pair who had evaded the Swarm hunters in the North had to be Tarathan of Ar and Jehane Mor. But who was this Emuun whose fist had failed to close around them? The speaker with the hissing voice had suggested that he had been close to the heralds for some time—and with Swarm facestealers in the game, that was entirely possible. It could be anyone, Kalan told himself, anyone at all.

*"Token-bearer."* The remote voice shivered through the mist and Kalan jumped, because no one had called him that since he left the Wall of Night. He waited, half dreading what the mist might reveal, but the whiteness remained blank.

The voice spoke again, cool across his dreaming mind: *"You need to impose your will on it."*

Kalan frowned, because that was not the Oakward way. *Then again,* his inward self pointed out, *you are not truly Oakward—are you?* Cautiously, he extended his awareness again, pressing against the white mist. At first he thought nothing was happening, then gradually the mist receded, its whiteness thinning. He saw a streetscape that he did not recognize between the strands, with a warrior in Darksworn armor sprawled on the pavement. Not Nherenor, he thought, puzzled: that's not even Caer Argent. And then he saw Orth approach, drawing a long, wickedly curved knife before he wrenched the fallen warrior's helmet off and cut his throat. Having made sure of his enemy's death, the Sword warrior proceeded to mutilate the face and sever the fallen warrior's ears, finally kicking the body before he walked away.

Serrut! thought Kalan: why do I need to see this? He prodded at the mist again and it boiled into his face, making him jerk back. When his vision cleared he found himself poised above a ruined hall, looking down at a tangled garden growing over fallen masonry and charred beams. He recognized the old Sondcendre mansion from the previous night, noting every overgrown walk and hiding place he had used to elude his Darksworn pursuers—and picking out the warriors who hunted there now. Darksworn again, he thought, seeing the lightning bolts on their helms. And Derai. He recognized Orth from his bulk and the knife he was using to cut another opponent's throat.

The moon over the broken garden was the same full, silvery orb he had seen from the Normarch town house, and Kalan guessed that one side must have pursued the other into the city tonight. Interpreting the truce as belonging to the tourney grounds, he supposed: the Darksworn leader had more or less said as much earlier. He was sure the Duke would not agree and wondered if this was where the ducal guards had been heading—but could see no sign of any others involved in the conflict. Nor could he believe that this was what he had been drawn into the Gate of Dreams to see, since the Sword warriors and the Darksworn were welcome to exterminate each other, as far as he was concerned.

Grimly, Kalan extended his awareness and his will again. A last tendril of mist wrapped itself around him, then drifted away, leaving him staring into the room beneath Imuln's dome. Jehane Mor was there, sitting cross-legged in the deep trance of one who holds a shield of concealment. But also protection, Kalan realized, a little puzzled by the shield's strength, even though Ghiselaine and Queen Zhineve-An *were* keeping their First Night vigil in the old chapel. He was not entirely sure that he could have generated and held so powerful a shield by himself—and where was Tarathan, who should have been protecting his herald partner while she was sunk in so profound a trance?

Kalan widened his vision and saw shadows slipping through the temple woodland toward the old chapel. Fear twisted in his stomach as he caught the Swarm taint and saw one of their number kneel, directing a long rod carved with runes, first at the main temple and then the courtyard where Rastem and his companions stood. Warding them out, Kalan thought. He could almost see the dark power emanating from the deeply carved rod.

He tried to reach through to Jehane Mor and Alianor first, but the mindcall fell away from him as though into a well, without any echo back. *Either the rod is blocking me even through the dream,* he thought, *or Jehane Mor's shield is too strong—or both.*

*Stay calm,* he told himself, and delved for Malian or Tarathan again, but only found the same uncanny absence. In the temple grounds, a cloaked figure halted in the bulk of the main precinct, studying the moon-bathed cupola of the old chapel. When he threw back his cloak and drew his sword, the blade gleamed beneath the moon—and Kalan saw that he was wearing parti-colored hose, one leg black as his cloak, the other royal blue.

*"Wake up, you fool!"* The remote voice cut like ice. *"You've no time to waste!"*

No time at all, Kalan agreed. He touched Girvase's sleeping thoughts with an Oakward alert and threw one last mindshout at Malian, as far as he could reach across the gulf that was the Gate of Dreams: *"Danger! Beware!"*

And then he was rolling to his feet in the Normarch town house and reaching for his sword.

# 46

## Moonset

**M**alian only *saw* the potential trap in the last searing flash before the fire of their seekers' powers, coming together as one, fused in light.

Along one path of seeing, the nightingale sang on, the scent of jasmine dizzying beneath the two luminous moons. Down the other, the moons dripped blood as serpents of power writhed from the ground and coiled around her, contracting into weighted chains that extinguished her fire to gray, cold ash. In that vision, the serpents twisted about Tarathan as well, igniting into flame that snapped whiplash strands in a second web across her chains. Malian's body arched against the searing pain, her mouth stretched into a rictus as the web scored fiery lines through flesh and soul until the core of her power was fused to his. His eyes, dark as the blindness that follows staring into the face of the sun, bored down into hers as he used the rite that had been powerful enough to save Jhaine from the Cataclysm to bind her in thrall to Haarth.

The darkness engulfed her and a potential third path opened up, fire exploding against fire as Tarathan tried to bind her and she fought back, the ritual worked far enough through that they killed each other, far down in the Gate of Dreams. And the world fell again, the binding that followed the Cataclysm torn apart by their death struggle.

Time hung suspended, poised around that single incandescent moment of *seeing,* and balanced on the knife edge of a rite that could be turned so easily to dark or light. And then Tarathan was moving in her, his eyes dark on hers as the heavy silk of his hair swung around them both. His lips found her mouth again and now Malian *was* on fire, only there was no pain—and somewhere beyond their conflagration the green world of Haarth sang to her with the voice of the nightingale.

Vision unfolded again on the other side of the fire, when they lay with their arms around each other and Malian's head close to Tarathan's heart. At first the *seeing* was simply whispers around his steady heartbeat, voices out of their shared past with the wisps of vision attached.

*"It was a long time ago,"* Jehane Mor's voice spoke gently as snow fell around them both, *"and it was not the two of you, or any of the Derai who live now, that destroyed Jaransor."*

And then Tarathan's voice: *"Be of good heart, Lira of the Derai. We will do all in our power to find your Heir and save her."* A pledge made to a dying Derai guard, again in Jaransor—and such promises were sacred in Jhaine and Emer, and on the River, just as they were amongst the Derai.

Another, clearer vision slipped through as Malian lay half sleeping, this time of a youthful warrior, his hair a twisting of chestnut braids, on his knees before a white-clad girl with his face buried in her lap. He lifted a fierce, passionate face.

*"We need to find her, this stranger, this power I have seen in my visions, and bring her to Haarth's song. But to take by force and fear what should only be given freely—that is* their *way."* He bowed his head again. *"I will not be what they are!"*

The girl bent her fair head over his, one hand light on the chestnut braids. *"You are not. And the paths of seeing are fluid, uncertain: you yourself have told me this. We must trust in Imuln to unfold another path."*

His lowered head did not stir. *"And if She does not?"*

For the briefest of instants, fear and doubt were cloud

shadow, chasing across the fair girl's face. *"The Goddess has made you the vessel for her vision. We must trust in that."* Her hands turned his face up to meet her gaze. *"As I have always trusted your true judgment and truer heart."* Her expression grew resolute. *"And if there is a price to be paid, we will pay it together."*

"You see us as we were long ago." Tarathan spoke quietly, into Malian's hair, and she realized that the link forged by the ritual still bound them and he was following her thoughts. Tentatively, she reached for his, and he did not draw away.

"I didn't know you had made that pledge to Lira." She watched the flow of events as he saw them, the ceaseless movement of the many strands that made up time and fate. She heard the whisper of his promise to Lira again and saw the strands of possibility drift apart and reform, a new channel opening for the river's flow. Jehane Mor's voice wove through it, out of their shared memories: *"Let there be no word of thanks between us, for are we not friends?"*

Malian recognized them as the last words the fair-haired herald had spoken, five years ago, before she and Kalan rode through Rowan Birchmoon's door into the Winter Country—but it was only now that she felt their weight.

"Yes." She could feel the waiting quietness within Tarathan again to her the same stillness as when they confronted the priestess-queens. "Whatever Zhehaamor—Jehane—and I may or may not have been able to do before coming to the Derai Wall, afterward it would have been a betrayal."

And that, Malian thought, listening to the rhythm of his heart, is not who you are—has *never* been who you are. She lifted her head and kissed him. "True," she whispered, the word a sigh from her mouth into his.

Yet they had called him an abomination.

"Because they finally realized it was I who was the seer and seeker, not Zhehaamor." His expression was stark, patterned by moonlight and shadow. "By the Goddess's law, they say, a man cannot be a seer at all—because the visions come from Imuln and so must be sacred to her consecrated priestesses. And above all else, a priestess-queen *must* be a seer, in order to absorb the great visions granted by the path of earth and moon. If the hierarchy had found out the truth when we were growing up—" He shrugged. "I would have been quartered alive and my remains purged in fire, while my six brothers of the Seven went to the headsman's axe. If Jehane had survived our deaths, which a queen who loses all her Seven rarely does, she would probably have been burned as well. That, or banished to an isolate's cell, far into the wilderness, to live out her life as a penitent, never again permitted speech with another human being."

Malian had raised her head and now stared into his eyes, appalled. She understood, too, what he did not say—that this could still be their fate, if either he or Jehane Mor were taken and brought back to Jhaine. Darkness draws darkness: she had heard Asantir say that in a dream, the one in which the Honor Captain slew a siren worm. Blood demands blood— and the priestess-queens had spilled a great deal of blood. The moon that rose with them had been black with it.

Yet were the Derai so different, with their great oath that forced anyone with old powers into the temple life? Malian felt a sudden helplessness: about her ability to change anything, or to convince the Lost that they should return to the Derai cause and the Wall of Night. Or even whether it was right, after all, that she should *try* to persuade them.

And yet I was promised, she thought wearily, that I would not have to be alone, as Yorindesarinen was when she fought the Chaos Worm. Tarathan's hand lifted, smoothing back her hair, and she closed her eyes momentarily, swallowing against the tightness in her throat.

*"Think it,"* he said. *"I can hear you."*

*"Even Kalan does not wish to return to the Wall. Why would he, when Emer has given him the life that he always wanted? The only problem is . . ."* She hesitated.

*"You have foreseen him there."* He was unsurprised, and she wondered if he had seen the same thing—and what else he might have foreseen with his falcon's sight.

*"But not with me."* There, she had said it at last. *"I saw him in Yorindesarinen's fire, the day we met, but I wasn't*

*with him in the vision. And even if I had been—I do not want him to be forced back against his will, serving my cause through constraint."*

Tarathan was silent, and when eventually he spoke, his mindvoice was almost gentle. *"If you do not wish it, then I doubt that will be why he returns."*

*"I wish,"* she began, and then fell silent herself. The nightingale, which had been quiet for some time, was singing again, and now the old Derai sorrow was all she heard of its song: Kerem the Dark Handed and Emeriath; Xeria's grief for Tasian; Yorindesarinen dying alone, her body hacked and riven, with the Chaos Worm's venom racking her veins.

Malian bent her head, her mouth seeking Tarathan's with something of his own fierceness. The green moon was rising higher above them, the blue moon sinking low; when the first horn of its crescent touched the horizon, then their time together would be done. But for now, his lips were still warm, answering hers, the touch of his hands sure.

The kiss lasted a long time, their bodies moving together in warmth and grace, and the lovemaking that followed was gentler than the fire and urgency of their first embrace. After, when they had dressed again, Malian helped Tarathan rebraid his hair, a task that took considerably longer than doing her own. She watched her fingers move, her mind carefully blank, as his was to her. But when it was done he took both her hands in his again and held them against his heart. She smiled at him: a little crookedly, she suspected, but a smile nonetheless.

*Take what you want.* The voice of Doria, her nurse, speaking out of memory. *And pay the price.* As I have, Malian thought, and will. But she kept her mind closed around that thought, an adept's subtle shielding. Her voice was steady, her eyes tranquil as they met his. "Will I see you again? Or do you return to the River now?"

"We still have business here, with Zhineve-An." Impossible to read his mind either, if he did not wish it, but his gaze was very dark as he touched his lips to hers. Malian's hands still lay within his and she did not want to draw them away—but she did, or he released them; she could not be sure which happened first.

Tarathan turned to study the blue moon, his profile as pure as that of Seruth on every temple frieze in the River lands. "Time to return," he said quietly, and she nodded, narrowing her eyes at the moon as though she could look through it to the temple garden and the pool.

And then she did *see,* as clearly as though she were gazing into a mirror: saw the bright light of the full moon and the tree shadows stretching black across the grass. Between the two, other shadows moved, slipping toward the old chapel of Imuln. Her mind flew to Jehane Mor, holding a protective shield over their rite—but unprotected herself.

A bank of mist boiled up, hiding the moon and the garden from Malian's sight. Kalan's voice spoke out of it, just two words cast toward her like a javelin, hurled as far through the Gate of Dreams as he could reach: *"Danger! Beware!"*

Tarathan's hand seized hers. "We must get back!" he said, and she felt the fire of his power buoying her strength, as it had when she walked the path of earth and moon. Malian glanced at the blue crescent and knew that it was not quite time, but she dared not wait. She threw her mind forward, focusing on that last vision of moon and woodland and pool, in the grounds of Imuln's temple.

"Now!" said Tarathan, his hand tightening on hers. Malian took a deep breath and opened her portal.

"Stay close," she said, and pulled them both into mist and darkness.

# 47

# The Old Chapel

*B*y the time Kalan reached the door, Girvase was already in the upper hall, dragging his mail shirt on over his head. "What's happening?" he demanded, banging on Audin's door as his arms came clear. Before Kalan told him, Audin was in the hall as well. He was fully dressed, and Kalan guessed that, like Girvase, he had lain down to sleep in his clothes.

"You need to get to your uncle," Kalan said, putting on his own armor as he spoke. "Get the guard turned out." He hesitated, then added, "Don't trust anyone else, *only* your uncle."

Audin nodded, his face twisting in pain as Girvase helped him into his jupon. "You don't trust Ombrose." His tone was flat.

"I don't." Kalan fastened the buckle on his sword belt. "I may be wrong but we can't afford to take that chance. And *make* your uncle listen, Audin, else Ghis and all the girls will be dead." He knew he did not need to tell the Duke's nephew that if anything happened to Queen Zhineve-An it could mean war with Jhaine, and possibly Ishnapur as well, given the longstanding alliance between the two. "Gir, the attackers are using some sort of ward to block awareness of what they're doing, so you need to get to the courtyard and raise the alarm there. I'll go in though the temple grounds."

"Rastem had three of his Seven on the postern entry there," Audin reminded him.

Kalan nodded. "If we can reach the chapel we may be able to hold it until the guards arrive. But we need more Oakward," he finished savagely. *Or Malian and Tarathan here where they're supposed to be,* he added silently, *not Nine knows where!*

The revelers were gone and the torches in the square doused when they reached the town house gate, but although the moon was sinking west it was still bright enough to see by. Girvase began to jog for the temple square, his boots echoing off the cobbles as Kalan and Audin turned toward the palace. "Is there another way in, besides the main gate?" Kalan asked. "Somewhere closer to the temple grounds?"

Audin nodded. "Try the stable gate. It's near to where the old mews begin, so you won't have the whole palace to tranverse. Get going," he added as Kalan hesitated. "Don't wait for me."

Kalan broke into the same jogging run as Girvase, heading toward the palace and the mews as fast as the day's stiffness would allow. The clang of his armor and weapons sounded loud to him, but no one chinked open a shutter as he passed by or called down a question. *Everyone's sound asleep,* he thought—*the ideal time for a surprise attack.* The bright moonlight made the contrasting shadows blacker, and Kalan kept one hand close to his sword hilt, but his route to the palace remained clear until he reached the stable gate. The sole sentry was slumped at the top of a short flight of stairs from the street, and at first Kalan thought he was asleep. A closer look revealed that the man's throat had been cut, and a partial boot print was smeared through the blood.

*A typical knight's boot,* thought Kalan, who did not need a torch or moonlight to make out details in the dark. He flattened himself to one side of the gate, creating a psychic shield of blended moonlight and shadow before slipping through, pressing close to the wall of the service alley on the far side. The stiffness in his muscles was easing by the time he reached the next door, which again stood open, with no sign of anyone on guard duty. The ribbon of greensward beyond was etched in black and silver, and Kalan kept to the deepest shadows as he moved along it. The night surrounding him was very quiet; even the normal chorus of insects had fallen silent.

The three Jhainarians at the postern gate were dead, shot with longbow arrows. The shafts of the arrows were painted with the same runes he had seen on the warding rod, and he wondered if the Jhainarians had even known an enemy was there. He strengthened his shield, but could detect no sign of hidden watchers. The apparent lack of rearguards bothered him, but he entered the temple grounds anyway, working his way into an overgrown corner.

Once there, Kalan stood motionless, listening. The temple's power thrummed through his boot soles, although with another note wound through it that he could not quite make out: moonlight shot through with the scent of jasmine, perhaps, while in the distance a nightingale sang.

He shook his head, the hairs on his nape rising, because there was no nightingale, although he thought there might be jasmine, spilling over the nearby wall. When he moved, he kept every step gentle, holding the tranquility of the night and trees around him as he slid from grove to thicket. Gradually, he felt the presence of other minds, pressing at the edge of his shield—and then a mindsweep washed across the night.

Not Nindorith, Kalan thought, when his heartbeat had slowed again. And not attacking me: not yet. He had stopped beneath a weeping birch and the tree's soft green trailed about him while his mind filtered new scents: the stink of rage and fear, and the metallic tang of blood. He could see the old chapel now, between gaps in the trees, and ghosted closer, crouching down beneath a gnarled elm. A few paces ahead of him, a body was sprawled on its back. It wore one of the bestial helmets favored by some Darksworn—a different lot than the lightning warriors? Kalan wondered—and had been killed by a crossbow quarrel through the eyeslit.

Good shooting, he thought, impressed. Kneeling at the

foot of the tree gave him a clear line of sight to the chapel entrance, where two great yews stood watch over a shadowed portico. Two more bodies in the bestial helms were slumped at the base of the trees, so clearly someone must be holding the door—or had been.

Jarna? Kalan wondered, or one of the damosels? He crept closer, alert for every twig or pebble that might give away an unwary step.

A warning feathered along his psychic shield an instant before he heard stealthy footfalls and the whisper of bodies through the brush. Four attackers broke cover, racing for either side of the portico, and a crossbow spat in answer. One runner gave a coughing cry and pitched forward, but his companions kept running—intending to close before the crossbow could be reloaded, Kalan guessed. He drew his sword.

The defender waited until the assailants were close enough to block the aim of any enemy archers, before stepping clear of the entrance. He was holding a ladyspike in a businesslike fashion and wearing one of the bestial helms—a contradiction Kalan was still trying to work out when the ladyspike severed one opponent's head, the return cut taking the next assailant at the knees. The fourth attacker swerved aside and rolled into the undergrowth as his comrade collapsed, screaming, and the defender retreated beneath the arch. A moment later another crossbow quarrel silenced the screams.

Where's Girvase? Kalan wondered. Surely he should have roused Rastem and the rest of the Seven by now?

The silence that followed the skirmish was intense, and he studied the surrounding grounds, stretching the edge of his shield to try and locate the seeker—who must be wielding considerable power through the warding rod, to have blocked out even the crippled warrior's screams.

A wave of red fury spat along the edge of Kalan's shield like another crossbow quarrel. He could not pinpoint the direction from which the mindsweep had come but guessed that it was intended to stun the defender. Time to act, he thought, and moved forward again, still careful not to break cover physically or release the chameleon dapple of his shield.

Darkness stirred at the edge of his eye and he whipped around, his sword blade arcing ahead of him and slicing a lurker in half as it dropped from the chapel eaves. The Swarm minion keened as the sword bit, a high thin wail abruptly cut off—and the garden around Kalan erupted as a wave of black-clad warriors surged toward the portico. There must be fifteen of them at least, maybe even twenty, he estimated, racing forward as well. Given those numbers, they must eventually overwhelm the lone defender, no matter how great his courage and skill.

The defending warrior came to meet his attackers with a sword in one hand and dagger in the other, wielding both like an extension of himself. He used the yews and the portico entrance to define the fighting space, limiting the number of enemies who could assail him at one time—but he was still going to be overrun. Kalan could see the Darksworn seeker now, a tall androgynous woman surrounded by power's aura, although its use had clearly failed against her opponent in the chapel entrance. Now she was coming at him though the Darksworn warriors instead, the steel rod she had used to ward the enclosed woodland and the chapel grasped like a weapon in her hands. More power shimmered along the hieroglyphs tempered into the metal, and one end was sharpened to a thrusting point.

And that, Kalan realized, is why the assailants are hemming their enemy in, rather than killing him outright—so their seeker can finish him with the sorcerous stake.

He shouted the Normarch battle cry, drawing some of the attackers onto himself, and sank into the seamless whole that was body and mindshield, sword and will, flowing together as one. He opened himself to the thrum of power beneath his feet and let the energy wash through him, erasing the aches and weariness of the past days and deflecting the sorcery the Swarm adept flung his way. A blur of cut and thrust followed, until the knot of attackers broke apart and Kalan saw that he was on the fringe of those surrounding the defending warrior. They had him pressed back against the wall now, and the nearest assailant had just aimed a massive blow at the bestial helmet.

If it connected, Kalan knew, it would crush both helm and skull—but the defender was already dropping and the blade glanced off the helmet's rim, pushing it askew. The warrior swept with his sword, trying to fend off antagonists and pull the helmet clear at the same time. Kalan shouted, attacking again, as the Darksworn seeker lunged for her enemy like a tiger, her teeth bared.

The defender flung the helm aside and Kalan shouted again as he recognized Ser Raven, then in denial as the seeker's eyes flamed, drawing back the rod for a death thrust. "Traitor!" she shrieked—even as Ser Raven's sword came back on line, forcing the rod aside. The sorcery that crackled from the runes flowed harmlessly to either side of his body, and the knight followed through without hesitation, driving his dagger up beneath the seeker's rib cage.

A direct thrust to the heart—she should be dead, Kalan thought, even as he downed another opponent himself. Yet impossibly, the Darksworn was still alive, staring into Ser Raven's face as confusion replaced the flame in her eyes.

"But—" Blood bubbled along her lips. "You're not . . ." Realization and shock followed in quick succession, and then an emotion that Kalan could not place before another Swarm warrior snarled into his face. The clash of sword meeting sword jarred along his arm as two more warriors came at him from the side, tying him up in a furious flurry of blows even as he became aware of another, more distant clangor of fighting.

*"She comes."* Cool fire brushed his mind as he dispatched another opponent—and almost checked his next stroke as the empathic link to Malian slid back into place. More voices shouted, this time from the direction of the postern, and now he and Ser Raven were fighting shoulder-to-shoulder with the portico behind them. They were still outnumbered, but the Darksworn warriors were falling back anyway.

That shouting must mean reinforcements, Kalan thought, even as the last of the attackers broke and ran. Ser Raven's face was stone as he watched them, the Darksworn seeker's body at his feet, but after a moment he stepped forward and began to remove another of the bestial helms from a dead warrior.

"They're good helmets," he said. "I got that first one from their rearguard by the postern."

So the Darksworn did leave a lookout, Kalan thought. "How did you know—" he began, but the knight cut him off.

"We need to find out what's happening in the courtyard." The sound of more distant fighting *was* coming from there, Kalan realized—but he had only heard it once the Darksworn seeker's spell dissipated, following her death.

"I'll go," Ser Raven told him. "Once you're sure it's friends at the postern, make sure all's well with Queen Zhineve-An and the Countess. The door was unguarded when I reached it," he added, "the attackers already coming through the grounds, but from what I could see at a quick glance, the damosels must have barricaded themselves into the cupola."

Kalan kept his sword in his hand as he watched Ser Raven disappear around the corner of the building and waited to see who would arrive from the postern. He risked a look inside the chapel, but could make out little beyond bare stone walls and a wooden altar. The silence weighed on him, and he drew back as Audin and a ragtag following appeared through the woodland, keeping to the more open areas between the trees.

No ducal guards, Kalan thought, his heart sinking, but Audin looked confident rather than harried, and a moment later he recognized Ser Alric on his friend's left. Those with them comprised a mix of knights and archers from the tourney camp, and even, he realized, blinking at the sight, Gol and a handful of the Sword warriors.

"My uncle took his personal guard and rode out," Audin told him. "No one knew where or why so I commandeered Ser Alric and his men—I'll explain later," he added quietly, seeing the glance Kalan shot toward the Derai.

Kalan nodded. "There's still fighting at the courtyard gate," he told them. "Ser Raven's gone to see what he can do, but could probably use help."

"We'll take care of it," Ser Alric said. "But I'll leave you some archers to watch this entrance and the perimeter of yon wood."

He organized the rest of the tourney camp company with a few quick words and they headed toward the courtyard. Kalan caught Audin's eye. "The northerners," he asked, low voiced. "How did that happen?" He could not add that his dream had shown him Sword warriors and Darksworn hunting each other through the old Sondcendre ruin.

"It's a little complicated," Audin replied, just as softly. "But they do seem willing to fight." He peered past Kalan's shoulder into the chapel interior. "Have you seen Ghis and the others yet?"

The silence inside the ancient walls was even more profound once they stood inside. Smoky light and ragged shadow leapt across stone as Audin lit a torch, illuminating the narrow windows and a door built into the tower wall, behind the altar. The door appeared intact, and Kalan guessed it must lead to the cupola.

Audin lifted the torch and examined the chapel again, but it was completely empty. "I suppose," he said, "we'll have to go through some form of cleansing rite, just for having been in here." His voice echoed softly off the surrounding stone.

"Not half so great a cleansing," Kalan replied grimly, "as if we let Ghis and the queen die out of respect for the sacred precinct." He could feel a draft of cool air, although the door behind the altar was closed. A heavy metal ring was set into the wood, but nothing happened when he turned it so he rapped against the timber with his sword hilt. "It's Hamar," he called, "and Audin. Is anyone in here?"

The silence resettled and he wondered if Ser Raven was wrong about the damosels barricading themselves in. A slight scratch sounded—or a scuff, he thought, someone creeping as silently as possible down stone stairs. He listened intently and felt the other's presence on the far side of the door, also tense with listening. "Alli," he guessed. "It's really us. You can come out now; the attackers have gone."

He heard a hiss of breath before Alianor called back. "What's the name of my horse?"

Kalan grinned. "Sable. Ask me something difficult, like Rolan, the name of your first puppy when you were a little girl."

"Hamar!" He heard the sound of bolts being drawn back and had to hold his sword as Alianor threw her arms around his neck.

"Where're the others?" he asked, seeing the empty stair behind her.

"Is Ghis there?" Audin spoke at the same time.

"I'm here." Ghiselaine came down the steps, sheathing her dagger as she saw them. Like Alianor, her expression was strained. "Aren't the others with you?"

"No." Kalan felt his heart begin to pound again as he turned, his gaze sweeping the empty chapel. "What happened? How did you get separated?"

"The ancient sanctuary's below us," Alianor said quickly. "In a cavern. The entrance is through the floor, at the other end of this chamber." Creating that draft I felt, he thought ,as Alianor pushed her hands wearily over her hair. "Everyone went down there except me. I stood guard up here, by the entrance to the cavern. For hours everything was quiet—and then Jarna yelled a warning and I heard Ilaise scream, 'Run!' "

"The chapel below is as big as this one," Ghiselaine put in, "so Jarna was on one side, Illy on the other near the stair. I heard a sound, but Jarna must have seen something because she was yelling a challenge, and then Iliase grabbed me and pushed me up the stairs. I thought she and Zhineve-An were just behind me as I went up."

"We ran for the door," Alianor said. She did not need to state the obvious: that her priority would have been to save Ghiselaine. She looked at Kalan, her eyes shadowed in the torchlight. "But I felt your warning, and the sense of danger from outside, so we shut ourselves into the tower instead. By that stage," she added, "we knew that only Ghiselaine had made it out of the sanctuary. And then we heard the fighting."

"Ser Raven," Kalan told them, "guarding the door." He thought about what might have happened if other attackers had come at the knight from behind. "Did no one pursue you?" he asked.

Ghiselaine glanced at Alianor. "We thought that was what the fighting was," she began slowly. "That it was Jarna and Illy holding them at bay—but Alianor wouldn't let me help them," she continued, biting off every word. "She shut me into the cupola itself until I promised to do as she said!"

If he hadn't been so worried, Kalan would have laughed. "You know she was right," he said to Ghiselaine, then looked at Audin. "We need to go down there, find out what's happened."

"I'm coming, too," Ghiselaine said with determination. "Illy and Jarna were only there because of me. And Zhineve-An is Emer's guest," she added.

Audin was shaking his head. "We'd just be putting you back in danger."

"And that can never be allowed to happen," she returned bitterly.

"Oh, Ghis," he said, and Kalan could hear the mix of fear and exasperation and love in his voice. "You know it can't. Not if we have any other choice."

"I'll go down," Kalan said to him. "Send someone after me as soon as you can, but one of us needs to get Ghis and Alli to safety as soon as possible. I'm sorry, Ghis," he added, seeing her bleak expression.

She just nodded, and he headed for the far end of the chapel without looking back. The grill made to fit over the opening still lay beside it, and the entrance in the floor gaped. Kalan strained both his eyesight and his hearing to discern what lay below, extending his psychic awareness at the same time, but everything was perfectly still. He could smell the hot wax of recently burning candles, but guessed they had been extinguished when Ilaise got Ghiselaine out.

But why didn't whoever attacked them follow? he wondered. This opening is easy enough to find.

The voice out of his dream whispered, cool as silver into his mind: *"As if I, who remained concealed from both Swarm and Derai for thousands of years, despite all their efforts to find me, could not deceive the weak-minded."* The trace of smugness in the voice deepened. *"Those who ward out others' minds should be more careful about protecting their own."*

This has to be Nhenir, Kalan thought. The moon-bright helm had never spoken to him before, but he knew Malian had been using it to help watch over Ghiselaine. *"Nhenir?"* he queried silently, and felt the ghost of an assent. *"Where's the queen? And Jarna and Illy?"*

The helm did not answer, and the muscles along Kalan's jaw clenched tight as he wove a shield cloaked in stone and dry, cold air, one that would deflect the eye away from his moving shadow. He listened again, and when he still heard nothing from below, began a cautious descent.

The cavern reminded him of the cave below the tower in Jaransor, although no ancient depiction of the Hunt of Mayanne flowed across its walls. The altar was a great slab of lichened stone, and the tall candlebras to either side had been knocked to the ground. Kalan could see the trail of congealed wax across the floor. But there must be another entrance, he thought—then whirled, his keen ears catching the almost soundless footstep behind him.

"There'll be concealed tunnels," Jehane Mor said, as though overhearing his thought. A match flared, lighting the torch in her hand. "All these ancient places have them—behind the stair most likely, as well as the altar. And probably one more."

Kalan stared at her, a number of thoughts chasing through his head: that she could not have been protecting Ghiselaine and Zhineve-An with her trance; that he had never seen her without Tarathan before; and that weariness had left its stamp on her habitual calm expression. In the end, he decided to keep them all to himself. "Not the stairs," he said, "because Ghiselaine said Illy was there and got her out. Jarna gave the alarm first and she was somewhere opposite Illy."

"So not the altar either." Jehane Mor crossed to the wall opposite the stairs and knelt down. "Here," she said. And then softly: "Kalan, I'm sorry."

This opening was in the floor as well, and an entire square of stone had been lifted out, revealing broad steps that descended to a circular room. Ilaise lay at the top of the steps, her long dagger fallen a few inches clear of her hand. Jarna was collapsed half over the foot of the stairs, half across the floor of the room below.

Kalan's first thought, seeing how much blood had soaked through her surcote, was that she couldn't possibly be alive. She had taken a sword cut through the shoulder that had severed bone as well as flesh, and another slash across the stomach—but when he dropped to his knees beside her and felt for a pulse, his fingers found the slightest of flutters. "She's alive," he whispered.

"Only just. And even moving her may kill her now." Jehane Mor was grim as she knelt opposite him. "Ilaise is alive, too," she added.

As if responding to her words, the damosel groaned, and they were both beside her in an instant. Ilaise moaned again and her eyelids lifted slowly, as though struggling to focus. Her lips moved. "Ser," she whispered. "Ser . . ."

Kalan wanted to encourage her, but held back, afraid that he would speak too roughly out of his anger and fear.

"Tell us," Jehane Mor said, in her voice that was cool as water.

Ilaise's eyes fixed on the herald as though she were a spar in a flooded river. "Ser Ombrose," she whispered. "It was . . . Ser . . . Ombrose . . . going to . . . kill Ghis."

"And Queen Zhineve-An?" the herald asked.

And Kalan realized that the Jhainarian queen was still missing.

# 48

# A Place for Troubled Times

Malian crossed from the Gate of Dreams into utter blackness, with Tarathan still at her side. At the last moment the Gate twisted, pulling them away from the sacred pool, which she was using as her focus point. She tightened her grip on Tarathan's hand, fighting to maintain their course, while a detached corner of her mind remembered every story of portal use gone awry. The Gate twisted again, like a horse trying to throw them off, but now Malian could feel the ropewalk path underfoot—and sense that it, too, was changing course, bringing them out someplace else.

Somewhere safer? she wondered, as the flow of power ebbed. Or where we are needed? Her instinct insisted that they had still emerged close to the temple woodland and the pool, but the darkness around them was so absolute that she could not be sure.

*"You must learn to eat the dark lest it eat you."* She recognized Nhenir's allusion to the long-ago dream when she had found the cave of sleepers, but the helm's voice sounded far too complacent to be a memory.

*"Or you could tell me where I am,"* she retorted, putting out her right hand and touching rock. The air here was cool, but dank. On brief reflection, she decided they must be close to the river. "We're underground," she said softly, and Tara-

than's hand tightened briefly on hers before he released it.

*"Think it,"* he told her. *"I will always hear you now, because of the rite."*

And she could hear him: the link was not only one way. She wondered if he would hear Nhenir as well, through her. *"Only if I choose to be heard,"* the helm informed her, sounding superior now, as well as complacent.

*"Ghiselaine?"* she queried back, but Nhenir's prompt assurance of the Countess's safety was so bland that she wondered what it was not passing on. Beside her, Tarathan had begun a delicate exploratory mindsearch, and she linked her own awareness to his, gradually realizing that they had come out in a network of tunnels.

*"Beneath the temple of Imuln, I think,"* Tarathan said. *"All the ancient temples have something of the kind, but Caer Argent's are extensive."*

*"Can we seek our way out? Or Jehane Mor guide us?"* She sensed rather than saw his head shake through the darkness.

*"We set aside our link for the duration of the rite,"* he replied, almost absently. *"A pity, because we're not alone down here."*

She let her seeker's sense follow his and detected someone hiding, frightened and alone, and a darker presence hunting through the tunnels. Her fear leapt instantly to Nindorith, but she quelled it, realizing that this power was subtle and focused, but not as strong. *"We shall have to be careful,"* Tarathan added, and she knew what he meant: without shielding, their seeking would be easily detected by a powerful opponent.

*"Your help would be appreciated,"* she said to Nhenir, and was almost surprised when the helm shielded them at once. Malian took a deep breath in and felt the quick shift of Tarathan's attention toward her—so she told him about Nhenir. To her surprise, he laughed softly when she explained how the helm pursued its own path. *"I suppose it is amusing,"* she conceded reluctantly.

*"I feel like I've just walked into a story I loved when I was*

*very young,"* he explained, *"the tale of the priestess-queen, Zharaan, and her First, Kiyan, in the early years after the Cataclysm. The world had stilled, but demons were slaying every priestess elected to the nine places left empty by the great rite. Zharaan was the third queen within a year in her temple, her Seven all just children like herself. But she was strong, and when the demons came, she tore open a portal and fled with Kiyan. They found themselves in a misterious cavern filled with sleeping warriors, one whom bore a sword on his breast that was possessed by a ghost. And the ghost told Kiyan how to use the weapon to defeat the demons. The sword had a will of its own, too,"* he added, when Malian remained silent, staring toward him through the darkness that concealed both their faces. *"Without the ghost it would never have answered to Kiyan's need, because it was sworn to another path."*

Malian's heart was hammering in slow painful thuds. She remembered standing in the same cave in her Winter Country dreaming five years ago, her hand stretching toward the sword on the sleeping captain's breast. Nhenir had not given any sign of recognizing the sword—and the presence had told her that it was not yet time for the Awakening. She had assumed it meant the sleepers, but even by speaking, she realized now, it had distracted her from the sword. She tried to keep her mindvoice easy. *"Does your story say why the ghost helped them?"*

*"According to the legend,"* Tarathan replied quietly, *"she said that she had done a great deal that she regretted, but had never condoned the murder of children."* He paused. *"The story has upset you."*

'She', Malian thought. *"Not the story,"* she said, keenly aware of the depth of Nhenir's silence, even though the helm continued to shield them both. With an effort, she pulled herself together. *"And we need to deal with whatever's happening down here."*

Creating a false impression, she thought, unhappy with herself—but felt his silent agreement and the flow of his power, searching the tunnels more aggressively. She let her seeker's sense remain linked to his, concealing the fact that they were two and not one. He was silent, his concentration fierce, and then she felt him pause. *"The one being hunted is Zhineve-An."*

She was unsure whether to ask how he recognized her so easily.

*"She is a queen of Jhaine,"* he said, answering her unspoken question. *"One without her Seven, which leaves her particularly vulnerable."*

Malian nodded, because walking the path of earth and moon had given her a better understanding of the bond between a queen and her Seven. *"Even on her own, she still has power."*

*"She is inexperienced—and not strong for a priestess-queen, in any case."* He hesitated, frowning. *"She may already be hurt in some way as well."*

Wounded, perhaps, and lost somewhere in the dark—as Malian herself had been once, in the Old Keep of Winds, until Kalan found her. *"I thought I told you to watch over them?"* she said to Nhenir. She thought the helm might not answer, knowing there was a reckoning coming because of the sword, but eventually it spoke, the silver voice distant.

*"You told me to watch over the countess—in part because you did not trust the queen. I did all that you asked and more: I kept the countess's enemies from her. Besides, only her life* need *be preserved to secure the information you require about the Lost."*

Can I blame the helm, Malian asked herself, for being what it is? She pushed aside her exasperation and concentrated on tracking down the hunter. Swarm, she thought, as the dark familiar taint assailed her senses. The quality of the hunter's power, coiled behind it, was seamless: she could almost see the sorcery's midnight sheen through her seeking. She could detect more of the sheen emotions as well, the pleasure taken from both the slow hunt and the prey's rising fear.

*"Cat and mouse,"* Tarathan agreed. *"He believes he has her beneath his paw. But she is still trying to seek out a path*

*to safety. It's bringing her to us,"* he added, steel whispering as he drew the swallowtail swords.

We need to move toward her, Malian thought, and intercept the hunter—except I'm blind in this blackness. *"I know,"* she said tartly, before Nhenir could make the observation again. *"I need to eat the dark."*

*"Or,"* Tarathan said mildly, *"you could draw on a little of the light that burns in you, the way you did in the Old Keep."*

Malian remained quite still, because she had been concealing the light that was part of her inheritance for so long, both in her first flight from the Swarm—which had used it to track her—and then to preserve the secret of her identity within the Shadow Band. Slowly, she lifted her arm, letting the sleeve fall back from Yorindesarinen's armring as she summoned light into her mind. She visualized a candle burning with a clear, steady flame, then mentally touched it to the surface of the armring. The fire bound into the metal danced into silver life, which Malian instantly muted to a glimmer. Just enough, she thought, to light a way for their feet while their minds were seeking ahead—and to reveal the shadow mask of Tarathan's face.

*"She's very close now,"* he said, and Malian nodded as they moved forward, each pressed close to either side of the tunnel. She, too, could sense the young queen, still doggedly deflecting her pursuer's tracking sorcery—and tell that she was flagging. The hunter would sense it, too, she knew, and the gap between pursuer and prey was closing. *"You get her away,"* Tarathan said. *"I'll stand as rearguard."*

For a priestess-queen of Jhaine who believes you to be an abomination, Malian thought, but she did not argue. The shimmer from the armring showed the tunnel ahead of them widening. A few footsteps more and they were in what looked like a small underground courtyard, with several passages opening off it. A mosaic of malachite and black marble paved the ground, while the columns holding up the vaulted roof were carved into robed and cowled priestesses, their hands raised in various forms of salutation or invocation. *"A place for troubled times,"* Tarathan observed, *"most likely where the high priestesses met the dukes."*

Malian did not need Kalan's acute hearing to pick up the gasp of approaching breath. She let her sleeve fall over the armring so only a faint gray relieved the gloom as she and Tarathan moved into the deeper shadows of the cowled pillars. The hunter's step had quickened but was still a short distance off. We just might, she thought, be able to get Zhineve-An clear.

The young queen appeared in the doorway, staggering as though it were an effort for her to stay on her feet. Her full robe was kilted to her knees for freer movement, but she kept her hand on the wall. Nearly done, Malian thought, and stepped forward with Tarathan behind her. As she moved, she let a little more of the silver light gleam from beneath her cuff. "Queen Zhineve-An—" she began, her tone reassuring.

Zhineve-An screamed, her face a white mask of terror. She whirled to run, but stumbled, half falling before she clutched at the wall. "The slayer," she panted, shaking her head from side to side as she pushed herself upright again. "No, no, no."

Tarathan rammed his swords back into their sheaths and sprang across the room, closing one hand across her mouth while his other arm clamped both hers tight to her body. Zhineve-An struggled wildly to be free, her eyes desperate, despairing, as Tarathan, impervious to the last ebb of power that she was hurling at him, hauled her bodily back across the chamber.

She's petrified of us, Malian thought. And then, fitting pieces from her visions and their conversation afterward together—no, of Tarathan. The other queens had called him the slayer, too: not just for killing a Seven, but because the queen they were bound to had also died. And the priestess-queens of Jhaine were conjoined, so Zhineve-An would recognize his face and the signature of his power through that link.

She shook her head, at a loss how best to calm the young queen and convince her she was safe after all.

*"She won't hear you."* Tarathan's expression was grim. *"Some of her Seven have died tonight. This close, I can feel*

*their loss through her; each death is a wound to her psychic
body. In the absence of her own Seven, I need to help her
close them off—if she will let me. But you will have to deal
with the Swarm hunter."*

"*Gladly,*" Malian said, and turned to meet Zhineve-An's
pursuer, the twist of her mouth half a smile, because this was
straightforward, something she knew how to fight.

"What have we here?" Arcolin stepped from the same
tunnel where Zhineve-An had appeared a few moments
before. "The little River maister. We did wonder about you,
after that business with the cup. And now here you are again."

The Darksworn had abandoned his formal robes for a
sleeveless black tunic and close-fitting hose, his long hair
woven into a braid that altered the angles of his face. *He
looks more like Rhike now,* Malian thought, rather than
Nherenor—or would, if his face weren't painted in runes.
The same intricate shapes swirled blackly down Arcolin's
arms and onto the backs of his hands. The brushstrokes
flickered with power, and when he moved she saw the same
magics dance across his palms. *Armored in sorcery,* she
thought, and let her lip curl, just a little.

He smiled in answer. "So what are you, then? *Not* a River
maister, I think. And not Nindorith's Derai spy either."

*So the rite has worked,* Malian thought. Clearly, Arcolin
had not recognized the armring as a Derai artifact either—
because of the rite, she wondered, or Nhenir's shielding
influence?

"I gather," she said, matching his tone, "that your deep
affection for Emer and Jhaine has just run out?"

The Darksworn laughed. "Were you there? I was willing
enough to go along with the alliance scheme while Nherenor
and his allies were in the mix, but with the boy dead—" He
shrugged. "War within and without will suit our purpose just
as well." His smile deepened. "A dead queen of Jhaine will
help immeasurably in achieving that. I take it," he added conversationally, "that you have no intention of standing aside?"

*He likes talking,* Malian thought, so she simply smiled
back, keeping her muscles and breathing relaxed, alert for

every subtle shift in his stance or across the scrawl of power on his skin.

"No," Arcolin said softly. "I didn't think so." He traced a sigil on the air and a knife materialized in his right hand. A blade made for throwing as well as cutting—and Malian's stomach tightened as she *saw* more black runes writhe along the tempered steel. The marks vanished in the instant she perceived them, but she was remembering both the poison cup and the night she had spied on Nherenor entering the Darksworn town house. Arcolin had come to the terrace door with a calligraphy brush in his hand—and Nherenor had turned away from him with an expression of distaste.

So is it lurker poison, Malian wondered, as Arcolin adopted a blade fighter's crouch, or something worse on the blade? The first of her own hideout knives flashed to intercept his strike—and she saw his disbelief surface when she blocked him. He was strong, but so was she, and she smiled again as she called shadows, the Band stock-in-trade, to smother the first flick of his sorcery.

"Who are you? What?" His lips smiled, too, as he came at her, but the words were at least half a snarl. They reminded her of the Malisande facestealer in the hill fort, and that Arcolin might well be linked to other Swarm—and she would not betray the Shadow Band through a careless word, anymore than she would own to being Derai.

The Darksworn shrugged, feinting, when she did not reply. Malian countered the slash that followed, leaping back as the tip twisted to catch her sleeve and tear the flesh beneath. Arcolin's expression darkened, his smile vanishing as voices shouted in the distance. She caught the flare in his eyes a second ahead of the sudden withdrawal and flick of the wrist that sent the knife hurtling past her toward Zhineve-An.

"It's poisoned!" she shouted, but dared not look away from Arcolin to see whether Tarathan had pulled the young queen clear. She followed the shout with her own strike as metal clattered against stone behind her, but Arcolin had already sprung back and pulled another weapon from the air. The sword's blade was incised with the same runes that had glistened on the knife, and the point described a gentle arc, keeping her at bay. She heard another shout as boots pounded in one of the tunnels.

A sorcerous penumbra rose from the runes painted onto Arcolin's skin, and Malian reached for the core of her own power as his eyes turned completely black. "Beware!" she shouted, releasing the last of her gathered shadows into his face. Just for an instant, she thought something moved in the tunnel behind him, the swirl of a cloak and a glint of color— but the sorcery around Arcolin was intensifying. She hurled herself back, anticipating a battery of power.

The assault never came. The concentration of sorcery was still present, but instead of exploding out, it began to spiral inward around the Darksworn. Malian frowned as the spiral revolved faster and Arcolin's eyes met hers, pits in which a reflected sorcery spun, and this time his smile promised revenge. She whispered to the dagger in her hand and threw—in the same instant as the spiral of power imploded, the figure within it vanished, and the resulting shock wave threw her off her feet.

# 49

# Healing

*B*y the time Malian got to her feet the underground courtyard was pandemonium. Rastem and the remaining four
members of Zhineve-An's Seven had dragged her away from
Tarathan and appeared to be doing their best to come at the
herald with swords, while Raven and Ser Alric were keeping them at bay with the blunt end of a pair of ladyspikes.
Girvase and Raher hovered as she dusted herself off, and
ducal guards, all carrying torches, were moving into the
other tunnels in a purposeful way. A blue-robed priestess,
whom Malian assumed had been the newcomers' guide to
this point, stood by a knight in ducal green and black. His
expression, as he surveyed the scene with the Jhainarians,
was an almost equal mix of grimness, exhaustion, and be-
musement. "Will someone tell me," he demanded, "what in
Imuln's name is going on?"

Her dagger had vanished with the portal, Malian noticed—
but she was more interested in the way everyone stopped
at the unmistakable ring of command in the new knight's
voice, even the Jhainarians. All four of the remaining seven
were white-faced and looked almost wild, while Zhineve-An
was leaning against the wall with her arms hugged around
her chest and her eyes closed. Without the regalia of priestess and queen, and with her hair straggling down her back,

she seemed absurdly young. And she had, Malian thought grimly, lost three of her Seven and been hunted through the dark by a Darksworn sorcerer, only to come face-to-face with one she knew only as the slayer of queens.

"I'm going over there," she said to Girvase and Raher, and they nodded, but she noted that they kept well back themselves. Where is Kalan, Malian wondered, and Jehane Mor? Her eyes met Tarathan's and she felt the brief touch of his mind, acknowledging her, although outwardly he remained impassive. Rastem was speaking rapidly, partly in Emerian but more often lapsing into Jhainarian, his fist clenched white around the hilt of his sword. She caught the words "Forsaken" and "Abjured" and something about a sacred rite.

"A rite's been profaned?" The newcomer looked at the priestess. "Does he mean the First Night vigil?" The woman shook her head, indicating incomprehension, and he looked around, as if for help. "I take it this *is* Queen Zhineve-An?" he said to Ser Alric, low voiced. He took off his helmet and tucked it under his arm, his brow furrowed. "It would help if someone else here spoke Jhainarian."

The young queen straightened, smoothing her hands over her hair and shaking out her kilted robe, and the remaining Seven grew calmer immediately, even before she spoke. "I *am* Queen Zhineve-An," she said, lifting her golden head as she turned to face the newcomer. "Who are you?"

He bowed, with a grace, Malian thought, that matched Audin at his courtier's best. "I am Hirluin Sondargent," he said, "the heir to Emer. My father, Duke Caril, sent me to find you and ensure your safety."

"And hunt down the traitor," Raher muttered behind Malian. He and Girvase had moved closer, and she did not think anyone else heard the comment.

Zhineve-An was still very pale, but she bowed in reply to Lord Hirluin's courtesy. "What happened?" he asked her. He glanced from Rastem and his companions, strung taut as bowstrings, to Tarathan's impassive face, then around at Malian. "We had barely finished clearing the courtyard when the priestesses told us that the tunnels had been broken into from the temple precinct. They were showing us the entrance that had been used when we heard someone scream. Your First says that was you?"

The young queen eased her hands over her robe, and Malian wondered what she was going to say. "I screamed because I saw something that frightened me," she said slowly, as though searching for the correct Emerian words. "But I was already afraid, and what I saw . . . was not what I first thought." Rastem opened his mouth as though to speak, but stopped when her eyes held his. "Armed men had entered the chapel from these tunnels, and brought a demon out of the dark years with them. I fled and the demon pursued me. Maister Carick and the . . . herald . . . came to my aid."

"I see." Lord Hirluin looked toward the spot where Arcolin had disappeared, his expression thoughtful. Even if he had not actually seen the envoy vanish, Malian thought, he and the others would certainly have felt the shock wave when the portal imploded. She braced herself for his next, logical demand—to know what she and Tarathan had been doing in the tunnels in the first place—but the Duke's son looked back at Zhineve-An. "Did you recognize any of those who attacked you?"

Zhineve-An hesitated, and her remaining Seven, who had still been watching Tarathan like cats at a mousehole, tensed at once. Eventually the young queen nodded. "The demon," she said, "wore the face of Lord Arcolin, the Many-As-One's envoy to Emer. Ser Ombrose, your father's champion, was with him, together with men wearing his wolf's head badge."

There's more to this, Malian thought, watching Zhineve-An: something she's not saying. Lord Hirluin simply nodded—because he already knew about Ser Ombrose, Malian guessed, or suspected, at least. "I may have seen him," she put in quietly. "In the tunnel over there, just before you arrived. The figure I glimpsed was hooded, but wearing parti-colored hose. One leg was black, the other royal blue."

"But he's the Duke's *champion*." Disillusion and disbelief roughened Girvase's voice.

Lord Hirluin nodded again, but Malian caught the flash of

grief before his expression settled back into weary grimness. "Ombrose has always been as much a Sondcendre as a Sondargent, and I knew that he had embraced their old enmity toward Ormond. I just didn't realize the hatred ran so deep."

The champion had also resented the Duke's intention to set aside the Sondargent name and adopt Sondemer instead, Malian thought, remembering the conversation in the Duke's study.

The Duke's son glanced at Zhineve-An again. "It seems he was more ambitious than we realized as well." The Jhainarian queen, her eyes cast down, did not see his look, but both Rastem and Zorem intercepted it and shifted closer to her. Malian glanced toward Tarathan and caught Raven's eye instead. His expression was so noncommittal that she felt sure he was considering every question Lord Hirluin had not yet asked about why she and Tarathan were here—and how they had known Zhineve-An needed help.

So why hasn't Lord Hirluin asked those questions? she wondered. And how is it that he's only arrived here tonight, despite being expected days ago?

"We should leave this for now," Lord Hirluin said. "I am sure my father will want to talk with you more later, Queen Zhineve-An and"—here his gaze considered them all—"we shall have questions for everyone involved tonight. But right now we need to see both you and Countess Ghiselaine safe, while the guards continue to search for my cousin and his men."

"They attacked us in the courtyard, too," Raher told Malian, as the Jhainarians maneuvered to make sure they were between Tarathan and their queen. He and Girvase waited while she stooped to pick up Arcolin's knife, but it was Raven who gave her his cloak to wrap the poisoned blade.

*"I'll retrieve you later,"* Malian told Nhenir.

"Not Ser Ombrose himself," Raher continued, as they hurried to catch up with the others, "but Emerians wearing his badge, together with some of the Lathayrans from the tourney camp. I still can't credit that," he added, shaking his head, "not after all Ser Ombrose did to them in the border war."

"Some of them," Girvase said dryly. "Lathayra's so divided that the enemies of those he put to fire and sword probably embraced him as their dearest friend."

"True enough," Raher agreed. "And I thought we might have been done for, except first you appeared, and then Duke Caril arrived with Lord Hirluin and the guard. Apparently the Duke received word tonight that Lord Hirluin had almost reached Caer Argent, but had been forced to travel in secret, so he rode out to meet him."

What word? Malian wondered. She recalled Ser Ombrose telling the Duke that he had sent his own men east—but perhaps that was why Lord Hirluin had been traveling in secret.

"Lord Falk was with them, too," Girvase told her.

"Lord Falk?" Malian almost stopped, she was so surprised. "I thought he was in the north?"

"We all did," Girvase replied. "But he must have decided that the attack on Ghiselaine could mean a threat to Lord Hirluin as well, so while we were on the road south, he went east."

And relied on us, Malian thought, to keep Ghiselaine safe—which suggests a high level of confidence in Kalan, Girvase, and Alianor, or a man who believes in taking risks. He had already known that the Swarm agents in the north must have had access to someone close to the inner circles of Emerian power, who had set them on to Normarch and the Oakward there. So by sending Ghiselaine to Caer Argent as though he believed it safe—and the Oakward's business all in the north still—he had lulled his enemies. And to a certain extent, used us all as bait to draw them out: clever fox, Malian thought reluctantly, as she had once before. *"Although,"* she added grimly, *"I'm growing tired of being bait."*

*"I think Lord Falk had confidence in your ability to bring down your enemies."* Tarathan mindspoke her for the first time since she had turned to face Arcolin. *"As well as in the younger Oakward he sent south."*

All the same, Malian reflected, he took an extraordinary risk. But then, maybe he felt he had to, rather than letting Ghiselaine's enemies continue to work from hiding. She

grimaced, because the risk had turned on a knife's blade—
but also because in flushing Ser Ombrose out, part of the
Swarm's objective of war within and without might have
been achieved. "So Ghiselaine's really all right, too?" she
asked abruptly.

"Yes," Girvase replied. "She, Audin, and Alli had just
joined the Duke when we came down here. From what they
said, we all owe a lot to Ser Raven, as well as Hamar for
rousing us all out." He told her as much of the story as he
knew, and Ser Alric added a little more, relating how Audin
had commandeered him in the palace courtyard.

"I've been wondering about that," Raven said. "Why you
rode in at all, let alone bringing the northerners with you?"

Ser Alric rubbed at his chin. "That's simple enough. Some
of the northerners were seen leaving the camp and heading
toward the city—bent on truce breaking we all thought. So I
decided enough was enough and went to hold the rest of them
to their oaths. They weren't happy, but eventually agreed to
take responsibility for their comrades. We were going to
the Duke first to let him know there might be trouble in the
city—and then Lord Audin, and the trouble, found us."

The Derai with him should have been happy anyway,
Malian thought, since it seems they found plenty of legitimate fighting to do. "So where is Hamar?" she asked. *"And
Jehane Mor,"* she queried Tarathan. *"Has your link reestab-
lished yet?"*

"Apparently the lad stayed at the chapel," Ser Alric said,
"to find the queen and the rest of the Countess's party. The
priestess is leading us that way now, so we can join up with
them."

*"Jehane Mor is with him,"* Tarathan told her. *"Malian,
it's not good news."*

*"Kalan?"* she asked, with a quick, sickening jerk of her
heart—and then they were filing into a small open area
and she saw that it was Jarna. And Ilaise, she added, an instant later, except that the yellow-haired damosel had been
wrapped in a gray cloak and appeared to be alive. Kalan and
Jehane Mor were kneeling on either side of Jarna, who was

soaked in blood, but they both looked up as the newcomers arrived.

"She's alive," Kalan told them harshly, "but she needs healing."

Lord Hirluin spoke quietly to the priestess, who nodded and went swiftly past them and up the stairs. At a jerk of the head from the Duke's heir, Lord Alric followed—for protection, Malian supposed, with the corner of her mind that was not focused on Kalan's face as he turned to Lord Hirluin. "We can't wait for the priestesses, ser. She's almost dead now."

Tarathan stepped forward, and Rastem made a half move as if to check him. The look the herald gave him was level, but the Jhainarian eased back and Tarathan settled onto his heels beside Kalan. He did not need to speak: the careful lack of expression on his face had already told Malian that Jarna's wounds must be very bad.

"Healing is in *her* gift," Zhineve-An said, almost as though the words were twisted out of her. Her eyes jerked from Jehane Mor to Tarathan. "And *he* gave me his strength." She shook her head as Rastem said something sharp and harsh in Jhainarian. "When I was almost done, to stanch the psychic wounds made by Arad and Zarn and Syrus's passing. But healing is *her* gift," she repeated. She took a step forward, her gaze falling to Jarna. "If it can be done at all."

Kalan's eyes were fixed on the heralds as well. "You healed Alli in the hill fort."

"This is much worse," Jehane Mor said, her voice full of regret. "And she has lost so much blood." She did not add that she and Tarathan had already expended a great deal of energy that night, but Malian knew it must affect what they could do now. And if she and Girvase helped as they had at the hill fort—or Kalan—it would mean revealing the Oakward to Ser Alric and the guards present. She did not think, though, that Kalan would care.

"Unless—" Jehane Mor raised her calm, gray-green gaze to meet Zhineve-An's. "It can be in your gift also," she said quietly, "if you were to join your ability and that of your remaining Seven to ours. We are beneath a sanctuary of Imuln and together may be able to draw on its well of power to mend what is broken here."

*To mend what is broken* . . . The words rang through Malian's seer's sense like the afternote of a bell, and she wondered how much of this Tarathan had foreseen. Zorem had clapped a hand to his sword at Jehane Mor's words, while another of the Seven snarled. Only Rastem remained still, and now he put an arm out, checking the others. His eyes had not left Tarathan since Zhineve-An said that he had given her his strength.

The young queen was staring at Jehane Mor, her hands clenched so tight the knuckles were white. "You are the Forsworn," she whispered, "your name ritually cursed in all Nine temples. And I know you have suborned the sacred rite, *felt* it, although I could do nothing—how can I join my power to yours?"

"Not suborned," Jehane Mor said gently. "Performed in its true form. And I do not ask for myself, but to save this young woman's life, which hangs in the balance."

"Just do it!" Kalan grated out "There's no *time,* Nine take you!"

Malian did not miss Raven's swift, blue-black stare, or Tarathan's hand, pressing into Kalan's shoulder. No one else seemed to have noticed the Derai oath; they were all watching Zhineve-An as her eyes remained locked on Jehane Mor.

"Please." Kalan whispered this time, and Malian felt the word swirl like autumn leaves: *please, please, please.*

Zhineve-An's eyes shifted to his, and Malian saw the war there, between loyalty to her fellow queens and the better instinct that wanted to save Jarna's life. Kalan reached out and closed his hand over the young queen's balled fist. "Please," he said again. "I beg you." And his eyes would not let hers go.

The fist beneath his hand stirred convulsively, and Malian could see the pulse in Zhineve-An's wrist, rapid as a frightened bird's. Then the priestess-queen gave a little nod and knelt beside Jarna as Kalan withdrew his hand. She pushed back her sleeves, her glance sliding quickly from Tarathan to Jehane Mor. "What must I do?" she asked.

# 50

# Duty and Honor

Jarna would live—although even with the power of the temple to draw on, Jehane Mor was gray with fatigue when she finally lifted her hands from the young knight's body. Zhineve-An and her remnant Seven simply seemed dazed, partly because of the sustained call on their strength, already depleted by the death of their companions, but also, Malian gathered, by the nature of the working. "I didn't know it could be like that," Rastem said finally, speaking to Tarathan but not quite meeting his eye.

"Well, now you do," Tarathan replied. The young First *did* meet his eyes then, before as quickly glancing away—ashamed, Malian thought, and looking as though he had a great deal to think about.

The slash across Jarna's stomach turned out to be shallow, and the healers who returned with the priestess said they would stitch it closed and set the broken collarbone as well, once back in the temple infirmary. But it was the initial healing, Malian knew, that had held Jarna's spirit to her body long enough for any subsequent treatment to occur. "The rest," Jehane Mor said softly, "we must leave to the body, and Jarna's will to live."

Malian thought she glanced at Kalan then, but it was so slight a look that she could not be sure. In any case, it was no secret that Kalan and Jarna were close friends, regardless of whether any of the Normarch company guessed at a deeper relationship. "We should find Ado at the infirmary, too." Girvase said, as the Normarchers helped lift the stretchers the healers had brought. "He turned his ankle and took a gash across the forearm during the courtyard fight. But he'll be all right," he added, as Kalan looked around quickly from his place beside Jarna.

Malian thought Zhineve-An hesitated momentarily, as though she wanted to go to the infirmary as well, but in the end she drew the remnant of her Seven around her like a cloak and departed with Lord Hirluin. The heralds left the infirmary soon after the healers had finished their work on Jarna, and Malian found time to slip aside and retrieve Nhenir from the old chapel while the rest of the Normarch company lingered, waiting for Ado. Guards were still coming and going from the tunnel network, but it seemed clear that Ser Ombrose and those of his men left alive had gotten away.

"We should get back," Girvase said, when Malian returned. "Find out what's happening."

No one seemed surprised when Kalan chose to remain in the infirmary with Jarna, because a close comrade would do that in Emer, as on the Wall of Night, so long as need allowed. Ado joined them, limping a little, as they farewelled Ilaise. She was still groggy from the blow to her head. "And needs *quiet*," a priestess told them firmly, adding that they could come back that evening so long as the damosel rested all day.

The search for Ser Ombrose was fanning out through the city, and Lord Falk had already taken men to the Swarm town house, but found it abandoned. The Duke had also sent messengers to the tourney camp, announcing that the finals had been postponed, for that day at least. "How can they continue at all," Girvase demanded bitterly, "with the champion's honor in the dust?"

"The Duke may need the men there in the field," Raven observed, "in order to bring Ser Ombrose to bay—depending on how many others he's drawn to his cause."

Many of the knights might need to sober up drastically first, Malian thought, judging by what Alianor had told her last night. The early arrivals looked sober enough, but they had not come from the camp. She recognized the Lords Bonamark and Tenneward arrving at the same time as a stooped, melancholy knight with shrewd eyes. "Lord Griffonmark's captain," Girvase said, when Malian asked. "He came with Lord Hirluin."

Lord Falk spoke with them briefly on his way to join the Duke's council of war, his expression bland as he glanced Malian's way. Fox, she thought again, not quite sure whether she meant it as an epithet or a compliment, although she had to admit that he looked like a man who had been driving himself hard. He gave them a quick account of his journey from the Eastern March with Lord Hirluin, an expedition beset by every kind of obstacle: flooded fords, trees fallen across roads, a hailstorm in Griffonmark with stones large enough to lacerate flesh. And finally, an armed force lying in wait at the last posting station in Azur forest, before the road ran clear to Caer Argent.

"Ser Ombrose's men?" Malian asked.

"It seems likely. We went the long way around them, rather than finding out." Lord Falk shrugged. "We've already sent word to Lady Azurward. She's loyal and will dispatch troops to round them up." He glanced toward the meeting chamber as Ser Alric and the Allerion knights came in. "I'll need Ser Raven with me, but the rest of you should get some rest. We will want to talk with you, although probably not before this afternoon."

So we will be called, Malian thought, as they got to their feet. She had looked around for the heralds several times—and been annoyed, each time, to have Raven catch her doing it. Tarathan and I said good-bye on the island, she reminded herself, but still felt as gray as the dawn that had greeted them when they left the old chapel for the infirmary.

They found Ghiselaine and Alianor back in the Gallery wing, which was bristling with ducal guards. Both young women were in a somber mood, as was Audin when he returned from the infirmary where he had spoken briefly with Kalan and looked in on a sleeping Ilaise. Malian was sure that most of their downcast looks were for the night's events—but part might be because Lord Hirluin had come to formally greet Ghiselaine before he joined his father.

"They spoke for a few minutes," Alianor told her, pretending to study the jostle of men and horses in the main courtyard below the window. "Just the expected courtesies, but it wasn't *too* stilted." She hesitated. "At least Lord Hirluin chose to come here first, before going to the council of war. He seemed kind," she added softly, "like Audin. And I think he wants to please her."

They might do well enough together, then, despite everything, Malian reflected: the heir of Emer and the heiress of Ormond. It would have been hard for Audin, though, if he had to stand by and smile. And for Ghiselaine, loving one cousin, but bound by politics, honor, and duty to marry the other—even if he was kind. Springtime love, she told herself, and sighed.

Ghiselaine caught the sound and turned. "You look exhausted, Maister Carick." Her gaze took in the remaining Normarch company. "We should all get some rest now, since there may not be time once we learn more of what's happening: whether the tourney will go ahead tomorrow, after all, or whether it's war again."

"Come with us to the Normarch town house," Audin said, and Malian was tempted just for the company, but the part of her that was Malian of Night, rather than Carro the scholar, or Carick the adept, needed to be alone. So she returned to her small rooms under the tower, setting Nhenir and the cloak-wrapped blade on the table while she sat on the bed, her elbows on her knees as she studied the helm. She focused her will to look through the layers of concealment to the moon-bright helm that lay at their heart. The dawn eyes on the visor gazed blindly back at her, opaque with secrets.

*"So it was the frost-fire sword all along,"* Malian said.

*"You deceived me through omission. Did you prevent the armring catching fire as well?"*

Nhenir said nothing, its silence as veiled as the eyes on its visor. *"The crow in Jaransor warned me to be wary of you."* Malian kept her mindtone dispassionate. *"So I should not be surprised to find you playing so deep a game. I am not inclined, though, to let the situation continue."* Still the helm remained silent, and she let the layered power within her uncoil. *"I could make you speak."*

Her truth sense shivered—telling her she could indeed break Nhenir and then remake it, as Yorindesarinen had done. Yet in the hero's case Nhenir had been broken in battle, she had not destroyed it herself.

*Is this the person you want to be? Or the leadership the Derai needs?* Yorindesarinen's questions, out of her dream.

No on both counts, Malian thought grimly. *"Consider yourself fortunate,"* she told Nhenir. *"But once we have found the Lost, then we will deal with this matter of the sword, you and I—and be warned, I will not accept either silence or deceit when that time comes."*

The helm did not reply, but there was a quality to its reserve that made her brows lift. Thoughtfully, she worked events back against the silence until eventually she nodded. *"You are suggesting that the heralds have done much the same by using my need to escape Nindorith to persuade me into their Great Marriage and so make me part of their world."* She made herself consider this. *"They are definitely playing the great game, with the fate of this world at stake. But they did not entrap me, they offered me a choice."* She smiled wryly. *"One I would likely have taken anyway, even without Nindorith to thwart."*

Nhenir did speak then, its voice moonlight on ice. *"This Tarathan is not for you."*

*"I know that."* And she did, having walked the path of earth and moon and absorbed its visions, including the nature of the rite. She understood that the Great Marriage was not intended to bind those who assumed the roles of priestess and king forever. It's not even as though I've never

had what the Emerians would call springtime loves before, she thought, or lain with a lover. Of course she had, since the Band taught that inexperience of love and the flesh made an adept as vulnerable as ignorance of death, or any other of the arts of Kan.

Yet understanding of the rite and adept's training or not, Malian was still intensely aware of the memory of Tarathan's skin, smooth beneath her hands, of his body beneath and above hers, and the fire of his mouth on her lips, his hands moving across her body. Similarly, seeing him working together with Jehane Mor as they healed Jarna, she had felt something quick and difficult turning in the region of her heart. It did not matter that she knew that Tarathan and Jehane Mor had always been together: sometime lovers perhaps, but always friends and comrades-in-arms, bound close by their bond as queen and First, as well as their herald's oath—and most of all by the purpose they had shared since they were younger than Rastem and Zhineve-An.

*He is not for you,* the helm had said, and it was right. She and Tarathan each had their own destinies to tread, driven by their foreseeing—and in the end she was Derai and he was not. It had not mattered on Imuln's Isle, and might not on the River, but it would on the Derai Wall, as her father had found to his cost.

Malian let her breath huff out as she lay down, falling almost instantly asleep. When she woke the shadows had moved past noon—and her mind was full, not of the sword or of Tarathan, as she would have expected, but of Zhineve-An. She was remembering the queen's constraint when she spoke of Ser Ombrose with Lord Hirluin—and also the way the champion had looked at the young golden girl who was also a queen, the first time they met by the Argenthithe bridge. Had he made overtures to her, Malian wondered, once he knew she saw completion of the Great Marriage as part of her embassy to Jhaine? And had she, far from certain of the Duke, encouraged those overtures? He was the champion, after all, and a Sondargent, both qualities that made him eligible for the rite.

But why, Great Year or not, did the ceremony need to be performed in Emer at all, when a Great Marriage could take place equally well in Jhaine? Malian sat up, frowning as she went over her visions from the path of earth and moon again, and everything, both obvious and subtle, that they had told her about Jhaine.

Nine men had died willingly during the great rite that was performed to bind the Cataclysm—and the nine high priestesses had died, too, draining their power and their lives with it, down to the lees. Yet in the generations that followed, as Jhaine closed in on itself, blood sacrifice had been twisted, through fear and the desire for control, into custom rather than a last desperate resort driven by great need. The victims were chosen by lot or taken by force—and families competed to give their sons to the Ishnapuri tribute.

I spoke truth during the rite, Malian thought. The serpent that is the priestess-queens' power is strangling Jhaine in its coils. Through perversion, the rite is losing its potency and Imuln has turned her face away. The queens know they must reach beyond Jhaine—for fresh blood, she concluded, disgusted. That's why they sent Zhineve-An, because they thought the Duke would be unable to resist her youth and beauty.

Malian shook her head, knowing it would never have worked even if the Duke had been dazzled and Zhineve-An had performed the perverted ritual. The Sondargents were not absolute rulers, and the lords and people of Emer would never accept a worship of Imuln turned to blood sacrifice. As for Zhineve-An, she might be young but she was by no means stupid. She had already been working out that the world beyond Jhaine was not as the priestess-queens thought.

Perhaps not quickly enough, though, Malian reflected. Had Zhineve-An allowed herself to be swayed by Ser Ombrose's ambitions and considered allying Jhaine to his cause? She felt sure the young queen had not plotted Ghiselaine's death—but did wonder whether the suggestion that the Countess of Ormond accompany her vigil might not have come first from Ser Ombrose. "Although how he thought she would react to seeing Ghiselaine murdered in front of her, I don't know," Malian said aloud.

Frowning again, she swung her feet to the floor. "Unless Ser Ombrose planned to kidnap the queen and marry her by force." The Sondargent wolf, she said to herself, thinking that it would fit with the open use of his own followers and allies in the courtyard, rather than relying on the Darksworn—who had betrayed him anyway.

"War within and without." She repeated Arcolin's words to the quiet room. "And Ser Ombrose abandoned once he had set their machinery in motion." She could not feel sorry for him: he had betrayed his honor and his kin. And would doubtless choose his allies more carefully in future, if he survived this setback.

Malian shrugged and stood up, wondering how much of her suspicions and conclusions she should repeat. In the end, she decided it might be best to let matters lie. If Zhineve-An had played a part in bringing about last night's events, then it was a relatively small one—and she had lost three of her Seven and would return to Jhaine having failed in the matter of the Great Marriage.

Not just failed, Malian reflected. Tarathan and Jehane Mor could well have opened another fissure in the hierarchy of Jhaine through involving her in the healing below the chapel.

Time would tell—but she felt sure that the Duke would want the Jhainarian alliance more than ever now, with a potential rebellion centered on Ser Ombrose and unrest with Lathayra. Another reason to let whatever part Zhineve-An might have played in last night's events lie.

Malian splashed water onto her face and decided that it was time to return to the Black Tower, even if she had not yet been summoned. When she reached it, the bustle outside was more purposeful, with a constant stream of messengers coming and going, but the Duke was still in council with his lords and captains. So Malian turned toward the Normarch town house and found Kalan there with the rest of the young knights.

"Jarn's sleeping," he said, when Malian asked. "They gave her poppy juice for the pain and said she'll probably need more when she wakes." He looked exhausted, with dark smudges beneath his eyes, but like the others he was checking over armor and weapons, preparing for whatever lay ahead.

"Ombrose has been sighted," Audin told her. "He was clear of the city and fleeing for the Cendreward with his followers, including the Lathayrans. Lord Bonamark's already in pursuit, with a force comprising his own men and about half the ducal guard. Ser Alric's gone with them, because Wymark and Cendreward have old ties and he knows something of the country and the people. And we need to act swiftly, to dissuade any of Ombrose's Sondcendre kin who are not currently with him from taking up his cause."

"I assume the Duke will follow?" Kalan said, tightening a rivet in a sword's haft.

"As soon as the Midsummer ceremonies are over," Audin replied. "From what I can gather, they're already marshaling the army, either to besiege Ombrose in his strongholds or force him across Emer's border and into Lathayra."

So Emer's peace looks set to be overturned again, Malian thought somberly.

"I heard a rumor," Kalan said, his eyes fixed on his hands, busy with the sword hilt, "that they may dispense with the formal rebetrothal tomorrow and hold the marriage instead."

"I think it likely," Audin said finally, his voice so neutral that Malian did not dare look at his face either. "The Ormondian peace is more vital than ever now, and we need to show that we're committed to it—not just to isolate Ombrose, but to prevent any hotheads in Ormond from trying to reopen old wounds."

Kalan finished his work on the sword and propped it against the wall. The blade was not long enough to be his, and Malian realized that he must have been repairing Jarna's sword, damaged in last night's encounter. Her eyes shifted to the mail shirt at his feet and she saw that it had been largely cleaned of blood, although the rent across the links still gaped.

Abruptly, Kalan stood up. "I'm going to the old Sondcendre mansion."

Raher looked up. "D'you think some of Ser Ombrose's men might be holed up there?"

"No," Kalan said. "I think that's where the missing northerners went. Rather than kicking my heels here, I'm going to find out."

"We'd better let the steward know where we're going," Audin said. "If my uncle does summon us, he won't want to be kept waiting."

They all went, though, and Malian guessed that they felt like Kalan, wanting to be on their feet and doing something. The sun was hot, the mood of the city subdued, except when people recognized Audin's Sondargent jupon and called out their support for the Duke. Although until yesterday they would have cheered for Ser Ombrose equally, throwing flowers to the Sondargent champion as he rode by.

Heat shimmered within the broken walls of the old mansion, and at first glance the overgrown ruins seemed peaceful, until they noticed the clouds of hovering flies. Malian turned away as the others went to investigate, making her way to the narrow lane where dried blood stained the cobbles and the cordite whiff of Nindorith's power lingered. She knelt down, touching a finger to the blood, and wondered why she still felt melancholy about Nherenor, when the Darksworn youth had clearly been an enemy.

"I thought I'd find you here." Kalan came along the lane, extending a hand to pull her to her feet. She took it and felt the old link between them reassert itself, stronger than it had been since they left the Wall.

"I'm glad Jarna will live," she said quietly.

He nodded, his hand tightening on hers. "I don't think I could have borne it if . . ."

"I know." His gauntlets were thrust into his belt and she could feel the swordsman's calluses on his palm. "Are there many dead here?" she asked, withdrawing her hand.

Kalan nodded again. "I think the Sword Derai had the worst of it, but there's enough of the lightning warriors to call the honors even. We haven't found Orth yet, but I'll let Gol and his lot know anyway, so they can bury their comrades."

Malian wondered if the remaining Sword warriors would return to the Wall now. Personally she considered their private bloodletting here a waste of energy and lives. "But they may have been right in one thing," she said. "Even if Nherenor was sincere in his embassy"—she paused, finding it difficult to imagine such an alliance really happening —"others within the Swarm are sowing chaos everywhere in Haarth that they can reach. We have to take the war to them, force them to fight on our terms. Otherwise what has happened here in Emer will go on until the whole of Haarth is one great conflagration."

*"I have been thinking that, too, while I sat with Jarna."* His mindtone was somber. *"And about why we left the Wall: not to find an easier situation for ourselves, but a place where we could survive and learn to better withstand the Swarm."*

Malian nodded. "You were right, though, to have reservations. Returning to the Wall means risking all that we have become. Because of our bond, I called you to my cause when Rowan Birchmoon died. But the greater part of that debt is mine, not yours, and you can still take the war to the Swarm here." She met his eyes squarely. "So I release you from any debt, Kalan of the Derai. I take it fully on my honor and my Blood as Heir of Night. You are free to choose your own path."

She had *seen* him back on the Wall, five years ago, but foreseeing was only ever about possibility—and now she had opened up another channel in its shifting river. What would he choose? she wondered, curiously detached. Even the day around them seemed to hang motionless, waiting.

Kalan shook his head. "Lesser part or not," he said, "I still owe a debt. And even the Heir cannot come between a warrior and his own honor. Captain Asantir said that, do you remember? And whether Kalan or Hamar, I know where duty and honor lie."

"Are you sure?" she asked.

"Quite certain," he assured her, his tone almost light as he took her hand again and raised it to his lips. Raher came around the corner in the same moment, accompanied by Girvase and Raven, and immediately stopped.

"What?" the Marcher youth demanded. "Why is Hamar kissing Maister Carick's hand—as if Carro were a girl?"

"Or a liege," Girvase observed, very quietly, but Raven was shaking his head.

"Raher," the knight said, his rare smile quirking, "you need to use those eyes of yours for seeing with. Our Maister Carick has always been a girl."

# 51

# Reports from the Wall

R aher exclaimed about Raven's revelation all the way
back to the palace. Malian was relieved to finally
escape his indignant disbelief, and the others' covert glances,
for whatever questions the Duke might have.

Raven had only been sent to fetch Kalan and herself,
because the Duke had spoken with both Ghiselaine and
Zhineve-An earlier in the afternoon. "So he knows their stories," Lord Falk said. He was waiting for them at the entrance
to the Black Tower, where Raven left them without a word. In
fact, Malian realized, the knight had not spoken at all on the
way back from the Sondcendre mansion. The whole journey
had been taken up by Raher's exclamations.

"I warned Hirluin that you were an adept of the Shadow
Band earlier," Lord Falk continued quietly. He was leading
them to the stairs that accessed the Duke's study, Malian realized, rather than to the main council chamber. "I didn't want
him to press you with questions in front of others," the Castellan added. She nodded, guessing that this was also why
they were being interviewed in private. "My foster brother
is unhappy that I kept your presence here secret, but not ungrateful for all you have done." Lord Falk glanced down at
her with a slight smile. "I have taken responsibility for the
former. The rest I have said, quite correctly, has all been your

and my young Normarchers work." His smile included Kalan, who nodded stiffly, although Malian could tell he was pleased.

Malian paused as they entered the hallway that led to the Duke's study, her eyes searching Lord Falk's. "Have I fulfilled my part of the bargain that we made in the hill fort?" she asked.

The Castellan bowed slightly. "You have. Come to me when you have spoken with the Duke and I will supply the information I owe." He paused, the expression in his light eyes quizzical. "I may have been ungenerous in my bargaining, given your great service to Emer. I fear that my information will not do you the good you hope."

She met his look steadily. "You are giving me the opportunity to find that out for myself. That is all I ever expected of our bargain."

He nodded. "And I will fulfill my part, as you have." He bowed to her again, but embraced Kalan. "I will see you after, too. But now," he added, with his fox's smile, "you must brace yourselves for my foster brother's questions."

Sunset was almost upon Caer Argent by the time the Duke let them go. Lord Hirluin had been with his father throughout, his steady, weary gaze assessing them both, although he rarely spoke. A little to Malian's surprise, Ghiselaine had been present as well, sitting across the table from the Duke's heir. No one could argue that she was not directly affected by the unfolding events. but she was not yet Duchesss-in-waiting to Emer, either. Perharps, Malian had concluded, keeping her face as gravely attentive as the young countess's, a message was being sent that the marriage between Hirliun and Ghiselaine was not to be mere sealing wax on the Ormodian treaty, but a union of equals. A bold move—if the Duke could pull it off in the face of Ser Ombrose's rebellion.

Whatever the intention behind her presence, Ghiselaine spoke even less than Hirluin, although she listened intently throughout. The Duke's questions had been searching rather than hostile, but he had wanted to know everything, from Malian's first mission to draw out the facestealers, to the detail of

Kalan's vision the previous night and his involvement in events at the old chapel. In the end, however, he had commended and thanked them both.

"Although," he added, his heavy gaze resting on Malian, "I would prefer to dispense with your services, Maister Adept. I understand the reasons Falk chose to enlist you in our cause, I even support them—but dancers of Kan, even those drawn from the Shadow Band, are not an aspect of River life I want to see take root in Emer."

"It's time for Maister Carick to quit the scene in any case," Malian told Kalan as they headed for the Normarch town house. "His usefulness is over following the open confrontation with Arcolin."

Kalan was frowning. "They didn't really ask about how Raven would have known that Ghis and Queen Zhineve-An were in danger. Maybe because he'd already accounted for it earlier. But what do you think?"

"He says he can smell magic," she said, waiting until they had passed the guard on the gate, although she still kept her voice low. "Perhaps the sorcery they were using alerted him."

"The Darksworn adept, the one who died, spoke to him at the last." Kalan was watching the first dance of moths through early shadow. " 'But you're not'—that's what she said. She seemed shocked, as though she had just realized something about him that she hadn't before. She'd called him a traitor earlier," he added, as they turned into the town house square. "But I don't think that was it."

Malian frowned, too, thinking about the two Darksworn she had overheard through the white mists. Rhike had certainly thought the warrior she spoke to on Summer's Eve was opposing her cause—and at The Leas, even the beast-men had seemed afraid of Raven. Which meant they *knew* to be afraid, Malian thought now. " 'But you're not,' " she repeated. "Not what, I wonder?"

Kalan stopped, staring past the everyday life around them. "I don't know," he said slowly. "But I think he must have some power beyond just sensing magic. I felt that last mindblast she hurled at him through my shield, and it should have knocked him cold, or killed him. But it didn't. And her last strike at him just deflected to either side."

I've seen something like that before, Malian thought, although the recollection eluded her. "Jehane Mor was holding a shield—" she began.

"I know. I saw her in my dream, under the great dome. I thought she was protecting the vigil, but when I got to the chapel there was no trace of her shield." Kalan shook his head. "So it had to be something else diverting the attack from Ser Raven."

But what? Malian thought. She had never detected any hint of power use around the knight at all. Yet Raven had seen through her Shadow Band illusions as well, either from their first meeting or over time, and known that the River maister was a young woman . . .

I need to work out where he fits into all this, she thought, but I'm too exhausted right now. She yawned mightily, and Kalan looked around with a wry grin. "I think I'll sleep like the dead tonight," he said.

Malian could not help herself: she made the River sign to avert ill luck, although she was careful not to let him see it. They walked the rest of the way across the square in mutual silence, although they both grinned when they passed a food vendor's stall and Kalan's stomach grumbled loudly. It did smell good, Malian thought, sniffing the tang of salt and frying oil appreciatively, but she knew there would be a meal provided in the town house—and plans to be made once she had spoken with Lord Falk.

The heralds were waiting for her in the town house forecourt, the late sunlight gilding their hair. "Another herald pair arrived at the Guild house here today," Jehane Mor told Malian, "They had come from Ar and one of their messages was for you, so we said we would deliver it."

She handed the roll in its sealed case to Malian, who did not need to look down to see Elite Cairon's secret mark amidst the scrolling on the heavy leather. "We have also," the herald added gently, "come to say good-bye. We have business in Port Farewell and will return to the River by ship."

So they were leaving: well, she had known they would.

Malian kept her face smooth, although she felt that quick pain again, in the region of her heart. Port Farewell, she thought—fitting! "I still have your medallion," she said, and made herself meet Tarathan's eyes, just for a moment. "I should give it back."

Jehane Mor's hand closed over hers, preventing her from reaching beneath the neck of her tunic. "Keep it," she said.

"But—" Malian shook her head. *"It's the insignia of a priestess-queen of Jhaine,"* she protested to Tarathan.

"You have earned it," their conjoined voice told her. Their eyes pierced her. *"You have walked the path of earth and moon and seen the visions that entails. You have heard the song of Haarth and will remain a priestess-queen. One who has passed through the sacred rite can never be unmade."*

It's not just Tarathan, Malian thought, a little shaken: I can hear them both. She remembered the young Zhehaamor, mind-speaking her fellow sovereigns in their temple strongholds, and supposed this must be part of being a priestess-queen of Jhaine.

"Keep it," Jehane Mor said again. "For my sake."

"For both our sakes," said Tarathan.

Malian nodded, if a little blindly, and was acutely aware of Kalan's presence, his face wiped clear of any expression at all. "Thank you," she managed, and realized that Jehane Mor was still watching her, something very close to diffidence in her eyes now.

"Are we friends?" asked the herald, who was also Zhehaamor of Jhaine.

Are we? Malian wondered. She felt the weight of the moon disc around her neck, balancing the fire of Yorindesarinen's armring on her wrist, and heard the hero's voice out of long ago: *There are many friends . . . some open and some still hidden from you.*

She heard a fair-haired herald speaking, too, the snow falling around them in Jaransor: *. . . are we not friends?*

"We are friends," Malian said, and in saying the words, recognized their truth. She clasped Jehane Mor's hand, and the herald kissed her on either cheek.

"Farewell, for now." She stepped back. *"May your nine gods watch over you."*

And then Malian was looking into Tarathan's dark eyes one more time. Let it not be a last time, she thought: let it never be that. "Farewell," he said aloud, and kissed her lips: *"Malian of Night."*

"Farewell," she said steadily, and inexplicably, the pain released its tight hold around her heart. The heralds stepped back, saluting her as one before walking away, their gray cloaks swinging across the tops of their boots. She watched them go, then turned to meet Kalan's carefully neutral gaze.

His hesitation was barely noticeable. "Do you think the scroll's important?"

Almost certainly, she thought. The Elite's mark on the casing told her it was something he believed she either needed or would want to know. "Let's find out," she said, keeping her voice as smooth as her face, although she caught Kalan's sideways glance all the same. As soon as they passed the door, she could hear the voices of the other young knights, talking somewhere in the upstairs region of the house. She ignored them, crossing to the brightest of the hall lamps before extracting the scroll and turning it to maximize the light. When she had read it through twice she rerolled the parchment and returned it to the case.

"Is it bad news?" Kalan asked.

"Fresh reports have come in from the Wall." She kept her voice low, aware of how speech could echo in the hall. "My father still mourns for Rowan Birchmoon. Some of the Band's sources even claim that he is mad with grief." She was silent, trying to think what that would mean if it were true. "But mad or not," she continued, unable to keep the irony from her voice, "a marriage has been arranged with a Daughter of Blood. There's to be a great festival of arms in the Red Keep at autumn's eve, to choose an honor guard and captain to escort her to the Keep of Winds."

She could see him waiting and met his eyes. "I foresaw Nherenor's death, five years ago," she told him, "when I looked into Yorindesarinen's fire. I saw you, too, in the same vision sequence. You were part of a wedding caravan."

*"So you want me to return, not just to the Wall of Night,*

*but to the House of Blood, and take part in this contest of arms?"* Kalan was expressionless again, his mindtone giving nothing away. *"Gain reentry to Night that way?"*

Do I just nod and say yes? Malian wondered. Instead she stepped close, her voice lower still. "I *saw* you in the wedding caravan, dressed as a warrior. I sense that it is vital you are there, although I don't know why."

*"So you purported to offer me a free choice earlier, when you already thought me fated."* She heard the iron in his mindtone and her heart sank. I should have explained about my vision before, she thought, cursing herself—but I wanted him to be free to choose.

Kalan stared into her eyes a moment longer, then gave a small jerk of his head. She recognized Girvase's gesture from the Rindle, signaling acceptance of Raven's leadership, however unpalatable the young knight had found his decisions. *"Everything I said then still holds true, regardless of your foreseeing,"* Kalan told her grimly. *"And if Rowan Birchmoon's death was plotted by those outside Night, a festival of arms may be a good place to pick up rumors."*

He paused, glancing toward the upstairs voices. "If I leave tonight I should catch up with the heralds. I can ride with them to Port Farewell and take ship for Grayharbor, then find another there to reach the Sea Keep. But I need to say goodbye to the others first, and see Jarn." He took the gauntlets from his belt, but did not put them on. "I will meet you back here afterward and we can settle any other plans before I leave." He paused again, his expression set as he regarded her. *"I take it that you will still seek the Lost?"*

Malian hesitated, but his unhappiness over the foreseeing had told her that she needed to be open with him now. I am sending him into danger as well, she thought. He needs to know that I trust him. "I will," she said. She kept her eyes and her voice steady. "But once I have done that, there is another path I must pursue."

And she told him about the sword.

# 52

## The Path of Return

"**I** still can't get over Maister Carick being a girl," Raher said, coming back to the subject after cancellation of the tournament finals had been thrashed out—together with the decision to share the prize money amongst the finalists so there would be no ill will. He paused as the young Normarch knights made their way through the main entrance of the temple complex, throwing out his arms. "And if Ser Raven knew all along, why didn't he say so?"

"None of his business?" Girvase volunteered, pointedly, but Raher went on muttering about it anyway as they walked around to the infirmary gate. "And is she a scholar or isn't she?" he asked, plaintive again. "He—she—seemed to know about book learning, but where does the knife-play in the tunnels come in?"

"Oh, for Imuln's sake!" Audin snapped. "Isn't it obvious? She's a dancer of Karn. And maybe a scholar as well," he added, making a visible effort to curb his irritation. "One doesn't necessarily rule out the other, I suppose."

They all exchanged careful glances behind his back. Not even Raher said anything, although Kalan knew they were all thinking about the formal announcement that Ghiselaine's wedding to Hirluin would take place the next evening. After a moment, Girvase threw an arm, sword-comrade fashion, across Audin's shoulders, and then Raher said, cautiously, that it looked like they would all be riding out with the Duke in the next few days. "So we won't have to worry about finding a place as a company until this business with Ser Ombrose is over."

"What about Jarna?" Ado asked. Kalan guessed that he was thinking about Ser Alric's comments yesterday. Girvase slanted a look at him but said nothing.

"She'll stay here, I suppose, until she's better." Raher sounded surprised. "And then she'll join us. But she'll be all right. The girls'll look after her."

The full moon of Midsummer was well up now, the pale light blanching Ado's fair hair to ash. "What if," he said, "we can't get a place as a company if she's part of it?"

Audin's lips pursed in a silent whistle. Girvase still said nothing, but Raher scowled. "What a cursed shabby trick!" he said, although it was unclear whether he meant no one taking them on, or the implication that they should abandon Jarna. "After Summer's Eve," he added, sounding less certain, "we swore to ride as a company."

They had reached the infirmary gates and stood beneath the shadowed arch, with its carved tracery of the poppy that eased pain. "We need to be sure about where we stand, that's all," Ado said. "Before the situation comes up."

He had spent most of his training years as Ser Rannart's squire, rather than at Normarch, Kalan reflected. It made sense that his bond to the group, and to Jarna, might not be as strong. Raher was scowling. "M'father says you should never abandon a sword comrade, even if you don't like them or the circumstances are not convenient to you. He says that's what it means, to be a knight of Emer."

"We rode as one at Summer's Eve," Girvase said quietly. "I'm with Raher's father."

Audin nodded. "It feels like that for me, too. As though I would be breaking faith, not just with Jarna, but with everyone who died if we broke our fellowship for advancement."

"Dishonored," said Girvase.

Audin looked at Kalan. "You're very quiet, Hamar. But no need to even ask you, I suppose."

"No," said Kalan, the word a weight. Girvase's head turned. "But not because I have always been Jarna's friend. I won't be riding with you. I'm leaving tonight."

The silence was so profound that he heard a priestess laugh softly, somewhere behind the temple walls. Much further off a nightingale was singing, at one with the night and the moon and every Emerian song of springtime love.

"You can't leave," Raher said. "You're one of us."

Kalan's mouth was very dry. "No," he said, for the second time. "I'm not. It's not for advancement," he added, reading Ado's expression. He wanted to laugh, entirely without mirth. "Almost the opposite in fact." He spread his hands, trying to explain to their incomprehension. "I'm not from Emer, although I was fostered here with Lord Falk. But now I've been called back."

"An older loyalty," Audin said, frowning and sounding unsure at the same time.

"Called by *her*," Raher said suddenly. "The maister— adept—whoever she is. Does your family serve hers, then, back on the River? Perhaps we could persuade her to forgive you the service?" His grin was mostly a baring of teeth.

Audin sighed. "Don't be a fool, Raher. She's an adept of Karn—and rode with us, too, at Summer's Eve." He looked at Kalan. "You're really leaving tonight?"

Kalan nodded, and they were all silent again. Despite his night vision, he found it impossible to read their expressions now. Finally, Audin stirred. "We still need to see how Illy is doing. Are you going to see Jarna?" he asked Kalan, who nodded. "We'll meet you out here afterward, then—see you off."

Kalan nodded again, and Audin left with Ado and an unusually quiet Raher. Girvase remained, standing a few paces away, but the distance, Kalan thought, might as well have been the full length of the road that stretched from Ij to Ishnapur.

"Lord Falk and Manan told me this might happen," Girvase said finally. "And that we were not to blame you."

Do you? Kalan wanted to ask, but he knew to wait, with Girvase. "I think," his friend said slowly, "that you are not from the River. And probably," he added shrewdly, "you're not even called Hamar. You're part of this northern business." He waited, but Kalan said nothing. "But you can't tell me that. Or your true name."

Kalan shook his head, although his throat burned with the longing to speak. "I'm sorry," he said.

"So am I," Girvase said. Something in the way he spoke made the words into an ending. But still he did not move. "And Jarna?"

The nightingale, Kalan noticed, had fallen silent, abandoning the moon and the night's warmth. "Will always be my true friend," he said stiffly. "As will you all."

Girvase was silent. He had a way, Kalan thought, of not saying anything that was annoyingly eloquent.

Ours is a just a springtime love grafted onto friendship, he wanted to reply, easy and confident: Jarn knows that. Except that suddenly he felt unsure. Jarna was so shy that sometimes it was hard to know what she truly thought. And she wasn't a damosel from one of the great families, who had grown up knowing that a springtime love could never be more than dalliance, before her family made her a marriage tied to wealth and land.

"The place I'm going," he said instead, "is brutal. Hostile to those from outside." He thought of Rowan Birchmoon as he had first seen her, amidst the falling snow in Jaransor, and grief caught in his throat. "Deadly, too, sometimes."

Perhaps he should have thought of that sooner, before he and Jarna took the step beyond straightforward friendship into something more. He had been a fool, hoping the Emerian life could last—but then, springtime love *meant* transience, coming into bloom and then gone again with the spring flowers. And already it was Midsummer, his and Jarna's fleeting springtime passed. "I have to leave Emer," he said to Girvase, his voice harsh. "But I'll see Jarna first and say good-bye, if she's awake."

"And if she's not?" That cursed, dispassionate tone.

"I still have to go." Girvase said nothing, but Kalan was aware of his friend's eyes at his back all the way across the courtyard and up the infirmary stair. It's none of his business anyway, Kalan thought, gritting his teeth. But he remembered Girvase at the fords of the Rindle, when he thought Alianor might be hurt or dead—and how there had been no doubt in him earlier either, when they spoke about sword comrades holding true to each other.

Jarna was awake, although the priestess keeping watch in her room said that she had been drifting in and out of consciousness and he could not stay long. "She's very weak," she said, "and we've had to give her more poppy, for the pain." But Jarna's eyes, though drowsy, were lucid when Kalan took the stool beside the bed. Someone had draped Ghiselaine's tourney favor across her pillow, the yellow rich in the plain room.

"The Countess herself brought it to me," she told him, when he asked. Her voice was a whisper. "Because of last night and not being at the wedding. She's kind," Jarna added, and Kalan nodded, because it was true. Gently, he picked up a strand of her hair and plaited it between his fingers. When he looked up, Jarna's eyes were fixed on him. "You want to say good-bye," she whispered. "Don't you?"

His fingers stilled. "Not want," he said, each word heavy as stone. He smoothed the hair out onto the pillow again, frowning. "How did you know?"

"I know you." Her eyelids sank down and he thought she might have slipped out of consciousness, but after a moment they rose again. "And I had a dream. Of white mist—and then the heralds with their one voice, saying you had begged for my life, but that your fate called you away from Emer." Her lips trembled and Kalan closed his eyes briefly, against the pain in hers. "They said . . . that where you are going, one of the great lords took an outsider consort and she was killed for it."

He nodded, seeing the falling snow again and a door opening into winter. "Your dream spoke truth. Where I'm going is no place for you, Jarn." It's no place for me either, he thought. "But I have to go."

Her eyes were fixed on his, huge in her white face. "Will you come back?"

He felt sure, then, that he never would, or not in any way that resembled the old life. Even if I live, Kalan thought, knowing there was a good chance that he would not. He wondered how much Malian and Tarathan had foreseen with regard to that, then shook his head: better not to know. He saw, too, that Jarna had read his expression. Her own grew bleak, gray as winter ashes, and he took her hands in his.

"You'll be all right, Jarn, you'll see. The others will all stand by you. Audin and Alli and Raher's families have influence, and there's Ghiselaine, too. She's already given you her favor to carry."

"But I don't want them," Jarna whispered, "only you." Kalan bowed his head, still holding her hands close in his, but could find no words to reply.

"You said . . ." Jarna's voice wavered, then steadied. "You said, when you hung the cherries in my ears, that you would buy me real jewels, after we'd won the tourney."

"Oh, Jarn," Kalan said. When he lifted his head, he saw that her eyes were closed, although the pinch to her mouth told him she was still awake. He leaned forward and placed his lips on hers. "*Be* well, Jarn," he breathed, as though he could will it into her. "Forget all about me."

Her eyelids lifted, her eyes meeting his. "I could never do that." He could see it was costing her to speak. "Take Madder. If it's as dangerous as you say where you're going, you'll need a good horse."

Kalan gave her hands a little shake. "Jarn, no. You've trained him from a foal."

"Take him. As my gift." She turned her face away, toward the wall—so he would not see her cry, Kalan guessed. How, he wondered, did you say either thank you or good-bye, in such a case? But he had to try. He put her hands down, bending close as he got to his feet. For the last time, he touched her hair.

"Thank you," he said softly. "For Madder. And for your true friendship, all these years. Farewell, my Jarna."

But although he stopped in the door to look back, Jarna did not turn her face from the wall and she did not speak.

The road east from Caer Argent was a silver ribbon in the moonlight, the outskirts of the city giving way to farmsteads and the black silhouettes of orchards as the horses' hooves drummed. Kalan was riding his own tall bay and leading Madder, with his armor and everything he needed for the road strapped across the roan's saddle. Soon it would be moonset, and then the early dawn of Midsummer, and he intended to get as far along the road as he could before stopping to eat or rest. He wanted to keep moving, outstripping the farewell to friends and his life in Emer, which rode close at his back. "The path of return," he said aloud, but the wind blew the words away.

A few miles further on the road dipped down to a ford, with the water stippled silver over stones and willow trees a dark fringe along either bank. A fine place for an ambush, he thought, but he slowed his horse anyway, approaching the uncertain footing of the ford at a walk. An owl hooted, and his keen sight caught movement along a hedgerow. A fox, he thought, looking more closely: Maister Fox, minding his own business—as I shall mind mine.

And below it all, the deep, wordless song of Emer that he loved.

The horses clipped closer to the ford and Madder snorted, his ears pricked forward. Kalan looked again, every sense alert—and this time he made out a cloaked shape standing amidst the willows closest to the road. His breath caught as he remembered another cloaked figure he had met once before amidst dark trees. But that had been deep within the Gate of Dreams, whereas this was the waking world. Kalan released the held breath and eased his power around him at the same time, his hand sliding close to his sword hilt as the bay closed the last few yards to the ford.

*"Kalan."* Tarathan of Ar's mindvoice spoke, and Kalan stopped the horses. He stared hard at the herald's face as Tarathan stepped forward into the moonlight. Although even seeing a face clearly, he reflected, would not help in the case of a facestealer.

*"We thought that you would take our road to Port Farewell."* The heralds' mindvoices wove together as one. *"We decided to wait for you."*

*"You mean Tarathan foresaw it."* Kalan knew they would hear his bitterness. *"Just as Malian has seen me back on the Wall."* He could make out Jehane Mor now, further back in the trees with the gray horses, all standing motionless as statues.

*"I cannot answer for what Malian sees."* Tarathan spoke alone this time. *"What I perceive is currents, the paths by which the stream flows, which can change at any time, just as this brook here may be dammed or switch course."*

Kalan frowned. *"So I can affect my own fate?"*

*"We all can."* The heralds spoke as one again. *"No one's path is ever graven in stone—or if it is, even stone may be eroded by weather and time."*

Kalan wondered if that was Malian's hope—that the Derai were not as rigidly bound by the Blood Oath, and to prophecy, as the tenets of the Wall life proclaimed. And if she was right . . . He took a deep breath, then let it silently out again. *"I wanted to stay here, to be Hamar in truth and live as an Emerian knight."*

Tarathan's eyes met his through moonlight and shadow, keen-edged as a lance. *"When honor and duty call, we cannot always have what we desire. But that is not the same thing as fate."*

Kalan gazed up at the vast river of stars overhead. The idea that he might not be bound by their patterns felt like the world falling away beneath his feet, with myriad possibilities twisting away into a vast unknown. Terrifying, yes—but exhilarating as well. He breathed out again, deep and soft, and felt the tension that he had not known was in his shoulders ease. Later he might talk with the heralds about the dream they had sent Jarna, and many other things besides, but not now. He looked away from the stars to where they waited, stillness spreading out from them like age rings in the heart of a tree.

*"Thank you,"* he said. *"Not least for waiting for me."* But mostly, he added to himself, for showing me that the road I take now is not about a destiny to fulfill, but one to make. He glanced back at the sky, then drew out Yorindesarinen's ring from where it hung concealed around his neck. The black pearl gleamed, a moon rising through midnight cloud, as he slid the plaited band onto his finger. *" 'A friend gave it to me, long ago . . .' "* Kalan repeated the hero's words, spoken out of his own past—then shook his head, clearing it of all thoughts of both past and future. *"We should press on, if we're to get clear of Caer Argent."*

Overhead, the stars continued their slow march west, traversing the short Midsummer night, while three riders and four horses crossed the ford and rode east, their backs to the slowly setting moon and their faces toward the dawn.

# PART V

## Summer's End

# 53

## The Solitary Tower

Malian worked her way east and south from Caer Argent, eating the road dust of summer as she rode toward the Ormondian hills and southern Aralorn beyond. Initially, the roads were clogged with Midsummer travelers, every inn overflowing with people talking about events in Caer Argent. Some of the merchants spoke of unrest everywhere, the Ijiri troubles earlier in the spring and conflict along the desert border of Ishnapur, but most of the Emerians simply viewed it as another chapter in their tumultuous history.

"The Cendreward won't follow Ombrose Sondargent, you'll see," one local knight asserted, as dusk settled around an innyard between Gulesward and Griffonmark. "If the Duke doesn't catch him first, he'll end up in Lathayra, causing the Castellan of the Southern March grief by raiding back across the border."

"Pity the Southern March then," a merchant said. "He didn't get the name 'wolf' for nothing in that last border war."

The talk, Malian found, was much the same in Griffonmark, but by the time she climbed into the Ormondian hills, keeping away from the densely settled valleys to the south and west, both the settlements and road traffic had grown sparse. The more isolated the land, the more suspicious of strangers those she met became, taking their time to look her over before coming close enough to exchange a greeting. She found herself sleeping in barns and copses more often, as both inns and temple guesthouses became rare.

She had left both Mallow and the identity of Carick behind in Caer Argent. Now she rode a sturdy gray cob and called herself Heris—a name that could equally well originate on the River or in northern Emer—an itinerant scribe on a pilgrimage to all the shrines of Serrut in Emer and Aralorn. And maybe Lathayra, although the shabby scribe was undecided on that point whenever his plans were discussed. Lathayra, he had heard, was a dangerous place for those not adept with the weapons of war.

"Perilous far, too," one farmer deep in the Ormondian hills opined. He had allowed Malian to sleep in his barn, which was little more than a drystone hut built into the side of a hill. The farmhouse, too, was small: both buildings and man dwarfed by the surrounding terrain. "Even Aralorn's a tidy step from here."

If Emer was not the River, Malian reflected, then the hills of northern Ormond were a vastly different world to Caer Argent. Farmsteads gave way to shepherd's cots, and fields to flocks dotted across the otherwise empty hills. A waist-high stone, sitting crookedly on the crest of a pass, marked the border into southern Aralorn. She camped that night beneath a spreading oak and studied the Aralorn sky, with constellations she had never seen before rising above the southern horizon.

Malian found it strange to reflect that the path she was following was the reverse of the route that Tarathan and Jehane Mor had traveled to reach the Guild house in Terebanth. The same path, she now knew, that brought the Derai fugitives south to the border country between southern Aralorn and Jhaine. And if what Lord Falk had told her was correct, the silent watchers who had come out of the woods the day that Tarathan and Jehane Mor crossed the boundary river must have been the Lost. Malian wondered, suddenly, if that was where the heralds had learned to speak Derai.

She stretched out on the hard ground, thinking about the network of contacts and safehouses that had passed the two Jhainarian fugitives north—a different kind of river, flowing strong and secret underground, but a route through Haarth nonetheless. For all these years it had been sweeping the lost Derai south as well, far from the Wall and anyone who might know to send word of the renegades there. She remembered the hill farmer and grinned, for if he thought Lathayra was perilous far, she doubted he would even comprehend the vast leagues that separated Aralorn and the Derai Wall.

So many people, though, must have been involved with this underground river: in Grayharbor and the River, Aeris—if she had gotten the route right, although there could well, she supposed, be more than one—and Emer, and finally Aralorn. Malian was amazed that the secret had remained so well kept. Although when she reflected again, between the Patrol and the Shadow Band, the Guild of Heralds and the Oakward, both Emer and the River were full of those whose business was the keeping of secrets.

And Elite Cairon? she wondered. For nearly five years I've been working the River every summer and hunting down trails that always came to nothing—yet he is an Elite of the Shadow Band, with its network of listeners and agents. All along, he *must* have known.

Bastard, Malian thought, entirely without surprise.

"Perhaps," Nhenir said coolly, "he distrusted your recklessness in those early years—the harm you might have done."

"And you?" Malian queried, just as cool. "How much have you known, all this time?" But Nhenir, of course, did not answer.

Was I reckless? Malian wondered. She supposed she might have been, in her determination to develop her strength and skills, marrying her Derai inheritance with the disciplines taught by the Shadow Band.

"As I said." Nhenir's mindvoice was very dry: "Reckless."

Malian grinned, just a little. "I've grown more responsible."

"*Like trying to* perceive *Nindorith's essence, that night in the garden?*"

Malian was silent, reliving that moment. *"You didn't exactly help,"* she observed.

*"I dared not. He would have known me."*

*"He goes back that far?"* Malian lay very still. *"To Yorindesarinen?"*

*"Farther. Look in the first annals of the Derai Alliance, Child of Night. You will find Nindorith there."*

Malian sat up, wrapping her hands around her knees as she stared into the warm night. *"That is why I need the Lost. We have let ourselves grow too weak, our powers fading further with every generation since the Great Betrayal. Even with Kalan—the two of us couldn't withstand a power like that, not on our own."*

*"You will need an army,"* Nhenir said simply, and Malian knew the helm did not mean warriors with swords. *"Or the Golden Fire of the Keeps as they used to be."*

"Ornorith always turning the face that smiles," Malian said—grimly, since fickleness was the innate nature of the Two-Faced Goddess. Yet even with the Lost, she still would not have the sort of strength that Nhenir meant. She rested her forehead against her knees, sitting like that for some time before lying down again.

Sleep eluded her, so she studied the new constellations instead, trying to see patterns in them. One, she thought, could be a swordsman raising his blade, like Telemanthar in the old stories, or Kalan at the Midsummer tourney, or— "Nherenor," she whispered, recalling how he had sprung down to meet her on the roof of the Sondcendre ruin. *"He was so young, yet he had an empathy link to Nindorith, whom you say is ancient."*

*"I did not know this Nherenor."* The helm was neutral. *"Or what he could have meant to Nindorith."*

All the same, Malian thought, there was something about him. *That I liked*, she wanted to say, but could not, even to herself.

Eventually she slept, although her dreams were jumbled,

showing her Kalan on a moonlit road, riding in company with the heralds. Even in sleep she veered away from that vision, because she had resolved, after Imuln's Isle, not to seek for Tarathan through the Gate of Dreams. Thwarted, her vision focused on another road, empty as the one she rode now but overhung by a storm's threatening gloom. Slowly, a darkness appeared on the road, and Malian thought she could detect the shape of a man at its heart.

She remembered both dreams when she woke and hoped that the dream of Kalan traveling with the heralds had been a true one. The second dream she found more problematic, because the figure in darkness did remind her of the shadow cloak and she had been thinking about Nherenor before she slept. The vision could simply have been a manifestation of that—but it could also be a warning. Malian checked her back trail with greater care as she rode on, and extended her seeker's sense, as unobtrusively as possible, over the terrain ahead. Once or twice she thought she caught the echo of a horse's hooves behind them, but although she lay in wait each time and continued to seek out vantage points with a wide view of the surrounding country, she saw no other rider.

Gradually, the high hills gave way to more rolling country, with villages clustered around crossroads and fords. Flocks of sheep still predominated, but Malian began to see geese grazing beside streams, and groves of olives and nut trees by farmhouses. Inns became more frequent, some little more than a village alehouse, while larger settlements boasted a secure stable and rooms for hire. Wherever possible she would stop: to water her horse and drink a mug of ale in the heat of the day, or to eat an evening meal and sleep afterward in the stable hayloft, avoiding the stiflingly hot attic rooms that were all an itinerant scribe could afford. At every halt, whether short or long, she would listen to the conversations around her, alert for any indication that there was more to this community than any other sleepy Aralorn village.

The language of Aralorn was yet another dialect of that spoken in Emer and on the River, although the accent was broad and she began to encounter unknown words. She was careful never to ask questions beyond directions to the nearest shrine of Serrut—or Serru, as they said it here, dropping the final consonant altogether. Instead she listened for any difference that rose naturally to the surface of local conversations. But the talk, Malian found, whether in Hayfield, or Oakwhistle, or Forge Crossing, was always the same. People discussed the weather and harvest prospects, and gave consideration, whether serious or idle, to the qualities of horses, dogs, and prize rams. Their outlook matched the Ormondian hill farmer's view of the world: "As far away as Ishnapur," they would say, giving it the same sound as "*beyond the rim of the world*." And they had never heard of the Derai Wall.

The shrines of Serru were isolated, often no more than a cairn at a lonely crossroads, or a small, lime-washed chapel tended by a lay priest from the nearest farm or village. Occasionally, Malian would be pointed to a temple more like those found in Emer and the River, with a community serving the god, but the priests were still drawn from the surrounding countryside. Two of these communities, she found, were sworn to serve the god in silence, which rather ruled out, she thought dryly, the possibility of listening in on their conversations.

*"And not one sign of the Lost yet,"* she said to Nhenir, *"although we must be very close to the border country now."*

Summer began its turn toward autumn, and now they passed harvesters in the small fields. Malian still sweated through the dusty days, but the nights held a hint of coolness, and the strange constellations rose higher as she rode even further south. The villages grew smaller again—more like those in Normarch, she thought: a straggle of cottages around a larger farmstead, or a knight's hold comprising a single stone tower. The shrines, too, grew sparse, and Crossgate directed her on to Hurdle, which in its turn sent her further east to Lowcliff.

She rode into Butterworth as the poplar leaves became gold tinted. The village had an alehouse as well as a forge, with a crumbling stone tower on the edge of the nearby chestnut woods. "Although only owls live there now," the girl who was sweeping the alehouse step told Malian, before bringing her a tankard of cool brown beer and filling the trough beside the step with water for the cob. "Shrines of Serru, is it?" She shooed away the hens that had come pecking around the door. "There's none here, nor as far as Thorpe, from what I hear." She gazed beyond the dusty yard and the hens to the nearby chestnut woods. "You could try the Ara-fyr, although—" She crinkled up her eyes, her tone growing apologetic, as if she feared disappointing her visitor. "They may not have shrines to Serru or even Imul. They're uncanny strange in their ways."

Malian took a long draught of the beer. "Worshippers of the . . . third?" she asked, letting herself sound surprised and a little nervous at the same time. She did not speak Kan's name, knowing that country folk on the River feared that it brought ill luck, the very act of naming drawing the dark god's attention.

The girl made a warding sign anyway. "Never say it!" she exclaimed, the words half a gasp, then twisted a finger in the strand of pale golden hair that had fallen free of her kerchief. "I don't know. The Ara-fyr keep to themselves, but Baz at the forge says . . ." She raised her shoulders high, then let them fall again. "I think they worship other gods."

A new voice spoke. "Mainly, Baz at the forge says that you talk too much, Jan Butterworth!"

The girl jumped, flushing crimson as a man limped around the corner of a lean-to shed. Despite his muscular build, he looked as though he had been badly injured once, and Malian could see the lines in his face left by old pain. His short bronze hair was dark with sweat; the eyes that regarded her were a vivid gray-hazel, but right now their expression was wary.

Malian eyed the smith's hammer in his right hand. "I meant no offense," she said, with the uneasiness a scribe might well display. "I'm on pilgrimage to shrines of Serru."

"I told him there's none in these parts," Jan put in quickly.

"That's not all I heard you saying," the smith said. His

vivid, wary gaze never left Malian, although he still spoke to the girl. "What questions did he ask you?"

She shook her head. "None. Just about the nearest shrine."

"Well, then." The smith addressed Malian directly this time. "Like Jan said, there's no shrines in these parts. Thorpe's the road you want—or Stoneford, although you'll find it a ride." He remained there, watching as she set the tankard down and remounted without a word. She bowed to Jan from the saddle—a scribe's awkward bob—before turning away.

Ara-fyr: Malian said the name silently as the cob clopped out of the village, following the Thorpe marker. *The* Ara-fyr, who must not be talked about and who worshipped strange gods. At last, she thought, as Butterworth disappeared behind a curve in the road.

She made camp that evening in a spinney with a clear view of the road, lighting no fire and setting trip wires for unwelcome visitors. Her seeker's sense could detect no enemies, but if Jan of Butterworth's Ara-fyr were the Lost, then she could not rule out the possibility of pursuers being shielded. Malian thought she might find sleep difficult, but instead dropped quickly into a dream of the solitary tower on the edge of the Butterworth woods. The wind, full of secrets, rattled through the nearby trees.

The next morning she rose before the sun and by the time the dawn chorus faded was already well into the wood. She let the horse pick its way along narrow deer tracks, her seeker's awareness fanning outward for any sign at all, physical or psychic, of the girl Jan's Ara-fyr. The Band's wards against scrying would offer some shielding, but without Kalan or Jehane Mor's level of protection there was no question: if the Ara-fyr were the Lost, they would know she was here.

As I want them to, Malian thought, stopping to eat a scant midday meal of stale bread and cheese among the roots of a forest giant. Her muscles ached, and she felt tired and keyed up at the same time. When she opened her awareness to the song of Haarth, she found the same quiet melody that prevailed throughout Aralorn, shot through with the chatter of birds, the shy movement of woodland animals, and the ceaseless rustle of leaves. If there was anything alien in the composition, it was very well concealed.

By the time evening fell she had reached the forest edge again and was gazing down on Butterworth with its solitary donjon. A few lights winked from the village, and she could sense the presence of people there—but nothing at all from the tower. The forest shadow lay black and impenetrable across the open ground, and every time her mind touched the donjon's periphery her awareness would slip away from it again. She narrowed her eyes, recalling what Kalan had told her about shielding and anomalies in the natural pattern, five years before.

Anomalies, she repeated to herself: an absence, rather than any more obvious sign—and turned her horse's head toward the tower.

Eastward, the fading moon was a chill paring of its former self, and a ground mist was rising across the fields as Malian circled the donjon. The entrance lay on the side farthest from the village, a crumbling arch with no door to bridge its span. She ground-tied her horse some distance away before approaching to within a few paces of the opening—and waited, patient as earth and stone, while both the mist and the paring of moon rose higher. An owl hooted softly from the nearby woods.

"I need to talk with you," Malian said, pitching her voice just loud enough to penetrate the darkness beyond the arch. "Is that so impossible?" She waited again, but nothing stirred and the silence wrapped around the tower remained as impervious and resolute as anything Nhenir could manage. Stubborn, she thought. Then again, she could be persistent—and had other resources at her command. Turning back to the cob, she removed Nhenir from the saddle, her breath catching as the phoenix wings gleamed silver and pearl, stripped of all illusion. *"You think they're here as well."*

Nhenir did not answer; it did not have to. Malian put the helm on her head and strode back to the tower, lowering the visor that had been crafted to resemble the dawn eyes of Terennin, the farseeing god. Seen through its medium, the donjon that rose before her was no longer crumbling, but sheer and smooth. A solid wooden door filled the entry arch, and robed and hooded figures crowded the tower height, many with owls perched on their shoulders. Three more hooded figures waited before the door, their faces concealed in shadow. Malian stopped at the same distance that she had before. "Was the walling out really necessary?" she asked, speaking in Derai. "What harm can it do, to hear me out?"

"We know who you are and what you want." The central figure of the three replied using the same language, his voice harsh. "Do you think you are the only one with prescience here? We foresaw your coming—but want no part of you, or your call to return to the Wall."

"A Derai who practices the arts of Ka." The second speaker used the Aralorn version of Kan's name, her voice sharp with contempt.

"Yet," the third speaker said, his tone more thoughtful, "her aura is also that of Haarth. Intriguing."

"I have walked the path of earth and moon," Malian replied, "and become part of this world as you have done, binding yourselves to this border country. But I am still Derai—and so are you."

"We do not deny it," the first speaker said coldly. "We know who we are, and what—the Ara-fyr, those who keep the hearthfires of Aralorn burning in this empty country, and hold the bloodlust of Jhaine and its queens at bay."

"Aralorn," the second speaker added, "has both offered sanctuary and given us purpose and a place of honor, as opposed to being immured and reviled on the Wall."

Malian waited, counting the voices of the night insects in hedgerow and field. " 'If Night falls, all fall,' " she quoted at last. "I, too, bear the old powers and am as much one of the reviled as any of you. But if the Derai and the Wall fall, the whole of Haarth will fall with it, including Aralorn."

"Perhaps the Derai should have thought about the Fall of Night before they swore their Blood Oath." The harsh voice dripped bitterness. "And who are you, when all's said and done, to demand such a sacrifice of us?"

He meant the question rhetorically, Malian knew, a challenge to the Derai hierarchy of Blood—but she would answer what was asked. She held up her arm, touching the fire of her mind to Yorindesarinen's armring. "I am Malian," she said clearly, "the Heir of the House of Night. I bear Yorindesarinen's armring and wear her helm, Nhenir, which is the first of the hero's lost arms to be found again. I have spoken with the hero herself, beyond the Gate of Dreams. The Swarm is rising, as I'm sure you know: duty and honor call all Derai to the Wall."

The woman laughed, but the sound was edged. "Duty and honor," she mocked. "We broke with Derai notions of that when we left the Wall—as did you, Heir of Night."

Malian bowed her head. Nhenir could be light as air, but she felt the helm's full weight as she raised her eyes to their shadowed hoods again. "I have also given my word to one who is now dead that I will do all that I can to save Haarth. But I cannot do it alone."

The Lost were silent, although she could feel their eyes fixed on her from within the concealing hoods. One of the owls cried, mournful, from the tower height.

"Ay," the first speaker said at last. "You need us: that is what this is all about. You will spend *our* lives and blood to honor *your* vow and defend a Wall that *we* disown."

The woman spoke again. "You may have the helm, but where are the sword and shield? Without all three of Yorindesarinen's arms, you are defeated before you begin."

"And we are just priest-kind," the third speaker added, although he sounded regretful. "Born to power, yes, but few of us have even a fraction of your strength. We have learned to achieve greater potency by working together. But for you to return to the Wall and deal as an equal with the Alliance, let alone hope to defeat the Swarm—Heir of Night, you do not need us. You need a House at your back."

"The whole of Night," the second speaker observed dryly. "And you will never have that while your father lives."

"So why should we sacrifice ourselves in vain?" the first concluded.

Is this what Yorindesarinen faced, Malian thought, when seeking allies to defeat the Chaos Worm? She studied the tower with its hooded figures, massed against her as surely as if they still held their shield in place, and wondered why she had ever thought they might consider, let alone answer, her call to sacrifice and duty. Just because a vow had seen made to Yorindesarinen as she lay dying—that her successor would not have to stand alone—did not mean that the Lost should sacrifice themselves to give it effect. Am I even right, she asked herself, to seek their aid?

Right or not, if she returned to the Wall with just Nhenir, there was every chance that she would be dooming both Kalan and herself—failing, Malian thought grimly, before I've even begun. Yet because of Kalan, she not only understood their reluctance, but empathized with it.

The silence stretched, filling the night while she tried to summon an argument that would bring them willingly to her cause. "Whether you and the rest of Haarth love or hate the Derai, this world will still fall with the Wall of Night." She spoke quietly, the way she had seen Asantir do. "And from Grayharbor to these hills, whether traders or Guild, Patrol or Oakward, Haarth has helped save you. I have made a vow to one who has died—but you also owe a debt."

"Which we repay here," the first speaker replied, swift and hard. "A service you would have us abandon, just like that!" He snapped his fingers. On the tower, the owls all turned their heads to gaze at Malian with glowing eyes.

"After all," the woman said in her edged voice. "Aralorn is not *Derai* business. What matter if its border lies open to the corrupt ambition of Jhaine's hierarchy?"

If I had not walked the path of earth and moon, Malian reflected, that is exactly what I might have said: that greater issues are at stake. But without the Ara-fyr here, their power a counterweight to the priestess-queens, what is to stop conflagration breaking out, one more conflict in the Swarm's harvest of war? *"Except this time,"* she said silently to Nhenir, *"I will have sown it. And the enemy I will set loose on these sleepy villages is the conjoined serpent of Jhaine, with its hunger for blood sacrifice."*

The helm's pause was ambivalent. *"Your choice,"* it replied at last. *"Because you* could *compel them. Even working together, which is their strength, they will be no match for you and the armring. And me."*

True, Malian thought. She also knew that she would not do it, because of the questions Yorindesarinen had put to her at Midsummer. *"That is not,"* she said, tasting the bitterness of defeat, *"the kind of leadership the Derai needs."* Something, she realized, understanding at last, that my father has known for a long time.

She had been standing silent, but the Ara-fyr were still watching: waiting for her next move. And fearing it, too; Malian could sense that now. Perhaps they had foreseen her compelling them—but were nonetheless determined to resist. She lowered her left arm and let the fire in the armring die, then raised Nhenir's visor. The Ara-fyr remained visible to her; they must have let their illusion wall go. "I will not compel anyone to serve me," she said tiredly. "And faith must be kept, even if it is a new one. Otherwise the Wall will fall as surely as if we abandoned the bastion keeps."

The Lost were quiet within their hoods. The owls shifted, restless on the shoulders that bore them, until the third speaker cleared his throat. "I believe you are right, Heir of Night. And we are not truly Derai anymore." Malian heard both loss and acceptance in his voice. "We have not been for many years. What we have left of the old sense of duty and honor now binds us to our service as Ara-fyr."

One by one the hooded figures withdrew into darkness, leaving her to the night and her defeat. Except that when she returned to the cob, she realized that she was still not alone. The smith, Baz, was standing beside the tower, his expression impossible to read beneath its shadow. Malian did not speak, and neither did he until she picked up the cob's reins and began leading it toward the village.

"There's an old woodcutter's cottage a mile or so down the Stoneford road," he said, "if you need somewhere to sleep the night."

Unutterably weary now, Malian simply nodded. The smith made a small gesture that she could not read, perhaps because he checked it so swiftly. He cleared his throat, much as the last Ara-fyr speaker had done. "I'm sorry," he said.

So am I, she thought, but just nodded again. What, after all, was there to say?

"Thank you," he said, exactly as if he had heard her silent question. And pressed his raised hands together and bowed, in the salute those in the southernmost realms used to honor a queen.

# 54

# Serru's Shrine

Malian's dreams later that night were shot through with visions of stone cairns and corvids' wings shrouding a lonely tower, while hoofbeats drummed steadily along a road she could not see. Kalan, she thought, rousing briefly, riding to meet the doom that she had made for him—or perhaps it had been the heralds on the road that first took them north.

When she slept again, her dream showed her the interior of the Keep of Winds for the first time since she had ridden through Rowan Birchmoon's door into winter, five years before. She saw her father sitting by a cold hearth, his shoulders slumped as though the armor he wore had grown too heavy. A grown-up Teron stood by the door, his face set like stone; his eyes, fixed on the Earl of Night, were full of pain. Malian's vision shifted and she saw Haimyr, his golden head bent over his harp while his hands drew a delicate wordless melody from the strings.

Blackness pressed in, blinding her, and the delicate melody became a woman wailing for the dead, her voice so full of sorrow and despair that Malian thought her own heart might break. The lament slowed into a formal dirge for a warrior slain, and a dark, wild, powerful voice wove through the woman's song until the dream echoed with their shared grief—and desire for revenge.

In the morning the weather had turned bleak, the wind sharp beneath gray skies. Malian turned north into it, her mood mournful as the day. Physically and mentally, she felt exhausted, her failure to persuade the Lost a vast weight on her spirit.

Baz had been right when he said that Stoneford was a long ride. By the time she reached the shrine in the early evening, untended amidst a grove of gnarled olives, pain was drilling into her temples and it was all she could do to slide out of the saddle. The wind's bluster had increased and a spattering of rain fell as she stepped onto the wide covered porch. The acrid scent of earth, touched by the rain's damp, rolled off the dry ground. Malian stopped, her hand on the latch and her forehead resting against the rough oak planks of the door.

The smell was all Aralorn—only she was back in the Gray Lands and it was not rain soaking into the earth, but blood. The wind crying around the shrine's eaves became a woman's disembodied voice: *"There is always a price . . ."*

"A price," Malian echoed. She sank to her knees, her hand sliding away from the bolt, and tears seeped from her eyes and down her cheeks. Her forehead still rested against the door, too heavy to lift clear.

I never mourned, she thought. They told me Rowan Birchmoon was dead and I felt nothing, because there was so much to be done and no time to feel . . . "Anything," she said aloud, and the pain in her temples pounded. The tears were trickling into the corners of her mouth now and she licked them away, tasting the bitter salt. She was the Chosen of Mhaelanar—but what merit was there in picking up the Defender's shield if she had grown arid as the Gray Lands, her feeling nature diverted into a persona such as Maister Carick, who was not real?

Is that why my father kept Rowan with him, Malian wondered, even when he knew that he should not—because without her the part of him that was still Tasarion, and not just the Earl of Night, would no longer exist? Is that why Rowan stayed, when she, too, must have understood the risk?

Only Yorindesarinen's voice answered, sadly weary, in her memory. *"You have grown to hard child, to sacrifice others so ruthlessly for your need. Is this the person you want to be?*

Tarathan showed his trust in me on Imuln's Isle, she told herself, a little desperately; Kalan answered honor and duty's call freely, in the end . . .And I did not compel the Ara-fyr.

She slumped against the door as emotion swirled like a flood, threatening to overwhelm her. The rain grew heavier and eventually she forced herself up and got the cob into the lee of the shrine. The eaves were wide enough that he would be all right there unless the weather really set in. She left her gear strapped behind the saddle, since she was shivering too much to get it down. The door, when she tried the latch, proved to be fastened from the inside, so she wrapped herself in her cloak and curled into the deepest corner of the porch.

The rain continued to fall as the dusk thickened into full night. Malian drifted in and out of an uneasy doze where the pain in her head became the tattoo of hoofbeats from last night's dream. Slipping beneath it, she found herself staring into the darkness-filled opening of a cairn, with Rowan Birchmoon standing just inside the low arch.

*"There is always a price,"* the Winter woman said gravely, before dissipating like blown mist. Malian was left gazing at the dark entrance, and wondered if it could be a portal in disguise. She tried to move forward, but found she couldn't. Dimly, she realized that the shivering had increased and her teeth were chattering.

A voice cursed through the pain in her head, and this time when the cairn appeared, the corvids' wings spiraled around Malian and beat her away from the opening. She heard a crack, like stone splitting, and felt a curious sensation against her forehead—as though someone were writing on it. When she forced her eyes open, all she could see was darkness, filled with the sound of rain, but the pain had receded and her teeth were no longer chattering. She drifted away again and this time she slept.

* * *

Malian woke to pale daylight. After a few puzzled seconds, she realized that she was looking up at a curved wooden ceiling. Someone had covered her with blankets, and when she put up a hand, she found a folded cloak beneath her head. I must be inside the shrine, she decided—although she felt sure the door had been locked. Water still dripped steadily, but she could no longer hear rain. She could smell smoke, though, and when she turned her head she saw that Raven was there.

The smoke curled up in a thin stream, drawn to an opening in the roof, and came from one of the braziers used in the shrines. Raven was sitting on his heels beside it, placing twigs on the glowing coals. Whatever the wood was, it burned with a sharp, aromatic scent. As though sensing her regard, he looked around and she met his darkly blue gaze. His expression was calm and a little considering, but without the sardonic edge she had come to expect. "So you're awake," he said.

"Yes." She supposed she should sit up and demand explanations. But she was warm beneath the blankets and felt oddly peaceful, listening to the drip-drip from the eaves. "I thought the door was locked."

"It was. But these country latches are simple enough to lever open if you have a dagger. You could have done it yourself if you'd been feeling better."

He seemed quieter, Malian thought, less hard. Different— although the edge, she suspected, was still there, just held beneath the surface more. "I imagine I could have." She continued to watch him, still reluctant to move. "You did something. Wrote on my forehead."

"I did. A rune of closing, for the third eye."

She remembered the opening in the cairn and the way she had been drawn to it. "What happened?" she asked. "Did someone work sorcery against me?" And if they did, she thought, why didn't either Nhenir or I sense it?

He shook his head. "I think you caught a fever. It can happen easily enough when you're tired and traveling rough. Some of the wayside inns are riskier still. But you must have been exhausted, because when you began feeling ill your innate power reacted as though you were being attacked on the psychic plane."

"So I turned on myself and the whole process kept escalating." She wanted to shake her head, but refrained in case the headache came back. "How did you know what was happening? Or what to do?"

Raven fed a few more scraps to the brazier, apparently absorbed by the task. "I've seen it before." He dusted his hands against each other. "Not often, though, because it usually only happens to those with very great power who may be at low ebb for other reasons—because of a battle wound, or grief."

Malian's heart lurched. He knows, she thought, every doubt of him rushing back. Or suspects, at least. She knew she should feel afraid and be reaching for her weapons or her power—but despite the initial lurch, she still felt that odd sense of peace. She closed her eyelids briefly, and when she lifted them again he was frowning at her. "The questions will keep," he said, with a trace of his old roughness. "You need to rest."

If he meant her harm, then he had already let ample opportunity pass by—which, Malian decided, made her as safe as she was likely to be in this world. This time, she let her eyes stay closed.

She dreamed of the solitary tower outside Butterworth with a chill wisp of moon rising overhead. When she called out, just as she had a day and a night ago, only silence answered. The season was later, she thought, noticing the spectral trees: this was autumn, the dying season of the year. My vision, Malian realized: I *saw* this, too, in Yorindesarinen's fire. Is that why I failed? she wondered. Would the Lost have answered differently if I had come to them in late autumn, rather than at summer's end?

Foreseeing is just possibility, she reminded herself—but cried out anyway, coming half awake with her need to change the vision, to make it work out this time. Gently, a hand pressed her back. "Let it go," Raven's voice said. "Sleep."

Malian sank down, and when she woke again watery sunshine was slanting through the open door of the shrine. She stretched beneath the blankets and saw that her gear had been stowed by the entrance. Nhenir—this time in the guise of the silver cap—was still tied to her saddlebow and the almost invisible Band sigils on ties and buckles were undisturbed. Raven was sitting on the threshold with his helmet between his hands and his face turned to the sun. His eyes were closed, although the line of his body told her that he was awake. He had woven fetishes of bone and feather into his helmet crest, she noticed, a style he had abandoned while serving Lord Falk.

" 'But you're not,' " she said quietly, meeting his eyes as they opened. "Kalan told me that's what Rhike said to you, before she died. What did she mean?"

"You know her name?" he asked, and she nodded, waiting. "Not what," he said after a moment. "Who. A case of mistaken identity."

"Who?" she echoed, making it another question.

Raven's answering look held a weighing quality. "Emuun, I imagine." His eyes never left hers. "My first kinsman. Our mothers were twins and we have always looked more alike than brothers, at least when he was wearing his own face." He shrugged. "Emuun is Nirn's hound, bringing down anyone the sorcerer names. He could well have been hunting in Emer—and none of the Swarm's other hunters would have expected to see me."

Darksworn, Malian thought, shaken. He really is Darksworn. It explained so much, particularly his knowledge of magic. Yet Lord Falk and Manan, and the rest of the Oakward in Normarch had seemed to trust him. What had Solaan said at The Leas—"*behold the raven of battle.*" As if, Malian thought now, she knew more of him than just the rough hedge knight.

Very slowly, she sat up, avoiding any gesture that might appear threatening. She still had her hideout weapons, she realized; he had not disarmed her. And he had not moved when she did, but remained seated in the doorway, his hands quiet on the helm with its fetish crest.

"So why are you here?" she asked. "What is your business with me?"

The look he gave her back was steady. "I have something that belongs to you," he said. "I wish to return it."

"To me?" she queried, genuinely puzzled now. To compound matters, her stomach rumbled sharply and he grinned, the old familiar twist to his mouth.

"Perhaps," he suggested, "I had better get some food into you first."

"No," she said, because she was still Heir of Night and would not let a Darksworn mock her, even if her memories called him a friend. She stood up, trying to think of what she might have lost. "What do *you* have that is mine?"

Raven rose to his feet as well, setting the helmet aside and keeping his hands in sight as he moved to his own gear, drawing out a leather-tied bundle. He sank onto his heels and untied the bundle with one hand, his eyes never leaving hers. "When your hero and the Chaos Worm both fell, fighting each other," he said, "it was our House, led by Khelor, who reached the battleground first."

"What House?" Lost, Malian thought, I sound lost.

"Fire," said Raven, and she shut her eyes. The House of Fire—but then she had stopped deluding herself that the Darksworn were anything but Derai who truly had gone over to the Swarm ever since se saw her own reflection in the planes of Nherenor's dead face. She drew her ragged breath and opened her eyes, because there must be no truth too hard to be faced, even an enemy wearing the face of a friend.

Nhenir spoke for the first time since Butterworth, its voice both ice and fire. *"Or a friend who wears the face of an enemy."*

Too difficult, Malian thought, and made herself concentrate on Raven.

"We reached the battleground first," he said again, "and since mutilating dead enemies was never Khelor's way, he gave orders that both bodies should be buried. Not together," he added, reading Malian's face. "We searched, but could not find the helm, and the shield was broken. But the hero's blade still lay beneath her hand."

Malian's heart began to slam, the blood like sea-surge in her ears as Raven rose and held out a sword. The scabbard and baldric were both plain black, and well worn; the hilt plaited black leather below a round pommel, with a simple guard. It *is* the sword from the cave, she thought. Despite the weapon's unadorned simplicity it still asked to be grasped in the way that she remembered—held aloft and wielded against one's foes. Yet the armring beneath her sleeve remained inert, and Nhenir, too, was silent. She stared at Raven. "What happened?" she asked, her voice a thread although her seer's sense was alight.

"Khelor took the sword." She recognized the expression on his face now, full of grief and weariness despite the underlying sternness. "It was the greatest prize of all our long war. Or should have been. But as soon as Khelor grasped it, the blade laid a geasa on him—and through him, on us all: to conceal and protect it until the hour it returned to the One-to-Come. The sword was made by a god," he finished grimly, reading Malian's doubt. "Do you think it could not do it?"

She shook her head, not knowing what to think. "You must have tried to break the geasa."

His brief smile was mirthless. "Yes. But also no. Amaliannarath felt that one reason it could place so strong a working on us was because we were already apt to its will. Weary to death of our endless war and its destruction."

Amaliannarath, Malian repeated to herself. She could feel Nhenir's waiting silence as Raven half drew the sword from its scabbard. If the helm had been animate, she would have sworn it was holding its breath. Like the unsheathed weapon in the cave of sleepers, the drawn blade was gray as pewter. "Are you sure?" she said at last. "Yorindesarinen's sword was known as the frost-fire blade."

Raven clicked the hilt home again. "It was like this when we found it. But we would not have held to our course so long for any lesser weapon."

Her thoughts whirled as she recalled the cave of sleepers:

row on row of armed warriors with their companion beasts, horses and hounds and hawks, sleeping beside them. She remembered the biers beneath the three banners as well, two empty and the third holding a captain with a stern face, his expression filled with weariness and grief.

"I *saw* you," she told Raven, "asleep with the sword on your breast. I spoke with the ghost that guarded you all. She told me that it was not yet time for you to wake." She thought about everything that the hedge knight had seemed to know, the years of his experience, glimpsed like a river below winter ice. And when she walked the path of earth and moon at Midsummer, the cave had been empty, the sleeping army gone. "What I saw was far back in time, but I think you have been awake for many years now." The disbelief caught in her throat. "Concealed in plain sight for over a thousand years," she whispered. "Yet no one knew you."

Raven's eyes held hers, a certain wryness in their depths. "No one saw our faces—and the Derai keep to themselves, in any case. But after we woke we saw an opportunity to help rebuild the world broken by their cataclysmic arrival."

Involuntarily, Malian touched the wall to steady herself. She had already guessed, but hearing him say it still set the day spinning around her—or perhaps that was her illness and lack of food. "I can't believe it," she breathed. "Almost since the Cataclysm, *Darksworn* have been keeping the River safe." And helping send the Derai Lost south: secrets within secrets, she thought dizzily.

He smiled, his face resembling that of the warrior in the cave far more than it did the hedge knight from the Long Pass. "We have not really been Darksworn for a very long time," he said. "More Forsworn, like Tarathan and Jehane Mor."

She stared at him, unable to look away, even to the sword he held between his hands. "So who are you," she asked, "when you are with the Patrol?"

"I am the Lord Captain—the last from all three lines of the Blood of Fire." His voice did not change, but she heard the depth of loss. "Raven is a shortening of my real name, which is Aravenor." He looked down at the weapon in his hands, then back up to meet her gaze. "We have kept this for you for a long time. Will you take custody of your sword, Heir of Night?"

Slowly, Malian took a step forward. She still felt light-headed and hesitated even when he extended the blade toward her. Nhenir remained silent and no fire blazed from Yorindesarinen's armring. Could the sword itself be a trap? she wondered. She studied Raven's—Aravenor's—face, but could read nothing there except patience. Delicately, she probed at the sword with her seeker's sense and felt the geasa bound into it. No, she thought after another moment, a geasa *within* a geasa: the first binding that had been placed on Khelor and his House; and a second that waited for her alone.

*"A promise made to the dying."* The mindvoice whispered out of the blade, but she recognized it from the cave of sleepers. *"I brought both the sword and the House of Fire here, to this world of Haarth, in exchange for a pledge."*

She raised her eyes to Aravenor's again, and now his look was quizzical as well as patient. He doesn't know about the second geasa, she thought, her truth sense sure. *"But you do,"* she added to Nhenir. *"It bound you to silence as well, didn't it? And through you, the armring."*

*"The arms of Yorindesarinen are one,"* Nhenir told her, *"as well as three. And a pledge made to the dying is binding across worlds and time."*

Malian was silent, her eyes fixed on the unadorned sword. In its way, it was as shabby as Raven had been, the day they first met in the Long Pass. Her stomach grumbled again and his lips moved, the slightest twitch, although he still said nothing, just waited for her to take back what was hers.

" 'I brought both the sword and the House of Fire here,' " she repeated aloud, and his brows arched up. The images replayed themselves in her mind: the cave of sleepers and then the secret helms of the Patrol, keeping Road and River safe for over a thousand years. *I am dead,* the ghost voice whispered out of memory. *I died a long time ago, so that they might live.*

"So now I can't have one without the other." Malian extended her hands and placed them beside Aravenor's on the scabbard. His eyes met hers again and she saw the dawn of understanding there. Her heart began to pound, because of the Ara-fyr, although she kept her voice steady. "But will you have me?" she asked. "That is the other part of why you rode into Emer, isn't it?"

Aravenor nodded. "As soon as I heard your name spoken by Jehane Mor in the very early spring, the sword woke and began to draw me to you. Yet we have served as the Patrol for a long time. Like the Ara-fyr, we have found a place in this world. And we have seen how far the Derai have fallen. The sword is yours by right—but the House of Fire is not for giving over to just anyone because of a title and a scrap of prophecy."

No, Malian thought. "And now?" she asked. "Having looked me over?"

His mouth twitched again, but his gaze did not waver. "I found a great deal to like in Carick the scholar, and I admired the Shadow Band adept's abilities. But I still needed to know more of who Malian of Night was."

Malian swallowed. She could not stop her hands tightening on the scabbard, even though he would see the sign of tension. Her mouth was dry, unable to frame another question. And if he refuses me, she thought, do I also lose the sword?

"I was there by the Butterworth tower," Aravenor continued. Her head jerked back and one of his hands shifted, closing over hers. "Your seeking would not have found me because I am largely immune to magic—that is one of the abilities Emuun and I share, and a major reason, I imagine, why Rhike mistook me for him."

Immune, Malian thought: of course—another thread out of the oldest histories. But if he had been in Butterworth, then he would have witnessed her failure. She was not surprised when he withdrew his hand.

"I was there," Aravenor repeated quietly. "As I said, I have admired your abilities for some time. But the night before last, in Butterworth, I admired you. I thought you just might be worth every scrap of that tattered prophecy." Raven's irony colored Aravenor's slight smile. "We are yours—if you will have *us*, Malian of Night."

A Darksworn House, Malian thought, and wondered if the world might shatter. But rainwater still dripped from the shrine's eaves and the rest of the Haarth day continued on its course, apparently untroubled.

Aravenor stepped back, lifting his hands from the sword, and Malian took it fully into her own. Slowly, she drew the weapon clear of its sheath, listening to Nhenir's deep silence as she tested the blade for weight and balance. Faith has been kept, she thought, remembering her conversation with the Ara-fyr. "I will honor the pledge made, so long ago," she said softly. "I take back what is rightfully mine—and will have the House of Fire as my own."

The answering shock of power jolted through the sword's hilt and up her arm. Silver fire blazed from her armring and along the blade, turning it to glittering frost—and Nhenir sang. The paean was an exultation of fire and moonlight and ice, and Malian's farseeing answered, clear as a winter dawn. Far away on the Wall of Night she saw her father's head lift from contemplation of a cold hearth, his shoulders straightening. In a hold close to the Gray Lands, in a room without windows, a huddled figure lifted a ravaged face, life creeping back into her lightless eyes as though she, too, heard Nhenir's song.

"Nhairin," Malian whispered, but the song was already fading and her farsight with it. She was shaking, too, from the aftermath of her illness, the shock of power, and the fire of her vision. Gently, Aravenor took the sword from her and sheathed it, then knelt and buckled belt and scabbard around her waist—a squire's duty, but she could not have managed it for herself just then. She rested a hand on his shoulder and the world steadied.

"I will have the House of Fire as my own," she repeated quietly. "For as long as you will freely follow me." And still the world stayed whole.

He stood up. "And I, Malian of Night," he said, in the voice that was both Raven's and a stranger's, "will ride in your shadow. Either until I meet my death, or together we find the far side of the long conflict between the Swarm and the Derai."

Here ends The Wall of Night Book Two,
*The Gathering of the Lost*;
To be continued in The Wall of Night Book Three,
*Daughter of Blood.*

# Glossary

**Abjured:** Jhainarian epithet for the renegade queen Zhe-haamor and her Seven

**Academy:** Ijiri Academy of Sages, one of the *Three of Ij*

**Academy Island:** one of the central islands forming the city if Ij; location of Academy of Sages

**Ado:** Emerian knight in training

**Aeln:** honor guard, serving House of Night

**Aenide:** younger sister to Jarna, a Normarch squire

**Aeris:** city kingdom in the lands beyond the River

**Aldermere:** liege-hold of Falk of Normarch, Castellan of Emer's Northern March

**Alianor:** companion of Ghiselaine, Countess of Ormond

**Alliance:** See *Derai*

**Alric of Vast:** Emerian knight, from the Wymark

**Amaliannarath:** a power of the Swarm

**Ambardi:** merchant family of Ij, of the lesser nobility

**Amarn:** Darkswarm adept, sworn to the sorcerer Nirn

**Annot:** damosel of Normarch

**Ar:** city of the River

**Arad:** one of Queen Zhineve-An's Seven

**Aralorn:** land south of the River

**Aranraith:** a leader of the Darkswarm

**Aravenor:** a captain of the Patrol

**Arcolin:** a Swarm envoy in Emer

**Argent:** one of the main rivers of Emer

**Arin:** lieutenant to the Lord Captain of the Patrol

**Arn:** Emerian knight in training

**Arun-En:** town on the Wildenrush

**Asantir:** formerly captain of the Earl of Night's *Honor Guard* and now *Commander of Night*

**Asha:** an honor guard serving House of Night

**Assassins:** see the *School of Assassins*

**Athiri:** princely family of Ij

**Audin Sondargent:** Emerian knight in training, nephew to the Duke of Emer

**Avice:** damosel of Normarch

**Aymil:** guard in the service of Normarch

**Barren Hills:** uninhabited hills to the south of the Border Mark

**Barrowdun:** clan territory of the Emerian Hill people

**Bartrand Ar-Griffon:** Captain of Normarch; see also *Ser Bartrand*

**Baz:** blacksmith in Butterworth

**bellbird:** songbird native to the Ij area

**black blades:** weapons of power, commonly associated with the hero Kerem

**black spear:** one of the legendary black blades

**Black Tower:** fortress and original ducal palace in Caer Argent; said to date back to the Old Empire

**blood oath, a:** powerful binding used by the Derai where the one swearing draws their own blood; it can never be broken

**Blood, the:** includes Earls of the Derai and any of their blood kin. Traditionally, the Blood have been closely linked to the power of the Golden Fire

**Blood Oath, the:** oath that has bound the Derai since the Time of Blood and institutionalizes the schism between the warrior and priestly castes

**Bonamark:** one of the seven marks of Emer; shortening of Bonacon Mark

**Boras:** priest of the House of Adamant, from the Keep of Stone

**Border Mark:** stone pillar that marks the boundary between the Gray Lands and the Barren Hills

**Brackwater:** islet on the seaward side of Ij

**Brania Sondmurre:** damosel of Normarch

**Bridge of Boats:** pontoon bridge in Ij, joining Minstrels' Island to *Landward*

**Butterworth:** village in southern Aralorn

**Caer Argent:** capital of Emer

**Carick Maister:** graduate of university in Ar, a city of the River lands, newly appointed as cartographer to Duke of Emer

**Caril Sondargent:** Duke of Emer

**Castellan:** ruler of an Emerian march

**Cataclysm:** period of extreme natural disaster, followed by war, that brought down the Old Empire; believed to have occurred as a result of the Derai's arrival on Haarth

**Cave of Sleepers:** cavern of sleeping warriors, deep within the Gate of Dreams

**Chaos Worm:** according to legend, the deadliest foe ever sent by the Swarm against the Derai

**Child of Night:** see *Malian*

**Chosen of Mhaelanar:** prophesied hero who will unite the Derai for the final victory, born of both the House of Stars and the House of Night

**Cloud Hold:** satellite fort of the Keep of Winds

**Col:** master archer at Normarch

**College:** Ijiri College of Minstrels, one of the Three of Ij

**Commander of Night:** overall military commander of the Keep of Winds and the House of Night

**Company of Engineers:** corps based in Ar, on the River, that maintains the great Main Road

**Conclave:** yearly meeting of the rulers of Ij

**Conservatory:** main performance hall of the College of Minstrels, in Ij

**Coreil:** noble family of Ij

**Count Ambard:** leader of Ambardi family of Ij

**Crosshills:** Emerian village, in the Northern March

**Cynithia Ambard:** Mykon Ambard's mother, Prince Ilvaine's niece

**Dame Nelys:** chaperone of the Girls' Dorter, at Normarch

**damosel:** young Emerian woman of knightly or noble birth

**Dancer in Shadows:** one of the three gods of Ij, patron of assassins; see also *Kan, Karn, Ka*

**Darin:** guard in the service of Normarch

**darkspawn:** term for minions of the Swarm of Dark

**Darkswarm:** another name for Swarm of Dark

**Darksworn:** vanguard of the Swarm of Dark

**Daughter of Blood:** title given to a daughter of the Earl of Blood

**Defender:** see *Mhaelanar*

**demonhunters:** servants of Ishnapuri magi who track and kill demons

**Denuli:** merchant clan of Ij

**Derai Alliance:** formal alliance of the nine Houses of the Derai

**Derai:** warlike race, alien to Haarth, comprising nine Houses and worshipping nine Gods. They arrived on Haarth fifteen hundred years before and brought with them their traditional enemy, the Swarm of Dark. The Derai, fighting an eons old war to stop the Swarm obliterating the universe, are divided into three societies or castes: warrior, priest, and a third caste that comprises both warrior and priestly talents but is focused on some other skill

**desmesne:** Emerian term for the holding of land, whether large or small, associated with a particular castle

**Doria:** Malian's nurse, killed in a surprise attack on the Keep of Winds, five years before

**dorter:** Emerian term for a hall or dormitory for either young men or women of the knightly and noble classes

**drinker of blood:** see *Kan*

**Ducal Guard:** the elite guard of the Duke's of Emer

**Duke of Emer:** ruler of Emer; see also *Caril Sondargent*

**Dunmuir Slough:** extensive wetland in the Emerian Hills

**Eanar:** honor guard, serving the House of Night

**Earl of Night:** hereditary ruler of the House of Night

**Earl of Swords:** hereditary ruler of the House of Swords

**eave owl:** small owl, native to the River, found in both city and countryside

**Eight:** ward, protective against magic

**Elite:** title for commanders in Ar's *Shadow Band*

**Elite Cairon:** a leader of the Shadow Band

**Emaln:** city of the River; feuding with Sirith

**Emalni:** citizens of Emaln

**Emer:** a land of Haarth, located south of the River

**Emeriath:** figure from Derai legend, who appears in the songs and stories concerning *Kerem the Dark Handed*

**empathy bond:** also *spirit bond*: an empathic/psychic link between two Derai that can be either one or two-way; usually occurs between two who are either blood kin, lovers, or very close friends

**Emuun:** Swarm agent

**Enna:** damosel of Normarch

**Ephors:** elected rulers of the River city of Terebanth

**Erennis:** prince of Ar, one of the major cities on the River

**Eria:** initiate priestess, serving in the Temple of Night

**Erron:** horsemaster at Normarch

**facestealer:** minion of the Swarm

**Fair Maid of Emer:** Ghiselaine, Countess of Ormond

**Falath:** one of Rowan Birchmoon's hounds

**Fall of Night:** feared twilight of the Derai and then all worlds, should the House of Night ever fall

**Farelle:** city of the River

**farsight:** power of farseeing, ability to see events across physical distance and time

**Festival of Masks:** spring festival of Ij

**First:** captain of a Jhainarain Seven

**First Kin:** first degree of kinship to the direct line of the Blood of any of the nine Houses of the Derai; common meaning is "cousin"

**First Night:** vigil, sacred to women, held on the first night of the Midsummer festival dedicated to the goddess Imuln

**Forsaken:** Jhainarian epithet for the renegade queen Zhehaamor and her Seven

**Garan:** honor guard, serving House of Night

**Gate of Dreams:** a place between worlds and times that can be reached through dreams or via mind- or spirit-walking

**Gate of Winds:** main entrance into the Keep of Winds, and a fortress in its own right

**Ghiselaine:** Countess of Ormond, a region of Emer

**Gille:** Emerian knight in training

**Girls' Dorter:** hall that houses the Normarch damosels

**Girvase:** Emerian knight in training

**Gol:** warrior of the House of Swords

**Golden Fire:** a power and strength of the Derai that once burned in the nine keeps, until the Great Betrayal

**Grayharbor:** northenmost settlement between the River and the Wall of Night

**Gray Lands:** desolate plains that adjoin Wall of Night

**Great Betrayal:** refers to the Derai civil war and its intended end when the peace feast turned into a night of slaughter between House and House, warrior and priest, kin and kin

**Guild House:** place where heralds reside, found in every River city

**Guild of Heralds:** society of messengers, said to have special powers, based in the River lands; see also *heralds*

**Guyon:** Emerian knight in training

**Haarth:** the world in which this story is set

**Haimyr the Golden:** minstrel of Ij, great-nephew to Prince Ilvaine; friend and retainer to the Earl of Night

**Hamar Sondsangre:** Emerian knight in training

**Hawk:** Emerian Hill chieftain

**Heir of Night:** designated successor of the Earl of the House of Night; see also *Malian*

**helm of concealment:** River phrase for the helmets used by the Patrol

**heralds:** messengers trained by and bound to the Guild of Heralds, based on the River; see also *Guild of Heralds*

**Heris:** itinerant scribe

**Herun:** tracker at Normarch

**High Hall:** main hall of a Derai fortress

**High Steward:** head steward, oversees most of the civilian affairs of a Derai keep; see also *Nhairin*

**High Tor:** landmark in the Emerian hills

**Highvert:** seat of the Lord Warden of Emer's Vertward

**Hillholt:** clan territory of Emerian Hill people

**Hills:** hill country lying partly in Emer, partly in Aralorn

**Hirluin Sondargent:** Duke of Emer's heir

**Hirn:** Emerian Hill chieftain

**hold:** satellite fort of the main Derai strongholds on the Wall

**Honor Captain:** captain of a Derai Honor Guard; see also *Asantir*

**Honor Guard:** an elite guard specially sworn to protect the lives of Derai leaders, mainly the Earls of the Nine Houses

**House of Adamant:** priestly House of the Derai Alliance

**House of Blood:** warrior House of the Derai Alliance

**House of Morning:** priestly House of the Derai Alliance

**House of Night:** warrior House of the Derai Alliance; claims to be the "first and oldest" of all the Nine Houses

**House of Peace:** priestly House of the Derai Alliance

**House of Swords:** warrior House of the Derai Alliance

**Houses:** name given by the Derai to the nine separate clans or peoples who comprise the Derai Alliance; see also *Nine Houses*

**Hunt of Mayanne:** a power that dwells beyond the Gate of Dreams

**Hunt, the:** see *Hunt of Mayanne*

**Hylcarian:** Golden Fire of the Keep of Winds; see *Golden Fire*

**Ij:** the Golden, greatest city of the River, built on the delta between the river Ijir and the sea

**Ijir:** the main river of the lands known as the River

**Ijiri:** person or thing native to Ij

**Ilaise:** damosel of Normarch

**Ileyra:** herald of the Guild house in Ishnapur; sister to Salan

**Ilkerineth:** a leader of the Darkswarm

**Ilvaine:** one of the great merchant families of Ij

**Imul:** southern Aralorn name for Imulun

**Imuln:** Emerian name for Imulun

**Imulun:** Mother Goddess, one of the three gods of the River and the lands beyond

**Innor:** honor guard, serving the House of Night

**Ishnapur:** fabled city and empire in the south of the known world, which borders the great western deserts of Haarth

**Isolt:** damosel of Normarch

**Isperia Katran:** Master of the Academy of Sages; kin to Prince Ilvaine

**J'mair:** famed poet of Ishnapur, whose work has survived down centuries

**Jan:** girl in the village of Butterworth, in Aralorn

**Jaransor:** range of uninhabited hills west of the Gray Lands

**Jarna:** Emerian knight in training

**Jehane Mor:** herald of the Guild, from the Guild House of Terebanth, a city on the River

**Jhaine:** a land of Haarth, located on the route to Ishnapur

**Jhainarians:** people hailing from Jhaine, also the Shah of Ishnapur's elite auxiliary troops; see also *Seven, a*

**Jharin:** Darkswarm adept, sworn to the sorcerer Nirn

**Ka:** Aralorn name for *Kan*

**Kalan:** friend of Malian's, born to the House of Blood

**Kan:** one of the three gods of the River and lands beyond; see also *Dancer in Shadow, drinker of blood*

**Karn:** Emerian name for *Kan*

**Katrani:** merchant family of Ij; allied to the Ilvaine

**Keep of Stone:** stronghold of the House of Adamant

**Keep of Winds:** stronghold of the House of Night

**Kelmé:** child prince in the history of Ar; the Shadow Band was formed to protect his life

**Kerem the Dark Handed:** ancient hero of the Derai

**Keron:** honor guard, serving the House of Night

**Khelor:** a Darksworn leader

**Kiyan:** First of Queen Zharaan of Jhaine, who lived in the years following the Cataclysm

**Kyr:** guard, formerly serving the House of Night

**Lady Bonamark:** wife of the Lord of Bonamark, in Emer

**Lady Sarifa:** demonhunter, from Ishnapur

**Land Marks:** Emerian administrative territories lying between the six inner wards and four outer marches, ruled by the Marklords. The marks are named for heraldic beasts: Allerion, Bonacon (called Bonamark), Chough, Griffon, Lyon, and Wyvern (called Wymark)

**Landward:** island in the city of Ij, immediately to the north of the river port and joined to Minstrels' Island by a pontoon bridge; see also *Bridge of Boats*

**Lannorth:** lieutenant of the Earl of Night's Honor Guard

**lantern boats:** river craft used in Ij; the annual races are held during the Festival of Masks

**Lathayra:** a land south of Emer

**Low of Meraun:** a code followed by the Derai House of Peace

**Lawr:** honor guard, serving the House of Night

**Leto Ilvaine:** grandson of Prince Ilvaine

**Lien:** assassin of Ij

**Lily of Ormond, the:** Ghiselaine, Countess of Ormond

**Linden:** Winter Country shaman and spring-singer for Rowan Birchmoon's clan

**Linnet:** companion to Ghiselaine, Countess of Ormond

**Lion Throne:** throne and also court of the Shah of Ishnapur

**Lira:** guard, formerly serving the House of Night

**Long Pass:** main pass into Emer when coming from the River

**Lord Bonamark:** Marklord of Bonamark, in Emer

**Lord Captain:** overall commander of the Patrol

**Lord Falk:** Castellan of the Northern March of Emer

**Lord Isrradin:** Ishnapur's ambassador to the River lands

**Lost:** Derai with old powers who have fled the Wall of Night and disappeared into Haarth

**Luin:** page in the ducal palace at Caer Argent

**lurkers:** common name for a species of Swarm minion; also *smotherers*

**Lyinor:** legendary lady of Emer and doomed springtime love of the hero *Rolan*; both are remembered in a *spring song*

**Madder:** red roan warhorse, belonging to the squire Jarna

**Madness:** condition associated with Jaransor

**Main Road:** road that runs the length of the River lands, maintained by the Company of Engineers from Ar and kept safe by the Patrol

**Maister:** Haarth term for a scholar or teacher

**Maister Carick:** see *Carick*

**Maister Gervon:** priest of Serrut and teacher at Normach

**Malian:** only child of the Earl of the House of Night, also known as *Heir of Night, Child of Night,* and *Daughter of Night*

**Malisande:** companion of Ghiselaine, Countess of Ormond

**Mallow:** Normarch horse, allocated to Carick

**Manan:** Normarch inn wife and healer

**Many-As-One:** name the Swarm of Dark's adherents call themselves

**march:** border territory of Emer

**mark:** see *Land Marks*

**Marten:** guard in the service of Normarch

**Masters of Ij:** heads of the Three of Ij; also includes the leaders of the princely and merchant houses

**Mayanne:** one of the Nine Gods of the Derai

**Meraun:** the Healer, one of the Nine Gods of the Derai

**messenger horses:** horses, usually black, belonging to the Derai messenger corps; famed for their endurance and speed

**Mhaelanar:** *Defender* (or Defender of Heaven), one of the Nine Gods of the Derai, also called the Beloved of the Nine, Great Strategist, and Shield of the Derai

**mindburned:** result of a form of psychic attack; see *mindsweep*

**mindspeech:** communicating directly from mind to mind, an old Derai power; see *powers*

**mindsweep:** a wave of psychic power, designed to sweep away any obstacle in its path

**Minstrels' Island:** one of the central islands forming the city if Ij; location of the College of Minstrels

**Miro:** assassin of Ij

**moon-bright helm:** part of the arms of the hero Yorindesarinen; see *Nhenir*

**Morin:** honor guard, serving the House of Night
**Mother Goddess:** see *Imulun*
**Mykon Ambard:** envoy of the Assassins' School and great-nephew to Prince Ilvaine
**Naia:** caretaker of the heralds' Guild House in Ij
**Nerion:** Malian's mother, the Earl of Night's former wife
**Nerys:** honor guard, serving the House of Night
**Nevi:** boatman of Ij
**New Keep:** newer, inhabited stronghold of the Keep of Winds
**Nhairin:** former High Steward of the Keep of Winds
**Nherenor:** a Swarm envoy in Emer
**Nhenir:** moon-bright helm, part of the arms of the hero Yorindesarinen
**Nindorith:** a power of the Darkswarm
**Nine Gods:** nine gods of the Derai: *Hurulth, Kharalth, Mayanne, Meraun, Mhaelenar, Ornorith, Tawr, Terennin, Thiandriath*
**Nine Houses:** nine Houses of the Derai Alliance
**Nine Queens:** nine priestess-queens who jointly rule Jhaine
**Nirn:** Swarm sorcerer
**Normarch:** stronghold of the Castellan of the Northern March
**North Gate:** northern exit from the city of Ij, on island known as The Sleeve
**Oakward:** secret society, said to exist in Emer to resist evil
**Oath, the:** see *Blood Oath*
**Old Earl:** current Earl of Night's father, Malian's grandfather, now deceased
**Old Empire:** empire said to have existed prior to the Derai arrival on Haarth, stretched from Jaransor to Ishnapur
**Old Keep:** original Keep of Winds, now abandoned
**One:** prophesied hero who will come to unite the Derai and defeat the Swarm, predicted to be born of the Blood of the Houses of Night and Stars
**One-to-Come:** see *One*
**one voice:** term for the herald habit of speaking in unison
**Onyx:** horse belonging to the Emerian squire Girvase
**Orn:** Swarm warrior

**Ornorith:** known as Ornorith of the Two Faces, one of the Nine Gods of the Derai, Goddess of Luck; depicted as having two, masked faces, looking in opposite directions

**Orth:** warrior of the House of Swords

**outsiders:** Derai term for the non-Derai peoples of Haarth

**Patrol:** corps that keeps the peace along road and river, between the independent cities of the River lands

**Perfumed City:** capital city of Ishnapur

**powers:** supernatural and magical powers of the Derai, once used to combat the Swarm of Darkness. They include: ability to command objects and forces, both natural and physical; understanding the speech of beasts and birds; acute eyesight and hearing, including seeing in the dark and hearing outside normal human range; chameleon ability to blend into surrounding materials and elements; dreaming; empathic spirit bond; farseeing and foreseeing; fire calling; illusion working; mindspeaking; mind- and spiritwalking; psychic shielding; prophecy; seeking; truthsaying; and weatherworking

**Prince Ath:** head of the Athiri, one of the princely families of Ij

**Prince Ilvaine:** head of the Ilvaine kin, one of the princely families of Ij

**Princess Coreil:** head of the Coreil kin, one of the princely families of Ij

**Raher:** Emerian knight in training

**Raptor of Darkness:** Swarm power, a psychic vampire and eater of souls

**Rastem:** First of a Jhainarian Seven, serving Queen Zhineve-An

**Raven:** hedge knight

**Rhike:** Swarm adept

**Rindle:** river in the Northern March of Emer

**River, the:** lands along the Ijir River system, mainly comprising city states such as Ij, Terebanth, and Ar. Also known as the River lands

**river port:** Ij's port for barges and galleys plying the Ijir and its tributaries

**Ro:** damosel of Normarch

**Road Gate:** gate where the great Main Road enters the city of Ij

**Rolan:** legendary hero of Emer and doomed springtime love of *Lyinor*; both are remembered in a *spring song*

**Rowan Birchmoon:** shaman of the Winter People, consort of the Earl of Night; see also *Winter Woman*

**Sable:** horse belonging to the damosel Alianor, in Emer

**Salan:** herald of the Guild house in Ishnapur, brother to *Ileyra*

**Sarathion:** lieutenant to the Lord Captain of the *Patrol*

**Sark:** guard in the service of Normarch

**Sarus:** veteran sergeant of the Earl of Night's Honor Guard

**School of Assassins:** Ijiri School of Assassins; one of the *Three of Ij*

**Sea House:** House of the Derai Alliance, traditionally known as "the navigators"

**Sea Keep:** stronghold of the *Sea House*

**Seasonal Analects:** rare work by the famed poet *J'mair* of Ishnapuri

**Secret Isle:** island of Ij, home of the School of Assassins

**seeing:** power to foretell and see future events

**seeker:** one with power to seek out the hidden and find the lost

**seeking:** active use of a seeker's power

**seer:** one who has the power to foretell and see into the future

**Selia:** damosel of Normarch

**Ser Alric:** knight of Wymark, in Emer

**Ser Amain:** captain of Lady Bonamark's knights-at-arms

**Ser Bartrand:** Bartrand Ar-Griffon, captain of Normarch

**Serinna Sondcendre:** queen of the Midsummer tourney in Emer; cousin to Ser Ombrose Sondargent, the Duke's champion

**Serivis:** toll clerk of Farelle, on the River

**Ser Ombrose Sondargent:** Duke of Emer's champion, but also his nephew; cousin to Audin Sondargent. Hirluin Sondargent

**Ser Rannart:** knight commander of Normarch

**Serru:** southern Aralorn name for Seruth

**Serrut:** Emerian name for Seruth

**Seruth:** one of the three gods of the River and lands beyond, the lightbringer and guardian of journeys

**Seven:** name of a power working, sacred to Imuln

**Seven, a:** elite *Jhainarian* warriors bound together in a unit; escort of the priestess-queens of Jhaine and may also be associated with the Ishnapuri magi

**Shadow Band:** initiates of Kan sworn to protect the Princes of Ar; not aligned with the Ijiri Assassins' School

**Shah:** title of the ruler of Ishnapur

**shielding:** power to conceal objects or people from both physical and psychic search

**siren worm:** powerful minion of the Swarm

**Sirith:** city of the River, feuding with Emaln

**smotherers:** see *lurkers*

**Solaan:** instructor for the squire training at Normarch

**Sondargent wolf:** nickname for Ser Ombrose Sondargent, the Duke of Emer's champion

**Sorriyith:** a captain of the Jhainarian Guard, from Ishnapur

**Southern Realms:** the lands of Haarth that lie between the great deserts beyond Ishnapur; also called the Southern Lands

**Stoners:** derogatory term for Derai from the House of Adamant

**spring song:** song form that celebrates Emer's tradition of *springtime love*

**springtime love:** Emerian tradition of romance between young men and women of the knightly and noble classes, where politics and family duty make marriage unlikely

**swallowtail swords:** twin swords with curved tips, favored in Haarth's South

**Swarm of Dark:** enemy of the Derai; a vast entity comprising many fell creatures; see also *darkspawn, Darkswarm, Darksworn, Many-As-One*

**Swift:** river in the Northern March of Emer

**Syrus:** one of Queen Zhineve-An's Seven

**Tarathan of Ar:** herald of the Guild, from the Guild House of Terebanth, a city on the River

**Tasarion:** current Earl, hereditary ruler of the House of Night

**Tasian:** Heir of Stars at the time of the Great Betrayal

**Telemanthar:** Swordsman of the Stars, an ancient hero of the Derai, twin brother of Errianthar the Priestess

**Temple in the Rock:** one of the oldest shrines to Imuln in Emer

**Temple quarter:** temple complex in a Derai keep, comprising the temples and adjunct buildings dedicated to all of the Nine Gods, plus living quarters of the priesthood

**Temple of Night:** the temple precinct in the Keep of Winds

**Temple of Seruth:** precinct in Ij dedicated to the god Seruth

**Teneseti:** noble family of Ij, allied to the Ilvaine

**Tenneward:** one of the six wards of Emer

**Ter:** honor guard, serving the House of Night

**Terebanth:** city of the River

**Terennin:** one of the Nine Gods of the Derai, known as both the Far-seeing and Farseer, also the Artisan or Artificer, as well as the Lord of the Dawn Eyes

**Teron:** follower of the Earl of Night

**The Leas:** a meadow area on Emer's nothern march and the site of a former village

**The Sleeve:** an island in the northern part of the city of Ij, where the North Gate is located

**Three:** common foreshortening of the *Three of Ij*

**Three of Ij:** the three main powers that rule the city of Ij: sages, minstrels, and assassins

**Tibalt:** Emerian knight in training

**Tirorn:** warrior of the House of Swords

**Token-bearer:** one who bears a ring said to have been made by Terennin, which is called the Token

**Torlun:** priest of the House of Adamant, from the Keep of Stone

**Two-Faced Goddess:** see *Ornorith*

**Var:** initiate priest, serving in the Temple of Night

**Vast:** Emerian town in Wymark, on the border with the Southern March

**Vern:** initiate priest, serving in the Temple of Night

**Vertward:** one of six inner wards of Emer, lying to the west and south of Caer Argent

**Vhirinal:** an Ephor of the city of Terebanth, on the River

**Wall:** common foreshortening of the *Wall of Night*

**Wall of Night:** vast mountain range that protects Haarth from the Swarm, garrisoned by the Derai Alliance, and said to have been created by the House of Night; also called Shield-wall of Night

**Wards:** six administrative territories surrounding Caer Argent in Emer, ruled by the Lords Warden and named for heraldic colors: Vertward, Gulesward, Azurward, Murreward, Tenneward, and Cendreward

**weirdling:** House of Swords term for a magic user

**Welun:** Normarch smith

**were-hunt:** a power of the Swarm

**were-hunters:** individuals that comprise a were-hunt

**Western Mountains:** range that froms the western border of Emer

**Westgate:** one of the largest islands forming the city of Ij, and the one closest to the western Road Gate; contains several market squares and a large warehouse quarter with headquarters of several major trading houses and embassies from other River cities

**Westwind Hold:** satellite fort of the Keep of Winds

**Wildenrush:** a major tributary of the river Ijir

**Winter Country:** vast steppes in the north of Haarth, inhabited by the Winter People

**Winter Woman:** see *Rowan Birchmoon*

**Wolf:** Winter Country shaman; Rowan Birchmoon's uncle

**wolfpack:** River and Emerian term for an outlaw band

**wolf's head:** an outlaw

**Wymark:** one of the six marks of Emer; shortening of Wyvern Mark

**wyr hounds:** hounds of the Derai, able to track psychic trails and those with psychic powers

**Xeria:** a priestess of the House of Stars at the time of the Great Betrayal, reputed to be one of the greatest power wielders born to the Derai; also called Star of the Derai

**Yorindesarinen:** greatest hero of the Derai. Heir of the House of Stars in her day, she slew the Worm of Chaos but died of the wounds received in that battle; also referred to as the Child of Stars

**Yris:** Patrol river pilot

**Zarn:** one of Queen Zhineve-An's Seven

**Zharaan:** a priestess-queen of Jhaine in the years following the Cataclysm

**Zhehaamor:** a priestess-queen of Jhaine

**Zhineve-An:** a priestess-queen of Jhaine

**Zorem:** one of Queen Zhineve-An's Seven

*If you haven't read the first
volume in the Wall of Night saga,
keep reading to see where it all began.*

THE HEIR OF NIGHT

*Available now wherever books are sold*

# 1

## The Keep of Winds

The wind blew out of the northwest in dry, fierce gusts, sweeping across the face of the Gray Lands. It clawed at the close-hauled shutters and billowed every tapestry and hanging banner in the keep. Loose tiles rattled and slid, bouncing off tall towers into the black depths below; as the wind whistled through the Old Keep, finding every crack and chink in its shutters and blowing the dust of years along the floors. It whispered in the tattered hangings that had once graced the High Hall, back in those far-off days when the hall had blazed with light and laughter, gleaming with jewel and sword. Now the cool, dry fingers of wind teased their frayed edges and banged a whole succession of doors that long neglect had loosened on their hinges. Stone and mortar were still strong, even here, and the shutters held against the elements, but everything else was given over to the slow corrosion of time.

Another tile banged and rattled its way down the roof as a slight figure swarmed up one of the massive stone pillars that marched along either side of the hall. There was an alarming creak as the climber swung up and over the balustrade of a wooden gallery, high above the hall floor—but the timbers held. The climber paused, looking around with satisfaction, and wiped dusty hands on the seat of her plain, black pants.

A narrow, wooden staircase twisted up toward another, even higher gallery of sculpted stone, but the treads stopped just short of the top. She studied the gap, her eyes narrowed as they traced the leap she would need to make: from the top of the stair to the gargoyles beneath the stone balcony, and then up, by a series of precarious finger- and toe-holds, onto the balcony itself.

The girl frowned, knowing that to miss that jump would mean plummeting to certain death, then shrugged and began to climb, testing each wooden tread before trusting her weight to it. She paused again on the topmost step, then sprang, her first hand slapping onto a corbel while the other grasped at a gargoyle's half-spread wing. She hung for a moment, swinging, then knifed her feet up onto the gargoyle's claws before scrambling over the high shoulder and into the gallery itself. Her eyes shone with triumph and excitement as she stared through the rear of the gallery into another hall.

Although smaller than the High Hall below, she could see that it had once been richer and more elegant. Beneath the dust, the floors were a mosaic of beasts, birds, and trailing vines; panels of metal and jeweled glass decorated the walls. There was a dais at the far end of the long room, with the fragile remains of a tapestry draped on the wall behind it. The hanging would have been bright with color once, the girl thought; the whole hall must have glowed with it, but it was a dim and lifeless place now.

She stepped forward, then jumped and swung around as her reflection leapt to life in the mirrored walls. A short, slightly built girl stared back at her out of eyes like smoke in a delicately chiseled face. She continued to stare for a moment, then poked her tongue out at the reflection, laughing at her own fright. "This must be the Hall of Mirrors," she said, pitching her voice against the silence. She knew that Yorindesarinen herself would have walked here once, if all the tales were true, and Telemanthar, the Swordsman of Stars. But now there was only emptiness and decay.

She walked the length of the hall and stepped onto the shallow dais. Most of the tapestry on the rear wall had de-

cayed into shreds or been eaten by moths, but part of the
central panel was still intact. The background was darkness, rimmed with fire, but the foreground was occupied by
a figure in hacked and riven armor, confronting a creature
that was as vast as the tapestry itself. Its flat, serpentine
head loomed out of the surrounding darkness, exuding
menace, and its bulk was doom. The figure of the hero,
dwarfed beneath its shadow, looked overmatched and very
much alone.

The girl touched the battered figure with her fingertips,
then pulled back as the fabric crumbled further. "The hero
Yorindesarinen," she whispered, "and the Worm of Chaos.
This should never have been left here, to fall into ruin." She
hummed a thread of tune that was first martial, then turned
to haunting sadness as she slid forward, raising an imaginary
sword against an unseen opponent. Her eyes were half closed
as she became the fated hero in her mind, watching the legendary frost-fire gleam along her blade.

Another door banged in the distance and a voice called,
echoing along silent corridors and through the dusty hall.
"Malian! Mal—lee-ee—aan, my poppet!" The Old Keep
caught the voice and tossed it into shadowy corners, bouncing echoes off stone and shutter while the wind whispered
all around. "Where are you-oo-oo? Is this fit behavior for a
Lady of Night? You are naught but an imp of wickedness,
child!"

The door banged again, cutting off the voice, but the
damage was done. The bright figure of Yorindesarinen faded
back into memory and Malian was no longer a hero of song
and story, but a half-grown girl in grubby clothes. Frowning, she smoothed her hands over her dark braid. The hero
Yorindesarinen, she thought, would not have been plagued
with nurses when she was a girl; she would have been too
busy learning hero craft and worm slaying.

Malian hummed the snatch of tune again and sighed,
walking back to the stone balcony—then froze at a suggestion of movement from the High Hall, two storeys below.
Crouching down, she peered between the stone balusters,

then smiled and stood up again as a shimmer of lilting sound followed the initial footfall. A slender, golden figure gazed up at her through the twilit gloom, his hands on his hips and his sleeves flared wide, casting a fantastic shadow to either side. One by one the tiny golden bells on his clothes fell silent.

"And how," asked Haimyr, the golden minstrel, the one bright, exotic note in her father's austere keep, "do you propose getting down from there? Just looking at you makes my blood run cold!"

Malian laughed. "It's easy," she said, "especially if you've been trained by Asantir." She slid over the balustrade and made her way back down the finger- and toe-holds to hang again from the gargoyle. She grinned down at the minstrel's upturned face while she swung backward and forward, gaining momentum, before arching out and dropping neatly to the stairs below. The staircase swayed a little, but held, and she ran lightly down, vaulting up and over the second balcony, then scrambled through its wooden trusses to descend the final pillar. The minstrel held open his golden sleeves, scalloped and edged and trailing almost to the floor, and she jumped the last few feet, straight into his arms. He reeled slightly, but kept his balance, catching her in a brocaded, musical embrace. A little trail of mortar slid down the pillar after her.

"I had no idea you were due back!" Malian exclaimed, her voice muffled by the brocade. "You have been away for-*ever*! You have no idea how tedious it has been without you."

Haimyr stepped back and held her at arm's length. His hair was a smooth curve along his shoulders and no less golden than his clothes, or the bright gleam of his eyes. "My dear child," he said, "you are entirely mistaken. I have every idea how tedious it has been, not to mention dull and entirely unleavened by culture, wit, or any other redeeming quality. But you—I go away for half a year and you shoot up like a weed in my absence."

She shook her head. "I'm still short, just not *quite* as short as I was."

"But," he said, "every bit as grubby and disheveled, which will not do, not if you expect to embrace me in this wild fashion." He looked around with the lazy, lambent gaze of a cat. "This is a strange place for your play, my Malian—and what of the danger to your father's only child and heir, climbing about in that reckless manner. What would any of us say to him if you were to fall and break your neck?"

"Oh, he is away at present, riding the bounds and inspecting the outposts," said Malian. "You would all have time to run away before he got back."

Haimyr regarded her with a satirical eye. "My dear child," he said, "why do you think your good nurse and the maids are all out hunting for you, high and low? Your father is back." Mockery glinted in his smile. "On the whole, my Malian, I think that it would be better for you and your household if you were on time for his returning feast."

Malian pulled a face. "We all thought the patrols would be away another week at least," she said, with feeling. "But thank you for coming in here after me. You're right, I don't think anyone in my household would brave it, even to prevent my father's anger." She grinned again. "That's why I like it, because no one else ever comes here and I can do what I want. They think it's haunted," she added.

"I know," said Haimyr. "They have been telling me so since before you were born." He shrugged, his tall, fantastic shadow shrugging with him on the wall. "Well, folk have always liked to frighten themselves, by daylight or by dark, but they may be partly right about this place. The shadows of memory lie very thick here."

"It is a strange place," Malian agreed, "but I don't think it's dangerous. It seems sad to me, because of the decay and the silence, rather than frightening. And the memories, of course, are very bitter."

The minstrel nodded. "All the histories of your people are tragic and shot through with darkness. But the memories here must rank among the darkest."

"You are not afraid to come here, though," she said.

Haimyr laughed, and the sound echoed in the high stone

vault overhead. "Afraid? Of the past's shadows? No. But then, they are not my shadows. They are your blood heritage, my Malian, not mine."

Malian frowned. "I am not afraid either," she declared, and Haimyr laughed again.

"Of course not, since you choose to come here," he said. "And rather often, too, I suspect."

Malian smiled in response, a small secret smile. "*Quite* a lot," she agreed, "especially when you and Asantir are away." She drew a pattern in the dust with her foot. "It has been very dull without you, Haimyr. Six months was far too long a time."

He smiled down at her. "I apologize for condemning you to a life of tedium. Will you forgive me if I say that I have brought back something you value, to make up for my neglect?"

Malian considered this. "New songs and stories?" she asked. "Then I may forgive you, but only if you promise to teach me every one."

Haimyr swept a low, extravagant bow, his sleeves tinkling and his golden eyes glinting into hers, one long slender hand placed over his heart. Malian smiled back at him.

"Every one, remember," she said again, and he laughed, promising nothing, as was his way.

It was only a few hundred paces from the old High Hall to the gate into the New Keep, which was barred and soldered closed, although there was a locked postern a few yards away. Malian's customary means of coming and going was a narrow gap between the apex of the gate and the corridor's arched roof, but she was resigned, rather than surprised, when Haimyr took the postern key from his pocket. "Oh dear," she murmured, "now I am in trouble."

Haimyr slanted her a mocking smile. "Didn't you hear poor Doria, calling to you? She summoned the courage to put her head around the postern for love of you, but even a lifetime's devotion wouldn't take her any further. Nhairin, of course, is made of sterner stuff, but we agreed that I was better suited to hunting you out."

"Because you could hope to catch me if I ran?" she inquired, with a smile as sly as his. "But I cannot see you scaling the walls, Haimyr, even to save me from my father's wrath."

He closed the postern behind them, locking it with a small, definite click. "You are quite right. Even the thought is an abhorrence. The ghosts of the past are one thing, but to scramble through the rafters like an Ishnapuri monkey, quite another. I would have absolutely no choice but to abandon you to your fate."

Malian laughed aloud, but sobered as they turned into the golden blaze of the New Keep. Darkness never fell in these corridors and halls where jewel-bright tapestries graced the walls and the floors were patterned with colored tiles. Pages sped by on their innumerable errands while soldiers marched with measured tread and the vaulted ceilings echoed with all the commotion of a busy keep. Malian's eyes lit up as the bustle surged around them. "It's always like this when my father comes home," she said. "He sets the entire keep in a flurry."

Haimyr's laugh was rueful. "Do I not know it? And now I must hurry, too, if I am to prepare my songs for the feast."

"Everyone will be eager for something new," Malian agreed. "But only after you have sung of the deeds and glory of the House of Night—for are we not first and oldest?"

"Oldest, first, and greatest of all the Derai Houses on the Wall, in deeds and duty if not in numbers," a new voice put in, as though reciting indisputable fact. A spare figure rose from an alcove seat and limped forward. She was as dark and reserved as the minstrel was golden and flamboyant, and her face was disfigured by the scar that slashed across it from temple to chin.

" *'For it is the House of Night that holds the Keep of Winds,'* " Malian chanted in reply, " *'foremost of all the strongholds on the Shield-wall of Night.'* It was you who first taught me that, Nhairin."

The newcomer's dark brows lifted. "I have not forgotten," she said, taking the postern key from Haimyr. She had soldiered once for the Earl of Night, until the fight in which she gained both limp and scar, and she liked to say that she soldiered still in the Earl's service, but as High Steward of the Keep of Winds, rather than with a sword. "I do not forget any of the few lessons that did not have to be beaten into you," she added meditatively.

"Nhair-*rin*!" said Malian, then a quick, guilty look crossed her face. "Have I caused you a great deal of trouble, having to look for me?"

The steward smiled, a slight twist of her mouth. "Trouble? Nay, I am not troubled. But I know who will be if you are not clean and in your place when the feast bell strikes." The smile widened at Malian's alarmed look. "That bell is not so very far off, so if I were you I should be running like the wind itself to my chamber, and the bath that is waiting there."

Haimyr clapped Malian on the shoulder. "The good steward is right, as always. So run now, my bold heart!"

Malian ran. Her father held strict views on the conduct appropriate to an Heir of Night, and exacted the same obedience from his daughter as he did from the warriors under his command. "We keep the long watch," he often said to Malian, "and that means we are a fighting House. The Wall itself is named for us, and of all the fortresses along its length, this one stands closest to our enemy. We cannot let our vigilance or discipline waver for an instant, and you and I must be the most vigilant of all, knowing all others look to us and will follow our example, whether good or bad."

Malian knew that upholding discipline included being on time for a formal Feast of Returning. Her nurse and the other maids knew it, too, for they did not stop to scold but descended on her as one when she ran through the door, hustling her out of her grimy clothes and into the tepid bathwater. Nesta, the most senior of the maids, caught Malian's eye as she opened her mouth to complain, and Malian immediately shut it again. Nesta came of a family that had served the Earls of Night for long generations, and she held views on the value of discipline, tradition, and truancy that were remarkably similar to those of Malian's father.

Doria, Malian's nurse, was more voluble. "An imp of

wickedness, that's what you are," she said. "Running here, and running there, and never in sight when wanted. You'll be the death of me yet, I swear—not to mention the wrath of the Earl, your father, if he ever finds out about your expeditions."

"We'll all die of fright on that day, sure enough," said Nesta, in her dry way, "if nothing worse happens first. But will our fine young lady care, that's what I ask? And none of your wheedling answers either, my girl!" She struck a stern attitude, with arms akimbo, and the younger maids giggled.

"Well," said Malian meekly, "it hasn't happened yet, has it? And you know I don't mean to be a trouble to you, Doria darling." She hugged and kissed her nurse, but poked her tongue out at Nesta over Doria's shoulder.

The maid made a snipping motion with her fingers, imitating scissors. "Ay, Doria knows you don't mean to cause her trouble, but it won't stop trouble coming—especially if we don't get you down to dinner on time." She held up an elaborate black velvet dress. "It had better be black, I suppose, since you welcome the Earl of Night."

"Black is good, thank you," agreed Malian, scrambling into it. She waited, as patiently as she could, while Doria bound her hair into a net of smoky pearls.

"You look just like the ladies in the old tapestries," the nurse sighed, as her fingers twisted and pinned. "You are growing up, my poppet. Nearly thirteen already! And in just a few more years you will be a grand lady of the Derai, in truth."

Malian made a face at the polished reflection in the mirror. "I do look like a scion of the oldest line, I suppose." She kicked the train out behind her. "But can you imagine Yorindesarinen wearing anything so restrictive?"

"That skirt would make worm slaying very difficult," Nesta observed, and Malian grinned.

Doria, however, frowned. "Yorindesarinen is nothing but a fable put about by the House of Stars to make themselves feel important." She sniffed. "Just like the length of their names. Ridiculous!"

"They're not all long," Malian pointed out. "What about Tasian and Xeria?"

The nurse made a sign against bad luck, while Nesta shook her head. "Shortened," the maid said. "Why should we honor that pair of ill omen with their full names?" She pulled a face. "Especially she who brought ruin upon us all."

Doria nodded, her mouth pursed as if she had filled it with pins. "Cursed be her name—and completely beneath the attention of the Heir of Night, so we will not sully our lips with it now!" She gave a last tweak to the gauze collar, so that it stood up like black butterfly wings on either side of Malian's face. "You look just as you should," she said, not without pride. "And if you hurry, you'll be on time as well."

Malian kissed her cheek. "Thank you," she said, with real gratitude. "I am sorry that I gave you all so much trouble."

Nesta rolled her eyes and Doria looked resigned. "You always are," she said, sighing. "But I don't like your gallivanting off into the Old Keep, nasty cold place that it is. Trouble will come of it—and then what the Earl will do to us all, I shudder to think."

Malian laughed. "You worry too much," she said. "But if I don't hurry I really will be late and my father will make us all shudder, sooner rather than later."

She blew a butterfly kiss back around the door and walked off as quickly as the black dress would allow, leaving Doria and Nesta to look at each other with a mixture of exasperation, resignation, and affection.

"Don't say it," the nurse said to the younger woman, sitting down with a sigh. "The fact is that she is just like her mother was at the same age—too much on her own and with a head filled with dreams of glory. Not to mention running wild, all over the New Keep and half the Old."

Nesta shook her head. "They've been at her since she was a babe with all their lessons, turning her into an earl in miniature, not to mention the swordplay and other skills required by a warrior House. I like it when she acts like a normal girl and plays truant, for all the anxiety it causes us."

Doria folded her arms across her chest. "But not into the

Old Keep," she said, troubled. "That was her mother's way, always mad for adventure and leading the others after her. We all know how that ended." She shook her head. "Malian is already too much her mother's daughter for my comfort."

Nesta frowned. "The trouble is," she said, pitching her voice so that no one else could hear her, "does the Earl realize that? And what will he do when he finds out?"

Doria sighed again, looking anxious. "I don't know," she replied. "I know that Nhairin sees it, plain as I do—and that outsider minstrel, too, I've no doubt. It's as though the Earl is the only person who does not see it."

"Or will not," Nesta said softly.

"Does not, will not," replied Doria, "the outcome is the same. Well, there's nothing we can do except our best for her, as we always have."

"Perhaps," agreed Nesta. Her dark eyes gazed into the fire. "Although what happens," she asked, "if your best is not enough?"

But neither the nurse nor the fire had any answer for her.

# THE CRITICALLY ACCLAIMED
## *SOLDIER SON* TRILOGY FROM
## *NEW YORK TIMES* BESTSELLING AUTHOR

# ROBIN
# HOBB

## SHAMAN'S CROSSING
978-0-06-075828-8

Nevare Burvelle was destined from birth to be a soldier in
service of the King of Gernia. Now he must face a forest-
dwelling folk who will not submit easily to a king's tyranny
and they possess a powerful sorcery that threatens to claim
Nevare Burvelle's soul and devastate his world.

## FOREST MAGE
978-0-06-075829-5

Freed from the Speck magic that infected him, Nevare Burvelle
is journeying home to Widevale, anticipating a tender reunion
with his fiancée, Carsina. But his nights are haunted by grim
visions of treachery, and his days are tormented by a strange
side-effect of the plague that shames his family and repulses
the lady of his heart.

## RENEGADE'S MAGIC
978-0-06-075830-1

Nevare Burvelle stands wrongly accused of unspeakable
crimes, including murder. Suddenly an outcast and a fugi-
tive, he remains hostage to the Speck magic that shackles
him to a savage alter ego who would destroy everything
Nevare holds dear.

HOB 0211